ELLIS KROSS

THE FIFTH

The Complete Edition

The V Trilogy

Published by Ellis Kross

. . .

First Edition, December 2013

Written by Ellis Kross

Edited by Sidonie Lailler

ISBN: 978-0-9894376-4-6

Cover and Design by Ellis Kross

. . .

C O N T E N T S

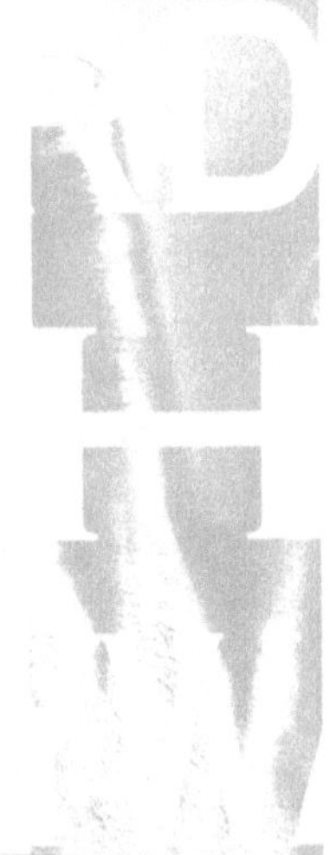

INTRODUCTION

SMALL BEGINNINGS

SOMEONE once told me that magic only exists in the movies. If I hadn't discovered Henry, then—for all I know—that person would've been about as right as the next. Sometimes things just happen. On any ordinary day, I would've easily agreed.

In the fall of 2011, I was wrapping up the last volume of an exhausting seven part series, which, relieved to say, I was ready to put behind me and move on to the next stage of my life. The Series was going to be my opus (at least that was what I thought), like my *Lord of the Rings*—only less fantasy, less hobbits, less Gandalfs, less dwarves, less elves, well, *Lord of the Rings* might've been a bad analogy. Nonetheless, the Series was very grandiose like Tolkien's trilogy or even Stephen King's *Dark Tower* novels. The Series took on a more modern approach, based around our time, in fact, 1959 (when the main character was a child) all the way up to present day. The heroine, more or less, the antihero was like a femme fatale, however, damaged and aloof like a John Constantine without the Silk Cut cigarettes. I decided to finish the ending the next morning after a round of coffee. Always does the trick. I remember it was sunny out—a Thursday, I believe—which, in my opinion, is a perfect day to get a lot of things done other than writing. I put Volume 7 of the Series on hold, let it mellow until I could get my hands around it that following day, and rummaged through a stack of old stories that I had written prior to the Series because, at the time, I was beginning to feel as if the Series was too dark for a debut novel, too disturbing, too weird, too political, too Biblical, too wordy, and *way* too long (the seven volumes altogether stood roughly over 1,000, 000 words—Yes, that's right. Seven figures!). I wanted to write a story that was inspiring, but still keep to that beloved mystery that makes a great story. I also wanted it to be sort of a coming of age story, stripped down to its bare bones, a story that, if you pressed your ear close enough to the pages of the book, you could hear a faint heartbeat. I narrowed down my search to around a dozen stories, all mediocre first drafts bleeding red with grammar corrections. Turns out none of them seemed fit for a debut—at least not the kind that sits nice and cozy in that ballpark of 80, 000 words. I was going through a strange time in my life as well. I was leaving behind one career as an engineer and focusing on another, my passion, my love, which was, of course, writing. But writing wasn't paying any bills or buying a roof over my head. I didn't have an agent or a publisher. I had about as many rejection letters as Franklin Roosevelt had stamps. Yada, yada, yada. . . The story's already been told before. So, later that afternoon, I ended my search and cleaned up the office area before I could enjoy the weather. Never a good sign when you have to hurdle over debris just to get to your own desk. As I was putting things back in their proper place—books, notes, and such—I moved to the closet or "The Black Hole," as I like to call it.

I wasn't so meticulous when it came to the closet. But I rolled up my sleeves anyway and tackled the task I had at hand. As I was moving junk out of the way, stuffing things in a garbage bag that I could haul to the nearest shelter, I came across the last remaining artifacts of musical equipment that had been collecting dust that past year on the top shelf (the rest, keyboards and samplers, had been sold due to financial reasons). I didn't know what happened at first. One second, I was thinking about whether or not I should pawn away a set of M-Audio speakers and the next I'm on my back with a pile of vinyl records on my chest. I wasn't hurt—just a nick on my elbow from where my arm caught most of the fall. After I regained my composure, I found a record from The Delfonics, the one with that one song, "Didn't I (Blow Your Mind This Time)," on the floor. The records belonged to my mother. My mother's name was even written along the thigh of one of the singer's legs. When I set my eyes on the singer in the middle, slightly standing in the shadows like a black John Wayne, the one they called Randy Cain, afro as round as a globe, hunched shoulders, both hands rested upon his hips, red floral pattern pants, dark silky shirt, brown vest jacket, I saw a story written along the lines of his face—not Mr. Cain's real life story but a story of my own, a story about a chivalrous man who was dealt a bad hand despite having shared the vast riches of stardom. Then, I saw a young man, the man's son, light in skin tone, no more than a stranger to his father. Like his father, his name was Henry, and he was going to be the next protagonist of my debut novel. I saw Henry's entire story laid out before me: his past, his present, and his future. Normally when I write, I wing it. Usually, I know the beginning and the end and I just fill the rest in the middle. Sometimes, I make ten different introductions before settling on the one I like the most. Not with Henry's story. He was me, he is you, he is every young man or woman out there who was once lost in a world that he/she didn't understand. When I found Henry, I found myself. I found my purpose. And I wanted to share it with the world. Call it what you like: coincidence, random luck, or whatever. I call it magic.

— E.K., December 5, 2013

To Monique,

for *always* being there, even when you weren't.

UNFINISHED BUSINESS

SHE never thought her boy saw what happened, not until he first developed a stutter at the age of six.

From the moment Henry spoke his first word, *jag-jag*, at three months, the doctors told his parents that their son was unlike any other baby his age.

Four months later, Henry was taking his first baby steps without any help, whereas most babies were taking their first steps between nine to twelve months.

When Henry turned two years old, he was going potty all by himself.

A month before Henry turned three, he was shooting hoops through a miniature basketball goal that his uncle had bought him for Christmas.

Not too long after that, Henry was speaking complete sentences like "Mama farts when she eats scetti."

It wasn't until the age of four when Henry finally pronounced the word *spaghetti* correctly, not scetti.

Despite his minor setbacks, by the rate Henry was going, he was either going to be a rocket scientist or a professional basketball player—rocket scientist from how easily he picked up on things or basketball player from how good of a shot he was.

Then, everything changed at the age of five, when Henry witnessed his mother commit murder.

The events that transpired on November 2, 1979—four minutes leading up to the crime—were nothing out of the ordinary. Henry was doing exactly what his mother had told him, which was to stay put and play with his toys. Before she closed the door behind her, she emphasized, "No matter what you hear behind this door, Henry, you are not, I repeat, not to open the door." Henry's mother had reiterated such demands, especially the part about not opening the door, until her boy agreed with the acknowledgment of a head nod and then the reply, "Yes ma'am."

While Henry was playing with his toy automobiles, skidding them around each groove and crack of the weathered hardwood floor like his favorite racecar driver, Dale the Tiger, from the animated television series, *Pluto's Vein*, the screaming started. Next, there was a loud *banging* noise coming from the end of the hallway, which was sending aftershocks across the racetrack of the floor. Henry listened closely to the sound, the furniture rattling. The banging was abrupt at first and then constant. Eventually, the banging stopped and Henry went back to playing with his toys. Then, more screaming followed. Henry's eyes suddenly flickered upward at the bedroom door and then pulled back to the mangled toys. The sound of a woman squealing pierced through the hallway. Once again, Henry removed his worried eyes from the toys and moved them toward the door, only this time Henry did so with a slow, cautious roll as if the door itself had eyes, as well as a particular interest in young boys, and if Henry dared to come near it, then the door would tattle about such insubordinate behavior to his mother. Henry's eyes steadied now. The door was closed as his mother had last left it, but Henry could still hear the screaming across the hallway. For several minutes it had gone on like this: two women screaming at one another, his mother's voice high and rancorous, while the other one's soft and slightly crippled. Henry's face was still bloodless, not from the women screaming, but from the latest encounter. His palms were sweaty. Hands shaking. He had tightness both in his gut and throat, which left his body—mostly his shoulders—in a curled and deflated state.

As he did with his eyes, Henry carefully rose from his crossed-legged seating position and sauntered over to a small television set and concluded, after a couple of attempts at switching it on, that it was broken.

The argument escalated outside the bedroom.

Henry hurried back to his toys and rammed two miniature trucks together; and by doing so, he hoped to erase the tarnished memory of the haggard woman from his thoughts (not his mother, of course, but the other much older woman). She was right there to easily access: her cancerous face, her glossy, marbled eyes sunken into the dark sockets of her skull, both cheekbones like doorknobs protruding from her face, her flaky lips as parched as a hardpan desert, and her sparse hair like wet shoelaces over her bald, scabrous scalp. Each penetrating scream brought forth vivid detail. The poor old woman had reached out to grab Henry with her trembling, liver spotted hand while stumbling through the bedroom. Reaching out for what, Henry wondered.

Particular smells in the air like the faint aroma of potpourri or the pungency of excrement absorbed in the autumn's breeze triggered the memory in Henry's mind: the same hand reaching out and grabbing him over the shoulder. Such an image came in violent waves—each one sending shivers throughout his body.

So, Henry did as his mother had told him and played with his toys. The harder he played, two trucks ramming into each other followed with hisses of explosions and the silent roars and cheers of an imaginary crowd from afar, the more comfort he found in them.

Where there was comfort, there was escape.

Soon, the image of the haggard woman dissolved away, so too did the echoing of her deathly voice.

Henry skidded the two trucks, leaving black streaks and serpentine patterns of tire tracks over the hardwood floor.

After another collision, a taut silence suddenly gripped the air and left Henry in a momentary state of standstill.

Again, his face went bloodless.

He honed in on the silence, creaking.

Then, he heard the sound of weeping coming from the other room.

More screaming pierced through the hallway and seeped through the cracks of the doorway.

Once more, Henry rammed the two toys together, harder this time, faster, but the screaming rang out like a battle cry.

—HOW COULD YOU DO THIS TO ME—

His mother's shouts were like needles prodding at his skin, now warm and damp.

The other voice was more subdued now, weak and gravelly.

Henry wiped the grimace from his face and then the sweat from his forehead. He listened more closely. Yet, he only made out fragments. He did, however, manage to catch the one word, the word *bitch*, within the argument. Nonetheless, the memory of the haggard woman was back. There she was, the poor old woman.

Easy access.

Henry placed his toys aside and glanced at the door.

Following the argument was a burst of laughter, extremely high in pitch.

The laughter was soon cut short from a loud thud over the headboard!

Curious of the noise (the *thud*, not the strange laughter), Henry slowly stood to his feet and cautiously walked over to the closed door.

Despite his mother's orders, Henry decided to open the door anyway.

No more yelling. . .

As Henry inched down the long and narrow hallway, he heard another sound: the utterance of struggle, muffled gargling, and deep moans.

He finally reached the master bedroom where he found his mother straddled over the other woman—the haggard one—on a king-sized bed.

The window was cracked open. Beige curtains were gracefully waving from a gentle breeze. The blankets had been thrashed around the bed as well as the floor. Bed sheets wrinkled. A couple of faded pillows, which were stained with brown rings and various red dots, were lying on the same aged hardwood floor. One of the pillows was held in his mother's hands and formed like a horseshoe. His mother violently struck downward on the woman's face, which caused the woman's boney arms to project outward like tree branches, making last-ditch efforts to grab hold of his mother's mane. The arms flailed around, hands yearning for something tangible to grab. Anything. A clock on the nightstand. The old woman was too weak, though. The clock slipped from her frail grip and fell to the floor. Henry cowered from the sudden *bang* of the clock striking the floor. Then, his mother fought off each swing and punch and slap that came her way and blocked her face with her elbows.

Henry vigilantly took a step back and hid behind the doorway.

With a final thrust downward, his mother rammed the nasty pillow into the woman's face. Her fingers erected and then slowly shriveled inward like dead spider legs. The gurgling ceased, so too did the struggle. Her two boney arms spilled over the bed. One of them lifelessly dangled over the side. Henry couldn't grasp what exactly his mother was doing to the other woman or what she *had* done.

Unaware of her son lingering behind the doorway, she pulled herself upright and took a moment to catch her breath.

Then, the pillow slid from the woman's dumb face.

The lifeless woman on the bed, Henry realized as he peered closely, was the same haggard woman from his thoughts.

Henry's attention was suddenly pulled to the front door closing downstairs, which gave way to another sound, a man's voice.

Before his mother turned her shoulder, Henry took cover behind the wall.

"I'm back!" the man exclaimed from below.

Henry caught a glimpse of a shadow of a strange man along the wall. He was holding a paper bag of groceries in his arms.

"Beatrice," the man said as he walked up the stairs. "You up here?"

When the man reached the top of the landing, Henry was back in the other bedroom.

As before, the bedroom door was closed as his mother had last left it.

With his eyes tightly shut and his cold, shivering hands cupped over his ears, Henry was curled in the corner of the bedroom. That shield of inert silence was suddenly breached by a thunderous bellow outside the master bedroom. He winced and pressed his icy hands harder over his ears not from the bellow, but from the sound of a paper bag of groceries crashing to the floor.

A gallon of milk, a loaf of bread, and a couple of Braeburn apples poured from the bag, one of them rolling from the landing and bouncing all the way down the stairs.

Even though both of his hands had masked the clamor across the hallway, Henry could still hear the two, now his mother and the man, as well as a repetitive beat of an apple bouncing farther down the staircase.

Over the soft, fading beat, Henry hummed the very first song that came to mind: "Mary Had A Little Lamb."

There was more screaming now, louder this time, followed with the man weeping, but Henry, of course, heard none of it.

BOOK ONE

THE SHADOW PLAYER

PART ONE

A CAW HEARD FROM THE GRAVE

ONE

THE last thing that Bryson and Kenzie expected to run into on their way home from school was another dead body.

This made two in only a month!

The first body freaked the two out so badly that they changed their route home from Luther Avenue to Josette Park. They spent days, even weeks, occupying their heads with other activities: every sport in the book (including bocce ball, if that even counted as a sport), video games, all of which didn't consist of shooting or killing zombies or zombie soldiers or zombie vampires, anything to keep their minds from the horrendous image of the dead clerk behind the Xpress Mart. On stormy nights while Kenzie cowered underneath a teepee of his own bed sheets with a flashlight gripped in hand, the clerk's dead eyes would spring open inside Kenzie's mind and force him to seek refuge in his parents' bedroom. The clerk had been shot twice, once in the back of the head and the second time in his gut as if the shot in the head didn't do the trick. Later, both parents found out that a former convicted felon, Clarence Mooney, robbed the convenient store and then killed the clerk out of fun. Pieces of the clerk's brain were painted over the alleyway like graffiti. The sight alone of the corpse prevented Kenzie from eating anything with red sauce like his mother's spaghetti or her chili con carne. Kenzie's friend, Bryson, didn't have as much difficulty in forgetting about the image of the corpse, although he'd be lying if he said he wasn't still dwelling about it in the back of his mind.

As Bryson rambled on about how much Coral was into Kenzie and yet Kenzie still didn't have the least amount of audacity to ask her out, Kenzie's face turned as white as milk, lips included, bloodless.

"Look out!" Kenzie yelled out and pointed below.

In half-strut, Bryson's eyes suddenly crossed the puddle of blood.

Before he could place his foot back on the ground, he stumbled forward. The heel of his sneakers landed over the puddle, which caused a couple of drops of blood to splash over the bottom lip of his blue jeans. Bryson recovered and tossed his book bag aside. He staggered closer to the body while Kenzie, as he did the first time around, remained in a state of shock.

"Is he really. . . "

"*Dead*," Bryson finished, his face pinched in sheer disgust.

"Again!"

"Oh geez. . . "

"That. . . that smell. . . " Kenzie said and covered both his nose and mouth with his sleeve, ". . . it's like my Aunt Koehler's bathroom after Chinese Night times ten."

"Relax, Kenzie."

"How can I relax, Bryson?" Kenzie argued, his voice growing louder. "We're like a magnet for dead bodies! We're we're we. . . we're. . . WE'RE CURSED!"

Bryson let out a sigh.

"We're not cursed," he droned.

"Yes we are!"

"Would you shut up?"

"YOU!"

Bryson rolled his eyes and then kneeled down over the body. The upper part of the body was lost in the shadows of the park bridge, which made it even more difficult to recognize the corpse's face. Underneath the corpse, a puddle of blood, now as dark as molasses, was circled in a three foot radius. Bryson, however, instantly recognized the bulky, curved object lying in the dead man's hand.

"What is it?"

"Looks like. . ."
No way.
"Like what?"
Bryson shook his head.
"I don't know," he said under his breath.
Without stepping in the puddle, Bryson placed his left hand over the wall in order to keep from falling forward, covered his other hand with the backside of his sleeve, and shoved the object from the corpse's grip. Bryson's hand suddenly slipped from the wall. He flopped forward, but Kenzie was there to grab his friend by the shirt and pull him backward.
"Thanks," Bryson said with great relief.
"No problem."
Kenzie nodded at the freed object below.
"What is it?"
Once more, Bryson kneeled down.
"A saxophone. . ." he read the name engraved on the side of the saxophone, ". . . a Jag. . . ger?"
"Jagger?"
"That's what is says."
Bryson reached out his hand.
Before he pried the saxophone from the corpse's cold dead hands, Kenzie blurted out, "DON'T TOUCH IT!"
"What? Why?"
"We can get in trouble."
"Lighten up, Kenzie," he mumbled. "I just want to see if it still works."
"You don't know where that thing's been." He waved his finger around the blood puddle and then the corpse. "I mean. . . you really want to put your mouth on the same piece that man had his mouth on? Do you?"
Bryson eyed the corpse's mouth or what was left of his mouth.
"I'll wipe it down," he said casually.
"But you can get like AIDS or something."
"AIDS?" Bryson snorted and shook his head. "That's through blood transfusion, you idiot."

As Bryson touched the saxophone, a jogger hollered from the end of the bridge's tunnel.

"What are you boys doing over there?"

Bryson and Kenzie slowly backed away from the corpse and faced the lanky silhouette.

"We didn't do anything," Kenzie whined, both of his hands held up in surrender. "We swear. We found him just like this."

The jogger hurried over to the two boys.

Once he saw the corpse, he proceeded forward with more caution, less urgency.

"Oh God," the jogger uttered and covered his mouth. "Is he alive?"

Bryson glowered at the jogger.

He said annoyingly, "Does he look like he's alive?"

The jogger inched closer to the lifeless body. He placed his hands over his knees and leaned forward.

"Now. . . now back away. . . " he said frantically as he studied the disfigured face before him. "You hear."

Part of the corpse's face was revealed in the dim light.

The jogger dropped his jaw in awe.

"I can't believe it."

"You know him, sir?"

"Yes. . . I do."

"Then who is he?"

"*Harry*. . . " he answered, ". . . his name is Harry."

"Does he have a last name?"

"Just Harry."

TWO

So, who is this Harry guy?

The question came like a passing car.

The detective asked once more.

. . . Harry?

Yet, he received no response from his partner.

Detective Donovan Backer, the "Don" or best known as "Donnie," was standing with both of his hands rested over his hips. Donnie carried a slight pouch on his abdomen and yet the rest of his body was well proportioned. He had bright blue eyes, easily mistaken as contacts. His cheeks were heavily scarred from acne, but even the week-old beard couldn't cover up the effects of his teenage years. His partner, Detective Albert Corpus, a couple of years older than Donnie, heard the question as soon as it left Donnie's lips, and yet he didn't comprehend a word that came from his mouth. His dark eyes were scattered among the scene: a barricade of cops, a small crowd of reporters and pedestrians, a Channel 9 news van, coroners, and CSI units. Corpus drifted farther into his daze. It was now becoming a ritual for Detective Corpus: moments like these where he would completely zone out. Throughout his eighteen years of being on the force, Corpus had seen the signs among his fellow detectives. It all started out with the afternoon headaches and then drinking more coffee—or anything with caffeine—to help dampen the headaches. For Corpus, the first sign was the early signs of gray hair. Each morning, he would look in the mirror and see more gray. At times, he would cut them out, the gray hairs. Other times, he was just too tired. Secondly, it was the moments when he would find himself staring at the pale outline over his ring finger, wondering what the hell went wrong. Thirdly, it was the irritability, the short tempers, coming home later to the misses. Hence why the third sign had driven him to a life of solitude and left him with a pale outline over his ring finger. And then, lastly, it was the apathy, a complete state of numbness. The great city of Lansford had a way of bringing out such signs as well as symptoms. Now, it was only a matter of time before Corpus could see himself becoming one of them, the jaded cop who everybody in the precinct avoided, that old dog.

And he dreaded it.

"*Hey, Corpus. . .*" Donnie said and snapped his fingers three times in front of his partner's face.

Corpus pulled himself from his daze.

"Earth to Al!"

"What?" Corpus said with a slight grimace.

"You feeling all right?"

"Just fine and dandy, Don."

"So, you know anything more about our victim other than what our witness said?"

"Just that he's been hanging around Josette for the past few years, playing his saxophone."

The two detectives walked away from the parked brown Ford LTD Crown Victoria, Crown Vic for short, and down the dirt pathway.

At the entrance of the bridge, Corpus came across a small pile of chewed up sunflower seeds. He took a mental note of this, the seeds, as he did with every bit of detail that seemed out of place.

They passed the three LPD cops. One of them was Donnie's younger brother, Ted, or Teddy, as the ones close to him called him (anybody who heard Ted reading the Miranda rights knew he was anything but cute and cuddly). As always, Ted wasn't doing much at all but just standing there looking like a brick wall. The other two, Officer Marson and Officer Wheaton, were keeping spectators at bay.

As the two detectives crossed the officer's path, Corpus couldn't help but notice the fresh bruises around Ted's knuckles.

He snorted and said to Donnie, "Times I wonder how in the hell your brother became a cop."

"I find myself asking that same question, Corpus," Donnie replied and forced a smirk on his face. "As long as he's keeping the crooks off the streets, then I can care less what he does in his spare time."

"Cops like him give us old folks a bad name."

"I'd be careful who you say that to."

Corpus glared at Donnie.

They shouldered their way through a crowd of pedestrians.

Donnie peeled back part of his trench coat and crouched under the yellow caution tape. Unlike his partner, Corpus entered the crime scene with a loud grunt. They finally arrived at the corpse. Both of them followed protocol as they had been doing for as long as they had known each other and put on standard police gloves and walked cautiously around the crime scene.

"Great way to kick off the first day of spring," Corpus mumbled.

Donnie didn't catch what his partner had said under his breath.

Instead, he was too focused on the corpse before him.

"Gunshot wound underneath chin," he said carefully while studying the mangled body. "Explains why half of his face is missing. Could be self-inflicted. Whoever did this didn't want to make it easy for us."

"You're telling me," Corpus mumbled to himself as he surveyed the corpse's wounds. "Looks like whoever did this didn't know what to do."

Donnie also noted the wounds around the corpse's abdomen, "Stab wounds, gunshot. What a complete fucking mess!" He studied the projection of blood splattered over the wall. Parts of brain matter were still hanging from the recesses of the mortar. The remaining parts were piled below. He shot a glance over at his partner. "So, the jogger said this Harry guy wasn't even that good at playing the sax. Said he was more of a disturbance than anything. Nonetheless, he said he was a nice fellow."

"They all seem nice, until you get to know them," Corpus said coldly. "Then, you find out what put them on the streets to begin with."

"I don't know, Corpus," Donnie said, his eyes scattered among the scene. "He could've picked up another hobby while he was living on the streets."

"Maybe a bad one."

Corpus witnessed the scars around the corpse's face. He also had track marks running down his forearms, as well as needle marks that had caught an early infection. There were red marks around his wrists, probably where he had been bound. Not far from the corpse, Corpus found a torn dog leash in the puddle of blood.

"Did our witness mention anything about a dog?"

"No," Donnie said over his shoulder. "Why?"

Corpus mumbled, "Just curious."

He directed his attention toward the Jagger saxophone and saw the initials, *H.M.*, at the base of the bow.

"Got initials here," Corpus said vacantly. "H.M."

"We already know what the *H* stands for," Donnie said, his voice trailing off as he sharpened his eyes over a recess in the tunnel's wall. "All we need now is the *M*."

Donnie spotted the four-inch barrel of a revolver protruding from the drain.

Corpus asked, "Got something?"

Donnie pulled out a pencil from his pocket, slid the eraser end through the trigger, and held up the revolver for Corpus to see.

"Indeed I do," he said. "Possible murder weapon."

"Will run it for prints," Corpus replied and drifted into another daze as he peered down at the corpse's body. "What's your story *Harry?*"

A sparkling glint pierced his eye, which temporarily pulled him from his train of thought.

Corpus kneeled closer without touching the blood patterns around the scene. He slid his gloved hand into the corpse's pocket and pulled out a silver crucifix.

THREE

As the minute hand moved closer to the twelve on the clock, the anticipation swelled within Henry. He assumed he'd have plenty of time to finish another song while his social studies teacher, Miss Sanders, was explaining to the class why President Lincoln ordered the Emancipation Proclamation during the American Civil War. If it wasn't for Jeffery, aka "Moby Dick," as the other ninth graders called him (most, if not all of them, made sure to stress the *Dick* part), due to his cruelty and, of course, portly frame, shooting spitballs through a straw, then Henry, or "Urethra," as Jeffery was mouthing under his breath, would've been well through the song.

One of the spitballs missed the mark and landed on the Uncle Sam poster with the famous line "I WANT YOU!"

Another spitball hit Henry on the shoulder.

The next spitball wasn't too far off from the second one. This one fell into Henry's shirt and caused him to squirm around in his desk. The tiny soggy ball of paper tickled him as it crawled down the spine of his back.

The following one was right on target.

Grimacing, Henry fingered the spitball from his ear and turned his shoulder.

Purposefully slouched over his desk with a stupid, animal-istic expression over his face, Jeffery mouthed the name, "*Urethra, Urethra, Urethra.*" A grin shaped over his face. "What are you going to do, da. . . da. . . dumbass?"

Henry rolled the wet ball around the edge of his fingertips (making it more compact) and then flicked the thing back at Jeffery, missing his face by only inches.

Miss Sanders withdrew her beady eyes from the chalkboard and glared at the two individuals in the back of the classroom. Both of her eyes were like menacing mechanisms, unnerving to some.

Jeffery quickly pulled his attention toward Miss Sanders while Henry directed his focus back on the song.

"Are you getting all of this, Mr. Burl?" Miss Sanders asked.

With his head buried in his composition notebook, Henry ignored Miss Sanders and wrote down the lyrics as quickly as they entered his thoughts.

Henry mouthing inaudibly: *Lincoln this, Lincoln that. . .*

While writing down his "rhymes," as he called them, the lights slowly dimmed in the classroom. The mood built romantically. Henry's eyes briefly moved away from the notebook and crossed Kerri Coleridge sitting in the front of the classroom. Her body was turned toward Henry, not Miss Sanders. Her hands were held closely in her lap. Her head was cocked to the side in wonder as she batted her eyelids like the smitten ones do in the cartoons. Her hair was seductively blowing around as if she was standing in front of a high-speed fan. The lights now darkened. One remaining light from above shined down on Henry, highlighting him like a star.

Lincoln this, Lincoln that, Henry wrote. *Lincoln in the papers. Lincoln on the tube. Lincoln in the movies?* (rest) *Child, please! How much Lincoln can you Lincoln with Lincoln to make a better Lincoln? See me, I'm not the chosen one, but I can't be the only one who's sick and tired of these pre* (the beat stops, skips, and continues) *pre, pre, pre pretentious clowns running out of ideas. Recycle your trash, not your stash. So listen up! I'm going to say it once. Twice if you're nice. Start your own thang. Make it the very best thang. Yeah! A revolution. Make it loud. Make it proud. Make it right. And grab your Everlasts cuz we be bringing the fight. Bringing the A. . .*

"Hey!" a voice interrupted the song.

Bringing the A. . .

"Hey, Mr. Burl?"

Hey!

Henry gazed out into the vast audience and saw Miss Sanders no longer perched on Jeffery's shoulders.

Instead, with a blank, angry stare, she was standing in the sparse audience with both of her arms crossed.

"Henry!" Miss Sanders called out.

Startled, Henry removed his eyes from his composition notebook and sat upright.

The song faded to black.

"Ye. . . yea. . . yes, Miss San. . . ders," he said, the classroom around him was back to normal.

Miss Sanders marched down the center aisle and stopped at Henry's desk. She picked up the notebook from the desk and skimmed through the pages, all rhymes and no notes from the lecture.

"I see you've been following along," she said and then faced the rest of the students in the classroom. "Would you like to stand up and share your notes with the rest of the class?"

"But. . ." Henry made an attempt to pluck the notebook from Miss Sanders' grip.

"I don't think so," Miss Sanders said and silently read some of Henry's scribbling to herself. "*Lincoln this, Lincoln that. . .*"

Henry blushed and dropped his head in embarrassment.

A couple of the students giggled behind Henry's back.

"Next time I see you doing this again in my classroom, then I'm sending you to the office," she said sternly while holding up Henry's notebook. "This can wait till after class. Do I make myself clear?"

Henry smacked his gums and rolled his eyes.

Miss Sanders sharpened her eyes and asked once more, "Do I make myself clear?"

"Yes, Miss San. . . ders."

"This is your last warning, Henry."

Henry bobbed his head.

The bell suddenly rang.

"All right, class!" Miss Sanders shouted out over the bell as well as the shuffling of students and squeaking of chairs and desks. "Remember to do your homework, ladies and gentlemen. We will go over the Chapter 4 questions at the beginning of class. And no copying from other students!" She directed her attention to Henry. "That includes you, Mr. Burl."

Henry packed his things into his backpack and was last to make his way to the exit.

Before Henry exited, Miss Sanders said from behind, "*Henry.*"

Henry swallowed the dry lump down his throat.

"May I have a word with you," she said, this time more sincerely.

Relieved from the tone of her voice, he ambled over to Miss Sanders.

"I just wanted to apologize," she said. "I didn't mean to make an example of you in front of the class."

He focused on the words.

Slow, he thought. *Just like Mrs. Haller taught me.*

"Th. . . th. . . th. . . th. . . th. . . tha. . . that's. . . o. . . kay. I'm. . .   I'm use too. . . to it."

"You shouldn't be, Henry." She sighed. "I noticed you've almost filled up your entire notebook. I didn't know you were a poet."

"It's not. . . po. . . poetry."

"I see," she said, bobbing her head. "Lyrics. These are musical lyrics."

Henry became embarrassed again and did the common reaction of hanging his head.

"This notebook is personal to you," she said. "I'm sorry for sticking my nose in your business. But you can't bring this to class anymore."

"Okay," he said clearly.

"Do you like to write?"

"A. . . a little," he said softly. "Yeah."

"Where did you learn how to write like that?"

"Wa. . . wa. . . wa. . . wa. . . watching. . . Teeee. . . TV li. . . li. . . li. . . lis. . . li listening to mu. . . music."

"What is a basketball player like yourself writing poetry?" She paused. "Sorry. I mean lyrics."

"I guess it's like a ha. . . ha. . . hobby of mine."

"Well, what I read was really good, Henry." She strolled around the desk. "What does your mother think about all of this?"

"Sh. . . she says I'm just going through another ph. . . ph. . . phase."

Thinking, Miss Sanders said, "We all have the right to dream, Henry. Some of us are dreamers and some of us are doers. When the time comes, you'll have to decide which one you want to become." She grabbed Henry's notebook and handed it back to him. "Nobody is born with talent, Henry. That's something you have to earn and work really hard to do. Some things we pick up easier than others. John Fitzgerald Kennedy, who was our. . . "

Miss Sanders waited for Henry to finish the sentence.

"Tha. . . tha. . . thurty-fourth presi. . . dant."

"Close," she said and cracked a smile. "Thirty-fifth president. He once said: '*All of us do not have equal talents, but all of us should have an equal opportunity to develop our talents.*' Think about that, will you?"

"Yes, Miss Sanders."

"Now, get out of here," Miss Sanders said, nodding toward the classroom exit.

After Henry gathered the rest of his supplies, a language arts textbook and a couple of extra pencils from the locker, which, by the way, had the word *Diarrhea* (one of the many nicknames drawn from his middle name, which was Uriah), written diagonally across the door with a black sharpie, Jeffery bumped shoulders with Henry and sent him staggering into another student.

The textbook slipped from Henry's hands and capered over the hallway floor until it openly came to rest.

As Henry reached down to pick up the textbook, Jeffery kicked it farther down the hallway.

"Go fetch, Urethra," Jeffery teased and gave his buddies high fives.

FOUR

DAY in and day out Henry surrounded himself with friends (mother's strict orders) and yet Henry was very much an introverted young man.

Everyday, Henry walked home from school, whereas most kids his age or around his age had their owns cars to drive to and from school. On some days, his friend, T.J., short for Tomas Johntavius, last name Livingston, most notably known as "Octopus," or "Octo," due to his long arms and legs and stubby, tree stump-like frame, who lived only four houses down from Henry, would tag along and keep Henry company. Of all Henry's friends, T.J. was the flashy one of the group (one of the few black kids who lived in the neighborhood), also the "don't-mess-wit-me" one of the group standing about seven inches taller than Henry, who was only 5 feet 6 inches. The others who knew T.J., like Henry, knew that he wasn't the way he had projected himself on the outside, a surly young man. He was outspoken, unlike Henry, the shy stutterer who operated, in *most* cases, on a similar wavelength as T.J. That was, of course, when T.J. could get Henry going without any pause or stammer. About three or four times a week—depending on the laundry schedule—T.J. would wear the same outfit: a pair of white Reeboks, black jeans with holes in them, a black tank top, and a gold chain around his neck. Same haircut too: a box haircut with a lighting bolt trimmed along the side of his head. Henry didn't mind T.J.'s company. In fact, of all his friends, except for Danny occasionally, T.J. was the only one whom he didn't mind hanging around with. Mostly, though, it was just Henry, a lone wolf at heart, and on the outside, a talented basketball player who had as many friends as the fingers he could count on his hand. Normally, whenever he walked home alone, he would take the longer way back home, which was straight down Main Street until it crossed over into Davidson Drive. Henry enjoyed the view, especially the colorful trees during spring. Enjoyed the quietude of the small town. But like most kids his age, he dreamed about leaving. Henry didn't know exactly where. There were so many places to see, so many places to go. Maybe one of those places he had seen or read about in the periodicals. Somewhere where people spoke a different language. Anywhere but here in Reddington. The population of Reddington was about 8,430. The small town was sixty-three miles from the capital, Lansford, the largest city in Peregrine. Since Reddington was an industrial town, it relied mostly on the steel industry, which, as of lately, hadn't been doing so well—not like it once was in the early 1950's. Two movies, both actions flicks, were shot right here in the town of Reddington. One called *Cheapskate* and another called *Montag's Profit*. There was something about Reddington's grittiest that drew in Hollywood producers like flies to a bad stench. The money, dirty or not, certainly helped out the small town. Plus, it invited other producers (not just Hollywood but from around the world). Except for the kids and the locals who played extras in the movies, nobody really cared when a movie was being shot in town. During production, most of Reddington was shut down. The roads blocked off. Schools delayed. However, everything one needed like groceries or medicine or supplies was a walking distance away. And everybody in Reddington practically knew each other by the first name, especially that one name in particular, *Henry*, not Urethra or Diarrhea or Henry Hurl or Henry You're Ah Ah Girl or, even worse, Oreo Cookie. Everywhere Henry roamed, he would carry around an old basketball. Part of the dry, coarse, crumbly leather was torn and peeled away from where Henry picked at it throughout the school day, but it still made a nice thunk when it struck the pavement. It became like a nervous tick for Henry. While others chewed on a pen or bit their fingernails or even sneaked into the boy's bathroom during third period to smoke a cigarette, Henry had that old, smelly, worn basketball at his disposal. Everyone in town could hear the young man coming. The sound of that basketball bouncing against the sidewalk could be heard at least four blocks away. At times, the sound would come in various rhythmical thunks, instead of the normal repetitive beat.

As Henry made his way down Main Street, which was lined with Bradford Pear trees, he made a right onto Billings Street and stopped in front of the pawnshop, Holiday's, which was next door to the town's only pharmacy, Fayette and Friends.

When Henry came across a strange instrument behind the front window, the first thing he thought about was the great Mr. Vortex. Henry literally shouted out the name in his mind, with extreme clarity too! His two eyes ballooned outward and just about popped from their sockets. *This is the first time. . .* For years, he had always wondered what it would be like to have one. *Man,* he thought as he pressed his forehead against the pane of glass, *just to wrap my hands around one!* Ever since Henry was eleven years old, he begged his mother every Christmas for one, but she didn't have enough money to afford one. For the time being, Henry had to make due with a toothbrush or a hair comb or anything long and curved from the garage to replicate the instrument. Over several occurrences, his mother, Abbey, waltzed into Henry's bedroom only to find him jumping up and down on the bed as if it was a trampoline, playing the air sax as a Mr. Vortex music video blasted over the television with the speaker all distorted and maxed to its highest level. Of course, his mother would storm. "Damn it, Henry! Would you turn that crap down?" For Christmas, his Uncle Charlie, who was much cooler than his younger sister, Abbey (Henry wondered at times how the two siblings were even blood related not only from the way the two interacted with one another, which was unlike any normal big brother-little sister bond, but also from the color of his skin and how—besides his particular taste in soul music—he was a white man without a single trace of black in him), bought him a Casio (CT-701). Henry's mother certainly didn't approve of the gift from her older brother. But anything to keep her boy out of trouble didn't bother her, just as long as it didn't interfere with his ABC's.

Of all the musical instruments, Henry imagined, the drums (which were *way* too loud for their 1,600 square feet home), the electric guitar (which looked way too complicated to play), the bass (like the electric guitar, way too complicated to play), this was the one and only instrument that gathered the most interest: the saxophone. Stylish and classy. Easy to carry around unlike the drums or any of those other instruments. *And I didn't need an amplifier*, he thought. He could play on the playground, on the courts, or in front of Kerri Coleridge's house!

Even though the saxophone in the display case was a hideous thing, filthy and tarnished and appeared as if it had just been unearthed by a team of archeologists, Henry was captivated from its unique appearance.

Man! If only. . .

Henry could hardly control the beam on his face.

As soon as his eyes crossed the price tag over the neck of the saxophone, however, that beam disappeared from his face.

Two hundred and fifty dollars. . .

Deflated from the price of the saxophone, Henry walked about halfway toward the next intersection when he paused and walked back to the pawnshop.

The storeowner, Holiday, was there to greet Henry.

"If it isn't my favorite customer," he said, acting like a car salesman ready to haggle.

"Wha. . . what's up, Holiday," Henry returned gladly.

"You sure are in a good mood, Henry," Holiday said and squinted his eyes. "You finally ask out what's her name? You know. . . the girl who lives across from you."

"Kerri?"

Holiday said, "Yeah, man."

"Sh. . . sh. . . she's still. . . wa. . . wa. . . wants nothin' to do wit meee."

"A handsome dude like yourself," the greasy storeowner said as he chewed on the toothpick in the side of his mouth. "She doesn't know what she's missing out."

"I guess," Henry uttered and shrugged his shoulders.

"So, you actually talked to her this time around?"

"No!"

"Then, how do you know?"

"How do I know wa. . . wa. . . what?"

"That she wants nothing to do with you," he replied. "That's how girls play nowadays. They like to play hard to get. You see." He leaned back against the counter and twirled the toothpick between his fingertips. "Me, I like my ladies to the point, if you know what I mean. A lady who knows what she wants and doesn't hesitate to ask."

"I know what you mean."

"I bet you do," Holiday said scathingly. "So, you here to buy something or are you 'just' looking?"

Henry craned his head around his shoulder and eyed the saxophone behind the front window.

"Ah ha!" Holiday blurted out with a smile gleaming across his face.

"Come on, Holiday," Henry begged. "You know I'm good for it. As soon as I get the ama. . . ma. . . money, I'll pay you back."

"It would take you ten years to pay me back, Henry," Holiday said, his voice high and girlish. "I'm sorry. You know how I run my business. And I swear." His voice shifted downward. "You better not be coming in here with your mother's stuff." With his eyes widened, he pointed at Henry in a fatherly way. "Last time, I caught hell from that damn woman."

Henry paused.

Holiday sighed and placed his arm around Henry's shoulder.

"Come," he said. "Let's take a look at her."

He walked Henry over to the front display case where the saxophone was perched and gently picked it up.

"Why you cha. . . cha. . . charging so much. . . "

Henry glanced over at Holiday.

"Well," he said and leaned closer, "this one here is special, Henry. It's a Jagger."

"To me, it lo. . . looks like you found it in a du. . . dum. . . dumpster."

Holiday tilted his head to the side.

"Then why you so interested in it, man? If you really want to buy a saxophone, we got Chessman's right around the corner. They got plenty of brass. Not a Jagger, though." He shrugged his shoulders. "Sure, you might find one cheaper than this one here, but, like I said, it's not a Jagger."

"I haven't seen one. . . like this be. . . be. . . before."

"Listen, Henry Man," Holiday said. "You don't buy an instrument like this from the way it looks. If you're going to fork out the money for this baby, then I want to hear you on the radio next week while I'm cruising to work with the top down. You feel me?"

"I feel you." He thought about Holiday's comment. "Ha. . . ha. . . how. . . how do I no. . . no. . . know what it sounds like?"

Holiday squared himself to Henry.

"You have to show me the money up front so I know you're interested in buying," he said. "You and me know, Henry, that you don't have this kind of money. But if you somehow 'magically' came up with the money—and not from your mother's things—I tell you what my man, the ladies will be dropping their panties for you, even that Kerri girl."

"Really?"

Henry drifted into a momentary trance.

"Wait a couple of years and you'll know what I'm talking about."

"She don't seem like that that ki. . . ki. . . kind of gir. . . girrrr. . . girl."

Holiday snorted.

"You see, Henry," he said, a grin growing across his face. "An instrument like this one is known to have a psychic power on the ladies. I've seen it before like in the music videos. The ladies go crazy for a man with an instrument. You learn how to play. Man oh man!" Holiday dementedly squinted one eye. "You could be like a real life Jedi Knight."

Henry had always been incredibly fascinated with the unknown, especially this so-called "force." However, being raised by such a practical woman—who had demonstrated to her son through her stern demeanor that she was very much grounded to reality—he learned at a young age the difference between movies and real life. Around the age of six, his mother took him to see the re-release of *Star Wars* for the first time. For the next two Saturdays, Henry begged and pleaded his mother to take him again. He ended up going one Saturday with his mother and another with his Uncle Charlie.

"Really?"

"Really *really*," Holiday said seriously.

There was a tense silence.

A loud howl of a laugh exploded from Holiday's chest.

"I had you going for a while," he said, laughing.

On a dime, his facial expression switched back over.

"But seriously."

"Can you hooo. . . hooo. . . ooo. . . ho. . . old it for me or not?"

"You know I can't do that, Henry," he said. "You know how merchandise comes and goes around here. If I hold it for you, then I got to hold something for every single person who comes in here who wants me to hold things, which, by the way, happens all the time. But I don't cave in. I tell them 'No! No holding!' You dig."

"Come on, Holiday!" he groaned. "Ja. . . jussst for the day!"

Holiday peered into Henry's puppy dog eyes and let out a sigh.

"Fine," he exclaimed. "But you better not be coming back here with your mother's things." He rubbed his fingers together as if he was rubbing invisible cash. "I want to see cash, papers, green. Capesh?"

"Capesh," Henry replied and exited the pawnshop.

As Henry rounded the pawnshop, he suddenly picked up a potent smell coming from the side alleyway. The smell was so foul that it forced Henry to cover his nose with the backside of his hand. Henry had smelled such awful odors before, especially in the gym locker room after recess. Never had he smelled something as awful as this.

"What the. . . " he uttered and inched closer.

With his hand shielded over his nose, he crept farther down the grungy alleyway. Next, he heard the buzzing of flies. There was a swarm of them, the flies. They were flying around a dog carcass. Some were crawling in and out of each orifice of its face, mostly the snout. Others were rubbing their tiny legs together in great delight, savoring the dog's rotting remains. Henry kneeled closer without touching anything and got a better look at the dead dog, the flies, especially the flies.

After a quick study, he realized it was a German shepherd (*a beautiful dog*, Henry wondered) and that it had been dead for some time now. Henry couldn't determine a cause of death. The dog didn't have any wounds, not on its body.

No leash either.

The only wound Henry could find was the one on its leg. Part of its bone was protruding from the skin.

Henry carefully placed the book bag on the ground and pulled out an instant camera from the side pocket. He leaned over the smelly dead dog. He leaned so close that the flies had accidentally mistaken him as the dead dog. Henry shooed away a couple of flies. But there was too many of them. They kept coming! Just when he thought they would fly away and leave him alone, one of them would land on his shoulder. Another one would zip by his ear.

As the flies buzzed around his ears (so close that he could feel the buzzes vibrating against his eardrums), Henry quickly took a snapshot of the German shepherd's face and backed away without tripping over that nasty wound on the dog's leg. He grabbed the book bag from the ground and then the self-developing film from the camera.

Standing at the edge of the alleyway, away from that awful stench, Henry waggled the film until an image was slowly brought forth.

An image, Henry wondered, so disturbing.

And yet so beautiful.

FIVE

IT was only a ten or fifteen minute walk from Graeme Park High School to Henry's house on Davie Morris Road. About twenty if he took the main roads.

After Henry crossed Main Street, he cut through the woods that ran behind his neighborhood, Glenn Forest. Ms. Marl Hamchild who lived across the street had warned Henry and his friends about cutting through the woods, as she did with most things that went against the norm like running in the middle of the street or throwing that damn football too close to the cars. Most of the kids who lived in Glenn Forest, Henry included, didn't quite understand half of what Ms. Hamchild said, nor did they pay much attention to her whenever she lectured. "There that nutty bitch goes again," the kids would speak among themselves, "babbling on about the end of days and how Jesus is going to come down from the heavens riding a white horse and rid all of us sinners." Two years ago, her husband, Bob, passed away from a massive stroke while the two were eating dinner and watching reruns of *Sanford and Son*. It happened right there in front of Marl, trying to revive her husband as he took his last breaths in a plate full of chicken tetrazzini. Now, as with most of the residents in Glenn Forest, Ms. Hamchild lived by the window and meddled into her neighbors' affairs. Like Mr. Hamchild, most of the residents in Glenn Forest used to work at the Smithen Steel Mill. Now, the mill was nothing more than a ghostly, rusty, derelict building—a Mecca for vandals. Parents warned their sons and daughters not to go near the old mill. Otherwise, they preached, you could catch lockjaw. Just the name alone, *lockjaw*, frightened the kids enough, but not all of them. The only downfall of the shortcut was that Henry had to creep through Ms. Craft's lawn, the house at the end of the street. During the ten years Henry had lived on Davie Morris, he hadn't even met Ms. Craft. Hadn't even given her that neighborly wave. That went for most of the residents on the street. About seven years ago (three years after Henry and his mother had moved to Reddington from Courier Point, a small town outside New Orleans) when Henry was around the age of eight, Ms. Craft moved from upstate New York to Glenn Forest—at least that was what Henry had heard from Ms. Hamchild. Yet, the house appeared as if it was abandoned from its overgrown shrubs and uncut grass in the front lawn to its molded siding and weathered shutters. Henry had only heard things from his mother, who would on several occasions complain about Ms. Craft's house being an "eye sore," as well as his small clique of friends, who lived no more than a few minutes away in either direction of his house. From the group of friends, T.J. was the only one who had actually *seen* Ms. Craft with his own two eyes. Others, including Henry himself, had only seen glimpses of Ms. Craft whenever she apprehensively poked her head out from the front doorway like a mouse from its hole or scuffled like a beetle toward the mailbox. However, his friends had never actually "seen" Ms. Craft up close, only from a distance. Another one of Henry's friends, Danny, the "big-boned" one of the group, once asked Henry if he knew anything about exorcists. Of course, Henry didn't have the slightest clue of what Danny was talking about. "When you look into her eyes," Danny explained, "you'll become possessed by demons. Your parents will need to call the best exorcist in town to cast out all of the demons trapped inside you. Pea soup, Henry," he emphasized. "Think about it. *Pea soup.*" Five years ago (when T.J. was around ten years old), he and his cousin from up North, also known as Snowbird, were wandering around Glenn Forest looking for adventures, when they crossed Ms. Craft's back lawn. In all fun, T.J.'s cousin from up North flipped off T.J.'s hat and threw it to the ground. When T.J. went to fetch the hat, he felt a mighty presence looming over his shoulder. He glanced up, eyes bulged like a bug, and witnessed Ms. Craft standing there behind the porch door. She was glaring down at him with these beady black eyes and expressionless face. T.J. was surprised; in fact, terrified. He and his cousin from up North darted into the woods and never looked back. That night, during a sleepover, T.J. told the rest of his friends, including Henry, about Ms. Craft. Somehow, the story had eventually turned into one of great horror. His cousin from up North was actually the one who started the rumors. From that point on, the gossip spread like wild crabgrass. A year later: "Did you hear about the woman who lives in the cul-de-sac? They say she's possessed by demons," or "She can strike terror into the hearts of young boys." Two years later: "They say she's got creatures living in her house. At nights, you can hear them banging around in the basement." Three years: "They say she *IS* a creature. . . half serpent, half spider!" Four: "She is *THE* face of evil." Whenever Henry or his friends passed Ms. Craft's house, they always did so with extra caution, mindful of this mythical presence or, as they presumed, this spawn from the depths of Hell.

As Henry passed Ms. Craft's house (not thinking much about the half serpent, half spider lady, but that dead dog from earlier), he shot a glance over at her house. She was somewhere there behind those windows, he thought, waiting and watching and listening. He thought he saw a pair of eyes behind the cracked blinds slightly bending farther downward. He didn't think twice about quickening his pace. And did so in a timely fashion.

*   *   *

When Henry arrived at his house, he marched straight up-stairs to his bedroom. Stationed around the room were a couple of keyboards, including the one Uncle Charlie had bought him, the Casio. He had a large bulletin board with comic book sketches and drawings that he had drawn when he was younger: Batman, Superman, and even his own creations like Saxophoneman. On the far corner of the board was a blue ribbon for second place in the science fair. Henry did a project on *How Much Force is Exerted To Break a Basketball Backboard?* He had gone through ten different basketball goals and ten different participants around Reddington, as well as Harrietsville, the town over, which shared the same county, Baritone County. On the drawer sat a novel by George Orwell called *Animal Farm*, which Henry had finished reading two summers ago. On the other side of the room, he had two Mr. Vortex posters hanging on the walls, a black and white one that was blown up from a concert performance in Nashville and the other from the cover of the *Sleepwalker* album. Below the posters sat a lava lamp. Next to that were an incense candle and a pack of matches, and then next to that was a lopsided bookshelf that he had painted scarlet red. On the shelves were VCR tapes, mostly horror and science fiction movies from the late 70's and early 80's.

Henry placed the photograph of the dead dog in a shoebox of similar photographs. Then, he grabbed the piggy bank from the nightstand and emptied it out onto his bed. What he thought was twenty-nine dollars and eighteen cents was actually *twenty-four* dollars and *two* cents. He completely forgot about buying T.J. and Skip a round of slushies from a dare that he lost, which cost him two dollars and sixteen cents. As far as the other three dollars, he had spent it on a nickel bag of marijuana that Danny had bought from his older brother, Andrew, who claimed it was middle grade, or mids, but was actually swag from a brick of Mexican weed. The stuff, grounded up like coffee beans, which Andrew swore wasn't oregano, smelled like dirt; and when they smoked it in a joint, the weed crackled and popped like Rice Krispies from all the seeds and stems in it. Henry ended up taking an aspirin from the nagging headache that he had gotten from the joint.

"Only two hundred," Henry sharpened his eyes inquisitively and solved the math in his head, "twenty-five dollars and ninety-eighth cents to go."

Even though his mother was at work, Henry tiptoed into her bedroom downstairs and rummaged through the chest of drawers. Above the chest, her diploma from Edmond High was suspended on a frame on the wall next to the brass Jesus crucifix. He wouldn't dare touch Jesus. Otherwise, his mother would probably ground him for an eternity. So, Henry started with the top drawer. He opened up the drawer, only to find a bunch of old and crinkled envelopes addressed to his mother, *Ms. Abbey Burl: 9832 Davie Morris Road, Reddington, Peregrine (PR) 39887*. Each envelope was from a person named Buddy Egghorn, who was from somewhere in Lansford. He moved down to the next drawer and then the bottom. At first, Henry wasn't aware of the purple, glossy, phallic-shaped device in his hand. The first thing that popped into Henry's mind was a Popsicle or a toy dagger, not the other thing. *Anything but the other thing*, Henry thought. The strange device was neither cold nor held on one of those sticks with a hidden fortune or, like the "other" thing, shaped like a rubber dildo.

It couldn't be?

Henry cautiously raised the tip of the device to his nose.

As he placed the device inches away from his face and caught a faint odor over the tip, he accidentally hit a switch on the bottom.

Henry drawled, "Oh God. . . "

As soon as he pulled the vibrating device from his nose, he realized exactly what he was holding in his hand. The distinct smell of the device brought forth a memory, one in which Henry would never forget. The movie *Predator* was released June of '87. Three weeks leading up to the big release date, Henry and T.J. had marked their calendars. What better way to kick off summer: a badass alien hunting Special Forces in the middle of a jungle! Even though there wasn't the slightest chance in the hell that they were going to be able to attend the movie nor was either of their parents going to buy them a ticket for the R-rated movie, they still kept their hopes up. So, in those three weeks prior to the movie release, it was like planning a bank robbery. Their friend down the street, Danny, knew a guy in fourth period who knew a guy who tore tickets at the Twin Falls Cinema. Danny told the guy about their dilemma and how they "needed" to be inside that movie theatre when the curtains lifted, the lights darkened, and the opening credits started to roll. Danny's guy came through as he said he would and hooked them up with seats away from the adults in the very back of the theatre. Toward the end of the movie, T.J. sneaked out with April Wallace, a ninth grader, where they fooled around behind the bushes in the back of the theatre. After the movie was over, Henry and his friends were all chilling in front of a gift shop next door when T.J. came barging into the rowdy group with his two fingers, index and middle, held closely in front of him while April Wallace was standing with her other girlfriends, all of whom were giggling at T.J. When asked where T.J. went during the movie, he teasingly waved his bloody fingers underneath Henry's nose, accidentally giving him a "Yosemite Sam." At the time, Henry had only rounded first base with a girl, so he didn't quite understand why T.J.'s fingers were all covered in blood and why they smelled almost like his mother's perch. Henry thought about the gorgeous Bradford Pear trees on Main Street. The tenth graders called them "Pussy Trees." At the time, most seventh graders—or soon to be eighth graders like Henry—were unaware of the meaning behind the name, the Pussy Tree, or the certain smell that the trees had given off every spring. When the evening was winding down and the rest of Henry's friends parted ways, T.J. finally broke the news to him. So that's what it means. . . The feel of the device, even the thought of where the device had been, made him gag. The peanut butter and jelly sandwich that he ate for lunch suddenly made an abrupt climb from his stomach. Henry covered his mouth and tried to think of something else, (FAST!) something boring like golf or a game of Scrabble or fishing, to prevent himself from blowing chunks all over his mother's underwear drawer. He quickly turned off the smelly device, threw it back into the drawer, and rushed to the sink where he scrubbed his hands with a bar of soap until they were nearly raw.

After the minor gross-out tapered off, Henry wandered over to the closet. He certainly couldn't sell any of his mother's dresses or coats or scarves, which she had a lot of. She knew her clothes down to the very fabric. He kept rummaging, though. During the whole time, he thought about items that would sell like hotcakes on the streets. What were everyday people interested in? The answer: jewelry. At least this was what he thought. The main difference between his mother's jewelry and the jewelry found downtown on Billings Street was that his mother's jewelry was real. He knew he could easily make enough money to buy the Jagger saxophone with his mother's jewelry. He walked back over to the drawer and opened up the chest of jewelry. His mother had so much, enough to please any long lost pirate. A beam from the sun sliced through the blinds and shone over the jewelry, now glistening in Henry's big round eyes. Most of the jewelry had been handed down from Henry's mother's mother and her mother before her—at least that was what she had said. *If I took two or three necklaces* that she never wears, he thought, maybe she wouldn't know. *I can easily replace them with fake ones. I've seen ones like these on the streets. The kind that make your neck turn green.* Two or three necklaces turned into a handful of necklaces, about five rings, and two golden bracelets. Just to be safe, Henry snooped around some more.

After he left his mother's bedroom, he moved the search into the upstairs hallway where he came across the attic.

With the jewelry stuffed securely in his pockets, he pulled down the attic door and hit the light switch on the side of the wall. The light never came on in the attic. Again, he hit the switch as if he was doing it all wrong the first time around. Again, the light never came on. Henry grabbed a flashlight from the closet and went back to the attic. The joints and springs on the ladder were all tarnished and corroded. In three forcible tugs, he yanked down the creaking ladder, carefully unfolded the ladder, and climbed up each step vigilantly and observantly. It was hard to see anything at all from the dust in the air.

After a thorough sweep, Henry stepped into the attic and inched his way through, clearing the dust from his face. He stumbled across several boxes of old toys that he used to play with when he was younger and came dangerously close to stepping through the pink insulation between the planks. From trucks to stuffed animals to action figures, they were all there collecting layers of dust. It didn't seem so long ago when Henry was playing with these very same toys. Times had gone. Interests had changed. Things had faded. Nonetheless, the sight of the toys brought a smile to his face, as well as a sudden emptiness that Henry couldn't explain.

Next, Henry came across yet another box. Inside were trophies, one from last year. He picked up the one trophy with a gold figure of a boy sculpted in a shooting stance. The silver plaque underneath read *"M.V.P. 1988."* Underneath that: *"Henry Uriah Burl."* He placed the trophy back into the box and snooped around some more. He shined the light on another dusty box with the word *MAGAZINES* written in capital letters on the side. He cracked open the torn flap and found a boxful of his mother's vintage *Vogue* magazines. She had every single issue up until 1978, the one with Rosie Vela on the front cover. Audrey Hepburn, Jacqueline Basset, Kelly Emberg—to name a few—were all women whom his mother had once adored. As he leafed through the magazines, he remembered his mother taking them everywhere they went: the doctor's office, the dentist, even the clinic, anywhere they had to wait for a good amount of time. Now, the magazines were put with the other "things." Henry moved the flashlight around the attic. The sharp beam of light cut through the darkness like a sword through the bloated belly of a beast and finally struck a mysterious box underneath the recess.

Intrigued, Henry shuffled over to the recess, pulled out the flimsy, partially ripped box, and shined the flashlight inside.

With his hand, he cleared the dust away and looked inside.

"*Records. . .*" Henry said with astonishment. "I. . . I've never seen these before. . . "

Henry moved the box away from the clutter of junk and planted himself over the clearing. There, he feverishly flipped through the records as if it was Christmas morning. His eyes landed on one name in particular. Gasping, he pulled the record from the collection and held it to his face. The record title was called *Hard Rider*. The artist's name: *Mr. Vortex*. He was wearing these big red sunglasses (futuristic-like) that looked like something one would see in a Stanley Kubrick movie. The white leather gloves were what really sent Henry over the edge. Same with the red leather jacket that he was wearing. Red shoulder pads like a hockey player. One of the shoulder pads was covered in metal spikes! Like Mad Max, Henry remembered. Rested against the other shoulder was the body of the saxophone. Mr. Vortex was holding the saxophone almost as if was a club. He had a precisely shaved beard that outlined his narrow face. Wide nose. Dark eyes. Sharp chin. As far as the rest of the band, they remained in the background like shadows. Henry wasn't the least interested in the band mates. He couldn't keep his eyes off the legendary Mr. Vortex, aka White Paw. Henry owned all of Mr. Vortex's cassette tapes. But never a record! His face lit up with incredible delight. Except for the fact that he hadn't heard of any of these other artists in the box, maybe the Doppler guy, Henry knew he was sitting on a gold mine. *Nobody really buys records like these anymore*, he thought as he flipped through the remaining records in the box, at least not the majority of people. *But for the people who still listen to vinyl, they'll pay a fortune! They will! I just know it!* Since they didn't own a record player, Henry and his mother, he couldn't find much use for the Mr. Vortex record other than hanging it up on the wall next to his other Mr. Vortex posters. Half of these records would be enough to buy the sax, *easily*. And the other half, well, Henry could just keep for himself. Who knows when they might come in handy one day? After the debate, Henry dusted off the box and lugged it downstairs without trying to trip over anything.

On the way out, Henry was left at a standstill from the disgruntled bellows of an untamed stomach rumbling throughout his body. He made a quick pit stop in the kitchen. *Who knows how long I was going to be out there?* Before he left the house, he scoured through the pantry for a bite to eat. With no luck, he moved his quest for food to the refrigerator. There was only an opened package of hot dogs and a couple of TV dinners. On a normal day, the hot dogs would seem appetizing: stick the weenies with a fork and hold them over the stovetop, cook until there was a fine char, douse them in yellow mustard, and then roll them up into a slice of white bread (no crust, of course). However, on a normal day, Henry wouldn't have come across his mother's "secret" toy. The sight alone of the hot dogs brought back the same grotesque feelings that he felt while snooping around his mother's dresser.

He tossed the package of hot dogs inside the refrigerator and wandered back over to the pantry. His eyes danced across each shelf. Henry couldn't go wrong with his favorite: Oreo cookies.

He grabbed a handful of cookies and stuffed them in his pocket.

Before Henry could cast out a single thought in his head from the recent discovery in the attic, he was on the corner of Main Street and Billings with a partially torn box of dusty records at his feet and both pockets full of his mother's jewelry and Oreo cookies. He took eight sellable necklaces (mainly, the heaviest ones) and hung them around his forearms, four on each. He received a couple of bites from a couple of people: one, a mother of two; and another an Asian man who was trying to haggle down a necklace for only ten bucks. Henry kept at it, though.

Exhausted from waiting around, Henry decided on a different approach, which was exactly that, to approach people, especially the ones who looked as if they had money, nice clothes, big hair, and nice cars. That was the key component: the nice cars.

As the day winded down, Henry ended up with not a cent to show. All he had received were cold shoulders, rolling eyes, and those two disheartening words *get lost.*

While Henry was quietly sitting on the curb of Main Street with his mother's jewelry dangling over his arms and cookie crumbs scattered over his pants, a couple of families, mothers and fathers and children, all in a state of elation, passed by. The sight of these families caused Henry to cringe in anger.

He didn't know why.

They just did.

SIX

IT was getting late, close to dinnertime.

Henry had eaten all of the cookies, mostly.

Leftover cookies, all without icing, were dispersed around him like dominoes.

In about an hour and an half, his mother was going to come home from work. If there wasn't something in the freezer to heat up like a TV dinner or a frozen pizza, then Mondays usually consisted of takeout, which had bought Henry an extra fifteen minutes or so. However, food was the last thing on his mind.

As Henry prepared to call it quits and head on back home, a handsome man with bleach blonde hair, who was wearing a

burgundy suit and a black turtleneck underneath, was towering over Henry.

"Hey you!" the man said superiorly, pulled one hand from
his pocket, and pointed at the torn box of records on the
sidewalk. Henry could already tell that the man had sifted
through the records from the disorganization as well the
longer tear in the box. "I see you got some nice records in
here. You trying to get rid of them?"

Startled, Henry anxiously rolled his eyes up at the tall,
well-dressed man.

"Eee. . . eee. . . efff. . . if the price is ra. . . ra. . . right."

Henry stood from the curb and faced the man.

The man pulled out a gator skin wallet and cracked it far
enough open for Henry to watch a tidal wave of hundreds
spill out.

"I'll give you one-fifty for the entire box."

Henry snorted.

"Th. . . th. . . three hundred," he said and glared at the
man.

"Okay," he said in disgust. "I see. How about two-
hundred?"

"Ta. . . ta. . . two se. . . se. . . eventy-five."

"What the hell's a matter with you, kid?"

"I ain't no kid."

"I can't understand you," the man exclaimed as the corners of his face turned red with anger. "Speak up."

"Two seven. . . "

The man was shaking his head and muttering under his
breath, "You gotta to be kidding me."

"Ta. . . two seventy-five!"

"Two-fifty," the man said austerely, placed one of his
hands over his hip as if he was going to be here for a while,
and glared back at Henry. "Take it or leave it."

The man held out his wallet in front of him, taunting
Henry—or at least that was what Henry thought. Of course,
this was not the man's intention at all, to taunt Henry. For
Henry, though, the man was practically telling him: "Go on.
Take it, you stupid punk. I dare you." Henry couldn't keep

his eyes from diving into the wad of cash inside the wallet. Plenty enough money to buy the Jagger.

Once more, Henry glanced down at the records below. That one particular record, *Hard Rider*, just so happened to be in the front.

Henry suddenly snatched the wallet from the man's hand.

The man shouted out, "HEY!"

Before the man could grab Henry by the collar, he picked up the box of records and sprinted down Main Street. The man followed Henry for about half a mile until he was out of breath.

After taking a left on Davidson Street, cutting through an alleyway, and then crossing a busy intersection, Henry finally made it to the woods. As he leaped over a damp trench on the side of the road, a couple of records slipped from the tear in the box. He didn't bother to turn back around. Yet, he kept running as if the man was still on his tail, even though the man had stopped some time ago. Henry ran deeper into the woods. The box was starting to wear him down. Over countless times, he had to readjust the box in his grip in order to keep it from falling. As his legs weakened, he suddenly stumbled over a severed tree stump. The records came pouring out over the ground while Henry landed face-first in the mud. Two of the records were completely ruined, one of them broken in half and the other caked with wet mud.

As Henry cleared the mud from his face, that same record, *Hard Rider*, was lying there on a patch of weeds. He pulled himself up, picked up the Mr. Vortex record, and left the rest of the records behind.

While he was both running and scraping the leftover mud from his face at the same time, he turned his shoulder and checked once more on the man's whereabouts in the distant woods. The man was nowhere around; in fact, the man had flagged down a police officer near Holiday's and was now giving a description of Henry's profile.

As Henry turned back around, he found two tiny white lights settled over a pair of red lights directly in front of him.

Before he had a chance to make out the alien light, he felt the warmth of an exhaust pipe blowing in his face.

His face went blank.

Eyes widened!

At the last second, Henry dove out of the way of the reversed car. His left leg made contact with the back of the car and flipped him like a coin in the air.

When he finally landed, he hit the side of his head on Ms. Craft's driveway.

The car slammed on its brakes, tires skidding over the pavement.

A car door swung open with a panicked woman hurrying outside.

The woman rushed over to Henry, who was lying on his back and drifting in and out of consciousness. The last thing Henry saw before blacking out was an older, graceful woman kneeling over him. She was wearing a black wool coat that stretched down to her ankles and a black knitted beret over her curly white hair. Her face was blurry and layered with a caramel color, her words distorted. She said her name was "Dolores" or something like that.

SEVEN

BY the time Henry woke from his nap, Abbey was already walking through the front door of the house. He listened carefully to the velocity of his mother's movements, wondering what kind of day she had (good or bad?), the keys jiggling and jangling and then being tossed over the kitchen table. Of all the sounds, including her oversized purse, which sounded like a maraca shaking everywhere she went, the jiggling of the keys had gathered most of his attention.

He cleared the blur from both of his weary eyes and rotated his head over his shoulder.

The time read "8:15."

For years, Henry had gotten used to the sounds of his mother, her patterns and routine. The one sound that drew the most interest was the purse and why it sounded exactly like a maraca. Henry once asked his mother about the purse and why it sounded the way it did and how it didn't sound like the other mothers' purses. She said it came from her medicine or "crazy pills," as T.J. called them (of course, behind Henry's back). Her most patent sound, besides the purse, was the way she walked up the stairs, how one step was louder than the other from her so-called natural limp. This time the sound of his mother strangely comforted Henry (not the jiggling sound or the rattling from her purse), whereas before it would send an alarming chill through his body.

At first, Henry didn't know how he ended up in his bedroom or on his bed for that matter. Once his fingers rubbed across the knot over his forehead, it took him a couple of seconds to realize that he was involved in a car accident. He also had a bandage on the side of his cheek. On the edge of the nightstand, a glass of water was perspiring over a napkin folded in a perfect triangle. Henry found a note next to the glass.

As Henry pulled himself across the bed, he heard his mother calling his name from outside the bedroom.

She was now rattling (?) closer.

Henry quickly rolled out of bed.

The sudden movement sent a rush of blood into his head.

Once the dizziness wore off a little, Henry read the note.

"*I have some items that belong. . .*" he read from the note.

"Henry!" Abbey exclaimed from behind the door. "You up here!"

Henry stuck the note in his pocket.

"Henry, why aren't you answering me?"

Two hard knocks on the door!

Suddenly, the door handle jiggled, which sent a ripple of fear through Henry's body.

As she opened the door, Henry turned the other way and plowed his bloodless face into the pillow.

Dressed in a purple blouse that she had worn to her job underneath the teal Depot apron, his mother stood at the doorway with her hands planted on her hips.

"What are you doing up here?" she asked with both relief and confusion from the sight of her son.

No response from Henry, who was now shaking from the sudden memory.

Abbey paused and foolishly tilted her head.

"Okay, you possum," she said sternly. "Play time is up. Go on now."

With his back turned to Abbey, Henry cracked open his eyes. He couldn't help but feel the presence of a corpse-like hand reaching over his shoulder. The hand was not his mother's. Yet, the hand was from *something* else. The veins of the hand were nearly black. The skin had a greenish tint, scabrous too. And the nails were long, brown, and gnarly like ones from a subterranean creature. Henry shivered and stirred, which brought relief to his mother.

"Henry please," she said and touched Henry over the shoulder. "It's been a long day."

Henry brushed away the sudden scare and slowly rotated his head around his shoulder only to find his mother.

"You're in bed early," she said, her concerned tone raised a bit. "Is everything all right?"

"Uh. . . " he uttered, ". . . fine."

Abbey squinted her eyes.

"What are you up to?" she asked, shifting her weight to one side of her body. "You're hiding something. Come on." She waved her hand as if she wanted something from her son. "Out with it."

Henry removed the pillow from his face, revealing his injuries.

"Henry!" Abbey cried out and limped around the bed.

She leaned closer to Henry.

"What in the world happened to your face?"

"I fell."

"You fell?"

"In the woods," Henry said with hesitation and yet somehow the words rolled fluently from his tongue. "I tripped over a log and fell."

"You got to be more careful, son." Abbey carefully hovered her hand over the wound and then ran her bare fingers over the knot.

Henry suddenly hissed in pain and pulled his head away from his mother's hand.

"Mom!"

Again, the words, or better yet, the word just came flowing from Henry's mouth without pause or stammer or lack of confidence.

"Sorry," Abbey said innocently and sat down next to Henry on the edge of the bed, which caused Henry to sit upright and slide to the other end of the bed. "Well, it's a good thing it's raised. Otherwise, we'd be at a hospital right about now." She sighed from her son's distance. "Was T.J. with you?"

He said under his breath, "Yeah."

"Were you two horsing around?"

Henry shook his head.

Abbey extended her head forward into Henry's range of vision.

"Henry? Were you?"

Henry saw his mother in the corner of his eye, the glare.

"No," he said.

"No what?"

"No, ma'am."

Abbey scanned over her son with suspicion.

With a closed mouth, she sighed and said, "Come on. I'll make you something to eat."

Henry responded with a nod.

Abbey let out a grunt as she stood to her feet.

"Come down when you're ready," she said.

Before Abbey left the bedroom, she glanced over her son once more and noticed something different about him. She didn't care to voice it. Yet, as she did with a lot of things, she kept it to herself and went on her way.

Henry pulled the note from his pocket and read the rest of the note.

It read: "*. . . You know where to find them.*"

Them, Henry thought as he pulled his eyes toward the floor. *The records and jewelry. . .*

Henry frantically searched around his pockets and came up empty.

. . . and the wallet!

After Abbey said goodnight, Henry piddled around his bedroom until his mother fell asleep. He had the process down to a science. For a single mother working two jobs, one as head cashier at the Depot five days a week and another as a front desk clerk at The Fifth Seasons Inn on Friday and Saturday nights, plus taking care of a teenager, which was, in a way, like a full time job, it didn't take long for Abbey to doze off.

Once Abbey turned out the light, she was *usually* out within five minutes, which was after she did her nightly routine: brush her teeth, floss, step on the scale to weigh herself, and then take her meds.

Tonight was different.

In the bathroom, Abbey carefully positioned all of her nightly pills like a front line on the edge of the vanity. She had white ones, blue ones, and even orange ones—each pill designated for a specific purpose.

As she downed the first pill—the white one—with a glass of water, a gentle breeze eased through the cracked bedroom window and grazed the backside of her neck. The breeze blew like a whisper in her ear. The cool touch of air suddenly pulled her from the sink. Both of her eyes crept toward the bathroom mirror. In the mirror's reflection, the curtains waved starting from the bottom to the top. As the curtains revealed the darkness of night outside the bedroom window, the night came alive, slipped over the windowsill, and slowly took shape over the floor. Abbey turned her shoulder and looked away from the reflection. The curtains were much calmer now—more or less, pulsing. Without looking at the reflection, Abbey grabbed the blue pill from the vanity and downed it without even a sip of water. Next, she downed the orange pill with a mouthful of saliva. When Abbey was done with the fourth pill—the one she saved for special occasions—her eyes mistakenly crossed the mirror. The night was closer now, more humanly. She heard a feeble moan in the night. The moan was resonant and broken and sounded like an old door squeaking open. She turned off the lights, exited the bathroom, locked the window, and slipped her body underneath the covers of her bed until the fourth pill worked its magic.

Six minutes later, Henry peeked over the banister and noticed that all the lights were off downstairs. Robotic in all his movements, he went back into his bedroom, cracked the window, and carefully scaled down the trellis along the peach-colored siding, which was cracked and weathered from years of wear. He practically knew each foot hole on the trellis as well as the ones that creaked. He knew that one creaked. Then. . . that one right there. . . wait a second. *Creak!* Henry hung on like a chameleon trying to blend into its environment. Hard to do, actually, considering he was wearing a sky blue shirt and black shorts and the trellis was all white. Since Henry wasn't much of a sleeper (in fact, he only caught a minimum of three hours a night), he learned how to master the skill of sneaking out. Over the years, he had tried the front door, the back door, the laundry window, and the garage, but failed. His mother's acute sense of hearing was like a hereditary power, a mutation similar to the comics Henry used to read. Through trial and error, the trellis was the only way of passage. Specific doors like the swoosh of the front door or the squeak of the back door or engine motors or footsteps or barking dogs, she could hear them all from the comfort of her bed. "Antennas," Henry explained to his other friends. On the nights he would sneak out, he would imagine them, his mother's ears like a serval cat, big and open, always twitching, even oscillating, as she tried to pick up the signals of a young teenager skipping out on sleep to attend nightly pranks and games with friends.

As Henry waited a minute on the trellis, he heard nothing, saw nothing either. Once it was clear, he leaped onto the lawn, which made the sound of a soft, squishing thud over the moist grass. He gazed around the street. Again, clear. Then, he set his sights on Ms. Craft's house. Nearly every light was off in every house, except for Ms. Craft's house. The blinds were also closed (not out of the ordinary).

Without any hesitation, Henry strolled up to Ms. Craft's house, rang the front doorbell, and then took several steps back from the door.

As he waited in his trembling stance, he thought he could hear the sound of an instrument playing from inside. *An organ?* Before he could pick up the song playing from inside, the instrument suddenly stopped after Henry rang the doorbell once more. Several tense moments expired. He heard the sound of footsteps behind the door and then a loud *crack*.

Slowly, the front door opened.

Ms. Craft stood close to the shadows of the door and never revealed her face.

"Can I help you?" she asked, her voice almost fragile.

"My name is Henry," he said with a tremor in his throat but no stammer, none whatsoever. "I just wanted to. . . to thank you for taking. . . for taking care of me." Ms. Craft waited there in the shadows as Henry tried to think of something else to say. "Are you going to tell my mom about what happened?"

"I've been thinking whether or not I should."

"Please don't," Henry begged abruptly. "If you don't mind."

Ms. Craft gave Henry a once over with her glistening eyes.

"I see you're doing well," she said. "You gave me quite a scare."

"If you tell my mom, I probably won't see the light of day anymore."

"I won't tell your mother, Henry," she said collectively. "But you have to do something for me."

Henry bobbed his head.

"Anything."

"You have to tell me why you stole the jewelry."

Henry grew more fidgety.

As Ms. Craft observed Henry's unsettled state (rubbing his hands, trying to clear the sweat from them), she cracked the door open wider, which caused Henry to take two more steps away from the door.

Ms. Craft said cordially, "I was going to make some hot chocolate."

Henry thought about what his mother always lectured about strangers—*Never to talk to them* or *keep your distance* or *if they offer you something to eat or drink, then you say no just like what your D.A.R.E. officer told you.* He studied Ms. Craft, her dark presence, mysterious and yet remarkably inviting. Then, Henry was thinking about all the other neighbors, a few of them as reserved as Ms. Craft. He knew them all, the reserved ones down to the first name and even the last name. He knew what most, if not all, of his neighbors did or used to do for a living. Yet, except for the awful names she had been given by the other kids, including Henry's friends, Henry knew absolutely nothing about Ms. Craft or what she did or what she used to do for a living.

Henry finally said, "Sure."

He cautiously stepped inside.

Ms. Craft closed the door behind him.

They made their way toward the living room. On the way, Henry looked over at a quiet Ms. Craft and carefully studied her face in the dim light. She was a healthy looking woman for her age. Her skin was smooth, without any sunspots (which was rare for her age), as if it had been dipped in butterscotch. She had a mole on the side of her chin, which matched the color of her eyes. Henry moved his eyes away from Ms. Craft and couldn't help but gaze at all of the memorabilia and Americana on the walls. There were old nineteen fifty and sixty and even seventy advertisements, old

Clover Soda signs and whatnot that she had collected from spending most of her young adult life on the road. There were more photographs of her and other people whom Henry did not know. There were nine of them, four of them women and the rest men. More photographs of these people standing around famous landmarks: the Grand Canyon, the Empire State Building, Stonehenge, the Great Wall of China, the Taj Mahal, several cathedrals in France and Italy, and then the Statue of Liberty. So many photographs, there were. Most of them were in black and white. However, each one brought extreme curiosity.

As Henry made his way down the hallway, he leaned in closer to one photo in particular.

"That's Cool Con and the Jimmies," he said ecstatically. "And Captain Smoothheart! And all five members of The Desolates!"

"That's right," Ms. Craft said, smirking.

"Were you famous?"

More photographs on the walls. Most of them were taken with a group of other musicians and rock stars. Most of them Henry knew from watching them perform on television.

Ms. Craft pointed at the couch.

"Have a seat, Henry."

Henry recognized the same gorgeous woman, who had that same mole as Ms. Craft, from all of the other pictures in the foyer behind Ms. Craft. She and another man were posing together in a photo booth, which had been blown up and framed on the wall. The man had a finely trimmed beard with long, lush hair that ran down his shoulders. The couple was posing in these goofy-looking faces with their tongues held outward and their eyes bulged.

On the way to the couch, Henry pointed at the photograph.

"Is this you?"

"That is me," she said casually and walked into the kitchen. "Well, that *was* me."

Henry glanced over at Ms. Craft and then at the photograph. After another glance, he could see her there, what her face used to look like. Now, it was hidden behind a thin layer of wrinkles and gray hair.

She placed a pot of milk over the stovetop and dialed up the heat.

While the milk was warming, not boiling, she walked over to the cabinet and pulled out two Christmas mugs.

"Do you like marshmallows, Henry?"

"I guess."

"Me," she said. "I can eat them straight from the bag."

Henry gazed around the living room and said, "So, do you ever sleep around here?"

"Not as well as I used to," she said smoothly. "Do you?"

Henry shrugged.

"Not really."

"We have something in common after all."

"What do you mean?"

"We're both night owls."

Henry chortled.

"Yeah," he said. "I guess so."

"A guy your age needs his sleep. It's all in the growing process. But. . ."

After she poured the warm milk into the mugs, she placed the hot chocolate mixture into the milk. Lastly, she dropped a handful of marshmallows into the mugs. She walked back into the living room and handed Henry the mug.

". . . but what do I know?" she said sarcastically. "I'm just a evil ole witch."

"You don't look evil to me."

Ms. Craft smiled.

For some reason, Henry felt comfort in the smile. It was like the awkward exchange of strangers had vanished.

He blew into the cup and then sipped from the hot chocolate.

"Thanks, Ms. Craft."

"You're welcome, Henry," she said. "You can call me Dolores."

With the cup of hot chocolate held closely with both hands, she sat down on a wooden bench.

Henry smiled back and sat down on the couch across from Ms. Craft.

"All right, Henry," she said with a sigh. "I know all that jewelry wasn't yours."

"It was my mom's," he answered solemnly and hung his head.

"And she doesn't know you have her jewelry."

"Yeah."

"It's a lot of jewelry," she said, thinking. "I could certainly make a lot of money out of it." She squinted her eyes and gazed upward. "Let's see. . . "

"You can't," Henry said suddenly. "You won't."

"Well, why not?"

"I was going to sell it," he said. "There's this saxophone at Holiday's Pawn Store. You know the store?"

She returned, "I do."

"Well, he's wanting two-fifty for the saxophone. Says it's a Jagger. Even showed me the name and everything."

"A Jagger. Huh? They make fine instruments."

"I figured I'd sell my mom's jewelry and then I would have enough to buy the saxophone."

Ms. Craft thought about Henry's comments.

He continued, "It's a really nice one too."

"I'll give you back the jewelry, Henry, but the wallet," she said, thinking again. "I'm definitely keeping the wallet."

"What wallet?"

"I'm not a fool, Henry, nor am I one of your little 'creatures' that you and your friends call me," she said and surprisingly remained calm. "When I was in the garden, I heard one of them call me '*Ms. Witchcraft*,' who just so happens to eat children." Ms. Craft chuckled. "I swear the kids nowadays are something else. They have quite the imagination. I have to remind myself that they're just kids. Shoot! I was probably like that at some point or another. But one thing was certain. I never disrespected my elders."

Henry threw his head in a nod.

"Do you have any children?"

"I do not."

"Ms. Craft, I mean, Dolores, I don't know why they call you those things," Henry said, his voice flattened. "They just don't really know you. That's all." He shrugged his shoulders. "Maybe they make fun of you because you're different. I don't know."

"Different?"

"Yeah."

She chuckled yet again.

"Hardly," she said and repositioned herself on the bench. "I'm a private person, Henry."

"Me too."

Again, Henry smiled at Ms. Craft and then looked around at the picture frames on the wall.

"But what about these pictures? You were famous or something? Right?"

"Or *something*," she answered and placed the coffee mug aside. "Do you really want to know who I was?"

Henry anxiously bobbed his head.

"Sure."

Ms. Craft carefully studied Henry.

"You're not like them, Henry. Your friends."

"I know," he said, hanging his head again. "They can be real bullies sometimes. Not T.J. or Danny or Arena, though. They straight. Sometimes. I guess."

"The others then," she said. "Why hang around them?"

Henry shrugged his shoulders yet again and gave her that I-don't-know kind of expression.

"Come," Ms. Craft said and walked from the living room. The layout of the house was identical to Henry's upstairs: one bedroom, a bathroom, and then a recreational room, which, at Henry's house, consisted of a miniature basketball hoop that his Uncle Charlie had bought him. Henry didn't know what to think of Ms. Craft, not yet. Not once did he seem frightened by her presence, especially the fact that she was taking him upstairs.

They both stopped at a closed door.

Then, she faced Henry.

"What I'm about to show you will change the way you think of me?"

"I'll keep it a secret," Henry said innocently. "Promise."

Ms. Craft extended her hand.

"Deal," she said and shook Henry's hand.

"So, where we going?"

"You'll see."

She opened the door and revealed the studio.

"No touching," she said sternly.

Henry was too amazed to speak. She showed him the organ (just as he thought!) as well as the piano next to a computer system. Next to the system, she had another keyboard.

"This is a Fairlight CMI!"

"You know your keyboards."

"I've seen Herbie Hancock with one of these!" Henry marveled at the keyboard. "Dang! That's off the hook!"

"Off the what?"

"It means it's cool."

Ms. Craft raised her chin.

"Ah," she uttered.

Henry hovered his hands over the keyboard.

"Remember," Ms. Craft said sternly. "No touching."

"Sure thing, Ms. Craft," Henry said and eased back his hands. "I mean, Dolores."

There were more of those photographs on the walls of Ms. Craft posing with other musicians at banquets, balls, and backstage at concerts. Then, he saw the still pictures of her singing on stage.

"You used to be a singer!"

"I was," she answered, nodding her head. "Yes. But that was a long, long time ago, Henry. Before you were even born."

Overwhelmed, Henry said, "Then why do you have all this equipment? I...I mean...this is some collection you got here."

"Most of this stuff was leftover from when we recorded *Roses For Judith*."

"Judy?"

"*Judith*," Ms. Craft corrected. "She was. . . "

Henry's eyes crossed a record hanging on the wall, which caused him to drop his jaw in awe. Ms. Craft didn't even have a chance to answer the question in its entirety. It wasn't that Henry didn't care. His attention was just all over the place. One second he was marveling over the Fairlight and the next second he was marveling over a record.

"This is a platinum record!"

Ms Craft sighed with relief, not stress.

"It is," she said humbly.

She walked over to a control board and grabbed the same record, *Hard Rider*, from the panel.

"I believe this belongs to you."

She handed Henry the record.

"Where did you get this?" she asked. "Mr. Vortex is a little old for you. Don't you think?"

"I found it in the attic," Henry answered. "I think it belonged to my mother."

"No offense, Henry," she said. "I'm not the type to judge. Trust me. I've been around my share of people throughout my career. But your mother doesn't strike me as a fan of Mr. Vortex."

"More like Aretha Franklin," he said with an edge in his voice. "Well, she was. I don't know how many times she used to sing R.E.S.P.E.C.T. to me."

Ms. Craft laughed, which caused Henry to laugh as well.

"That's a wonderful song," Ms. Craft said. "Uplifted an entire generation. I think your friends should listen to a more Aretha Franklin." Her face grew long. She mumbled, "Maybe we all need to."

"That was her favorite," he said, wandering around the studio. "But she doesn't listen to much music anymore. Not like she used to. After the cancer, all she talks about now is the ABC's."

"ABC's?"

"Academics, Basketball, and Church."

"What kind of cancer did your mother have, Henry?"

"Breast cancer," he answered. "The doctors removed her. . . you know. . . before the cancer could spread any farther."

"She had a mastectomy?"

"Yeah."

"I'm sorry to hear that, Henry," Ms. Craft said genuinely. "It sounds like your mother has been through a lot."

"She has," he said soberly. "I just wish she'd stop forcing me to do things I don't want to do."

"Like the ABC's?"

"Yeah."

"Well, she's just trying to do what's best I guess," Ms. Craft said optimistically. "And she's also entitled to her faith. We all have some kind of beliefs." She quickly changed her thought. "So, Henry, you're really serious about your music, about this saxophone. . . "

"Yeah."

Ms. Craft drifted in thought.

"I tell you what," she said suddenly and walked over to the piano. "I will pay for your saxophone, only if you return Mr. Gerry Walter's wallet as well as your mother's jewelry."

"You would do that?"

"Absolutely."

"But you don't even know me."

"No," she said. "But some people deserve a second chance. Not everybody. But some."

Ms. Craft displayed another one of those charming smiles. She dug out a wad of cash from a Japanese-designed vase on top of the piano.

"How much is the saxophone again?"

"Two hundred and fifty dollars. . . "

Ms. Craft said quietly, "That's a lot for a used saxophone."

"That what I said, but Holiday said it was 'special.'"

"Right," Ms. Craft said under her voice.

She counted two hundred and fifty dollars, placed the rest of the cash back inside the vase, and then handed the correct amount of money to Henry.

"Thank you, Dolores," Henry said gladly. "I promise I'll pay you back."

"That won't be necessary," she said flatly. "Now go on before your mother finds out that you were here. I reckon she wouldn't approve of you being here, especially at this time of night."

Henry took his belongings.

Before he exited the studio, he turned back around at Ms. Craft.

"Thanks again, Dolores."

"You're welcome, Henry."

"Well," Henry said and gazed around the studio, "good night."

Ms. Craft smiled.

"Good night, Henry."

Henry walked back downstairs and exited the house.

EIGHT

WITH only catching an hour, or two at best, of sleep, Corpus was trying to keep pace with Lieutenant Louis Reed as they shouldered their way through the crowded precinct and toward the lieutenant's office.

"I don't want to hear it, Corpus," Reed said through his resonant voice and made it to a clearing in a hallway.

Corpus returned, "Are you forgetting something?"

"What, Corpus?"

"About the gun. . . " Corpus said, ". . . and how it ended up at the crime scene?"

"I'm having lunch with Laverne in ten minutes." Reed quickened his pace. "Whatever it is, it'd better be quick."

"I traced the serial number on the Smith and Wesson Model 19 back to Dominic Gaines."

Reed abruptly stopped in his tracks.

"So where is this Gaines guy now?"

"Mason County Penitentiary," Corpus informed. "He was arrested five years ago for armed robbery. He's currently serving a twelve-year sentence behind bars."

"Then how did his gun end up on the streets, Detective?"

"It never reached the streets, Lieutenant," Corpus answered candidly. "The gun's been right here in evidence."

The comment created a globe of silence.

Reed groaned.

"I got IA crawling all over my fucking back, Detective," Reed seethed. "The last thing we need right now is to jeopardize the department's future on some. . . some lousy. . . bum. Not to mention, your job."

Reed made an attempt to flee back to his office.

With a lunge forward, Corpus suddenly stepped in his way.

"He wasn't just some lousy bum, Lieutenant."

Reed rolled his tongue around the base of his inner lip and glared at Corpus.

"Does the name Henry McClintock sound familiar?"

"Is that name supposed to mean anything to me, Detective?"

Corpus held up the file in his hand and waggled it in front of Reed's stony face.

"You might know him by his stage name: Mr. Vortex."

Reed snorted in disbelief.

"Are you serious?"

"I shit you not."

"The musician?"

"That's right," Corpus said and tilted his head. "*The* musician."

"I thought his name was Harry."

"Must've changed it while living on the streets," Corpus said casually. "Who knows? Two years ago, Mr. McClintock was arrested for disorderly conduct. Ten years prior, he was involved in an altercation with another man. He messed the guy up so bad that he had to have reconstructive surgery.

Mr. McClintock was fine. Walked away from the fight without a single scratch."

"A real contributor to society, this Mr. Vortex was."

"After he went separate ways with his band, he spent a year in Cedar Hall."

"So," Reed said under his breath, "he was a nut."

"Contacted his doctor. . . " Corpus skimmed over the file in his hand, ". . . Doctor Lowe."

"And what'd he have to say?"

"Couldn't get a hold of him."

Reed snorted.

Then, Corpus said, "Good thing we had his fingerprints on record; otherwise we'd probably never identify the body considering the condition it was in. . . "

"Did you contact the family?"

"His sister," Corpus answered. "Well," he corrected, "stepsister, Hannah Glover. She was recently released from Staten Correctional. Served a two-year sentence for possession of narcotics. It gets better. Prior to the arrest, her stepbrother slapped a restraining order on her."

"Restraining order? Sounds like one big happy family."

Corpus held up the folder and said, "Well, not big anymore. Besides having several children born out of wedlock—none of who were mentioned in the will—Mr. McClintock's stepsister is the only surviving member of his family."

"What else do we know about this Ms. Glover?"

"Well, according to the will, Hannah got all of her stepbrother's possessions, including the saxophone found at the crime scene."

"Possessions?" Reed said with his face squinting. "The man didn't have a dime to his name." The lieutenant sighed and shifted his weight in thought. "If Mr. Vortex hated his stepsister so goddamn much, enough to file a restraining order on her, then why in God's name would she be in his will?"

"The hell if I know, Lieutenant."

Once more, Reed glared at the exhausted detective.

"A high profile case like this, we can't afford to have any unwanted guests sticking their noses where they don't belong. If you know what I mean. . . "

Corpus slowly and steadily bobbed his head in agreement.

"Face it, Louis. You have a bad seed in your department."

Reed sighed once more, this time of great unease.

"Tell me something I don't know," he said and stormed off. Before he entered his office, he turned back around. "Just take my advice, Corpus. Let this one go, at least for now."

Reed hurried into his office and slammed the door behind him while Corpus stood there in the hallway with the case file in his hand. The one question that had been bothering him all day finally surfaced.

As the detective stood there in a complete state of numbness, he glanced down at the badge on his belt and asked himself, "What am I doing here?"

NINE

TO save money, Henry called a taxi from the telephone inside *Jean's Pizzeria* and spent his entire twenty-four dollars and two cents on the cab fair, which cost him just under twenty-two dollars. He used the change to tip the driver.

After Henry thanked the taxi driver and strolled through the lawn of the two-story stucco house, he pulled out the wallet from his book bag and slid out the driver's license from the holder. He compared the address from the license to the address on the front of the house. *A match*. During the trip over here, Henry thought about what to say to Mr. Walter. He mostly thought about whether he should be apologetic or should he be cold like a reptile. Most likely, Mr. Walter was at work. How else could the jerk afford a suit like that? Plus, the wallet! Made out of some kind of weird skin. The thing had to cost as much as Henry's entire outfit combined. Henry decided to stick the wallet underneath the WEL-COME doormat.

Next, he rang the doorbell.

Before the doorbell finished ringing throughout the house, he bolted like a skittish burglar from the front porch, sprinted through the front lawn, and then hurdled over the shrubbery, which was trimmed into a perfect rectangle. Mr. Walter, who was still wearing his bathrobe, a black one, finally opened the door. He checked the lawn, but Henry was already on his way to the closest bus stop. Mr. Walter glanced at his leather slippers and saw the wallet sticking out from the doormat. He picked up the wallet and counted the money inside. It was all there, every dollar bill, every credit card, every condom.

"Damn, kid." Mr. Walter pushed out a sigh, one that had been building up in his chest from the night before. He shook his head in surprise and said to himself, "Some guilty conscience." He smacked the wallet in his hand and snorted. "Some guilty conscience."

The bus stopped two blocks away from Holiday's. Henry stepped off the bus and, as he did with the taxi driver, thanked the bus driver for letting him ride. The bus driver, a stout fellow with a bushy mustache and a comb-over, wagged his finger at Henry.

"This is the last time, Henry," he scolded. "Am I making myself clear? Next time, you're going have to pay like everyone else."

With his head held downward, Henry said, "Okay, Mr. Pendergrass."

"Well, all. . . all right then," the bus driver replied, the anger easing from his voice. "I'm glad we have an understanding."

"Won't happen again."

"Good."

The bus driver closed the door.

Everything was now lined up in order: the wallet was returned to its rightful owner; the transportation was taken care of; all Henry had to do was purchase the Jagger saxophone. With the two hundred and fifty dollars that Ms. Craft gave him securely in his pocket, Henry mistakenly found himself speed walking toward Holiday's. At one point, he was actually skipping, of course, when nobody was looking.

Once he arrived at Holiday's, he went straight up to the front display glass. He saw the saxophone sitting there, part of the horn glistening from the beating sun above. His eyes traced down the neck of the saxophone and landed on the price tag. The excitement slowly wore off. Henry's face turned pale and slack.

What? Why would he do such a thing?

Henry suddenly clinched his teeth with inexhaustible rage.

Moments later, Henry was storming inside the pawnshop. His shoulders were all raised in defense. His chest was puffed out. His hands were balled into fists, ready to punch.

As always, Holiday was there to greet him.

"If it isn't my favorite—"

Before Holiday could push out another word, Henry blurted out, "Why. . . why did you change the price?"

Holiday froze with guilt.

"*Price?* Price for what?"

"The Jagger!"

"Relax, Henry," he said and held out his hands. "I never changed the price of the saxophone."

With both his hands and voice trembling from the immense anger, Henry exclaimed, "Just the other day you. . ." he paused and breathed deeply, ". . . it was two hundred and fifty dollars. Now, look at it."

"Two hundred and fifty dollars?" Holiday said with his voice chiseled with anger as well. "You need to get your eyes checked, man."

Again, Henry's chest swelled up.

"Eyes checked?"

"You heard me," Holiday said, taking a couple steps forward. "That price has been the same ever since I put it up there."

Henry turned away from Holiday.

It was two hundred and fifty dollars, he thought.

"Is everything okay, Henry?"

Henry ignored Holiday.

"No," he said. "It's not okay."

Henry stormed through the pawnshop.

Holiday tried to wave him down.

On the way to the exit, Henry glanced at the price tag.

Again, he clinched his teeth in inexhaustible rage.

"Hey, Henry!" he shouted out from behind. "Don't be doing anything stupid! You hear!"

Henry was already out the door.

TEN

AT the local Green City grocery store, Henry and T.J. were sampling from the trays of hors d'oeuvres that the local chefs and restaurateurs brought from their restaurants. For Henry and T.J., this was about as good as the two ate. Forget TV dinners or frozen pizzas. They even had caviar, both salmon roe and sturgeon, served on thinly sliced bread. For Henry and T.J., this was the only time they felt like royalty, like they belonged. The only downfall was that they had to be really quick about the process. No time to savor. One grabbed and ate while the other one stayed on the lookout for the store manager, whom they called Bigfoot due to his full beard and hairy arms and, of course, his colossal size. Danny had told the two about the legend of Bigfoot, not the mythical Sasquatch, but the "real life" Bigfoot right here in Reddington, and how he once caught eighth grader, Tad Shepard, grabbing more than his share of hors d'oeuvres. Bigfoot found out about Tad and how he nearly cleared out an entire tray of escargot. Two weeks later, Tad was still wearing Bigfoot's handprint over his arm like a brand. And that wasn't even the best part of the story. As soon as Bigfoot chased down Tad through the store and grabbed him by the arm, Tad turned around and vomited all over Bigfoot's apron. After that, it was like a chain reaction throughout the grocery store. Each customer, either standing in the checkout line or in the produce aisle or even entering the store, was vomiting from the sight of the slimy pile of snails. Some were doing it in secret behind an aisle or magazine rack while others were puking right on the produce or even on that conveyor belt thingy in the checkout line. It was quite a mess. They even had to close the store for the remainder of the day.

"Hey!" a heavyset man screamed to the top of his lungs. "This is the last time I'm going to tell you kids!"

T.J. yelled out, "Bigfoot!"

Henry stuffed the rest of the hors d'oeuvre in his mouth, turned his shoulder, and saw the colossal store manager charging at the two.

With his mouth full of hors d'oeuvres, Henry mumbled, "Rnnn, Octtttooooo. . . "

Henry and T.J. grabbed a handful of hors d'oeuvres—crackers with layers of sliced prosciutto and Gorgonzola cheese, a popular appetizer from a local restaurant called *C'est Si Bon*. The server stood there shaking his head while Henry and T.J. dashed from the grocery store with handfuls of food.

"Works every time." T.J. turned his shoulder. Bigfoot threw down his hands and shook his head in disgust as he helplessly stood at the entrance of the grocery store. T.J. turned back around at Henry. "So, you didn't answer my question. You really gonna do it?"

Henry stuffed another hors d'oeuvre in his mouth.

"Henry. . . "

With a mouthful, he muttered, "Whhhht?"

"You never answer my question."

"This prosciutto is delicious."

"Pro what?"

"Prosciutto," Henry said. "I think it's like ham."
"Gimme," T.J. said and reached for the cracker.
Henry pulled away.
"Get your own."
T.J. smacked his gums.
"Be like that," T.J. said under his breath.
"So, what do you think she'll say?"
"Who?"
"Dolores. . . "
"You mean Ms. Craft?"
"Yeah."
"Sumwhere 'long the lines 'get lost.'"
"I don't know," Henry said. "She doesn't strike me as that kind of woman."
"How you know?"
"You should've seen her house, Octo. It was like a museum. She even had a photograph of Audrey Hepburn."
"Get outta here, man," T.J. said with a laid back tone. "She used to be like an actress or sumtin?"
"I'm not supposed to say."
"I'm ya best friend, Henry. You can tell me."
"I pinkie swear."
"You done a pinkie swear wit that old lady?"
"I sure did."
"And by the way," T.J. said. "When did you start talkin' like that?"
"Like what?"
"That!" T.J. pointed at Henry's mouth. "That right there!"
"Right where?"
"Your stutta, man," T.J. said. "It gone."
"It is," he said. "Isn't it? I guess when Dolores hit me with her car, it sort of went away."
"She hit you wit her car? That's messed up."
"It was accident," he said. "She was backing up. Next thing I know, I ran into her."
"When did this happen?"
"Just the other day."

"Wondered where you got that cut on your face," T.J. said. "Does your moms know?"

"Nah," Henry said. "I just told her that you pushed me into a bush."

"Me? Why'd you go and do that?"

Henry shrugged his shoulders.

"Cuz she likes you, Octo," Henry said. "And she knows we were just horsing around."

"But we wasn't horsin' around!"

"Not what she thinks."

"You haves to tell her the truf."

"Nuh uh."

"Is to! I don't want to get on your mom's bad side."

T.J. shoved Henry.

"Don't sweat it, T.J.," he said, laughing. "You're on her good side, man."

Not too long after Henry split with T.J., he was standing on Ms. Craft's front porch repeatedly ringing the doorbell while simultaneously pounding away at the door.

The door violently swung opened.

Henry flinched.

Once he saw the strange man standing at the doorway, his face dropped in confusion.

He had to be in his thirties, he thought. *Whoever he was, he didn't look like Dolores's son.* The man at the doorway wasn't wearing a shirt. He was ripped too and looked as if he did over two hundred push-ups and sit-ups a day.

"What are you selling, kid?" the man asked coldly and slowly, grabbing the side of his head as if he just woke up from a nap.

"I'm . . . I'm not selling anything."

"Then what do you want?"

"I'm looking for Ms. Craft," he said, not showing the least amount of intimidation.

"Who?"

"Dolores. Is she home?"

"She isn't here," he said.

"Can I come in?"

Henry made an attempt to squeeze by the man.

"Whoa!"   The man threw out his arm.   "Hold up, kid. . ."

"I'm a friend of hers."

"Well, she isn't here," the man said and closed the door.

"Wait!" Henry yelled out. At the last second before the door closed, he stuck his foot alongside the doorway panel. "Where is she?"

The man glared at Henry's foot.

"She's at work," he said, his beady eyes peering into Henry's.

"And where does she work at?"

"She's doing a thing up at the church."

"Which one?"

The man sighed.

"Sister of Grace I think."

Henry didn't even say thank you to the man.

Instead, he took off running.

By car, Sister of Grace was about five minutes away. On foot, he could make it there in roughly twenty minutes.

As Henry approached Sister of Grace, he heard the organ playing from inside.

Mesmerized from the sound of the organ playing, as well as the choir singing, he moved furtively inside the church and respectfully sat down in the back pew. Henry searched for Ms. Craft, but she was nowhere around. He gazed upward at the organ pipes rising over the nave. The pipes were enormous things, like nothing he had ever seen before—at least not like the ones at his church, Reddington Baptist, which was about the size of his living room. Then, as he sharpened his peer, he thought he saw a person behind the pipes. From where Henry was sitting, the strange person appeared no darker than a silhouette.

*　　*　　*

Mass was finally over.

Henry paced around Ms. Craft's Cadillac until she finally showed up.

Dumbfounded from the sight of Henry next to her car, she uttered, "Henry?"

"Hey," Henry said unsteadily.

"What are you doing here?"

"I went to your house. . ."

A sigh shamefully pulled down her shoulders as well as her eyes and left her in a state of surrender. Her eyes inched back upward and landed on Henry.

"I reckon you met Jodi," she said disappointedly and slowly approached Henry.

"Is he your. . . your son? I thought. . ."

Ms. Craft snorted and disgracefully dropped her head.

"He is not, Henry," she answered and stood next to Henry and stared out into the pink sunset behind the church. "He is just a friend. That's all."

"You mean. . . like a boyfriend."

Ms. Craft quietly sighed.

"When you get older, Henry, you sometimes get lonely."

"You're talking about sex. Aren't you?"

Ms. Craft's eyes grew in embarrassment.

"It's all good, Ms. Craft," Henry said. "It's not my position to judge. I mean, you got to do what you got to do. Right?"

Once more, Ms. Craft snorted.

"Me," Henry said apathetically. "When I was ten, I learned about the birds and the bees the hard way. I walked in on my friend's mom doing *it* with another man."

"Henry!"

"Yeah," Henry said. "*It*."

"Oh," Ms. Craft said, her voice slightly restrained. "It. Huh?"

"I don't have a father," Henry said bluntly. "So, Mr. Cherry told me all about the birds and the bees." He rolled his eyes. "You know. . . sex."

Ms. Craft interrupted, "Why are you here, Henry?"

"Say, was that you up there playing?"

"It was."

"But I thought you didn't go to church?"

"I never said that."

"You didn't. . . " he said with confusion. "I don't know. You just don't seem like a religious woman."

Ms. Craft burst out laughing.

"You're much smarter than your age, Henry," she said. "So, why do you say that, that I'm not religious?"

"I don't know." He paused and gave his shoulders a sharp shrug. "I mean, the things in your house. I didn't see a cross or Bible. I mean, you don't seem like the rest of them."

"Rest of who?"

"Like everybody else in Reddington."

"You have keen awareness, Henry," Ms. Craft said. "That's rare nowadays, especially for a guy your age. Religion is a hard conversation. It's best that you leave it alone and just let it be whatever it wants to be. Besides, Henry, I don't mind playing for these good folks. If it helps them believe in something or if it helps them uplift their spirits, then it's all right with me." Her eyes sharpened. "It's better to believe something than nothing."

"So," Henry said, "what do you believe in?"

Once again, Ms. Craft sighed.

"To answer your question, Henry," she said patiently. "No. I don't go to church. I just play on the side."

"Why?"

"It's good money."

"About that," Henry said and grimaced a little. "The money part."

"Did you return Mr. Walter's wallet as we agreed?"

"I. . . I did," he said with his shoulders tightly raised in the air, facial expression too. "But the saxophone turned out to be more expensive than I thought."

Ms. Craft tilted her head to the side.

"How much more expensive?"

"Like two thousand more dollars expensive. . . "

"That must be some saxophone," she said and turned to Henry. "Well, if I'm going to fork out the money for this thing, I need to see it first."

Before Henry could wrap his head around the situation, Ms. Craft and Henry were strolling into Holiday's pawnshop. At the same time, Holiday was pacing over to them from the back of the store. He even ignored a customer—nearly pushed him aside—in order to stop Henry and Ms. Craft from entering the store.

"I'm so sorry, Henry," he said, the guilt worn like a mask over his face. "Right after you left, a man came in the store and bought the Jagger."

The muscles in Henry's body tightened and left him as still as a frame. Parts of his face moved and quaked. The jaw line around both sides of his face flexed into these tiny fists. His eyes were like daggers. Henry hurried over to the front display case and saw that the Jagger saxophone was no longer there, as Holiday had said.

Henry spun around to Holiday.

"You said. . . "

"I know, Henry," he said, holding out his hands. "I'm sorry. He had the money up front. What else was I supposed to do?"

"Let's go, Henry," Ms. Craft said disappointedly and then cautiously. "Let's not make a scene."

She walked Henry from the store.

"Hey!" Holiday cried out. "I'm sorry, Henry! I mean it!"

When Ms. Craft got back into the car, Henry was in the passenger seat with the side of his head pressed against the window. Ashamed to acknowledge Ms. Craft, Henry's right hand was shielding his face, mostly eyes and nose. Ms. Craft could hear the sniffling, the phlegm being sucked back into his nose, underneath the curled hand. Then, she witnessed the tears flowing down the sides of his cheeks.

Ms. Craft suddenly turned off the ignition.

"Wait here," she said, keeping that same sternness over her face.

Ms. Craft marched up to Holiday's.

Before she made it halfway to the store, Holiday greeted her outside on the sidewalk.

All Henry could see was a lot of finger pointing from Ms. Craft. In return, Holiday was doing that thing where he innocently held up his shoulders, as well as hands, as if he had been accused of a horrible crime. From what Henry observed, Ms. Craft was making Holiday appear like a fool. He was left in a state of humiliation like a dog that had just made a mess of things in a kitchen, trashed spilled out all over the floor, food thrown everywhere, and was now hearing an earful from its master. After the argument, Holiday walked back inside with his head held downward. Ms. Craft glanced over at Henry in the car and gave him a thumbs up. With the tears still glazed like icing over his cheeks, Henry tried to conceal the sudden chuckle. He wiped some of the tears from his cheeks with the backside of his hand. Struggling to look Ms. Craft in the eye, Holiday walked back outside and blindly handed a napkin to Ms. Craft. Henry rolled down the window and tried to listen in on the conversation. All he could make out before Ms. Craft marched away was the word *asshole* projecting like a missile from Ms. Craft's lips. She got back inside the car.

"What's that?" Henry asked.

She handed him the napkin.

"Just the address of the man who bought *your* saxophone."

"We can't go to his house!" Henry exclaimed. "He already bought the Jagger!"

"And I'm going to buy the Jagger from him."

"You can't do that!"

"Watch me, Henry," Ms. Craft said confidently.

The neighborhood that the buyer lived in was the kind Abbey and Henry drove through during the weekend. The houses were doubled, even tripled, the size of Henry's house. Abbey had dreams about living in Corner Heights. Every once and awhile, Abbey and Henry would pass another couple, usually mother and son, driving through the wealthy neighborhood.

Ms. Craft arrived at a Spanish style mansion with a brown tile roof and a well-manicured lawn. The driveway was guarded by two large columns and wrapped around the front of the mansion in an arch-like pattern.

As Henry gazed at the mansion in awe, he drawled, "What's his name?"

"He said his name was Simon."

"Simon?"

"That's right."

"He didn't even give you a last name?"

"Just Simon," she said and sighed. She too was left in awe from the sight of the mansion. "Nice place."

"Tell me about it."

She cut off the engine and turned to Henry, who, again, was still left in awe.

"Do you watch movies, Henry?"

"Yeah."

"The people in the movies you watch," she said. "What do they do?"

"Well, there's this one, Johnny Lame," he said as he bolted upright in the seat. "He's like a modern day Charles Bronson. In the movie *Johnny Seeing Red*, Johnny goes after these mobsters who have captured his girlfriend. He goes after each and every one of them, kills them in the most brutal way, ends up saving the girl. . . "

"That's not what I meant, Henry." Ms. Craft rolled her eyes. "What I'm trying to say is that these people, these actors like this Johnny Loser character. . . "

"*Lame*," Henry corrected. "Johnny Lame."

"Whatever," she said. "What are they really doing when you see them in the movies?"

Henry gave the question some thought.

"They're acting."

"That's right, Henry," she said. "They *are* acting. So, can you act for me?"

"I can try," he said. "Octo and I used to play cops and robbers. But that was like a long time ago."

"Octo?"

"That's my friend, T.J.," Henry said. "I'd always be the cop. Octo would be the robber. He'd end up getting away every time."

"I'm going to do a little acting, Henry," she said closely. "And I want you to play along. Can you do that?"

"Sure," Henry said innocently.

"All right," she said and leaned upright in her seat. "Here's what we're going to do. . . "

On the front doorstep of Simon's house, Ms. Craft brushed a piece of lint from her coat and made a couple of last second adjustments by lining up her collar and primping her hair.

Finally, she rang the doorbell.

"Remember," she whispered to Henry. "Johnny Lame just lost his girlfriend in a terrible boat explosion."

"Easy enough," he said and frowned.

A polished man with a finely trimmed mustache that appeared as if it was drawn on with a pencil answered the door.

"Can I help you?" he said curiously.

"Are you Simon?"

"Yes," he said tentatively and occasionally moved his eyes down at Henry. "Do I know you?"

"You don't," Ms. Craft said somberly. "But my son and I were sadly informed that you purchased a certain instrument at a pawnshop."

Simon's attention was drawn to Henry, who was loudly weeping. It had gotten to the point where the man could hardly hear what Ms. Craft was saying.

"The saxophone," he said over Henry. "Yes. Is there a problem?"

"No problem at all, sir," she said. "My son here was saving up money for months to buy that saxophone. See, the owner of the pawnshop, Holiday, was supposed to be holding the saxophone for my son. But he turned out to be a lying, mistrustful fool.”

“I would love to help, ma’am,” Simon said genuinely. “I really would. But you see, my son, I was going to give the saxophone to him as I birthday present.”

“I see,” Ms. Craft said emotionlessly, turning away from Simon. Her spirits suddenly rose. “I will pay the same price, the two thousand and fifty dollars!” She reached down into her purse. “I have the money right here. . . ”

“Wait just a minute,” Simon interrupted and extended his hand. “I didn’t pay that much money for that thing. The man charged me a hundred bucks for it. He said originally it was a different price than the one you’re asking for, the two thousand and fifty dollars.”

“Really?”

Simon said, “He thinks someone changed the price tag to a hundred dollars. He said it might’ve been one of his employees. He wasn’t sure. Anyway, he had to sell it for the price on the tag. He didn’t want to come off as some kind of ‘scammer.’”

“I see,” Ms. Craft said, thinking. “Then, today is your lucky day.”

“Listen, lady,” he said and stepped from the doorway. “It’s not about the money. My son’s been bugging me all week about this damn thing. I’m sure you understand how that must feel.”

He stepped back inside the mansion.

“Goodbye,” he said dourly and closed the door.

“But. . . ”

There was a brief silence.

Ms. Craft turned to Henry and said sincerely, “We tried, Henry.”

They both quietly walked back to the car.

As Ms. Craft pulled out of the driveway, Simon stepped in front of her car. At the same time, Ms. Craft jerked the steering wheel and slammed on the brakes.

“Are you crazy?” she cried out.

"Here," he said, carrying a leather case in his hand. He walked up to Ms. Craft's window and held out the case.

"Take it," he said.

"I don't understand."

"I said 'take it.'"

"Are you sure?"

"Take it before I change my mind," he said once more.

Ms. Craft grabbed the case and handed it to Henry. Henry opened up the case and lit up with joy, which caused Simon to smile. There it was, the Jagger saxophone, just as he imagined.

Ms. Craft dug in her purse and pulled out a check.

"Who do I make the check out to?"

Simon shook his head.

"You don't owe me a penny."

"But I have to give you something."

"Don't worry about it."

Ms. Craft pulled out a pen.

"Here. . ."

"I said 'don't worry about it,'" Simon said grimly. "My son doesn't even like music. He's more like his old man. He just wants it to show off in front of his friends."

"That is very nice of you, sir, but—"

"Forget about it," he said overpoweringly. "That's final."

"Thank you," Ms. Craft said quietly and turned to Henry.

"You're welcome," Simon replied, his eyes attached on Henry as well. "From his looks, I can tell your son will enjoy it more than mine."

"What do you say to the nice man?"

Henry said, "Thank you, sir."

Simon said, "You two take care."

Henry was so fascinated from the sight of the Jagger saxophone that he didn't have anything to say in return.

Simon walked back to his mansion.

"So," Ms. Craft said and nodded at the saxophone, "how about that?"

"I can't believe we pulled it off."

"We work well as a team, you and I."

Henry bobbed his head.

"Yeah," he said. "We do. Don't we?"

"So, what are you going to name it, the Jagger?"

Henry moved his eyes away from the Jagger and with bafflement, settled them on Ms. Craft.

"Every instrument has to have a name."

"I don't know. . . "

Henry pulled his attention back to the case and carefully thought about what to call the saxophone.

The entire ride home, Henry was thinking about what to call the Jagger saxophone. He had so many names, most of them from his favorite movies (*Johnny Lame* being one of them). Not only that, he was so fascinated by the Jagger that he was afraid to even touch the thing. His hands were hovered over the case as if he was using the case as a hand warmer.

It was night when Ms. Craft finally arrived at Henry's house. The lights were off inside, which was a good sign. Henry stepped out of the car, looked down at the case, and then at Ms. Craft. He stepped back inside the car.

"Thank you, Dolores."

He leaned forward and hugged Ms. Craft.

"You're very welcome, Henry." She embraced Henry. "You take care of it just as Simon said."

"I will," Henry said gladly.

He pulled himself away, stepped from the car, and waved goodbye.

"See you around, Dolores."

Intoxicated from Henry's excitement, Ms. Craft waved goodbye as well and said softly, "Bye, Henry."

ELEVEN

AFTER Corpus and his partner, Donnie Backer, left Josette Park in a last attempt at finding the missing bullet from Dominic Gaines' Smith and Wesson Model 19 revolver, Corpus parked the car in the desolate parking lot of a closed movie theater. On the façade of the rundown building, the N from the sign Crown was burned out as well as the C, E, M, A, S, and 22 from Cinemas 22. Some of the letters had been shattered from rocks and other projectiles. The letter N was spray painted above the burned out E of the word *Cinema*. The "SPACE FOR RENT" sign was partially torn from the front door. Vandals had kicked in the front windows and anything that broke or shattered. Crushed beer cans and broken beer bottles and marijuana roaches and cigarette butts and used needles were all peppered around the movie theatre.

Donnie wondered why Corpus stopped the car, especially in a territory that was notoriously known for criminal activity.

He asked Corpus, "Why are we stopped?"

Corpus paused and said mindfully, "How long have we been partners, Donnie?"

"Going on eight years now," he said, furrowing his brows.

"I want you to hear me out," Corpus said. "Your brother is a murderer."

"This is what you wanted to talk about: my brother?"

"I know he stole that gun from evidence, same one that was found at the crime scene."

"What are you trying to say, Al? That my brother killed this Henry McClintock guy?"

Corpus let out a sigh, loud enough for Donnie to hear, over the repetitive beat of rain as well as the constant back and forth squeak of the windshield wipers.

"I know my brother's dirty, Al," Donnie seethed with his voice climbing higher over the name *Al.* "Hell! This entire fucking department is dirty. Listen to me. I know my brother. All right! I know he wouldn't kill anybody."

"How do you explain the bruises on his knuckles?"

"What bruises?" Donnie paused. "You're opening a door, Corpus," he said as a seed of anger formed lines over his reddening face. "Wherever you're going with this, I suggest you back off before you do something that you may later regret."

"Is that a threat, Don?"

Donnie grimaced, the anger forming more clearly. He kicked open the passenger door and stepped out.

Before he stormed away, he stuck his head inside the car.

"Me and my brother have our share of problems, but I would never, I mean, *never* rat out my brother." Donnie looked over at his partner in repulsion. "Of course, you would know nothing about that."

Donnie slammed the passenger door, popped his collar, hunched over his shoulders, and walked through the rain.

As Corpus listened to the beating of the rain against the windshield, he thought about chasing after Donnie and kicking his teeth down his throat. He'd be lying if he said it wasn't the first time he thought about doing violent acts to his partner. Instead, as he always did whenever he found himself in a bind, he pulled out the photograph from his pocket. A wave of calmness washed over his face as he peered at the photograph: a beach off the Caribbean Sea, sugary white sand, palms trees, and ocean water as blue as the sky. All the violence went away. He was left with that one thought, the only one that he thought about whenever he looked at the serene photograph. For Corpus, retirement couldn't come soon enough. But would he ever find his paradise? That tranquility, once worn over the detective's face, soon melted away. Now, it was replaced with a scowl.

Corpus crumbled up the photograph, rolled down the window, and tossed it outside in the rain.

TWELVE

THE following morning, one of Henry's favorite songs was playing on MTV. When they debuted their first album *After Dark* in 1964, they were originally called Mr. Vortex and the Flying Pigs. The whole concept behind the name was briefly explained in their first music video, "From Lamb to Lion." The low budget video was done like a parody of the movie *Wizard of Oz*. Instead, Mr. Vortex (twenty-nine at the time), known as a kind of genie in the bottle type of character around the small farming town of May View, was spawned from a puddle of tears made from a young boy, not girl. Mr. Vortex swept through May View where he came across a pig farm; pigs were hoisted into the sky from Mr. Vortex's unspeakable power; the pigs grew wings as well as human qualities; Mr. Vortex supplied them with instruments; then the pigs rocked out on the peak of a mountain surrounded by raining bolts of lighting; at the end of the song the pigs returned to normal and wound up back on the farm; the sun lifted over the dark clouds; the boy suddenly woke up; the end. After *much* criticism, the band ended up ditching the Flying Pigs part and stuck with Mr. Vortex, just Mr. Vortex.

Henry turned up the volume until the speakers rattled and distorted. In one swift movement, Henry picked up the saxophone from the chair, strapped the instrument around his shoulder, and inaudibly played the bridge of the song "Lying Face," which was from Mr. Vortex's last album before the band split. The album was called *Under the Table*, which *Sphere Weekly* called "one of the most disturbing and yet beautiful Vortex records to date." The bridge was played with a staccato-like rhythm with Mr. Vortex brutishly shrieking, *"I said 'Go! Go! Go! Go! Go on, girl!' You better pack your things! Head to the door! Don't want to see your lying face no. . ."* the song abruptly came to a Grand Pause. Mr. Vortex then shrieked, *". . . NOOOOOOOOO! NO MORE!"* Mr. Vortex wiped the saxophone around his body (so did Henry) and played alongside a guitar solo. On a normal morning, Henry's mother would have to drag her son from bed. Not this morning. This morning, Henry was amped up like a Peavey. He mimicked Mr. Vortex's every movement, every detail—even down to playing back to back with the guitarists, which, in Henry's case, was a dresser. Henry swung the saxophone in front of his body, jumped back onto his bed, and played without any sound whatsoever. He didn't even blow into the saxophone, yet he acted as if he was blowing with his two cheeks ballooned out like a puffer fish.

Before Henry could really get into the crescendo, there was a sudden *pound* at the door!

Henry suddenly withdrew from character and quickly slid the saxophone underneath the bed.

Abbey barked, "Henry, what is going on in there?"

Out of breath, Henry stood upright and readjusted his clothes.

"Nuttin," he mumbled.

Abbey opened the door and found Henry standing with his hands down by his side and a guilty expression on his face.

"Shouldn't you be getting ready for school?" she asked, her voice growing louder. "And get off that bed!" She directed her attention toward the television and saw that one song, "Lying Face," playing. The sides of her face flexed in rage. "Didn't I tell you about that garbage!" She marched through Henry's bedroom and switched off the television. "Not in my house! You hear me! I don't want that man's noise in my house!"

Henry pointed to the posters on the wall and said innocently, "But it's Mr. Vortex. I thought you said. . ."

"I don't care who it is! Not in my house!"

Henry smacked his gums.

Abbey's hands fell upon her hips as she shifted her weight to one side of her body.

"What was that that just came out of your mouth?"

"Nuttin."

"You mean nothing, not *nuttin*."

"Yeah."

"Boy. . ." she said and shook her head, ". . . You better get your act together."

Henry mistakenly rolled his eyes.

"Don't roll your eyes at me!" she barked. "Watch it now before you get popped! And didn't I tell you to get off that bed and get ready!"

"Yes, Mom," he said, hanging his head.

Henry did as his mother demanded, stepped from the bed, and sauntered over to the closet. Somewhere beneath that now somber expression a smile was growing and the words *go, go, go, go* were blaring in his head.

Around lunchtime, Sergeant Stallings stopped at Reed's office.

Paranoid, the sergeant gazed around the offices behind him.

Once it was all clear and everybody seemed to be involved in other matters like bookings and working on other cases, he knocked on the lieutenant's door.

"Come in," Reed said from behind the door.

Without making any sound, Stallings cautiously entered the dark office. The blinds were almost closed and yet the little sunlight that came through the slits of the blinds shone over the lieutenant's stony face in striped horizontal lines.

"We need to seal any loose ends to this case before the press gets a hold of it," Reed said with his back facing the sergeant. "I already have Warble on my back. Says he's going to go public if we don't wrap this thing up soon."

Stallings took a seat in front of the desk.

"Can Corpus prove Backer was responsible?"

"He knows Teddy checked out the gun," Stallings informed. "However, Marson says Teddy was with him all night. His alibi just might hold up in court."

"But what about the gun, Stallings? That can't look good for our department."

"Listen, Reed," Stallings said. "I know you've practically raised that kid. After his father's death, you and Donnie were the only two people there for him. I can make this go away. I just need the green light."

Reed spun around in his chair, leaned forward over the desk—away from the light pouring in through the cracked blinds—and faced Stallings. His face was now cloaked in the shadows of the room.

"What about Corpus?"

"Corpus is harmless," Stallings said. "I wouldn't worry about him."

"Do what you have to." Reed leaned back in the chair and sipped from the steaming cup of coffee. Those lines of sunlight highlighted his sharp eyes. "But if anything happens. . . " he said, ". . . it's your ass."

In the cafeteria, Henry sat quietly at the lunch table while his closest friends, T.J., Skip, Armani, and Danny, discussed what part of the country had the best emcees (East Coast or West Coast?). His other friends, Jesse, Arena, and Devon, were sitting at the far end of the table and joking about Ms. Kilter and how she ripped a wet, nasty fart in the middle of chemistry class. Henry wasn't paying attention to either the discussion from one side or the ridicule on the other, yet he continued to sit there, quietly.

Armani noticed Henry wasn't saying much at all. In fact, he seemed as if he was trapped in his own world. *I said 'Go! Go! Go! Go!'* The peanut butter and jelly sandwich had one bite mark and was sitting there on the torn brown lunch bag.

"Hey, Henry!" Armani said and nodded at Henry. "You got the bug?"

A couple of other students directed their attention toward Henry. Again, he wasn't saying a word.

"He's probably still thinking about the saxophone that Ms. Witchcraft 'supposedly' bought for him."

"She did buy it for me, Skip," Henry said abruptly. "And her name is Dolores."

Skip mocked, "*Her name is Dolores.*"

"Chill, Henry," T.J. said. "Ain't no reason to get all mad."

"The Creature from the Cul-de-sac bought you a saxophone?"

"I swear the house is haunted," Danny interrupted and crammed the ham and cheese sandwich in his mouth. "The other day," he said while chewing, "I walked by her house and I literally felt colder. And it was like ninety degrees outside!"

"Makes sense," Armani said under his breath, took a bite of the squared pizza in his hand, and then tossed in back on the plate. While chewing the rest of the bite of pizza in the corner of his mouth, Armani leaned closer to Henry, "He just wants the saxophone so he can get some from Kerri."

Henry blurted out, "No! I don't!"

"Why not, Henry?" Armani shrugged his shoulders as he finished swallowing the bite of pizza. "I would. I'd be standing in front of her house, playing the sax like that one guy from that LL Cool J video. You know which one I'm talking about?"

"You mean 'Going Back to Cali'?"

"That's it!"

Armani acted as if he was scratching on a turntable. He even provided a scratching sound effect as well.

"That dude's only in the music video for like a second," Skip said next to Armani.

"Man! Don't be hatin'!"

"Plus that dude ain't really attracting the ladies. . . "

"He and Danny should hang out more," T.J. teased and gripped the air saxophone in his hands. "Even tilted the screen when he dipped down and hit them low notes."

"Low notes?"

"Whatever, T.J.!"

". . . not like Cool," Skip drawling out the *cool*, "J."

"Ladies love the cool J like Henry loves the K."

"That's right." Skip giggled. "Henry 'Elephant Juices' Kerri."

"Shut up."

Skip was mouthing those words *elephant juice*, which to the eye, appeared as if he was mouthing the words *I love you*.

T.J. said to the others, "That girl fine. But she a poser."

"Big time!"

Danny said over the chatter, "Did you guys see her wearing that tight spandex the other day?"

"Look at Danny over here drooling."

Danny wiped the side of his mouth.

"I'm not drooling!"

A burst of laughter.

"I be tellin' Henry that all the time."

"Whatever. . ."

"Poser or not, I'd still tap it from behind."

"Yeah, man!" Armani suddenly mocked Skip in his best Skip voice. "I'd tap that, man! Yeah, man! I do it from behind doggy style!" He rolled his eyes and waved off the cheap impersonation. "Yeah right!"

"Quit it, dude."

Armani pushed Skip on the shoulder.

"Watch it! You're going to make me spill my soup."

"By the way, who in the hell brings soup to school."

"Apparently, Skip does." Armani puckered his face. His voice was high and girly. "His mommy made it for him. His mommy says it's good for him. His mommy says it will make his bones big and strong."

Skip mumbled, "Shut up."

"So, really, Henry. How'd you get the saxophone?"

"Ms. Craft. . ."

"*Witchcraft*," Danny said over a cough.

"Ms. Craft," Henry emphasized, "she was going to buy it from Holiday's, but Holiday already sold it to some rich guy across town. She drove me all the way to Corner Heights."

"Corner Heights? No way!"

"Yes way," Henry returned. "You should've seen her. She made up this crazy story about how she was my mother and I was her poor ole son who was desperately saving up cash for the saxophone."

"Get outta here."

"It's true," Henry said. "*And* she's not what you guys think. She's nice. She used to be. . . "

"Used to be what?"

Henry completely forgot. The words simply slipped from his tongue. He tried to retrace his thoughts.

"Uh," Henry uttered. "She used to be a music teacher."

"Music teacher?"

"Well, she's still a freaking creature."

"She's not a creature," Henry said, his voice raised.

"Looks like you hit a sore spot."

"So, this 'nice' lady magically gets rid of your stutter and then buys you a brand new saxophone. Something just ain't right here. Sounds a little fishy to me."

"Yeah, Henry." Armani leaned closer. "*Fishy.*"

"Henry, you got a thing for Ms. Witchcraft?"

"No. . . "

"So, what do your moms think 'bout this sax?"

"She doesn't know."

"You know she'd kill you if she finds out."

"Like I don't know that already, Octo," Henry said. "After she left for work, I tried playing a little. It's way harder than I thought."

"What'd you think, Henry? You could jus pick up the saxophone and start playin' like Mr. Vortex or Da Blue Doppler? It takes p-r-a-t-i-c-e."

Danny mumbled, "You missed a letter, buddy."

Armani shoved Danny.

"All right, wise guy," he said. "Quit being a dick."

"Speaking of The Blue Doppler," Skip interrupted. "I found one of his records in the woods the other day, along with a whole bunch of these other oldies, half of them I haven't even heard of."

"Records?"

"Yep," Skip said to Henry. "I took them down to Holiday's and got almost three hundred bucks for them. Can you believe that? Three hundred big ones for a bunch of garbage."

"Hey!" Henry shouted out. "Those were my records!"

"Not anymore. They ain't."

"I dropped them when I was being chased."

"Chased? By who?"

"Mr. Walter."

"Who's Mr. Walter?"

"Henry stole his wallet," T.J. said. "And then took off in the woods."

Henry elbowed T.J. in the arm.

"What?"

"It all makes sense now," Danny said. "You were being chased by this supposed 'Mr. Walter' in the woods and then Ms. Witchcraft 'accidentally' ran into you with her car." Danny's voice turned sarcastic. "Yeah. That does make a lot of sense."

Henry hesitated.

"That's not what happened, Danny."

"You know, Skip. You should give Henry at leas haf of that money. I mean. They is his records."

Danny rolled his eyes.

"Change the subject," he said and cringed his teeth. "This is a conspiracy. This is what this is."

"Finder's keepers, Octo."

"He's got you there."

Henry sighed.

"About this saxophone, Henry," Armani said. "When we going to see it?"

* * *

When school was over, Henry took his friends back to his house.

Gathered around Henry's bed, Skip, Armani, and Danny were passing around a joint of swag that Skip had rolled over a grammar textbook. Since T.J. didn't have a hard surface to play on as he usually did during school (mainly his wrists and knuckles pounding over any hard surface that he could find like a desk or a lunch table), he supplied a generic beat with his mouth for Skip and Armani to rhyme over. Danny didn't rhyme. Wasn't the type. Instead, Danny sat there on the floor (eyes red and squinting from the weed) and stuffed his face with barbeque potato chips and provided commentary.

Armani led: "*It's Armani. That's right. But not like the fashion designer. I'm a designer, however, a designer of lyrics, spitting from my lips, seeping directly into your cerebellum.*"

"Weak," Skip blurted out and slowly dragged from the joint.

"You try then, Brainiac," Armani said.

Skip blew a couple of smoke rings from his mouth.

"Dude!" Henry suddenly blurted out from his bed. "How many times do I have to tell you? Through the filter."

Danny said, "Yeah, Skip. If Henry's mom finds out that we were smoking in here, she would string us up by our freaking balls, man."

"Nah, boy!" Armani said with his best Ms. Burl impression. "She's gonna go to her room and get the shoe on you, boy!"

With a trace of sarcasm, Henry said under his breath, "And you sound just like her, Armani."

"Scary."

"Good thing I brought Visine."

"And cologne."

"If you're so worried about Henry's mom, then why don't we just go to Danny's house? His parents went to Woodstock."

"That was a long time ago, Armani," Danny said. "They would flip if they caught us smoking weed inside."

Skip said under his breath, "They just tell us to go outside."

"You serious about her stringing us up by our balls?"

"Find out for yourself and then get back to me, Skip."

"That's if he's still alive."

The others laughed while Skip frantically waved the smoke from the room and then tried to guide it through the cracked window. Next, he picked up the filter, which was an empty toilet paper roll with three fabric softener sheets stuffed inside. After he took another drag from the joint, he placed his lips over the circular end of the roll and blew the smoke through the fabric softener sheets.

"See," Henry said. "Can't smell a thang."

"Yeah," T.J. said under his breath. "Room smells like one of them Laundromats."

"Here I go now," Skip said and nodded at T.J. "Bring the beat back."

T.J. got to work on the beat.

Bhhm, Chht, Ah Bhhm-Bhhm, Chht. . .

"*Your clothing line is trash. I woke up this morning in your mother's bed and tried to get rid of this itchy rash. On my, yep, that's right. Then, I found a tick. And not from strolling through a forest.*"

"Oh! Damn!" Danny cried out, wiping his greasy fingers over his shirt. "He went after your mom."

"Don't be talking shit about my mom," Armani said, building red with anger.

"*How about we shake hands and call it square,*" Skip rhymed. "*Sike! If you can't stand the heat, then stay out of the kitchen, little tick. Why don't you run back home and tell your mommy how much she enjoyed my di—*"

"That's it!" Armani shouted out and grabbed Skip by the throat.

T.J. stopped the beat while Henry and Danny burst out laughing.

"Chill you two," T.J. said and pulled Armani from Skip.

"Just joking, Armani," Skip said, fixing his crinkled collar. "Damn."

"That ain't funny. Yo!"

"New deal," T.J. said. "No battle rap."

T.J. put the cassette tape, *Future Shock*, into the stereo and turned up the volume to its highest level.

"This is my fav right here. Yeah!"

"I swear. You and Herbie Hancock, Octo."

"He da bomb."

"*The* bomb?"

"No," T.J. returned. "Da bomb. Duh? Best damn keyboard player on the planet earf. That's fo sho!"

"Would you turn it down a little," Henry said from the bed as he studied the Jagger saxophone in his lap.

"You're starting to sound like Arena over there."

"Shut up, Skip."

"By the way, where is Arena?"

"With her goth friends. . ."

"Like *yeah*," Armani teased, "I'm going to go hang out behind the cave and smoke some cigarettes and paint my nails black and talk about how miserable life is."

"You're stupid."

Danny picked up the flashlight from the nightstand and mouthed the lyrics into the flashlight as if it was a microphone.

As the chorus played, "*Future Shock*," the rest of Henry's friends straightened their frames and violently shook and convulsed as if they were being shocked; and yet it looked more as if they were having seizures. New dance: "The Seizure Dance." Skip even rolled onto the floor and did "The Seizure Dance" while Armani acted as if he put his finger into the wall outlet. There, he was doing "The Seizure Dance."

Henry strapped the saxophone over his arm and said to T.J., "You suckers haven't heard nothing yet."

"Uh oh," Danny teased and turned down the volume halfway. "Henry is finally going to bust a rhyme."

Henry adjusted the saxophone around his shoulder.

"Yeah right!" T.J. yelled and covered his mouth. "Henry's 'bout to bust a solo!"

Henry let the beat of the song sink in. He blew into the mouthpiece of the saxophone. The sound was piercing. Henry couldn't hit a single note. The Jagger sounded like a wounded animal crying out for help. Everyone around Henry covered their ears and grimaced.

"You suck, Henry!"

"I told you it wasn't easy," Henry said bashfully and tried yet again.

They covered their ears again.

"Enough, Henry!"

"Let me give it a try."

Skip grabbed the saxophone from Henry's grip.

"But. . . just be careful with it. . . "

Skip said, "Watch this," to the others and played the saxophone. He was just as pathetic as Henry. Except for Henry, everyone else was laughing at Skip and his inept saxophone skills. Skip tried once more. When he went to blow into the reed, his eyes suddenly bulged. Then, he gagged as if he was going to vomit right there in front of Armani and T.J. He quickly pulled the mouthpiece away and dropped the saxophone over the floor.

Henry picked up the saxophone from the floor and shouted out, "Be careful with it!"

Skip's eyes were filled with great panic now. He tried to utter something from his mouth, but something was obstructing his air passage. His face turned a pastel blue.

Henry said urgently, "Cut it out, Skip."

"What's wrong with him?"

"He's got the 'Future Shock' fever."

"No," Danny said urgently. "He's not playing guys."

"Skip?"

Skip quickly motioned to his throat.

"I think he's choking," Armani said, his face expressionless.

T.J. turned off the stereo.

"Skip?"

With his eyes bulging in fear, Skip rose to his feet. He grabbed his throat with one hand while the other one motioned to the others. T.J. suddenly pounced to his feet and wrapped his arms around Skip's abdomen and held them there as tightly as he could. He proceeded to give Skip the Heimlich maneuver. On the third push, Skip violently coughed.

"Help him, Octo."

"I'm tryin'!"

"Try harder."

"Come on, Skip," T.J. forced. "Spit it out, man!"

T.J. gave another thrust into Skip's abdomen.

Skip finally spat out a piece of debris from his throat. The slimy piece hit Henry on the foot.

"Are you okay, Skip?" Danny asked, leaning over Skip.

While kneeling over the floor, Skip took a moment to catch his breath. The color in his face finally returned back to normal.

"You idiots," he seethed, his breath still labored. "Didn't. . . didn't you see I was. . . I was choking?"

"What was that?"

He pushed Henry.

"What I do?"

"What the fuck, man?"

Henry ignored Skip and carefully picked up the piece, which was covered in a dark resin, slimy and slightly gummy. After he cleaned away the tarry substance with his fingers, he held the piece up to the natural light from the window.

Danny asked, "What is it, Henry?"

"It's a bullet," he drawled.

"Bullet? What the hell is a bullet doing in your saxophone?"

"I don't know," Henry said blankly.

"You fucker," Skip groaned. "That thing could've killed me."

"I didn't know there was a bullet inside!"

Danny chimed in, "That's what you get for buying it at a pawnshop."

"Forget this shit," Skip whispered and tramped through the bedroom.

"Where you going?"

"I'm out of here," he said and nodded at the others. "*Donkey Kong* anyone?" His voice started to trail off as he exited the bedroom. "Do yourself a favor and throw that piece of shit in the trash. . . Bonehead. . . " Typical Skip. He always swore or said something unusually harsh underneath his voice whenever he walked away.

"I got first dibs," Danny said excitedly and quickly got up from the floor.

"Second dibs," Armani said and got up after Danny.

T.J. stayed behind with Henry.

"Don't worry 'bout Skip," T.J. said to Henry. "He can be a real dick sumtimes."

Henry was still baffled from the bullet.

"How did a bullet get into the saxophone?"

"That's a good question, Henry."

With a blank expression, Henry stared at the bullet in his palm and then the shade of red over his skin.

"It looks like it's got blood on it."

"Listen, Henry," T.J. said sincerely. "I'm gonna take off. I gotta go to the store and pickup sum milk."

"I thought you were going to go over to Ms. Craft's house with me."

"Maybe sum otha time."

Henry continued to stare at the bullet in his palm. He didn't have anything to say. Yet, he still tried to find an answer to that one question: How did a bullet get in the saxophone? Like his words, he had nothing.

"See ya 'round," T.J. said and left the bedroom.

"Yeah," Henry said thoughtlessly. "See ya."

THIRTEEN

For the rest of the afternoon, Henry spent most of his time pacing around his bedroom and biting his fingernails.

After an hour or two of unanswered questions, mainly about the bullet that was lodged inside the saxophone, his thoughts moved to what Skip had said to him: "You suck, Henry." And worst of all, Skip said the insult in front of Henry's friends, T.J. and Danny. Henry wasn't that close to Skip or Armani, not like he was with T.J. or Danny. In the back of his mind, he wondered if T.J. or Danny would think less of him now or if they really cared what Skip had said. After all, it was *just* Skip. And Henry wasn't that close to him, not enough to consider him a friend—more so a presence. In fact, it was his mother, Abbey, who introduced her son to Skip a couple of years ago. Henry's mother knew Skip's mother from church. They weren't tight like Henry and T.J. or Danny, but they still talked to one another every time they bumped into each other. The word *suck* lingered with Henry. Such an ambiguous word as *sucked*, groveling, poisonous, pleasurable, deviant, most symbolized as marks of failure, ended up staying with Henry for the remainder of the day like an uninvited guest encroaching on his privacy. Such a demoralizing word like *sucked* had fangs, sharp ones too. The deeper the word dug its fangs into Henry's mind, the more furious he became. "Failure," the word screamed at him. "YOU ARE A FAILURE! YOU. . . YOU SUCK!"

Pacing back and forth in his bedroom, Henry said under his huffing breath, "I'll show him." He paced faster. Face tightened into a grimace. "I'll show that Skip, that little. . . that little. . . pissant. . . "

Before Abbey came home from the Depot, Henry spent the entire afternoon practicing on the saxophone and trying his best to prove Skip wrong. Still, he couldn't hit a single note correctly. The pitch was off. There was no fluidity with his playing. Each time he played, it sounded like a frog croaking in a swamp. Toward the end of his practice, he involuntarily screamed out to the top of his lungs and chucked the saxophone against the wall. While the sax was in midair, Henry had already felt the regret. The saxophone struck the wall and left a hole in the wall. Small chips of drywall fell to the carpet. Henry rushed over to the Jagger, picked it up, and saw a dent over the bow and bell. Several of the keys were bent. One was dangling from a tiny rod. The slightest movement could've easily loosened the key. Where there was anger, there was sadness, so much sadness bottled up inside him. The sight alone of the damaged Jagger released every single emotion he had in his body. Henry dropped to his knees and cried, softly at first and then loudly.

With his teeth clinched together (any harder they would've shattered like glass), Henry screamed. The scream was a gravelly and demonic one. Nothing like he had heard before.

Suddenly, the sound of a car door slamming shut from outside halted the pain pouring from Henry's voice.

He immediately opened up his ears and listened closer.

After he heard the faint sounds of keys jiggling, he sprang to his feet, ran to the window, and spotted his mother's car, the "Jelly Bean," as he had called it, parked in the driveway. He turned to the large puncture in the wall. He quickly tossed the saxophone, as well as the saxophone case, in the closet, threw a sheet over it, kicked some of the crumbled up drywall under the bed, and then moved a lamp in front of the hole in the wall.

Finally, he hid the bullet casing in the Bible in his desk drawer.

Henry hurried downstairs and opened the front door before his mother could slide the key inside the knob.

"Well," he said, out of breath, "you're home early."

Abbey grabbed her chest in surprise.

"Henry..." she said, "...you're going to give your mother a heart attack."

Henry stood in the middle of the doorway.

"Sorry."

She pointed inside the house.

"May I come in?"

"Oh," Henry uttered and stepped out of the way. "Right."

He noticed the Pizza Cave box in her hand.

"I picked up some pizza."

The first thing Abbey noticed when she saw Henry were his eyes and how red they were.

"Are you feeling okay?" she asked, staring at his bloodshot eyes.

"I'm fine," he replied and shrugged his shoulders.

"You don't look fine."

"I... I was taking a nap."

Henry closed the door behind his mother.

"Nap?" she said, her voice altered with confusion. "That's twice in one week. Are you sure you're feeling okay?"

"I told you 'I'm fine.'"

"I heard you," she said, her eyes widening. "I don't understand you, Henry. First, your stutter goes away. And now, you're sleeping more than usual. Something is going on with you."

She reached down and felt Henry's forehead with the backside of her hand. Next, she patted his cheeks.

Henry pulled his face away.

"I'm fine."

"I can't afford for you to get sick, Henry," she said. "I don't have that kind of money. You know doctor visits come straight out of my pocket."

"I know," he groaned. "I was just tired."

"From what?"

Once more, Henry shrugged his shoulders.

Abbey studied her son's face.

"You've been cooped up in that pigsty of a room for the past few days, which reminds me," she said sharply. "Have you cleaned your room yet?"

"No," he said hesitantly. "But I will."

With a closed mouth, she sighed.

"I'm giving you to the end of the week, boy," she said sternly and then paused. "If that room isn't clean by Sunday, then you are *grounded*. You hear me?"

Henry rolled his eyes.

"Don't you roll your eyes at me."

"All right. Geez," he said and followed his mother into the kitchen where she placed the slender box of pizza on the dinner table.

While Abbey removed her jacket and placed it in the hallway closet, Henry made himself a drink, a glass of Clover for himself with two cubes of ice from the ice tray. One of the ice cubes accidentally slipped from the tray and fell onto the floor. Without his mother looking, Henry kicked the ice cube underneath the refrigerator.

"What was that?"

Henry shrugged his shoulders.

"Nut. . . nothing."

From the hallway, she asked, "How was school?"

"Fine."

"Just fine."

"Yeah."

Abbey walked back into the kitchen and switched on the television across from the kitchen table.

"*This afternoon, police arrested Timothy Snead,*" the anchorman said. "*Mr. Snead was charged with the murder of fifty-four year old, Henry—*"

Abbey instantly recognized the photograph of the black man on the television. Not the Snead fellow, but the other one. Her face slackened. Henry grabbed a plate from the cabinet, placed two slices of pizza on the plate, and then made an attempt to flee from the kitchen. Abbey quickly switched off the television before the entire name, *Henry McClintock,* could be revealed.

"Hey!" she blurted out and turned her shoulder. "Where are you going?"

"My room."

"No," she said. "You're going to eat right here at the table. Enough of this eating in your room stuff."

Henry rolled his eyes.

"Come on now," she said and waved over Henry. "You're going to eat with your mother."

Henry stood in the same exact position: not moving, not talking.

"What happened to us, Henry?" she asked as she stood over the kitchen table. "We used to be friends. Are we not friends anymore?"

Henry mumbled, "I don't know."

Abbey walked over to Henry and grabbed the plate of pizza as well as the drink from his hands and placed them both on the table.

"This is a family, Henry," she said. "Families eat together."

Henry ambled over to the kitchen table and sat down in the chair.

"Did you wash your hands?"

"Yeah," he said and took a bite of pepperoni pizza. "Did you?"

"I am right now," she said zestfully and proceeded to wash her hands over the sink.

With the corner of her eyes, Abbey looked at her son suspiciously as if she knew something that he didn't know, or at least he did know but he wasn't being forthright with his mother.

Abbey asked Henry more questions about his day. *How was lunch? What did you learn in Miss Sanders' class?* In return, Henry was short, as usual. Abbey didn't speak a word about her job. Like Henry, she was short in the matter. Even if Henry asked or persisted, as he almost never did, Abbey would keep the answer as short as possible.

After they were both settled at the table, they ate dinner in silence. Henry ate as quickly as he could. After every other bite, he would wash down the pizza with a swig of soda. Abbey ate from a salad that she made from a wedge of iceberg lettuce and some farm fresh onions and tomatoes that she had bought from the market.

"When I came home from work, I almost tripped over your basketball in the yard," she said, keeping to her austere manner. "Are you not taking it to school anymore?"

Henry shrugged one shoulder, not two.

"Sometimes," he answered and took another bite of pizza.

Abbey sighed.

"Sometimes? Is there something you're not telling me, Henry?"

Henry slowed his chewing and then innocently shook his head no.

"The other day, I talked to Mr. Clydesdale down at the courts," she said. "He says he hasn't seen you in some time. Plus, I received a call from Miss Sanders. She says she wants to schedule a parent conference. You want to explain to me what's really going on?"

Henry shrugged his shoulder, this time the both of them.

"I've just been busy."

"Busy?" she said sharply and leaned upright. "Busy doing what?"

"Things," Henry answered vaguely.

"What kind of things?"

Disgruntled from his mother's questions, Henry said, "*Things.*"

"Don't get an attitude with me, boy," she said, pointing the fork at Henry. "One day, that basketball is going to pay for your college. Do you understand me?"

Henry paused and thought about the consequences of his next remark.

He mumbled, "I don't want to go to college."

"Excuse me," she said in a high tone and dropped the fork into the bowl, which made a piercing sound throughout the kitchen. "You want to run that by me again."

Henry glared into his mother's eyes.

"I don't want to go to college," he said, this time loud enough for his mother to hear despite the fact that she heard him as clear as day the first time around.

"You *will* go to college," she fumed. "And you *will* play basketball. No ifs, ands, or buts."

"Why do I have to do everything you want me to do?" he said, the appetite he once had went away. "What about me? Why can't you let me do what I want to do?"

Abbey folded her arms.

"And what do you want to do, Henry? Tell me."

Henry paused once more.

"I don't know," he muttered.

"Speak up, boy."

"I don't know," he said, this time louder.

"What do you mean you don't know?"

"I like music," Henry said with a tremor in his voice. "What if I wanted to be a musician?"

Abbey burst out laughing.

Henry sharpened his icy glare.

"Musician?" she returned. "You aren't a musician, Henry."

"How you know?"

"Well, let me think," she said casually. "Last year it was a marine biologist. The year before that it was a professional wrestler like the ones on the television. This year it's a musician. What is it going to be next year, Henry? A comedian?"

"Why do you always do this to me?"

She picked up her fork and took a bite of her salad.

"You're meant to play basketball, Henry," she said after she carefully swallowed her food. "Think about all of those other kids out there who would kill to have your talent. If you don't play basketball, then you're practically spitting in the Lord's face."

"I don't care," Henry said loudly.

"Watch your tone," Abbey said sharply, keeping her fork in her hand. This time she pointed it toward Henry's face. "Tomorrow I'm going to talk with Mr. Clydesdale," she said, her eyes flaring. "And if tells me that you never showed up at the courts, then we are going to have a serious conversation."

Henry shouted out, "It's always serious with you!"

Abbey dropped the fork. Her finger was like a sharp knife held in front of Henry's grill. Her voice was tightly squeezed, chilling.

"Don't raise your tone toward me. Don't you dare. . . "

Henry threw down his slice of pizza and rushed upstairs.

Abbey pounded her fist over the table.

"You get back here!"

Henry never turned back around.

"Henry!"

In return, Henry pounded each heel into the stairs on the way up to his bedroom.

FOURTEEN

ONCE bedtime was near (which was usually around ten o'clock during the weekdays, depending on what mood Abbey was in), Abbey didn't even say goodnight to her son. Instead, she went straight to bed and fell asleep.

As for Henry, he wasn't doing much sleeping at all. And if he did manage to rest, it was during each break from tossing and turning and searching for the coolest spot on the bed. This went on for a couple of hours, Henry trying to find a cool spot to sleep. Ever since he closed his eyes, his mind was like a neglected engine constantly running. Every spot his face or body would touch, the sheets or pillows underneath him would warm like a heating pad. And it wasn't just from the argument at the dinner table, which was causing the blood in his veins to boil. It was a whole accumulation of things: the condition of the Jagger saxophone; Skip and what he had said in front of his other friends; his mother and how persistent she was about him going to college. They would never stop running, his thoughts.

As Henry thrashed around the damp sheets, he heard the jiggling of a door handle. The sound was as faint as a whisper.

The handle jiggled once more.

The sheets suddenly wrapped around his face, smothering him like his thoughts. Henry opened his eyes, only to witness a dull shade of white over his body. The faster he moved, the harder the sheets beat down on him, creasing, wrinkling, and tightening. The warm blood raced through his veins, pulsing. His chest tightened, breath labored. The bed sheets were now suffocating his every breath. That was when panic set in and then the screaming and crying, but the sheets didn't care.

With one last surge upward, Henry woke from his sleep and turned to the door.

The jiggling had stopped.

The damp sheets were scattered over the bed and not on him. A draft of cool air washed over his body, which made him more at ease. *It's happening again*, he thought as he finally caught his breath. There was a week's stretch where he didn't dream at all. Just blackness. Then, after the blackness, there would be a burst of light from where he woke the next morning. In a way, he yearned for the blackness— closing his eyes at night and then opening them the next morning. No dreams, no horror. She was gone, he knew, but not entirely. Now, the dreams were back, the horror. Most importantly, *she* was back. As long as he could remember, he dreamt the same dream: a door handle jiggling, the faint gasps and gurgles of a dying woman coming from behind a closed door, and then him waking up in a strange room with a television set and a vanity table and a mirror. At times, she would come in various forms: eyeless or without teeth, just slimy gums and drool dripping from the corners of her mouth. At times, the poor old woman would make her way to young Henry when he least expected it and startle him by pressing her pale and clammy face against his and moaning like a diseased-riddled whore and tonguing the side of his cheek.

Soon, she would come. She would climb from the sounds of death and stalk through the darkness of night and surface over the bright moonlight. Henry didn't quite know when or how, but soon, she *would* come.

Aggravated from the lack of sleep, he flung the remaining sheets aside and checked the clock on the nightstand.

The time read: 12:03.

With hours now spent tossing and turning in bed, Henry knew he wasn't going to get that good night sleep, the one where he sunk into a sea of blackness and surfaced over a tide of brilliant sunlight. So, he decided to roll out of bed. He grabbed the flashlight from his drawer, cleared his eyes, and ambled over to the closet. Once he arrived at the closet, he pulled off the sheet from the saxophone and shined the light on the dent. Henry's face became long and ghostly pale. He cleared his eyes once more. Maybe his weary eyes were fooling him. He kept shining the light over the dent, hoping he could find one. He couldn't. Not even a single scratch on the Jagger saxophone. It was as if he never threw it against the wall!

"*Impossible. . .* " Henry mumbled.

Another hour passed.

Henry decided to sneak out of the bedroom window with the saxophone case. He tossed the case in a bush that helped soften the impact and carefully climbed down the trellis.

He crept over to Ms. Craft's house. This time the lights were off. Henry rang the doorbell anyway.

The same man from the other day—Ms. Craft's "friend" named Jodi—answered the door. He was holding a beer as well as a cigarette in the same hand and wiping the phlegm from his nose with the other.

"Jesus," he said, sniffling. "You again. She's sleeping."

"Can you wake her up?"

"I'm not in the mood to deal with you, kid. . . "

He made an attempt to close the door.

"It's an emergency!" Henry exclaimed and then scanned around the empty street in paranoia.

Jodi pulled back the door and looked down at the case in Henry's hand.

"Wait here," he said.

Before he closed the door, he looked down to see if Henry was going to stick his foot inside the doorway.

A couple of minutes went by.

Finally, the door opened.

Ms. Craft was standing there in a white robe.

Worried, she said, "Henry, you can't keep coming over here as you please, especially at this hour of the night. Your mother would have my head on a spear."

"I know," Henry said. "But I've been trying all day. I can't play. I'm no good."

"Nobody can pick up an instrument for the first time and instantly know how to play," she said sharply. "It takes practice, Henry. Lots and lots of practice."

"Can you teach me how to play?"

"I can't, Henry."

Henry begged, "*Please.*"

Ms. Craft took a couple of seconds to ponder about Henry's proposition. With a keen eye, she observed the frustration on Henry's face.

"I'll tell you what, Henry," she said and crossed her arms. "I'll make another deal with you."

"I'll do anything!"

Ms. Craft leaned in closer.

"You're going to wake the neighbors."

Henry whispered, "I'll do anything. I swear."

"After you get out of school, I'll teach you how to play the saxophone."

"I have basketball tomorrow, but I can practice the day after."

"I have a gig up at Central Reserve Stadium."

"You mean you play for the Black Bears too?"

"Just for the seventh inning stretch."

"Really?"

"It pays the bills, Henry," she said and then thought carefully. "I'm free on Thursday. How about Thursday?"

Henry bobbed his head.

"Okay," he said.

"But in return, you have to do some chores around the house for me. Can you do that?"

Once more, Henry bobbed his head.

"I can do that."

"I'll see you Thursday then."

"Thursday it is."

As Henry walked away, Ms. Craft said cautiously in a loud whisper, "Say, Henry! Did you ever find a name for your saxophone?"

"Adrian," he said after a sudden pause. "Its name is Adrian."

"Interesting name," Ms. Craft said, keeping the volume of her voice as low as possible. "Where did you come up with a name like that?"

"*Rocky*," he said with a half shrug, half smirk.

"The movie?"

"Yeah."

"That's a great movie. What's not to love? A local underdog who comes from nowhere and goes toe to toe with the undefeated heavyweight champion and gives him a run for his money. Not only that, Rocky gets the girl at the end of the story."

"But he doesn't win the fight."

"But he sure did fight like a true champion despite the loss," she said. "Listen, Henry. Not all heroes win in the end. Sometimes, it's the journey they're willing to embark on that makes them the *real* hero. And if they give it their all and come up short in the end, then they keep trying."

Henry took a moment to absorb the comment.

She asked, "Would you like me to be your Mickey?"

"No, Dolores," he said thoughtfully. "I want you to be you. Not Mickey."

"I can do that," Ms. Craft said and folded her arms together from the chill of the night. "Remember, Henry. Thursday."

Henry bobbed his head yet again.

THE FIFTH

He hurried back to his house, hid the saxophone case be-
hind the bushes, and entered the same way that he exited.
He didn't even dream that night.
He didn't think much about anything.
Henry slept. . .

. . . finally.

PART TWO

ROSES FOR JUDITH

FIFTEEN

HENRY removed the reed of the saxophone from his lips.

"I can't do it," he said.

"Let's try again, Henry."

"I don't understand what I'm doing wrong!"

"Remember your posture."

Henry smacked his gums.

"*Posture.*"

"Yes, ma'am."

"Dolores."

"Yes. . . Dolores."

Henry straightened his shoulders, his neck.

"Good," she said. "Now, try again."

A sigh.

"Don't give me that."

"Give you wha. . . "

"Try again, Henry."

Next, Henry adjusted the strap around his neck, made sure his head was pointed ahead and his neck straight so that there was no obstruction in his throat, and placed both of his hands around the saxophone accordingly.

Ms. Craft carefully listened to Henry blow into the saxophone, Adrian. The sound was remarkably inconsistent and extremely unpleasant to the ears.

"I know what your problem is."

Ms. Craft stood from the seat.

"Where are you go—"

"Wait right here," Ms. Craft interrupted.

She went to the kitchen, filled up two glasses of water from the sink, and walked back into the living room.

"Put down the saxophone for a minute."

Henry did as he was told and rested the saxophone over the couch.

Ms. Craft handed Henry the glass of tepid water.

Instinctively, Henry took a sip from the glass.

"I didn't say drink," she said snappishly.

Embarrassed, Henry pulled the glass from his mouth.

"Sorry."

She pulled out two straws, keeping one for herself and then handing the other one to Henry.

"Let's see who can blow the biggest bubbles."

"Bubbles? You serious?"

"I bet I can blow them bigger than you."

Ms. Craft blew into the straw while Henry sat there in a haze.

"Are you too old to blow bubbles?"

"*Yeah*."

"I see how it is."

Ms. Craft continued to blow bubbles.

Once more, Henry smacked his gums as he watched the bubbles boiling over like scolding water from the glass. In the back of his mind, he knew she wasn't going to stop until he followed along. So, he placed the straw in the glass of water and blew bubbles with Ms. Craft just as he was told.

Ms. Craft's bubbles were twice the size of Henry's bubbles. Water was splashing all over the floor as well as her hands and wrists.

Henry pulled his lips from the straw and asked, "How'd you do that?"

"Your problem is, Henry," Ms. Craft said and wagged the water from her hand like a dog wagging its wet tail, "you're letting out too much air from the sides of your mouth. That's why the sound is so thin. I want you to try and blow through the straw with your lower lip slightly over your lower teeth and the corners of your mouth completely closed. Like this."

Ms. Craft demonstrated for Henry. The bubbles in her cup brimmed over and splashed over the carpet. She couldn't help but laugh as the water trickled down the side of her chin.

"Now, you try," she said and wiped the water from her face with a washcloth.

Henry did as Ms. Craft showed him (lower lip over teeth, corners of mouth *completely* closed) and blew into the straw. His bubbles were just as big as Ms. Craft's. Some even twice as big! They too splashed over the carpet.

"See, Henry," Ms. Craft said, laughing. "That's how you should play Adrian." She grabbed the cup from Henry's hand and placed it on the coffee table next to the piano. "Now, pick up Adrian. I want you to go up the scale just like I showed you."

Henry picked up the Jagger from the couch. He placed his left hand on the upper body of the saxophone and then his right hand on the lower body. He pressed down on both keys and blew into the mouthpiece the same way he blew into the straw. The sound came out much broader and cleaner. Henry pulled his mouth away from the mouthpiece.

"See!" Ms. Craft said excitedly. "How much better did that sound?"

"A lot better," he said with a smile.

"Now, let's take five."

"Five?"

"Yes," she said. "I mean a five minute break."

"But we haven't even played a song yet!"

"We'll get there, Henry," she said reassuringly. "Be patient."

Ms. Craft grabbed the glasses of water and took them back into the kitchen where she placed them both in the sink. Meanwhile, Henry waited patiently in his seat and thought more about the songs he could now play. *It just takes more practice, more time*, he thought. *Man! I could even play the solo in "Prom Night."*

"To be honest, Henry," Ms. Craft said as she carefully rinsed out the glass in the sink. "You're in a much better mood than I thought you would be."

Henry heard his name being spoken, the name *Henry*, and pulled himself from his thoughts.

"What. . ."

"Excuse me."

"Huh?"

"Don't say 'what,'" she said motherly. "It's rude. Instead, say excuse me."

"*Oh*." Then, Henry said under his breath, "Excuse me."

"So, I said that you're in a better mode than I thought you would be."

Henry asked, "What do you mean?"

"You haven't heard. Have you?"

"Heard about what?"

Ms. Craft placed her hand over her mouth in surprise.

"Oh dear."

"What happened?"

"Mr. Vortex," she said and stood by the kitchen counter. "You haven't heard what happened to him?"

"No."

Ms. Craft strolled over to Henry.

"It's been all over the news," she said and paused in thought. "Let me think. It was in Tuesday's or Wednesday's paper, I believe. I thought you might've known."

"Known what?"

Ms. Craft sighed and then answered bluntly, "Well, he died, Henry. His body was found in Josette Park last Monday. They said he was homeless."

"Mr. Vortex is dead?"

"I'm so sorry, Henry."

"I don't under. . . stand," Henry said while clearing his throat.

The blood suddenly rushed through his veins.

Soon, his skin, mostly the areas in which the eye couldn't see like his armpits and such, perspired like a cool glass of water left to bake in the summer heat.

"What. . . what. . . " Henry said as his thoughts began to race, ". . . what was he doing in Josette Park?"

"That's where he was living, Henry."

The fame, he thought. *The money, all the girls, the big hair, the lavish suits, the diamond rings, the jewelry. . .*

"But he used to be famous," Henry exclaimed, his eyes watering a little. "What about all the records he used to sell? Surely, he made lots of money."

"I hate to bring such bad news to you, Henry," Ms. Craft said despairingly. "I really do. Being an admirer of his, I just thought you knew. That's all."

"We," he mumbled, his eyes trailing toward the floor. "We never got the newspaper. . . that. . . day. . . "

Ms. Craft kneeled down to Henry's level.

"Sometimes in life bad things just happen," she said. "Sometimes they make us worse and other times they make us better, stronger. Do you understand?"

Henry sniffled, bobbed his head, and said, "Yeah."

For three weeks straight, Ms. Craft went over the fundamentals with Henry: how to hold the saxophone in the correct position, where his hands should be, how to use the reed, even went over every little detail of the design of the saxophone, the keys, the key guard, the octave pin, the ligature, the bell, and the rest of *her* body. Henry let the first one slide. Maybe Dolores's tongue slipped and she meant to say it, not *her*. Then, the old woman kept calling the saxophone "her." "Be gentle with *her*" or "Take good care of *her*" or "Make sure to put *her* away when you're done playing *her*." Henry couldn't take it much longer. He decided to ask her, Ms. Craft that is. Ms. Craft's response: "If you're going to give an instrument a woman's name, Henry, then you must treat the instrument the same way you would treat a woman."

On the second day of tutorials, Ms. Craft accidentally walked in on Henry using brasso to clean Adrian. Henry's first reaction: bafflement. "I thought. . . treat her like a woman." Ms. Craft hollered out as if the young man was committing a mortal sin, "STOP! PLEASE! STOP!" The old woman went on a rambling fit about what brasso does to lacquer, even went down to the science of aging—as if a lady who had as many wrinkles as a bed sheet knew a thing or two about aging. At the end of her rambling, Henry learned a simple and yet quick fix. "Nothing more than a little elbow grease," she preached and handed Henry a dry washcloth. By the time Henry got done cleaning Adrian, his arm felt as if it was going to fall off. The payoff: Adrian was now glistening to a blinding shine. Now that Henry knew the ins and outs of the saxophone, he let *her* loose, really let her go wild. Adrian that is. At first, it wasn't like he imagined in the glamorous music videos with all that reverb and effects layered throughout the sound, adding more depth and sensualism. The sound was raw, untouched, nothing added, which, to Henry, sounded in the vein of the older jazz musicians like John Coltrane or Miles Davis, two legends who, through his eye, stood shoulder to shoulder with his favorite saxophonist, Mr. Vortex (R.I.P.).

Either way, Henry was hooked.

Most certainly.

Some days, Ms. Craft drove Henry to the edge with her dedication and assiduity. Having a competitive nature, Henry strove for perfection, as did Ms. Craft. For instance, when Henry was playing basketball, he always wanted the ball like Jordan; and if the other teammates didn't pass him the "rock," then he would somehow find a way to steal the rock from the opponent or the cherry pickers and score a basket on his own. Henry kept at it, though, and really took to heart what Ms. Craft preached: "Right now, there is a man out there—just like you Henry—who is practicing till all hours, trying to be the next great saxophonist." On some nights before Henry's mother arrived home from work, Ms. Craft could hear Henry playing from his bedroom. It wasn't just Ms. Craft either. In fact, the entire neighborhood could hear Henry playing. At times, she could hear him pounding on the walls (with his fists) from missing a note or not hitting a note the way he wanted to. On many occasions, Henry felt the urge to smash Adrian on the ground until there was nothing left of her but bits and pieces, food for trashcans. Over time, Ms. Craft trained Henry how to control the urges, the temper, and funnel them all into his playing. The process was what Ms. Craft called "the art of contortion," contorting one's body, mentally and physically, to the material world (in Henry's case, Adrian). The art of contortion, Ms. Craft explained to Henry, was either complex or rudimentary, depending on the artist. For Henry, the art form relied heavily on emotional response. The way of thinking certainly liberated the one unparalleled quality that either made or broke a novel saxophonist: *improvisation*. One wouldn't have to travel down a dusky back alley in Parker Square to pocket such a secret of a great saxophonist. Improvisation came from within, Ms. Craft preached, that meaty place God-fearing men called a soul. Once Henry finally caught on, each major and minor scale became that much easier. Ms. Craft used videotapes to help guide Henry such as *The Sound of Music*. The song "Do-Re-Mi" was a good way to start. From there, the range grew, so too did Henry's taste in music. Henry was now getting the hang of terms like "tonguing" and "slurring." By the fifth week, Henry was learning the most elementary songs. And by the beginning of the third month, Henry learned to play the opening solo from one of his favorite Mr. Vortex's songs, "Prom Night." Overall, Henry was a quick learner, quicker than most his age. Over breaks, Ms. Craft would help him with his homework. She enforced education. Said, "Knowledge is power. Even more powerful than Superman." During study, she would play classical music like Bach or Chopin or Beethoven over the record player, which helped relax Henry as well as open up his mind. Abbey saw the change in grades that her son was bringing home. She posted the A's and B's on the refrigerator door. Not once did Henry ever bring home a grade lower than a B. Even Jodi, Ms. Craft's "friend," or what Henry liked to call her "boy toy," took notice of Henry's improvement and, on many instances, voiced the progress to Ms.

Craft. On rainy days where time felt as if it didn't exist, Henry and Ms. Craft danced to Frankie Avalon, Bobby Darin, and The Beatles. She taught Henry some moves that she learned when she was younger, including "The Dip" and several others. In return, Henry taught Ms. Craft some moves of his own like "The Seizure Dance." Whenever Henry wasn't practicing on the saxophone or studying for school or even dancing with his mentor, Ms. Craft— according to the deal—Henry did chores around the house such as mowing the lawn, painting, vacuuming, and dusting the furniture, even the music equipment in the studio. On other days when they finished up early, Ms. Craft would take Henry to a local record store, Milly and Munford's Discs, and buy him Mr. Vortex vinyl records, posters, and cassette tapes (Henry's bedroom started to look like a Mr. Vortex museum). Ms. Craft even bought Henry two Herbie Hancock concert tickets and told him to take one of his friends. So, what better person to ask than Mr. Hancock's number one fan? Henry and T.J. ended up using the movies as an excuse to tell their parents, which never failed. Ms. Craft was generous enough to drive them to Fairmont Hall in Harrietsville and pick them up when the concert was over. On several occasions, Abbey grew suspicious of what Henry was doing behind her back. When Abbey asked Henry where he got all of these things such as the records or the music posters in his bedroom, he told her that he bought them from selling lemonade and merchandise from 2 Hot 2 Handle, he and T.J.'s so-called "band," including demo tapes, stickers, and plain black tee shirts with *2 Hot 2 Handle* written in red, white, and blue on the front. The demo tape consisted of four tracks, "Four Score," "The Minotaur Vs. Da Boy From Davie Morris," "Putting Out Us Fires," and "The Crown." At first trial, Henry dissembled one of his speakers (as he had done with almost all of the electronics in the house including the radios, the televisions, and so forth and, of course, without his mother's consent) and dummied the speaker into a microphone. Henry's voice turned out sounding like a Chipmunk. Cool effect, they thought. However, not quite the sound Henry and T.J. were going for. Despite their many hitches, they never quit. They decided to ask Ms. Craft about their dilemma. Without thinking twice, she agreed to buy them a microphone, a really nice one too! The employee at Chessman's claimed it was the same kind that the professionals used. "Studio quality," so he claimed. Abbey didn't take them too seriously, Henry or T.J and their so-called band. Henry didn't make any money from the lemonade or the 2 Hot 2 Handle merchandise, maybe enough to buy a couple of boxes of Jr. Mints and a round of sodas for his friends at the Twin Falls Cinema. Nonetheless, Abbey fell for the lie. And that was what it was: one ongoing lie. One day when Henry was at "the movies with T.J.," Abbey sneaked into his bedroom and found one of Henry's demo tapes that he had made with T.J., just the four songs with he and T.J. rapping—and singing—over a sampled beat and a synthesizer. She listened to the tape on the way to the Depot. Halfway through the first song called "Four Score," she tossed the cassette tape out the window where two other cars ended up playing shuffle puck with it until it was flicked into a sewer drain. When the weekends arrived, Abbey and Henry remained fairly busy. Saturday mornings usually consisted of Abbey mowing the lawn, not Henry. In the afternoon, she would take Henry and his teammates to AAU games in the Jelly Bean. Abbey always kept Henry within smacking reach if he ever got out of line in the car—especially with six teenagers, all jacked up on pre-game adrenaline and packed into a Volkswagen Golf. Henry made sure to keep basketball in rotation in order to stay out of trouble. Abbey, being Henry's number one fan, was *always* there to keep her son in line. When Henry was playing, he could hear his mother across the court, cheering away, screaming over all of the other parents on the bleachers. Sunday nights, best known around April as "Playoff Nights" around the Burl household, were usually spent with Henry's closest friends. Abbey would make a pan of lasagna for the gang while they rooted for Magic "Showtime" Johnson and the Los Angeles Lakers or Jordan and the Bulls. Danny was a huge Larry Bird fan and always sported the green number 33 jersey and Boston Celtics hat whenever a game aired on television. So, whenever the L.A. Lakers battled the Boston Celtics or the "Bad Boys" of Detroit, there was almost always a heated exchange among the others. The arguments never came down to fisticuffs. Just talking smack. "Bird would beat Magic any day of the week," Danny argued. "You can't stop the three, my brother from another mother!" Then, T.J. would come in. "You *IS* crazy! Magic would take dat white fool to school!"

For sometime, Henry had kept up this routine of squeezing basketball practice into his busy schedule so that Mr. Clydesdale wouldn't nark him out while his mother was at work. In the back of her mind, Abbey had an idea of what was going on behind her back. However, she never quite looked into it.

And things went on like this.

For Henry, it was a good time.

SIXTEEN

AFTER Henry finished a late afternoon session with Ms. Craft, Ms. Craft pulled Henry aside into the kitchen before he had a chance to say goodbye.

Henry asked, "What's wrong, Dolores?"

"Have a seat," she said flatly and pointed at the kitchen table.

"Oh. . . okay," he said unsteadily and sat down.

Ms. Craft sat down across from him.

"I've heard you've taken an interest in the house across the street when you were cutting the grass."

Henry swallowed the dry lump down his throat.

"You. . . you were watching me?"

"No," she said innocently. "Of course not. But Jodi told me all about it."

"Right."

Henry depressingly hung his head.

"What's her name?"

"Kerri," he said. "Her name is Kerri."

"I see," Ms. Craft said. "You like her. Don't you?"

Henry blushed.

"No," he said, his voice drawn out. "Not really."

"There's no shame in admitting you have a crush on another person, Henry."

"But I don't have a crush on her," Henry said, louder. "She's just a girl who lives across the street. Nothing else."

"Are you sure?"

Henry hesitated.

"*Yeah.*"

"All right." Ms. Craft leaned back in the chair. "But just hear me out on this one because I know it can be a hard subject for a guy your age. The last thing you want to be is somebody else, Henry."

Henry drifted in thought.

"She's not even my type. . ." Henry said mindfully, ". . . and yet. . . "

". . . And yet you can't get her out of your head."

"Yeah," Henry said softly, struggling to pull his eyes up at Ms. Craft. "How'd you know?"

Ms. Craft gradually smiled.

"I know a lot of things, Henry, especially when it comes to love."

Henry interrupted, "I don't love her."

"But you like her. Right?"

"Yeah."

"*Love* and *like* are very similar," she said. "Sometimes, they're the same."

"They are?"

"Of course."

His face washed over with misery.

"What does it mean?"

"It means you're human, Henry," Ms. Craft said and leaned over the table. "You wouldn't be thinking about her if you didn't like her. Tell me. What is one thing you do like about her?"

"She's pretty."

"Okay," Ms. Craft said, closer now. "That's a good place to start. Besides that, what else do you like about her?"

"She has a nice smile."

"What else?"

"She has nice hair."

Ms. Craft chortled.

"Try not to think about her physical appearance, Henry," she said. "What do you really like about her?"

"She's. . . she likes to play."

"There you go!" Ms. Craft said ecstatically. "So, she likes to have fun. That's a good trait in a girl. Good trait in anyone, the way I look at it. Now, tell me one thing you don't like about her."

"She. . . she   seems   conceited. . . snobbish. . . I   don't know. . . " Henry said with a slight anger increasing throughout his voice, ". . . she acts like she's better than everyone."

"How can you say that when you don't even talk to her, Henry?" Ms. Craft tried to find Henry's eyes, which were scattered over the table. "To me, it just seems like she has more bad qualities than good."

He squared his shoulders to Ms. Craft as he looked her in the eye.

"But I do talk to her."

Ms. Craft tilted her head.

"When?"

"In class."

"And what do you two talk about?"

Henry paused.

"I've never actually talked to her face to face."

Ms. Craft sighed and sat back in her chair.

"You have to talk to her, Henry."

"I guess it shouldn't be *that* hard," he said. "You can hear her from a mile away. It's not like she hides who she is."

"And neither should you, Henry," Ms. Craft emphasized. "There is a difference in hiding who you are and exaggerating who you are." Ms. Craft cleared her throat. "I was once like Kerri."

"You were?"

Ms. Craft drawled, "Sure." She cleared her throat. "Then, I finally got over myself and learned that the world doesn't revolve around me, Henry. Some girls grow up and others don't. Just remember that there is at least one girl out there who likes you, Henry, and likes you for who you are. I know it might be hard to swallow. This Kerri girl might not be the right one for you, and you might think right now that she's the only one for you, but you have to feel it, Henry." She placed her hand over her heart. "Here, in your heart. You have to remove everything around you, the materials, the amenities, necessities, strip all of that stuff away, Henry, and find out what *you* really want."

"What about the art of contortion?"

"I'm afraid this process doesn't involve materials, just you and this. . ." she said and pointed once more at her heart, ". . . your heart. Henry, if you can't feel it here, deep down in your heart, then, well, it's just a little crush. We all go through them. Some we learn to get over. Others stay with us for as long as we live. One thing is certain, Henry. You must listen to your heart. Then, you will know what to do." She leaned even closer. "So, Henry, what does your heart tell you?"

Henry calmed his breathing and sat in a radiating silence. He did as Ms. Craft told him to do and removed all surroundings, walls, furniture, that glass of milk from the coffee table, and listened closely to his heart.

"Maybe," he said faintly. "Maybe I like her because she doesn't like me."

"How do you know she doesn't like you, Henry?"

"For one thing, she can't even bring herself to look at me," he said vacantly. "Times, it's like I'm a ghost. Other times, it feels like *she's* the ghost. Like I'm trying to reach out to her, but I can't because she doesn't exist."

"But she does exist, Henry," Ms. Craft said closely. "And so do you. Maybe she's just scared of you, scared to like you."

"It's like I want to prove to her that I'm a good person, that I will be there for her no matter what, that I. . . that I. . . I would treat her exactly the way she wanted to be treated, but. . ."

"But what?"

Henry hung his head and said, "But I can't, Dolores. It's so hard."

"Listen to me, Henry," Ms. Craft said and took a hold of Henry's hand. "You *are* a good person, Henry. Where would you get an idea like that? Believe me, Henry. They don't get any better than you. So, don't you go and try to be the bad boy. Trust me. Girls don't like the bad boy. You might think they do. But they don't."

"Really," Henry said, his eyes filling with tears.

"*Really*," Ms. Craft said fiercely. "I think that's just the athlete coming out of you. You know you don't have to look at life as a competition." Ms. Craft found herself in a state of reflection. "When I first started singing, I was the same way. I wanted to be 'unique.' I didn't want anyone to be like me. Then, another singer came onto the scene. She sounded similar to me. Over time, I learned to deal with her. This was *my* voice. I had to make the best I could from this voice. So, I did. I put all the negativity aside and sang the way I wanted to sing. Forgot what everyone else said. I gave it my all. And I stayed true to myself. That's how you should look at this 'Kerri Situation.' Be yourself, Henry. Be unique. Remember. You don't have to prove anything to anybody. You understand?"

Henry bobbed his head.

"If she can't accept you for who *you* are, Henry, then forget about her," Ms. Craft exclaimed and pointed at Henry's chest, his heart. "Move on! Life is too short! And trust me. There are too many girls out there."

Henry remained quiet.

Ms. Craft peered into Henry's droopy eyes and found them slowly looking back at her.

"Okay, Henry?"

Henry bobbed his head.

"Yeah," he said. "Okay."

The next day, Henry stormed straight home from school and skipped basketball practice. Right before he walked inside the house, he spotted in the corner of his eye Kerri and two of her friends practicing their cheerleading moves outside Kerri's house. He tossed the smelly book bag on the front porch and let it dry out. It was another one of those days. Moby Dick was at it again. A minute before the lunch bell rang, the Dick stole Henry's book bag when Henry was asking the English teacher, Mr. Stoker, a question about last night's homework. As soon as Henry found out about what the Dick had done, he chased him down into the girls' restroom where he found the Dick standing next to the last stall on the left. Henry noticed the sign, OUT OF ORDER, taped on the front of the door. At that moment, he knew the outcome was going to be bad, really bad. The Dick threw Henry's book bag into the clogged toilet. "Go fetch, Urethra," he said and then shoved Henry out of the way as he exited the restroom. Henry never ate lunch. Even if Henry had the opportunity to eat, he was so disgusted from the condition of the book bag that he didn't have any appetite whatsoever. Instead, he spent the rest of the school day cleaning the feces and soggy toilet paper from his book bag.

For about an hour, Henry paced around in the kitchen and thought about what to say to Kerri. Occasionally, he glanced out the window and made sure that she was still there. From the looks of it, she was going to be there for quite some time. He thought *maybe* she would be gone by the time he gathered enough nerve to speak to her. He found himself standing in front of the bathroom mirror going over lines like: "Hi," he said, pushing a smile from his face. "I'm Henry." Henry sighed with frustration and paced around the bathroom. "Dork!" He tried yet again: "Hello, Kerri." He shook his head once more and said to himself, "Creep." Next, he peered seductively into the mirror and said, "Name's Burl, Henry Burl." Henry cried out, "I'm not James Bond! I'm unique! Remember!" Again: "Hi there, good looking," he said in a southern voice and winked at himself as he held his hand like a pistol and bent down his thumb as if it was cocking a hammer. "What do you say, me and you hitch a ride on the *Loveboat* and sail to a little place I like to call Mexico." Again: "What's up!" And again: "Howdy!" And then again: "How about this weather?" He shouted out, "Idiot! Who talks about the weather?" FINALLY: "I. . . I can't do this," he said and made an effort to look himself in the mirror. He could hardly recognize the fifteen-year-old looking back at him. In that final moment of surrender, he reached the point where he didn't care anymore.

Moments later, Henry was tramping from his house and down the driveway with Adrian strapped over his shoulder and mumbling to himself, ". . . what the hell does she know about love. . . art of. . . of contort. . . my ass. . . I'll show her. . . Dolores." His sweaty palms were clutched against the neck and bow of the saxophone. Occasionally, he had to readjust Adrian in order to keep it from slipping from his fingers. The color had emptied from his face. His stomach was doing pull-ups against his chest. He could hardly walk a straight line, even though the street that separated Henry's house from Kerri's house was as straight as an arrow. His legs were like two wet noodles, both ready to give out on him. For years, Henry had dreamt about this day, wondering what it would be like to have a meaningful conversation with Kerri, which, to Henry, seemed to go as smooth as suede in his head. No pause or stammer or hesitation. Standing with the most upright posture. The words flowing ever so fluently from his lips, hitting the right tunes, right phrases, right everything. Perfection!

As Henry crossed the street, he heard a couple of giggles coming from the side of Kerri's house.

As Henry stepped onto the driveway, he witnessed Kerri joking around with a couple of her friends in the driveway.

Kerri cupped her hand over her breast and shouted out, "That hurt, you bitch!"

"I barely even hit you," her friend returned.

Again, Henry could hardly stand straight. His knees were about to buckle. Heart racing. Senses heightened. Not only that, he had tunnel vision. He took in a deep breath and marched through Kerri's lawn.

Kerri and her friends turned to Henry approaching. Their laughter suddenly came to a halt.

"Hey, Kerri," Henry said with a tremble in his voice.

At first, Kerri acted as if she wasn't interested in a single word that he had to say.

She didn't even respond to Henry.

"I'm Henry," Henry said and pointed at his house over his shoulder. "I live across the street."

"I know," she said, her voice more whinny than from the voice in class.

"I'm in your social studies class," he said as the tremble finally calmed. "I sit in the back."

"So," Kerri said, causing a couple of giggles from her other friends.

One of Kerri's friends was whispering into another friend's ear.

Henry only made out parts.

"—*at a loser*—"

"—*What does he wan*—"

"—*don't know*—"

"—*hy is he acting so weir*—"

"Let's get out of here," Kerri said to her other friends.

"Wait," Henry blurted out. "Don't be scared."

"Scared? Who said I was scared?"

"Here," Henry said and placed the reed of the saxophone against his lips.

He played the solo from "Prom Night" and he completely nailed it too!

"What are you doing?" Kerri asked and glowered at Henry as he played the solo. "Can you stop doing that?" She covered her ears with her hands. "It's like hurting my ears."

Her friends couldn't stop laughing at Henry.

"What do you think?"

"It's annoying," she said, rolling her eyes.

The sweat beads formed around the sides of Henry's face. He peered around the street and saw the basketball against the curb.

"Do you like basketball?"

"It's okay," she said with a shrug.

Henry hurried over to the basketball. He placed Adrian in the grass, picked up the basketball, and dribbled across the street. On the way, he dribbled underneath his legs and around his body. Next, he twirled the ball over his index finger, which gathered the most attention from Kerri's friends.

"You're pretty good," Kerri said, drawing several *ahs* from her friends.

Their eyes were fascinated from Henry's slick and stylish movements, unconventional.

"You wanna play?"

"Maybe," she said. "Yeah."

Henry's eyes widened with joy.

"*Catch*," he said teasingly and passed the ball to Kerri as if she was one of the guys.

Kerri stood there stupidly. She didn't even make an attempt to catch the ball. The ball smacked her directly over the bridge of her nose. Her head snapped backward. Blood squirted out from the gash on her nose. She suddenly bellowed out and immediately grabbed her gushing nose and lunged toward the ground.

"You jerk!" one of her friends blurted out. "What are you doing?"

"I'm sor. . ."

"Kerri," Kerri's friend said and wrapped her arm around Kerri's shoulder, "are you okay, sweetie?"

She cried out, "No! I'm not okay! Look at me!"

"Look at what that jerk did to Kerri's face. . ."

Another friend: "Oh my god!"

With both of her hands cupped over her bloody nose, Kerri cried, "Why don't you just leave me alone?"

Occasionally, she pulled her hands from her nose, which caused the blood to drip all over the driveway.

"Look at all the blood!"

Her friends turned to Henry and looked at him as if he was the scum of the earth.

"I didn't mean to. . . " he uttered and hurried over to Kerri, ". . . I. . . I was just ma. . . ma. . . maaaa. . . messing around. . . she was supposed to. . . "

One of her friends stepped in front of Kerri and pushed Henry away.

"What the hell is your problem, asshole?" one of her friends said coldly, both of her hands planted on her hips.

As Kerri was rushed inside her house, Henry stood there alone and tormented.

While Henry was washing the dishes, the doorbell rang.

Abbey answered the door.

The sound of his mother, the strange greeting outside the doorway, the deflation in her voice, forced Henry to stop what he was doing and dash upstairs. He didn't wash the soap from his hands. Didn't even put up the rest of the dishes.

Once the two parents were finished talking, Henry carefully closed the bedroom window and darted back to his bed where the pounding started. The sound was hollow like the head of a hammer striking an empty wooden box, and yet at the same time, it was rich and reverberant. He couldn't distinguish the two sounds, blending over one another.

Henry breathed deeply.

Counted to ten.

By the time he reached eight, the pounding in his chest calmed a little and brought forth clarity, now two distinct sounds, the sound of his beating heart and the sound of his mother's footsteps.

The pounding eventually stopped.

Now, he could feel *her* presence looming behind the door, as well as her shadow darkening the bedroom.

The door squeaked open.

Abbey found her son sitting on the edge of the bed with his head held downward.

She asked from behind, "Do you want to talk about it?"

Henry sniffled.

"No," he mumbled.

Abbey sat down next to Henry on the bed.

"They took her to the emergency room," Abbey said quietly. "She said Kerri had to have eleven stitches."

Henry wiped away the tear from his cheek and turned to his mother.

"I didn't mean to. . . " he cried, ". . . I swear."

"I know you didn't, Henry."

"You do?"

Abbey said sternly, "It's a good thing she's not going to press any charges. She said her father was pretty upset."

"Mom, it was an accident. . . "

Abbey sighed and kissed Henry on the forehead. She got up from the bed and stopped at the doorway.

She said, "I want you to go over there tomorrow and apologize to that girl."

Before Abbey could finish her sentence, Henry was already standing on his feet.

"But I didn't. . . "

"I don't want to hear it, Henry," Abbey said, her eyes sharpening. "It's the least you can do."

Before Henry had a chance to respond, his mother was already out the door.

SEVENTEEN

AT the start of the next session, Ms. Craft could sense that there was something wrong with Henry. Whenever she got a chance to look into Henry's eyes, which were mostly held toward the floor, she recognized the torment in them, almost as if a different, much darker person had taken over his body.

She pulled her hands away from the piano keys and faced Henry.

In one sweeping motion, she folded her legs and then placed her hands over her knees as if she was going to be in that position for the remainder of the afternoon.

Ms. Craft asked sternly, "Do you want to talk about it?"

Henry snorted.

"Talk about what?"

Again, his eyes were attached to the floor.

"You know."

Henry said, "I don't know."

Ms. Craft leaned forward and tried to make eye contact with Henry.

In return, Henry adjusted the saxophone in his lap.

After he observed Ms. Craft's eyes beating down on him, he mumbled, "I don't want to talk about her anymore. I'm done with her."

Ms. Craft leaned back and sat in that same position: legs folded with both hands rested over her knees.

Henry ignored Ms. Craft, her still posture, and warmed up with Adrian. He only got through two notes before he stopped and pulled the saxophone from his lips.

131

Ms. Craft leaned closer and asked, "What's on your mind, Henry?"

As his eyes watered, Henry pulled away from Ms. Craft.

"She thinks I'm a monster," Henry said, his head pointing to the cracked window. "I went to her house to apologize. She slammed the door on my face."

"Apologize for what, Henry?" Ms. Craft said and touched Henry on the shoulder. "Look at me, Henry." Henry slowly pulled his attention toward Ms. Craft. His eyes were now attached to Ms. Craft's eyes. As always, he found comfort in them. "Why are you sorry?"

Henry didn't answer.

"Are you really sorry for what you did to this girl?"

"Ye. . . yeah. . . " he said and shrugged his shoulders, ". . . I mean. . . I don't know."

Ms. Craft reached around the piano, grabbed the green mug, which was rested on a white lace coaster, and took a small sip of coffee.

"Any girl who finds you to be a monster needs to get her head checked," she said as she held the warm mug in her hands. "You're a nice, handsome young man who is wise beyond his years."

"Why can't more girls be like. . . " Henry cautiously looked into Ms. Craft's eyes, ". . . like you, except more younger."

Ms. Craft dropped her jaw in astonishment and asked, "What do you mean, Henry?"

"I mean girls who don't play games, girls who don't make fun of me."

Ms. Craft placed the mug onto the coaster.

"Well, that all comes with age, Henry," she said and smiled. "I must say, Henry. You are an old soul. That sure is rare to find nowadays."

"Whatever," Henry said with disgust.

"It's not a bad thing," she said. "It's a good trait to have. It means you're very mature for your age and that you appreciate the very things that make us human and don't take everything for granted. So, yeah, I would say it's a wonderful trait to have. I wish there were more men out there like you, Henry."

Henry thought about Ms. Craft's comments.

"Tell me, Henry," she said. "What's on your mind? I take it things didn't go quite well with Kerri. . . "

Henry interrupted, "I told you I'm done with her."

Ms. Craft eased away from Henry.

"Okay," she said.

A sudden tension built over the conversation.

Henry remained in thought, distant.

He finally said, "I. . . "

"You what, Henry?"

"I had a dream last night."

"What kind of dream?"

"I dreamt of fire," Henry said, thinking. "And wind. I remember waking up in my dream and walking to the window and seeing a tower of flames over the streets. The wind blew open the window. The fire was rising to the sky. Burning everything it touched. Houses. The trees. The gust nearly blew me over. Then, I heard this. . . this song across the neighborhood, beyond the wall of fire. I never had a dream like that before. It was so. . . so real."

Ms. Craft listened closely.

"The song got louder, almost deafening, in my head," Henry said, motioning toward his temple. "I can feel it still there, getting stronger. After I woke, I couldn't go back to sleep. It's like. . . it's like it keeps pounding in my head."

"This song," Ms. Craft said, "what kind of a song was it?"

"I don't know," Henry replied. "I can't explain it."

"Interesting," she said and thought more about Henry's dream.

Henry nodded his head.

"You know some of the best songs ever written are about girls. . . or guys," Ms. Craft said with a slight grin. "You have to embrace that song from your dreams, channel it, and project it through your music."

"But you said. . . "

"When the art of contortion works hand in hand with the heart, well, that's where a real musician creates his magic. Remember, Henry. Love is a powerful thing. Everybody can relate to love." She pointed to her heart. "Remember. It all starts in here, the emotion, the drive, the love." She moved her finger from her chest to her temple. "Then, it takes shape in here. Science will tell us that love doesn't start in the heart, but, in fact, it starts in the brain, the mind. My grandmother once said, 'Don't believe what you hear and half what you see.'" Once more, she pointed to her chest. "But believe this, Henry. This right here. If you do, you'll be okay."

Ms. Craft unfolded her legs and quickly got up from her seat.

"Where are you going?"

"Come," she said, waving to Henry across the room. "You're ready."

Henry got up.

"Ready for what?"

"Leave the sax here," she said, not looking back.

They went upstairs into the studio. Ms. Craft had Henry close the door behind him. Henry picked up a sudden change in mood: affable to reticent. She hardly spoke a word to Henry, and whenever she did, she was very short and stern. With her back turned to Henry, she pointed to an old movie projector tucked away in the corner of the room and had Henry lug the dusty thing across the studio. She told him to place the projector on a table in the middle of the studio. Once the projector was securely on the table, Ms. Craft pulled out the circular casing of a 16 mm film reel labeled THE GALLERY OF STARS. She removed the cover from the casing and attached the film reel to the projector. Then, she had Henry cut off the lights.

"What is this?" he asked anxiously.

"You'll see," she said mysteriously. "Take a seat."

Henry sat down on a large beanbag while Ms. Craft played the show from a spot on the wall that was bare.

"I was thirty-four at the time," Ms. Craft said nostalgically. "We just recorded our fifth studio album, *Don't Wait Up*." Ms. Craft walked over to the section of keyboards and recording equipment and pulled out a vinyl record from the shelf. She handed the record to Henry, who immediately eyed the record.

"You were gorgeous," he said, the fuzzy light from the projector glazed over his face.

"I was," she said. "Wasn't I?"

Henry read the names of each Dove. He read the name *Gloria Silk* out loud.

"That was my stage name," Ms. Craft said. "Some people called me *Silk* like the fabric. They said my voice was as smooth as the texture of silk. I loved the way the name sounded, Silk. Dolores Craft certainly didn't come close to sounding as catchy as Silk."

"You're the same woman, though," he said. "You just have more wrinkles."

"Indeed I do," she said. "But don't let the wrinkles fool you, Henry. I'm still the same woman, only much more older."

Henry smiled.

"And more wrinkly."

"Yes," Ms. Craft said and carefully bobbed her head. "And more wrinkly."

With her glossy eyes glistening from the projector, Ms. Craft sat down on the recliner and didn't say much after that.

A few seconds went by without the two saying anything.

"I didn't mean," Henry said abruptly and witnessed the change in Ms. Craft's behavior. "I. . . I just know a lot of old people and they aren't half as nice as you. I. . . I mean. . . there's Ms. Hamchild down the street. If you ever met Ms. Hamchild, you know she can be a pit bull."

"It's all right, Henry," Ms. Craft said, smiling. "I know my body is old. There's no hiding that. No surgery can make a woman look younger. I don't care what they say." Then, she directed her attention to the still projection on the wall. "The night before the show, I broke up with my longtime boyfriend. His name was Sebastian. He was a great man. He was the kind of man who would go into battle for me. He could've been outnumbered by at least a hundred men and yet he would fight for me, die for me. We met while I was recording *Roses for Judith*, a record I wrote after my mother's passing. Sebastian and I certainly had our share of fights. But the night before this one show in particular, he wanted me to quit the band and start a family with him. He called me 'the most selfish woman on the planet.' That was when he gave me an ultimatum: either quit The Doves of Saturn or he was going to leave forever. He was so sick and tired of all the attention I was getting. The jealously was consuming his body, suffocating him."

Intrigued, Henry asked, "What did Sebastian do for a living?"

"Believe it or not, he was a producer," she answered. "At the time, he was having trouble with a couple other bands. He had enough of the industry. There was a song on the album called 'Empty House.' I wrote the song about Sebastian." Ms. Craft looked up at the projection on the wall. "This was my performance."

The Doves of Saturn played.

She turned up the volume.

The passion and aggression was immense. Gloria Silk sang with a deep, bottomless anger, visceral. She sang: *"I don't want your diamond ring. I don't want your picket fence. I don't want that pink Ferrari. If this is too hard to ask, then go 'head and leave. That's right. Leave! Go 'head. And leave! Take everything that you've ever given me and leave! You can't buy your way into my heart! So don't dare lie your way into my heart! 'Cuz I just want you! Is that so hard to ask? I just want you! Nothing more! Nothing less!* (Tambourine shaking, building) *Don't want your diamond ring! And leave! Don't want your picket fence! And leave! Don't want that pink Ferrari! I don't want! I don't want! So leave! And leave! AND LEAVE!"* Henry was amazed and yet shocked from the performance. Halfway through the performance, when the song suddenly slowed and Ms. Craft was repeatedly singing, *"What have I done? There goes another man on the run. Alone now in this room. Alone now in this empty house,"* the tears flowed down his eyes, Henry's. When the performance was over, Ms. Craft turned to Henry, who was trying to wipe the tears from his cheeks before Ms. Craft had a chance to look.

"What do you think?" Ms. Craft asked, holding her hands together.

Henry said, "I. . . I. . . I can't believe that was you."

"I know."

"It was amazing, Dolores."

"Thank you, Henry."

Ms. Craft suddenly got up from the recliner and turned off the projector. She turned the light back on.

"I tell you what, Henry," she said with a bit of excitement in her voice. "How about I take you out for ice cream?"

"I would like that."

Ms. Craft wrapped her arm around Henry.

"You're buying," Henry joked.

"Then it looks like you're going to have to clean up my garage," she said and pulled Henry closer. "It's getting pretty messy in there."

After they ate ice cream at a local ice cream parlor called Two Scoops where Ms. Craft shared valuable information about Adrian and how she was one with him now and how he must listen to his heart and find his song, deep within, despite all the outside noise that might come his way, like the imposters, like the copycats, like the critics—"the power of your sound lies within yourself and now you are the captain of your own ship," she preached—Ms. Craft dropped off Henry at the house. Henry thanked Ms. Craft, not only for the orange sherbet ice cream, but also for letting him borrow her record player from her vast collection. This one so happened to be a suitcase-style Crosley with three speeds, portable too. Henry went back inside his house and went directly upstairs to his bedroom and set up the Crosley on the bed. Next, he carefully pulled the vinyl record, *Roses for Judith*, from the sleeve, held the record in his hands as if it was a holy artifact, and read the *Gloria Silk* autograph, as well as the personal note (*To my good friend, Henry*) on the front cover.

As he removed the vinyl from the sleeve, he carefully placed the record on the turntable.

During the second track, he heard the sound of giggling over the steady vinyl crackle. He sprang from the bed and peered out the window. Kerri and her friends were sprinting back to Kerri's house. Henry thought he heard one of her friends shouting out across the street, "Now you two love birds can fly away together!"

Stricken with outrage, Henry removed the needle from the record and went downstairs to check out the commotion outside.

Once he saw the object lying over the front steps of the porch, he realized the joke was now on him and would be for the rest of the school year, which was still a couple of weeks away. All of the ridicule, the jeering and sneering, as well as the harsh and demoralizing names that were ignorantly thrown at Ms. Craft, were now headed in Henry's direction.

He eased himself through the front door and cautiously picked up the weathered broomstick from the steps.

From now on, Henry was known as. . . "Igor, the Witch's Apprentice.

EIGHTEEN

WHILE Henry was drifting in and out of sleep, a strange whispering caused him to stir. The whispering was now piercing to his ears. The door handle jiggled, slow at first and then violently. Sweating profusely, Henry rolled back and forth as the damp bed sheets strangled his body. The muddled voice was now screaming in Henry's ears. Louder! However, the voice was different from the one before. Not womanly or deathly like the other dreams, but masculine. And the door handle, it was *still* jiggling, causing the screws to loosen. One screw fell from the door and landed on the floor. Suddenly, a fist pounded against the door and caused the bed to shake. Henry's eyes bolted open. The sheets were now pulled away from Henry's body, leaving him room to breath. In a daze, he scanned the empty bedroom and realized he was in a different room, which, with the exception of a couple pieces of girl's furniture (vanity table and dresser), was empty. The walls were plain and solid green. No pictures hanging on the wall. One mirror. Henry's reflection in the mirror was as dark as a shadow, unrecognizable, even from the glow of snow on the antique television. There wasn't any sound coming from the television. No white noise. The hardwood cracked from the cold breeze of air coming from the open bedroom window. The bottom half of a moonlit curtain was gently waving around like a weightless hand. The whispering remained intact, not as penetrating, yet soft and delicate. Henry soon realized the whispering wasn't coming from outside the window! He untangled his feet from the bed covers, rolled out of bed, and searched for the source of the whispering. *Behind the door*, he drew his attention toward the door, which was now still, not rattling. He strolled through the familiar bedroom and eased his hand over the door handle, which was loose and wobbly. He cautiously opened the door. A gasp ran like a dull blade over the hair of his neck and brought her to life. He canceled her out with other thoughts: baseball, Scrabble, golf, or something boring or mundane. She went retreating back into his mind. However, he didn't know how much longer he could hold her off. The darkness had a way of bringing out such ghosts. A narrow hallway stretching into a wall of darkness was revealed. He poked his head from the bedroom and found another room across the hallway, the master bedroom. He tiptoed down the creaking hallway and then entered the other bedroom, the master bedroom, which was twice as big as the room he was just in. The comforter was lying on the floor. Flattened pillows too. Dark stains covered the white sheets in continent-like shapes. *It's coming from the closet*, the whispering. Henry stumbled his way through the strange bedroom and opened the closet door. The whispering was even louder now, beating like a piston, and yet he still couldn't make out a single word. He followed the whispering to a leather case, his saxophone case. For a second, the case shifted and then moved inches away from its resting place. For a second, Henry thought there was some kind of rabid animal inside the case! His heart sank into his stomach, which prompted him to tightly roll his hand into a fist.

With one of his hands balled up, he popped open the case with his other hand.

"Adrian," he mumbled with his hand unfolding.

Just Adrian.

He pulled out Adrian and held the saxophone closely in his hands. He leaned his head closer to the bell and heard the same masculine voice coming within the saxophone.

"*Lover, rider, fighter of the night,*" the smooth and layered and resonant voice sang from the darkness of the bell. "*Show me the way to the forgotten land. Set your sights on the light.*"

Henry stepped back in confusion and pulled Adrian away from his body. The lyrics were from a Mr. Vortex's record, he concluded. In fact, the song was the title song from the record *Hard Rider*. The voice kept crackling and repeating over and over. "*Lover, rider, fighter of the night. Show me the way to the forgotten land. Set your sights on the light.*" Henry pulled his ear away from the saxophone and peered into the dark hollowness of the bell. Suddenly, a maddening eye opened inside the darkness!

Henry gasped and ripped through his bed covers.

Sweating, he slowly gathered his surroundings and realized he was back in his own bed, his own bedroom. He glanced over at the time on the nightstand. The clock read 2:37.

He turned to the closet across the bedroom.

The doors were the same as when he fell asleep: closed.

The window was closed as well.

There was no whispering either.

No song playing.

No Mr. Vortex.

The only noise coming from the bedroom was the constant humming of an air conditioner overhead.

NINETEEN

WHEN summer finally came, Henry went through a metamorphosis in his attitude toward music and the way he carried himself, which impressed most, if not all, of his teachers. He was down to only three friends, T.J., Danny, and Arena, a tenth (now eleventh) grader who lived on the next street, Gabi Orchard Road. Although the rumors about "Igor" and his new friend, Ms. Witchcraft, were traveling around the school like the Monday gossip after the weekend, he wasn't bothered—at least not all the time. There were times when Henry felt dejected and isolated and pushed into a corner. Most of the time, however, Henry just simply brushed off the rumors, the name calling, whatever, as if he was brushing a piece of felt from his shoulder. "They say he's sacrificing goats for her over there," one rumor spread around the school. "And she makes him drink the blood!" Another one: "They're reanimating the living dead." And then another: "That dude, Jodi, rumor has it is that he's going to be their next test subject for this so called 'Cyborg Project.'" It was true, but not all of it. Henry and Ms. Craft were delving into the realm of cyborgs, at least not the kind the other students were gossiping about. Out of good fun, they recorded an instrumental song together. The conception of the song came from Henry himself. He said, "I want it to sound like a soundtrack for a B-rated horror movie." Since Henry was fairly knowledgeable when it came to 1970's and 80's horror movies, mostly 80's—or so he thought—he wanted to do a creepy song that would scare the living hell out of people, especially with Halloween four months away, which, to

Henry, was right around the corner. The purpose of the song was to throw all the rumors back in the other students' faces and pretty much say, "Yeah. Ms. Craft and I are friends. Yeah. She's like fifty or sixty years older than me. We hang out from time to time. So what? Got a problem?" The song was recorded in Ms. Craft's studio upstairs. She ended up playing most of the instruments on the song, including the Fairlight as well as the organ, a Vox Super Continental. Henry, of course, improvised with a solo of his own, which Ms. Craft called "awfully wicked." T.J. was also asked to join in on the song. So, he provided some factory sounds (mostly ambience with distant shrieks and whatnot) that were taken from a sound library, as well as the beat and an introductory sample borrowed from the movie *Frankenstein* (1931). The famous line: "It's alive!" Henry Frankenstein, who was played by Actor Colin Clive, hysterically shouted over the claps of thunder as he witnessed his creation's hand slowly rise above the operation table. The sample was played over the Vox. Then, T.J. created a beat. "IT'S ALIVE!" After the song was recorded onto cassette tape, Ms. Craft asked Henry and T.J. what they should call the song. "Call it 'Cyborg,'" Henry said. T.J. was instantly sold. As for Skip and Armani, they were afraid of ruining their reputation. So, they decided to make new friends with the football players. Again, Henry didn't care. Not one bit. Once when Henry was ready to embrace the liberation that was summer—and not to mention, no more homework—Abbey hit him with bad news. Surely, Henry wasn't going to get a free ride and spend his whole summer at Ms. Craft's house. Henry *had* to work. Abbey found a part time job at the local newspaper. On weekdays, Abbey and Henry got up at three o'clock in the morning and delivered newspapers. Henry was in charge of rolling up the newspapers and fastening them with rubberbands while Abbey was in charge of placing the newspaper on each doormat. Since Abbey quit her job at Fifth Seasons, she and Henry watched every purchase they made. During the summers, every penny counted. The electric bill was almost always higher, car payments. Henry rode the bike more often than none, despite the heat. They also kept as many lights off in the house as possible to save money. "Each light counts." Abbey compared the lights to meals. "Each light you turn off saves money, which very well means you got a meal on the table at the end of the day." Henry was relieved to say that basketball season was over. And the season didn't start back up until next fall. He had taken his AAU team to the State Finals where they won victoriously, which was no surprise. Henry came out as M.V.P. of the tournament. Had the trophy to show. Each year, Abbey displayed the trophies over the fireplace mantle and then took them down and replaced them with new ones. Whenever Henry wasn't practicing with Ms. Craft, he hung around T.J. and his other two friends—but mostly T.J. During the afternoon, they practically lived at Water Mountain, a popular water park located in Lansford. At times, Arena—if she wasn't too busy going on missionary trips with the church—would "borrow" her father's car (even though she only had her learner's permit) and take them to Water Mountain. Other times, T.J.'s stay-at-home mother, Mrs. Livingston (Henry didn't exactly know her first name), would take them and then chaperone. By mistake—actually a slip of the tongue—Mrs. Livingston found out about Henry and Ms. Craft. In fact, she already knew about the two. So, when T.J. slipped his tongue, it was no surprise to her. Even though Henry wasn't a boy scout (never thought about becoming one or got pressured into joining the organization), he made a scout's honor with T.J.'s mother not to tell Abbey about the relationship.

So, she didn't.

At least that was what Henry thought.

Besides Christmas and his birthday, Halloween was one of Henry's favorite days of the year. Christmas had the presents and stuff—same with his birthday—as well as Santa Clause, the sleigh, and his reindeer (at the age of two the gig was blown when Henry caught his mother cramming presents underneath the Christmas tree in the middle of the night), and then Rudolph and those stop-motion animation television specials, Frosty the talking snowman, the Christmas decorations, the Christmas lights, more Christmas decorations, the Christmas commercials (*The California Raisins* being one of them), Grandma's house, and the snow, or at least the idea of a white Christmas. On neither of those days, though, Henry couldn't dress up as a monster or see how much candy he could fit into his pillowcase or have a legitimate excuse to stay up late or watch horror movies with his friends. Since he was fifteen—going on sixteen next January—and now a tenth grader, he knew that this was going to be the last year for trick-or-treating. After tenth grade (which was really pushing the bar), it seemed odd to the other high school students. Not like Henry cared. He was at that age where he was more excited about the parties than the trick-or-treating. So, Henry wanted to go out with a bang.

The week building up toward Halloween was always like being trapped in a fog, unlike Christmas or his birthday where he was in the company of his family. Most of the time was filled with sketches and doodles of what his next costume would *or* could look like, preparations of costume gear, trial runs of various costumes, gutting pumpkins over old newspaper and carving jack-o-lanterns into the most ridiculous faces, using the rest of the pumpkin to make pumpkin pie and roast pumpkin seeds. When his Uncle Charlie from California (who was planning on moving to Lansford next spring) came to visit Henry three Halloweens ago, he took Henry to the local costume store, The Attic. Initially, Abbey sent Uncle Charlie and Henry on an errand run: two bottles of Pinot Noir, one bottle of white face paint for Henry's skeleton costume, the same one that he wore trick-or-treating several years before, and an economy sized bag of Candy Teeth and Peanut Butter Cups for the trick-or-treaters. Then, Henry saw it there mounted on the wall along with all of the other masks underneath those bright spotlights. On the way to The Attic, Henry was raving about this one movie that he and T.J. had sneaked into at Twin Falls, which played Halloween movies throughout the entire month of October. Henry was telling Uncle Charlie how he didn't sleep for two nights straight. The movie was called *The Howling* (1981).

Uncle Charlie, being a movie buff like Henry, had seen the movie as well. During the road trip, they talked forever about that one scene where Eddie Quist, a serial killer played by Actor Robert Picardo, transformed into a werewolf (Henry: "Similar to the one in *American Werewolf in London*, but way much more rad." Uncle Charlie: "What? You crazy!" Henry: "Yeah uh!" Uncle Charlie: "I don't know, Henry. The one in *American Werewolf* was pretty sick. You have to admit. That jaw, how it stretched out into a snout. Pretty sick, Henry.") When Henry's eyes crossed that one particular mask among the other gruesome masks on the wall, he immediately turned to Uncle Charlie in a state of rapture. After a minute of begging and pleading and tugging on his coat, Uncle Charlie caved in and said in a long, drawn out tone, "You win, Henry." The mask had long salt and pepper hair—which his friends later teased about being made up of a Chinaman's pubic hair when, in fact, it was only faux fur—and a drooling snout with fangs as long as fingers and two little holes as eyes. Abbey, as usual, didn't approve of the mask and hid it in her closet throughout the winter. She claimed it was "too mature for a twelve year old!" Although Henry never dressed up as a werewolf that year (he went as a skeleton with his skeleton suit and skeleton face paint, which, to Abbey, was more appropriate due to his skinny frame), he convinced his mother into dressing up as a werewolf the following year. From there, Henry went as a werewolf. A couple of weeks prior to last year's Halloween, he altered the look of the werewolf and tried to make it creepier than the trial before. The first trial: just a mask and a pair of white briefs. The second: the mask with a tee shirt and sweat pants and a pair of yellow cat-like contacts. The third (and final): the mask with his grandfather's Mr. Brawny Man-like flannel shirt ripped at the sleeves and a pair of blue jeans shredded and frayed around the knees to make him look as if his skinny frame changed over into this stocky, bowlegged beast. T.J. said that Henry was like a "hairier Incredible Hulk." So, Henry kept at it until he got the costume just right.

*   *   *

The meteorologist predicted that winds would reach up to thirty miles per hour from Hurricane Jacob, which was currently cutting its way through the Gulf Coast of Mexico, but it never stopped Henry from his favorite holiday of the year.

As Henry stood in front of the bedroom mirror with his nerves spinning around his body like a turbine, each pass sending a combination of chilling anxiety and radiating excitement, and the last bit of sun wincing through the window, he couldn't believe that he actually pulled off the greatest costume ever. *By far, this was the best costume*, he thought. *Perfection.* Henry was wearing a full-on werewolf suit. All week, he had searched around from costume store to costume store looking for the suit. The day before Halloween, he finally found one across town at a hole in the wall shop that had the same salt and pepper hair as the mask.

While Henry went over every single detail of the suit, every hair and claw, Abbey knocked on the door.

Another knock.

"Come in," he said behind the mask.

Abbey poked her head into the bedroom.

"Whoa! Whoa! Whoa!" she said, stepping into the room. "Go on now!" She studied Henry's costume, even the contacts in his eyes. "What did you do to my Henry? Oh my Lord! My poor Henry!"

Her eyes were filled with both wonder and terror (orchestrated, of course). Prior to the fitting, she had only seen the suit folded up in bag.

"Funny, Mom," Henry said, as his voice dampened underneath the mask. "So, what do you think?"

She set the bowl of candy teeth on the table and folded her arms over her chest.

"It's a bit too much, but. . . " she puckered her lips to the side and studied the costume closer in both surprise and confusion, ". . . if that's what you want to go as. So be it."

Henry scanned over the costume.

"It's perfect."

"Has T.J. or Danny seen the costume?"

"Not yet," he said.

A wave of excitement flooded over her voice.

"Well, go on then! You got to show them!"

Henry didn't move an inch. He was too enthralled from the costume as well as his mother's rare even-tempered state.

"I'm gonna get my camera. . ."

Moments later, Henry and Abbey were making their way downstairs into the living room where T.J. and Danny were both sitting on the couch. T.J. was dressed up as Frankenstein's monster. He and his father spent all afternoon constructing the outfit. Most of the time was spent trying to get those rubber bolts to stick to T.J.'s neck. They even contemplated stapling down the bolts. Mrs. Livingston actually thought the two jokesters were being serious. As for Danny, he went as the Count himself, Count Dracula. Henry could smell Danny's sour hair gel from halfway across the living room. Everything else from the plastic vampire fangs, which made the gap in his teeth more disguisable, to the black polyester cape and pale makeup were from one of those prepackaged stock costumes Henry had seen numerous times at the local drugstore.

Danny said, "I thought you were going as Igor this year."

"Yeah," T.J. whined. "That's why I went as the Frankenstein."

"And I thought you were going as the Blob."

"Very funny, Henry," Danny said, rolling his eyes.

"Yeah, Count," T.J. teased as well. "They even named a cereal after you. It's called *Count Chocula*."

"Shut up, Octo!"

"Vampires are supposed to drink blood, not eat the entire body."

"Cut it out, you two," Abbey said sullenly and then pointed at T.J.'s costume. "By the way, T.J., it's Frankenstein's monster. Frankenstein is the name of the scientist."

T.J. smacked his gums.

"I ain't never heard of that."

"Well, that's what it is," she said and then nodded at Danny. "So, what's the story with Igor? The other day I heard that girl across the street, Mrs. Coleridge's daughter, yelling out that name for everybody on the entire street to hear."

"It's. . . " Henry said abruptly. "She's ah. . . ah. . . she has Tourette's syndrome."

"Tourette's syndrome?" Abbey drawled. "How come I've never heard of that?"

Both T.J. and Danny followed along with Henry's concealment.

Danny said, "It's where you yell out names and curse words, Ms. Burl."

T.J. followed, "Yeah. That's right. The otha day, she was even yellin' out letters from the alfabet."

"I wasn't born yesterday, T.J.," Abbey interrupted. "I've never heard Mrs. Coleridge say anything about her daughter having Tourette's."

"She thinks she's like from the future, Ms. Burl."

"Yeah."

"Don't get smart with me," she said, sharpening her eyes. "The both of you."

"Sorry, Ms. Burl."

Danny slightly hung his head.

Abbey asked cheerfully, "So, are you guys ready?"

T.J. got into character and stood up from the couch like a walking stiff, with his arms extended out in front of him, his head upright, and his eyes opened widely. When T.J. walked with his knees locked and his legs straight, he looked more like a North Korean solider marching than Mary Shelley's monster.

"Hey, boner!" Danny cried out. "You're doing it all wrong."

Next thing Danny knew, he was stumbling forward from a swift *smack* in the back of the head. Danny grimaced and grabbed the backside of his head.

Abbey was looming over him.

"No boner talk in my house, boy," she said, her sharp finger aimed at Danny.

"Sorry, Ms. Burl."

"Pee-you!"

T.J. sniffed his armpit and then smelled the air around Danny.

"Who done farted?"

"Not me," Henry said.

Danny disgracefully shrugged his shoulders.

"Danny!"

"What?"

Henry said to T.J., "S.B.D."

"S.B.D.?"

"Silent But Deadly."

"Dang, Danny Boy! What'd you eat?"

"It slipped," Danny said innocently. "I swear!"

"Yeah! Whatever. . . "

"All right, you three!" Abbey exclaimed. "Outside! Now!"

As Abbey walked the three monsters outside, she gathered them around the front lawn and took a picture with the instant camera. The wind picked up and blew around the fallen leaves as well as some of the spooky decorations around the front of the house.

"One more," she said and then waited until the wind subsided. "This wind is something else."

"Do you have to?"

"Be a good sport, Henry," she said and guided Henry back into the frame. "Now, give me your meanest monster poses."

"Really?"

"Don't be such a grouch, Henry," Abbey exclaimed. "You love Halloween."

The wind finally died down.

Henry and his other two friends posed for the picture. Henry arched upward in an attack position while T.J. got back into a Korean solider stance and Danny hissed, revealing those cheap plastic fangs.

Abbey took the picture.

"All right now," she said ecstatically. "That's good."

"Can we go now?"

"Yeah." She sighed. "You can go now." Abbey shooed away Henry and his two friends. "Have fun! And don't eat too much candy! And no later than nine o'clock! Some people have to go to work tomorrow! And if it gets too windy, you hurry back home! You hear!"

Henry shouted back, "All right!"

As the final glimpse of sun flirted with the horizon, the three monsters walked down the street and met up with Arena, who was dressed up as Alice from *Alice in Wonderland*, on the corner of Arthur Belk and Gabi Orchard Road. She was wearing a blonde wig with a black bow, same blue dress, white stockings, and slippers. She was holding hands with a white rabbit as tall as her waist. The rabbit was wearing the same red suit and bowtie and carrying the same large clock like the white rabbit from *Alice in Wonderland*.

"Wow, Arena!" Henry studied Arena's costume in wonder. "Nice costume!"

"Who in the hell you supposed to be?"

"Watch the language," Arena said and nodded at the rabbit next to her.

"Alice, of course," Henry spoke for her.

"So, what do you think?" she said, wearing a beam across her face. She flaunted the dress, as well as the wig, and did a little twirl for the three.

"Not bad," Danny said impressively, his lips bent with a frown. "So, who's the rabbit?"

"This is my little brother, David," she answered. "My mom said he had to come with us."

T.J. groaned.

"Only for like an hour," Arena said anxiously. "Then I have to take him back home."

"Why is he all dressed up like it's Easter?"

"Yeah, David," T.J. said jokingly. "Where's your basket of Easta eggs?"

"Don't you guys ever read?" Henry said annoyingly. "He's the white rabbit from *Alice in Wonderland*. Get it. She's Alice. He's the white rabbit."

"Oh yeah," T.J. said. "Now I see. I 'member seein' him that one time in them cartoons."

"Nothing scary about a little ole bunny."

Arena rolled her eyes and said, "He's only four years old, Danny."

"Whatever," Danny whined. "Are we going to get some candy or what? I'm dying over here."

"I'm sure you is, Danny Boy."

"By the way, I brought a little something for the road," Danny said and reached into the pillowcase. "I could only get six. Plus, the stuff in the liquor cabinet was all watered down."

Danny pulled out six airplane bottles of Jim Bean as well as three Cherry cigarettes.

T.J. hollered out, "Now, this is what I'm talkin' 'bout."

"Where'd you get the smokes?"

"Stole 'em from my older brother."

"Your older brother smokes Cherry cigarettes?"

"Aren't those girl cigarettes?"

Danny smacked his gums.

"What's the difference?" he whined. "A cigarette is a cigarette."

"Nah. I'm pretty sure Cherry cigarettes is for girls."

T.J. snatched the pack of cigarettes from Danny's hand and handed them to Arena.

"Here, Arena," he said. "Danny brought you a present."

Danny grabbed the pack from T.J.

"Give them back."

"Chillz."

"I didn't know cigarettes had a gender."

"They don't. But Cherry's do."

"Whatever," Danny said under his breath. "That completely makes no sense at all."

He twisted open the cap from the airplane bottle and took a baby sip.

"What if your dad finds out? Six bottles is a lot to go missing."

"He hasn't drank these things in years," Danny said to Arena. "They've been sitting there for as long as I can remember. Besides, if he finds out I'll just tell him that T.J. stole them."

"No you ain't!"

"I'm just teasing," he said. "I'll fill them back up with apple juice or something."

"Yeah," T.J. said. "Like that's gonna work."

"It will," he said. "Trust me."

"You mean you had them in there the entire time?"

"Yeah," Danny shrugged his shoulders. "So."

"What if my mom found out?"

"But she didn't, Henry," Danny said casually. "Relax."

Danny handed T.J. and Arena each an airplane bottle.

"Your lil brother ain't gonna tell your parents. Is he?"

"Like I said, he's only four, T.J."

"Aight," he said. "But if he rats us out, then. . . "

"Then what, T.J.?"

"I'm jus sayin'."

"He won't rat us out, T.J."

Danny took a swig from the airplane bottle.

"Yuck!" he said, grimacing.

"Pussy."

"It ain't that bad," T.J. said and sipped from the airplane bottle.

"You try then, Henry."

Danny handed Henry an airplane bottle.

"I don't know, guys," he said.

"Quit being such a pussy."

Henry smacked his gums.

"I'm not a pussy."

"Then prove it."

Henry lifted up the werewolf mask and sipped from the airplane bottle. His face went sour. His eyes watered and then burned from the contacts.

"He's going to hurl."

"I'm good," Henry said and breathed a sigh of relief.

Danny patted Henry on the back.

"See," he said. "Told you."

"That a boy, Henry."

The five walked off into the sunset, Arena and David holding hands while the other three were stumbling around from the alcohol. The sky above them displayed a brilliant wash of reds and pinks. Their costumed bodies (Werewolf, Dracula, Frankenstein's monster, Alice, and the White Rabbit) were like silhouettes marked across the colorful horizon.

"Hey, guys," Danny said and downed the rest of the airplane bottle and then let out a loud *burp*, "if a vampire bites a werewolf, does the werewolf turn into a vampire or is it immune to vampires?"

"I don't know, Danny," Henry said. "But that would make one killer movie."

"It sure would."

"If Danny bit you, Henry, I'd think you catch diabetes."

"Hey!" Danny cried out and opened up another airplane bottle. "Not funny."

"Danny might end up eating you, Henry!"

The others burst out laughing.

Since T.J. was the closest, Danny pushed T.J. for laughing.

As they walked down Gabi Orchard, Danny reached over and acted as if he was about to bite Henry on the neck.

Henry pushed him aside.

"Cut it out, Fatcula."

"I got a question," Arena said curiously. "What if a werewolf bit a vampire?"

"That would make it more beast than bat," Danny wondered out loud. "Talk about one hairy bat!"

Arena exclaimed, "Now that would be a killer movie!"

"How about this?" Henry said blissfully. "What if a werewolf got bit by a vampire," he touched Danny on the shoulder, "not you Danny, but like that vampire from *Nosferatu*. Then, this half werewolf half vampire got *it* on with a Lamia. And then, they had a baby."

T.J. butted in, "How do you think Danny Boy was born."

Danny groaned and rolled his eyes.

Arena asked, "And what is a Lamia?"

"She's from Greek mythology," Henry explained. "According to myth, she eats children."

"Really?" Danny whined. "This is coming from the same person who got all over me for claiming Ms. Witchcraft ate other kids."

Henry said angrily, "That's because she doesn't, Danny."

"Does to."

"She don't, Danny Boy."

"You're one to talk, Octo."

T.J. groaned, "Can we jus drop the whole eaten children conversation please? It's freakin' me out big time."

They all agreed for the time being.

Toward the end of the night, they all grew tired of David's whining, including Henry.

It was getting late, close to nine o'clock, and Henry and his friends were due back in about twenty minutes. At this point in the night, Henry didn't care much about the candy anymore. Henry and the gang would've easily picked up more candy along the way, but they ended up taking a detour back to Arena's house off Gabi Orchard and dropping off Arena's little brother ten minutes earlier from all of his complaining about the stuffiness of that rabbit costume. "I want to go home!" he kept whining every ten seconds while yanking on Arena's skirt. Not only that, they had to wait for Danny, who ended up vomiting behind a bush after taking two drags from a Cherry cigarette. The others were pretty tipsy but held their own. Arena was known for pretending to be drunk when, in fact, she wasn't. Example: Last summer, Danny stole a half gallon of Aristocrap from his father's cabinet. What Danny didn't realize (at least not until he took a swig from the bottle) was that he completely forgot that he filled up nearly the entire thing with water two weeks prior. He and T.J. decided to play a prank on Arena. So, that night they went out to a friend's house. They passed around the half gallon and acted as if they were drunk when, in fact, they were as sober as a couple of Mormons. After they finished the entire bottle, Arena was stumbling around and slurring, "I'm soooooooo wasted," to the others. Later, Danny broke the news to Arena. Instant poker face followed with a swift smack across Danny's face.

After David made it safely back home, the others were relieved to say the least. Unlike Dracula or Frankenstein's monster or Alice, who were all wearing costumes that could breathe, Henry shared the same difficulty as David. During David's fit, Henry bit his tongue. Not once did he ever complain about how tropical it was inside the costume despite the windy conditions. Each inhale was like breathing the steam from a pot of boiling water. And the sweat was acting like an adhesive against the costume. Once during the stroll back home, it crossed his mind that maybe the costume would be permanently stuck to his body and Abbey would have to call the fire department and tell them to bring the jaws of life. The werewolf costume might have been a poor choice, he thought, especially on such a warm and humid night.

Despite losing around two pounds of sweat now, Henry stayed in character and yearned for each gust of wind.

Only a couple of houses left now, Mr. Quail's house and then Mr. and Mrs. Livingston's house, which was always in full supply of candy. Last year, it was Ring Bites. This year it was Magic Beans. They decided, however, not to stop at Mr. and Mrs. Livingston's house due to Danny's current state as well as their own. Plus, they reeked like bourbon whiskey and artificial cherry-flavored cigarettes.

As Henry swayed back and forth, he pursued one more house, which was still lit up like Christmas with at least a dozen jack-o-lanterns scattered around the front porch and red lights lighting up the interior, while most of the other houses had their lights off, which pretty well meant the residents were through with trick-or-treaters. In prior years, Henry and the other trick-or-treaters were told not to go to Ms. Craft's house and if they did, their parents threw away the candy that was left on the front porch. Some said that

Ms. Craft stuck razors inside the candy, which wasn't true. These were, of course, just rumors.

As they strolled down Davie Morris, Henry and the others passed a couple of other seventh and eighth graders from school. Their fathers were chaperoning them.

Danny, who was starting to slow down in his walk, nodded at Henry.

"Where are we going, Henry?" he asked.

Henry struggled to pull off the werewolf mask. When he finally did with two strenuous tugs, the warm air was like a cool breeze against his skin. The wind picked up again and blew over Henry's face, comforting him greatly.

"Are we just going to stand here all night?"

Henry finished savoring the cool gust of air and pointed at Ms. Craft's house.

He returned, "What do you think, Danny?"

"Ah no!" Weary eyed, Danny stopped and then sat down on the curb. "I'm not going over there. No way!"

As he was known to do, T.J. smacked his gums together.

"It's cool, Danny Boy," he said. "She ain't like what others say 'bout her. She nice." He motioned to Henry. "Ax Henry yourself."

"You've met her?"

T.J. moaned.

"Yeah," he said. "The time she drove me and Henry to the Herbie Hancock concert."

"Hold up, Octo," Danny said and stood to his feet. "You said you went with your dad."

T.J. shrugged his shoulders.

"I lied."

Danny's shoulders inflated.

"What do you mean?" he said, his tone rising.

"Come on, Danny. . . "

"Friends don't lie to each other."

"The only reason we told you that we went with Octo's dad was because we didn't want to get in trouble."

"You thought I would nark on you?"

Danny stood in the same position: shoulders inflated with a betrayed expression on his face.

"Remember that time when Octo accidentally broke your mom's blender."

"I was. . . " he stuttered, ". . . I was getting back at him for what he did to Frosty."

"Come on, Danny Boy," T.J. drawled. "It was jus a prank."

Danny didn't say anything in return.

Henry and T.J. were staring at Danny.

"All right," Danny said with irritation and followed Henry and T.J. to Ms. Craft's house. During the whole time, Henry had a time putting his mask back on. "But if she starts chanting in Latin or speaking in tongues, then I'm out of there."

"Witches don't speak in Latin," Arena said, rolling her eyes.

Henry finally stuck on the mask and shouted out through the snout, "She's not a witch, you guys!"

"All right," Arena said in defeat.

"She's jus an old lady, Danny *and* Arena," T.J said. "You guys call her names and yet you haven't even met her."

On the way to Ms. Craft's house, Danny spotted someone from their grade, who was dressed in scruffy jeans and a solid black long sleeve shirt and wearing a sinister, Pennywise-esque clown mask over his head and carrying an armful of what he thought were candles, and then another kid, also with no chaperone, who was dressed up in skin tight jeans and a red shirt and blue sweat jacket and wearing a Pumpkinhead mask over his head, sneaking behind Ms. Craft's house.

"Hey," Danny said as he gazed farther down the street. "Isn't that Skip and Armani?"

T.J. saw Pumpkinhead creeping behind the house.

"I think so."

Henry recognized Jesse, who wasn't dressed up at all, standing on the curb across from Ms. Craft's house and smoking a cigarette.

"Look," he said and nodded at Jesse. "It's Jesse."

"Looks like he went as himself."

"He too cool for Halloween."

"Talk about scary," Danny teased, gathering a couple of laughs.

Halfway toward Ms. Craft's house, Henry glanced back over at Jesse, who was acting extremely paranoid, glancing back and forth around the street. As soon as he pulled his attention toward Henry and the others approaching, he placed his index finger and thumb inside his mouth and whistled to Skip and Armani, who were already behind Ms. Craft's house. Henry didn't think too much of the strange reaction. He thought that they were cutting through the woods, as most kids did around here, and Jesse was just giving his friends a heads up.

A couple of houses down, Abbey stepped outside on the porch and blew out the flame from the jack-o-lantern.

As she went to pick up a few crumbled-up candy wrappers from the front lawn and sidewalk, she heard a commotion coming from Ms. Craft's house.

The front door of Ms. Craft's house slowly creaked open. The door opened entirely. Nobody was there behind or around the door. A fog machine was pumping out thick bands of fog over the porch.

Abbey stopped what she was doing and focused on Ms. Craft's house.

She suddenly heard the kids yell out, "*Trick or treat!*"

Ms. Craft inched from the shadows and crept toward the open door. The bright red light coming from the inside of the house was glazed over one side of her cloaked body. The other side was covered in the shadows. She was wearing this dark robe down to her ankles and a pointy hat (like a witch!). Her face drifted closer into the red light, revealing slowly. The gang noticed her ugly face (the makeup, the nose!). Then, they gasped in horror. Her face was a shade of pale green. Her nose was long and sharp like a bird's beak. Her eyes wide and menacing. She stepped from the shadows and revealed her costume.

Ms. Craft said in a high pitch voice, "Hello, my pretties!"

"WITCH!" Danny screamed. "I TOLD YOU!"

As Danny alone made it halfway down the stairs with his arms flailed out while the others remained on the porch, Henry along with T.J. and Arena nearly fell to the ground laughing.

Henry hollered out, "Where you going, Fatcula?"

Ms. Craft asked, "Henry, is that you under there?"

"Yeah," he said as he yanked the mask from his face. "What do you think?"

After a once over, she said, "I love it! Especially the eyes!"

As soon as Danny realized that Ms. Craft's costume was only a costume (which Henry made abundantly clear, "only a costume") and that Ms. Craft wasn't really a witch or a creature, he rotated back around and sauntered to the others with his head held down in humiliation.

Ms. Craft said, "I didn't mean to frighten you, young man."

"That's Danny," Henry said calmly. "Don't worry about him. He thinks you're a witch."

"Well, I am a witch," she said directly as she motioned to Henry. "How can you breathe in that thing?"

"I can't," Henry said, displaying the mask for Ms. Craft.

Danny suddenly paused.

A smile grew over Ms. Craft's face, eyes wide and maddening.

The others laughed again.

"Hello, Danny," Ms. Craft said and held out a plate of peanut butter cookies. "My name's Dolores."

Danny was hesitant to grab a cookie. The others grabbed a peanut butter cookie from the plate and stuffed them in their mouths. When they reached forward to grab more cookies from the plate, Ms. Craft leaned her head back in repulsion and waved her hand around her pointy nose.

"Hi," Danny said bashfully and struggled to make eye contact with Ms. Craft.

"Don't mind him."

Ms. Craft leaned in closer to Henry and took a whiff.

As cookie crumbs fell from the corners of Henry's mouth, he said, "Maybe you should've gone as the Cowardly Lion, Danny."

"Shut up," Danny exclaimed and pushed Henry.

Henry found himself pausing like Danny as he noticed Ms. Craft's strange behavior.

"What?"

He innocently shrugged his shoulders.

"Henry," Ms. Craft pulled her nose away from Henry, "you stink."

Henry smelled his armpit.

"No," she said. "Not like that."

He sniffed the werewolf costume and then cupped his hand over his mouth and blew.

"Yes," Ms. Craft said. "I can smell it a mile away."

"But Dolores. . ."

"I'm not going to tell your mother, Henry," she said. "But if she smells that stuff on your breath, then I take it she won't be a happy camper."

"You think."

T.J. tapped Danny on the shoulder.

"What she sayin'?"

"I don't know."

"How about I fix you guys a cup of coffee? You can't go back home smelling like that, especially you Henry."

"Thanks," he said, "but we have to get back at nine. I'll just stuff a whole bunch of candy in my mouth."

"What about your costume?"

"Hey, Ms. Craft," T.J. interrupted. "I like your costume."

"Thanks, T.J.," she replied and glanced around at the decorations on the porch, the cobwebs hanging from the corners of the doorway, the plastic spiders, and the fake human skull perched on the mantle. "This year, I decided to get in the Halloween spirit. I can say the same about your costumes.   I love what you did here.   Let me guess. . . Frankenstein's monster."

"That's right," he said, grinning.

"And who are you supposed to be?" Ms. Craft said and pointed at Arena.

"Alice from *Alice in Wonderland*."

Ms. Craft lit up in delight.

"That's a great story!"

"This is Arena," Henry introduced Arena to Ms. Craft. "Arena, this is Dolores."

Ms. Craft extended her hand and shook Arena's hand.

"It's a pleasure to meet you, Arena."

"Likewise."

"You can't go home smelling like that Henry."

Danny said from behind, "Smelling like what?"

Henry turned to Danny.

"She can smell. . . you know."

Both T.J and Danny whiffed their costumes.

"Don't worry," he said. "Danny's got cologne."

Danny shook his head.

"I. . . I forgot it."

"Whatcha mean you forgot it?"

"Don't worry," Ms. Craft said over T.J. "I got something even better."

Ms. Craft went back inside the house and ripped out the strip of cologne from an advertisement in a fashion magazine on the coffee table. She suddenly heard a racket coming from the back porch. She went to check out the noise, but nobody was there.

On the way back to the front porch, Ms. Craft suddenly stopped in the foyer. Her right arm erected upward in thought. Then, she snapped her two fingers, middle finger and thumb, in the air. She scuttled over to the boom box near the front window, inserted a cassette tape with the name CYBORG, and pressed the play button.

The song came on, now playing louder throughout the house.

"What is she doing?" Danny asked Henry.

"I don't know."

Henry paused and listened carefully.

"Listen. . . "

"What is it?"

"Hey," he said to T.J., "that's our song!"

Listening closely to the organ on the track, Arena asked, "The one you played with Ms. Craft?"

T.J. hollered out, "Yeah boy!"

Once more, Danny smelled his Dracula costume.

"We don't really smell. Do we?"

"Here you go," Ms. Craft said from the doorway. She handed Henry the strip of cologne. "Now you guys will smell like a Clarke Bass model."

"Perfect," he said and dragged the thin strip of cologne over his werewolf costume. "Now, I'm going to smell sexy!"

"Yeah, baby!"

"I see you be playin' the song we made," T.J. said to Ms. Craft.

"It really sets the mood," she said. "Doesn't it?"

"Give it here," Danny said and reached over Henry's shoulder.

Henry handed the strip to Danny.

Like Henry, he wiped the strip over his costume.

As Abbey suspiciously ambled back toward the front door while keeping her eyes on Ms. Craft's house, she suddenly heard one loud bang after another. Her first inkling: gunshots. Startled, Abbey darted back onto the porch. The sounds were soon lifted with screams and wails of fireworks shooting in the air. A thick cloud of smoke lifted from behind Ms. Craft's house, as well as all sorts of bright colors flashing like a rave throughout the clouds.

On Ms. Craft's front porch, Henry and his friends were pale and frozen.

"It's coming from behind the house," Henry uttered.

The fireworks soon fizzled out like hot kernels with one or two *pops* or *cracks* before silence filled the neighborhood. One of the fireworks shot from the pile, crashed through Ms. Craft's kitchen window, and skipped onto the living room carpet. Shattered glass fell down into the garbage disposal in the sink and over the tile floor. As the firework came to rest at the base of the wool couch, a small fire ignited over the beige shag carpet. Not too long after, the fire spread over the skirt of the couch. And then not too long after that, the entire couch was engulfed in flames. A gust of wind picked up from the West and sent the rising clouds of smoke over the backyard and into the house. The wind caused the fire to build inside the living room, now covering the walls.

Abbey hurried onto the sidewalk.

"Henry, T.J., Danny, Arena!" she yelled from a couple of houses down. "Get over here!"

Smoke was now pouring around the sides of the house.

"We're just talking to Ms. Craft!"

"I thought I told you not to go over there!" she yelled, this time louder. "Now come here!"

T.J. shouted out, "It jus fireworks, Ms. Burl."

"All of you get over here now!"

"But we didn't do anything. . . "

"Now!"

"Listen to your mother, Henry," Ms. Craft said somberly. "I better go check the back."

"I'm not going to tell you again!"

"Why's your mom being such a stick in the mud?"

"I don't know," Henry mumbled and hung his head.

Arena asked, "What's that smell?"

Danny checked his armpits and then his boxers.

"Not me," he said sheepishly.

As Ms. Craft stepped back inside, the thick black smoke was pouring from the living room. Ms. Craft hurried through the hallway and witnessed the flames scattered around the living room. The fire was spreading farther up the walls. The wallpaper peeled from the wall, exposing the burgundy paint underneath. Soon, the paint peeled as well and bubbled and cracked. One by one, the picture frames fell from the wall. The photographs inside burned and curled into ash while the glass blackened. Then, the lively fire crawled onto the ceiling above like an arm reaching out, burning everything it touched.

Ms. Craft ripped the prosthetic nose from her face and then removed the witch hat and wig. She tossed them both aside and hurried back outside with her arms raised in the air.

She shouted out to the closest person she could find, "Call 911!"

Henry walked back to Ms. Craft's house and said, "What's wrong?"

"There's a fire!" she said with panic in her eyes. "The whole living room is on fire!"

"Man!" Danny blurted out. "This is like the best Halloween ever."

"It's not funny, Danny!"

As T.J. dropped his pillowcase of candy and ran over to Abbey, Skip and Armani sped away on their bikes and howled and hooted out loudly in rebellion.

Abbey grabbed T.J. by the shoulders.

"What's going on, T.J.?"

"There's a fire. . ." he said and tried to catch his breath, ". . . at Ms. Craft's house."

Abbey could easily smell the liquor on T.J.'s breath. She scowled at him and then glanced over at Ms. Craft's house. Smoke was now pouring from the front door, not fog.

"Henry!" she shouted. "Get away from there!"

Abbey turned to T.J.

"You stay right here, mister!"

Abbey ran inside and called the police.

When she rushed back outside, the flames were twice the size as they were before she called the police.

The track, "Cyborg," skipped and stuttered and then finally died out (the cassette tape now melted, the speakers warbled the words *It's alllaiivaaveeeee*) as the flames consumed the entire boom box.

Abbey sprinted over to the burning house and tried to find Henry.

By then, a small crowd gathered on the street. Some of the spectators were trick-or-treaters. Others were curious neighbors dressed up in pajamas who wanted to see what all the excitement was about.

"Where's Henry?" Abbey said frantically as she shouldered her way through the thickening crowd. She found Ms. Craft standing near the front porch and grabbed her by the arm, which forced Ms. Craft forward. "Where's my son?" Abbey's grip tightened. She asked once more, "Where is he?"

In a daze, Ms. Craft pointed inside the house.

"I tried to stop him," she cried. "He wouldn't listen to me."

The flames were slowly making their way to the second floor.

As Henry darted up the stairs, the flames caught the faux hair of his costume and sent the costume ablaze. As Henry flailed around on the landing, the fire spread up the werewolf costume. The faster Henry moved, the quicker the flames spread. Before the flames could overtake him, Henry removed the costume from his body and beat out the fire against the floor. Now dressed in only a white tee and pair of blue boxers, Henry hurried to the studio. He used the werewolf mask to shield both his nose and mouth from the smoke, which was now filling the entire house. It had gotten so bad that Henry could only see a couple of feet in front of him. Nonetheless, he kept moving. With resilience, Henry fought through the thick smoke and dashed into Ms. Craft's studio. Coughing and waving his hand around, Henry scoured around and found the one reel, THE GALLERY OF STARS, perched in a box of other 16 mm films. He grabbed the reel. Eventually, the flames overtook the studio. Henry absorbed it all, the flames spreading over the music equipment (the Fairlight!), the platinum records, the photographs on the walls; all of it had gone up in flames. Years and years of memories were now ashes. As the fire grew all around him, he thought about other things to take like the Vox or the Doves of Saturn collection. But the fire was spreading too fast.

Maybe I could grab just a few more records, he thought.

As Henry rushed back to the studio, the flames shot up around him and prevented him from entering. He turned to the staircase, which, like the studio, was engulfed in flames.

With no other way to go, he hurried to the master bedroom, which was directly above the living room, and went to the window. He tried to open the window, but the window was stuck; therefore, he grabbed the nearest object, a wooden chair from a desk, and flung the thing through the window. The glass shattered. Parts of jagged glass rained down on the crowd below and forced several neighbors to take cover.

After Henry cleared away the glass with the werewolf mask, he poked his head outside and cried out from above, "I can't breath!"

Holding his head outside the window, he embraced the fresh air.

Abbey shouted out from below, "Henry!" She ran over to where she could see her son and shouted out from below, "Hold on!"

"Mom, there's no way out!"

"Wait there!" Abbey shouted up at her son. "I'm coming for you!"

A couple of the neighbors stood in front of Abbey.

"Get out of my way!" she screamed, the veins swelling over her forehead. "That's my son!"

"You won't make it!" one neighbor shouted.

A burst of flames filled the front doorway.

Abbey pushed her way through the crowd and ran into the house, but the flames were too big. The staircase suddenly collapsed, which forced Abbey back to the front lawn. Below, she shouted up at her son, "You're gonna have to jump, Henry! The window is the only way down!"

"But it's too high!" Henry shouted back, studying the distance between the window and the ground.

T.J. was pacing around Danny.

"*Mattress. . .*"

Still in a state of shock, Danny was speechless.

"Come on, Danny!" He hit Danny on the arm. "Follow me!"

While T.J. and Danny ran over to T.J.'s house (T.J. mostly dragging Danny along), Henry searched around the bedroom and thought about the next course of action. His options were scanty. Then, he wondered what they would do in the movies. What would Johnny Lame do? His eyes crossed the bed. That's it! Henry ripped off the bed sheets, took the ends of the two sheets, quickly tied them together, and made himself a rope.

"That should be long enough. . . " he said to himself.

Suddenly, the hallway floor outside the bedroom collapsed. The ceiling below the hallway dipped down into an arch. Pieces of the foundation cracked like twigs. Part of the room shifted and nearly came down with the hallway and forced Henry to brace himself against the dresser. As more thick, black smoke poured into the master bedroom, Henry placed the collar of his white tee shirt over his mouth. Finally, he took in one last breath and held it in just like he and T.J. would do underwater at the public pool during the summer.

With his hands trembling, Henry tied the end of the sheet to the bed's leg and made a double knot.

Next, he stuck the werewolf mask underneath the waistband of his blue boxers.

While all of this was going on, T.J. and Danny were racing toward Ms. Craft's house with T.J.'s queen size bed mattress, all stripped. They tripped several times from the awkwardness and bulkiness of the mattress. One of the neighbors saw the two struggling and decided to help.

Once they made it to Ms. Craft's house, they ended up placing the mattress directly underneath the second story window.

Henry spotted the mattress over the lawn.

"All right, Henry!" Abbey shouted out from below. "We'll catch you!"

While keeping the reel tightly in his hand, Henry wrapped his hand around the sheet, gave the sheet a tug to make sure it was secure around the bed, and repelled from the window. Once he was clear from the smoke, he could finally breathe. And when he finally did, it wasn't just any other breath. It was of great relief. A quarter of the way down, the master bedroom suddenly collapsed! The bed, which was keeping

Henry secure, fell directly through the floor and into the living room below.

"Oh God!"

In a matter of seconds, Henry propelled upward, the window acting like a pulley. He lost his grip from the sheet.

Abbey yelled out, "LET GO, HENRY!"

He dropped about twelve feet. A couple of the neighbors were on either side of the mattress, which was kept directly underneath Henry.

One neighbor screamed, "Catch him!"

Henry landed safely on the mattress. The reel spilled from Henry's hand and rolled onto the lawn while the werewolf mask remained securely underneath his waistband. His ankle ended up taking most of the fall. Except for a sprained ankle and a little smoke inhalation, Henry would live.

As the neighbors helped Henry to his feet, the crowd cheered in both excitement and relief. Once Abbey realized that her boy was all right, she embraced him in her arms and held him there as long as the cheers carried through the night. A couple of minutes passed, and the fire department finally arrived at Glenn Forest. The sirens from the fire trucks made the roars of joy sound like murmurs. Abbey pulled herself from her son and glared through the crowd at Ms. Craft, who had her hands cupped over her chest in solace. Strangely enough, the house seemed like the least of her worries.

After the paramedics tended to Henry in the back of the ambulance and provided him with oxygen and sent him on his way with the recommendation of plenty of rest for the night, the firefighters were still putting out the fire. Henry mostly stayed in his bedroom and only left twice, once to use the bathroom and another time to hawk into a wad of toilet paper. Most of the time, however, Henry couldn't sleep, not from the sugar rush of candy, which, in fact, his mother had stashed on top of the refrigerator, or the creeping headache from the alcohol, but from the one thought that had been nagging away at him while he was racing through Ms. Craft's house. He couldn't help but wonder what it was like to burn. One time he burned his fingertip when he was lighting a bottle rocket on the Fourth of July. Then, there was that one time when he accidentally touched the side of a hot clothing iron. He received no pleasure from being burned. The pain alone from both instances was unbearable. But for the entire body to burn, to catch on fire, Henry couldn't imagine the pain. The warmness of the room pressed against his body forced him to remove the sheets from the bed. He left the bedroom (this being a third time now) and turned down the temperature on the thermostat in the hallway.

As the air conditioner ran at a cool sixty-six degrees throughout the upstairs of the house (he could hear it now: his mother yelling at him after receiving the monthly electrical bill), Henry plumped himself back on the bed and propped two pillows behind his head. Eventually, the room cooled down. And finally, he found a bit of comfort in his rest. Whiling resting, his eyes were glued to the television screen. He was watching the horror movie, *Halloween 2*. On any other Halloween night, he would've been terrified. His face partially covered with a pillow. Occasionally, he would take peeks at the movie. The iconic stalker, Michael Myers, entered the screen. His masked face was lit with a red light. Now, he was stalking, slowly and yet somehow cornering his victim. None of this, the vacant face of Michael Myers, the stalking, the grisly screams of "Help" from our iconic stalker's sister ringing out over a synthesized score seaming effortlessly throughout the scene, had affected Henry. The highlight of suspense brought no emotion. No excitement or fear. He just lay there and stared at the television screen. Henry finally switched off the television, rolled out of bed with a loud grunt, and shuffled over to the bedroom window where the red lights from the fire trucks flashed over his steely face, his eyes. Now, only a couple of firefighters were watering down the last flames with a hose. In the corner of his eye, Henry saw a tiny movement. He directed his attention across the street and noticed Kerri sitting on the porch. In all the years he had lived on Davie Morris, he had never seen Kerri like this. From what Henry could see, she looked almost worried (hand cupper over chin, her body leaned forward from the chair, eyes fixated on the fire).

As Henry pulled his eyes back on the remaining flames, he couldn't help but draw his eyes back to Kerri, who had pulled her attention toward Henry's bedroom window and waved, not openly, but subtly. A surge of exhilaration swept over his body, his thoughts. In return, he raised his hand and waved back at Kerri, openly. Too much? *All this time*, however, Henry wondered, *she never acknowledged me*. Why now? Was it from the fire? Was it from barely escaping death? Did she have different feelings towards me now? Would she talk to me now? Was it because she wasn't around her friends? *Maybe* they had some influence on her. What about the stitches? She didn't wear a scar on her face. But nonetheless, she did go through quite an ordeal. Henry would never find out even though the questions would be there, eating away at him throughout the night. Kerri lowered her hand and smiled, closed and not openly, at Henry and walked back inside the house.

Before Henry went back to bed, he spotted Ms. Craft and Jodi standing on the sidewalk outside the destroyed house. The flames were glistening in their orange eyes. On a whim, Ms. Craft moved her orange eyes toward Henry's house. Then, her eyes trailed upward, slowly and patiently. She found Henry standing behind the bedroom window. Both of their eyes connected like magnets. Jodi followed Ms. Craft's eyes up at Henry's bedroom and moved his arm around her shoulder and pulled her closer to his body.

TWENTY

FOR the rest of the night and into the early hours of morning, Henry slept with the image of Kerri close to his mind.

The image was so close to his mind that he could literally feel it pressed against his skin, her hand waving at him, his fingers carefully sliding into the gaps of her hands, now interlocking. He pulled his hand over his chest, making sure that Kerri could feel his beating heart. And that was how he slept: with Kerri's body curled around his body and her hand placed over his heart. Henry hadn't slept that good in years. "Like a baby," he told his mother the next morning over breakfast. Even though they didn't say much to one another throughout the entire breakfast, Abbey mentioned that she was taking the day off to make sure Henry was okay. In the back of Henry's mind, he knew the real reason why his mother was taking off work and it wasn't his health. Let the interrogation begin.

"Where did you get it?" she asked him.

Henry sipped from the glass of orange juice and swallowed the bite of toast with grape jelly.

"Get what?"

"Don't act like you don't know what I'm talking about," she seethed. "I could practically taste the liquor on your breath last night. How much did you drink?"

Henry didn't respond.

"Where did you get it?"

Again, Henry didn't respond.

"Was it from Danny? T.J.?" Abbey snorted in disbelief. "It was Danny. Wasn't it?"

"I only had a couple of sips," Henry said with his head down.

"You must play me for a fool, Henry."

"It's not a big deal."

"Not a big deal?" Abbey returned, her face like stone. "You could've gotten yourself killed, boy. Don't you realize that? What was so important in that house that you just had to go inside?"

Henry sighed and tossed the toast over the plate.

With his head down, he mumbled, "You would never understand."

"Try me."

Henry looked into his mother's eyes, sharpening.

He thought carefully, especially about Dolores.

"She used to be a singer."

"Who? Ms. Craft?"

"Yeah."

"A singer?"

Abbey squared her shoulders.

"Have you been over to her house before?"

Again, there was no response from her son.

"Have you?" she asked, this time raising her voice.

Henry shrugged his shoulders.

"Just once or twice," he said innocently.

"That's all?"

"Yeah," Henry mumbled and shrugged his shoulders once more. "She showed me a reel of her singing."

"Showed you what?"

"A reel of her singing."

"When?"

"I don't know," Henry said. "It meant a lot to her. So, I saved it for her."

"You risked your life over a. . . a reel?"

Abbey's eyes wandered around the table and nowhere near her son.

"I don't even want to see your face for the rest of the day," she said distantly and got up from the kitchen table. She walked over to the sink and placed her plate inside, which made a thunderous *clunk* throughout the kitchen. "And I'm going to have a little chat with Danny's mother. That will be the last time you hang out with that boy."

Henry sprang up from his chair.

"But he didn't do anything!" he blurted out.

Abbey ignored her son and continued to scrub the dishes in the sink.

Henry shoved the chair back under the table and stomped away from the kitchen.

TWENTY-ONE

A full two weeks passed and still no sign of Ms. Craft or Jodi.

In the early part of November when the autumn colors painted over Reddington and the leaves started to drop from the trees and pile up over the front lawns, Henry kept mostly to himself. After school whenever he wasn't playing basketball, he would take long walks through town. Whenever he was driven inside from the cold, he didn't do much at all around the house but piddle. He would do his homework (mostly skimming through it) and even some chores around the house like cleaning his room or washing the Jelly Bean whenever the weather was tolerable, but mostly he did as quickly and neglectfully as he could so he could get back to watching television. Henry wasn't all there, though, even while watching television. Last week, he tried out for varsity basketball and ended up making the team with flying colors. Later that night, Abbey treated Henry and his closest friends to dinner at KFS (Kentucky Fried Steak). Danny worked out his issues with Henry's mother and was able to join them for dinner. Still, Henry wasn't *all* there. He felt as if he had taken so many steps backward and now he was at that place where he felt as if he didn't belong anymore. From time to time, he would find himself thinking about her, about Ms. Craft. Whenever Henry wasn't practicing with the basketball team, T.J. would stop by Henry's house after school and see how he was doing. So much had gone on in the past two weeks that he and T.J. didn't even have a chance to talk about the fire and what it was like to come *that* close to death. Henry would give T.J. the same response: "Not in the mood." At times, Henry wouldn't even answer the door whenever T.J. stopped by the house to say hello. Instead, he sat by his window and gazed at the neighborhood street. As for Kerri, she was nowhere around. At first, Henry wondered if he had scared her off. The wave she had given him was maybe a way of her saying her final goodbyes. The days after the fire, he hoped that maybe she would come around and the two might turn a corner. Times after school, he would wait for a knock at the door, hoping that Kerri would be there, waiting. Then, she stopped coming around. Even at school she was nowhere around. Eventually, Henry heard from a neighbor that she and her family were gone on vacation: Key West. At least Henry didn't have to look his best in front of Kerri or try to impress her with his basketball skills. And finally Dolores, he wondered, where was she? How was she doing? So many questions there were, all without answers. Maybe she would stop by the old house, or what was left of it. And then maybe she would stop by Henry's house and ask how he was doing. Over that stretch of two weeks, she never came. At other times, Henry rode his bike to places that he thought Ms. Craft would be at like Sister of Grace or Central Reserve Stadium or even Milly and Munford's Discs. Maybe he would bump into her while riffling through used CDs or cassette tapes or vinyl records, as she almost always did every Tuesday and Sunday. Henry never found her, though. He wondered if she was still in town or if she had moved away without saying goodbye or if she was dead. Was he chasing after a ghost? The thought of losing his friend, Dolores, left him in an unsettled state. At night, Henry cried himself to sleep over the thought of never seeing his friend again. And during the day, he did all he could to hold the tears inside and not expose them for his other classmates to see. Henry was good at hiding, good at playing the part of the shy young man by putting on a mask in front of all the other students, as well as his teammates, and covering up how he truly felt. For Henry, those two weeks were the longest he had ever experienced. In the back of his mind, he wished someone would wake him up from this terrible nightmare. Nobody would, though. And Henry kept drifting along like a log down a river.

A couple of days before Thanksgiving break, as Henry was strolling home from school after basketball practice, a Cadillac pulled up beside him.

"*Hey, stranger*," a familiar voice said from inside the car.

As Henry did his best to hide the emotion over his face, Henry peeked over his shoulder and saw her there sitting behind the steering wheel wearing the same dark coat and beret.

"Dolores. . . " he said in surprise.

Ms. Craft parked the car next to Henry.

With his face long and empty, Henry walked up to the passenger side and leaned through the open window.

Ms. Craft said, "I've been thinking a lot about you."

A coy smile rose over Henry's face.

"I've been thinking about you too."

"Do you have a minute?"

Henry gazed around the quiet street.

"Yeah," he said.

Ms. Craft got out of the car and walked over to Henry.

"I heard those two who started the fire got into some big trouble."

"Yeah," Henry said anxiously. "Police came to their houses. Jesse ratted out them both. It didn't even take them that long to find Skip or Armani. They just followed the trail of broken mailboxes."

"Is that so?"

"If I were you, I would've pressed charges. My mom said that if they were a couple of years older, then they might have gone to jail."

"I'm sure their parents were pretty upset."

"Let's just say I don't plan on seeing Skip or Armani around any time soon."

"Well, hopefully, they learned their lesson."

"I know them, Dolores," Henry said sympathetically. "I don't know why they set your house on fire."

Ms. Craft returned calmly, "I'm sure it was just an accident, Henry."

"You're not mad?"

"Of course not."

"But what about all of your records. . . the pictures. . . the Fairlight?"

"They're just possessions, Henry," she said thoughtfully. "For years, I've kept the past in my rear view mirror, always taking a look every chance I was able to. It's time to start a new chapter in my life. I've. . . " like Henry before, she gazed around the street, ". . . I've reminisced long enough. All that matters now is that you're safe."

"Are you staying with anyone?"

"I'm currently living with Jodi on Grand Park."

"Grand Park?"

"That's right."

"My mom always tells me to stay away from that place. I hear there's a lot of gangs in that neighborhood."

"I reckoned she said the same about my house, but that never kept you from coming over."

Henry chortled.

"There's even a Momma Demeter down the street from Jodi's house," she said, growing excited. "I remember you talking about how much you loved their food."

"I've never been to that one there," he said. "Me and my mom usually go to the one off Lexington. It's much nicer. They even have leather seats inside."

"Leather seats. Huh? Nice."

"You should check it out sometime."

"Maybe I will."

"You know, Dolores, I would let you stay with me, but my mom. . . she. . . "

"That's kind of you, Henry," she said, "but I'll be fine. This is just a little bump in the road. That's all. Just a little bump. The road wouldn't be worth traveling if it wasn't bumpy every now and then. Am I right?"

"I guess so."

"You travel down a smooth road in life, well, you sort of miss out on the things that make us human. Let's just say the bumps have a way of bringing out the best in us."

"Or worse?"

"Or worse, Henry," Ms. Craft said as she placed her hands over Henry's shoulders. "But don't you worry about me, Henry. I'll be just fine."

"You know I can talk her into you staying."

"Don't do that. I'm fine, Henry. Really."

"Are you sure? I mean I'm a good actor. Aren't I?"

"You are indeed, Henry," Ms. Craft said. "But I'll be fine."

Henry said under his breath, "Okay."

Ms. Craft snapped her finger in the air.

"I almost forgot," she said and reached inside the Cadillac. She pulled out the 16mm reel from the passenger seat and handed it to Henry. "I want you to have this. After all, you were the one who risked his life in order to save my film reel."

"But it's more than a reel, Dolores." Henry's eyes traced over the reel. "I can't take this," he said and tried to hand the reel back to Ms. Craft.

With her gloved hand, she pushed the reel away.

"I want you to have it, Henry."

He looked up at Ms. Craft.

"I don't know what to say."

"Just say 'thank you.'"

"Thank you," he said and hugged Ms. Craft.

"By the way, have you been practicing?"

"Lately," he said and pulled himself away from Ms. Craft's grip. "No. Honestly, I wanted to. But. . . "

Ms. Craft ran her hand over Henry's cheek.

"You don't have to explain, Henry." She moved her hand over Henry's shoulder and said, "You will, Henry. Just give it time."

Ms. Craft grabbed a handkerchief from her pocket and violently coughed into the handkerchief.

"Are you okay?"

"I'll live."   She folded up the wet handkerchief and crammed it back in her pocket. "Every now and then, I get these coughing spells." She glanced around the street. Except for a couple of cars passing by, it was still quiet. "Well, I guess I'd better get going."

She walked to the driver's side of the car.

"Goodbye, Henry."

"Wait!" Henry shouted out.

"What if I still want lessons?"

Ms. Craft mused over the question.

"That's all right with me, but. . . " she said, ". . . only with your mother's permission."

"But she won't let me play. You know her."

"Right," Ms. Craft said. "The ABC's."

"Yeah."

"I'm sorry, Henry, but that's how it has to be," Ms. Craft said sternly. "If you don't ask your mother, then I can't help you out."

Henry paused in thought.

"Okay," he said. "I'll ask her."

"You will?"

Henry bobbed his head.

"Be honest with her, Henry," Ms. Craft said in a motherly way and pointed at Henry. "Tell her how *you* feel about playing. Tell her the truth."

"How?"

"Remember," Ms. Craft placed her hand over her chest, "here. Listen here, Henry," she moved her hand upward and pointed at her temple, "and then speak from here."

She stepped inside the car, found a pen from the glove compartment, and wrote down her number on a piece of paper.

"This is my telephone number," she said and handed Henry the piece of paper through the passenger side window. "Let me know what your mother says."

Henry smiled and said, "I will."

Before Ms. Craft drove off, Henry waved her down.

"By the way," he said, "I have a basketball game next Thursday after break. I would like for you to come."

"Really?"

"Yeah."

"I would love to, Henry."

"Okay," Henry said as he cracked a smile. "Then, it's done. I'll call you."

"Goodbye, Henry."

"Bye."

TWENTY-TWO

WITH Christmas break just around the corner, Henry and T.J. decided to take a night off. They spent the evening watching the movie *The Secret of NIMH*. Except for final exams, which were scheduled for the next couple of weeks, the two didn't have much homework. A night of no homework was like a night to do whatever they wanted—almost everything. They could stay up a little later than usual. They could watch more movies or television shows. Play more video games. Since his mother was still awake, Henry had to make sure to keep the volume low. Abbey wasn't too far away from her son and his friend. In fact, she was in the laundry room—just within listening distance—folding the last items of clothing, a navy blue sweatshirt and a flannel shirt, from the final load.

After Abbey finished folding the clothes, she placed them on top of the stack of already folded clothes, passed her son and his friend in the living room, and carried the stack to Henry's bedroom where she placed them on the edge of his bed. She noticed that the closet door was cracked open. So, Abbey went to close the door. There was a sudden restriction, though. A worn leather case was obstructing the pathway of the door. She pushed the black case farther into the closet with the heel of her foot and closed the door. Curious, she opened the closet once more and then the case on the floor. There, Abbey saw the saxophone, Adrian, with the initials *H.M.* on the bottom. Her hand covered her gaping mouth. Soon, her gaping eyes shriveled down like raisins. She forced herself into a yielding state of calmness when, in fact, she was fuming inside. Her greatest suspicion had finally come true. It had all started with the dirty toothbrush in Henry's bathroom. She wondered why it smelled like brasso. Then, it was Henry's strange behavior and Ms. Craft showing up more frequently to Henry's basketball games. The calmness in her eyes died and birthed with bitterness.

Moments later, Abbey was standing at the base of the stairs with her arms folded over her chest.

"Go on home, T.J.," she said shortly to T.J. "I need to have a talk with my son."

Henry turned toward his mother, removed the bowl of popcorn from his lap, and witnessed the look on her face.

"But Ms. Burl. . . " T.J. said and wiped his buttery fingers over his pants, ". . . the movie's almost over."

Abbey didn't even have to speak. She looked at T.J. with that animalistic glare, "The Look." T.J. had witnessed the look once before. They were in sixth grade at the time. Henry and T.J. found a stray basset hound roaming around the woods. They brought the poor dog back to Henry's house, gave it a bath, combed its hair, clipped its nails, and then fed the dog an entire package of hot dogs. When Abbey came home from work, she found the basset hound in the living room, sitting between Henry and T.J., all cleaned and manicured. All Abbey had to do was give Henry and T.J. that "look," arms folded across chest, eyes wide and glaring, and a wraith of snarl hiding underneath her crinkled lips. Before Henry could mouth the words *can we keep it,* the dog was back in the woods.

T.J. got up from the living room floor and hurried from the house.

Henry gradually eased himself onto the couch. His eyes trailed downward at his mother's feet as she slid the saxophone case in front of her.

"That's not yours," he said unsteadily.

"How long have you had this thing?"

Henry didn't answer.

"ANSWER ME!"

Henry flinched from her roaring tone and pulled his eyes away from the case.

"I don't know," he mumbled, his head cocked to the side.

"You don't know." She snorted in a kind of maddening way. "It's that sneaking snake, Ms. Craft, who lived down the street. She's been brainwashing you. Hasn't she?"

Henry stood up from the couch.

"Don't talk about Dolores like that."

"You even know her first name," Abbey said comically. "Isn't that something?"

"She's my friend."

"Not for long, she isn't."

"Why do you hate her so much?"

Abbey threw down her foot.

"Don't question me, boy," she seethed and took another step forward. "Now, I'm going to ask you one last time. Where did you get this?"

Henry mumbled, "Holiday's."

"I can't hear you." Her voice rose. "Speak up!"

Henry said louder, "Holiday's."

"And where did you get the money?"

"Dolores."

"She bought you this?"

"Yeah."

"Nobody gives us anything for free. You got that?"

Abbey picked up the case and handed the heavy thing to Henry.

"Go on," she said, her voice like nails piercing into Henry. "*Take it.*"

Henry flinched and grabbed the case.

"Either you find Ms. Craft and give it back to her or toss it in the trash," she said. "Either way, it better be gone by tomorrow. Am I making myself clear?"

Henry hung his head.

Abbey pinched Henry's chin and lifted his head upward.

"Do you understand me, boy?"

"Yeah," Henry said, grimacing with rage.

"Yeah?"

"Yes."

Her fingers tightened over Henry's chin, which caused him to grimace even more.

"Yes what?"

"Yes, ma'am," he answered, struggling to focus his eyes on his mother.

Abbey let out a sigh, sharp like a gust of wind.

"Let me tell you something, boy," she said with her breath labored. "You better wake up. You hear me. It's time to stop living in this fantasyland of yours! Do you understand me, boy? The world doesn't give a shit about you or your lousy music! Do you understand me? You're nothing to them. Just another fool to throw peanuts at, to dance around on stage like ah. . . like a. . . puppet. Is that what you want to be: another one of their puppets, Henry? You're going to stick with basketball. End of story."

Henry puckered his face into a sneer and pulled his chin from his mother's grip. His shoulders hunched over. His head arched forward like a turtle. The sneer on his face became more prominent to his mother.

"What happened to you?" he said, his voice honing into a blade. "What made you so. . . mean all the time?"

"Mean? Oh! You haven't seen mean yet, boy."

Henry shouted, "I hate you!"

"What did you say?"

"I wish you were dead!"

"Go. . . go to your room. . ." Abbey said, her voice trampled with a sense of defeat. "Now, Henry."

Henry remained in the same position.

With her widening eyes, she yelled out, "I said 'Go to your damn room!'"

"Fine!" Henry yelled back.

"Go on! Before I take off my shoe!"

With his head hung down, Henry carried Adrian upstairs.

He knew exactly what that meant, the shoe.

He didn't want to be anywhere near his mother when the shoe came off. That was for sure.

TWENTY-THREE

THE next morning, Henry woke up with the comforter and sheets liberated from his curled body. The indigo comforter was dangling from the chair beside the desk. The bed linens, which, as of lately, had become both his best friend and his worst enemy, were scattered across the carpet as if they had been thrown from the bed. As a glow of reds and oranges and pinks brightened over the closed blinds before him, Henry rolled out of his naked bed and reached inside his backpack on the dresser. He fished his hand around the backpack until he pulled out a frosty blue flyer that he had grabbed from the cafeteria bulletin board the other day. The flyer read: "THE ANNUAL WINTER TALENT SHOW HAS ARRIVED! THIS FRIDAY IN MISSION'S AUDITORIUM!" Henry got dressed for school in his normal Thursday clothing (a burgundy schematic-like sweatshirt similar to the one Rick Deckard wore in the movie *Blade Runner*, brown corduroys, and beige dress shoes to match the designs in the sweatshirt), pocketed the flyer, and went to the bathroom to wash up.

As Henry brushed his teeth, both quietly and quickly, Abbey gently knocked on the door before she poked her head inside. He didn't acknowledge his mother, who was standing at the doorway in the same position that he saw her last night: arms folded against her chest. The only thing missing was that she didn't have *the* look on her face. A couple of seconds passed before Abbey cleared her throat. Henry heard his mother, the clearing of her throat as well as the tapping of her shoe against the tile, behind him and yet he kept brushing his teeth.

"About last night. . . " she said patiently.

Without looking at his mother, Henry spat out the mouthful of foamy toothpaste into the sink and closed the door.

". . . I'm—"

Abbey marched away. She grabbed her things for work, coat from the hallway closet, purse and keys from the kitchen table, and slammed the front door on her way out.

After school, Henry rode his bike over to Jodi's house as he had done every Monday, Wednesday, and Friday for the past month.

On the second attempt to ring the doorbell, Jodi answered the door with a bowl of cereal in his hand.

Jodi didn't say a word. Instead, he was too busy chewing the crunchy cereal in his mouth. He left the door open and turned the other way.

A couple of seconds later, Ms. Craft approached Henry on the front porch.

"Henry," she said gladly. "It's Thursday. I wasn't expecting you today."

Henry pulled out the flyer from his pocket, unfolded it, and then showed it to Ms. Craft.

"I know, but there's a big talent show tomorrow night."

Ms. Craft glanced over at Jodi, who was now sitting at the kitchen table with his arms crossed in frustration. Not chewing.

"Come in," she said expressionlessly and nodded at Henry.

Ms. Craft stepped from the doorway as Henry entered the house.

*   *   *

On the way home from work, Abbey passed a family owned restaurant called Momma Demeter. The slogan underneath the purple sign read *"Voted Best Tacos in Peregrine!"* In deep thought, Abbey cruised on by the restaurant. Before she took a right onto the highway, she suddenly slammed on the brakes and crossed over the median. A car swerved around, nearly missed her, and blew the horn. Abbey regained control of the Jelly Bean and pulled into the drive-thru lane.

As Abbey sat at the stop light with a picnic box of warm chicken tacos on soft corn tortillas and corn cakes topped with a blueberry sauce, as well as two ice cold grape sodas, one for Abbey and the other for Henry, she heard the faint sounds of a lawnmower running next to her car. As usual, the air conditioner wasn't working properly—even after a combination of jabs against the dial. Frustrated, Abbey cracked the window and grabbed some fresh air. The air wasn't really that fresh or soothing, as she had anticipated. Yet, the air was smelly and fumy. The noise both from the traffic and the lawnmower was like a grinder to her ears. She couldn't help but glance through the cracked window at the familiar teenager pushing the rusty lawnmower through the dense grass. An oily red shirt was wrapped around the top of the teenager's head like a turban. She could only see one side of the teenager's face. Abbey didn't put too much stock into the teenager—at least not until she took another glance at him and saw the scar, long and jagged, on the side of his ribcage.

The light turned green.

A car behind Abbey honked the horn, which drew the teenager's attention toward Abbey.

"Henry?" Abbey uttered with confusion.

Henry's face went slack as his fingers freed from the handlebar, which caused the lawnmower to shut off.

Abbey jerked the wheel to the left and parked the car on the side of the street. She got out. Then, a loud *thud* of a car door slamming swiftly followed. As she marched through the partially cut front lawn, Henry slowly backpedaled from his mother.

"What the hell are you doing here?" she asked, the anger flooding her eyes.

"Maa. . . Ma. . . Ma. . . Ms. Craft waaaaa. . . wa. . . was giving me lessons."

Abbey pointed to the brick ranch style house behind Henry.

"Who lives here?"

"Ja. . . Ja. . . Jod. . . di. . . "

The front door swung open and then the screen door.

At the doorway, Ms. Craft was quickly tying a knot over her purple bathrobe.

Once she was decent, she scuttled over to Abbey.

"Is there a problem?" Ms. Craft asked, her eyes racing around in confusion as well.

Abbey said angrily, "What are you doing with my son?"

"Well, I was giving him saxophone lessons."

She carefully eyed Ms. Craft's outfit and then her bare feet.

"Saxophone lessons? I don't know anything about saxophone lessons."

Ms. Craft followed, "Henry said you gave him permission."

Abbey seethed, "I did NOT give Henry permission to come over here."

With her eyebrows furrowed, Ms. Craft glanced over at Henry.

"I'm sorry, Dolores," he said to her.

"Henry. . . "

"How long has this been going on?"

Henry barged between the two, "You don't have to answer her, Dolores."

Abbey grabbed Henry by the arm and yanked him away from Ms. Craft.

"Easy, Ms. Burl," Ms. Craft said and held out her hands. "Please. You don't have to be so rough with him."

"How dare you talk to me that way? Don't tell me how to parent my son."

Abbey flexed her jaw. Her eyes were flaring.

The look. . .

"Get in the car," she said to Henry.

Henry tugged his arm away from his mother's grip.

"Go to hell!" he shouted out.

"Henry," Ms. Craft said, her voice drawn out. "Don't talk to your mother that way."

"I said '*Get in the car!*'"

Ms. Craft held out her hand, closer now.

"Henry," she said, "you listen to your mother."

"How can you do this to me?" Henry exclaimed to Ms. Craft. "Why don't you stand up to her?"

Ms. Craft let out a sigh in front of Henry.

"You're being too hard on him, Ms. Burl," she said confidently to Abbey. "As responsible adults, we should be there for these kids and teach them about the world, not hold them back from it."

"Excuse me," Abbey said, her tone slanting. "You think your God. Isn't that right? You think you can patronize me?"

"I just think it's time for you to accept what your son wants to do with his life," Ms. Craft replied, her composure held tightly in front of the seething mad woman. "It's time for you to embrace his passion for music."

"Passion for music?" Abbey returned, almost hysterically. "He's only fifteen years old. It's just another one of his 'phases'. Besides, you're *not*. . . you're not. . . his goddamn mother. Quit acting like it." Abbey waggled her finger at Jodi's house. "So, why don't you do everyone a favor and go crawling back to that hole you came from? You little bug!"

Henry grunted.

He ran over to his bike and rode away.

Abbey hollered out, "Get back here, boy! Henry!"

Before Abbey chased after Henry, she pointed her finger in Ms. Craft's face, held it there like she would do with Henry, like a blade, and whispered, "You stay away from my son or so help me God. . . "

Abbey rushed back to her car and chased after Henry.

After crossing a busy intersection, Henry managed to lose his mother at the next stoplight. He took several shortcuts—one through a dilapidated industrial park and the other through Snake's Trail in the woods—and beat her back to the house.

As soon as Henry swung open the front door, which created a small puncture the size of a door handle over the wall, he didn't even bother to close the door. Behind him, he heard the Jelly Bean skidding into the driveway. He darted toward his bedroom—this time slamming the door behind him—and plumped himself onto the bed where he buried his face into the pillow and softly wept. *She would not get to me in here*, the devil, he thought as he threw the covers over his body. *I don't care about living here anymore, the money. I wish she were. . . she were. . .*

There were three knocks at the door, gentle.

"Go away!" he cried into the pillow, his voice was strained and raspy.

Abbey carefully opened the door.

"Come downstairs, Henry," she said quietly from the doorway. "There's something I need to show you."

Abbey went downstairs, quietly, not marching, and waited at the kitchen table until Henry arrived. On the table, the basketball and Adrian sat on either side of her. Henry rolled out of bed, cleaned up, including wiping the tears from his face, and finally went downstairs. There, he stood at the edge of the kitchen.

"Have a seat," Abbey said sternly.

She got up from the chair, walked around the table, and politely held out the chair for Henry.

With his head hung down in his chest, Henry sat down in the chair across from his mother.

"Look at me, Henry."

Henry sniffled up the loose phlegm from his nose and raised his head.

Abbey shifted her chair closer to Henry.

"I come home early from work to take my son on a picnic and this is what I get: you mowing some stranger's lawn."

"Jodi's not some stranger—"

"I thought I taught you better, Henry."

Henry hung his head and struggled to look his mother in the eye.

"Look at me in the eye." She flipped up his chin with her finger. "I don't want you hanging around that woman or that man anymore. You have no business being over there (Period!)"

"She cares about—"

"Women like that are *sick* and *dangerous* and they don't need to be filling my son's head with sick and dangerous ideas."

"Why do hate everybody who's different from you? You never have anything good to say about anybody."

Abbey didn't respond to Henry's comment. The only response Henry gathered was the grimace meticulously forming over her face. Her eyes flared, as they had been doing occasionally throughout the argument.

"Who is this Jodi guy?" she asked, her eyes suddenly squinting. "Is that one of her boyfriends?"

"You're never here," Henry said dauntlessly. "So, why should I tell you anythi—"

"—Because I'm your mother and I know what's best for my son!" she said over Henry's voice, now shrinking. "Do you hear me? You wouldn't be here if it wasn't for me!" Her voice built with steam. "I'm out there in the real world, Henry. Do you understand me? I'm out there busting my butt so you can have a roof over your goddamn head! So, answer my question!"

Henry said loudly, "Yes."

"Yes what?"

"Yes," he said. "Jodi is her boyfriend. So what?"

Abbey's breath was heavy like a running tailpipe.

"I saw that man standing by the doorway," she said bitterly. Henry could feel the warmth of her breath on his face. "He looked half her age. You don't need to be hanging out with losers like that. You should be with people your own age, like T.J. or Jason or even that, that oriental one. . ."

"Don't call her that. . ."

"Whatever," she said callously. "I hardly see them around here anymore. What's going on with you? Are you on drugs?"

"No. . ."

"Then, what is it? T.J. used to come over for dinner all the time. Practically lived over here. Now, I hardly see him here anymore. Not to mention, you. You never want to talk to me. It's like pulling strings to get you to eat with me. I thought your friends liked coming over here."

"Not anymore they don't," Henry argued. "Because you find a way to run them off. And it's not just T.J. They don't like you. You're always watching over them, waiting for them to do something they're not supposed to do. Danny, Arena. . . they're afraid to say anything whenever you're here. They're all scared of you."

"Good!" Abbey shouted, her eyes flaring brightly. "LET THEM BE SCARED!"

The anger was breathing in her eyes now. Eventually, the anger took hold of Abbey, sapping every bit of her strength. She took a moment to catch her breath, her thoughts. She turned away and then faced Henry.

Her voice calmed.

"Did she touch you?"

"*No*," Henry said emphatically.

"Why were you cutting that Jodi man's lawn?" Abbey asked in a surrendering tone. "You can cut his grass and yet you can't even lift a finger around here. How many times have I asked you to clean your room?"

"I did that one time."

"Wow, Henry," Abbey exclaimed. "One time out of how many times?"

"Dolores was giving me lessons. . ."

"And all that garbage in your room," she said over Henry. "She paid for that as well? She must have because there's no way anyone would want to buy those silly tapes of yours."

Henry grimaced and shot daggers at his mother. His eyes were as keen as a reptile.

"It's time for you to make a decision," Abbey said and pushed the two objects, basketball and saxophone, closer to Henry. "Choose one."

Henry looked over the two. He didn't think too long. He nodded at Adrian.

"That's too bad," Abbey said and pulled the saxophone case from the table and placed it on the floor. "You're going to play basketball, *just* basketball."

"But you just said I had a choice!"

"And I was hoping you would choose basketball," she said. "Now, you leave me with no other option. You can't afford the distractions."

"I'm not going to play basketball!"

"Excuse me?"

He repeated, but this time louder, "I'm not going to play basketball!"

"You *will* play."

"Why?"

"Because I'm your mother."

"Well, that's not good enough!" Henry shouted out. "I want to know why!"

The tears were pouring down Henry's eyes.

"What about the records in the attic?" he whined. "You once loved music."

"I did, Henry," she said solemnly. "But I grew up. And soon, you will to and you'll thank me for all I've done for you. I'm doing this because I don't want you to go down the same. . . " Abbey suddenly grimaced ". . . You are going to play basketball. End of story."

"No!"

"Quit defying me!" she yelled out.

A hand lifted up and came violently across Henry's face. His head jerked to the side. Henry grabbed the side of his reddening face.

Strangely, he stopped crying.

He got up from his chair.

"I'm sorry, Henry."

Henry reached into his pocket.

"You want to talk about earning your own money around here," he said, his voice trembling.

He pulled out an envelope from his pocket and threw it on the table.

"Looks like I'm not. . . I'm not the only one around here with secrets."

Surprised, Abbey said, "Where did you get this?"

"In the drawer upstairs."

She grabbed the envelope and said dolefully, "Go to your room."

Henry asked, "Who is Buddy Egghorn?"

The steaming anger suddenly lifted in her face, a hideous mask.

"GO TO YOUR ROOM! RIGHT NOW!"

Henry didn't move a muscle.

Abbey's eyes pounded away at him.

"I SAID 'NOW!'"

He bolted from the kitchen.

While Henry hurried upstairs toward his bedroom, Abbey grabbed the saxophone case from the kitchen floor and exited from the house (stomping, door slamming, everything done so loud enough for her son to hear). In return, Henry slammed the bedroom door behind him and not just once. Over and over again, he slammed the door against the doorway until one of the hinges fell off. After he wore himself out from beating the door against the panel, he plumped himself on his bed. Abbey took a drive around town to cool off. Henry had other ways of cooling off. During the process, he felt a weight pressed against his chest as if he was being smothered. He had trouble catching his breath. As Uncle Charlie had taught him when he was younger, he slowly breathed in through his nose and out through his mouth—*deep breaths*, Uncle Charlie had showed him—and then stopped thinking, mainly about his mother, her words, her screams, her stares, and her abuse. He concentrated on the saxophone, Adrian. It was at that moment when Henry no longer felt the pain in his chest. Now, he could finally breathe clearly.

TWENTY-FOUR

WHEN Abbey returned, it was already dinnertime.

Henry stirred in his bed until he found a comfortable position to listen closely to his mother's movements. The soft pitter-patter of her footsteps trailed across the living room and into her bedroom. Henry paid closer attention now. Soon, the sounds of her movements faded out. So, Henry leaped from his bed without making a thud over the floor, eased himself over the banister near the landing, and heard his mother placing a bulky object (most likely, the saxophone case) underneath her bed. Abbey exited the bedroom and made her way to the base of the staircase. Before she went upstairs, Henry quietly rushed back to his bedroom, slipped underneath the covers, and acted as if he was sleeping with his back, of course, facing the doorway. His heart was racing, skin crawling. He wondered if *she* would come again, not his mother, but her. Would her scabrous hand reach out and grab him by the shoulder and drag him down into the dank shadows in which she dwelled? Would she come, the old haggard woman? If she did, would Henry finally confront her? A sudden flash of her sunken eyes penetrated through Henry's mind. The strain in his head was tightening and becoming more resilient like a headache. He turned his thoughts to his mother, not *her*, but his mother. The thought alone of his mother like a merciless predator occupying, plotting, attacking his mind, made him queasy to his stomach.

Abbey opened the door.

The squeak alone was like teeth digging into his skin.

As she strolled toward the bed, she witnessed her fragile son, bruised and deflated (almost frightened), lying on his side. Henry opened his tightly sealed eyes and gazed at all the Mr. Vortex posters on the walls, the memorabilia. And just like that, the two women drifted from his mind. The hand gone. The sunken eyes gone. The bed behind Henry gradually sank down a little from where Abbey sat down on the edge of the bed. The drive around town had cleared the anger from her face, voice, and manner. The anger was still there, though, on standby.

"His name isn't really Buddy Egghorn," Abbey said soothingly from behind. "His name is Henry McClintock. He *was. . .*" she sighed, ". . . he was your father, Henry."

Henry remained on his side with his head rested against the pillow. His attention was still on the Mr. Vortex posters on the wall.

"What really happened to him?"

"Last spring, this. . . this big city detective visited me at the house," she said. "He informed me about your father. Said that these two kids found him dead in a park. He was murdered, Henry."

"Murdered?"

Abbey said, "The detective said whoever did it really had it in for him. Your father didn't have a single enemy, Henry."

He turned his head briefly.

"Did they ever catch who killed him?"

"Yes," Abbey answered quietly. "They said a man named Timothy Snead killed him. Said he was arrested before on drug charges. He's now serving a life sentence in jail." She cleared her throat and leaned back against the headboard. "I spent days thinking about the man who had done those awful things to your father." For a moment, Abbey hung her head in solace. "I can't imagine a person doing what they did to your father. It just didn't make any sense." Her face curtained over with emptiness. She looked upward, pulled her eyes to the back of her son's head. "But that's what the streets will do to a man, Henry. They will drag you down with them. You understand?" Henry barely moved his head over the pillow. "The detective also said your father had been living under another name. Harry, I believe." Abbey shook her head with sheer disgust. "He was a drifter. A loser, Henry. He was a musician like you. Look what happened to him, Henry. He ended up living the remainder of his days on the streets with strangers, criminals, no home, no money, alone, and then just like that, he was swept under the rug like a piece of dirt." Abbey did her best to hide the emotions from spilling over into her empty expression. Some emotion crept through, which caused Abbey to grimace slightly. "Now do you see why I'm so protective?" She stroked the top of Henry's head. "I don't want to see you waste your life as your father did."

"Why didn't you tell me this sooner?"

"One day, I was going to tell you," she answered. "When you were ready."

"But we could've helped him," Henry said sorely. "He was out there alone. We could've helped him, Mom."

"No," she said and stroked the back of Henry's head. "We couldn't help him, Henry. He left me. He left *us*, Henry. You know this." She paused. "In the end, he turned out to be an incompetent. . . no-good. . . " Abbey quickly changed her thought, ". . . he lost his mind, Henry. It had gotten so bad to the point where he couldn't even understand what was real or not. He became obsessed and began to hallucinate and see things that weren't even there."

Henry asked, "What kind of things?"

"He talked about this. . . *darkness* like people around him weren't themselves anymore but these. . . these shadows." Abbey's eyes swelled with conviction. "He was crazy, Henry. Ever. . . " Abbey suddenly pulled back her thoughts once more, carefully, ". . . The only good he ever did in our lives was send these checks in the mail every month. Eventually, the checks stopped coming. That's when I knew. I knew he was gone from our lives. . . for good." She grabbed Henry's shoulder. "Listen to me, Henry. You're not going to be like your father. Do you understand me, Henry?" The emotions finally flooded through her voice and face. Tears formed in the corners of her eyes. A tremor escaped from her chest and scampered up Abbey's throat, squeezing now like a fist. "You can't. You won't go down the same road as your father did. . ."

Henry felt the urge to revolt, to question his mother, but he could sense the aftermath of the slap echoing against his cheek. Plus, he had never seen his mother so upset before. He sat upright and forced himself to look at his mother, who was now wiping the tears from her cheeks.

". . . And you're not going to play dress up anymore. You're not going to play that saxophone anymore. You're going to go to college. You're going to get an education. And you're going to be a successful basketball player. Do you understand?"

Henry ignored the end of what his mother said, about the basketball, and focused on the records, one in particular, *Hard Rider*.

H.M., Henry thought, *the initials on the saxophone.*

"I want you to say it back to me," she said clearly and leaned her head forward into Henry's vision. "You're not going to go to Jodi's house anymore either. That goes for Ms. Craft. I don't want you seeing that woman anymore."

Henry drifted into a daze.

The Jagger, he thought. *Could it really?*

"Henry. . ."

He answered robotically, "Yes. I won't go to Jodi's house anymore."

"And Ms. Craft?"

"We're through."

Abbey reached over, hugged Henry, and said into his shoulder, "I love you, Henry."

As always, Henry never said it back.

During dinner, Henry remained fairly quiet. He didn't eat much—only half an egg roll and a couple of bites from the sweet and sour chicken that Abbey picked up at a local Chinese takeout.

Throughout the entire meal, as short-lived as it was, Abbey never spoke of Henry's father. Surely, he had so many questions about him, his father, and his murderer, Timothy Snead. Not once did Henry ever question his mother about his father or his father's killer, Mr. Snead. Instead, he sat there thinking about all the questions he wanted to ask his mother.

After dinner, Henry went back to his bedroom with those initials, *H.M.*, on his mind. It could've been a coincidence, Henry thought over dinner. And he was found at the park too! He remembered Ms. Craft talking about Mr. Vortex, his death, how two kids discovered his dead body underneath a bridge in Josette Park.

Henry searched around his closet and found a box of old toys. He came across those very same initials, H.M., etched on the bottom of the toys. There was one toy in particular, a miniature red truck blemished with a little bit of rust and dirt buildup along the sides. When Henry was younger, he carried this one truck everywhere he went.

Now, one of the tires was missing.

Years ago, Abbey had told Henry to throw the nasty thing in the trash. She said it was a "source of bacteria," and "make sure you wash your hands afterwards." Henry never threw the toy in the trash, obviously. Nonetheless, the toy had been tampered with and not by Henry.

Someone else had tried to etch away the M from the bottom of the red truck and replace it with the letter B.

TWENTY-FIVE

AFTER Henry climbed his way through the entire school day, he hitched a ride back home with Arena, who had recently acquired her driver's license.

Since Henry wasn't in the mood to hang out with Arena—and even if they did hang out either at the mall or at the courts or at Milly and Munford's Discs, Henry wouldn't be much company—he told Arena to drop him off at the house.

Once Henry tossed his book bag over the couch, he went straight to the telephone in the kitchen where he called his Uncle Charlie.

In an upbeat tone, his Uncle Charlie answered the phone, "Charlie here."

Henry could hear a frantic man whispering in the background.

"Uncle Charlie," Henry said over the phone. "It's Henry."

"Henry!" Uncle Charlie chirped. "What's up, my man?"

"Not much," he said. "I know you're probably busy."

"I always have time for my nephew," he said, as the whispering was cut off from the sound of a sturdy wooden door shutting. "So, what's up, Henry? Your mother tells me how good you're doing in basketball. She tells me that you guys are undefeated."

"We are," Henry said, "but that's not what I want to talk about."

"What do you want to talk about, Henry?"

"I need to ask you about my father."

Uncle Charlie said with curiosity, "Is your mother home?"

"No," Henry answered.

"Does she know you're calling me?"

"I know his name was Henry McClintock," Henry said abruptly.

"Where did you hear that name, Henry?" Uncle Charlie said, his tone suddenly changing from ecstatic to grim.

"Mom told me," he said. "She said he was murdered."

"I heard," Uncle Charlie said. "I'm sorry to hear."

"So, you *did* know him?"

Uncle Charlie was hesitant to answer.

"Listen, Uncle Charlie. . . "

"Yes, Henry."

"Did you know anything about my father?"

A sigh breezed through the receiver.

"I know he was in the music business," he said casually. "That's about it."

"Did he go by another name?"

There was no answer over the phone.

"Uncle Charlie?"

"I'm really not supposed to say, Henry."

Henry begged, "I won't tell anybody, Uncle Charlie. I promise."

He could hear another sigh, this time a loud one rattling through the telephone.

"This is between you and me, Henry," Uncle Charlie said carefully. "You can't tell anybody, even your mother."

"I won't," Henry said. "I swear. Cross my heart and hope to die."

"He went by his stage name. . . Mr. Vortex." The other end of the phone made a couple of clicking noises like the phone was being thrashed around. "Henry?" Uncle Charlie said. "You there?"

"*Yeah*," Henry said, his voice trailing.

"You're not going to tell anybody about this. Are you?"

"No, Uncle Charlie."

"Good," he said with relief.

There was a loud banging noise over the phone, which Henry thought was knocking on a door.

A strange man was franitcally yelling from a distance. More knocking.

Then, Henry heard a calm woman's voice saying from behind the door, "*Doctor Lowe, I need you to take a look at this. We have a situation out here.*"

"Is everything okay, Uncle Charlie?"

"Yeah, Henry," he said quickly. "Everything's fine. Listen, Henry. I gotta split. I want you to do me a favor and tell your mother to call me as soon as she gets home from work. All right?"

"Sure. . ." Henry said suspiciously.

"It was nice talking to you, Henry."

"Nice talking to you, Uncle Charlie," Henry said and then hung up the phone.

TWENTY-SIX

IN about two hours, Abbey was going to come through that door—and more than likely, she was going to be in a foul mood.

Without squandering over another second, Henry pocketed the flyer in his hand and hurried over to Abbey's bed. There she was, Adrian. Henry reached underneath the bed and pulled out the saxophone case. He opened the case to make sure Adrian was there, fully intact.

Next, Henry hurried to his bedroom and searched around his closet for something to wear. He only had five or six outfits, one for each day of the week. Monday usually consisted of an unbuttoned red flannel shirt, both sleeves rolled up to his forearms, a solid black shirt underneath, black jeans—skinny not baggy—and a pair of black and white off-brand Converse Chuck Taylor All Stars called Chucky T's. Tuesday: a pea green shirt with a yellow Adidas logo, blue jeans—folded over the bottom—black Ray-Ban Wayfarer, same Chucky T's. Wednesday: a black polo with a cigarette hole in the back, same blue jeans, Vans Slip-Ons. Thursday: Rick Deckard. Friday: a gray *Hawk* hoody, blue jeans, Chucky T's. The following week, Henry would switch up the clothes: red flannel over green Adidas shirt or black polo with brown corduroys. The last two remaining pieces of clothing in his closet, which hung at the very end (feet away from the other clothes), was a black blazer, a pair of black slacks, and a plain white dress shirt. By far, it was the most expensive outfit in his closet. Saved up for two months to buy it. He carefully removed the blazer from the clothes hanger and laid it out over his bed.

Behind the closed curtain, Henry paced back and forth with Adrian strapped over his neck. He was dressed in Sunday's best: a black blazer with a pair of black slacks and black dress shoes that he usually wore to Mass. Instead of a black tie, he was wearing a white dress shirt with the top two buttons unbuttoned and black Wayfarer sunglasses like Bob Dylan and a piece of paper with the number 5 over the breast pocket of his blazer. Number 4 was finishing his performance, which made Henry even more nervous. After every magic trick, the members of the audience *ewwed* and *ahed* and clapped like synchronized penguins. *How could I follow a magician who made exotic animals with balloons?* The audience, which mostly consisted of juniors and seniors (however, parents and school faculty were there as well), completely adored him. Plus, the little magician had spunk and personality too. What was not to like? Then, more questions came Henry's way. What if I mess up? What if Kerri is here? What if I trip and fall on stage? What if. . . what if I puke all over the front row? Henry frequently patted the sweat from his forehead with the backside of his hand. Each time he glanced at the magician, the audience, the many faces, the lights, the sweat dripped faster from his forehead and was followed with peculiar hot flashes.

Shortly following Henry's breakdown, T.J. finally found Ms. Craft sitting in the third row.

Ms. Craft noticed T.J. shuffling closer.

She quickly rose from her seat.

"He's freaking out," T.J. whispered in Ms. Craft's ear.

"Oh dear," she mumbled with a long expression over her face.

T.J. guided her backstage.

When the two arrived backstage, Henry was already crouched in the corner near a speaker.

"I. . . I can't do it, Dolores. . . "

"Sure you can, Henry," Ms. Craft said with reassurance. "If I had a nickel every time I said those exact words before I performed, I'd be a millionaire."

"I can't do it. . . "

Ms. Craft kneeled down to Henry's level.

"Henry," she exclaimed as her eyes narrowed, "look at me."

Henry cleared his throat and looked into Ms. Craft's piercing eyes.

"I've seen greatness in you," she said closely. "This is nothing, Henry. This is no different than you playing in your bedroom."

"But look at all those people. . . "

"So what? They're *just* people, Henry."

"What if. . . "

"I don't want to hear 'what if,'" she said over Henry's deflating voice. "'What if' doesn't live in the now." She placed the tip of her finger on her temple. "It only exists in here, in your mind. 'What if' is just another way of saying that you're scared. And there's absolutely nothing wrong with being scared, Henry. We all get scared. It's okay to be scared. Think about *Rocky*. Think about how scared he was when he finally stepped inside that ring with Apollo Creed. All the training, the preparation for that one moment."

Henry thought about *Rocky*, that one fight.

"It's time to confront your fear, Henry," Ms. Craft said.

Henry focused on his fear, not the audience, but his real fear.

"Close your eyes."

Henry was hesitant to close his eyes.

"Go on, Henry," she said with a nod. "Close them."

Henry closed his eyes.

"Imagine your worst fear behind the darkness of your eyelids."

A brass door handle jingling. . .

"Now, let it in."

. . . Henry opened the door. . .

"Stand your ground."

. . . A scabrous hand reaching through a moonlit bedroom. . .

"Embrace it, Henry."

. . . Sunken eyes. . .

"Nurture it."

. . . The haggard woman grabbed Henry's forearm. . .

"It's scared like you, Henry."

. . . She pulled herself closer, her smelly body now hugging Henry. . .

"It grows weaker."

. . . One side of her skeletal face pressed against his shoulder. . .

"Feel your fear's strength draining like water from a punctured balloon."

A gravelly voice: *I'm scared.*

"Now, let it go."

. . . Her upper body suddenly thrust backward from a swift blow across the jaw. . .

Focus, Henry.

. . . She plummeted back into the shadows.

Henry said vacantly, "It worked."

Ms. Craft smiled.

"Of course, it did."

She touched Henry on the shoulder.

Henry looked up at Ms. Craft with big eyes.

"You *can* do this, Henry," she said confidently and pointed her finger at Henry's chest. "Clear your mind and play from here." She then waved Henry closer and whispered into his ear, "Pretend as if the people in the audience were all naked."

"Naked? How the heck am I supposed to do that?"

"Here," she said and pointed to Henry's head. Her hand moved down to Henry's chest. "And then play from here."

"Naked? Really?"

Ms. Craft laughed.

"How embarrassing that would be. Right?"

"I guess so. Yeah."

"They look at you standing there, dressed nicely in that nice blazer of yours, looking as sharp as a tack, ready to entertain them with your music. Not so embarrassing after all."

"No," Henry said, shaking his head.

With a pen in her hand, the stage director pointed at Henry.

"You're up, Number 5," she said.

"Remember," Ms. Craft said. "They're all naked."

Henry sighed and bobbed his head.

"Okay," he said to himself. "I can do this."

The curtains pulled away, revealing a strobe light above. Henry drunkenly made his way to the center of the stage. The pale bluish light was flashing over him, making his walk appear static as if he was teleporting from one space to another. Then, as he approached the front of the stage, the strobe suddenly cut off. The spotlights above came on over the darkness and temporarily blinded Henry. After the fuzzy glare vanished from his eyes, he did as Ms. Craft told him and pretended that each audience member was naked. For Henry, it wasn't that hard. He just closed his eyes and then reopened them and then. . . naked. Henry couldn't help but laugh to himself from the sight of the audience. Members of the audience turned to their partners or friends or family in extreme bafflement.

As Henry placed his lip over the reed, he peered into the audience and observed Kerri and her friends staring back at him. The only person from the group of cheerleaders who wasn't giggling at Henry was, in fact, Kerri. She was sitting there, almost in a state of suspense with her keen eyes attached to Henry. All of sudden, the suit became uncomfortable, itchy almost. Other areas of his body, mainly underneath his slacks, collected with perspiration. *Not here*, he thought, *anywhere but here.* Henry blushed from her nakedness, which, after a couple of seconds of realizing that he was standing on stage, looking as sharp as a tack—as Ms. Craft told him—and she was out there with the naked barbarians, didn't seem to bother him one bit. However, he was more interested in why Kerri was so interested in him, that moment of suspense. As Henry got ready to play the song, he moved his eyes to the back of the auditorium. There, he suddenly caught a glimpse of a familiar woman standing in the very back near the entrance. He turned ghostly, expressionless. He pulled Adrian from his lips and stood frozen.

From backstage, Ms. Craft had her hands balled into fists and was urging Henry to play.

Henry glanced over at Ms. Craft and then directed his attention back to the familiar woman who was standing with her arms crossed and that "look" over her face. He observed the jaw muscles flexing on the sides of her face in anger.

Henry removed the dark sunglasses from his face and uttered to the crowd, "I'm so. . . so. . . so. . . sorry."

Then, he pulled Adrian from his shoulder, dropped the saxophone on the stage, and slowly backed away from the stage.

As he backed away, his eyes crossed the front of the audience.

Kerri was shaking her head in disappointment while her friends seated on either side of her were laughing hysterically and cackling like babies and pointing at Henry and hollering out phrases like "What a coward?" or "Igor got a case of stage fright!" Henry witnessed one of Kerri's friends pouting her face with great exaggeration and saying to the other students around her, "Aw!" More students around the clique of cheerleaders, including the footballs players, the jocks, burst out in an irrefutable laughter. T.J. ran onto the stage, picked up Adrian, and then hurried off the stage as Henry stumbled and tripped his way backstage.

Outside, Henry shouldered open the backdoor of the gymnasium and sprinted into the parking lot. His breath was like steam pouring from a pipe. He paced back and forth in the parking lot and tried to catch his breath while Abbey wandered around in search for her son. She found Henry pacing through the parking lot and then flagged him down.

"Henry!" she shouted, her breath visible from the frigid air. "Wait!"

Angered from his mother's appearance, Henry spun around.

"Henry!"

Abbey ran up to Henry.

"What are you doing here?"

"I heard from one of the neighbors."

"Who?"

Abbey didn't answer.

"Who told you?"

"It doesn't matter who told me."

Abbey grabbed hold of Henry's arm.

Before she could pull her son closer, he retracted his arm from his mother's grip.

"Please don't do this," she said with restraint. "Not here."

"Do you know what they're going to think of me now?"

"What did you think was going to happen, Henry?" Abbey said. "You think those people out there care about you? Well, they don't—"

Henry interrupted, "You weren't supposed to be here!"

"If I knew that you didn't want me here, then I wouldn't have come, Henry."

"No," Henry said with a frown. Tears swelled in his eyes. "You did this on purpose! You wanted to watch me fail!"

"Listen to me, Henry," Abbey grilled, her eyes sharpening. "Is this what you really want to do?"

Henry didn't answer. Yet, he was too embarrassed to look his mother in the eye, too angry, too betrayed.

"I love you to death, Henry." Abbey leaned in closer to Henry. "Do you understand me?"

Henry tried to catch his breath.

"If you really love me," he paused, "then you would let me play."

"I just want you to do the right thing, Henry. If this is what you want to do, then we can find a way to make it work around basketball."

"What do you know about doing the right thing?" Henry seethed and stepped forward, dangerously close to his mother. "The right thing would be for me to have a father in my life, a person who can be there for me, a person who can support me! And you're never there!"

"But I'm here now, Henry," she exclaimed and towered over Henry. "Aren't I?"

Henry grimaced in rage and ran away.

"Henry!" Abbey hollered out. "You get back here!"

After the talent show was over, Abbey spotted Ms. Craft making her way to the parked Cadillac in the parking lot.

Abbey marched up to Ms. Craft, caught her off guard, and shoved her against a parked car.

"I thought I told you to stay away from my son," she said, her teeth bared like a junkyard dog.

"*You*," Ms. Craft said, her voice quaking with anger, "you don't know anything about your son. You!" This time she stuck her finger in Abbey's face, held it there like a blade. "You don't know how to be a mother!"

With her eyes glazed over from the cold of the night, Abbey stepped closer and stuck her face inches away from Ms. Craft's face, close enough to smell what she had eaten earlier that day.

She said, "If I catch you hanging around my son ever again. . . I'll kill you."

TWENTY-SEVEN

THE very next morning, Henry skipped breakfast and played a game of H.O.R.S.E. with T.J. and Danny (even though Henry was not permitted to hang around Danny without a parent around). Throughout the game, Henry never said much, only short responses to their inquires like "What did you end up doing after the show?" Henry answered, "Went home. Went to bed." T.J.: "Did you get in trouble?" Henry: "Don't care." The conversations were kept to a minimum. As both T.J. and Danny could tell, Henry wasn't one to be messed with. There was something building inside him, something dark. So, the two eased back and kept their distance from Henry. None of them mentioned what happened at the talent show last night, the part where Henry froze on stage. Only twelve hours after the show, the nicknames were already circulating around Glenn Forest. And it wasn't even a school day! A couple of eleventh graders joked about Henry's "new" talent. *Hey! Look at me. My name's Henry. This is my talent.* On the basketball courts, Jeffery (who had, over the summer, chiseled away at all of that ninth grade baby fat and shaped his body into lean muscle) strolled up to Henry and stood gaping like a museum sculpture. "You call this a talent!" Jeffery cried out. Henry was tempted to kick the Dick where the sun didn't shine—really hard too as if there was a cute prize waiting for him on the other side like a pink bunny stuffed animal that he could give to Kerri. Jeffery, along with his football buddies, branded Henry with the new nickname, one that Henry would *never* hear the end of. That name was Popsicle.

A couple of neighbors called out the name "Popsicle" on their bikes as they rode past the courts. Henry tried to ignore the insults, but their persistence was starting to get the best of him. T.J. and Danny witnessed the escape in Henry's eyes, as if he was being backed against a wall, a crushed teenager sentenced to life where he would serve the rest of his dying days in his own jail cell with bars and no keyhole.

After they finished playing H.O.R.S.E., Henry never said goodbye to his friends. Instead, he gave them a nod—which was his way of saying goodbye. He left the courts and moped around the woods behind the neighborhood before he finally dragged himself back home where Abbey made ham sandwiches for herself and Henry. As Abbey brought the sandwich to the porch, Henry was sitting on the steps and marveling at the record, *Hard Rider*, in his hands and visualizing himself in Mr. Vortex's face. Henry didn't see it at first, the resemblance. He had been told by many of his friends around the neighborhood that he didn't have a black nose. Some of the other kids didn't know exactly what race Henry was. Same went for his mother. His hair was curly and dark, nearly jet-black, and yet his skin was neither black nor white. Not once did Henry ever think about his racial background or his heritage, even though he didn't exactly know *what* he was: white or black? Whenever Henry took a test or exam, Abbey told him to fill in the multiracial circle, not the African American or the Caucasian one. Henry never questioned why? "It is what it is," his mother always told him. Now that Henry knew who Mr. Vortex was, he could see a piece of himself in the picture—only the face was more mature. Henry had his father's hazel eyes, his smile.

With a plate in her hands, Abbey patiently stood behind her son. On the plate was a ham sandwich made the way Henry liked: a little bit of mayonnaise, no crust, cut in wedges.

Abbey asked carefully, "Do you want to talk?"

Henry didn't respond.

She placed the plate on the railing of the porch and noticed Henry holding the *Hard Rider* record in his hand.

"You know," she said and nodded at the record, "I used to listen to that record all day long. It never got old. I mean *never*."

"I know who he is."

Abbey didn't respond from the remark. Yet, she sat down next to her son on the front steps and curled her hands around her knees.

"Yes," she said casually. "I had a little chat with Uncle Charlie over the telephone. He said he felt bad about telling you. But he did the right thing, Henry." Abbey reverently gazed around the street. "You don't know how many times I wanted to tell you. Maybe if I told you, then, well, then maybe you would think differently of him." She pulled her attention back to her son. "I know how much you enjoyed listening to his music. Now," her voice rose with a hint of excitement, "I'm sure you're going to brag to all your friends about it, how your father was a famous musician."

"No," Henry mumbled.

"Yeah, right," Abbey said sarcastically.

"He may be my blood," he said. "But he's not my father."

"But he *was* your father, Henry."

Henry said mindfully, "When I listen to Mr. Vortex, I feel like he's speaking to me in his music like he knows everything about me and I know everything about him like we are connected in some way. For once in my life, I actually felt like I belonged, like I was normal. I know now. He wasn't speaking to me. He wanted *nothing* to do with me." Henry eyed over the record once more. "If he cared, he would've been there for me. He wouldn't have left us."

Abbey found herself looking at the steps below. She regained her composure and looked Henry in the eyes.

"The closest I get to my father is from some stupid ass record."

Abbey let out a sigh.

Then, Henry flung the record on the sidewalk.

"I can't stand it here," he said, frowning. "Everyone thinks I'm a joke. Girls even laugh at me now. And Kerri, she thinks I'm a creep."

"Forget about her, Henry. You deserve much better. Believe me."

"But you don't even know her."

"I know enough, son." Abbey wrapped her arm around Henry. "You still have me and T.J. and that Arena girl. She seems nice."

Henry stressed, "I don't like it here anymore!"

Abbey sighed once more and pulled Henry closer.

"What if I said that we don't have to live here anymore, Henry?" Abbey said and pulled her son's attention toward hers.

"What do you mean?"

"Last week, I was offered a managerial position, one that pays a lot more than my current position at the Depot," she said. "If I take it, Henry, I will be transferred to a Depot in Lansford. It's only about an hour or so away from here. You could still see T.J. and Arena, but it would have to be on the weekends. Henry," she tightened her grip around her son, "I won't have to work two jobs anymore! That way I could spend more time with you. Isn't that great? I wasn't going to take it if you didn't want me to."

Henry thought over the new job.

"No," he said clearly. "*Take it.*"

"Are you sure?"

"Yeah."

"You know we still haven't discussed what we're going to do with that saxophone."

"It was his," Henry said. "Wasn't it?"

"You mean your father's?"

Henry said coldly, "I mean Mr. Vortex."

Abbey sighed.

"I don't know," she said solemnly. "It could be anybody's. There's a lot of people with the initials, H.M. But if it *was* your father's, then maybe it's best you hang onto it. You know. Something to remember him by."

Without anymore thought, Henry said, "I'll throw it away."

"If you really want to play it on the side, then I will let you, Henry," Abbey said and then her voice rose. "As long as it doesn't interfere with basketball or homework. You understand?"

During his mother's proposal, Henry was shaking his head.

"I don't want to play anymore."

"Are you sure?"

"Yes."

Abbey pulled her son even closer, kissed him on the cheek, and said, "I love you so much, Henry." She smiled and lifted Henry's face upward. "To new beginnings."

Henry bobbed his head and barely cracked a smile.

"To new beginnings," he said.

After the talk with his mother, Henry didn't bother to eat lunch. Instead, he went straight to his bedroom and gathered all of the records, Ms. Craft's record player, the cassette tapes, the 2 Hot 2 Handle merchandise, the drum machines, keyboards, and samplers that were scattered around his bedroom. Next, he tore down the posters of Mr. Vortex, the bobble head dolls, the toys, the comic books, the video games, the Mr. V tees and belt buckles, all Mr. Vortex memorabilia, and dumped everything in a storage bin. When he came across the film reel—THE GALLERY OF STARS—he decided to put it aside in the closet and leave it be. Last but not least, he grabbed Adrian as well as the leather saxophone case.

With his arms full of music equipment, Henry went outside and threw everything in the trashcan, including Adrian and the storage bin of Mr. Vortex memorabilia.

To new beginnings, he thought.

FROM inside the car, Abbey asked, "Are you ready, Henry?"

Standing on the curb of their old house, Henry was hesitant to get inside the Jelly Bean. He absorbed the scenery: the Mayflower truck all loaded up, the SOLD sign in the front lawn, and the now empty house.

He said under his voice, "Good riddance."

Before Henry stepped foot into the Jelly Bean, he directed his attention across the street and saw Kerri sitting alone on the front porch. She was reading a book, which Henry thought was out of the ordinary. In all the years Henry had known Kerri or at least thought he had known her, he had never seen her reading a book or doing homework or anything that required a moment of reflection.

"Henry," Abbey said from inside the car. "We have to get going."

Henry ignored his mother and continued to stare at Kerri on the porch. At times, Kerri would pull her gliding eyes away from the book and shoot a glance toward Henry and the empty house behind him. Henry wiped the sweat from his palms over his blue jeans and bit down on his bottom lip and tried to think of something to say to Kerri, something for her to remember him by, something romantic like he was going to drive away and never come back and this was his last stance to win her over. Henry was tempted to do all of those things—most importantly, to walk over to her, unruffled, and express how he truly felt about her, how no other girl made him feel they way she made him feel inside, how she was the reason why he took more time getting dressed in the morning. Then, after Henry pulled his thoughts from the current situation and imagined the confession through another person's perspective, an onlooker, the reality set in, the doubts. After all that Kerri had put him through, the stress, the pain, the sleepless nights, the weight loss, the rejection, the name calling, the teasing, the games, Henry decided it was best to say what was *really* on his mind.

As he made an attempt toward Kerri's house, his mother said once more from the car, "Henry. . ."

Henry turned to the car and then glanced at Kerri's house. He looked once more. Kerri was nowhere around. The rocking chair was rocking back and forth, but there wasn't anybody sitting in the chair. So, Henry got into the Jelly Bean and they drove away.

After the movers finished unloading the truck, Abbey and Henry stood in front of a ranch style house, all brick with blue shutters. The front yard was twice as big as their previous yard in Glenn Forest. The backyard was mostly woods. Even the air smelled much cleaner. The city alone, Lansford, was much different than Reddington. Being a big banking city (and having one the tallest skyscrapers in the country), Lansford attracted a diversity of people. Abbey called them "transplants." The accents were hard to distinguish. It was like a hodgepodge of all accents: Northern, Southern, or Western, all wrapped into one. Most of the residents who lived in the melting pot that was Lansford acted much more differently than the ones in Reddington. In addition, they drove much nicer cars (Abbey and Henry even passed a red Ferrari Testarossa and a Pontiac Trans Am like KITT from the television show *Knight Rider*!) and wore lots of hair gel and jewelry and suits and sunglasses and big hair. While they cruised through Lansford before arriving at their new house, Henry could sense the waft of arrogance floating in the air like a cloud of smog. The kids who were his age, fifteen going on sixteen, didn't talk to many other kids outside their cliques. The adults weren't that friendly either, he observed.

"What do you think?" she asked, standing proudly with one of her hands over her hip.

"It's nice." Henry peered around the neighborhood. There were no kids playing on the street like there were on Davie Morris. In fact, the street was completely desolated. No sounds of cars or laughter. Fallen leaves were piled up in neighbors' lawns. The dogwood trees lined on each side of the street were stripped bare from the change in season.

"What's a matter, Henry?"

"It's. . . it's quiet."

"Well, moms and dads are at work and kids are at school," she said. "That reminds me. The other day, I talked with the principal at Marilee Anne High over the phone, Principal Teague. I asked him if there were any amusement parks around the city. He said there was a shopping mall not too far from here."

"I'm kind of tired," Henry said somberly.

"Oh. . . okay," Abbey said. "Why don't you take a nap and then when you wake we'll start unpacking the rest of the stuff."

Abbey and Henry walked through the front lawn and into their new house.

TWENTY-NINE

EVEN though Henry wasn't so adamant about sleeping during the day, he surprisingly caught two solid hours of sleep without any interruptions. Henry woke from his nap, refreshed like the morning sun, and wandered downstairs into the kitchen where his mother was busy unpacking a box of plates and silverware and placing them as quietly as possible in the overhead cabinets.

"Hey, Henry," Abbey said excitedly over her shoulder. "Did you sleep well?"

"Yeah," he said with a shrug. "Sort of."

"Well. . ." Abbey said as she moved her eyes toward the many boxes stacked on the marble countertop, ". . . take your pick."

"If it's okay, I was going to check out the backyard."

"Sure," she said, her voice still filled with excitement. "But don't wander too far. I want to get this done by the end of the day."

Before Henry exited the house, Abbey said from behind, "Henry. . ."

As Henry cracked up the backdoor, he turned around.

"Yeah, Mom."

"We did the right thing," she said. "Didn't we?"

Henry replied, "Of course," and walked through the back-door.

As Henry took another step into the woods, he glanced over his shoulder in curiosity and barely recognized his new house through the narrow cracks of the trees.

For about a quarter of a mile, he followed a running creek through the woods until he had nowhere to go but across. He rested at the creek for a minute and searched for any fish or reptiles underneath the murky water, but he couldn't find any. The water also had a strange smell to it, almost like sewage. Henry mapped out the rocks along the creek, which was about seven or eight feet wide, and used them to cross. Halfway across the creek, he kneeled down and eased his hand into the water. Suddenly, a water moccasin, dark with age, came slithering by Henry's hand. He quickly pulled his hand from the frigid water and accidentally splashed the sides of his Air Jordan's. Henry didn't care much about the shoes, at least not until he made it safely across the creek.

Then, Henry vented.

"God. . ." he muttered, ". . . fucking. . . little piece of shit. . ."

As he wiped his wet hand over his blue jeans and finally regained his composure, he watched the snake moving franitcally down the stream.

"That's right," he said to himself. "Run off, you coward. . . "

After Henry did his best to clean his shoes (by mostly using dried leaves scattered around the woods to wipe away all the mud and even then, once he was done with the leaves, there was nothing left of them but these tiny flakes from where they crumbled apart), he moved his journey farther into the colorful woods. Most of the trees were pine, some of them oak. Besides a couple of leaves clinging onto the branches, most of the trees were exposed. The trunks of the trees were old and hearty, nothing like the withered, scrawny trees back in Reddington. Each step Henry took was crunchy from the crisp leaves, which covered the ground like a blanket. At least if Henry dirtied up his Air Jordan's again, he didn't have to worry about running out of cleaning supplies. Strangely, though, the woods were quiet too like the neighborhood.

As Henry made a detour around a couple of fallen trees, which had been uprooted from a terrible storm, he heard another pair of footsteps, only smaller in size, coming from afar. A crunch here and a crunch there. The sounds or lack of them made him wonder about the woods—most importantly, the silence.

Not too far ahead, the sun shone over a clearing and revealed an open stretch of land.

As Henry found the clearing, the reclusive sun pulled back behind the clouds and darkened the land. Periodically poking its brilliant face behind the clouds, the sun lit up the land and revealed a slope leading up to a set of rusty railroad tracks.

Intrigued, Henry pursued through the woods until he reached the clearing.

Before him was a railroad track that stretched as far as the eye could see in either direction. There was a small embankment on each side of the tracks, which had cut through the middle of the woods. He trekked along the embankment and stood on the sturdy tracks. Curious, he kneeled down and hovered his ear along the track and listened for any upcoming trains. No vibrations. No sounds. Silence. The atmosphere was somewhat eerie and hard to explain. For a moment, Henry wondered about this foreign place. He had been in similar places before, similar woods. But the life, Henry knew, it was as if the life that inhabited these lands, the birds or the squirrels (both creatures he routinely crossed throughout the day) or the deer or the raccoons or even that one water moccasin in the creek, was suddenly scared of something, not Henry, but something. . .

As he wandered over the railroad tracks for about half of a mile and played soccer with a couple of pebbles across the wooden planks, a tiny, almost grain-like glint of sunlight caught his eyes. At first, Henry thought it was just his eyes fooling him—like whenever he got lightheaded from hanging upside down or getting up too quickly and those tiny flashing stars would flicker across his vision. The same went for whenever he stared at the television screen for so long and a floater would dance across the corner of his eye. The glint appeared too exclusive to touch. Like the stars or the floaters in his eyes, the glint came from within.

Then, he looked closer.

The glint took shape, now tangible.

He wasn't lightheaded, that Henry knew.

The sharp glint was coming from the middle of the track, not above, not from either one of his eyes! The closer he crept to the glint, the brighter the glint appeared.

The glint was so bright now that he had to momentarily shield his eyes.

A lone cloud briefly grazed across the brilliant sun and dampened the tiny glint before him.

He pulled his hand from his face and peered closely. For a second, he thought he saw an opened saxophone case on the tracks.

He increased the speed of his walk, now a jog.

The sun shone across the familiar object inside the case, which forced Henry to shield his eyes once more.

As Henry stared through the cracks of his hands, his heart raced against his chest.

He stood a few feet away now.

Inches.

His face slackened.

His jaw gradually dropped.

With fear speeding throughout his veins, Henry inched closer to the open case and kneeled over the saxophone inside.

Carefully, he reached down and turned the saxophone over on its side.

There, he saw the initials, *H.M.*, over Adrian's bow!

Henry gasped in horror and stumbled over the tracks.

When Henry finally found his feet, he sprinted through the woods without looking over his shoulder. He ran so fast and hard until the silence was no more. All he could hear was the sound of his heart pounding like a drum. The sound rippled throughout his body, which caused him to run faster and harder.

The pounding didn't stop, even when he returned home from his trek.

When his mother asked what was the matter, he told her it was nothing and he went to his bedroom where he unpacked his boxes.

The pounding was still there, though, but it wasn't from his heart.

PART THREE

THE HOLLOWS OF SINCLAIR LEPRIEUR

THIRTY

THE weekend after Christmas, Henry had talked his mother into driving him to T.J.'s, which was a little over an hour away. About fifty-eight minutes without traffic. And Abbey was an aggressive driver too. She dropped Henry off on a Friday afternoon and planned on picking him up on Sunday. Before she said her goodbyes to her son, she warned him to stay away from Jodi's house, most importantly, Ms. Craft. "Don't even go *near* that place!" Abbey warned. Henry made a promise not to visit Ms. Craft and even shook on it with his mother.

The first thing Henry and T.J. did when Henry arrived that Friday afternoon was pay a visit to Holiday. Along the way, Henry told T.J. all about the new hood, about Adrian, and how he found her sitting on the train tracks.

"A saxophone stalking you, Henry?" T.J. said, trying to hold in his laughter.

"It's true, Octo," Henry exclaimed. "And I'm not crazy."

"I never said you was."

"So. . . " he said, ". . . you believe me."

"You know your moms put it on them tracks for you to find."

"Why would she do that?" Henry asked himself and then squared his shoulders in front of T.J. "She wouldn't do that, Octo. Plus, I watched the garbage man pick up Adrian the next day. I swear. Saw it with my own eyes."

"Could've fallen off a train or sumtin."

"Really, Octo," Henry said and rolled his eyes. "A train carrying a load of garbage."

"Maybe like one of them trains goin' to one of them, you know, one of them what-do-you-call-its. . . " the word finally came to T.J., ". . . like a. . . like a landfill."

"I know what I saw," Henry said louder, more serious. "Adrian was sitting there like she was. . . I don't know. . . waiting for me."

"Waiting for you?"

"Yeah!"

T.J. smacked his gums.

"I don't even know why you went and throw it away in the first place?"

Henry mumbled, "I don't know."

"After all you went through to buy that thing. . . " T.J. said, ". . . it jus don't make any sense, Henry."

"Doesn't matter anyway," he said. "I got it back."

"You play it yet?"

Henry smacked his gums.

"Hell no," he said. "I got it chained up in my closet."

"Chained up? Whatchu mean chained up?"

"I mean '*chained up.*'"

"Chained up?"

"Yeah." Henry shrugged his shoulders. "So."

Like Henry, T.J. smacked his gums.

"I take that back, Henry," he said. "You is crazy. . . "

After hours of strolling through town, they finally arrived at Holiday's.

"So, you really gonna do this?" T.J. asked as Henry paced around the front of the shop. He walked past the front display case behind the front window. There were other things set up on the display like a set of golf clubs and crossbows and antique clocks, but no musical instruments.

Henry turned away from the front window and walked over to T.J.

"What else is there to do, Octo?"

"He gonna flip when he sees you. You know this. Right?"

"That's why you're here," Henry said and patted T.J. on the shoulder. "Right?"

"You better not be tryin' to start sum trouble, Henry."

"No trouble," he said. "This is a recon mission."

"Recon? Whatchu talkin' 'bout '*recon*'?"

All of a sudden, Henry acted as if he didn't have a tongue to speak. He returned with a simple shrug of his shoulders, which left T.J. that much more frustrated from Henry's inquisitiveness. Like T.J., Henry didn't exactly know what the word *recon* meant. He had heard people (mostly, the military types) say it in the movies or on the televisions shows before an enemy or ally was about to go to war or do something strategic that required a great deal of patience and secrecy. After all, Henry just thought the word *recon* sounded pretty cool.

They confidently strolled inside the pawnshop. The cowbell above rang out louder and more fitful than the regulars and instantly pulled Holiday's attention from behind the front counter to the front door.

The moment Holiday saw the two, mainly Henry and the grin he was wearing on his face, he waved and shouted out, "No! No! No! I want you kids out of my store!"

"Just give me a second, Holiday."

"NO!" Holiday guided both Henry and T.J. toward the entrance without touching them. "You're not allowed in here anymore."

Henry exclaimed, "The saxophone is haunted!"

Holiday suddenly froze.

"Haunted?" he said eagerly. "What do you mean haunted?"

"Yeah," Henry replied and pointed at T.J. "Haunted! Right, Octo?"

"He be tellin' the truf, man."

"And who are you?"

"Me. . . " T.J. stuck one hand into his pocket while the other one did most of the talking, ". . . I'm T.J., but my friends call me Octo."

"Octo?" Holiday snorted. "Is this some kind of joke, Henry?"

"No joke," he said without missing a beat. "I just want to know where you got the Jagger. Then, we'll leave."

"For good?"

"I swear you'll never see our faces ever again."

Holiday put more thought into the dilemma.

"I'm sorry, Henry," he said finally while shaking his head. "I can't give out customer information."

"Then, I'll be back."

Holiday asked cautiously, "Where. . . where are you going?"

"I'm going to get my friend."

"Your friend? What friend?"

Henry said, "You know. *My* friend."

"You mean that old bag? Don't you?"

"Yep," Henry said and made his way to the door. "*That old bag.*"

"Her name is Hannah," Holiday suddenly blurted out and waved down Henry. "I don't know her last name. She told me that her brother was a famous musician, traveled around the world. One man's trash is another man's treasure. Right?"

With a smile creeping on his face, Henry spun around and walked back into the pawnshop.

He asked, "Where does she live?"

"You know I can't tell you that, Henry."

Henry spun around yet again and made an attempt toward the door.

"Then, you can tell that to my friend."

"All right!" Holiday let out a moan loud enough for both Henry and T.J. to hear. He muttered, "Wait here."

While Henry and T.J. waited patiently, Holiday went to the back of the store and grabbed the record book.

They left with a name and address written down on the back of a crumpled Black Caves brochure.

"So, Henry, what 'xactly did Ms. Craft say to Holiday?"

"I don't know," he said. "But it must've been something."

T.J. laughed in Henry's face.

"You tellin' me." A beam widened over T.J.'s face. "Did you see that man's face? The last time I seen someone that scared was when you put that plastic black widow spider inside Arena's locker."

"Remember her reaction?"

T.J. postured up and animatedly threw his hands to his cheeks.

"Oh my god! Spider! Get it away! Get it away!"

Henry laughed alongside T.J.

Since the address wasn't too far from Holiday's, they ended up going by foot. They both traveled down Main Street until it turned into R. Reynolds Avenue, which then turned into the projects, Raven Heights, one of the roughest, crime-infested neighborhoods in Reddington. They found themselves walking closer together—close enough to hold hands. The two were more aware, more vigilant, more cautious, more everything. A block away from Hannah's house, they passed a couple of thugs perched on the street corner. One of them was keeping it "gangster," or so he thought (a white tee wrapped around his neck like a towel, displaying the gang symbols tattooed over his bare stomach like a fragmented black rainbow and pretending like it was summer, even though winter was weeks away from showing its teeth). The real alpha of the two was the one staying nice and cozy in the jacket, gold teeth, a pistol concealed underneath his belt buckle, and holding a leash in his hand.

In the corner of his eye, Henry witnessed the pit bull perched like a courthouse statue next to the two thugs. Not once did Henry or T.J. ever turn and direct their attention toward the pit bull.

"You little homies lost?" one of them said over the low growl of the pit bull.

Henry and T.J. ignored the thug, mainly the pit bull, kept their heads down at their feet, hands in their pockets, and quickened their pace.

*   *   *

They finally arrived at Hannah's house.

Henry said, "This is it?"

He matched the address with the one on the brochure.

"Are you sure?" T.J. asked.

"1832 Briar Hill Lane," he read and then looked at the crooked numbers *1832* on the side of the front doorway, as well as the cocked mailbox at the end of the driveway. Every single window around the house was boarded up with plywood. Drawings of a bug-eyed woman, as well as words like *devil's lair* or *spawn* or *psycho bitch,* were spray-painted in black over the plywood. No grass. The front lawn was all dirt and rubble. There was an out of place tree in the shape of a giant stickman in the middle of the lawn. The branches were all warped and overgrown—some of them had even snapped off from a recent storm and fallen over the clogged gutters of the house and were hanging there like ornaments. The trunk was covered with a powdery dust and was starting to rot from the inside. The front door was covered with strips of yellow caution tape.

"Do you think she's in there?"

Henry glanced around the desolate neighborhood street and said, "I don't know about this, Octo." Somewhere in the distance the sound of a baby crying pierced over a fading police siren. Henry turned to T.J. "There's only one way to find out."

"Say, Henry," T.J. said unsteadily. "Let's get the hell outta here."

"We didn't come all the way out here for nothing."

Henry took a couple of steps forward and realized T.J. was standing in the exact same position.

"Are you coming or not?"

T.J. shook his head.

"Stop being a wuss."

"What if she like dead inside?"

"She's not dead, Octo."

"How you know?" he said frantically. "Look at that door. That's the same 'xact tape the police use for them crime scenes."

"Maybe she doesn't want to be disturbed. I don't know."

Henry proceeded forward.

"Henry!" T.J. whispered. "Come on, man."

"I guess I'm going in alone," Henry said calmly. "If I don't make it out alive, then you're going to be the one who has to explain to my mother what happened. . ."

"No thank you," T.J. said and sighed.

He followed Henry to the front door.

They tried to ring the doorbell, but the housing was torn away. All kinds of wires were sticking out. With no other option, Henry decided to knock on the front door. There were sudden movements inside, almost like things fleeing away. For a moment, it sounded like children randomly clapping.

"What was that?"

"Birds. I think"

Henry walked around the side of the house.

"Where you goin'?"

"To try and find a way in."

Henry made it to the back, which, like the front yard, was completely bare.

Again, T.J. was closely following behind him.

They ended up hurdling over a chain link fence and sneaking through a broken window in the back of the house.

"You know how much trouble we can get into?" T.J. said as he cleared the dusty debris from his shoulders.

"You're starting to sound like Danny."

"I'm serious, Henry," T.J. complained and closely followed Henry. "She obviously not home."

"I know that, T.J.," Henry whispered annoyingly. "Quit talking."

They snooped around the dim, powerless house. The sharp beams of sunlight cut through the boarded windows and highlighted the years of thick dust that was finally liberated into the air. The smell was horrendous too. Henry and

T.J. covered the bottom half of their faces from the terrible funk inside the shadowy kitchen. From what they could tell, there was food still lying around on the countertops. Most of the food now was moldy and black like compost. Next, Henry came across a basket of apples, all of which were shriveled and pruned from decay. As he got a closer look at the basket, he observed these specks of white spiraling around the apples. At first, he thought that maybe he had a sudden dizzy spell and that he was seeing stars floating around his head (like with the glint from the train tracks). Then, he got an even closer look. He gagged from the sight of the apples, not the actual apples themselves, but the maggots crawling in and out of them. Even the sound of them, the maggots, making all kinds of squishy sounds, forced Henry from the smelly kitchen. Henry and T.J. made their way into the living room where a black tar-like substance was splattered over the walls and couch. The stench in the air was different, more synthetic as if it had been repeatedly sprayed with chemicals and air fresheners in order to eliminate the once awful smell. The bitter smell was still there, though, lingering underneath all the chemicals. Once more, they covered the bottom half of their faces with the bend of their arms. However, the smell was still there, lingering—even after the two curious teenagers trained themselves to breathe through their mouths. They aimlessly walked through the living room, mainly around the center of the room. The furniture was covered in floral bed sheets riddled with long lacerations. Some of that same black substance had splattered over the sheets. A ceiling fan was partially fractured down the middle, but not entirely broken.

T.J. looked above and asked, "What happened here?"

"Not anything good," Henry drawled and searched around. "That's for sure."

They suddenly heard a noise coming from upstairs.

"What was that?" T.J. said abruptly.

With Henry cautiously leading the way, T.J., who was franitcally jolting from every minuscule sound, every creak or crack, closely followed him up the aged wooden stairs and into a bedroom.

After a quick scour through the empty room, Henry noticed a doll on the dresser. He picked up the handmade doll and held it up to the dusty beam of sunlight. Its eyes were made from black buttons. The joints, as well as the mouth, had x-shaped stitch marks. There were three needles protruding from the doll's abdomen. Bits and pieces of its face had been pecked away—from foul play or even a crow perhaps. He placed the strange doll back into the box and walked around some more.

Standing at the doorway, T.J. asked, "Can we leave already?"

Henry ignored T.J. and came across an old business card in the drawer of an armoire.

The business card read "Witch For Hire."

Underneath, an address: "6115 Wilshire Road."

Henry noticed the city, Sinclair Leprieur.

"*Louisiana*," he said to himself.

"What'd you got?"

"A card."

"Lemme see."

Henry showed T.J. the card.

"Witch for hire? I don't like this, Henry. Not one bit."

Henry scanned around the desolate room.

"Me either," he said.

T.J. handed the card back to Henry, who, after careful thought, ended up pocketing the card.

"Come on, Henry," T.J. said and grabbed Henry by the arm. "Let's get out of here."

They walked downstairs into the kitchen.

A hollow *thud* rang out!

Henry turned to the broken window only to find himself face to face with the same growling pit bull from before: white with brown spots and a long pink scar running down the side of its face. One canine was raised slightly over its bottom lip like a tiny dagger ready to pierce Henry's skin. The pit bull's growls suddenly turned to barks.

Henry stumbled backward and accidentally tripped over T.J.

"What you little homies doin' in here?" the throaty voice of a man said from behind the window.

Startled, Henry and T.J. inched toward the broken window. The man, who turned out being the same golden tooth thug from before, yanked the pit bull from the window.

"We were just. . . just. . . "

"Jus leavin'," the thug interrupted and nodded toward the outside.

Henry and T.J couldn't quite see the thug's face from both the dust and the hazy darkness. From the depth of his voice, they knew that he was much more older and stronger.

Without cutting themselves on the shards of glass scattered around the windowsill, Henry and T.J. carefully exited from the window and followed the thug outside. The thug grabbed the leash from the ionized spicket on the side of the house and walked the pit bull back to the sidewalk where the other thug was smoking a blunt.

"You two ain't supposed to be up in there," he said in a fatherly manner.

Henry and T.J. were somewhat frightened from his rough appearance, but mainly from the pit bull standing inches away from their feet.

Henry was first to respond: "Sorry."

"You damn right you sorry."

"We. . . we were just looking for someone. . . "

"Yeah," T.J. followed.

Like a owl, the thug chirped, "Who?"

They finally made it back to the sidewalk where the one thug was eyeing down Henry and T.J., mostly Henry.

"Hannah," Henry said clearly and pulled out the brochure from his pocket.

"You mean Hannah McClintock?"

"Yeah," Henry replied and displayed the address on the brochure. "Do you know her?"

The thug pushed Henry's hand away.

"This ain't no tourist attraction, fool."

The other thug chimed in, "What's it to you?"

Henry said, "We just wanted to know what happened to her. We swear."

"Ms. McClintock, she was my neighbor," the other one nodded to the house next to the dilapidated house, which, except for the boarded windows and caution tape over the front door and that strange-looking tree in the front lawn, was just about as dilapidated as Hannah's house. "See," he said, "I live over in that house there."

"Does she still live here? Ms. McClintock?"

"Ms. McClintock, she passed away a few months back."

The other one mumbled, "Not even that long."

T.J. asked, "So, what happened to her?"

The thug scowled at T.J.

"Why the fuck you care, nigga?"

Henry was quick to point at T.J.

"My friend, T.J.," he said abruptly. "She was his aunt."

T.J. whispered through the corner of his mouth, "*Henry. . .*"

The other thug smacked his gums and said sardonically, "Yeah right."

The other one with the gold teeth glared at T.J. and then moved his eyes back on Henry.

"Then you should know that, like most around her, she had her own problems."

Henry said, "That's why we came here. To see how she was doing. We were worried about her."

"Hold up," the thug said abruptly. "You mean you don't even know what happen to your own aunt?"

No response.

"I'm talkin' to you, nigga," he said and pointed at T.J.

"Nah," T.J. said and innocently shook his head.

The other thug with the shirt wrapped around his shoulders smacked his gums again, carefully eyed T.J., and said, "You clearly didn't know your aunt that well."

T.J. said, "What you mean?"

"Her problems," the other one said, "you see, hers were a bit more complicated. I would say ones that she ain't really have any control over. But you wouldn't know anything 'bout that. Would you?"

Henry and T.J. glanced over at one another in confusion.

"Shit," the thug said and paused, "I mean. . . I ain't normally call the po-po. As far as I'm concerned, those pigs ain't welcome up in Raven Heights. But I can smell a dead body from a mile away. For months, Ms. McClintock was locked up in that house. Never came out." He moved his attention toward T.J. "Didn't have any visitors. When the po-po came, it was already too late. They found Ms. McClintock dangling from a ceiling fan like a goddamn slave nigga hangin' from a tree." Considering Henry and T.J. were much younger than the thug (around nine or ten years), he figured it was best to keep out the part about how the flies had gotten to Hannah first and then the crows. And when the police found her body, there was hardly anything left of her. Mostly bone. He cleared his throat and said, "Crazy shit, man."

Again, the two looked at one another in both confusion and now shock.

"I didn't mean to scare you little homies," he said with a grin. "Hey! You wanted to know."

"You mean she killed herself. . . "

The thug returned bitterly, "What part of 'hung herself' don't you understand, little homie?"

"She must've got her hands on the Jagger beforehand," Henry accidentally said out loud.

"Jagger?" the thug said. "What you mean 'Jagger'?"

The other one returned, "Like the saxophone, nigga."

"Yeah."

"You see I knew her brother," the thug said over a sudden thought. "Me and him were tight."

The other thug smacked his gums as he had been doing throughout the conversation and waved his hand.

"You didn't know that fool. So, quit actin' like you did."

"I did too," he returned.

"Who was her brutha?"

"You her nephew. You should know."

T.J. replied, "She ain't never really tell me much 'bout her brutha. Only that he was. . . that he used to work at the factory."

"Factory?"

"What factory?"

"The one where they make. . ." T.J. searched for the right word. He couldn't help but notice the one thug with his shirt off. ". . . Shirts!" he blurted out. "A shirt factory. That's where he used to work."

"Shirt factory?"

"Yeah," T.J. said. "I 'member Hannah tellin' me 'bout how he used to come home wit all these free shirts."

"I ain't never heard anything about The V Man working at a shirt factory before."

"V Man? Who's the V man?"

"Mr. Vortex, nigga," the thug said bluntly. "You know, your aunt's brother. He the one with that '*Hard Rider*' jam."

Henry asked curiously, "Did you know Mr. Vortex's real name?"

"Yeah, man," he said. "It's Henry. Henry McClintock."

"Hey," T.J. said and nudged Henry on the shoulder. "He's got the same name as you, Henry."

Henry squinted his eyes at T.J.

T.J. was unaware of the full name.

"He's right, T.J.," Henry said, clearing his throat. "Henry McClintock was Mr. Vortex."

T.J. blurted out, "You serious?"

"You see," the thug said, "me, I was the one who actually came up with the idea for that one song, 'Stilts.' You've probably heard it on the radio before." He sang: "*She got hips like waves in the ocean. Legs like stilts. . .*"

"Man," the other one suddenly hollered out and shoved his friend, "he full of shit! He be tellin' people the same bullshit to everyone else. But it ain't true."

The thug rolled his eyes.

T.J. asked Henry, "How you know her brother is Mr. Vortex?"

"I didn't know Hannah was his sister," Henry said to T.J. "But my mother told me about the name, *Henry McClintock*. I didn't believe it at first. But then she showed me the obituary section in the newspaper. Mr. Vortex was just his stage name. The real Mr. Vortex died last spring."

"But you should know that," the thug said to T.J. "Right, nigga?"

"Yeah," T.J. said, furrowing his eyebrows. Then, he turned to Henry. "Henry!" he blurted out and held out his arms in elation. "The saxophone! All this time you been playin' the same saxophone Mr. Vortex played!"

"You don't know that," he said callously and suspiciously glanced over at the thug as if his friend didn't know what he was talking about.

"Then, how did his sister. . . "

The thug said suspiciously, "You mean your aunt?"

"Yeah," T.J. corrected. "I mean how did my Aunt Hannah get a hold of that saxophone? He must've given it to her like as a gift or sumtin."

"Sounds like this homie here knows more about Ms. McClintock than this nigga does," the thug said quietly to his friend.

"Octo," Henry said, "Mr. Vortex plays an alto, not a soprano."

"Yeah, but still, Henry. . ." he tried to gather himself, ". . . maybe he had other ones."

"Doubt it."

"She could've gotten the sax after he died. . . " T.J. said, his voice trailing off. Suddenly, he blurted out, "Hey, Henry! What if that's the same saxophone he played on *Hard Rider*?"

"Would you chill out, Octo?" Henry said, turning upset. "For the last time, Mr. Vortex played an alto, not a soprano!"

"I'm jus sayin'."

"Hey, nigga," the other thug said sternly. "Thought you said you was Hannah's nephew."

Henry cut in, "They're not that close."

"Yeah right."

"As long as I've known T.J., he's only mentioned Hannah's name once."

The other thug snorted.

Over an awkward silence, the thug said, "I can remember the day Mr. Vortex died. Ms. McClintock started actin' strangely and shit. Like I was sayin' before, she ain't never really leave her house. Remember the po-po comin' over to Ms. McClintock's house all the time." He briefly reflected. "Times I wondered what in the hell was goin' on inside that house. It ain't really none of my business. So, I don't know. I guess everybody has their demons, sum jus different than others."

"Demons?"

"Dats what he said, homie."

"What kind of demons?"

"The kind of demons one usually keep in they closet, them kind."

THIRTY-ONE

LATE Saturday night, Henry had a nightmare about Hannah.

It all started with Henry strolling past one of the girls on the sidewalk whom he and T.J. had met earlier that day at the food court in the Peregrine Place Mall. Henry remembered the girl's legs and how they appeared as if they had stretched for miles, as well as the cute dimples she presented on either side of her face when her lips parted ways and formed into a smile. Not only that, what the thug from Raven Heights had sung about in his Otis Redding-like voice (Mr. Vortex song "Stilts," about this fine looking gal having 'hips like waves in the ocean' and 'legs like stilts') most definitely played a factor in the young girl's appearance. In the nightmare, the girl was eight feet tall, give or take, had legs like five-foot stilts, and waddled without any balance or bend in her knees. Henry looked twice at the girl, once when he passed her and another time when she was halfway down the block. Next, he was pulling away the yellow police tape and entering Hannah's house through the front door—not sneaking in through the back as he did the first time around. The inside was teeming with streaks of pale moonlight. Even the awful smell that he and T.J. had gathered from the house on Friday afternoon was still lingering on his clothes, which were scattered across T.J.'s bedroom floor, and seeping into his vivid nightmares. T.J. wasn't in the nightmare. Nor were the same two thugs on the street corner. Henry was *not* alone, though. He listened closely to the sound of a dog chain clanking outside the house. The clanking was faint at first and then noisy. He turned to the direction of the sound and saw a small shadow scurrying by the window. The clanking noise was followed with a soft growl. The dog, Henry wondered, was probably that pit bull with the pink scar on the side of its face. However, the pit bull was the least of his worries. Henry wandered into the open living room where he found Hannah's lifeless body dangling from a noose on the ceiling fan. Her body was gently swaying. Her head was drooped to the side, away from Henry. Both of her colorless eyes were stapled open, not closed. Henry inched closer to the body, her feet just inches away from his face. She had tiny gashes—all bloodless—over her neck, chest, and arms from where the crows had recently picked away at her flesh. A couple of bloated crows (one of them letting out a loud *caw*) were perched on top of the bookshelves of the living room. The crows were staring down at Henry with their black glossy eyes. Henry ignored the crows and inspected Hannah's body. Her legs were shapeless like sausages. Even her feet were twice the average size from where gravity had pulled all the blood from her body.

In a sudden burst of life, Hannah rolled her head toward Henry and said vacantly, "Hello there, Henry." Her ghostly voice echoed throughout the old house, now creaking and cracking. A wicked smile lifted in a sharp arch across her deathly face. "He looks just like his father." Her dead eyes slowly followed the grotesque figure looming behind Henry. She said haughtily not to Henry, but to the figure behind him, *"Don't you think, Claudia?"*

Before Henry could spin around, a gnarly hand grabbed him by the shoulder!

"Henry," a muddled voice said.

As the colorful shades of dawn shone over the bedroom, Henry woke with the tip of his nose as cold as ice and T.J. crouched over his body.

Once more, T.J. shook Henry's arm.

"You snorin', man," T.J. said quietly.

It took a few moments for Henry to absorb his surroundings.

"Henry. . ."

"Sorry," Henry mumbled.

As T.J. went back to bed, Henry balled himself up in the sleeping bag. T.J.'s parents, Mr. and Mrs. Livingston, kept the house around sixty-seven degrees at night to save money on the electric bill. But Henry had slept in colder conditions. The rest of the morning consisted of him rolling around in the sleeping bag and thinking about the saxophone, Adrian, and how she wound up on the train tracks over sixty miles away from where he had last left her. Abbey was scheduled to pick up Henry around noon. With this in mind, Henry forced himself back into bed, zipped up the sleeping bag, and shut his eyes. No luck. He spent another hour rolling around over the carpet. For the remainder of the morning, he peddled around T.J.'s bedroom, mostly reminiscing over the used Casio that T.J. had borrowed from Henry before he moved to Lansford. Henry meandered over to the bedroom window and found himself gazing at what used to be Ms. Craft's house. Now, the space was a vacant lot.

During the entire car ride home from Reddington, Henry opened up his mouth only a few times to speak when his mother asked him what kind of activities he did with T.J. or what they ate or where they spent most of their time. On many occasions, Abbey tried to spark up a conversation with her son. Henry returned with short answers and killed any chances of a decent conversation. At times, he responded with a nod.

As they crossed the small city of Saint Thomas, just fifteen miles outside Lansford, Henry decided to voice what had been on his mind ever since he left Holiday's.

He turned to his mother and asked, "Did you know Mr. Vortex's sister?"

Abbey readjusted the grip around the steering wheel.

"You mean your father?" she asked uneasily and then cleared her throat.

"*No*," Henry said, keeping a forbidding composure. "I mean Mr. Vortex. He had a sister. Her name was Hannah. Did you know her?"

Abbey now tightened her hands over the steering wheel until her knuckles turned pale and bloodless.

She asked, "Where did you hear that name?"

"Holiday told me."

Abbey forced out a sigh.

"Barely," she said and shot a glance over at Henry. "I barely knew the woman. She wasn't even your father's sister. She was his stepsister, Henry. They weren't even blood related."

"What do you mean?"

"They weren't related, Henry."

"Her last name, though," he said foolishly. "It was McClintock."

"Is that what Holiday said?"

"Yeah."

"Well, she probably used it because of your father's fame."

"Why?"

"Because that's the way some people are, Henry," she answered and shot yet another glance over at her son, who was still in a state of bewilderment. "Some people like to leech off others."

"Leech? You mean like sucking other people's blood?"

"No, Henry," Abbey said with a less serious tone. "Like taking advantage of others."

"Oh. . ."

"You'd be amazed how many people come out of the woodwork once you get famous," she said. "Some people you don't even know. And Hannah, well, she was one of them. She. . ." Abbey paused and thought carefully, ". . . she liked the attention."

"What was she like?"

"I only met her once or twice," Abbey said nonchalantly. "I remember the first time I met her was right before one of your *father's* concerts." Her voice rose slightly whenever she spoke of Henry's father. "She was sickly. Looked as if she hadn't eaten in days. She and Henry, the Fourth that is— *your* father—didn't get along at all. There was a rift between the two. Hardly spoke about her. When I asked about her, he said that they were always fighting. He said she had her run-ins with the law. He even got a restraining order on her."

"Restraining order?"

"It's when you try to keep someone away from you," she explained. "And if that person comes within a certain distance from you, then you're obligated to call the police and have them arrested." Intrigued, she glanced over at her son. This time, her eyes remained on her son, not the road, but her son. She studied his facial expressions, his still eyes. She asked sharply, "Why are you so interested, Henry?"

Henry shrugged his shoulders.

"Just curious."

A fraught silence filled the car.

"Did you go to a lot of his concerts?"

"I did," she answered cautiously.

"And where did you meet Hannah?"

"In Baton Rouge I believe," his mother said, again with uneasiness in her voice. "I remember she said she was passing through, but I didn't believe her. I think she had another agenda on her mind."

Henry asked, "What kind of agenda?"

She forced out yet another sigh.

"To destroy your father," Abbey said emotionlessly. "To take his money, all of his possessions. I don't know."

"She don't sound like. . . "

Abbey interrupted, "Don't?"

Her son corrected, "I mean she doesn't sound like a very nice woman."

"When you enter the real world, Henry, you'll find out that there's a lot of bad people out there."

"But," Henry followed quickly, "but people can change."

A snort slipped from Abbey's mouth.

"Right. . . " she said sarcastically with her voice slowly trailing off.

Abbey briefly drifted inward and thought about her son's comment, not the one about the bad people in the world, but the one about how people can change.

Another wave of silence washed over the car.

"Besides all of his issues—and I mean, he had *a lot* of issues—if there was one thing I admired about your father, it was that he always put on one heck of a show," she said with her eyes glazed over the interstate. "The way he played. . . it was. . . it was magic. I swear your father didn't go anywhere without that saxophone."

"So it's true," Henry said. "The saxophone, it belonged to my. . . Mr. Vortex?"

"I don't know, Henry," Abbey said quietly and drifted in thought. "But I do know that your father always had a way of marking his territory." A smile flashed over the side of her face. "So," she shrugged her shoulders, "it may be his or may not. I don't know, Henry. I wish I could tell you."

Henry said mindfully, "I think it belonged to him."

"How do you know?"

"I don't know," he said. "I just know."

Abbey cracked another smile.

"You're afraid I'm going to be like him. Aren't you?"

"Yes," she said softly, not angrily as Henry expected her to. "There's a reason why your father was living on the streets."

"Why?"

Abbey rolled her eyes over at Henry.

"He went crazy, Henry."

"Yeah, but. . . "

"But nothing," Abbey said sternly. "I didn't want to be-lieve it. It was like being trapped in a nightmare. I wanted to wake up from it all. But it's true, Henry. Your father did go insane."

Henry pulled his attention toward the passenger window and stared at the passing trees next to the interstate, each one the same as before.

"Back then, I guess I would listen to about anything." Her thoughts were brought back to the night of the concert, *that one night*. "When the show was over in Baton Rouge, I met up with your father backstage. At the time, we were sort of a couple. Nobody really knew what to think of us. I knew what we were. Henry knew what we were, but he wasn't the type to be so candid as I was."

"Candid?"

"Honest," she said, swallowing. "To be honest. Anyway, as we were about to leave, a fan I believe or one of your fa-ther's past lovers—and there were quite few of them—ran up to him. I will never forget that night. She was upset, scream-ing at him. I was coming back from the restroom. So, I missed what had happened. But Henry's manager told me all about it. He said this older woman charged at Henry and she was speaking in a different language. . . like tongues."

"Really. . . " Henry uttered and suddenly thought about the business card in his pocket.

"Whatever language it was, it wasn't anything he'd ever heard before. He said her eyes were rolled back in her head. All white. She was holding a strange object in her hand. Hannah was standing there next to her. He couldn't make out any of the words, although, when I got back from the restroom, I remember the look on your father's face. I'll never forget such a look." Abbey pondered briefly. "A week later, he went to do a tour in Europe. The first couple of shows were delayed. Your father came down with a terrible bug. Doctors couldn't explain what was wrong with him. They were just as confused as the rest of the band. When he came back from overseas, he wasn't the same man I fell in love with. It was like he was always walking around with this. . . this black cloud over his head. Never had fun. Never smiled. He said he didn't have the luxury of friends. I could see his transformation before my eyes. After a while, he became this ghost. Didn't eat. Hardly slept. Didn't talk to anyone. And whenever he did talk, it was a command or 'What are you doing?' or 'Where are you going?' Every time you talked to him, it was like something had suddenly come up and he didn't want to hear it. It's like he wanted me all to himself. It got to the point where it was hard to be in the same room with him, with Henry, your father. I couldn't. . . " Abbey caught her breath. Her eyes watered. She never really shed any tears, at least not in front of Henry. ". . . I couldn't stand to watch your father deteriorate like that. Then, he started to lose it. That's when he went crazy. He kept going on about this darkness inside him, taking over."

Henry said, "That's when he saw the shadows?"

"Yes," Abbey answered timidly. "He tried to seek help, but nobody could explain what was going on with your father. Even your. . . " She corrected, ". . . even his doctor couldn't help him." She shot another glance over at her son, almost of sympathy, and cracked yet another smile. "You listen to me, Henry, and you listen carefully. Nobody wants to be around someone like that. All they're good at is bringing you down with them."

After some thought, Henry said, "And that's when he left us?"

Abbey's eyes crossed the rear view mirror and stayed there until the car began to slowly drift over the white line of the passing lane.

"Yes, Henry," she said flatly, pulled her eyes back to the interstate, and corrected the steering wheel. "That was when he left us."

*   *   *

Henry sat on his bed and thought: *speaking in tongues.*

He pulled the Witch For Hire card from his face and tried to make sense of what his mother had told him about his father and how something really bad happened to him after the concert in Baton Rouge, something that had to do with the card in his hand.

Could it be from the same person, he thought, *this Witch For Hire?*

Was it because of Hannah?

Did she have something to do with it?

After spending hours of sitting on his bed and wondering whether or not his father was cursed, Henry decided to go downstairs and throw a TV dinner in the microwave.

Once the dinner cooled, he took it upstairs to his bedroom where he only ate a couple of bites before he began to feel ill. Henry turned his focus back to the card and studied it carefully.

He rolled out of bed, pulled out a map of the United States from his desk drawer, and spread it out over the base of the bed.

There, he traced his finger over the map and found Sinclair Leprieur, a small town outside Baton Rouge.

THIRTY-TWO

HENRY started back to school on a Wednesday, two days after New Years.

Before Henry left the house that morning, he emptied out his textbooks, as well as his binders and notebooks—including that one composition notebook—from the inside of his book bag, and packed an extra pair of clothes, socks, and the same toothbrush that he had been using for the past six years, along with a coiled tube of toothpaste. Next, he packed a map of the United States. Stuck it in the side pocket of the book bag where he normally placed his pens and pencils. Last but not least, he packed a steak knife that he had stolen from the kitchen downstairs. He securely wrapped the sharp blade in a hand towel and left the handle exposed just in case he ran into any witches in Louisiana.

A sudden *knock* at the door!

Henry stopped what he was doing.

"Yeah!" he hollered out and then quickly zipped up the stuffed book bag.

Abbey asked from behind the bedroom door, "Are you ready for school?"

"Just about," Henry said, breathing a sigh of relief.

"May I come in?"

Henry combed through the bedroom and made sure he didn't leave anything out for his mother to see.

"Henry. . . "

"Just a minute!"

"What's going on in there?"

"Yeah!"

At the last second before his mother opened the door, Henry placed the book bag behind the bed.

"Henry," she said and gradually eased herself into the bed-room, "I just wanted to tell you that your father. . . despite all those things I said to you in the car, he wasn't a bad man. Sure, he had a lot of issues. But he had a good heart. It's just. . . "

Henry hung his head in thought.

". . . he changed, Henry," Abbey said. "And I didn't like the man he was changing into." She stepped closer. "You must understand that sometimes when you get older you grow apart from the ones you love."

"Do you think he was cursed?" Henry asked, his voice slow and unsteady.

Abbey's facial expression went blank and lifeless.

"Cursed?"

"Yeah."

Abbey's eyes flared, the pupils like daggers.

"What do you mean 'cursed'?"

"Like from a necromancer."

"Necro what!"

"A witch."

"Where. . ." she cleared her throat, ". . . where would you get such a ridiculous idea like that?"

Henry shrugged his shoulders.

"I don't know," he said. "What would make him change like that? My father was Mr. Vortex, one of greatest saxophonists ever!" He retraced his thoughts to what his mother had said in the car. "The old woman," he said, "the one speaking in tongues."

"You listen to me, Henry," Abbey said and pointed her finger at Henry. "There's no such thing. So you better get that out of your head. You understand me?"

Henry responded with a stern *yeah* and waited for his mother to exit the bedroom until he could recheck the belongings in his book bag.

Throughout her shift at the Depot, Abbey couldn't stop thinking about what her son had said to her in his bedroom. Since she wasn't in the mood to deal with any griping customers ("That wasn't the same price on the display!" or "In your ad, it says that this washing machine is twenty percent off, not ten!"), she decided to take off work early to set the record straight once and for all. When she got back home, Henry was nowhere around. She went over to the neighbor's house and asked the neighbor if she had seen her son. The neighbor hadn't seen Henry. That went for everybody else in the neighborhood.

By the time she got back from asking the neighbors about the whereabouts of her son, it was already dusk. She called Henry's school, Marilee Anne High, and spoke to Principal Teague, who told Abbey that he was just heading out the door and needed to be somewhere. She threatened the principal. She said things to him that would make a grown man fall to his knees and cry. Although the principal never fell to his knees or cried—the temptation was certainly there—he did as Abbey ordered and checked the daily attendance. He discovered that Henry never showed up for all of his classes, not even his first period class. When Abbey got off the phone with Principal Teague, a gnawing sensation was throbbing inside her gut. The sensation had been slowly building up all afternoon. At times, stabbing. The feeling alone sent Abbey staggering away from the kitchen counter. She braced herself against the sink. There was nothing else like a mother's intuition. Abbey knew from the second she saw her son that morning that he was hiding something. She could see it on his face, his manner. Plus, what he had said, about this witch character. He had his *bags packed* this morning, she thought, while taking a sip from the glass of warm water. Either Henry went somewhere else or something happened to him before he got on the bus. Then, she went over the options where Henry might be. The questions kept coming at her like a swarm of locusts in an open field: *What if he was abducted? What if there was a car accident? What if he was struck by a car and left for dead? What if he's hurt somewhere? What if my boy's lying in a ditch? What if he ran. . .* Abbey canceled the thought before she could think about it any longer and grabbed a flashlight from the drawer. In a state of panic, she hurried from the house and sprinted through the woods in the backyard. As the beam of light swiftly carved through the dark woods, she shouted out Henry's name three times but received no answer. Having no luck with the neighborhood, she decided to get in her car and drive around the city of Lansford. There were a couple of places, one being the basketball courts at the local park and the other being the movie theatre inside the shopping mall. She even stopped locals and showed them a current photograph of Henry and asked them if they had seen her boy, "Henry." She received nothing. No indication. It was like Henry disappeared from the face of the earth. Abbey called off the search and went back home. Exhausted, she had no other option. It was already eleven o'clock in the evening, just past Henry's bedtime. She picked up the telephone, dialed 911, and reported a missing child.

When the police arrived at Abbey's house, she had given the two officers a photograph of Henry that she had taken from a frame, as well as his body description. She also informed the officers that Henry had his book bag packed and was getting ready for school and that she had called the school and spoke to Principal Teague as well as Henry's teachers. Before the officers left, they asked Abbey one last question. In the back of her mind, she knew the question would be asked.

The officer asked, "Have you been having any problems at home, ones that would cause your son to run away?"

Abbey foolishly shook her head.

"Not that I'm aware of," she said innocently and cleared away the running mascara from her face. "I mean we have our share of arguments. But he would never do such a thing. Not my Henry."

At the crack of dawn, Abbey called out sick and drove to Henry's school. Principal Teague showed Abbey Henry's locker. Running off no sleep, Abbey frantically searched through the locker but couldn't find anything useful. Most of his books and school things were piled inside, which told Abbey a different story, one that had been eating away at her all night as she tossed and turned through the wee hours. Abbey knew the cop was right last night, about her son being a runaway. She just couldn't accept the fact. After she left Marilee Anne, she drove to the police station and talked to the same police officer from last night. Took down his badge number and everything. He gave Abbey the runaround, how he had filed the report, as well as Henry's name in the database. The officer wasn't so inclined to do as Abbey demanded right then and there in that very moment, which was to put together a search party for her son, release the hounds, and do whatever it took to find her son. Instead, the officer stuck to protocol and sat in his seat and listened to Abbey pleading for help.

With no luck at the police station (her voice now hoarse from all the yelling and screaming she was doing in front of the officer, Officer Patterson was his name), Abbey drove to Reddington and found T.J. and Danny shooting hoops on the courts.

"Ain't that Henry's mom?" Danny said to T.J.

T.J. stopped dribbling the basketball and rotated toward the woman marching at them. Her eyes were like tiny slits, shoulders hunched over, and jaw protruding forward in rage.

"She don't look too happy," he uttered and slowly took a couple of steps backward.

"Hey, Ms. Burl," Danny said charmingly and waved at Abbey.

Danny didn't receive a hand wave, yet a steaming mother marching faster toward him.

Abbey seethed, "Where is he?"

"Where's who?"

"My son!" She grabbed Danny by the collar. "Where is he?"

With his eyes swollen, Danny shook his head.

"I. . . I haven't seen Henry," he stuttered. "I promise."

"T.J.," she said and released Danny from her grip, "do you know where he could be?"

"No, ma'am."

Abbey pointed her finger at T.J. and held it there, as she was known to do.

"Don't lie to me, boy! He must've said something to you the other day!"

With his eyes squinted—not swollen—T.J. shook his head as well.

"He didn't," he said honestly.

Abbey grabbed T.J. by the mouth and squeezed his cheeks.

"You tell me now or I'll make you wish you were never born, boy!"

T.J. pulled his face from Abbey's grip.

"I ain't tellin' you nuttin!"

Abbey's eyes flared. Her index finger eased back into her hand, which now tightened into a fist.

"Try me, boy," she seethed, her eyes still flaring. "Don't think I won't knock your lights out. Go on, boy. Try me."

T.J. puffed out, chest now deflated.

"He found a card," he mumbled and turned away from Abbey.

"Speak up!"

T.J. pulled his eyes up into Abbey's.

"We went to this woman's house," he said, his voice slightly shaking. "Her name was Hannah McClintock. She wasn't there. She died sum time ago."

The sound of the name sent another sensation into Abbey's gut, stabbing.

T.J. said, "Henry found this card in her room."

Abbey exclaimed, "You went inside her house?"

"Yeah," T.J. said, shrinking. "We didn't touch anything. I swear. . ."

"What did the card say?"

T.J. didn't answer.

"You tell me. . ."

"It said something like 'Witch For Hire' or sum bullshit like that."

"What was that that just came out of your mouth?"

"But it's the truf, Ms. Burl," T.J. said, his voice slightly louder. "For the rest of the day, Henry be talkin' 'bout goin' there. I didn't know what he was sayin', Ms, Burl. I didn't think he was bein' serious. We know Henry," T.J. turned to Danny, "we know he wouldn't go there."

"Go where?"

"Some place in Louisiana."

"Where, T.J.?"

"I don't remember."

Abbey reared back her fist.

"Leepair," he said abruptly. "Sinclair Leepair I think."

"Sinclair Leprieur?"

"That's it," he said. "That's the place."

For a second, the wind was knocked out of Abbey.

Worried about his friend's safety, Danny leaned forward and said, "Ms. Burl? Is Henry all right?"

"You two. . . this is only between the three of us," she said sternly and regained her composure. "Is that clear?"

"Yes, Ms. Burl," Danny said.

"T.J.?"

"Did sumtin happen to Henry?"

Abbey loomed over T.J. Her voice rose over his, squashing him like a bug.

"I said 'Is that clear?'"

"Yeah," T.J. said and rolled his eyes.

"Now, you two go on back home," Abbey said and shooed the two away from the basketball courts. "You speak to no one about this."

T.J. and Danny gathered their things and did as Abbey demanded.

On the way back home from Reddington, Abbey broke every speed limit and law.

She couldn't afford to be pulled over by the police, but each second was absolutely critical. Each second spent, Abbey realized while trying her best not to make any erratic maneuvers or anything that would draw attention to herself, meant that her boy was that much closer to death. During the drive to Lansford—whenever Abbey wasn't too busy veering around cars or weaving in and out of traffic—she would frantically move her eyes from the road and glance in the rear view mirror not to see if any cops were on her tail, but to see if *she* would come. Five hours had passed since Abbey had taken her last medication and her medicine bottle—the one with her magic pills, the orange ones—was back at home.

As soon as she arrived at her house in record time, she rushed upstairs to her bedroom, fell to her knees in front of the dresser, and then dropped her purse, as well as the car keys, beside her.

With her hands shaking uncontrollably, Abbey removed the entire bottom drawer from the track.

Next, she dumped the clothes and underwear and every article inside over the carpet and used her knuckles to find the hollow spot over the bottom panel. She knocked twice, both equally sounding the same. On the third knock closest to the middle of the panel, she received a more reverberated return, hollow. She reached up, grabbed the Jesus statue from the top of the dresser, and stabbed the blunt side through the hollow recess. She cleared away the debris with her hands and pulled out an old wooden box from the secret compartment. She placed the box beside her, away from all the debris. Inside, there was a small stack of newspaper articles and old photographs, all faded and brown with age. On top of the articles and photographs lay a pistol, a 9 mm Beretta from the 92 series, as well as a magazine of ammunition.

Suddenly, a shadow manifested over the wall behind her.

A tiny *squeak* of a door slowly closing. . .

Then, a gravelly voice from behind the door: "You're running out of time."

Every ounce, every muscle, every pulse in Abbey's body, froze.

Her heart punched against her chest, making her gasp.

Then, her hands started to tremble again.

She glanced over her shoulder and saw a corpse-like woman standing in the corner of the bedroom. The woman was the same haggard one from Henry's nightmares, only less haggard and her skin was as black as charcoal, not pale or green as he had witnessed in the darkness of night, and wrinkled too, especially around the curves of her face. The woman also had more hair than the haggard one from her son's nightmares. Her skeleton was exposed underneath her leathery skin. She was dressed in all black. Her clothes, however, were old, worn, and delicate as if they carried a century of dust on them. She casually stood there with her left shoulder rested against the wall, arms folded across her flat chest, and gave Abbey that same icy glare—*the* look—only her dark, raven-like eyes were sunken into the sockets of her own skull.

Abbey quickly shut her eyes and then opened them below.

After she checked the safety and made sure it was off, and *not* on, she grabbed the Beretta and loaded the magazine inside until she heard a click.

From the shadows: "You know what he'll do to him."

"There's still a chance for my boy," Abbey said angrily.

"He will tear your boy apart. . . "

She shot her eyes up at the corpse-like woman who was no longer standing in the corner of the bedroom.

Abbey looked around the room.

The woman was nowhere to be found.

Next, Abbey rushed to the bathroom (mouthing those words, *she doesn't exist, she doesn't exist*, over and over to herself), grabbed a medicine bottle from the cabinet, and downed a pill—the orange one—with a sip of faucet water. She hurried back into the bedroom, grabbed a tote bag from the closet, and packed for two days. She placed the handgun inside the side pocket of the bag, gathered her purse and keys, as well as that bottle of pills, and turned off the lights in the house. She hurried from the house and locked the door behind her.

From a distance, she heard the sound of police sirens cutting through the streets outside the neighborhood. Strangely, the sirens grew louder and louder. The alarming sound came closer to the neighborhood, her street. That stabbing sensation was back in Abbey's gut. She made it three steps into her driveway when suddenly two police cruisers came speeding toward the house. Abbey's initial reaction: *Not for my Henry.* Her heart sank into her aching stomach. Her face was left pale and forlorn. Her limbs went weak and numb, causing her to drop the bag from her loose grip.

As she stood there with her shoulders slouched downward, the officers cut the sirens from their cruisers and greeted Abbey in the driveway. They were wearing no expressions over their faces. Abbey knew the look. Seen it before.

"What happened to him?" she asked, her face growing long and sad.

"You need to come with us, ma'am," one officer said.

"Where is he?"

"We found a body off Johnston Road."

She whined, "What happened to my boy? YOU TELL ME!"

"We don't know," the officer said and extended his hand toward Abbey. "Please, you need to come with us."

At the city morgue, Abbey stood over the covered body on the table.

"We think it was a hit and run," the examiner said.

Abbey stood in a state of shock, not crying.

"Are you ready?"

She returned with a nod of her head.

The examiner slowly pulled back the white sheet from the upper part of the body.

Abbey closely studied the side of the body, which had been stripped for investigators. A wave of relief washed over Abbey, nearly drowning her.

As her legs wobbled, she braced the side of the table.

One of the detectives rushed toward Abbey and caught her before her knees buckled.

"I'm okay," she said and waved off the detective. "Give me a minute."

As the wave of relief pulled back like a strong current, dragging along all emotion with it, Abbey stood upright and studied the pale body once more. The body matched Henry's description, mainly height and weight, but the face was completely unrecognizable. Her eyes fell upon the body's ribcage and then the unmarked skin around the bone.

"When my Henry was eight years old, he and his friend, T.J., were playing around on the basketball court," she said, her eyes glazing with tears. "Whenever the two got bored from playing, they would climb things: trees, houses, lampposts, fences. After school, he and T.J. made a bet on who could make it to the top of this one raggedy, rusty fence on the blacktop behind Graeme Park. When Henry reached the top of the fence, T.J. was halfway up the fence. Henry lost his grip from the bar. On the way down, the side of his body scraped against the fence. I ended up leaving work early to take Henry to the hospital where he received thirty-seven stitches and a tetanus shot. But no broken bones. Just a nasty scar to show how reckless he was."

"I know how hard this may be. . . " the examiner said.

"That's not my boy," Abbey interrupted, her tone as cold as the stiff before her.

THIRTY-THREE

YESTERDAY morning before the school bus arrived at the end of Henry's street where four other students, one a ninth grader and the others from his grade, waited, Henry cut through the woods behind his neighborhood and followed the railroad tracks until he reached Delaney Avenue.

While glancing over his shoulder from time to time (cops were especially known for picking up kids skipping school around here), Henry traveled down Delaney Avenue and crossed over to Ford's Street where he used the money that he had earned from rolling up newspapers during last summer and bought a one-way ticket to Baton Rouge at the nearest greyhound station. It was a twelve-hour drive from Lansford to Baton Rouge. They were scheduled for three stops, two to use the restroom and the other for food and gas. As the bus was loading up, Henry managed to grab a window seat in the middle of the bus. Luckily for him, he didn't have to seat next to anybody. The last thing Henry wanted right now was to start small talk with a stranger. He had too much on his mind. Too much at risk. The only thing that kept his mind occupied throughout the entire trip was the one card in his hand, the one with the name "Witch For Hire."

When the bus arrived in Baton Rouge, it was night.

Weary from the trip, Henry found a cheap motel nearby. He only had ninety dollars and some change left, just enough to buy a bus ticket back to Lansford and a couple of meals if he was lucky. He was walking past the main lobby of the motel when he noticed the clerk watching television in the back room. His feet were kicked up on a table. A can of beer rested over his belly. Some basketball game was playing, Henry realized. He couldn't tell who the teams were. At this point, he really didn't care. It was the perfect opportunity. While keeping his eyes on the clerk, Henry sneaked inside the lobby and grabbed the doorbell above before it could make a soft *ding*. Henry shouldered his way inside and gently closed the door behind him, all done without a single sound. He found the room keys hanging on the wall behind the counter. With his eyes never leaving the clerk in the back room, Henry slipped past the counter. He reached in his pocket and pulled out a pair of keys. He tried to find the closest key that resembled the motel key. Turns out that his house key was the only key that matched the motel key. With the clerk distracted from television (the broadcaster yelling out, *"Jordan takes the shot!"*), Henry grabbed the key for Room #37. He carefully removed the tag #37 from the motel room key and replaced it with the house key and then hung it back on the wall in its rightful place without being detected. Once he acquired the key, he exited the lobby as if he was never even there. Henry just hoped the clerk didn't check out room #37 to any other customers. From the looks of the motel, Henry wasn't too concerned.

The next morning, Henry left the room before the maid came by. He hit the road with a stomach full of cherry pastries, as well as a book bag full of at least half a dozen single serving cereal boxes that he stole from the motel's continental breakfast.

After two hours of walking alongside the highway (ten minutes being spent using nature's own front step as a restroom), Henry finally made it to the port city of Sinclair

Leprieur. Alongside Churner River, which appeared as black as tar from where Henry was standing, a row of chimneys and industrial plants guarded the small city. Massive smokestacks were oozing from the tops of the chimneys as if the dark clouds above were funneling down into the chimneys like a vacuum and not the other way around. Henry carefully climbed down an embankment off the highway and walked alongside the polluted river. He found a couple of beached fishes wiggling around on top of the muddy bank from where an early tide had come in. An oily sheen, parts of it as colorful as a rainbow, was covered over the surface of the water. Orange clumps of what appeared like oil were floating over the water as well. And the smell, a combination of dead fish and oil, was unbearable. Henry couldn't make it into town soon enough.

When he finally reached the downtown area, which was made up of one long street with local businesses on either side, he stopped twice, once at an Italian restaurant and the other at a pawnshop, and asked the locals if they knew anything about a so-called *"Witch For Hire."* The locals responded with churlish laughs. Once they found out that Henry wasn't joking from the look on his face, they immediately sent him on his way and did so without a smile on their faces.

Lastly, Henry stopped at a local convenient store called AM (Aunt Monty) and bought a pack of Oreo cookies and two grape sodas for the road. This time he decided to ask about the address, not the witch. At first, the mousy clerk refused to help out Henry with the address. His face got all ghostly white. His throat tightened up all of a sudden as if an invisible hand had mysteriously clutched him around his neck. He bawled like a minister giving a sermon, "No, sir!" and followed by saying that the address was strictly "off limits" and then later he corrected himself (this was after Henry paid the clerk exactly eighty-seven dollars, fifty for directions and the other remaining money from the eighty-seven dollars to tell him about this *"Witch For Hire"*) by generously shrugging his shoulders and saying that it was "doable."

Money was a valuable commodity, especially in the art of persuasion.

The clerk wrote down the directions on a napkin for Henry.

"Okay," Henry said as he pocketed the greasy napkin. "Now, who is this Witch For Hire?"

The acne-faced clerk suddenly hushed Henry and then leaned over the counter, dangerously close to Henry. He carried a slight knot underneath his bottom lip. His teeth, long and slanted like Kansas road signs, were stained with dark tar; and a dribble of brown spit was caked over the corner of his mouth.

Henry carefully backed away from the clerk and covered his nose from the man's awful breath.

"You best be careful saying that name out loud 'round here, son."

"Who is she?"

The clerk gazed around the desolate store. His eyes rapidly flickered around like an insect's.

"Her name is Claudia Rampar," he whispered.

The name. . . *Claudia*. . . repeated once more in his mind. He had heard the name before, but he didn't know where.

"Claudia. . . "

"Don't!" the clerk suddenly shouted out and then placed his stick-like finger over his mouth before Henry could even speak another word. "If you're looking for her, then you're out of luck. She'll find you. That's how this thing works."

"What thing?"

The clerk pulled himself from the counter and replied, "The story, of course."

"Story? What story?"

"You ain't listening, son," the clerk said and leaned away from Henry. "Claudia ain't the type to be found. You got that? She used to live at the Rampar Plantation off Wilshire until the caretaker found her. . . dead. . . "

"Dead?"

The clerk followed, "Now, she's nothing more than a ghost, a legend 'round here. They say her spirit wanders these very swamps."

Henry asked, "Where is this plantation?"

"On the map, just as I showed you," the clerk said. "Like I've been saying, son, you ain't gonna find her. So, you best do yourself a favor and quit while you is ahead."

"Thanks for the advice," Henry said annoyingly and walked out of the convenient store.

The clerk furrowed his brows and said behind Henry, "You best be careful out there, son."

As Henry exited AM, his eyes were drawn toward the entire pane of glass on the side of the store, which was decorated with a collage of MISSING signs and posters. So many faces there were, some old and others recent. Most of them were taken from school yearbooks while others were snipped out from portraits or family gatherings. Henry stood in front of the window and closely studied the faces and descriptions on the signs. Like a detective, Henry gradually picked up the pattern, the clues. All of the children were between the ages of 8 and 12 years old. Before Henry pulled himself away from the window, a familiar face behind a couple of other photographs grabbed his attention. Without anybody looking (after all, the only person around was that one mousy clerk and he was out of sight—at least from Henry's point of view), he peeled away the two crinkled photographs, which revealed an aged black and white photograph underneath. The face was much younger, of course. But the similarities, they were uncanny.

"No way. . . " Henry said under his breath and then gazed around the desolate gas station.

He folded the partially torn photograph from the glass and stuck it in his pocket.

Meanwhile, the clerk was standing with his forehead pressed against the pane of glass and watching the young man's every move.

Without the young man looking, he peeled his face from the window and carefully observed a paranoid Henry exit the parking lot and then take a right on Kernel Road where he would make a couple more turns until he reached his destination: Wilshire.

The clerk got on the telephone.

A groggy man with a resonant voice picked up the phone and answered, "What?"

"Hey, Fox," the clerk said with a tremble in his throat. "You busy?"

"What now, Beaumont?"

"There was a kid in here asking 'bout Wilshire."

"What'd you tell him?"

"I sent him on his way. Best be getting there shortly."

"Alone?"

"He was indeed," the clerk said and grinded his stained teeth together in arousal. "A lone wolf, this one was. Just a couple of years older. . . "

There was a sharp *click* on the other end of the line.

"Fox? You there?"

The clerk sighed, hung up the phone, and causally went back to his business.

After Henry made a left on Wilshire Road, as the clerk had written down in his child-like handwriting on the napkin, he zipped up his book bag and flung it over his right shoulder. Then, he glanced down at his ankle and made sure there wasn't any protrusion. There wasn't any. And he was somewhat amazed by the concealment.

With a mile down and about nine more to go, Henry passed a giant mailbox on the side of the road. The strange mailbox—like most things around here—aged with rust and overgrown vines, was nearly the size of a small billboard. The red flag on the side was sticking toward the overcast sky. Henry was momentarily struck by a sudden case of déjà vu. He had seen this before, the mailbox, that red flag, this dirt road, this scenery, not in a dream but in real life. Before the memory came back to Henry, he shook off the strange feeling and kept on walking. The farther he made it down the road, the denser the vegetation got. Swamps covered each side of the road now. The walk was serene or eerie, if one believed in such stories like what the clerk, Beaumont, had told Henry. As of now, Henry wasn't entirely convinced about this Claudia woman. For all he knew, she could've been the same old lady that his mother had spoken of, the one from the concert in Baton Rouge. Henry wasn't entirely convinced, at least not until he saw Claudia with his own eyes.

Two miles later, a cardinal red 1962 Chevrolet truck approached Henry from behind.

The truck pulled up to Henry.

A scruffy-looking man said from inside the truck, "You need a lift, young man?"

"No thanks," Henry said distantly and looked around the eerie woods.

"Where you headed?"

Again, Henry looked around the woods.

"I don't mind giving you a lift," the man said. "I was actually on my way into town."

Henry replied vacantly, "I'm not going into town."

"All right then," the man said calmly. "So, where you headed? There ain't nothing out there but wetlands."

"I'm looking for Claudia Rampar."

The man's facial expression went blank.

"Claudia, huh?"

"You know her?"

"I reckoned everybody 'round here knows a thing or two 'bout Claudia."

"Can you take me to her?"

"And what exactly you expect to find, young man? If you don't mind me asking. . . "

Henry said toughly, "It's personal."

"All right then," the man replied with a well-trained restraint in his voice. "Just so you know. Claudia's been dead for over ten years. But. . . but something tells me that you already know that. Am I right?"

Henry reached in his pocket and pulled out the "Witch For Hire" card.

"I found this card," he said and showed the man the card from the passenger side window.

"I see. . . "

After Henry studied the man's interest in the card, he got a closer look at his face. The left side of his face was covered with old scars that ran like rills over his pallid skin. One scar jaggedly ran over his left cheek, socket, and brow, but not his eye, which was all white. The other one was as blue as the ocean. His hair was white and long and greasy and curled behind his pointy ears.

"Where'd you get that card?"

"It doesn't matter where I got it," Henry said confidently.

"Hey," the man said with surrender. "I'm just tryin' to help."

"I think this address has something to do with my father's death."

"Is that right?"

Henry eased away from the truck and stood defensively on the side of the road.

"I tell you what," the man said and placed the gear in park. "Her place ain't too far from here. I'll take you there and let you see for yourself, if it brings you any closure. But I must warn you, son. There ain't nothing there but an empty house. So, if I was you, I wouldn't get my hopes up."

"I just want to look around," Henry said. "That's all."

The man reached over and opened the passenger door for Henry.

"Well, hop on in then," he said charmingly.

The road had opened up briefly to a vast everglade, but then went back into the dense woods.

Throughout the drive, Henry picked up a strange vibe from the man like he had met him before.

Henry nodded at the man's black leather gloves gripped over the steering wheel and asked, "What's up with the gloves?"

The man carefully lifted up his hand—the other one still tightly gripped around the steering wheel—and mechanically moved his fingers around.

"Accident," he said.

"What kind of accident?"

"I was badly burned."

"How'd you get. . . "

"So," the man interrupted, "you live around here?"

"No," he answered.

Henry thought about asking more questions about the man's hands and how they got burned, but then he took one glance at the man's scars on his face as well as that white eye and decided not to.

"Where you from?"

"Lansford."

"Long way from home."

Henry didn't respond.

"You said your looking for some answers to your father's death?"

"Yeah," he drawled.

"When did he pass? If you don't mind me asking."

"Earlier this year."

"How did he die?"

"He was murdered."

"Murdered, huh? How was he murdered?"

"So," Henry interrupted, almost in a mocking way, just like the strange man did when Henry wanted to know more about his burns, "you said you knew Claudia."

Henry could hear the leather cracking as the man gripped the steering wheel even tighter.

"Barely," he said, once more showing a well-trained restraint in his voice. The man robotically glanced over at Henry; and like a robot, he didn't have a single expression on his face. "I live just a couple of miles from where she stayed. She was a very private person like myself."

"So, is it true?"

"Is what true?"

"About Claudia," Henry said. "Is she really a witch?"

The man laughed merrily, which caused Henry to ease his hand down by his ankle. He kept his hand there just in case.

"I don't know too many people who call them witches anymore, but she definitely did have a dark side. So," the man said and paused, "I never got your name."

Over second thought, Henry said, "Henry. . ."

"Are you sure?"

"Yeah."

"It's nice to meet you, Henry."

The man reached out his gloved hand.

Henry removed his hand from his ankle and shook the man's delicate hand.

"Name's Harvey," the man said with both clarity and conviction, "but you can call me Fox."

"Nice meeting you," Henry said cautiously.

"So, your father, what do you think he had to do with Ms. Rampar?"

"I think she put a curse on him."

"A curse?" Fox said and snorted. "Someone must've really had it in for him."

"Something like that," Henry said quietly. "My father didn't exactly get along with his stepsister."

Fox asked curiously, "And what was your father's name?"

"Henry," Henry said like before, with hesitation. "Like myself."

Fox squinted his eyes in suspicion.

"I see."

"And his stepsister?"

"Hannah."

"Did you say Hannah?"

"Yeah."

Once more, Fox suspiciously glanced over at Henry. The restraint, which he once held onto like a secret, nearly slipped from his eyes.

"I'd be. . ."

Fox drifted into thought.

Henry directed his attention toward Fox and witnessed the salacious grin shaping the side of his face.

He asked, "Did you know her?"

"No," Fox corrected and quickly removed the grin from his face. "Not personally. But I heard Claudia speak her name once or twice like she knew her."

"I thought. . . I thought you just said that you barely knew Claudia. . . "

Fox hesitated.

"I did," he said and cleared his throat. "Well, we were civil to one another. After all, Claudia was my neighbor. Conversations never went past small talk, though. Ever since the murders. . . well, she just hadn't been the same."

"What murders?"

"Personally, I didn't think a person was capable of such a horrendous crime," Fox said and focused on the road ahead. Hands tightening. "She was only eight years old when it happened." Occasionally throughout the story, the man pulled his eyes from the road and shot glances over at Henry. "Claudia was a troubled young girl. I mean troubled. They say she was born and raised in darkness. Me, the only time I got to know her was when she was older. I asked once about the murders, but she didn't like speaking about what happened that day. Claudia's father, Neal Rampar, he was a slave owner. He had a dozen or so slaves working on his plantation. After slavery ended in 1865, the slaves were free to leave as they pleased. Most of them had gotten so used to working on the plantation that they ended up staying. So they stayed. The fact of the matter was that Mr. Rampar didn't want to see his slaves go. After 1865, it was considered illegal to be holding onto former slaves. But Mr. Rampar kept his slaves anyway. One day, Mr. Rampar accidentally impregnated one of them slaves. Natasha was her name. Then, on February 2nd, 1881, Natasha had a baby. She named the baby after Natasha's mother, Claudia. Eight years went on by. That's when the murders took place." Henry remained still in the seat—intrigued and yet horrified at the same time. "Little Claudia discovered what her father had been doing to his slaves, especially her mother. If they had gotten out of line, Mr. Rampar stuck 'em down in the basement, chained 'em up like dogs, and used that summer heat like a punishment. Let them sweat out all the wrong they'd done. Now, if you ever lived here in the summers you know the heat can get pretty intolerable. I seen some good folks die, healthy folks, pass out from exhaustion. I seen it with my own eyes." During the story, Henry's hand slowly moved down his leg. His hand stayed there—slightly above his right ankle—until Fox made a move at him. "Mr. Rampar," Fox said and cleared his throat, "he had left 'em down there in the darkness for days, even weeks, until there was hardly anything left of them but skin and bones. Well, now, Claudia found her mother in the basement, the same place she was born, in the darkness, locked up in chains like a dog. The poor girl tried to free her mother, but her father found out what she was doing. He tried to catch her, but he couldn't keep up with Claudia. She was too fast for the old devil. So, he went back to the main house while Claudia went to the authorities. And then later that night, the authorities found out about Mr. Rampar and the slaves he was holding captive in his basement. The story goes that Mr. Rampar went to the shed before the authorities arrived, grabbed hedge clippers from the storage, and went to each and every slave. Well, you get the picture." Henry carefully peeled down his sock. "When the authorities found Mr. Rampar, he was sitting in his room with a bullet in his head. His body spilled over his desk. His mind sprayed over the walls. But Mr. Rampar, he wasn't the only dead body the authorities found in the house. There were many more bodies, all decapitated. All of them slaves. Supposedly, Mr. Rampar just didn't end with the slaves. The old devil even killed Claudia's mother too, Natasha. They found her down there in basement, locked up in chains, with her head severed from her body. Claudia found her mother, her head. That was when she ran away in the swamps with all the other creatures. The town found out what had happened on Mr. Rampar's plantation and they sent out the bloodhounds in hopes of finding little Claudia. After days of searching, Claudia was nowhere to be found. And they never found her either, even till this day. Eventually, she came back some days later when the house was all boarded up and left to rot. But the girl who came back wasn't a girl anymore, but something else entirely. Authorities, they don't even come near this place anymore. After awhile, folks had just given up on her. Ain't nobody ever step foot in these lands every since."

"If you knew that Claudia came back, then why not tell the people that she was found, that she was okay. . . " Henry said, ". . . you know. . . for reassurance?"

"But she wasn't okay," Fox said grimly. "It was best to let her be."

"Yeah, but still. . . "

"Like I said, son, she was just an old lady by the time I met her," he said. "By then, Claudia seemed like she didn't want to be found. The poor old lady had already seen enough. I figure it was best to leave her alone."

"It doesn't make any sense!" The volume of Henry's voice rose a little. "What if she was the one responsible for putting a curse on my father?"

"I wouldn't go as far as saying that, son," Fox said, almost angrily from the passenger's persistence. "Claudia had her skeletons, but she was no witch."

"How do explain the card then?"

Fox didn't answer the question.

"Doesn't it bother you," Henry said, "to live near a place with such bad history?"

Fox stepped on the gas pedal a little and increased the speed of the truck.

"Any person who lives out here is running from something," he said, his eyes swelling. "This place, son, it's a place where the world can't touch you. You see, son, that's the thing about stories. They're best left untouched. Sometimes, it's best to leave the past in the past. Otherwise, you may dig up a story that you may not like."

Without Fox looking, Henry grabbed the protrusion over his ankle.

"So, what exactly are you running from, Fox?"

The front end of the truck suddenly dipped down.

The tire struck a pothole.

As Fox swerved the truck, Henry removed his hand from the protrusion underneath the sock and braced himself over the dashboard.

Eventually, Fox regained control of the truck.

"Shit," Fox whispered and checked the rear view mirror. "I think it's a flat." He parked the truck on the side of the road. "You wait here."

Henry stuttered, "I. . . I . . . think it's better if I. . . if I just walk from here. . ."

He cracked open the door.

"Suit yourself," Fox said flatly and tended to the flat tire.

As Henry grabbed his book bag and made it as quickly as possible toward the road without running, Fox hollered out from behind, "Say, Henry! I need a hand over here! You can't just leave me stranded like this!"

Henry paused and glanced over his shoulder.

Fox had his arms out as if he had done nothing wrong.

"It'll only take a second! I just need help with the jack!"

Henry kept on walking.

"I didn't mean to scare you, son," he said, his voice eased back. "There just stories. Ain't nobody really knows what really happened out here." Fox pointed in the opposite direc-tion from where Henry was walking. "Besides, you're going the wrong way. Claudia's house is back that way. All there is over there is swamps and more swamps." Henry stopped walking. "I'll take you to the house once I get the tire fix." Henry turned around only to see Fox pointing at the tire. "See for yourself."

Henry gazed around the wetlands and didn't see a soul in sight. In the back of his mind, he knew something wasn't quite right. *If I keep going*, he thought, *I should be fine. I'll find the highway and hitch a ride back to the station and forget I even came out here.* Henry didn't quite know if this Fox guy was telling the truth and how there was nothing that way but swamps. He moved his attention toward the vivid sky and oddly enough found a sense of peace as if the flat didn't mat-ter, the stories, the saxophone, Hannah, Claudia and what she might have done to his father. The sun was just about to set, which cast a brilliant red light over the parting clouds.

After relishing the timeless view, he cautiously walked back toward the truck.

"I think I ran over a nail," Fox said optimistically and then placed the jack on the ground. "I just need you to move the jack underneath the truck. I would, but I can't because of my bad back."

As Henry kneeled down over the ground and carefully moved the jack farther underneath the truck, his eyes mistakenly fell over the tire, which wasn't flat. In fact, it was still inflated. No nail. No flat! His eyes widened and then slowly moved around his shoulder. Behind him, Fox pulled a crowbar from behind his back. Before Henry could make a run for it, Fox struck him in the back of the head with the crowbar. The last thing Henry saw was Fox towering over his body. He was saying something like "making it too easy for me," and then his voice became muffled and distorted.

As Henry's head bobbed around like a buoy in a rough ocean, he honed into what Fox said.

"Didn't your mother warn you not to get into cars with strangers?" Fox said callously and then his voice drifted off into a dull silence.

Henry's head fell against the asphalt.

Then, two dark curtains slowly shut over his eyes.

THIRTY-FOUR

THE curtains lifted, unsteadily at first and then gradually.

Somewhere in the musty darkness, Henry heard the sound of Steve Urkel's nasally voice crying out. . .

. . . *Did I do that?*

The question was followed with a burst of audience laughter, which had fizzled out over the ringing in his head. He closed both of his eyes, the curtains. Another sound: a *clink* from above! The sharp sound compelled Henry to open his eyes yet again, even though a gesture as simple as opening one's eyes seemed unfeasible. Henry's eyelids were now open, both of them. The stage was set up before him. Yet, his eyes felt as if they were still shut. Henry carefully focused on the darkness around him. A couple of minutes passed until a soft light, geometrical, blushed over the darkness. In a sudden jolt, Henry moved his arms around, but he couldn't move them farther than a foot or two in either direction. The materials around him were slowly brought forth. The darkness finally lifted. Henry ran his cold hand across his other wrist and felt an iron bracelet and then the chain attached to the wall. He did so with the other wrist and felt the same iron bracelet and chain. He gave a slight tug on the chains, only to be caught in a dead stop. So, he used the chain and pulled himself across the coarse floor until he reached the brick wall.

With the chain now wrapped several times over his hands, he yanked and pulled and tugged as hard as his body would let him, but the chains attached to the brick wall weren't budging.

I'm going to become one of them, he thought. *Another face posted on a window.*

"This can't be real," Henry said and slapped himself across the face. "Wake up," he told himself. "*Wake up. . .*"

Once more, he slapped himself in the face.

Henry now thinking: the flat tire, the shadow on the dirt road. . .

He touched the backside of his head and then hissed from the tenderness of the knot.

Then, he moved his eyes upward.

In the darkness, Henry caught a glowing outline of a doorway above a narrow staircase. Another sudden burst of laughter, this time coming from the same man who had struck him in the back of the head with a crowbar.

Henry said softly, "Hello?"

More laughter.

"Hello?" Henry said, more loudly. "Where am I?"

The television suddenly muted.

Henry heard footsteps coming from above the basement. Another door, smaller in size and volume, opened from upstairs. The door slammed shut, but did so quietly. More footsteps! More creaks! Much closer now! He carefully followed the creaks of footsteps until they reached the glowing door above the darkness.

There was a momentary silence. . . building louder now. . . a slow hum. . . and then the blood pounding in Henry's head! The inexorable sounds around Henry were suddenly shattered by the sting of the basement door squeaking open, revealing a silhouette of a man standing in the middle of the glowing doorway.

"Hello, Henry," Fox said resonantly as he walked down the stairs.

Each step that he made was heavy and loud.

"Help!" Henry suddenly cried out. "Somebody help me!"

Once more, he tried to free himself from the wall.

While doing so, he nearly ripped off his wrists.

"You can shout all you want, Henry," Fox said calmly from above. "Nobody can hear you."

Henry backed up against the wall.

"What do you want from me?" he asked, his breath labored.

"You're here to keep the legend alive, Henry."

Trembling, not only his body, but also his voice, he asked, "Where is she? Where's Claudia?"

"Like I told you, Henry, Claudia is dead," Fox said and made it to the base of the wooden stairs. "But her spirit. . . her spirit is alive and well."

"You're full of shit!"

"Am I, Henry?" He strolled from the darkness and kneeled down to Henry's level where a beam of light escaped from the doorway. "Why don't you ask her yourself?" His pale face was revealed in the dim light. Henry flinched, not from the sight of his face but from his jet black eyes, which were like tiny night skies glistening from the reflection of light.

Once more, Henry braced himself against the wall and struggled to make eye contact with the strange old man. Without the man looking, he picked up the chain from below and wrapped it around his knuckles.

In great fascination, Fox gazed around the dark basement.

"This is where it all happened, Henry," he said, almost in a trance. "You're a lucky boy. Not many people get a chance to visit the birthplace of a legend. If it weren't for her father then—who knows—perhaps she wouldn't have been the legend she is today. Shit!" Fox chuckled. "Perhaps Claudia would've been just another ordinary girl with ordinary problems." The amusement slowly washed from his pale, scarred, wrinkled face. "No," he said gravely. "I like to think Claudia died down here when the murders took place. She died with her mother." He turned his attention back to Henry. "I wish I could've been down here when it happened."

"Like you would've made any difference. . . " Henry interrupted and then cowered closer to the wall, ". . . you can't even pick on someone your own size. So, what makes you think you could've stopped Claudia's father?"

"That's the thing, Henry." Fox rotated his head toward Henry. "I *wouldn't* have stopped him." His eyes sharpened, appearing like two quills. "No," he said quietly, "I would've watched him kill every single one of them." The comment sent Henry even closer to the wall. "If you close your eyes, you could almost see it." Fox briefly closed both of his eyes and took in a deep breath through his nose, which gave Henry an opportunity to do what he had considered doing ever since he witnessed those two black eyes. Certainly, he was much stronger than Henry. But he appeared weaponless. On the other hand, Henry had a weapon of his own (in fact, two weapons: one attached to his wrist and the other hidden next to his ankle), which could've been used to his advantage. Fox exhaled, loudly. In a state of arousal, he ran his tongue over his colorless lips. As Henry reared back, Fox reopened his black eyes, pointed them at Henry, who was now doing all he could to look away. The eyes were still, two faint beacons floating in a sea of darkness. "When I was seven years old, Claudia found me on the side of the road like a lost puppy. At the time, she was much older than me, old enough to be my mother, hell, even my grandmother—it wasn't until some years later when she told me how old she really was. Not once did I ever think about how old she was because she was the most beautiful woman I had ever laid my eyes on. She looked like. . ." a smile crept over his face for a second and then receded back into his coarse face, ". . . like a black angel sent down by God. She took me in. Gave me food and shelter," Fox said nostalgically. "I was a runaway like yourself, Henry."

Henry returned, "Who. . . whooooo. . . who said I ran away?"

"What other reason would you be here, Henry?" he said amusingly, stood upright, and paced around the dank room. "Your father? Really? Because you found a business card with Mr. Rampar's address on it?" He drawled, almost sadistically. "Trying to dig up old skeletonszzzz." A snort. "You best be careful, Henry. Sometimes a father's skeletons come back to life and bite you right in the ass. I mean, what good did you ever expect from coming down here in my city, Henry?"

Henry responded with a scowl.

"Right," Fox said, paused, and studied the lines over Henry's face. "Makes sense." He pulled his eyes from Henry. "People don't know how good they got it until everything is taken away from them. When my Claudia found me, I had nothing. No family. No friends. I was *alone*, Henry," Fox said with reflection. "Claudia, she very well could've tossed me back on the road and sent me on my way. But she didn't, Henry. She raised me like I was one of her own. She took care of me, loved me." Fox strolled back over to Henry and kneeled down before him, which caused Henry to defensively ease back against the wall. "By the time I was fifteen, we were traveling around the entire country. I drove her from city to city. . . from San Diego to Topeka. . . it's like we were on top of the world and nobody could touch us. The things, the things she could do, Henry," his voice suddenly filled with great excitement, "her fortitude, her powers," his hand curled into a fist, "her ability to defy nature! Claudia was indeed one of a kind." He paused briefly. His tone became more soft and sympathetic. "I remember there was this one job in Pensacola. A wife, a nurse, Mrs. Rachel Salinger, would come home from work to a man who would get drunk all day and then slap her 'round if she didn't do as she was told. She grew tired of waking up next to a smelly lush and looking at the bruises in the mirror from the night before. Mrs. Salinger grew sick and tired of the abuse, the suffering. After awhile, she couldn't even recognize the person looking back at her in the mirror. That was when she acquired our services through a friend of a friend." His black eyes squinted. "I've seen it with my own eyes, Henry, a man growing gills on each side of his face. I. . . I've watched the horror consume his eyes," Fox's eyes widened with awe, "*the fear*. It was like. . . like watching a man's soul deteriorate right before my eyes. One second, Mr. Salinger was a king in his own castle. All the problems he carried around with him day in and day out would all be taken out on his poor ole wife. The next second, Mr. Salinger was a toddler who acted as if he just. . . broken the television remote." He chortled yet again. "I heard Mrs. Salinger's husband paid several visits to doctors who tried to stitch up his new gills. They kept growing back, wider and deeper. The gills had gotten so wide that they stretched across his entire head. After awhile, well, Mr. Salinger lost his head." Fox stood and paced around a baffled Henry. "I watched a man's head shrink to the size of a peanut. I watched a woman's hair fall out and turn to dust. I've seen what others have not. . ."

"You're full of shit!" Henry suddenly cried out. "All you are. . . is a killer. . . a killer like Claudia!"

"Claudia got paid money to kill, Henry," Fox said and shrugged his shoulders. "I don't. I do it for much bigger purposes." Fox kneeled back down and ran his hands across Henry's chains. "You can call her a witch. You can call her a demon, monster. Call her. . . a murderer. Call her what you like. It's doesn't make any difference to me. I know what kind of woman she was." Without showing a hint of emotion, Fox leaned even closer. "A friend, a lover." He paused and pictured Claudia in his mind—*that one night*, he thought, *in Manhattan*. "We were doing a thing in New York. I was seventeen at the time. Never owned my own tuxedo before. We were at this ball, some charity thing for politicians. Claudia was wearing this white dress with diamonds on it. I remember all the men, even some of the women, couldn't take their eyes off us, mainly Claudia. She looked like a princess." Fox thinking from that one night: And yet, *even though all the men wanted to be with her and all the women wanted to be just like her, she was mine, my ebony princess, and I was hers and together we were inseparable.* He moved his eyes down at Henry. "She was. . . my everything." A grimace. "And then she was taken away from me." Once more, his dark eyes drifted into a state of reflection. "After her death, she paid me a visit when I was asleep. I've seen her face like I see yours right now, as if she was there inches away from my face. She told me about my purpose in life and what I had to do from that day forward." Another grimace crept onto his face. "For ten years, I've been carrying out my mission. I've done what she has told me to do. I never questioned her. I never tried to reason with her. I did it. . . " Fox snapped his head away and frantically scratched the side of his face with his trembling hand, ". . . I do it because I love. . . d her. This place is special, Henry," he looked around the basement, "It's a place where no one, I mean, no one can touch you."

Henry thought more about the MISSING signs at the convenient store.

"All. . . all those kids," Henry said, his voice shaking.

Fox smirked.

"You catch on quick, Henry." He witnessed the anger building in Henry's reddening face. The anger was like a train gathering speed, trying to break through. Henry thought of something quick, something calming like Ms. Craft's words or Saturday nights at the movies, something to slow down the train before he lost control and did something that he might later regret. Strangely enough, Fox found peace and comfort in watching Henry, the anger, and how he wore it like a mask over his face. "This house was built in 1854, a few years before the Greek Revival swept across the South," he said casually, studying the lines and cracks over Henry's face. "During the day, you can hear her spirit roaming the hallways, protecting this place, making sure everything is going according to plan, making sure the mission is carried out. . ."

Henry suddenly reared back and swung at Fox, but Fox grabbed Henry's fist before it could land over his chin.

"Ah, ah, ah," Fox said tediously.

"You!" Henry shouted. "You're the one who killed them, you son of a bitch!"

Fox forced Henry's arms to the floor where Henry kicked and squirmed around. However, he was no match for Fox's strength.

"When Claudia returned after her death, she specifically told me that the children helped keep the spirit alive." Fox scanned Henry's body, the muscles flexing over his forearms. "You, well, you're a little too old for her taste. But, nonetheless, the legend must go on, Henry. And Claudia, she is a hungry woman. If it weren't for you, Henry, then it would be some other poor child. As far as I see it, you're doing civilization a favor. You're helping keep the sheep in order."

The veins swelled in Henry's forehead as he whined, "By killing me? What difference will it make?"

"You mention the name *Claudia* in town and everybody runs for cover," Fox explained. "Even after death, she still has control over the human spirit." He waved his hand around in arrogance. "Their will, it's broken. Imagine, Henry, a world without fear, without tradition. This is how we keep order, Henry, balance. Without fear, the world would slowly rot like a piece of old fruit."

Fox patted Henry on the leg, which caused Henry to shiver from the coldness of his hand.

"What. . . what about what you said in the truck. . ."

"And what exactly did I say, Henry?"

"The past," he cried, "leaving the past in the past."

"This is different."

"How so?" Henry yelled closely. "It's time to live up to your word! Me and you, we're both alike! We both lost someone who we cared about! If you let me go, I won't tell anybody about this place." He suddenly grabbed Fox's leg. "I swear I won't! I'll forget I even came here!"

Fox removed Henry's hand from his leg and towered over his curled body.

As he strolled away in the darkness, he said coldly, "Tomorrow, you're going to be a hero, Henry. You're going to be famous. . ."

After Fox left the basement, Henry curled himself into a fetal position over the floor and tried to keep warm. He still couldn't believe what was actually happening. It had been years since Henry had prayed. That night, he did so. He asked the Lord to protect him and give him the strength to escape this horrible place. Once he finished praying, he thought about the one thing that had comforted him the most.

In the darkness, Henry quietly sang to himself, "Lover, rider, fighter of the night. Show me the way to the forgotten land. Set your sights on the light. . ."

By the time she reached Arkansas, the rain started.

Abbey rolled up the window before the rain soaked her clothes.

Lover, rider, fighter of the night. . .

Then, she cut off the radio and tucked the thermos of coffee in the side compartment of the door. She had been driving all night and now she was working her way through a cup of coffee that she had bought at a gas station just off the interstate.

A pair of headlights flashed over her eyes, now crossing the rear view mirror.

"You're boy is weak, Beatrice," the same sickly woman from before said in a gravelly voice from the shadows of the backseat. "He doesn't stand a chance."

Abbey flinched from the dark woman's presence, calmed her breathing, and then seethed, "You don't exist. . ."

"Yet," the woman rolled her head away from the window, the drops of rain running across the glass, and glared into the rear view mirror, "here I am."

Abbey's eyes flickered into the mirror.

"What do you want from me?" she asked, her voice louder.

The woman returned, "What do you want for yourself?"

"For you to leave me the hell alone, you bitch!"

"Good. . ." the woman drawled, raised her chin in superiority, and cracked open her lips, the faintest breath spilling from her mouth, ". . . I like it when you're angry. I like it. . ."

She pulled her beady black eyes from the mirror and watched the cars passing by as Abbey weaved in and out of traffic.

Set your eyes on the light. . .

Henry, now shaking from the coldness of night, suddenly flinched from the flash of lightning and then the explosive crash of thunder that followed. He got up from his curled position, looked out the basement window, and watched the flashes of lightning flicker across the dim woods outside. Another crash of thunder sent his blood racing through his veins. He curled himself against the wall and covered his ears, now singing louder, "*Lover, rider, fighter of the night. . .*

After she downed another pill with a sip of coffee, the woman was gone from the backseat.

"I'm coming for you, Henry," Abbey whispered to herself. "Hang on. . ."

Once more, she found her eyes slowly moving toward the rear view mirror. . .

Lover, rider, fighter of the night. . .

. . . Blue flashes of lightning soften over the dank darkness. . . an audience of claps trail off. . . a sudden flicker of light, a tiny flame over a match. . . Henry removes both hands from his ears. . . the light from the flame flashes over a lanky black woman, naked and nearly rawboned, without a head and chained against the wall. . . she places the flame inside a lantern on the ground. . . her stick-like arms reach around her lifeless body (while doing so, she makes all sorts of sounds as if bones are being ripped from joints). . . places a head on top of her severed neck. . . she moves the newly acquired head around. . . a couple of *cracks*. . . and then the black woman turns her attention to a frightened young man, who is seated frozenly on the cold ground. . . the shackles over his wrists are now gone, the chains scatter away from him. . . *You there,* the black woman whispers to the young man. . . she raises the lantern to her gaunt face, close enough to show the young man that she means no harm. . . *Come here, boy,* she says, her voice trembling. . . *I needs ya body heat.* . . "Are you. . . are you cold too?" Henry asks. . . *Froze.* . . her parched lips quiver. . . Henry removes the shirt from his body and crawls over to the black woman who, like Henry, is shaking uncontrollably from the coldness of night. . . "Here," he says and gives the shirt to the black woman. . . *Much obliged.* . . she places the shirt over her chest, secures it around her shoulders, and wears it like a shawl. . . more flashes of lightning, now bring out the ashen shades of the haggard woman, now hastily twisting her limbs and head and rhythmically contorting her body, from the darkest corners of the basement. . . a tear drops from the black woman's eye. . . a narrow trail of white tears paints over her cheek. . . finally, a smile breaks through the rigid skin of her face. . . Henry keeps close to the frightened black woman, ignores the haggard one from afar, and rests inside her bony arms. . . the shivering stops.

When Henry asks what her name is, the slave, she tells him *Natasha*. . .

THIRTY-FIVE

FOX woke an hour before dawn.

As he did almost every morning, he went downstairs in the kitchen where he fried an egg—sunny side up—in a cast iron skillet along with three thick slices of Canadian bacon and boiled a pot of grits and brewed a batch of House coffee. He ate in the rocking chair on the front porch and listened to the vast wildlife around him.

For the rest of daybreak, Fox spent his time honing a hunter's knife in front of the kitchen window. He spent about hour or two on that blade, making sure it was sharp enough to cut through steel.

After he was done with the blade, he grabbed Henry's book bag from the stool and dumped the articles inside over the kitchen counter. He picked up Henry's shirt and took a big whiff of it. Then, he unrolled a hand towel, set it aside, and skimmed through the other belongings inside the bag.

Streaks of sunlight pierced through the cracks and openings of the live oak lining the driveway—the branches stretched out over the long, narrow driveway like frozen tentacles—as well as the hickory and sycamore trees, and maneuvered into the old house and then finally, by the time the sunlight made it through the entire house and toward the basement, the streaks were nothing more than a pale gleam over the tiny window. The daylight brought Henry's bleak surroundings to light.

As Henry finally woke (the entire night had been spent with rapid images of a frail corpse in its latter stages of decomposition shuffling toward him and not through his dreams or nightmares, but just images, flickering through his mind's eye), he found a rat resting upon his shoulder. What Henry thought was a hand, Natasha's hand, on his shoulder, was, in fact, a rat, a really fat and smelly one too. Henry quickly brushed off the rat, which sent the squishy thing squealing away. He surveyed the basement. He noticed shackles and other rusty chains hanging from the wall. The story of Claudia's father, he remembered, chaining his slaves to the walls out of punishment. *Like dogs,* he recalled what Fox had said. Dark bloodstains were scattered over the floor. There was a worktable with rusty tools on top. Next to the tools lay a doll with curly red hair dressed in a dotted gown, ripped and frayed around the end. One of the doll's eyes was missing as well. In his thorough survey, a strange object caught the corner of his eye. Henry faced the wall and looked closer at the object in a crack. However, he couldn't quite make out the object in its entirety. The object was red. Other than that, Henry didn't have the slightest clue as to what the object was or if that red was from blood. He searched around his thoughts until the one thought that had been with him all day yesterday suddenly surfaced. He completely forgot about it, that steak knife holstered in his sock. He assumed it was from the shock. Now, for some reason, the shock was gone. Now, he saw things more clearly.

With the chains restricting his movement to only a couple of feet, Henry reached down and pulled the knife from his sock and loosened the object from the crack in the wall. He reached inside the crack and fingered out a red shoe covered in dirt. The shoe was only three or four inches long. Something only a little boy or girl would wear. *Not even eight years old*, Henry thought, his eyes shrinking, *but much younger.* Right then and there, Henry's eyes swelled with understanding.

Suddenly, the basement door squeaked open from above.

Henry crawled back toward the wall and stuffed the shoe inside the crack.

As Fox made his way down the stairs, Henry slid the knife back into his sock.

"It's time," Fox said vacantly and unlocked the chains around Henry's wrists.

He pulled a black rag from his back pocket and held it down by his side.

"No, no, no, no. . ." Henry cried, ". . . Please, don't do this. . . I swear I won't tell anybody. . . please. . ."

Fox grabbed Henry by the throat. His grip tightened. Henry tried to breathe, but Fox was cutting off his oxygen.

He asked, "Are you going to behave?"

Henry tried to speak, but the two words came out short and mostly raspy with a strained gargle. Fox leaned closer and with his big black eyes stared at Henry. Henry wasn't the least frightened of them, the eyes, not anymore.

While Fox tightened his grip around Henry's throat, Henry grabbed the chain below and whacked Fox over the head. Fox's head jolted to the right. His left eye was back to normal (all white) while the other one remained black. Henry looked into his eyes, especially that white one in the middle of the jagged scar. Henry pulled his eyes downward and found a black contact on the ground.

Henry said sarcastically, "Looks like you dropped something."

Fox scowled.

"You like playing dress up," Henry said bravely.

Fox yanked Henry closer.

"You're gonna wish you hadn't said that, son. . ."

Fox reared back and punched Henry directly in the middle of his face. Next thing Henry knew a black rag was being tied around his eyes.

Over the soothing darkness, Henry heard the sound of leaves rustling.

Henry opened his eyes as before, delicately, and peered through the tiny crack of light. Below him were twigs and leaves and torturous branches, some covered in scabs of moss. There was a tightening around his throat, but not like a hand. In fact, it was the collar of his shirt. In a daze, he reached behind his neck and grazed another hand, a smooth and leathery one, gripped around the backside of the collar.

"Get up on your feet," Fox commanded.

Henry did as he was told and stumbled to his feet.

Fox repositioned himself and now stood behind Henry.

"Now walk," he said and pushed Henry forward.

Henry staggered and fell to the soft ground.

The black rag over his eyes suddenly came loose. Then, he found himself below a black pile of rubble, which was shaped precisely in a circle. His hand brushed over the soot and charred wood below him. In the debris, Henry found a golden bracelet. He fished his finger through the bracelet and brought it closer to his eyes. Before he could look at it any closer, Fox grabbed him by the collar and jerked him to his feet. He retied the rag over Henry's eyes, this time much tighter.

Then, once more, he pushed Henry forward.

"*Walk*," he said more sternly.

Henry stumbled his way through the woods.

As the tempo of his walk steadied, his foot suddenly snagged a fallen tree branch. Henry flopped forward—his hands mostly catching the fall. Fox was there to pick up the frustrated teenager and push him in the right direction. It went on like this several times: Henry falling, Fox picking him up like a rag doll, and then toying him around as if he received pleasure by doing so. Henry's palms bled from cutting them over bark. Throughout the walk, he cried not from the pain, but from the realization of death and how imminent it was.

"Stop your crying," Fox said from behind. "We're here."

Fox grabbed Henry by the arm and tugged him toward the ground. He pulled a piece of rope from his back pocket and tied Henry's wrists together. Next, he tied the rope around a tree and made a double knot.

"Just in case you find your legs," he said jokingly.

Henry didn't know exactly what Fox was doing. All he could hear was him moving around a bulky object, like a piece of plywood or some kind of large board. Once the object was flung aside with a loud grunt coming from Fox, Fox wiped his gloves clean. Henry couldn't see exactly what had been unearthed in the woods. The air felt colder, the stench much stronger. Fox quietly stood over the massive hole in the ground and gazed below. Then, he pulled the rag from Henry's eyes. After the light from the sun softened over his tender eyes, he frantically looked around the woods until he came across the board with leaves stapled on top over the ground and then that massive hole right next to it.

A *gasp* escaped from his mouth. . .

Thousands of human bones, Henry witnessed, some white and spotless while others chipped and weathered. Some of the bones could've easily passed off as twigs or tree branches, but Henry couldn't tell the difference. There were at least forty to fifty skulls that he could count on the surface of the bones, but many more underneath the pile. All he saw was death and what used to be someone's son or daughter, brother or sister. Years of pain and suffering, Henry witnessed. He couldn't help but think about all of the families and the ones who had lost loved ones. They would never know what happened to their children or brothers or sisters. One day, their loved ones were there as they always were, laughing or playing or simply talking. The next, they were removed from all existence without a single trace as if they were plucked from the earth the same way a farmer would pluck a crop from his or her farm.

"Welcome to the Hollow," Fox said and revealed the sharp hunting knife in his hand.

As Fox made a move toward Henry, whose face was now empty and bloodless, he heard a sudden car door slam in front of the house.

Fox paused and then looked down at Henry in surprise.

"Must be Beaumont," he said curiously and pointed the knife at Henry. He stuck it real close, close enough that Henry could feel the sharpness of it. "If you so much as make a sound, I will gut you like a pig and make you watch. Do you understand me?"

With his eyes bulged in fear, Henry bobbed his head.

As Abbey prowled down the driveway of Rampar Plantation (her purse strapped diagonally across her chest, not over her left shoulder as she normally would carry the purse), she checked the chamber of the Beretta and made sure she had a round inside.

Safety: *on*, of course.

Halfway down the driveway, she paused and took a brief moment to gaze around the land, the woods, the swamps not too far away, and then the main house, which was once a blinding white, now off-white from the owner's neglect. The colonnade of the front exterior of the house consisted of six Corinthian columns, all but one supporting the entablature. One of the columns, the one on the far right, was broken in half from where a sycamore had fallen across the front of the house during a devastating hurricane. It took Abbey many years—in fact, every bit of seven long years—to erase this place from her mind, especially the events that transpired on November 2, 1979. She couldn't believe she was back at the one place that she thought she would never see again. So much pain had resided here. So much misery. Just the thought of being back here made her extremely nauseous. The cool air was almost dead around the house. She spotted the red Chevrolet parked next to the house.

Once more, she checked the chamber and then the safety.

With caution, Abbey walked up the stairs of the front porch. Except for one, all of the rocking chairs were toppled over on the porch. One of them was rested on its side against a column. The front door was all boarded up. She managed to find a shattered window.

Trying not to cut herself over the sharp, dirty glass, she sneaked through the window. The inside of the house was just like the air outside, dead. Sunrays poured in through the shattered windows, as well as the cracks and holes in the roof, and cast a little light. She made it to the kitchen and came across three large shelves on the side of the wall. All the shelves were empty except for one, which had a couple of cans of Spam and other boxed foods like crackers or cookies. Most of the cabinets were like the other two shelves, gutted. She exited the kitchen and strolled down a long hallway with the Beretta kept closely in hand. Toward the end of the hallway rested a wooden table with a couple of overturned picture frames. She flipped over one of the picture frames with a loud sigh and saw a picture of a little girl, possibly eight or nine years old, maybe ten. She grimaced and immediately turned over the frame before the memory could take any more shape. She proceeded farther down the hallway until she came across the basement next to the living room. She cracked open the door. Another wave of memories came back to her, none of them good. She remembered the darkness, how she was frightened of it as if the darkness was a singular presence, a beast. The beast, she remembered, *the basement was where the beast lived,* as well as the ghosts of the plantation. She tightened the grip around the Beretta and slowly walked down the staircase.

When Abbey arrived at the basement, she noticed the chains on the walls and that faint and yet sour stench of death in the air. Her eyes wandered around and then finally landed on a basement window. She ambled over to the window.

As she peered around the woods, her eyes crossed a young man tied to a tree.

Her eyes widened. . .

"*Henry,*" she said with tremendous relief.

As a sense of hope flashed through her mind, she suddenly staggered forward. The blood rushed through her veins and spiraled Abbey into a complete state of disorientation. She glanced down at her abdomen and then at the bloodstain spreading over her beige shirt. She reached down, touched the wet stain, and lifted her hand to her face. The blood was covering her palm.

Her blood.

My blood?

The handgun slipped from her fingertips and fell to the floor.

She lurched forward and shouldered the wall, which momentarily kept her upright.

Fox stepped forward into a beam of sunlight. His face was filled with incredible astonishment.

"Well, well, well," he said, trying to force a smile over his face. "Look who decided to show up. . ."

"You. . ." Abbey uttered, ". . . what are you doing with my boy?"

"All this time," Fox said with fascination. "I knew it was him. At first, I thought to myself: there ain't no way that kid would've came back here, not after what happened. But then he told me his name. I just knew."

"Leave him out of this. You hear. . . "

"Mr. Henry's been chosen to take part in the reformation of America," Fox said calmly as he stepped closer to Abbey. "After Sinclair Leprieur, it's Baton Rouge, New Orleans, and then Nebraska, Oklahoma, and then the entire East Coast. Soon, this country will be ours again."

"When are you ever going to learn," Abbey said, grimacing from the sharp pain in her side. "It was never yours to begin with, you piece of shit. You, you're just another angry white man. That's all you'll ever be to me, to her, to everyone."

"We'll just see about that."

"You're insane just like her," Abbey said faintly.

"Beatrice," Fox said sincerely and kneeled down as Abbey slid to the floor, leaving a blood trail over the wall behind her, "my little Bee Bee. You should've done yourself a favor and never come out of that room."

"But I did," Abbey said, both of her eyes rolling around her head. "And I saw the world and the beauty that awaits for my boy. I will watch him grow up to be a man and start a family of his own. He still has a chance out there."

"I'm sorry, Bee Bee," Fox said, "but soon, your son will join the rest of them."

"Please," Abbey begged, "whatever you plan on doing to my boy, please leave him out of this. This is between you and me. So, go on. Do it. Take my life. If that's what you wanted all along, then do it." Abbey nodded her head at Fox. "Go on, fool. What are you waiting for, you coward? You hear me. You little coward. That's all you are. You are a coward living in his own bubble. Soon, that bubble. . . it's going to pop. You hear. And the world will finally see who you truly are."

Fox traced the blade over Abbey's cheek.

"I won't even give you the satisfaction, my little Bee Bee," he said as his eyes ran over Abbey's breasts. The blunt side of the blade ran down her neck, now her breasts. "You should've killed me when you had the chance."

Abbey pulled her eyes away from the blade.

"I'm afraid your death will be a slow one." He picked up Abbey's Beretta from the floor and then checked the contents inside Abbey's purse. Most of the contents were cosmetic supplies, mascara, lipstick, and whatnot. The only item from the purse that piqued Fox's interest was the bottle of prescription medication. He read the name of drug to himself and then carefully eyed Abbey. "Murder can put a lot of stress on the mind." He winked at Abbey. "I'll make sure your boy gets a quick death." Then, he tossed the bottle of pills at Abbey and walked away. As he made his way up the stairs, he said mockingly, "Don't go anywhere. You hear? This party is just gettin' started."

As Fox made it to the first floor, Abbey's head flopped over her shoulder. Her eyes went still, so too did her breath. Once it was all clear, Abbey breathed a sigh of relief. She lifted her head and got up from the floor, slowly at first and then quickly. The stab missed any vital organs, she realized; instead, the blade went directly through tissue and muscle. She hurried over to the worktable and found a full roll of duck tape. She tore off several strips with her teeth and placed them over the wound to stop the bleeding. The tape worked for the time being. Next, she grabbed the bottle of pills from the floor. After that, she grabbed the end of the worktable and slid it over to the window. She found a crowbar hung over the wall and used it to break the window. She cleared the jagged glass from the window and then placed her black leather jacket along the bottom window panel.

Above, Abbey heard sudden footsteps scampering across the upstairs and heading toward the basement.

As she climbed up the wall and squeezed through the window without cutting herself, the basement door squeaked open!

Fox came sprinting down the stairs.

"You fuckin' bitch!" he shouted out as Abbey pushed her way through the window.

Meanwhile, Henry was trying to cut away the rope around his wrists with the steak knife. He heard the shattering of glass. Then, her saw her face. At first, he thought it was a hallucination or something. He peered closer and saw his mother now crawling from the window.

"*Mom. . .* " he said confusedly.

As Abbey slithered her way out, Henry shouted out, "Mom!"

"Henry!" she said, grabbing her side. "Hang on!"

Henry cut faster, but he couldn't get a good angle on the rope.

As Abbey rushed through the woods, the backdoor of the house flung open.

At the doorway, Fox was scanning around the woods until he finally spotted Abbey hobbling over to her son.

Henry embraced his mother.

"How did you find me?" he asked.

"We don't have much time. . . " she said with her breath labored, ". . . He's coming for us."

She grabbed the knife from Henry's hand and cut away the rope from his wrists.

"Let's go," she said.

As the two made a run for it, a gunshot rang out!

The bullet grazed the tree behind them, sending shards of bark over their shoulders.

"This way," Abbey said and ran with Henry deeper into the woods.

Another gunshot rang out!

Abbey ducked behind a sturdy southern pine and peeked around the trunk, only to find Fox stalking through the woods with her gun aimed in their direction. The man wasn't going to stop, Abbey realized, not until we were both dead.

"Keep up," Abbey said to Henry.

She took in a deep breath as if she was about to swim underwater and grabbed her son by the shoulder and sprinted through the woods. They weaved around the trees and led Fox deeper into the woods. They made sure to stay close to the trees—Abbey had specifically told her son with sudden explosions from her chest. Henry could only make out a couple of the words, *close* and *trees*. The rest of what Abbey said sounded like hiccups. She didn't have to explain why. And even if Henry questioned his mother, she would not answer him. As of now, every bit of strength counted. Instead, Henry did as his mother said and followed her lead and stayed close to the trees. As with Abbey, Henry's focus was mainly on both of his feet and legs and making sure to keep them moving. If they let up for a second, then he would catch them. Not only did he know this, but also so did his mother. Unlike her son, Abbey knew he wouldn't just kill them quickly or shoot them or stab them. Fox would take his good easy time with the two of them, especially Abbey. All of those rusty tools that she came across in the basement would finally come to good use. And that was what kept Abbey going. Both mother and son acted in unison and used the trees to their advantage like shields, ducking and diving around them.

When they reached a clearing, they took a detour around a swamp where Fox lost some ground due to the muddiness of the land.

Two more gunshots rang out, one of them catching Abbey in the sleeve.

Henry asked, "Are you shot?"

"Just a graze," she said and pointed ahead.

They found a shortcut back to the house, which was partially visible through the trees.

Fox was still behind them, though, but this time much farther away.

Abbey and Henry decided to find cover back in the main house.

Once inside, they went directly upstairs.

The climb up the stairs acquired most, if not all, of the strength in their bodies. By the time they both reached the top of the landing, their lungs were grasping for oxygen. Their legs were incredibly numb and felt twice as heavy as they normally were. Even the mud on both of their shoes was like carrying around ten pound weights. Both mother and son were hunched over in their own way. Abbey was hunched over—both hands clutching her knees—while Henry was hunched over the banister of the stairs.

"You. . . you. . . you distract him. . ." Henry said and then grabbed the knife from Abbey's grip. ". . . And I'll sneak up on him. . ."

Abbey's eyes fell on her shoes, the mud, and then the tracks that both she and her son were leaving behind.

"Don't be a fool, Henry," Abbey said, trying to catch her breath. "He's got about six shots left in the gun." She took off her shoes and looked around the dimly lit hallway. Henry didn't even need to ask his mother as to why she was taking off her shoes. He went ahead and took his off as well. "We need to hide."

As Fox kicked open the door from downstairs, Abbey came across a familiar bedroom. The furniture, even the cherry wood dresser and vanity mirror, was still intact. Nothing had been moved. Even the stale smell of the room was the exact same.

Henry followed his mother into the bedroom.

Inside, she opened the closet doors and waved over her son.

However, Henry was left at a standstill. He couldn't help but look to the floor, the dark streaks zigzagging over the hardwood and the sounds of toy trucks colliding together echoing throughout his head.

"*Henry. . .*"

Henry remained in a trance.

His eyes came across the door, the door handle, now *jiggling.*

"*. . . he's coming for us.*"

Henry snapped from his trance and hurried over to the bedroom closet where his mother was anxiously standing.

She kneeled down over the floor, accidentally leaving a smudge of mud over the hardwood.

"Here," she said, mindless of the stain.

Abbey opened a secret door on the floor.

Henry, again, was left at a standstill. He squinted his eyes in suspicion from his mother's knowledge of the house, especially the secret room.

"Get in. . . hurry. . ."

Abbey helped Henry down into the secret room, which was roughly four feet in height, width, and length.

Henry squatted inside the small room, looked up at his mother, and said, "Where are you going?"

"I'm going to end this once and for all." She heard the sound of Fox casually walking up the stairs. His footsteps were loud and heavy. "I love you, Henry."

"Mom. . . " Henry whispered.

"Hand me the knife."

Henry handed Abbey the knife.

In return, she handed Henry the purse.

"Stay here," she said, out of breath.

Abbey stuck the knife behind the belt around her back and closed the door.

Fox was closer now, making his way up the last two stairs. On the last stair, Abbey darted into yet another room, the master bedroom, across the hallway. The sight alone of the immaculate king-sized bed caused Abbey, like Henry previously, to freeze in her stance. The bed was made. The bed sheets were tightly tucked underneath the mattress. The comforter was precisely spread across the mattress, no humps or creases or folds. The pillows were plump and nestled at the head of the bed, tucked underneath the green comforter. Past images, some hazy while others fragmented, flashed across her mind. Images of smothering, Abbey mentally saw, images of a frail hand reaching out to grab her hair; then, she saw one last image, an image of her little boy who was no older than five years old at the time, ducking behind the doorway. Before the images could take shape, she immediately blocked them out. Her eyes traced along that bed, over the set of pillows, plump, not stained or flattened, and then once more, across the comforter, which was immaculate. She shook another sudden memory from her head and hurried to the closet.

"Please be in here," she whispered to herself as Fox crept down the hallway with the Beretta drawn to his side.

Abbey ran her hand across the top shelf. Her fingers struck the end of a double barrel shotgun. She grabbed the double barrel and then a worn box of slugs next to it. Kneeling over the floor, she proceeded to place the two shells inside the shotgun. During the load, one of them slipped from her trembling, muddy hands and fell underneath the bed. Footsteps came closer now! She dropped to her knees, reached under the bed. . . the same frail, gnarly hand from earlier reached out to grab her mane. . . all five fingers flexed and curled inward like a spider's legs. . . behind the grotesque hand, a gaunt face was brought into view, *her* face. . . the shadows fell into the passing sunlight. . . her eyes, like Fox, Abbey witnessed, were as dark as space. . . her brown teeth were bared too. Abbey flinched from her presence and shook the haunting image of the corpse-like woman from her mind. Another footstep at the door! Abbey picked up the shell from the floor and inserted the shell inside the shotgun.

As soon as she snapped close the shotgun, a voice said from the doorway, "There you are, Bee. . . "

Fox's eyes swelled open.

Abbey, who was kneeled down beside the bed, pulled the trigger.

At the very last second, Fox jerked backward from the shotgun blast, which ripped through the side of the door panel. Tiny shards of wood exploded in the air, a couple of them catching Fox in the side of the face.

Abbey grabbed the shells from the box and stuffed them in her pockets.

Nobody would've survived that, she thought as she sauntered through the bedroom.

As Abbey reached the chewed up doorway, another gunshot rang out! This one, of course, wasn't as thunderous as the shotgun. However, it could've done just as much damage. The bullet struck the wall next to Abbey as she ducked back inside the master bedroom. She peeked through the doorway and saw Fox's shoulder sticking out from the doorway of the other bedroom.

"I see you found, Old Nelly," Fox said from behind the wall as he wiped the blood from his face. "We use to go squirrel hunting with her. Remember, Bee Bee?"

"Yeah," Abbey said and snorted. "I remember you were a horrible shot."

"I was," he said, thinking. "Wasn't I? But I can't say the same about you. But with age comes rust, Bee Bee. Your reaction slows. Your focus wanders. Your joints become stiffer."

"Why don't you crawl out from where you're hiding and we'll see how good of a shot I am?"

"Can I take a rain check?"

"I don't think so, Harvey."

Throughout the standoff, Henry was listening to the conversation inside the secret room. Their voices were muffled, but he could make out what they were saying.

"*Tell me. Why did you do it, Bee Bee?*"

Abbey tried to catch her breath.

"The question is: Why. . . why didn't you do it before me?"

Fox paused in thought.

Abbey continued: "Do you remember the way she treated you? What she did to your face?"

"She was my life," Fox answered and moved the Beretta toward his lap. "She was the closest thing to a mother. She took care of me. . . looked after me." He clinched his jaw in anger. "And you. . . you took her away from me. . ."

Fox stepped from the doorway and fired three more shots. All of the shots caught the wall, which sent Abbey farther into the master bedroom. She heard Fox running in the opposite direction. She hurried to her feet and poked her head past the doorway and caught Fox darting into another room. In return, she fired but missed. She emptied out the smoking shells from the barrel and slid two more shells inside the barrels.

A *squeak* at the end of the hallway!

As Abbey snapped close the barrel, she said, "You never were good at playing hide and seek."

More squeaks, now from above.

Abbey's eyes trailed upward.

She heard the sound of footsteps, creaking and cracking. She passed the bedroom and then made it to another room where the attic ladder had been pulled down to the floor. She readjusted the shotgun in her hands and entered the guest room. The whole time, she kept the double barrel aimed at the ladder—wondering whether or not Fox was going to leap from the darkness at any moment and pounce on her like a lion to a gazelle. Abbey finally reached the base of the ladder, but Fox was nowhere to be found. She held the shotgun upward, into the darkness of the attic, and climbed up the ladder.

When Abbey reached the top and searched through the thick haze of dust, she saw another attic door open. The dim light from below was barely shining through the attic darkness.

Two doors, she remembered, *one here and the other in the guest room.*

As Abbey climbed back down the ladder and rushed back into the hallway, she was greeted by the butt of a gun handle. She fell backward and grabbed a hold of her numb face. Fox kicked the shotgun from her grip, out of arm's reach, and pounced on top of her body. His body was now squared over her body, knees pinned over her shoulders. The Beretta was pressed against the side of her cheek. Abbey knew, however, that he wouldn't shoot. He wouldn't kill her like this. As before, Abbey knew that hell awaited her, torture, and suffering, but not here in the hallway. Fox was a private man, that she knew, and he worked best in comfortable surroundings. Just the thought alone of having Harvey pick apart her body forced her to fight, despite all of the blood, which was now gushing down the curves of her nose and into her mouth and causing her to gag and choke. Somehow, she managed to free an arm from Fox's knee. She punched at Fox, but Fox grabbed her by her weak wrist with his other hand and forced the wrist to the floor. He holstered the Beretta behind his belt—his other hand holding down Abbey's wrist—and smacked her across the face with the backside of his fist. Abbey then cried out in agony, defeat. Her weary eyes slowly drifted toward the right, toward the room where Henry was hiding.

"I win," Fox said sinisterly and heedfully followed Abbey's glossy eyes.

As Abbey drifted in and out of consciousness, Fox strolled into the bedroom.

"I almost forgot," he said and kept to his calm nature as he strolled directly to the closet.

Fox opened up the closet, saw the smudge of mud on the hardwood floor, and then opened up the secret door.

There, Henry was sitting with his knees pressed against his chest and the purse in his lap. He warily looked up and found Fox towering over his vulnerable body.

"Where were we, Henry," he said with a sinister grin on his face and pulled the hunting knife from his holster.

As they moved through the house, Henry was still baffled from his mother's remarkable resilience. She had taken a knife to the stomach, a shot to the arm, and then pistol whipped across the face, and yet she carried on.

Fox pushed both Abbey and Henry from the backdoor of the house.

"Move it, you two," he said as he stuck the muzzle of the shotgun in Henry's back, while, with the other hand, he kept the Beretta aimed at Abbey.

Abbey fell to the ground and wiped the blood from her face with the backside of her hand.

Henry moved his arm around Abbey's shoulder and helped her up to her feet.

"Don't let him break you, Henry," she muttered as her eyes wandered around her head. "Whatever he does, don't let him break you."

"Come on," Henry said and helped walk his mother to the hollow, not the basement as Abbey had expected.

Fox said from behind, "Less talking, more walking."

They finally arrived at the hollow.

Abbey lifelessly dropped to her knees.

"Mom," Henry said, crying.

He followed his mother to the ground and looked her square in the eyes.

"I love you," he said as he hugged his mother. "I know I haven't said it such a long time. I always have, Mom. I. . . I always wanted your strength."

"You do have my strength, Henry," she said weakly and placed her bloody, muddy hand on his cheek. "You have it here," she pointed to Henry's heart, "inside. You just haven't found it yet. But you will." Abbey pulled Henry closer and hugged him tightly. The tears ran from her eyes and mixed with the blood over her lips. "You're the best thing that ever happened in my life. I love you, Henry. . . I love you so much. . ."

Henry too tightened his grip around his mother.

"Are you two finished?" Fox said as he aimed both the shotgun and the Beretta at the two of them. "Get up. The both of you."

Both Henry and Abbey didn't move, not an inch.

"I said, 'Get up!' Now!"

Fox holstered the Beretta, grabbed Henry by the arm, and forced him to his feet. He pushed him closer to the hollow.

"Now your turn," he said to Abbey.

He grabbed Abbey by the arm.

"You're going to watch your son die and then me and you are going to finish some business."

Abbey's eyes flickered toward her son.

In that moment—as brief as it was—Abbey witnessed the expression on his face, his great anger, as if he hated every ounce of the man and wanted him gone forever. The sight alone of her boy's face, that anger, the hatred, and his desire to survive, sent a ripple of energy throughout her body. Her skin was tingling. Her hand gripped the soggy earth beneath her. The hand now flexed into a fist.

Abbey mumbled, "No. . . "

"I didn't quite catch that, Beatrice," Fox said and leaned in closer.

"*No,*" she said gutturally and pulled out the steak knife from behind her back and plunged the blade into Fox's chest before he could get a shot off. She grabbed the handle of the Beretta and tugged the pistol from his belt buckle. She lowered her right shoulder like a linebacker and drove her shoulder into Fox. He staggered away, toward the hollow, and dropped the shotgun from his grip. Just two feet away from the hollow now! He removed the knife from his chest and tossed it to the ground. Swaying back and forth, inches away from taking one last step toward his final demise, he pulled out the hunting knife (twice the size as the steak knife) and spun around toward Henry, who had a bat-sized branch in his hand. Henry swung the branch at Fox, hitting him directly in the nose. The sudden blow lifted Fox from his feet. He soared into the hollow and fell about ten feet before landing in the stack of bones. Fox let out a grunt on impact, then a moan. His eyes flashed with panic, moving toward his chest and then settling on the two, mother and son, towering above.

As Fox robotically squirmed around over the pile of bones, his hands crossed his body and then the broken femur bone protruding from his chest.

His eyes closed.

Then, his head flopped backward.

Above, Abbey was slow to stand to her feet.

Henry tossed the branch into the hollow and turned to his mother.

"Nice swing," she said, smiling. "Maybe you should've been a baseball player."

"And maybe you should've been an actor."

Henry smiled as well.

Clutching her side, Abbey strolled over to her son.

She tossed the Beretta on the ground.

Henry embraced his mother once more.

"Are you hurt?"

"Me," she said. "I'll live. How about you?"

Henry burst into tears.

Abbey held her son's head against her chest. She glanced down at all of the bones inside the hollow.

"Are those what I think they are?"

"He killed them, Mom," Henry said, crying. "He killed all those kids."

"It's all right, Henry," she said tenderly and pulled Henry closer. "It's over now."

Henry sniffled and glanced down at Fox's body.

"What are we going to do about him?"

"We leave him," she said and picked up the steak knife and then the Beretta from the ground. "There's nothing we can do." With the steak knife in her right hand and the Beretta in the other, Abbey looked around the eerie woods and pulled Henry even closer and said to her son, "Let's go home. First, I need to grab my purse."

Henry pointed to the house.

He said, "Back in there?"

"Unfortunately."

They made a few steps toward the house before a shrill voice shouted out from the driveway, "Harvey! You back here!"

Both Abbey and Henry suddenly came to a halt.

"Did you hear that?"

Henry feverishly bobbed his head.

"Harvey!" the voice said, closer now. "Thought you said you weren't going to start the party without me!" The slender man rounded the house. "Say, who's that P.O.S. parked in the drive. . ."

Like Abbey and Henry did from the sudden voice across the woods, the man came to a halt. The six-pack of beer slipped from his grip. One of the canned beers burst open. Foamy beer sprayed the side of the man's leg. The man wasn't so quick to clean up the mess. He was more concerned with the two trespassers, mother and son, who were standing about twenty yards ahead of him.

"I know him," Henry whispered to Abbey. "He's the same man from the convenient store."

"The clerk?"

"Yeah," Henry mumbled. "How'd you know?"

"Wild guess." She held her hand in front of Henry. Her other hand, the left one, which was holding the Beretta, eased behind her back, away from Beaumont's line of sight. "I'll take care of this. . ."

"Say," Beaumont said genuinely to Henry and picked up the remaining beers from the ground, "I see you found your way to the house. Did you find what you were looking for, son?" Then, he noticed Abbey's injuries, the cut over the bridge of her nose, and then the blood soaked over her shirt. "Say, is that your car parked in front?"

"What concern is it to you?"

He pointed at Abbey's abdomen.

"Are you okay?"

"Fine," she said vacantly.

"I don't think those wounds you got there are going to lick themselves, ma'am," he said and turned toward the driveway. "I got a first aid kit in my van. I can treat that wound if you like."

"It's not necessary."

"I don't mind at all," Beaumont said eagerly. "In fact, I insist."

He made an attempt toward an old, dirty white van parked at the edge of the driveway.

"Wait," Abbey hollered out. "I said, 'I'm fine.'"

"But you don't look fine, ma'am," he said, now more sternly. "I assure you. It's no problem at all. I got the first aid kit right here. Let me go get it for you."

Beaumont quickened his pace toward the van as both Abbey and Henry remained in the woods.

"I don't trust him," Henry said closely and quietly. "He's the one who gave me directions out here. He's working with him, with Fox. I say we just run, Mom."

With her eyes never leaving the mousy fellow, Abbey said to her son, "I'm sick and tired of running, Henry."

When Beaumont reached the van, he quickly grabbed the pump-action shotgun from behind the passenger seat.

"This fuckin' bitch don't know who she fuckin' with," he muttered while reaching inside the glove compartment.

He grabbed the remaining shells, dropped a couple of them on the floor mat of the van, and then loaded them up into the shotgun.

After the shotgun was all loaded up, Beaumont slid the forestock down and then up the action bar, making an unnerving *chh-chht* sound. He spun around only to find the young man's mother standing ten feet away with a Beretta aimed directly at his chest. She didn't waste a second of Beaumont's time. She didn't even give the man a chance to draw the shotgun. Abbey aimed once. Then, fired twice. Two bullets struck the upper part of his body, one in the shoulder, which threw him to the side of the van, and the other in the chest. The shotgun fell from his hands as he slid across the side of the van, leaving a long smear of blood across the white paint.

With the handgun now empty, Abbey cautiously approached a lifeless Beaumont. Other than using the pistol to smack Beaumont over the head, using it like a fist and making sure he was completely dead, the pistol was now unless. So, she tossed it to the ground. The only weapons she had now were the steak knife in one hand and her fist in the other, which, in her eyes, was better than an empty pistol. Abbey kneeled down to Beaumont's level. His chest was still, she observed. No heartbeat. If he had one, a heartbeat, it was faint. Abbey checked the pulse on the side of his neck. The knife was held directly in front of Beaumont's face. If the pervert did wake, Abbey realized, he would wake to the sharp end of a blade in his face. She made sure of it. . . then, for a brief second, her eyes were drawn to Henry, who was slowly approaching the van. Just as she removed her fingers from Beaumont's neck, a bloody hand suddenly wrenched her wrist and forced the knife away. Abbey attempted to stab Beaumont exactly where she had planned if he had awakened, which was in the face, but the slightest interruption of her son diverted her plans. The blade struck the van behind Beaumont. The sudden recoil caused the knife to slip from Abbey's hand. Beaumont—with his eyes now bolted open— jerked Abbey forward and head butted her in the side of the face. He threw her to the ground and they rolled and wrestled around with one another until Beaumont was on top of Abbey. He battered her across the face, the first blow dazed her, while the others caught the sides of her head. She did all she could to shield the wild punches. Then, she smuggled in a blow of her own: a knee to the groin. Directly on the sack, right between the balls too. Beaumont fell forward, his face squinted, his lips puckered like a sphincter, and he howled out like a wolf, "Youuuuu *bitch!*" He scrambled from Abbey and grabbed the knife from the ground.

As she made a sudden run to the woods, Beaumont tackled her to the ground. He was now straddled over top of Abbey. Like Fox in the hallway, both of his knees were pinned over her shoulders. He was now holding the knife in both hands, rearing them back over his head. Abbey gazed up into the mad eyes of her soon-to-be killer and put her struggle to an end. Her shoulders relaxed now. Her arms extended outward, both of them stretched horizontally from her body.

Beaumont's arms reared farther back over his head. . .

A shotgun *blast* pierced out!

Henry, who was standing several feet away, lowered the shotgun from the sky and pointed it at Beaumont.

He yelled, "Let her go. . . or. . . "

The shotgun was trembling in his hands.

"Or what. . . "

Both of Beaumont's arms were still arched above his head. The knife was aimed directly at Abbey's heart. For a moment, his eyes flickered toward Henry's way.

In that moment, Abbey saw opportunity.

". . . You. . . you don't. . . have. . . the guts to kill me, boy. . . "

What Beaumont didn't realize was that Abbey had grabbed a branch beside her.

"But I do," she said from below.

She freed her right shoulder from Beaumont's knee and rammed the sharp end of the tree branch into his jugular.

Beaumont flopped backward like a whale over the driveway. He did all he could to stop the bleeding in his throat. Both hands now curled around his throat, now streaming with strings of blood. There was so much that his shirt had gone from white to red in a matter of seconds. He desperately crawled toward the open van door. Mostly, he was just kicking his way over the driveway.

With the hair on one side of her scalp all jacked up from the recent grapple, Abbey stumbled over to Henry.

"Give me the shotgun. . . "

Henry didn't budge or waver.

The shotgun remained on Abbey, not Beaumont, who was now bleeding out.

To Henry, the woman teetering before him appeared nothing like his mother. Instead, she appeared like a devil with her hair spiked up, her eyes like rings of fire, and her teeth bared like a vicious animal.

"Henry. . ."

Henry's finger tightened over the trigger.

"Goddamn it, Henry!" Abbey screamed. "Give me the fucking shotgun!"

Abbey lunged forward and snatched the shotgun from Henry's hands.

Pump action.

"Look away, Henry," she said and walked over to Beaumont.

Henry did as his mother commanded and looked away.

As Abbey towered over Beaumont, who was now taking his final breaths—for real this time—she aimed the shotgun at his head and pulled the trigger.

No hesitation.

None whatsoever.

THIRTY-SIX

WHEN they returned from Sinclair Leprieur, Abbey had the wounds over her face, the broken nose, and the gash in her stomach looked at by her primary care doctor, Doctor Township. Of course, Doctor Township asked Abbey how she obtained her injuries, especially that gash in her gut. She simply told her doctor, "Hit and run." Then, Abbey later explained: One of those expensive cars with those fancy emblem thingies on the front hood. One minute, she was crossing the street. The next, she saw two headlights bearing down on her. After that, Abbey was seeing stars. Doctor Township bought the story, even though it was exactly that, just a story. She decided not to show him the graze on her arm (from the bullet, of course). Otherwise, she would've been trying to explain to the authorities not only about a hit and run ("Did you happen to get the license's plate number?" or "Description of the suspect?" and so forth), but also the person who shot her and why exactly an accidental hit and run had strangely turned into an attempted murder. Was it dark out? Did the driver think you were a deer and he just wanted to put you out of your misery? The questions would come. So many of them that Abbey didn't have an answer. There would be a thorough investigation, as well as detectives snooping around her personal life, which was the last thing Abbey wanted right about now. So, she thought it was best to treat the graze on her arm herself.

After they returned home (during the entire drive Henry didn't speak one word to his mother, even when she asked him how he was doing or if he wanted something to eat), Abbey called Principal Teague at his home, as well as the police, and told them about her son and how she found him at his uncle's house and other than a nice whopping he received, he was doing just fine, even though he really wasn't. It was the nightmares. They were happening again and continued happening through the entire Saturday.

As always, the nightmares started out with the *jiggling* of a door handle.

Then, the rest of the nightmare was the same as before. On several occasions, she came and went. At times, she would creep into Henry's bedroom like a shadow on the wall. Other times, she would show her face, her teeth, or her black eyes.

"No," Henry muttered as he stirred through his bed. "Not again."

As before, the bedroom door slowly opened.

Henry's eyes bolted open.

The figure at the door was as boney as a corpse.

As Henry rolled around in the bed, his eyes glazed over with fear. There she was again, hobbling over to him. Her skin was pale, almost a green color. The frayed dress that she wore was long and black. Her hair was like shoelaces. Parts of her scalp were exposed from where all the hair had fallen out; and her eyes were sunken into her skull and appeared like a pair of glistening marbles. Henry cautiously slid from the covers and backed toward the bedroom window as the haggard woman inched closer to him.

"Henry. . ." she groaned.

With his back against the wall, Henry closed his eyes and tried to wake up.

"Don't be afraid, Henry," she said, her voice weak and raspy.

Henry gagged from her pungent stench.

In one swift stroke, she grabbed Henry's wrist and pulled him closer toward her body. Henry refused and tried to pull himself from the nightmare. He could feel the pillow pressed against his cheek, the bed underneath him, and the photograph tightly gripped in his hand, and yet he couldn't pull himself from the sickly woman. His limbs suddenly went numb.

Another hand, healthy and light skinned, grazed over his shoulder.

His eyes flickered open.

"No!" he yelled out and shot up from the damp bed.

"Henry," Abbey said as she sat next to Henry on the bed. "It's just another nightmare. . ."

Henry embraced his mother. His eyes moved from hers and crossed the window, which cast a gray tint over the bedroom from the overcast sky.

"Here," she said, holding a white pill in her palm.

"I don't want it," Henry said, turning away.

His mother tried once more.

"You need your rest, Henry."

"I said, 'No.'"

In return, Abbey sighed and placed the pill next to the glass of water on the nightstand.

"I remember now," Henry said slowly and wiped the sweat from his forehead.

"Remember what?" Abbey said, stroking the side of her son's head. She stopped for a moment and noticed the photograph underneath the sheets. She pulled her hand from Henry and peeled the old brownish photograph from the sheets. Her face went slack. She said urgently to Henry, "Where did you get this?"

"When you weren't around, I went into your room," he said. "I found that picture along with others like that one in your drawer?"

Abbey sighed and held her head downward.

"That's you in that picture. Isn't it? And that man, Fox, you knew him."

Abbey's eyes briefly flashed with rage, some of the emotion still lingering from the trip to Sinclair Leprieur. She breathed slowly, which made the anger retreat back into that murky place inside.

Henry sat against the headboard of his bed and innocently glanced at his mother.

"Something happened when I was there," he said mindfully. "It was like I've been there before. Then, when we went into that house, that one room where you hid me, that was when it came back to me. I remember I tried so hard to block out that one day. I remember being so scared. The sitter called out sick or something. You were hardly around."

"I'm here, Henry," Abbey said closely. "And I'm not going anywhere."

Henry's eyes crossed his mother's.

"The sitter, Annie," he said. "I remember we became good friends. We used to go to the park all the time. She would always find something fun to do, even if it didn't seem fun at all." A smile eased over Henry's face. "I never saw Annie after that one day you drove me to that one house, just like the one in Sinclair Leprieur. You told me to play with my toys and that no matter what I heard to stay put and never come out of that one room. I remember hearing a woman moaning. Then, a door opening. She was standing there at the doorway reaching out to me. I didn't know if she wanted my help or to hurt me. I didn't know if she was real or not. It was like she was straight out of a movie. Then. . ." Henry focused, ". . . then, then you came running upstairs. You walked the woman back to another room. I. . . I remember hearing your voice. You were yelling at her.

I can't remember what." Henry snorted. "I've been thinking these past couple of days. How you found me in the woods. Thinking about that old woman." He looked into his mother's eyes, this time keeping them there long enough to witness the pain in her eyes. "She's the one from the picture. Isn't she?"

Abbey stood to her feet and strolled over to the window. She sat down on a cushioned bench behind the window and gazed at the gray sky spreading out over the treetops of the neighborhood.

"You weren't supposed to see her like that, Henry," she said vacantly as she stared out the window. "You were only five years old. I. . . I didn't want to expose you to that side of life."

"Who was she?"

Abbey shot a glance at Henry.

"She was your grandmother, Henry."

Henry didn't respond.

Yet, he thought about the comment.

Abbey directed her attention back to the window.

"When I was your age, I dreamt of being a singer," she said and kept to her stern composure. There wasn't even a glimpse of delight from her faint remembrance. "As I got older, I soon realized that these dreams I had of being a singer were just fantasies, a way of escape, my release from reality." Her eyes almost darkened. Henry knew exactly where she was going with the story, nowhere pleasant. "When I turned twenty-four, I finally woke up, Henry. All the time I wasted on dreaming of becoming a singer was gone. Once it was gone," Abbey paused, "there was no way of getting it back. It is gone, Henry. *Forever*." Her eyes brimmed with tears, now glistening from the clouded sunlight. "When I was child, she would lock me up in my bedroom and I wouldn't be able to come out until dinnertime. There were times when I went to bed without any dinner at all. Other times, when she would go away for days, weeks, I would be there in that big house. Alone. I didn't know where she went. I remember seeing her when she came back. It was like looking at a person with no soul or heart. No feeling. No emotion. I remember the days and how long they were. I did all that I could to keep my mind busy: making forts in the woods. I even had a name for every single insect, every reptile. There was Oscar, the alligator." A smile flashed over her face—small enough to go unnoticed. "There was a caretaker who watched over me and kept me company."

"Fox," Henry said with clarity. "You're talking about that man, Fox. You really did know him."

"Yes," she mumbled and once more hung her head. "I remember I had this one TV set. I would watch it all day long, dreaming of one day being in that TV like Patsy Cline or Doris Day or Sarah Vaughan. They were all so beautiful like. . . like angels to one day fly me away from that horrible place." She pulled her eyes toward Henry. "I grew up in that house. That was my room. That was my secret little hiding place."

"Claudia. . ." Henry said, the breath nearly escaping from his chest, ". . . she was your mother. . ."

"For as long as I can remember, Henry, I did everything— I mean *everything*—in my power to try to escape from that house," she said. "Once when I was a little girl." Abbey pulled out the black and white photograph of the young girl from her pocket and showed the crinkled up photograph to Henry. "Before I was about to wash your jeans, I found this in your pocket."

"I knew," Henry said suddenly. "I knew it was you the moment I saw it."

"They found me hiding out near a dumpster in the back of a grocery store," Abbey said vacantly. "That was one of the worst days of my life. I wished they hadn't found me. I wished they had forgotten all about me. Another time, I was nineteen years old. Your father was playing at a small club outside Sinclair Leprieur. After the show was over, I bumped into him on the street. I had never met a man like your father, the way he looked at life. It was like he was. . ." she searched for the right word, ". . . *fearless*," Abbey said. "It was like whatever happened, the world would never get to him, never hurt him, never lock him up, never yell at him, never call him names. And even if they did, he would shrug them off. That night. . . that night was the best night of my life. I wished it had never ended. That night, Henry, I fell in love with the one man I wanted to spend the rest of my life with. He rescued me from that horrible place and showed me the world. He saved my life, Henry." She sniffled and calmed her breathing. *Just like Charles showed me*, she thought. "We were going to get married in Saint Martin. He proposed to me a week before the show in Baton Rouge. Then, a week later, your father changed—" Abbey snapped her fingers, which made a sharp *smack* "—like that. In the back of my mind, I knew it was because of her, your grandmother. After awhile, I stopped questioning myself whether or not she had anything to do with it or, in fact, your father really did go crazy." Abbey turned to Henry. "I had to leave him, Henry. I had no other choice." Her voice gradually rose. "I chose you, Henry. I chose a better life for us."

"But you said he left us. . ."

"I did, Henry," Abbey said solemnly. "And I'm sorry. I'm so sorry. I couldn't live that way anymore. It was too hard on me, too hard on us, Henry. But. . . but don't you see why I tried to protect you from that place, from her, your grand-mother?"

Henry asked, "Then why did you go back?"

"She was sick," Abbey said with a slight pause. "Fox couldn't take care of her on his own."

"Where was Uncle Charlie? Why couldn't he have taken care of her? Why you?"

"You don't have a Uncle Charlie, Henry," she said bluntly.

Henry's face lit up with anger.

"What. . . " he said, ". . . what do you mean?"

"He's not your uncle."

"No more lies," he cried out and stood from the bed.

"Uncle Charlie is Doctor Charles Lowe, my shrink."

". . . shrink?"

"It's the truth, Henry!" she shouted out, her voice overpowering Henry's. "What difference does it make if he's your uncle or not? Charles will always be there for—"

Henry interrupted, "What did you do to her?"

"Don't. . ."

"What did you do?"

"I did what was necessary," Abbey said sternly and stood from the bench. "It was me. . ." she pointed at her chest, ". . . I killed her, Henry." Her face puckered as if she was biting down on something awfully sour. "You remember. You! You saw the way she was. If I didn't do it, then who knows what she would've done to you. . . to us!"

Once more, Henry interrupted, "How did you do it?"

"Does it matter?" Abbey asked as the tears raced down her face. "I did the right thing. And I have no regrets."

Henry suddenly dashed toward the bedroom door.

"Henry. . ." she said as Henry sped down the stairs, ". . . you have to forgive me. You have to believe me! Please, Henry! I was only trying to protect you! Henry!"

Henry darted from the house and ran as fast as he could. He ran for miles through Lansford until his legs would take him no farther. He stopped at the nearest park and sat on the bench and looked at the stars. For hours, he thought about what his mother had done, what she had said. In some way or another, he knew she *had* done the right thing, that she was only trying to protect him from the evil that raised her and that she was a good person and her intentions were good and that she would never harm him like Claudia had harmed her.

Once Henry cooled off from the previous conversation with his mother, he went back home.

By then, it was already around midnight. When he saw the fire flickering through the living room window, he was confused, but also curious. Ever since they moved to Lansford, his mother had never used that fireplace. The two of them used to have fires regularly when he was younger, especially during the winter times to save money.

Henry cautiously opened up the front door and then closed the door behind him. *She must be asleep*, he thought over the crackling silence.

In the living room, he discovered his mother standing motionless in front of the fireplace. Not once did she turn and acknowledge her exhausted son. Yet, she stared into the fire.

Upset from his mother's state, Henry ambled over toward the couch and sat down without making much sound.

"You should be in bed," Henry said to his mother.

"I couldn't sleep," she said flatly while staring into the fire.

From behind, Henry asked, "Was it true?"

"Was what true?"

"What Claudia's father did to all those slaves?"

"I don't know, Henry," Abbey replied with the fire glistening in her glossy eyes. "I heard about the rumors, the stories about her. I never wanted to believe them. I guess I just got out of there before finding out the real truth about her. There was a part of me that didn't want to know, that didn't care. The way she treated me. . . I didn't care. I just wanted to run, Henry. I wanted to run far away and never look back. There are some things. . . I guess. . . you just can't run away from." Abbey turned her shoulder at Henry. "Sooner or later, your past will catch up with you." She wiped the tears from her face. For the first time in the conversation, she looked her son in the eyes. "You don't know how good you got it, boy. I've given you everything. . . "

Henry said innocently to his mother, "I know you have. I'm sorry."

Abbey shot another glance at Henry, penetrating.

"The only way we can get through this is by doing it together," she said as a teardrop fell from her eye and slithered down the side of her cheek. She never wiped the tear away. Instead, she reached out her hand.

Henry was hesitant to grab his mother's hand.

Then, she nodded.

He sighed and grabbed her hand.

With her other hand, she pulled out from her pocket an old and grainy and discolored photograph of herself (when she was around fifteen years old), the caretaker, Fox, and her mother, Claudia, posing in front of the main house of Rampar Plantation.

"Here." She nodded to the fire, extended the photograph toward Henry, and said, "I want you to do it."

Henry asked, "Do what?"

"Burn it," his mother said expressionlessly.

Henry stood from the couch and grabbed the old photograph from his mother's hand.

Without getting too close to the fire, he kneeled over the brick hearth, placed the photograph over the three burning logs on the grate, and then sat back down on the couch. Shortly after, Abbey sat down beside Henry and held him close enough to feel his strong heart beating against his chest.

As the two sat in silence, they both listened to the crackle of fire and watched the photograph curl and blacken until there was nothing left of it but a tiny flake of ash. As much as Henry disagreed with Fox, he was right about one thing and one thing only. Henry remembered what Fox had said before he woke up in the basement. "Sometimes," Fox said to Henry, "it's best to leave the past in the past."

And that was exactly what Henry was going to do, at least for the time being.

BOOK TWO

UNTIL THE SON RISES

PROLOGUE from Starlet Rollinson's *Missing the Edges: A Memoir (New York: Titled Hat Press, 2045, 1ˢᵗ Edition)*

I was on stage when it happened. We were in St. Louis, second to last show on tour before we hit the West Coast. Three minutes into the show while we were playing the opening song "Happy Trails," an unreleased track that Henry and I had thrown together in only two days at my home studio after the *Machine Mistress* recordings, all hell broke loose. Our backup drummer, Big Ray, was sprinting from the stage. Socks and Deon were next to leave the performance. At first, I didn't understand what was happening or why they were running or why I was still standing there like a clueless stooge on stage with thousands of Mona's Arch fans staring at me. Then, as William's bass struck the monitor and the set was left in a disturbing silence, I heard it, the guttural screams of what sounded like some kind of creature coming from backstage. My first reaction: one of the roadies was pulling a prank, as they had been known to do. What did the boys do this time? Did it involve a wild animal? Then, the screams sliced like razor blades through my ears. The screaming intensified, barbaric, almost demonic. I couldn't exactly pinpoint the screams. Were they running toward the screams or away from them?

As I stood on stage, I could literally feel my skin turning inside out, revealing all the pink underneath, the blood and veins and whatnot. For a moment, I thought a member of the audience was performing an exorcism. That was what it sounded like, the screams. They sounded like that one poor girl from the film, *The Exorcist*, shrieking out every single curse word from George Carlin's dictionary. I soon realized—after gazing out into the audience and witnessing our fans' eyes, all mournful like a funeral—that the screams weren't coming from the audience. They certainly weren't coming from a strange creature either. They were coming from Omar, our saxophonist who was filling in for Henry. Next thing I knew, William was gawking at me. He suddenly darted from the stage toward the direction of the screaming. I followed William backstage where Omar was rolling around next to a subwoofer and screaming to the top of his lungs. His hands were clutching his face. Harry was lying right beside him. One of the roadies, Edgar, was holding a towel against Omar's mouth. Three more roadies were trying to calm down Omar. The blood kept coming. The road crew, engineers, managers, and local journalists were scurrying all around me as if they were ants fleeing a destroyed anthill. In a matter of seconds, the towel went from a creamy white color to crimson red. I have never seen so much blood, so much horror being expelled from a person. Everything was so surreal, like a movie.

As I stood there, still clueless, I was waiting for the director to jump out from behind the cameras and shout out, "*Cut.*" I never heard the word, only more screams, more cries, more horror.

Before I could make any sense of what happened, James sprinted toward me with the speaker end of his cell phone over his shoulder. The expression over his face was one I will never forget. Even now, the details of that one night still remain blurry. I can see James now looking at me with this apocalyptic stare as if the world was hanging on the balance of a thread, and that thread slowly unraveling was moments away from snapping. James told me Henry was on the other end of the phone and that he was calling from Lansford Medical Center. The next words that came from James's mouth, not only brought tears to my eyes, but also brought me to my knees. It felt as if I had been struck by a sledge-hammer. Later, I was told that our guitarist, Deon, who was closest to me during the pandemonium, swooped in like a guardian angel and caught me before the side of my head struck the floor. In the blink of an eye, my world had suddenly snapped in two. That thread had given way. The ground beneath my feet was cracking and slowly breaking apart. I was now left standing alone on the edge of a cliff, peering across the violent sea before me and at the rising storm that awaited me. Somewhere in my thoughts, I was still waiting to hear that one word.

PART FOUR

GHOST NOTE

ONE

FOX murmuring in the cool darkness: "*Henry. . .*"

A shiver.

He felt a tight grasp over his wrists.

The voice was closer.

"Oh Henry," Fox said girlishly.

The wood let out a *creak* from above!

Then, a bone cracked from inside the darkness. . .

A feeble chuckle.

"Like the candy bar."

The voice was now more sonorous.

A sudden explosion of laughter burst from his chest, almost pompously.

Henry's eyes quickly bolted open, only to find that they were still closed—at least that was Henry's first conclusion. Another survey. Darkness. Warmer now. His eyes finally readjusted to the darkness, which gradually lifted into the dusty air. Snakes, Henry saw. A dozen of them! No! Two dozen! The darkness now softened from the pale nightlight easing through the tiny windows above. Even more snakes, Henry saw, scattered around the floor. He rolled from his curled position and scuffled toward the nearest wall. The snakes moved from each jerk and twitch that he made. No snakes, he realized. He peered closer at the floor and recognized the many rusty chains, occasionally limping closer from his response. The grip around both of his wrists tightened and cut against the bone.

"Ahhhhh. . . " Henry let out as he ran his coarse hands over his wrists and felt the shackles over them and then the rusty chains attached to the shackles.

I'm. . . I'm back in the basement. . .

"What do you see now, Henry?" another voice said over his shoulder.

The voice wasn't Fox's voice or the distant voice inside his mind.

The voice was smooth and comforting, familiar.

Uncle Charlie, Henry thought, *Charles.*

"I'm right here, Henry," Charles said. "Tell me. What do you see?"

Chains. I see chains, lots of them. . . and darkness. . .

Fox said from above, "Here I come, Henry. . . "

His voice was sharper now, mischievous.

Henry heard footsteps overhead.

Another *creak*. . . followed by a *squeak*!

The basement door opened from above and cast a faint light over Henry's clothed legs and feet, both covered with dirty socks.

Above Henry, the silhouette of a lanky man stood at the lit doorway. His shadow appeared as if it stretched across the entire staircase.

Terrified from the man's presence, Henry braced himself against the wall.

His breath grew labored.

Heart raced.

"Long time, no see," Fox said nonchalantly as he walked down the steep staircase.

Each step he took was heavy.

The weathered wood creaked from each step.

"I see you've shed some weight."

His shadow was now shrinking into his body.

Henry didn't respond.

He's coming for me.

What is he saying, Henry?

I don't know.

Concentrate, Henry.

Snake. . . he's saying something about a snake.

"What else," Fox said flatly as he made his way farther down the staircase.

The air tightened in Henry's chest, now throat.

Something's happened.

"Concentrate on my voice, Henry," Fox said strangely as he approached Henry. "Tell me what you see."

It's Fox. . .

"In the flesh." Fox arrived at the base of the stairs. He trudged through the basement. The soles of his boots slid against the grit of the concrete floor. He stopped in front of Henry and glanced over his shoulder. He said tediously, "Come give your grandmother a hug, Henry."

There's someone else in the room!

Henry followed Fox's eyes until he found an ashen body standing in the corner of the basement. She was hiding in the shadows. Unclear. *Woman*, though, he recognized, as thin as a corpse. Her bones, mostly skeletal structure, were slightly protruding from her pasty skin. She was wearing a long backless black dress, frayed around the edges. She had dark eyes, as black and glossy as a raven's eyes. Devil eyes. The haggard woman was standing still. However, when she studied Henry's interest with her black eyes, her devil eyes, she was subtle in her head movements like a robot.

It's her.

No!

Him.

The haggard woman was no longer standing there in the shadows.

Now, the clerk from the convenient store had taken the woman's place. The man was gaping at Henry and making all kinds of guttural noises. Clumps of his brain were dripping from the depression in his head and splashing onto the floor beneath him.

Fox said next to Henry, "Who?"

His voice was altered a bit, a combination of Charles's laid back California accent and Fox's Louisiana drawl.

Beaumont. . .

Fox kneeled down into the sharp beam of light in the darkness.

Henry gasped!

The face was not Fox's, but Charles's.

One of his eyes was white, without an iris, and glossy from where the lit doorway shined upon the basement below. He had a pink scar running down the side of his face.

Charles reached down and touched Henry's arm.

"Henry," he said and shook Henry on the arm. "Wake up."

Henry suddenly choked!

Once more, his eyes bolted open.

Now, he found himself in an office. Pale blue walls. An oak desk with a telephone and a folder on top. Two oak bookshelves to match the desk, which were all filled with hardbacks, mostly books about the brain, doctor books, science books, neurology, and psychology. His eyes traced his body, which lay on a hard leather couch. To the side of him, he glided his fingers across the tiny brass balls on the stitching of the armrest. He pulled his wandering eyes in front and settled them on the gold wristwatch, the brown khakis, the white dress shirt with each sleeve rolled over the forearm, the solid blue tie, and then the face of the red headed white man looming over.

Charles?

In a state of confusion, Henry tried to catch his breath.

"You're safe," Charles said patiently. "Just breathe."

Henry said unsteadily, "It's happening again."

"Catch your breath first, Henry."

Charles, who was perched on the footstool next to the couch, helped Henry to an upright position on the couch.

"She was right there," he said frantically. "I saw her."

"Easy now."

Henry bobbed his head.

"Count to ten, Henry," Charles said. "Remember. Just like I showed you."

He did as Charles instructed.

"Slowly. . ."

As Henry counted to ten out loud, he took long slow breaths as Charles had taught him after the incident in Sinclair Leprieur. Finally, the panic cleared from his thoughts. He eased back into the seat and sipped from the glass of lukewarm water.

Charles stood up from the footstool and sat back in his chair next to the couch.

"Better now," he said.

"Better."

"So, Henry," Charles said as he crossed one leg over the other, "what else do you remember from that night in Sinclair Leprieur?"

Henry didn't respond.

"This is a safe place, Henry," he said. "You can tell me anything." He looked around the large office. "Think of this room as. . . as a refuge. Anything you say doesn't leave this room."

The royal blue curtain next to the window stirred.

The window was closed, Henry realized.

It could've been a possible draft?

He looked to the floor below the curtain and didn't see any vents. Like the floor, the ceiling was bare too.

No vent.

Then where was the breeze coming from?

As Henry embraced another long, slow, deep breath, he reached to his side and took another sip of water from the glass.

Charles cleared his throat, uncrossed his legs, and leaned forward.

"Henry," he said and carefully sighed, "I'm going to try something different if that's okay with you. I'm not Doctor Lowe anymore. I'm not Uncle Charlie. So, right now, just think of me as your friend. Nothing more. Nothing less. Charles Lowe, a friend. Okay, Henry?"

"Yeah," Henry said slowly, "okay."

Charles got up from his seat and paced around the office with his hands in his pockets.

"You keep having these dreams, Henry, because you're unable to accept what happened to you," he said. "In order to move on from the past, sometimes it's best to talk about it. It will only get worse if you keep it inside. Tell me what's bothering you, Henry."

"I. . ."

"Remember, Henry," Charles said as he sat back down in his chair. "I'm your friend. What do friends do?"

Henry didn't respond.

Charles answered, "They trust each other, Henry."

Henry moved his eyes to his left.

He suddenly gasped!

His skin went bloodless.

A dead Beaumont was standing there, like the haggard woman before, still behind Charles's oak desk. The darkness softened around him and brought out the color of his skin, which was the color of ash. He was also standing next to a floor lamp, which was turned off and tucked away like a shadow. The daylight from outside the windows cast light over his body, his mutilated face, and yet he still remained as dark as a shadow.

"She's here," Charles said as he leaned over the edge of his chair. "Isn't she?"

Henry pulled his eyes toward Charles and then gradually shook his head.

"No," he drawled.

"Who is it, Henry?"

"Bea. . . Beauu. . . Beaumont. . . "

"And what is Beaumont doing?"

The beads of sweat swelled over Henry's forehead.

With his trembling hand, he took another sip of water.

"Calm your thoughts, Henry," Charles said, closer now. Then, again: "What is he doing at this very moment?"

Henry glanced over to the corner of the office.

A smile slowly crept over the man's face, which was half missing from the gun blast of a shotgun.

"He's. . . he's smiling at me," Henry said, his heart beating faster.

Intrigued, Charles got up from his chair and walked over to the corner of the office.

He pointed to the corner of the office and then glanced over at Henry.

In return, Henry bobbed his head.

"He's standing right here?" Charles asked and pointed to the ashen figure next to him.

Henry bobbed his head, but this time more rapidly.

"Yes," he said, his voice quivering.

Charles switched on the floor lamp, which brought out the dead man's face, his wounds, parts of his skull.

The light shined over his dead eyes, mainly the one that was still together.

"No. . ." Henry cried, ". . . he's still there."

"What does he want, Henry?"

"I don't know. . ."

Beaumont placed his frail hand over Charles's left shoulder.

"Charles!"

A loud grunt spilled from his lips!

"Look out!"

Charles suddenly stumbled forward into the lamp.

He grimaced in agony and eyed the bloodstain forming over his white shirt.

A string of blood ran from his lips and trickled down the side of his chin.

Henry slid farther across the couch and cowered against the cushions while Beaumont removed the steak knife from Charles's back and licked away the blood. By the time the dead clerk reached the tip, the sharpness of the blade split his tongue in two halves—a snake's tongue, now wiggling.

"*I promise you*, Henry." Charles's voice came from the side. Like before, Charles was still seated in the chair next to the couch. One leg was crossed over the other. He had a pen in his hand. A notepad in the other. He said carefully, "Nothing leaves this room."

"Nothing?"

"You have my word, Henry," Charles said.

Henry counted to ten once more, but this time he did so mentally.

TWO

SOMEWHERE in his thoughts, a door was squeaking open.

Not wooden, he perceived, metallic.

Before the heavy door closed, a delicate voice of an aged woman slithered through the cold openness.

"*What will your song* be, Henry?" the voice said over the humming silence.

The voice dwindled into a near whisper.

Before the voice retreated entirely inside Henry's mind, the voice suddenly transformed and multiplied into something inhuman and automated.

As the pulsing of the alarm amplified, Henry struggled to pull himself from his semiconscious state. A sudden rush of pain seeped behind his shiftless eyes, which forced him to crane his heavy palm over the snooze button and then drop it like an anchor. His roommate, Afed, was snoring in the bed next to his. A pins and needles sensation suddenly ran up Henry's left arm and sent him into a state of panic. He slipped his dead arm from underneath the naked girl who had one of her legs entangled around his and squeezed the numbness from his hand.

As he raised his head from the pillow (the one side of his face nearly paralyzed), he gazed around his blurry surroundings. His head was now splitting in two, stomach burning like a bed of hot coals. He felt nauseous and yet ravenous at the same time.

Once Henry finally came to, he realized that the girl was wasted behind comprehension.

He quickly checked her pulse to make sure she was still alive. He found a tiny pulse pecking away at the warm skin of her neck. The strange thing: Henry didn't exactly know who the girl was. Strange? Yes. Didn't even know her last name. Cassandra, he replayed over his mind.

Cassandra Whatever, he thought. *Trilby is gonna kill me.*

As Henry pulled his face away from the girl, he caught a stench of her breath. He picked up the smell of limes underneath a faint, hovering waft of an already ingested vegan burger crawling up her throat. She never blew chunks—at least not on Henry's bed. And her hair reeked like an ashtray. The smells combined—including that pungent smell coming from her crotch—caused him to gag. Like the girl, he never blew chunks—at least not all over his bed. Henry sluggishly pulled his face away from hers and rolled out of bed. He let out a moan from the ache in his hips. His skin was sticky and musty too, as if he spent the night camping in a forest. His foot grazed a half empty bottle of Vodka, which sent him stumbling across the room. Henry regained his footing, braced himself over a computer desk, and gazed around the bedroom. Beer cans—some squashed like pancakes, others smashed—were strewed all over the floor like rubble after a mortar attack. A bag of leftover mushrooms was wedged underneath the overturned television set. Several crumbled up stems and caps were also strewed over the floor. There were even a couple of holes in the wall.

"Jesus," Henry muttered while observing the two naked ladies—both asleep—on his roommate's bed. "Looks like someone finally got lucky last night." His voice trailed off. "Way to go, Afed. It's about time. . . "

He staggered to the window and gazed over the tree line at the bell tower situated in the middle of the courtyard of Haddon University.

The question came to him without any hesitation.

"What am I doing here?" Henry asked himself, trying to pull his thoughts back to that one strange dream.

After Henry threw on some clothes—a gray flannel over a solid black tee shirt with PUBLIC ENEMY across the chest, as well as a pair of raggedy jeans—he exited the room without waking his roommate or the other girls.

As Henry arrived at Wilkinson Clark Building (roughly a five minute walk from where he was currently residing), he bumped into his girlfriend, Trilby, whom he had met during his freshman year at Haddon. Her round face was full and easy on the eyes. She had dirty blonde hair—still wet from the morning shower—combed over one of her shoulders. She was a fairly slender junior with a couple of extra pounds of college fat on her hips. Dressed mostly in denim.

"Well, you look like you just got flushed down a toilet, Henry," she said bitterly and didn't bother to hug her boy-friend. Instead, Trilby readjusted the textbooks in her arms and moved them to the other side of her body. From the bit-terness in her tone, Henry gathered, Trilby appeared as if she had been waiting on Henry for quite some time. "So, what did you do last night?" she asked. "I called you like a million times."

"Nuttin'," Henry replied, scratching the backside of his head.

Trilby snorted and rolled her blue eyes.

"It doesn't look like you did 'nothing,'" she said sharply as her fingers quoted the word *nothing*. Next, Trilby took a big whiff of the potent odor around Henry. "Who was she, Henry?"

Henry paused halfway toward the elevator.

"Listen, Trilby," he said seriously. "I don't know if this is going to work out."

"What are you saying?"

"All I'm saying is that I need a little space," Henry said without a hitch. "You can't keep checking up on me like some kind of parole officer."

"Parole officer?" she groaned. "That's what I am to you. A parole officer? I can't believe I'm actually talking to you right now."

Henry sighed.

The elevator doors opened.

A portly student with glasses was patiently waiting inside. The student was about to exit, but Henry and Trilby were standing in his way.

"You know, Henry," she said, her voice drawn out with great frustration. "I really thought you enjoyed 'fucking my brains out.'"

Henry glanced over at the student inside the elevator.

"Can we just talk about this later?"

"No, Henry!" Trilby shouted out. "We can't talk about this later!"

Henry whispered closely, "Please, Trill. . ."

"You're an asshole. You know that."

Henry moved aside and let the student out of the elevator while Trilby stepped inside the elevator.

"Sorry, man," he said quietly to the student.

"So, what?" she fumed. "You did this to me to get back at me. Is that it?"

Speechless, Henry was shaking his head.

"I admit I screwed up once, Henry," she whined. "You get all over me, threaten me, and yet it's all right when you fool around behind my back."

Trilby struck the close door button on the side panel.

Before the doors closed, she said angrily, "You can take the stairs, asshole. From the looks of you," her eyes grazed over Henry's groin, "you probably need to stretch out that groin of yours." She tilted her head in curiosity and sharpened her eyes. As the elevator doors closed, she said, "You think I didn't notice the way you were walking." Her tone honed with mockery. "Bravo, King Henry. That little slut must've been worth it." Before the doors closed: "Tell me, Henry. Was she a good f—"

Over the past year, Henry had learned how to master the art of napping in class without getting caught.

The trick: grab the seat closest to the window, slightly lean toward the wall, keep the left hand directly above the left brow, fingers held in front of the closed eyes, and keep the head positioned upright, not sloped over. That was the key part, keeping the head upright. Otherwise, the gig was up.

A few minutes expired from his nap. Professor Carter's voice became nothing more than a cave echo. Origin unknown. The other students were like these sentinel beings keenly watching their leader speaking.

While the professor was giving a lecture on one of the earliest civilizations, Mesopotamia—Henry only caught the *Meso* part, so the professor could've very well been lecturing about Mesoamerica or a mesosaur or even mesoblast and Henry wouldn't have had the slightest idea of what he was babbling about—Henry was stuck in his own world, mainly replaying the events from last night. The images were right there, so close to grasp. All he could remember was inviting Cassandra (?), the girl whom he had woken up next to, and her friends, the two naked ones on Afed's bed, over to the house for drinks. Henry thought they played the game spin the bottle or something of that nature. Perhaps truth or dare? Perhaps twister? A card game as well? Things got real loose. The clothes came flying off, Henry remembered. Skin was exposed, underwear. Body shots. Then, after the shots, the hormones took over like a parasitic host. Henry remembered gently whispering something into Cassandra's ear, something like "Why don't we go upstairs?" He didn't know if Cassandra kissed him first or what. As of now, it didn't really matter. From the time they went into Henry's bedroom, the night remained in fragments. Each time he focused his mind on the reoccurring images of last night's dream—not the rough sex—a pair of nipples grazed across his chest.

As Henry stirred in the classroom seat, he readjusted his tee shirt. His armpits perspired. He focused on Professor Carter's voice, his words, *the* words. Another vivid image was brought forth from the hint of citrus shampoo that the girl seated next to Henry was still wearing: Cassandra's lush brown hair grazing across his face. More images: Cassandra's slender face; her smile; her upper set of teeth, the one snaggletooth, ivory white, glimmering in the smile; her eyes sharpening; and the innocence once held nicely inside now stripping away from them. Henry's heart fluttered. Even more images: Cassandra's perky breasts bouncing over his chin, smothering him. The images, so stark and palpable, sparked familiar sensations over Henry's skin, tingling now. Her aroused nipples were like two positive terminals of a battery against his chest with each graze or pinch sending explosive shocks through her body.

Henry quickly covered his nose and breathed through his mouth and focused on the professor's voice, his words, *the* words.

As best Henry could, he warded off the racy images, now overlapping and playing out in a sequence. They kept nagging away at him: Cassandra's eyelashes batting, the tips of them brushing across the side of his flushed cheek; now, her nibbling on the skin of his neck. In a playful, childish manner, she maneuvered her hard, charged nipples around his as if she was driving the two nipples around a test track. More images and sensations: more swerving of her breasts; Henry's hands cupping over them, caressing them softly as well as aggressively; his moist lips working their way down her firm abdomen, scaling the hill of her hip; her thighs, as smooth as silk, like a safety harness over Henry's shoulders; Henry kissing them ever so patiently; his lips detouring; his steamy breath blowing over the more sensitive parts of her inner thighs, sending violent waves of excitement throughout her body; perspiring; lubricating; his tongue now swirling, penetrating, and then palpitating like a tiny heart over the tip of her clit; searching for her right notes with his versatile tongue and then hitting them with remarkable precision like a skilled violinist; sucking, kissing, now from the inside; painfully deep; almost cannibalistic; her fingernails scraping along his scalp, digging into the roots of his hair; her toned abdomen pumping, faster; breath labored; more perspiring; moans rolling and rumbling like roars of thunder; the craving; her hips convulsing, jerking up and down, pulling farther away; holding off; surrendering; holding off yet again; surrendering; Cassandra howling out satanically, "Smite me with your devil tongue!

Fuck yeah! Fuck yeah! Fuck yeah! Right there, fucking Romeo!"

A weight suddenly settled over Henry's chest. His face went pallid. A couple of students seated next to him were aware of Henry's alarming state.

Finally: Henry using both of her thighs like handlebars to steer as well as locate her orgasms, the right notes; and then, their wet bodies moving in unison now; climax!

A sudden wave of nausea crossed over Henry's feverish body.

Breathe, he thought.

Remember. . . Charles. . .

As his nerves calmed a little, he focused on the strange dream, not the sex. The images gradually became nebulous and harder to visualize. Soon, the images ran into his other thoughts, more clear and dominating ones. From the fallout, he could only remember an older light skinned woman sitting in what looked like a living room (the house perhaps built in the 1960's). The older woman's face was marked with wrinkles and yet she was very healthy and free spirited. There was also a piano there, he thought, picture frames. Some of them were hung on the walls while others were perched on flat surfaces. Nonetheless, the other, more palpable images from last night, mostly the thrusting and then the explosions over Cassandra's breasts, aroused Henry so much that he was driven to reposition his pants. The powerful tastes of Cassandra were lounging on his lips, tongue, breath, and skin. The dream dispersed from his thoughts. No detail whatsoever. Would the dream ever return? The two images of the dream, the woman and piano, were now replaced with the recent events of last night, which came back in full capacity.

Fragments were connecting themselves properly, nature correcting its course.

Mindful of the predicament, Henry moved his arms and hands below the desk and covered up the bulge projecting from his pants.

Paranoid, Henry glanced around the classroom.

As before, the students were like these sentinel beings, all staring at Professor Carter. Henry's eyes traced over his shoulder. There, he witnessed another student, not so sentinel, sitting only two desks away. She had wavy strawberry blonde hair that flowed like a waterfall over her bare back, porcelain-like skin—like a doll's skin—with a sparse patch of freckles around the top of her cheeks and nose, a shade of coral shadowing around her dark, earthy eyes. The student was wearing a couple of hemp necklaces, one around her neck and the other around her ankle.

Flushed from the sight of Henry, her glittery lips peeled open and released the faintest breath. She carefully ran the tip of her tongue around the rim of her upper lip, now, like Henry's erection, bulging slightly. Next, she winked at the aroused sophomore before her.

As of now, Henry couldn't tell if the girl had an involuntary twitch in her right eye or if she really did wink at him. Nonetheless, his suspicions were soon evident once she repositioned her legs underneath the desk. Henry cautiously looked ahead and then once more looked over his shoulder. His eyes fell below the cute girl's breasts, down her blouse. Henry jerked his eyes away and then suddenly pulled them back to the girl's skirt, her thighs slowly opening like a set of doors. Like a dog to a bone. His smile was wide and yet closed, obedient.

As he pulled his attention toward the front of the class and slid farther down into his chair, he couldn't stop thinking about those very same words that he had woken up to, as well as Cassandra from last night (or whatever her name was) and, of course, that awfully cute girl behind him who wasn't wearing any panties.

Henry didn't know what her name was, the cute girl.

But soon, he would. . .

. . . or not.

THREE

ON the way to Saber Coliseum, Henry was quietly sitting in the back of the bus and mentally preparing for the upcoming conference finals against Madison College until a sequence of images rapidly flashed through his mind. The images were the same as the ones from last night's dream (and not of Cassandra Whatever), an older woman and her piano. The old woman was speaking to him, teaching him the art of music, patience, balance, and control. However, the images were all tangled together like a lock of hair and extremely hard to make out. Henry focused. Another image: a pair of frail, papery hands gracefully capering across the keys of a piano like dandelion seeds over a pond.

As the old woman played, she was gazing at Henry with a smile pulling across her face. Her eyes were bright, beautiful.

Henry lost himself in her eyes.

Before the melody rose from the background, there was a heavy knock at the door, metallic.

The old woman's head was like a bust.

The melody faded away over both the chatter of teammates and the hum of the bus's engine.

The old woman's facial expression livened as she turned her shoulder and directed her attention back to the young man, Henry, who was now gaping and sitting with his legs crossed on the carpet of her living room. Not once did he look toward the door, the loud knock. Yet, he sat there, gaping, like the old woman's head prior to interruption, as if his head was sculpted into a bust.

"*You don't have much time, Henry,*" she said with urgency.

Then, Henry snapped from his daydream.

From *Missing the Edges,* page 8:

The great thing about Berksville was its scenery, as well as its people.

Before my success with Mona's Arch, I frequently visited Berksville until developers found out about the land. It was a magical place where one could really do a lot of soul searching. For me, it was the perfect place to escape the material world and recharge the batteries, especially after touring with Like Heroin. The land stretched out until the horizon eventually swallowed it up. Miles and miles of land, once untouched, were now plagued with commercial businesses: cheap cookie cutter houses built by men who all looked the same, Do-Marts, McVille's, and other fast-food restaurants. Prior to the invasion, the sunsets alone were worth the mileage and gas money combined. If there was such a thing as God or an Almighty Creator, then Berksville was certainly His greatest creation (next to coffee beans, of course). I'm sure Berksville still is a decent place with decent people. But it's not the same. It's bloated, commercialized; and with all things big and corporate comes corruption. The last time I visited Berksville, which was several years after the reformation, I could hardly recognize the place or the people. Mostly, it was business types: the slicked back hair, nice suits, nice cars, and a wad of dirty cash in their pockets. I talked to an older fellow who, for thirty years, had been visiting the same diner, The Sunny Egg, every morning. He told me that most of the natives sold their land to developers and relocated. Every now and then, I could imagine them, the natives, sitting on a beach somewhere, sipping cocktails with one of those tiny umbrellas hanging from the glass. The thought of Berksville being consumed with commercial businesses, even till this day, breaks my heart. For me, those lands were sacred. Meant to be untouched.

I was born May 13, 1965, and raised in a household where a little thing called music seemed unobtainable. Most of the music around us came from the sounds of the land, "the salt of the earth," my father said, the workingman, the whistling postman, the humming farmer, or the church. Unlike most musicians, I accidentally stumbled into music. My parents weren't musicians, nor were they music lovers by any means. Going to church every Sunday morning and listening to the choir sing psalms from the gospel were about all the music they had ever known. My father, who worked as a dairy farmer, once told me about "The Voice of the Land." If you traveled through the desolate roads of Wellbird County, he preached, through the small town of Berksville, you could hear that voice scattered over the land, through the pastures or cornfields. If you listened closely, it was there in different shapes and sizes. My father didn't know much about anything outside Berksville (naïve, I might say), but he certainly knew the land and how to nurture it and live off it and how not to rely on anyone but yourself and the land. The Voice was there, as my father preached. Sometimes that voice didn't consists of words at all but took the form of a whistle or a hum or a chant. Other times, that voice was rich and hearty; it sang with stripes, the laws of the land. If you traveled down Ridgemont, the town over, you could hear one particular voice, my father's. His voice would spread like wildfire over a wheat field. Mostly, he sang church songs. It was a treat to hear that voice, either coming from my father or even my mother hanging up soggy clothes on the laundry wire. It was a way of saying, "I'm here, contributing, providing, belonging, working to the sound of my own beat."

When my cousin Renée and I went into the city for the first time, I caught a glimpse of the music outside Wellbird. And it wasn't far off from my father's Voice of the Land.

One day, I found that voice and so too did a recluse man who went by the name of Benny Jacobs. It was getting late into the afternoon. I was taking one of my daily walks through the fields when I heard a crack below my feet. I couldn't remember anything from the moment I fell until the moment I woke up in a dark entrapment. I fell at least twenty feet into the earth. A couple of days later after I recovered, I found out that the hole was used as a passage during slavery. The passage was no longer accessible. Over time, each tunnel had collapsed from the weight of the earth. If I had known that men and women, brothers and sisters, resided in these very dark quarters of the earth, I don't know if I would've survived. The trauma would've been too hard on me. Hours dragged on. The moon was out, giving little light. The loneliness woke up something inside of me. . . that voice. The only thing I remember about that night was singing about not being scared. Growing up as a shy girl, the idea of singing out loud was daunting enough. But I sang! My voice was rich and hearty like my father's. I didn't care who heard me. I just sang from the top of my lungs. Somehow, our neighbor, Benny, heard that voice, my voice. I remember hearing the sound of footsteps. I looked up through the glistening hole above. There it was, Benny's gauntly face trapped in the moonlight. He said he heard an angel singing from over the hill. Benny followed the singing, this so called "angel." Somehow, my voice led him to me. Once I was safely brought home (besides the state of shock I was in, I only suffered a bruised knee), Benny went on about this singing angel to my parents. They thought Benny was sort of nuts, in a way. He lost his wife to tuberculosis. He was a faithless man, an untrustworthy man who didn't talk to many people. My parents didn't believe Benny. But they didn't ignore what Benny explained to them. They decided to make me join the local church choir. At first, I didn't know how to sing. When I was alone in the hole, I didn't have anyone around me to judge me. I took that same approach to singing. Apparently, I was good at something. Prior to falling in that hole, I was always good at being "The Pest" or "The Girl Who Chases Chickens" or "The Trespasser." Now, I was a "singer." It went on like this for about ten years: singing in choir, going to school, studying, playing with friends, experimenting with other instruments, and then, not to mention, singing in the choir. Nothing really changed for me. When I was around the age of seventeen, these twin pale-looking brothers approached me after Sunday Mass. They said they were looking for a soulful voice and that I was just whom they were looking for. I went back to their house and listened to their own music in their parents' attic. A month later, we went on to create a band. That band was called Like Heroin. Again, I started to fall into another routine: singing in a band now, serving coffee on the side, bartending at night. There was still a hole in my life, one that could easily swallow me whole if I wasn't careful.

Before Henry sprinted from the locker room, Coach Boland pulled him aside as the other teammates flooded the court.

He tentatively asked, "Are you sure you can play?"

"Of course, Coach," Henry responded, his breath increasing from the adrenaline. "I'm good. She'd want me to play."

The coach smiled.

"Forget what I told you earlier," Coach Boland said to Henry. "Pretend like he's not even here."

Henry bobbed his head.

"Yes, Coach."

"Then, you go give 'em hell!"

Coach Boland slapped Henry on the back.

Henry ran onto the court with his arms raised in the air. He pumped his fist above his head, which caused a sudden uproar from the crowd, one side cheering and the other booing.

In the last remaining quarter, Henry was a foul away from fouling out of the game. He only had ten points and three rebounds, which, to him, was a bad game. Most of the opposing players were double-teaming Henry and leaving him no room to score a basket. However, his defense was absolutely stellar. He had six blocked shots and eight steals.

The Haddon Big Cats had the ball with eleven seconds left on the clock.

The score: HADDON 84 MADISON 86.

As Coach Boland mapped out the play on the sidelines, Henry suddenly drifted off into a trance.

The strange melody from last night's dream was gradually coming back to him.

Before he could put his ears to it, a beat had taken over.

At first, it sounded as if someone was pounding away at a door.

A loud *thud* and rattle.

Then, the pounding gained rhythm and vitality.

For the entire game, it had been there, that beat, slowly and yet constantly *click*, *click*, *click* clicking away. He could hear that beat as if it was inches away from his ear, a tiny drummer boy with some teeth on him.

Henry pulled himself from the huddle and gazed around the courts in paranoia.

The atmosphere darkened.

Lights dimmed.

A sudden breeze, blowing around the basketball nets, poured into the openings of the coliseum.

The breeze whispered. . .

". . . *Henry*. . ." Coach Boland slapped his hand over his knee. "Are you with us?"

Henry snapped from his trance.

The breeze suddenly stopped.

"Yeah, Coach," he said, shaking his head. "I'm here."

"The second you get open, you take the shot," Coach Boland said, his eyes wide and engaging.

Henry was slow to bob his head.

"I won't let you down, Coach."

"All right." The coach put his hand in the middle of the huddle. "Put it in, guys."

The rest of the team put their hands over one another.

The coach shouted, "Big Cats on three!"

They pushed down three times into the pile of sweaty hands and furiously yelled out, "BIG CATS!"

The shooting guard, Wyllie Randall, inbounded the ball to center, Jackson, nicknamed "The Hurt," who waited for Mansard to set the pick for Henry.

Once Mansard set a pick, Henry, who was wearing the number 5 over his beige and burgundy jersey, juked around from an opposing player and found himself wide open.

Three seconds remained on the clock.

Two. . .

The Hurt passed the ball to Henry.

One. . .

Unmanned, Henry squared his shoulders to the basket and shot the three pointer.

As the ball soared through the air, the crowd went dead silent.

The basketball hit the backside of the rim and fell to the court.

Before the Hurt could tap the ball into the basket, the buzzer suddenly went off!

Hands went flying in the air like synchronized swimmers.

The hometown crowd erupted with a deafening roar of victory.

As players drifted back toward their opposing benches, a stampede of fans rushed onto the court while Henry stood there in shock with his head hanging downward.

Fans darted past a deflated Henry, shoving him around like a pinball.

Once the security guards cleared a path for the coaches and other players, Coach Boland approached a stocky man who was dressed in all black.

"I really thought he was going to make that shot," the stocky man said to Coach Boland.

"What can you do?" Coach Boland said, shrugging his shoulders. "You win some. You lose some. You can't always count on one man to win the ballgame for you."

"He's got the skill to play for the NBA, Kip," Tom, the scout, said closely. "There's no question about that. I just don't know if he's quite ready to roll with the big dogs."

Coach Boland pulled the scout closer—fans moving and cheering all around them.

"Listen, Tom," the coach whispered into his ear. "How long have we known each other?"

A grin flashed over the corner of Tom's face.

"Too long," he said.

"Give the kid another chance."

The scout paused for a moment.

"I'll think about it," he said.

"Kid's mother is sick, Tom," Coach Boland said. "He's got a lot on his mind. Show a little compassion."

"That's no excuse for losing," the scout said callously as he walked off.

Not a peep in the team locker room.

Coach Boland sat down next to Henry on the bench. A damp towel was hanging over Henry's head and eyes.

"It's happens to the best of us, Henry," the coach said as he patted Henry on the knee.

Henry sniffled.

"I blew it, Coach," he said to the floor.

Coach Boland breathed out a sigh and threw his lucky pink hand towel over his shoulder.

"I know you are going through a lot right now, Henry," he said and then paused. "But let me ask you something. Are you having fun out there?"

Henry slowly raised his head from his curled shoulders and glared at the coach. His eyes were like red dots underneath the lip of the white towel.

"What I meant to say, Henry, is that for the entire season you looked as if you were going through the motions," he said. "Where is that drive that you had last year? You almost look like. . . a completely different ball player out there."

"Maybe I am going through the motions," Henry said soberly. "I guess. . . I'm just confused."

"Confused about what?"

Henry didn't have an answer for the coach's question.

"The talent is there, son," Coach Boland said closely as he pointed his finger at Henry's chest. "But talent, talent doesn't mean a damn thing when your heart is not working on the same page."

FOUR

FOR the rest of the night, Henry pondered over Coach Boland's remark about his dedication to basketball.

In the back of his mind, he knew Coach was right about everything, his talent, and most importantly, his heart, and how he wasn't into the sport that he had grown to both love and hate.

During his junior and senior year in high school, Henry had become close to Coach Boland. Back then, the greasy haired man who wore way too much aftershave was known as Kip, not Coach Boland or simply Coach. Kip and Henry frequently talked over the telephone like old pals catching up. Kip would check up on him to make sure he was staying out of trouble, making good grades, studying, that sort of thing. On more than one occasion, Kip visited Henry at his home and ate diner with him and his mother. But what Kip didn't know was that Henry wasn't being completely honest with him when he asked Henry what other hobbies or interests he had as a child.

"Basketball," Henry told Kip with a straight face. "All I did as a kid was play basketball. Playing was like tying my shoes."

The following day the coach's remark gnawed away at Henry and left him in a vanquished state. The night before he didn't get any sleep. When he got ready for class, he did exactly what Coach Boland mentioned to him in the locker room and went through the motions. Henry went to class. He took notes. He left class. He talked to a couple of his friends in the courtyard. Most of the time he ate his lunch on the go. Henry drifted through all of these things, but he wasn't *all* there.

When the day finally ended, Henry decided to pack for the weekend and pay a visit to his mother in Queens Dive, a small town on the outskirts of Lansford.

On the way back home, Henry took a detour through Reddington. He cruised by their old house on Davie Morris, which looked nothing like he remembered. There was a family with younger kids who lived there. Toys and plastic play sets were piled and scattered around the backyard like a junkyard. The owners even added on a separate garage next to the house, as well as cast iron bars around the windows. The owners also painted the siding from the old color, which was peach, to lime green. Then, Henry saw Kerri's house across the street. It remained just the way he had remembered (yellow with black shutters), although it appeared much smaller. Henry was astonished how things appeared so much bigger when he was younger, even Holiday's. When he was younger, Holiday's was like a museum of ancient belongings and lost treasures. Earlier, when he drove past Holiday's, it looked like a storage room of clutter, a hoarder's wet dream. The sight of the house brought back a ripple of memories, none of them any good.

On some nights when Henry was alone, he would sit on the porch or around the porch or on the roof of his house or on the front lawn, gaze at the stars above or read comic books or scour for lizards or spiders or crickets to keep in his bedroom aquarium, which, within a day or two ended up going right back outside followed with his mother barking "Those damn things belong outside, not in my house!" As time went by, which, when Henry was a kid, seemed as if it couldn't go by quick enough, he always wondered if Kerri would have the nerve to take the next step, forget about his stutter or the accident with the basketball, and finally cross the street with genial exchange. Her father, Roy Coleridge, who played seven years as a defensive linebacker in the NFL until a three hundred pound guard came crashing down on his leg during a fumble and sent his knee ninety degrees in the opposite direction, didn't care much for Henry nor any of his friends for that matter. Her father was a Herculean man who walked around with a chip on his shoulder (the kids in the neighborhood had plenty of nicknames for him like *Meathead* or *No Neck*, but they never dared to say those names in front of him). At times, Henry, who, unlike the other kids on Davie Morris, wasn't the least scared of Mr. Coleridge (only false impressions), wondered if he was the reason why his daughter seemed so uninterested. Breaking his daughter's nose didn't earn him any points either. With the accident aside, Henry thought maybe he had a short leash on Kerri to keep her in line. After all, she was only fifteen years old. Regardless, Henry's intentions were always good. The word *sex* didn't even cross Henry's mind until the age of sixteen or seventeen. Back then, it was like a murmur or a distorted moan or a scrambling television screen on one of those higher channels, and the most that he and his friends had ever seen was a nipple or a bush or a resemblance of a leg. Throughout the day, he would always leave an invitation open for Kerri: a promising smile, a long gaze, a wave, a signal to play with his other friends, or an attempt to impress her with his amazing dribbling skills. Twice, he had knocked on Kerri's front door, once a couple of weeks after the accident and another before he left Reddington, but there was no answer. His mother was well aware of the feelings that her son had for Kerri (days after they left Reddington, it had all become clear to her when she witnessed the withdrawal symptoms: her son's loss of weight, the irritability, never leaving his bedroom). Whenever his mother was at home taking care of Henry, she did everything in her power to keep his mind on basketball and not on the "immature white girl across the street," such as calling out "supper" whenever she saw the two together outside, when, in fact, supper wasn't close to being ready, or patrolling the front lawn like some kind of savage predator whenever Kerri was playing with her friends, or keeping her distance from Mr. and Mrs. Coleridge. Maybe she knew something that I didn't know. Maybe she knew that Kerri wasn't interested in me and, if she was, she was just leading me on for fun, something to tell her friends about over a sleepover, some kind of sick joke. *Games*, he reminded himself. *It was all a game.* At times, Henry felt like a prisoner, smothering and suffocating from his mother's mental grip over him. Many times, he thought about suicide. Even the word *suicide* was like tittle-tattle around the other kids. They had heard the word before in the news or in the papers, but they didn't know people could actually do it. Once or twice, Henry thought about the steak knife in the kitchen drawer downstairs. Thought about sliding it vertically across his wrist and watching all the blood in his body pour out. He could do it like they do in the movies, Henry thought, and do it in the bathtub. Then when his mother found him, the water would be stained with red. Another time, he thought about going to the Smithen Steel Mill, climbing up to the top of the building, and jumping off. Then, she would finally leave Henry alone and not force anything on him. There would be no more pressure, no more pain, most importantly, no more smothering. Then, there were those thoughts of running away. Many times, he thought about staying at Uncle Charlie's house. Sooner or later, Charles would have to tell Abbey about her son, her Henry. Many nights, though, it had been exactly that, contemplating or planning or just wondering "what if." Kerri was probably *engaged* now, he thought, probably *to a rich man* (appeared like the type) who would treat her like the Queen of England. Wherever Kerri may be in life, Henry wondered, he hoped she was happy with her life. You know. The whole package: husband, dog, children, and job. Happy.

Last but not least, he drove by Ms. Craft's house, which appeared abandoned and different from what he imagined. The house was now a one-story house, not two. The previous owners were planning on adding another section to the house, but the job was postponed. Reasons unknown.

Henry parked the car and stepped out.

He saw a FORECLOSURE sign on the front lawn.

As he stepped into the lawn, a middle-aged woman, who was taking a nightly walk, passed by Henry's car.

"Excuse me, ma'am," Henry said, turning around.

"Yes," she said cautiously.

"Did you know the people who used to live in this house?" he asked, pointing at the house.

"Mr. and Mrs. Ellington."

"How long have they lived here?"

"No more than a year I suppose," she answered. "Ever since I moved here four years ago, at least three other families have lived in that house there. Between you and me, I think it's, " the woman carefully glanced around the dark street, "haunted."

"Haunted?"

"Strange," she said. "Isn't it?"

"Yeah," Henry said sarcastically. "That is strange."

"So, do you live around here?"

"Yeah," Henry answered. "I did. I used to live in that house over there."

Henry motioned to his old house.

"Taking a trip down memory lane."

Henry was somewhat turned off by the woman's assumptions.

"I guess you could say that," he said vacantly.

"So, what's your interest in this house?" she asked as she pointed at the house.

"I used to know the woman who lived here."

"You must mean Dolores Craft."

"That's right," Henry said curiously.

"The neighbors who have been here longer than me told me about her. They said she did strange things over there, rituals. They think she belonged to. . . " the woman leaned in closer, ". . . a cult." Henry couldn't believe what he was hearing. "They also told me about the fire. Said it was her goat that caused the fire."

"Goat?" Henry uttered, his cheeks flushed.

The woman whispered, "You know. . . like witchcraft. She was actually sacrificing the goat. Pretty scary, huh? I tell you. You have to be careful out there. There are a lot of creeps nowadays. I even get the goosebumps every time I walk by that house." She leaned in ever closer. "That's between you and me."

Henry shook his head in disgust and walked to his car.

The woman stood in bafflement.

Before Henry stepped back into his car, he spun around and clinched his jaw in rage.

"It's people like you. . . " Henry seethed, ". . . forget it." His voice trailed off. "You're not even worth it."

Henry got inside the car and slammed the door.

FIVE

OVER an hour later, Henry found himself parked outside Charles's office building on the outskirts of downtown Lansford.

Drumming his fingers against the steering wheel, he said to himself, "This is crazy."

He finally decided to shut off the ignition.

"Fuck it," he whispered and got out of the car.

Henry walked up to the large building and entered via a revolving door. A hunchback janitor, who was waxing the marble floors with a professional buffer, acknowledged Henry through his thick bifocals.

"Good evening, sir," he said over the noisy buffer and moved his way across the lobby like a turtle.

As Henry went to push the UP button on the metallic panel on the wall, the triangular light above the elevator lit up red.

A loud *ding* followed!

The two elevator doors to the far left opened. Henry eased his way over to the open elevator. There he was, Charles, with satchel in hand, ready to exit the elevator. His eyes trailed from the floor and up at Henry.

Dumbfounded, Charles said, "Henry? What. . . this is a surprise. What brings you here?"

Henry was looking around, mainly at the exotic plants perched in the corners of the lobby.

"I see you spruced up the place a bit," he said with a tremor in his voice.

Charles observed Henry's unsettled state and stepped from the elevator.

"Is something wrong, Henry?"

In response, Henry shook his head and said, "I. . . I just need. . . needed someone to talk to."

"I see. . . " Charles trailed off and then paused in thought. He pointed to the revolving doors. "I was just on the way out. How about a cup of coffee? I know a great place just down the street. They have the best coffee."

"Yeah," Henry said with a shrug. "Sure."

Since the family owned coffee shop, Cup of Joe, a popular hangout among the locals and late night business types, was only a block away from the office and, unlike the chained coffee shops, stayed open for twenty-four hours a day (Joe Burke, the owner who opened Cup of Joe after he left Wall Street in 1985, ran the coffee shop during the day while his two sons, Dean and Carl, ran the coffee shop at night), Charles and Henry decided to walk. "Besides," Charles told Henry, "I've been sitting all day and I could really stretch out my legs." On the walk over to Cup of Joe, they didn't really say much at all. Mostly, it was small talk. Henry had never expressed what had been bothering him for these past couple of days. Not yet. They kept it simple: catching up on how they had been doing or how Abbey had been holding up or talking about basketball or Henry's grades.

When they arrived at Cup of Joe, Charles ordered two large cups of coffee, one for Henry and the other for himself, as well as a cinnamon roll. At the serving station, Henry loaded up his cup of coffee with cream and sugar whereas Charles drank his black. They picked a booth near the back of the shop where Charles removed his trench coat and placed it over the seat next to his satchel. For a couple of minutes, they sat mostly in silence and sipped from their steaming coffee. Henry was pinching off pieces of the cinnamon roll and placing them into his mouth. Mostly, nibbling. He followed each nibble with a sip of coffee.

"So, Henry," Charles said finally and kept his hands warm around the cup of coffee, "what's been bothering you?"

Henry mumbled, "Nothing."

"You sure?"

Henry responded with a shrug of his shoulders.

"Henry, I haven't seen you in four years," Charles said. "Now, you show up out of the blue at my office. How are you sleeping?"

"Good," he said quietly. "I guess."

"It's the dreams," Charles said, tilting his head. "You're having the dreams again. Aren't you?"

"No," he said. "I mean. . . not like I had before. These are different."

"Different how?"

Henry didn't respond.

"What is it, Henry?"

"I don't know," he said with his eyes glazing over. He took two more nibbles from the cinnamon roll and washed the bites down with a sip of coffee. "I just. . . I feel like I'm. . . like. . . like I'm lost again. Like I'm that fifteen year old kid again who doesn't have a fucking clue what he wants to do with his life."

"What about basketball?"

Henry shook his head.

"I don't know," he mumbled.

Charles leaned forward and looked into Henry's eyes, which were scattered around the table. Henry briefly pulled them up at Charles. In that moment of recollection, Charles witnessed the emptiness inside Henry's eyes as though whatever soul he had behind the eyes was drifting through purgatory.

"Listen, Henry," he said over a drawn out sigh, "I know the last time we spoke. . . it wasn't the most pleasant. A lot of things were said about your mother, about what she did, about her past, your father's, about my past, none of which I've shared with anybody."

"So," Henry said, his eyes sharpening as he shot upright in his seat, "you think because you told me all those things about you and my mother, how you two were once a couple, that. . . what. . . it's supposed to make our relationship better."

"I didn't say that, Henry," Charles said calmly. "I told you the truth."

"You think what you did to me was right?"

"No, Henry," Charles said and moved the cup of coffee aside. "It wasn't right what we did to you." He placed his hand over his chest. "What I did to you," he said clearly. "But things just happened. I fell. . ." he cleared his throat, ". . . I wanted to turn your mother in, Henry. By law, if someone admits to committing a murder I have to report it to the authorities. You don't know how many nights I spent awake, thinking about going to the authorities, but I didn't, Henry. I could've, but I didn't because. . ."

"Because what?"

"I loved your mother, Henry," Charles said, his eyes glazed like Henry's. "And I did all that I could to protect her even if it meant telling her son that I was his uncle because she was too ashamed to admit to him that she was clinically insane. That's why it's so hard to see her, especially like that. . . I'm sorry, Henry. I truly am."

Henry leaned over the table.

"How do you think I feel, Charles?" he asked as he furrowed his brows into a sharp angle. "You think I like seeing her that way. Well, I don't."

Charles let out another sigh, shorter.

"Listen, Henry," he said, "I know our relationship hasn't been the same ever since. . . I got myself caught up in a lie, Henry. If I knew it was going to affect our friendship the way it did, then I would've never lied to you." Charles reached across the table and held out his hand. "I want to be your friend again, Henry. If you'll let me. . . "

Henry glanced down at Charles's open palm.

"Thanks for the coffee, Charles," Henry said, exaggerating the name *Charles*.

Next, Henry got up from the booth and exited the coffee shop.

By the time Henry arrived at the townhouse, his mother was already asleep. Without making any noise, he carefully opened the front door and carried his things inside.

After he settled his things on the floor, he accidentally shut the front door harder than expected.

In the wake of the door closing, he heard a person stirring upstairs.

Two tiny thuds followed.

"Henry. . ." a strung out voice said from the top of the landing.

"It's me, Mom," he said quietly and found his mother slouching forward over the landing.

From where he stood, she remained nothing more than a dark silhouette, a frail and wretched one.

"Wha. . . whaaa. . . what are you doing home, Henry?" Abbey whined, scratchy her crusty eyes. "You didn't call."

Henry walked up the stairs and embraced his mother at the top of the landing.

"I wanted to surprise you."

"Henry. . ."

"I'm here, Mom," he said into his mother's shoulder. He could feel her skeleton in his arms. The odor on her body was unnatural and synthetic. "I didn't mean to wake you. You should be in bed." He gazed around the bedroom. "Where's the aide?"

"I sent Odyssey home," Abbey said, grimacing. "She was getting on my damn nerves. Trying to tell me what to do all the damn time. I swear. 'Don't tell me what to do.' I don't take orders from some fat white girl! As a matter of fact, I've about had it with her!"

"I thought you two were close."

"Not anymore."

"That's not the first time I've heard you say that."

"Well, no more!" she exclaimed. "I've had it!"

"She's just trying to help, Mom."

"I don't need her damn help."

"Yes," Henry said with frustration. "You most certainly do. You can't do this on your own." Henry walked his mother to the bed. "Trust me," he said. "Things will be better tomorrow. You just need to get some sleep."

The excitement briefly flashed over Abbey's face.

"Maybe I can move closer to you, Henry."

"Near Haddon?" Henry snorted and eased his mother's puny body into bed. "Don't think so."

Abbey said weakly, "It's just nice to see you, Henry."

As Henry tucked Abbey into the covers, she grabbed a hold of Henry's hand.

"You know I wanted to go so badly," she said with the anguish carefully etched in her face. "I didn't have the strength."

"It's okay," he said stiffly. "It wasn't much of a game anyway."

"I heard it on the radio," Abbey said and rubbed the top of Henry's hand. "You have nothing to be ashamed of."

Henry paused.

"My team was counting on me," he said, the tears building in his eyes.

"Don't talk like that, Henry."

Abbey studied the disappointment in her son's face.

"Henry, listen to me," Abbey said. "Nobody is perfect." Her glossy eyes drifted into a state of reflection. "For the longest time, I've been running away from myself, my past. I never had a chance to face that woman. I left her in the dust. Alone, Henry. Starving." Her pale eyes drifted toward the bedroom window and stayed there. "I have regrets, Henry, so many regrets."

"I thought. . ."

"I do, Henry," Abbey whined and faced Henry. "I never want you to feel like this, to live with regret. It is a cancer. And if you let it, it will eat away everything that was once good inside."

In her older age, Abbey had a way of carefully explaining things to her son. She told him about the cancer and how it was like a spider slowly crawling through her body.

Abbey squeezed Henry's hand.

"What is it, Mom?"

"Don't be so hard on yourself."

"Mom. . ."

"I'm sorry, Henry," Abbey cried. "I just wanted what was best for you."

"Don't do this. . . not now. . ."

"It's your time, Henry," she said convincingly. "Soon, you will be a man. The question is: What kind of man will you be?"

That night, Henry hit the streets of uptown Lansford.

It was a perfect spring night for a stroll.

Not too cold.

Not too hot.

Just perfect.

The air was unseasonably dry.

The plants and trees around Henry, like dogwoods and azaleas, were in the early stages of blooming.

He came across a bright neon flyer stapled to a wooden street post.

The flyer read: "Open Mike Night at Hot Foxy Saturday Night!"

Henry plucked the flyer from the post.

Once more, he scanned over the enticing flyer.

An image ran like a shiver through his mind, same one from earlier. The image nearly knocked the wind out of him. It was that same image of an older woman, still pretty with age, who was sitting on a bench in front of a piano. The detail filled around her, black and white picture frames on the walls, and old advertisement signs in the corners. He saw one in particular: *Clover Soda.* As he had seen before, the woman wasn't sitting with her back toward him. Yet, she was staring at him with big, bright eyes. However, the eyes weren't terrifying. They were calm and reassuring. And Henry was only a young boy. Fourteen or fifteen, he believed. After Henry shook the image from his mind, he stuck the flyer in his pocket and went on his way.

It was her, Henry thought, the *older woman in my dreams. She was trying to tell me something.*

Around midnight, Henry arrived back at the townhouse. His legs were tired from walking all night. He was starving too. He hadn't eaten a thing for dinner, only a granola bar he ate on the ride over.

With the stars glimmering above, he stood at the front steps of the townhouse and wondered where all of the images came from, the dreams, *that beat.* Now, that beat was as hot as fire. Throughout his teenage years, as well as the start of his freshman year at Haddon University, that beat had been there—slowly burning away. Soon, he realized, the fire would die out if he didn't channel that beat into something physical, something audible. Soon, he realized, everything that he had dreamed of as a child, the music, the spotlights, the fame, the glory, and the girls would all die out with the fire. Henry couldn't see himself becoming his mother, a shriveled down person who lived with regret, a victim. Now, he had a chance to make things right, to live without regrets, to *not* be a victim.

The fire was back all right, blazing, crisping into an undefiled beat again.

Without waking his mother, Henry tiptoed to his old bedroom and carefully opened the closet door.

His moonlit eyes grew in wonderful madness.

Henry kneeled down to the shaggy carpet floor and removed his mother's floral bed sheet from the case.

A cloud of dust kicked up into the air and caused Henry to momentarily shield his face with the backside of his forearm.

As he concealed his cough with his arm, he waved away the cloud of dust with his other hand.

After the dust cleared, he grabbed the key from his piggy bank and unlocked the padlock over the leather case, now chapped like winter lips.

He untwined and then peeled away the rusty galvanized chains from the case.

As Henry held in his breath (both from the dust particles and the anticipation), he cautiously opened the saxophone case.

Adrian was revealed before his eyes, waiting, glistening in the brilliant moonlight. Brand new!

He reached inside and carefully removed Adrian from the case and cradled the saxophone in his arms as if it was a newborn baby.

From *Missing the Edges*, page 28:

The great singers I listened to when I was a little girl played at least one instrument. Growing up outside the plains of Wellbird County where microwaves didn't yet exist (televisions were rare like Loch Ness Monsters in the Hudson River and radios were the only mediums to the outside world), I yearned to be among that superlative group of singers: Hendrix and his guitar, Dylan and his harmonica, me and my bagpipes. Soon, it went from bagpipes to the accordion. Then, the flute. At the age of seventeen, I gave up trying to fit an instrument on my belt and concentrated on something that I was good at.

Every Saturday afternoon, Renée would drive forty minutes from the small town of Collinsville and take me to the local record store in town. The first time I saw Bob Dylan was when he was a poster hanging on the wall like a god of Olympia next to a couple of other musicians whom I didn't know at the time. I remember Bob Dylan from that patent black suit and Wayfarer shades and his skinny, Casper-like appearance. Renée told me who the "handsome, Elvis-looking man" was next to Mr. Dylan. She told me his name was Conway Twitty.

At the time, I didn't know exactly who the man was or what kind of music he sang or what instrument he played. Whoever this Conway Twitty man was, he was somebody who was admired, worshiped.

Later that evening, I skipped dinner and spent hours gazing at the stars, trying to imagine my poster next to Mr. Dylan and Mr. Twitty and all of the other great musicians on that wall.

SIX

SOMEWHERE, the dust was still loitering.

Henry woke to a sharp, hoarse voice screaming out his name. Even though the voice was so far away (like several miles away), the voice penetrated his ears like a drop of water through a sieve.

Shivering, he shot upright from bed.

The atmosphere was different from when he lay himself down to sleep: warm with a strange stench in the air. *Sulfur,* he thought. He knew that stench all too well, the sulfur. When he was younger, his mother brought him to the Depot on father appreciation day. Since he didn't have a father, his mother filled both shoes. There, his mother introduced Henry to the other employees around the warehouse, including Tony, aka "The Tiger" due to his heavily built upper frame. Tony worked in receiving, which was located in the back of the store near the loading docks where the shipping trucks would drop off all of the merchandise. The stench, Henry remembered. *How could I forget?* Tony said it was the sulfur from the forklift charger and that every now and then the "god, I mean, the gosh darn thing leaks."

The smell was strong enough to burn the hairs from his nostrils.

That smell, he realized, was the same smell in the air.

The smell, however, was indistinct and somewhat tolerable.

Somewhere, though, the dust was still lingering. The air was heavy, not only from the sulfur, but also from the dust. His face, especially the tip of his nose, was as cold as a glacier. A warm breeze was building around him.

The heat, he thought. *Then why am I so cold?*

The strange air had a thickness, one that was coming from the land.

The dust, Henry assumed.

His eyes traced along the comforter and fell to the shag. He soon realized there was no floor, no shag, only dirt and rubble. His feet were bare.

No! Shoes. . . now steel-toed boots!

The sound of a generator was purring from a distance.

Henry moved his eyes around the vast open land.

The same breeze from before was building now.

Warmer.

Eventually, Henry's body thawed, including his nose and fingertips. The tip of his nose was now runny with phlegm. His entire bedroom was no more. But. . . gone?

The walls had been pulled back.

The clouds were masking the moon and stars, leaving just enough light to see the open land.

He sharpened his peer.

All Henry could see was the land, a barren, debris-filled land, a gray desert that stretched as far as he could see, covered in the thickening dust.

No sign of civilization for miles.

The only material that remained in his bedroom was, in fact, his bed.

Everything was. . . gone.

What is going on?

How did my bed get all the way out here?

Henry stepped onto the rugged ground blemished with broken boards and rocks and all kinds of foreign debris.

For miles, Henry wandered through the desert.

During his travels, he protected his face from the dust. So sharp it was, the dust, like thorns over his skin. Still, he hadn't seen an iota of life anywhere around. He could only see about twenty or so feet ahead of him.

The land was death, no vegetation, no life.

Just death.

Along the journey across the deserted land, he tripped over a hard object protruding from the parched earth. He kneeled down and saw a pile of scattered bones. He inched closer. The bones were from an animal. He recognized the long snout, the canine, the claws. Whatever the thing was, it had shared the same fate as the land.

After two more miles of wandering, Henry came across a glimmer of light inside the cloud of dust.

The dust cleared enough for Henry to see the alluring light residing over a hill. The light was coming from a concrete structure, he thought, small in size.

Henry quickened his walk.

He finally arrived at the perfectly squared structure that was no bigger than a small shed.

The door was open and cast a brilliant white light from inside. About a hundred feet to his right, he spotted a massive vent in the ground.

Curious, Henry walked inside the facility.

Eventually, his eyes adjusted to the bright light of the white hallway, which trailed downward into another hallway. There were automatic doors lining each side of the hallway.

A prison, he thought.

As a looming suspicion crept over his thoughts, Henry suddenly turned to his immediate right and flinched.

A guard was standing frozenly next to the open door.

Once he realized the guard was artificial, as if the thing had been pulled from a television, he breathed a sigh of relief.

The guard was dressed in black Kevlar. Its skin was pallid and grainy like an old television screen.

He reached out and carefully brushed his finger through the hologram. The frame shifted and scrambled a bit, but then returned to its normal pose.

Henry snorted.

"You gotta to be kidding me," he said to himself.

As Henry made his way down the steps (an underground facility, he acknowledged) and into yet another hallway, the hologram's eyes turned toward Henry's back.

Henry got halfway down the hallway until that looming suspicion crept back over him.

His palms became sweaty while other parts of his body became swampy.

Henry pulled his eyes down to the glistening white floor and witnessed a dark blood trail. The blood was old and yet smelly.

He followed the trail up the wall.

The blood took the shape of a handprint near a keypad.

Henry asked himself, "What the hell happened here?"

Behind Henry, the eye of the hologram pulled from the socket and took dimensionality.

The eye madly spun around.

Eventually, the eye stabilized and inaudibly hovered down the steps and into the same hallway.

As the eye idled above Henry, Henry glanced inside the window of a cell and witnessed a bald man sitting in the corner with his back facing the door. He was crazily rocking back and forth, bashing the side of his fist against the center of his forehead. Henry only caught a glimpse of his face. A pink scar ran like a lightning bolt down the side of his face. His left eye was all white and glossy. The strange man suddenly turned his shoulder and revealed his entire face to Henry.

Before Henry could make out the face in its entirety, he pulled himself away from the window and followed the blood trail down the hallway.

The holographic eye kept a distance as it followed the visitor through the hallway.

Henry rounded a corner, which caused the eye to reroute.

The blood trail led to a thin Native American man who was curled over the floor. His clothes were casual: blue flannel with jeans. Behind his ear, he had a hawk's feather beaded around his tightly braided ponytail.

"Hello. . . " Henry said softly.

The man grunted and slowly came to.

He looked around with urgency. It took him some time to understand that Henry was standing there, waiting for the man to say something, anything.

The man drew his eyes on Henry and said frantically, "Who are you?"

"I'm Henry."

"Henry? You're not Henry."

"Of course I am."

"Did He bring you here too?"

The eye reached the end of the hallway where it mounted over a tiny fixture inside a keypad. A mechanical arm projected from the keypad and scanned the eye. Once the scan was COMPLETE (followed with a green light flashing merrily over the screen), the device automatically folded back into the wall.

There was a click and then a sharp hiss!

A curling smoke poured from an opening panel.

"Who?"

The man's eyes widened with fear.

Behind Henry, a tall silhouette stepped away from the wall. The tall robotic thing was stalking down the hallway. The man was too afraid to speak from the sight of the strange thing creeping closer to Henry. He quickly curled up against the wall and bawled. He tried to scream, but he was left in shock, gasping.

Henry exclaimed, "Who brought me here?"

"It's already too late," the man whined.

In the corner of Henry's eye, he saw a young man, possibly the one "who" the frightened man was rambling on about.

As the tall figure stalked closer to Henry, he glanced through the window of the cell.

The room was familiar, homey.

Ms. Craft was sitting behind a piano, giving lessons to a young man sitting with his legs crossed on the carpet.

Next, Henry noticed the black and white picture frames on the wall.

Before he could make sense of what was going on, the hologram, the prisoner, the bloody man, the young man, he suddenly found himself sitting on a carpet.

Henry glanced over his hands in awe. They were much smaller, shrunken. He was also wearing a red striped long sleeve tee shirt and a pair of blue jeans. And his legs were crossed in an Indian style position. The things around the homey room appeared much larger in size: those black and white picture frames, the product advertisements.

"I remember when I was your age, I wanted to be a nurse just like my mother," Ms. Craft said to young Henry. "She was my hero. She was the kind of woman who would take care of another person before taking care of herself. She truly loved helping people." Ms. Craft tilted her head in deep thought. "I got to thinking about what I wanted to do when I grew up. I finally came to the conclusion that I was not my mother. I was my own person. So, I asked myself: 'What if there was a way I could take care of people, as my mother did, but without following in my mother's footsteps?' That was when I journeyed inward. Music." Her voice climbed with passion. "Music is the one pastime that will always nourish the human spirit. Music is life. It's all around us. It's in the air we breathe, Henry. The sounds of nature." Ms. Craft's face filled with great wonder. "It's power! Music, Henry, music has the power to bring all walks of life together! So what better way to help people than to make timeless music for them and, of course, rule the world?" The comment provoked a chuckle from young Henry, mainly the *"rule the world"* part. "Sure. It would take hard work and responsibility. But it would most certainly be worth it." Her voice dampened, almost in reflection. "Over time, I felt like giving up. Then, it came to me, my voice. Like my soul was holding on to this new energy source, my voice. I discovered my voice when I was at my lowest state. It was always in there, lurking around. I just had to find it. And when I did, I was complete. I never did it for the money. Most of the money I earned went to charities and hospitals. Nowadays, it's different. You see these musicians doing commercials, acting in movies, coming up with their own clothing lines. We've lost touch." Mrs. Craft pointed to her chest. "I, Henry," she said, "I lost touch. Then. . ." a smile crept onto her face, ". . . then, I met you." Her voice dampened yet again, reflective. "Sebastian and I, we tried many times to have children. Over many attempts, a harrowing feeling came over me. We visited doctors. Not just one. They all told me the same thing: I was barren. For so long, I cursed God. 'Why me?' I asked. But then you came into my life." Her eyes sharpened. "Now, it's time for the son to rise. So, I ask you." Her eyes sharpened. "What will your song be, Henry?"

Ms. Craft waited for an answer. As she waited patiently, she pulled her narrow eyes away from Henry and glanced at the doorway.

She turned back at Henry.

"You don't have much time, Henry," she said calmly.

The door violently shook.

The top hinge popped off.

Two now remained.

More shaking.

The middle hinge loosened.

Just as the door was about to pop off, the shaking finally ceased.

Now, someone or something was relentlessly pounding at the door.

A draft of heat ran over Henry's skin, perspiring.

The pounding developed shape, rhythm. . . that beat!

That was when Henry woke from his sleep, when that beat had gotten so loud that it distorted.

*   *   *

The strange dream had stayed with Henry from the time he woke the next morning until the sun finally set. All day he thought about where such a dream had come from. Was it from a movie he watched when he was younger? A television show? So vivid the dream was.

As Henry sat on the edge of the bed and watched the red sun creep over the jagged horizon through the bedroom window, he pulled out the flyer from his pocket.

The words of his mother replayed over and over in his head.

"It's your time, Henry," she said to him.

It's your time.

After Henry gave the flyer a once over with his eyes, the answer was clear.

He placed the flyer on his dresser and exited the bedroom.

Before Henry hit the streets, he stopped by his mother's bedroom, kissed her on the forehead, and said his goodbyes while she slept soundlessly. Henry exited the same way as his mother slept—soundlessly—and yet she still woke after the door closed.

From *Missing the Edges,* page 92:

When Like Heroin first started out, we were just a couple of eager teenagers trying to make a name for ourselves. I was completely ignorant as to how the music industry worked. Henry compared the industry to the stock market, always fluctuating, at the top one day and in the pits the other. If I only met Henry earlier in my life, but I could go all day with "if only." So, I'll spare you the trouble. Surely, I thought, we would be on the billboards after Like Heroin's debut album *Fists For Breakfast.* I was so proud of FFB. The album was like giving birth to my own child. Like most kids at that age, I learned the most important lesson of them all: life painted a different story from the one designed in your head. That was what I deserved when I came from nowhere and the people who supported me and puffed me up like a small town hero turned out not knowing anything at all about the world outside. What these people, parents included, didn't know was that the world outside Wellbird grew up and changed without them. The rat race was real all right, volatile, and scary too. Peregrine was spitting out one artist after another as if there was an underground assembly line of musicians somewhere that I didn't know about. And I was another pretty face with a pretty voice. That was all we had going for us. We were hungry! Starved! Our appetites were great and plentiful. When I was fourteen, I suffered from an eating disorder. It wasn't that I didn't like food. I just didn't like eating in front of other people. I think something else was to blame, but I'll touch up on that later in the book. Like my mother, I had high metabolism. But that hunger, it all changed when we started Like Heroin. We were all alike and yet we came from different parts of the country. For once, I felt comfortable in my own skin. And that hunger! Did it change into something else or what? I was as hungry for fame as water was to a dying beached whale. A year prior to our success, I was searching for an edge, a look, something to drag me from that just-another-pretty-face-singer category. When our guitarist, André Greene, asked me if I would like to play the tambourine, I was a bit skeptical. I told him about the bagpipes and the flute, which, at first, he thought I was joking. After trial and error, I gave up on trying to play an instrument. André convinced me that it was only a tambourine. Anybody could play one. André, or Philly, as the other boys called him, compared it to rubbing your belly and patting the top of your head at the same time. That was all the talent you needed to play the tambourine. After the first trial, I soon realized that at the end of the day I was just another sleeveless singer, a pretty face. André, not having much of a filter, insisted I give it another shot, told me to "play that fucking thing until the disks fall off." That was exactly what I did. The discs fell off. And then, I finally let my hair down.

When Henry played one of his demo songs for me, it changed my way of thinking in general. Everything I thought about when it came to great singers was completely tossed out the window. Without question, Henry was at the top of that list. Even above Hendrix and Dylan. I'm sure other members of Mona's Arch would disagree. I've heard earfuls from Deon especially. But the bond shared between Henry and Harry was one I had never seen before. He would hit notes that I thought never existed on the musical scale. He could literally shape his voice through Harry. It was magical, to say the least.

After my first recording session with Mona's Arch, I asked Henry where he came up with such a name as Harry. That was when he told me about the saxophone's previous name, Adrian. In this kind of reluctant, exuberant secrecy, he told me, "The movie *Rocky*." I never watched the flick. Frankly, I didn't care much for movies. I didn't have time to sit around, kick my feet back, and act like a couch potato. When the flick first came out, I was probably somewhere in a cornfield chasing butterflies. Over time, Henry and I became closer. His knowledge of pop culture was like a boundless frontier. He was the only man whom I had ever met who found beauty in everything (and not just nature). Believe it or not, he didn't *not* like anything. Even if something was garbage—I mean the worse possible movie or song or commercial or piece of art or whatever—he would still find a way to convince me that it was somewhat cool in its own way. He certainly had a way about him, as if he never carried one negative thought in his head. Never a critic. On the Bound and Dangerous Tour, we would take advantage of the free time before sound check and visit the local museums. He would find the most hideous piece of art and mentally take a scalpel to it and try to find the meaning behind it, wear down each possible detail until it was depleted. I asked Henry where all of this came from, the openness. That was when he told me about his mentor and best friend, Dolores Craft.

SEVEN

HENRY prowled down Faulkner Street until he reached the South End district, a trendy hangout where scruffy college grads and dog lovers frequently rubbed shoulders with the CEOs and millionaire business types of Lansford. Most of the district consisted of rival art galleries (one called The Gauche Lion, which always drew a decent-sized crowd on Thursday nights), local coffee shops, Internet cafés, editing suites, and high-end clothing outlets. During the daytime, South End was fairly quiet. "Dead," some might say. Most of the local metropolitans who lived in South End were most likely confined to a dark room, somewhere technically creating the next big thing. At night, when the six o'clock shadows cast from the uptown Lansford cityscape loomed over, South End came alive. The arrogance was like a cloud of smog trickling down from corporate Lansford into South End, taking hold of everything it touched.

As Henry rounded Dow Street, he caught the bright strobe light flickering at the end of the block along with the sign HOT FOXY next to the marquee. Even though the club was only several blocks away, the walk felt like miles. The light brightened over his eyes, sharpening like a tiger's eyes. The area between his two eyebrows shriveled into a narrow crease. He arrived at Hot Foxy right when the Open Mike Night was just getting started. The outside was teeming with eager partygoers and musicians alike, all as hungry as Henry. Their eyes, the seduction, Henry noticed, carried that same focus and resilience.

Henry loitered behind the stocky bouncer, who was checking ID's, and waited for the right moment to slip past the distracted bouncer at the entrance.

He was like a cool breeze in the night grazing across the backside of the bouncer's neck.

Before the bouncer turned his shoulder, Henry was already inside.

The inside of the club was thriving in all directions. The carefree song "I Love Music" by Rozalla was playing overhead. The club was extremely diverse in both atmosphere and décor. There were two bars, one on each side of the club, both crowded, a couple of billiard tables, a dartboard, a dance floor, and a sitting area in front of the stage. Occasionally, a young server dressed in neon lights and carrying a tray of drinks would effortlessly coast through the rowdy club without spilling a single drop of alcohol.

As Henry shouldered his way through the crowd, he felt an uprising in his stomach. He suddenly clinched his jaw and breathed slowly through his nose. On the back of his tongue, he could taste the vomit crawling up his throat. As quickly as he could, he tried to think of something else besides playing in front of a full crowd. Strangely enough, he thought about what Ms. Craft had told him a long time ago. "Imagine they are all naked," she once told him. And that was exactly what Henry did. They were all naked, every single one of them.

The attractive brunette, svelte and shaped like a model, standing next to the billiard table: naked.

Her Ken boyfriend, or what Henry thought, playing 8-ball with another woman: naked.

The two girls smoking cigarettes next to her: naked.

The older fellow with greased back hair: naked.

As Henry walked past the older fellow (his two tits sagging like waterbags), he turned his head away and immediately put clothes on the man. The nerves calmed a bit, but he was still jacked about going on stage. Four people were waiting in line to take the stage.

Henry took a number from the emcee.

After Henry took a number from the emcee (his number no other than number 5), he decided to take a seat at the bar until his number was called to the stage.

He placed Adrian on the stool next to him and carefully observed the way the other barflies were sitting at the bar: shoulders slouching with eyes slightly squinting in agony. He mimicked their steely demeanor and sat with his shoulders slouching and his eyes squinting in agony.

Across from him moved a bartender—naked, of course. She was a rather stout woman, but not overwhelmingly fat. Big boned by nature. For eight hours, she stayed on her feet and worked way too hard to let herself go. Her breasts were plump without much sag. The sides of her body were tight and linear, no sag.

With his eyes fixed on the bartender, Henry flagged her down.

Smoothly and gracefully, she moved over to Henry.

On the way over, she stopped twice, once to fill another man's drink and another to crack open a bottle of beer with a bottle opener that she carried over her forearm.

"What will it be, cutie?" the bartender asked and then planted herself in front of Henry.

Henry confidently ordered a shot of vodka—his voice much deeper than usual. There were so many brands and types of vodka to choose from. Must've been at least fifty bottles, flavors from apple to mango, peppermint, triple distilled, one-eighty proof, another sixty proof, another this and another that.

Henry decided to let the bartender choose.

She gave Henry a once over, especially the way he was sitting.

"I got just the thing," the bartender said with a wink.

She went with the brand Viktor, an imported bottle from Russia. Henry quickly downed the shot before he even had a chance to taste the vodka. He ordered one more shot. Again, he let the vodka roll down his throat. The two shots really didn't do much for Henry. The nerves were still there, reeking havoc with his insides. The person who was on before him, Number 4, was reading free verse poetry to the audience. Henry didn't have the slightest clue about what the poet was trying to say. He heard something like "*I clean you off with alcohol. . . then I slide you around both eyelids. . . peel them back like curtains for the world to see. . .*"

After Number 4 was finished talking about sliding things over his eyelids, he received a standing ovation.

While Henry made his way toward the stage, the emcee for the night jogged from the backstage and grabbed the microphone.

"What a performance!" the emcee blared out as Henry, who couldn't quite tell if the emcee was being sarcastic or not, paced around backstage. "Let's give another warm hand for my man, CAPS." He pointed at the poet strolling off the stage. The poet was dressed in all black, black turtleneck and jeans, heavy mascara, and had dyed black hair combed over one side of his face. "CAPS everybody!" The audience applauded. "All right! Next, we have a little brass for all you jazz enthusiasts out there. Please put your hands together for. . . " he read from the card, ". . . Henry the Fifth."

The audience applauded.

With Adrian held closely to his body, Henry steadily moved his way onto the stage. The audience was no longer naked. His knees buckled a bit. Then, he concentrated on what Ms. Craft had told him. He steadied his walk and made it to the center of the stage. He shuffled toward the microphone and leaned over.

"Name's Henry the Fif', *not* Fifth," he said, the tremble in his voice brought out with a daunting lucidity over the microphone. Henry glared over at the supercilious emcee, who was wearing this "whatever" kind of expression on his face: eyes rolling, one half of his mouth puckered. Henry moved his eyes toward the audience and couldn't help but smirk from their primordial appearance. His heart skipped a beat from the same brunette in the front row, the svelte one who was hanging around the billiard table. *That's what I'm talking*, he thought. *Soon, I'm going have you jumping in the air, screaming my name.* His eyes crossed the back of the audience, near the entrance. A lump in his throat dropped into his stomach. There she was standing (with her clothes on!) holding her frail hands together over her chest, waiting, anticipating for Henry to play.

Henry felt his hands turn stiff and cold.

Do something. . .

He tried to move, but he couldn't.

. . . Anything.

He stayed there, frozen.

Then, his mother mouthed those very words to her son, "Break a leg, Henry."

A grin eased over Henry's face.

He regained feeling back into his limbs, thoughts.

With a rush of energy, he grabbed the microphone and said smoothly, "This gem right here is called 'Captured by Light.' Enjoy."

Henry placed his lips to the reed.

The trembling was gone, the crowd, the eyes. He imagined himself practicing inside Ms. Craft's living room. The furniture, aged and yet homey. . . timeless picture frames hanging on the walls. . . black and white pictures of The Doves of Saturn. . . Gloria Silk posed with other famous celebrities. . . Americana. . . the piano. . . the organ. . . two steaming cups of hot chocolate sitting on the coffee table. . . and then, there she was, Ms. Craft, once, in her prime, known as the great Gloria Silk, graciously observing Henry behind the piano. "You finally done it, Henry," she said and smiled. "Now, let's see who can blow the biggest bubbles." Henry focused on the crowd before him. At first, the song was slow. He hit every single note. After a minute into the song, the tempo increased. Right under his eyes, the soprano suddenly warped! The mechanics of the saxophone popped and swelled. He played harder, faster. The keys transformed. He played faster, stronger, improvising along the way. Right before the crowd's eyes, the little soprano saxophone transformed into a masculine alto saxophone. The crowd was stunned from the performance. Gasps rose like fledglings from the crowd. They didn't know how an instrument could completely switch ranges and shape as it did! One spectator was checking his bifocals. Another spectator was scratching his eyes, wondering if that was even possible. Henry was on the same page as the audience. However, he kept playing, aggressively too. The music sent feverish chills through the audience, goosebumps.

As the song finally ended after eleven minutes, which, by the way, left the audience craving for more, Henry stood in a daze. Adrian, which was slightly larger now, hung over his hip like a giant holster. The audience sprang to its feet and shook the entire club with cheers and roars and whistles and applause. The ladies were waving the heat from their bodies. Henry shook from his trance and stared at the audience, all clothed now.

"Give it up for the Henry the Fif'!" the emcee cried out and sprinted out onto the stage. "I tell you. I will never forget that name again." He patted Henry on the back and whispered into his ear, "Hey. Nice job, kid." The emcee directed his attention toward the crowd. "What a show, huh?" he shouted out over the house music. "Damn! We got some real talent in the room tonight! We're going to take a ten minute break, but don't go too far because next we have the young and talented siren, Gunna! So, you guys stick around, especially all you Romeos out there. . . "

Henry could hardly control the beam over his face. He made his way from the stage with the saxophone case in hand and received pats on the back as well as handshakes of congratulations from the participants waiting in line. A slender, ruffled hair man in a suit barged through a couple of socialites and walked up to Henry with his hand stretched out for Henry to shake.

"Some playing, Henry the Fif'."

"And you are?" Henry asked and shook the man's hand.

"Name's Mort Rockwell," he said. "Producer for Phat Stacks. I like your style."

"The record label?"

"That's right, Henry," he said. "Nowadays the old is the new. . . new, if you get my drift."

"Not really," Henry said and looked around the crowd.

"Anyway, I'd like to hear more of your work."

He handed Henry a business card.

"Uh. . . " he said over thought, ". . . Yeah." He grabbed the card from his hand and looked it over. "Sure."

"Do you have a demo I can take with me?"

"No, sir," Henry said eagerly. "But I can make one. . . "

"You put a demo together and you give me a call. Okay?"

"Okay," Henry said, keeping that same wide smile on his face.

Henry shouldered his way through the crowd and kept the card gripped tightly in his hand. As he made his way toward the back of the club, he spotted his sickly mother standing there. She too was wearing a smile over her face, one that Henry hadn't seen in a long time. Tears were traced around her eyes.

"You should be in bed, Mom," he said and hugged his mother.

"I had to know," Abbey said with her chin rested over his shoulder. "I just had to know, Henry."

"I did pretty good. Didn't I?"

"You were more than pretty good," she said, her voice cracking a little. "You were phenomenal."

"And I didn't freeze up."

"You certainly didn't, Henry," she said and faced Henry. "All this time, I never took your music seriously, Henry. I just wanted to say that I'm sorry. I just wanted to see you do well."

"It's all right, Mom," he said over a sudden roar from the crowd. "I forgive you."

A hint of relief lifted over her gauntly face.

"You do?"

"Of course I do."

She pulled her son close to her frail body and hugged him once more.

"I'm so proud of you, Henry," she said as the tears rolled down both cheeks.

"By the way," Henry said curiously into her shoulder, "how did you get here?"

"A friend," she answered bluntly. "I think you might know her."

Henry pulled himself away from his mother.

"What friend?"

His face went slack.

"A person who I was wrong about. . . "

With a smile, Abbey nodded over Henry's shoulder.

Henry turned and spotted Ms. Craft sitting at the end of the bar. She was sipping from a glass of gin and tonic and looking directly at Henry. There was an empty stool next to her.

"How. . . "

He quickly turned back around to his mother.

"I found her name in the yellow pages," Abbey said. "It was much easier than I thought." Once more, she nodded toward the crowded bar. "Well, go on. What are you waiting for? I suppose you two have a lot of catching up to do."

Smiling ear from ear, Henry strolled over to Ms. Craft. She hadn't aged that much. Her hair was whiter, though. Except for a couple of dropped pounds and the change in hair color, she appeared about the same. She was wearing a silk white dress shirt with a frayed gray scarf over her shoulders. Her black trench and beret were hanging over the coat rack at the other end of the bar.

"When your mother called me, I came as soon as I could," Ms. Craft said and stood up from the stool.

For a moment, Henry hesitated to hug her.

"I. . . I can't believe you're here."

"I wouldn't miss it for the world, Henry."

"How did you get here so fast?"

"Well, I only live a half hour away from here," she said. "Your mother said she got my number from the yellow pages. You can find my name under 'piano instructors.'"

Henry placed the saxophone case over the bar and hugged Ms. Craft.

"It's so good to see you, Henry," she said over a sigh of relief.

"It's good to see you," Henry replied.

Ms. Craft pulled herself away from Henry and studied his body.

"You've grown so much," she said in awe. "Last time I saw you, you were so little. Now, look at you. You're a grown man."

"I guess," Henry said. "Yeah."

"I'm proud of you, Henry."

"Thanks," he said bashfully. "So, how are things with you?"

"Good," Ms. Craft answered. "They're good."

"You still with Jodi?"

"Nah," she waved her hand, "after a while, we got sick of each other. He went back to his same ole ways. We were moving in different directions, Henry. I quit the job at the church. I've been saving up money. I was thinking about maybe traveling again. Maybe go somewhere exotic. I don't know. I miss it. I miss traveling." Her eyes drifted in thought. She looked around the rowdy club. Her eyes connected with Henry's. "I miss you, Henry."

"I miss you too, Dolores," he said and cleared his throat. "I wish things didn't end the way they. . . "

"It's okay, Henry," she interrupted. "I see your mother finally came through."

"It only took her like ten years."

Ms. Craft touched Henry on the shoulder.

"How is she doing, Henry?" she asked tenderly.

Henry said, "It's hard to say really."

"She told me about her treatment, the chemotherapy."

"Yeah," Henry said depressingly and glanced over at his sickly mother across the crowd. "She isn't doing that well. I mean. . . she has her good days and her bad days. Seems like now the bad days outweigh the good."

"Things will get better, Henry," Ms. Craft said and removed her hand from Henry's shoulder. "You just have to have faith."

Henry looked at Ms. Craft with a strange expression.

"Thought you didn't believe in that kind of stuff."

"I don't," she said. "But, like they say, things do happen for a reason." Her eyes trailed across the bar, across the gin and tonic, and landed on the saxophone case. "I see you got a new saxophone."

"Uh. . ." Henry said, his voice faltering from Ms. Craft's comment, ". . . yeah."

Ms. Craft nodded at the case.

"May I?"

"Sure," Henry said unsteadily.

Ms. Craft opened up the case, which revealed the alto—not soprano—saxophone before her eyes.

"What's her name?"

"He," Henry said confidently. "It's a he."

"Really?"

"Harry," Henry said over brief thought. "His name is Harry."

"Harry, huh?" Ms. Craft said with surprise. "That's a good name. Like Harry Houdini."

"Yeah," Henry said with his eyes falling over the alto saxophone, "Just like Harry Houdini."

EIGHT

EXCERPT from Starlet Rollinson's *Missing the Edges: A Memoir (New York: Snow Globe Industries, 2049, 2nd Edition)*, page 332:

Before I had a chance to take it all in (the past couple of days were like a chronic hangover from spending hours in the waiting room, staring at the blank powder blue walls, listening to the constant sobbing of mothers and fathers and sons and daughters as their loved ones remained in critical condition, not eating, not sleeping, and then sneaking into the bathroom to cry), Henry and I were smoking cigarettes in bed and telling road stories. I was doing most of the talking. Henry was doing that thing where he was playing it cool like James Dean, taking long drags from his cigarette, even though I knew there was a storm brewing somewhere underneath his eyes. As I had a tendency to do whenever the two of us got together, I interrogated him. I always played the good cop, the compassionate one. Never the bad one. Usually the second I got Henry going—to the point where I thought twice about asking the question in the first place—it was hard for him to stop. Sometimes it was like breaking a dam with Henry. First, I'd chip away at him with a chisel. Ask him the easy questions. Then, I'd find the right spot, the softest spot, what made him tick, and then take a hammer to it. Once the dam was broken, all the sorrow and pain and every single emotion that Henry kept bottled up inside came spurting out in a steady stream. When Henry performed on stage, the stage was his chair and the crowd was his shrink. The man poured out his heart on stage. The cycle would continue, over and over, city to city. After all the release on stage and off, there was still something deep trapped inside him, sucking away at him like a leech. Henry never shared that something with me, let alone, a stranger. At times, he would wear it in his eyes, the sorrow and pain brought on from the early demise of his father. Most of the time, he concealed all of the emotion as if he was wearing a mask over his face. When the cigarettes finally burned out, so too did the fond conversation. The second I saw Harry scattered over the carpet, I knew something was up. A chalk line tracing a dead body. Above the debris, there were three holes from where Henry rammed his fists into the wall.

Ever since I stumbled into the music industry (that was when I weighed around a buck ten with the bird chest of a young scrawny boy, freakishly wide shoulders, and an ego as tall as the Statue of Liberty), I dragged around a seething darkness inside me. Those who knew me well could always sense it there, the darkness, like a foreign entity, undetected like a germ but there all right, hiding in its callus, infrangible shell, waiting to strike at the first sign of intrusion. Back then anything could've driven me to the edge: a wrong note or chord, an empty high hat, even a heckler in the audience. I guess it was from being raised in a household of perfectionists.

On a humid night in October '94, my band mates in Like Heroin, as well as the thirty or forty something patrons in the club, had gotten free admission to this darkness. We were doing a show in Swanson. Over half of the people in the club were there for Tiny Sylvester and the Grunts, a Goth band and local favorite. The other half were there for the cheap dollar beer on draft. We were fairly new to the scene (about six or seven years), eager to get our feet wet, traveling from town to town in Billy's pale blue 1989 Chevrolet Astro with a cardboard box of demo tapes. At the time, the money was flowing pretty steadily. Most of the money we made was from performing. It wasn't much. But it was better than nothing. I quit my job at the café and bartended every now and then whenever we couldn't find a gig. I mainly focused on the music. We hadn't really made a name for ourselves yet. But I felt it in my bones. Soon, I kept telling myself, it was going to happen. Like cheese dangling over a hungry mouse. Soon, the mouse was going to reach up and take a nibble. We were opening up for small bands, which pretty much made us unknowns, especially in the big cities. The locale was a hole in the wall nightclub called The Squat. Fitting name. I swear the temperature inside the club had to be at least a hundred degrees. The band was wearing thin, which was never a good sign, especially when you work in the entertainment business. People just want to be entertained, not put to sleep. Halfway during the show while we were into the bridge of "Count Your Cards," the engineer behind the board must've accidentally hit a wrong button. One of the speakers blew. I remember my ears ringing for the next two days. I don't, however, remember exactly what happened. The guys said I switched over into a woman possessed. The critics called it the "Blood of a Peregrinian." The next morning, there was a review in the local newspaper,

the *Low Down.* They said it was one of our best perform-
ances—"visceral. . . and enchanting," they wrote. In all the
years of traveling from one shitty club to another, we've never
been called enchanting. I took it as a compliment. The
other band mates not so much. Like it or not, Peregrinians
all had it in them, the darkness. I'd like to think that the
cloudy weather had something to do with it, the darkness.
Somewhere in Peregrine, it was raining. And somewhere in
Peregrine, a kid was locked up in a bedroom, stashed far away
from his or her parents, pouring his or her soul into an instrument, resurrecting a music scene or starting a brand new
one. At times, I swear I didn't know who was on stage. It
went on like this for the next couple of years until I met
Henry. I sang about the trials and tribulations one goes
through in order to find, or better yet, stumble into true love.
Most of the time, I was singing about my past experiences,
the flings, the romances (some rather dirty at the time), the
bad dates, the waiting-by-the-phone game (driving myself literally sick!), the stand-ups, the hardship from break ups (all
punch lines for my unwelcoming guest), finding what you
thought could be the one, not eating or sleeping (the toilet
becoming your new best friend), putting on weight, losing
weight, thinking all day about this *possible* one, getting
worked up, and then being let down, the crying (going
through so many boxes of tissues), and finally that void, a devoted companion of my guest, the darkness, a sanctuary inside my heart yearning to be filled with the company of the
one, not some pretentious asshole. The darkness wanted
nothing of it. It loved the void, the loneliness. It took joy
relishing such emptiness and yet longing. Just the utterance
of love was like nails on a chalkboard. The darkness wanted
to keep me behind that windowsill by throwing a doubt or
two my way so it could rejoice and bask in my own misery.
Every now and then, I found myself wondering whether or
not this opposing entity would consume my body and take
over all that was once pure. And then, I met him, Henry, and
he changed my life forever.

After I fell witness to the destruction, I stopped trying to put together what had happened with the saxophone, as well as T.J. Soon, the grieving would stop. They said it was like a virus and that it just needed to run its course. "The first forty-eight hours are the worse," they said. Then, they said its gets better. "But," they went on to say, "only after acceptance." What did they know, especially when it came to acceptance? It was easy to accept the breakup of Mona's Arch or the path Henry had chosen for himself. With T.J., it was out of my hands. I felt powerless. The word *acceptance* hadn't seemed so hard to embrace and conquer. I wondered whether or not I could ever accept what had happened to T.J. Was he going to survive? Who knows how long it would take him to recover from his injuries? Was his condition ever going to improve? The doctors told us that it could take days, weeks, months, even years. Throughout the many questions and concerns I had for T.J., the instrument that Henry had grown to love was now destroyed. As with T.J., the questions would come and go. The answers, however, were ones I wished not to hear or ones I never expected. Most importantly, I wondered why. Why would Henry destroy something so priceless after all these years? It got to the point where I stopped asking questions. The answers would come after the grieving had run its course—at least that was what I thought. I turned my eyes to Henry's trembling hands and then up to his eyes. I could see the hurt in them, both of his eyes filled with anger. It was as if another person had taken over his body. The Wind, my Wind, was gone for who knows how long. Then, as I gazed deeper into the reflection of his glossy eyes, I witnessed the anger melt away. Right then and there, I knew it was replaced with something else, my own worst enemy.

The next day, Henry didn't do much but spend most of his time locked in his bedroom trying to figure out how Adrian transformed from a soprano to an alto saxophone, which, by the way, was now called Harry according to last night's conversation with Ms. Craft. The brass appeared like new, versation with Ms. Craft. The brass appeared like new, not damaged or stretched or cracked.

Late afternoon, while his mother was receiving a chemotherapy treatment at Lansford Medical Center, Henry decided to take Harry to Stanley's, the local music store. He found an engineer on staff, a lissome man with a weasel-like face and greasy blonde hair tied in a ponytail, and asked him to take a quick look at the saxophone. After about an hour of examining Harry with a magnifying glass as large as Henry's head, the engineer found nothing wrong with it.

The engineer shook his elephantine head behind the magnifying glass.

"Nope," he said and pulled his face away from the magnifying glass. "I can't find anything wrong with your instrument."

Perplexed from Henry's claim, he removed the purple John Lennon glasses from his pointy nose.

"You're serious," Henry said, dumbfounded. "I saw it with my own eyes." His voice rose higher. "It came alive, you see!"

"If you don't mind me asking, amigo," the engineer drawled with the glasses dangling from his limp hand, "but what kind of drugs were you on last night?"

"None," Henry said honestly and scowled at the engineer.

"Sure about that?"

"I swear!"

The engineer slid the saxophone back to Henry.

"Listen, amigo," he said and sighed as if he was about to drop some knowledge on Henry. "A man and his instrument share a tight bond. In a way, the instrument can become a part of its user." He pointed his finger at Henry. "But just remember. It's not flesh and blood. It's just an instrument."

As baffled as Henry was before, he left Stanley's without a proper explanation on how a saxophone could change like that and walked for miles through a small art district in Queens Dive. Kicking around objects on the sidewalk from boredom, Henry reached into his pocket and pulled out the producer's business card. He eyed over the card for a long time until he finally realized what he was meant to do. When Henry was younger, he was told countless times that it was just a whim, another one of his fantasies. Last night *was* real, Henry realized.

Henry hurried to the nearest payphone. He tried to remember the phone number. *74. . . 8, no*, he thought, *2, 742.* He had dialed the number so many times when he was younger that the number was there on the tip of his tongue. In fact, he once knew the number as well as he knew his own. After a moment of thought, the number came to Henry.

"742-5354," he said jubilantly.

As Henry slid a quarter into the payphone and dialed the number, he repeated the telephone number, *742-5354*, over and over in his mind. The phone rang three times before a person picked up on the other line.

"Hello," an aged voice said carefully over the telephone.

"May I speak to T.J.?"

"T.J. doesn't live here anymore," the woman answered. "May I ask who's calling?"

"Mrs. Livingston?"

"Yes," she said, her tone shifting to a spirit of inquiry.

"It's Henry," he said, "from Reddington."

"Henry!" she blurted out, her voice nearly leaping through the payphone's shoddy receiver. "How have you been?"

"Good," he answered shortly.

"Me and T.J.'s father have been listening to you play over the radio," Mrs. Livingston said. "I'm sorry to hear about your loss against Madison. You must be devastated."

"Not really," he said. "It's just a game."

"Well, I wanted to tell you that we've been thinking about you," she said gladly. "And we miss having you around."

"Thanks."

"So, when was the last time you talked to T.J.?"

"Two years I think," he answered. "I really need to get in touch with him. Do you know a number where I can reach him at?"

"Well, he doesn't have a phone," she replied with a sudden pause. "But you should pay him a visit." Her voice grew with optimism. "He would really like that."

"You wouldn't know the address. Would you?"

"Sure," she said, her voice extending. "I got it right here."

By car, the address was only twenty minutes away from Stanley's. Henry used the ten dollars that he stole from his mother's purse, filled up the Jelly Bean with regular, which was only going for a dollar and ten cents a gallon nowadays, and decided to pay a visit to T.J. All through high school, Henry was told to avoid a certain part of the city. "The rough part," he was warned, "a jungle." And not just from his mother. When Mrs. Livingston read the address over the telephone, Henry was shocked, to say the least, that T.J. would move to such a forlorn place as Parker Square, also known as P.S. "Stay Out of Parker Square," or P.S. "Proceed With Extreme Caution." The suburb, which was in the process of becoming its own town, sat on the edge of Queens Dive, closest to Lansford. The police routinely patrolled Parker Square. Each night, there was something going on—a shooting or a stabbing either domestically or from a turf war between the two rival gangs, *The Cueballs*, which had been taken from the Dick Tracy comic strip, and *7th Ward*, a vicious gang notorious for hustling drugs, mostly crack rock, in and out of Parker Square. The years had gone by. As Bob Dylan once sang, "The times are ah-changing." And some people grew up and got a job while others stayed the same.

After driving through a labyrinth of streets, some with the same exact street names, stopping at a local convenient store for directions (while Henry was asking the clerk for directions, the clerk had his right hand wrapped around a twelve gage shotgun underneath the counter), Henry finally found the correct apartment complex. The barred windows were riddled with bullet holes, Henry noticed as he warily made his way through the complex. Along the way, he acknowledged the struggle, the broken families, families trying to make ends meet. He witnessed a part of the city that he had never seen before, only heard about from his friends and family.

After walking up seven flights of stairs, Henry arrived at his destination. In the hallway, he stumbled across an obese child—*probably no older than four years old*, he wondered—carrying a famished baby in his arms. Along the way, an elderly man, who was wearing a thick pair of sunglasses and a worn beige Panama hat, grabbed Henry by the arm.

"You ain't allowed up in here," he barked, his teeth skewed forward over his upper lip. "You take your scrawny ass somewhere else to buy drugs. We don't want your kind here."

Henry brushed off the man's hand.

"Do you mind?" he said and kept walking.

"I'll pray for you!" the intrusive man shouted down the hallway. "You hear! I'll be praying for you! You just remember! You can't escape God's wrath! God is always watching. . ."

As Henry walked past apartment 5B, he heard a sudden rattling noise coming from two apartments down. The doorway panels of each apartment suddenly vibrated. Door handles jiggled. The foundation of the ceiling cracked and sounded as if it was about to give way. Henry's first thought: she was back. After all these years, he had forgotten about her. She was back. Then, the noise boomed! The noise slowly developed into what Henry thought was a jet flying overhead and then music. Somewhere underneath all the bass, a harp was playing. Henry listened closely and pinpointed the music. The music wasn't that much more distinguishable from the bass. From what Henry gathered, the music was a combination of different genres: rap, electronic, and trance. Henry wasn't too familiar with the style of music. The only time he had heard such music was when a thuggish man from Parker Square named Glow randomly showed up with pockets full of drugs at his friend's dorm room last year. With his headphones, the thug was listening to music, similar to the kind being played across the hallway. Henry remembered asking the lazy-eyed thug what kind of music he was listening to. He told him it was called "White Ballin'."

Henry glanced down at the sliver of yellow paper that he tore from the phonebook.

"Apartment 7B," he read.

He arrived at 7B, the source of the loud music.

"Some things never change," he said jokingly to himself.

He knocked on the door.

No answer.

The knock sounded like a pulse over the throbbing music.

He decided to bang on the door.

The music suddenly came to a halt.

He heard a voice saying, "the dough man," from behind the door.

A skinny, hollow eyed man with a shaved head flung open the door. On the front right side of his scalp was a white circular spot caused from vitiligo. He had almost the same frame as Henry; however, he was more strung out than built, similar profile, only his skin was much darker than Henry's. He had all kinds of creature tattoos (dragons and scorpions) over his arms and wrists and even knuckles. He had one tattoo on his chest (some kind of creature perhaps), which was covered up by a white tank top. Henry couldn't quite make out what the tattoo was. All Henry could see were these dark red claws running up the side of his neck.

With his eyebrows furrowed, the skinny, hollow eyed man looked Henry over, starting from his head down to his shoes.

The man asked angrily, "What the fuck do you want, half breed?"

"I'm looking for T.J.," Henry said, his voice trembling a bit.

"Who?"

"I said I'm looking for. . . "

"Henry?" a voice called out from inside the grungy apartment. "Is that really you?"

"You know this fool?"

He cracked open the door.

"I can't believe my own eyez."

T.J. removed the headphones from his ears, walked over to the door, and shoved the other man out of the way.

"Chill," the man whined.

Like the man before him, T.J.'s eyes fell on Henry. A smile gradually stretched across his face.

"It's really you?"

"What's up, T.J.?"

They shook hands.

"How you doin', brotha?"

Then, they hugged.

"I've been better, I guess," Henry replied and peeked inside the apartment. He saw the many drum machines and samplers on a table. T.J. even had a Casio SK-1 that he had kept from his childhood. He threw his head in a nod. "I see you're still messing with them beats and stuff."

"Hells yeah," T.J. said as his eyes trailed down to Henry's hand, the case. "Adrian?"

"That's right," he said, reading T.J.'s thoughts. "Well, Harry. I call him Harry now."

"Harry? What up wit the sex change?"

"Long story," he said.

T.J. squinted his eyes in suspicion.

He smiled again and shook Henry's hand.

"We gotta lots of catchin' up to do," T.J. said and wrapped his arm around Henry's neck and guided Henry into the apartment. "By the way, how'd you find me?"

"Your mom said you'd be here," he said and shot his eyes toward the hallway from behind. "I was meaning to ask you. Who's the old man at the end of the hallway? That old man was tripping on me."

"You talkin' 'bout Cranky Calvin," T.J. said. "Don't you be worryin' 'bout the Crank. He's jus an old man wit nuttin else better to do but pester us hard workin' folks."

Henry glanced over the wide variety of drugs on the coffee table. There was a kilogram of cocaine, uncut, a handful of crack rocks scattered over the table like marbles, and at least two pounds of marijuana.

So, he thought, *that's why.*

"Right," Henry said insecurely.

NINE

FOR the rest of the afternoon, Henry and T.J. talked about what they had been doing for the last couple of years. Henry told T.J. what it was like being a sophomore in college: playing basketball and his team losing in the conference finals; going to parties, so many wild parties; and then hooking up with all the fine college girls. T.J. told Henry about how he moved from his parents' house and met up with Screw at a friend's house. At the time, T.J. needed a place to stay. So, Screw made a deal with T.J., a deal that T.J. never told Henry about—at least, not then.

Henry asked, "You keep in touch with anyone from school?"

With one side of his face puckering in thought, T.J. shook his head.

"Nah," he drawled and passed the wet, smelly joint. Henry placed the joint up to his nose and jarred from the potent smell. "I seen that one girl you used to be head over heels for. What's her name?" T.J. placed his hand over his temple. "Shit! What's that girl's name?" His eyes widened. "Kerri! That's it!"

"Really? Kerri? You mean the girl who used to live across our old street?"

"You remember?"

"Of course," Henry said excitedly. "I mean. . ." he suddenly changed his tone and manner from excited to calm, now restrained, ". . . yeah. So. . . what's she up to these days?"

"She's into like clothes and shit, like a fashion designer or sumtin fancy like that," T.J. answered. "Graduated early from Peregrine State. And from what I can tell, she be makin' sum killer bank. Said she was movin' to the Big Apple. She acted like she in a hurry when I talks to her up by the Red Rabbit."

"Did she ask about me?"

"You?" T.J. said laid back. "Nah."

"Conceited as usual." Once more, Henry held up the joint to his face. "You know. . . " he glanced over the joint. He didn't know exactly what was in the joint, most likely swag from Mexico or "dirt," which was what most of the people around here called it. ". . . I shouldn't be doing this, but. . . "

"But basketball season's over, my brotha," T.J. finished. "Ain't like you gonna get drug tested."

"I was going to say 'But I've done worse,'" Henry said, grinning.

T.J. pounded his knuckles over Henry's.

"That's my boy right there!" he exclaimed in front of Screw.

Henry took a drag from the joint. He held the smoke in his lungs until his chest burned. He violently coughed, which generated some laughter between T.J. and Screw, who had been sitting there all uptight on the couch.

"So why is you really here, Henry?"

"Yeah," Screw said. "And what up with the saxophone? The eighties are over, kid."

Henry ignored Screw and said to T.J., "I need a backbone."

"I'd say you haf a good one," T.J. said. "You know, from coming up in here. Ain't nobody really come here unless. . . "

"That's not what I meant."

"Then what did you mean, foo?"

"I mean I need a man who can lay down some beats for me."

Screw interrupted, "T.J.'s your right man, then."

"And why exactly would I do that?"

Henry pulled out the business card from his pocket and handed it to T.J.

"Where did you get this?" T.J. asked, glancing over the record label on the card.

"It was given to me."

T.J. read the name on the card.

"By Mort. . . Mort Rockwell? You be shittin' me." T.J. eyed over Henry with confusion. "But how? You still in school. I don't. . . what does one of the top producers in the industree want wit a hotshot athlete like yourself?"

"I went to Hot Foxy last night, T.J.," Henry said and leaned over the coffee table. "I took Harry here with me, if you feel me."

Screw asked, "And who the fuck is Harry?"

Henry glared over at Screw and directed his attention toward T.J.

"I hadn't played like this before, T.J.," he said convincingly. "I mean. . . I killed it, T.J. Even got a standing ovation."

"No shit!"

"Believe," Henry said. "I want to make a demo for Mr. Rockwell."

Henry took a hit and then passed the joint back to T.J.

"Are you in or not?"

"Hells yeah," T.J. said, bobbing his head in total agreement. "All the ways, Henry."

Screw remained mean and quiet.

At sunset, Henry and T.J. stumbled from the apartment complex with a forty-ounce bottle of Sherman's malt liquor in their hands.

Henry took a swig of the malt liquor.

He grimaced and said sourly, "This crap tastes like piss."

"Hey," T.J. said with a shrug, "you get used to it."

"We're not going to get anywhere with work," Henry slurred. "Are we?"

"Nah, nigga," T.J. said animatedly.

"Come on, T.J.," Henry said. "You know I don't like that word."

"Why?" T.J. returned. "Cuz you ain't really a real nigga, like I'm talking about a real *Roots* nigga like myself?"

"The last time I checked slavery was over like a hundred years ago," Henry said sharply. "You weren't even born. I take that back. You weren't even a little sperm swimming around in your daddy's nuts."

"Goddamn, Henry," T.J. mumbled as he leaned back in surprise.

Henry glared at T.J.

"It represents our struggle, Henry," T.J. said. "Where we came from, our history, our repressions—"

"—Yeah," Henry interrupted. "You really struggling."

"What you mean?"

Henry's glare tightened on his face.

"All that equipment I saw in there."

T.J. smacked his gums.

"It's not like you don't have a roof over your head, T.J."

"Damn, Henry!" T.J. blurted out. "You still that same uptight muthafucka from when we was kids!"

"Only this time I can kick your ass."

"You be trippin', nigga," T.J. said, exaggerating the word *nigga.*

Henry chortled to himself.

"This right here, Henry, this is a part of the whole process," T.J. said and smacked Henry on the shoulder. "You know what I means. First, we gets super loaded. You feel me. Then, we find sum hoes. You feel me."

"I most definitely feel you," Henry said and grazed T.J.'s shoulder. "But not like the ones who be starting all kinds of drama and shit."

"I gotcha covered, homie."

"Then, what. . . "

"Then, we go back the apartment and hit the studio."

"A little late to be playing music," Henry said. "Won't we wake your neighbors?"

"Them!" T.J. shouted out, his wandering eyes sharpening over Henry's. "They don't give a shit, Henry. Half of these people who live up in here walk around like they in a fuckin' coma. They like zombies and shit. There was these couple of times when the cops came up in here." T.J. awkwardly leaned over and whispered, "What else is new?" He waved his hand and raised his voice to normal level. "But they didn't do nuttin, Henry. Besides, Screw's got these people on lockdown."

"Lockdown, huh?"

"Damn straight."

Henry said sternly, "Can I be honest with you, T.J.?"

"I know," he said, not giving Henry a chance to finish his thought. "You hate that muthafucka."

"I wouldn't say 'hate.'"

"Hate, don't like," T.J. said. "What's the difference?"

"Okay," Henry said. "I don't care much for him."

T.J. laughed obnoxiously.

"You crazy, Henry."

"So, how'd you know?"

"Know what?"

"That I didn't like Screw."

"I seen it in your face."

"But. . . "

"But nuttin." T.J. tapped Henry on the chest. "It's all good, homie," he drawled. "To tell you the truf. I don't like him neither. It's jus another roof over my head. You know. It could be worse."

"Will Harry be safe with him?"

As before, T.J. smacked his gums.

"Please," he said, his voice laid back. "Screw don't care about that shit. All he cares about is the green. Screw, he's a high roller."

"So, what if he goes behind my back and pawns Harry for some *green*?"

"He won't do you like that, Henry."

"How do you know?"

T.J. smacked his gums yet again.

"All right," Henry said warily.

There was a brief pause.

"What's his game?"

T.J.'s facial expression went slack.

"Listen, Henry Man," T.J. said seriously. "I was gonna tell you. You've been gone for a long time. You know. Things ain't like they used to be."

"What's he selling, T.J.? The stuff on the coffee table?"

"That right there is jus an appetizer," T.J. answered, slightly embarrassed. "He pretty much sells anything that's a hot item. Last week, it was dust. This week it's rocks. Next week it might be X, smack. Who the hell knows?"

"And he has you selling his stuff," Henry said. "That's the deal?"

T.J. nodded his head yes.

"You see, Henry," he nudged Henry on the arm, "there's nuttin to hustlin'."

"You won't be saying that when you get a knife pulled on you or even worse. . . "

"It ain't like that, Henry."

"Then what is it like, T.J.?"

"Check it," T.J. said. "It's simple. You buy in bulk, right. You take a little itty bitty from your stash, a couple of grams or two," he pointed to the complex behind him, "these people don't know the fuckin' difference—then you make your profit, Henry, you buy more, then you do the same goddamn thing over and over again, make more profit. Supply and demand. See, you give the people what they want. In return, you make a lil' chedda. I mean most of these people who lives 'round here in the P.S. need an escape, a fuckin' release. You feel me. Sum snort it. Others smoke it, shoot it. You know." He shrugged his shoulders. "Whatever."

"Yeah," Henry drawled. "You're really starting to sound like the corporate pig."

"Huh?"

"One day," Henry said, "Uncle Sam is going to come knocking on your door."

T.J. waved off Henry's comment.

"Whatever that fuck means," T.J. mumbled. "It's all economics, street knowledge. Nuttin you would know 'bout, Henry." T.J. finished his thought. "You know! And this be comin' straight from the same dude who be drinkin' Sherman's malt liquor. That my friend, that right there is a corporation. And you the dude who be tryin' to take a bite from the hand that feeds you."

"Different story."

"How the fuck so?"

"I'm sure Sherman was some guy like us who was trying to make a name for himself. It's not like he started his own empire. He just. . . " Henry glanced over the bottle in his hand, ". . . he makes malt liquor that taste like piss."

"But he is a household name. Am I right? And by the way, how do you know what piss taste like?"

There was another brief pause.

Henry smacked his gums like T.J.

"I'm just drinking it because I didn't want to hurt your feelings."

T.J. shoved Henry.

"Get outta here, man! Hurt my feelings?"

After the playful shoving match, Henry turned serious.

"You're going to tell Screw that you're not selling for him anymore."

"Hold up. . . "

"You heard me."

"You fuckin' serious!" T.J. hollered out. "You can't jus show up out of the blue and start tellin' me what to do wit my life. Who made you Saint Henry?"

"I came to you because we were friends."

"Yeah," T.J said. "*Were.*"

"Come on, T.J.," Henry said. "Don't be like that. I'm just looking out for you, man. That's all."

"I can take care of myself, Henry."

There was another silence, but this time longer and tenser.

"Are you really sure 'bout this Rockwell guy? I mean. . . if he's 'xpectin' a couple of songs from you, then it can't be sum half-ass bullshit. It has to be sumtin new and fresh."

"What? Like White Ballin'?"

"Not like White Ballin'," T.J. returned. "I mean sumtin that ain't nobody eva heard before. I've been workin' on sum new things on my own."

"You promise me to stop selling," Henry said sternly and stopped in his tracks. "If you do, we can really go all the way with this thing."

T.J. didn't respond.

Henry extended his hand.

"This is a once and a lifetime opportunity, T.J. Things like this don't happen for folks like us. What do you say?"

T.J. asked, "What am I gonna say to Screw? He's countin' on me."

"It's easy, T.J.," Henry said. "You just tell him that you're out."

"And where the hell am I gonna live?"

"I got a few more months left until the end of semester," Henry explained. "What better place to make a demo than a house full of drunken college students?"

"You talkin' 'bout a dorm room?"

"No," Henry said. "I stay with three other guys in a two story house right off campus." He nudged T.J. on the arm. "Think about it. We can play until the sun rises and we don't have to worry about the police busting down our door."

"Sounds nice, Henry," T.J. said. "It really does. But I can't go back wit you. I mean. . . college!"

"You're not going to college, dude," he said. "You'll just be staying with me. It's just me and my roommates. Two of them you'll hardly even see. So, really it's just me and Afed."

"Afed? What the hell kind of name is Afed?"

"He's straight, T.J.," he said. "Down for whatever."

"What's the deal wit your landlord?"

"Straight," Henry said again. "He even parties with us. Comes over once a week just to see if the place is still standing."

"I don't know, Henry. *College.* I mean. . . there's going to be a lot of distractions."

A car suddenly sped away.

The passenger in the car was firing a gun in the air.

Henry and T.J. suddenly ducked behind a dumpster.

"Distractions," Henry whispered closely to T.J.

"Like I said," T.J. said and looked around. "You get use to it."

"I'll be there to make sure you don't slip on me."

"Aight," T.J. said over some thought.

He shook Henry's hand.

"So, what we gonna write 'bout?"

"This," Henry said, stood, and then pointed around the neighborhood.

"Too many people have written songs 'bout '*this*,'" T.J. said sarcastically and used his fingers as quotation marks, "*the* struggle. Besides, it ain't like we had it that bad growing up as kids. We both had hard workin' parents who made sure we had food on the table, shelter over our heads. Some of the lil' kids around here ain't as fortunate as we was."

"That's not what I mean."

"Then what you mean?"

"Life, T.J.," Henry said. "Plain and simple."

"Man!" T.J. cried out. "You gotta be way more specific than that."

"This," Henry specified for T.J., "this is going to be our *Purple Rain*."

"Get the fuck outta here!" He leaned close to Henry. "You jus want to write 'bout that Kerri girl. You know you do." T.J. was wearing a grin over his face. "Don't you?"

"Hell nah!" Henry blurted out. "I'm over her. Besides, that was like five years ago."

"Then, why'd you ask 'bout her early today."

"Shit," Henry drawled and then laughed. "It was *you* who told *me* about Kerri. Don't be twisted my words around."

"So, what then? It can't be like when we was kids. Back in the day, it was jus one big ass jam session. We need structure."

"Oh please, dude," Henry said girlishly. "What do you know about song structure?"

"I like to think I know a lot 'bout song structure."

Henry smacked his gums.

"What we need to do, T.J., is take this thing to the next level."

"Like how?"

"I got some ideas."

The two stumbled from a long alleyway and came across a rundown building that was boarded up. A tarnished sign on the top of the building read: POSTAL OFFICE.

T.J. picked up a rock from the street and chucked it at the window that wasn't boarded.

The glass shattered.

Jagged pieces of glass danced over the asphalt.

"What the fuck, T.J.?"

T.J. said, "Relax, niggarella."

"What?"

"Jus fuckin' wit you, Henry."

"Why'd you go and do that?"

"The city is gonna demolish this building any day now. What's sum rock gonna do?"

"It's public property."

"See, Henry," T.J. said. "This is what our song should be about."

"'Bout vandalizing shit that isn't ours?"

"If this building right here belong to the city, then it sure as hell belong to the people of the city," T.J. said as he pointed at the old building. "Beside, that ain't the point."

"Then what's the point?"

"Throwing rocks," T.J. said proudly. "The poor man's weapon."

"Poor man's weapon?"

"Yeah."

"Then why throw them?" Henry asked. "Thought you was a 'high roller.'"

"Oh," T.J. said. "They ain't get higher than me."

"You the top dog. Huh?"

"Fucking rottweiler."

"Throwing rocks is our way of stickin' it to the Man."

"*The* Man?"

"That's right," he said. "*Da* Man."

"You crazy," Henry said under his breath and waved off T.J.'s comments.

"Am I now?"

T.J. tossed Henry a rock and sang, "*We be throwin' these muthafuckin' rocks. Revamping these old dilapidated blocks. Makin' brand new ones without any locks.*"

Henry chortled and shook his head in disgust.

"You're not better than us. Are you, Saint Henry?"

Henry reared back and threw the rock through the window. As before, the glass shattered from the window and crashed toward the ground.

"You're one of us now, Henry," T.J. announced and patted Henry on the shoulder.

A tiny spotlight glimmered from the end of the desolate street.

"*Cops.*"

"What do we do?"

T.J. sobered up and looked Henry directly in the eyes.

"Run," he said with wide eyes.

Henry didn't move.

"RUN DAMN IT!"

T.J. took off running.

Henry quickly followed.

The cop behind the wheel of the cruiser switched on the siren and chased the two. After running through three different alleyways and hiding behind a dumpster, Henry and T.J. finally ditched the cops.

"All clear. . . "

"That was a fucking buzz kill."

Henry tried to catch his breath.

"But gave me another song idea," T.J. said, resting his hands over his knees. He too was trying to catch his breath, especially with Sherman's malt liquor churning in his belly. "*Running from cops. Run, run, running from da cops. Can't stop or you're stupid ass is gonna get caught.*"

"Very original, T.J.," Henry said annoyingly and walked off down the alleyway.

"Where you goin', Henry?"

"*I'm hun, hun, hungry,*" Henry sang. "*Better eat some food or I'm going to get real, real angry.*"

"See, you hippo," T.J. teased. "Now, you catchin' on."

"Yeah, T.J.," Henry said with frustration. "Everybody can relate to food. Why don't we write an album about food? It could be like our own modern take on a cookbook. That would be a real hit."

In a joking manner, T.J. grabbed Henry by the back of the neck.

"Aight, smart ass," he said. "I know jus the place."

From *Missing the Edges*, page 12:

When I was a little girl, my father and I used to play a game of chess on the front porch every Sunday morning after church.

At the time (thirteen or fourteen I believe?), I hardly saw him around. I was off doing my own thing either running around in the fields or getting into trouble with Mr. Ardsley's son, Adam, who lived down the road, or singing to the stars at night. During the week, I was at school. My father who was at the farm was making sure that, at the end of the day, we had shelter over our heads. He was a provider, my father was, and a man of wisdom, which was hard to believe from a man who spent most of his days milking cows. My father had a way of making things easy for me, teaching me how to be a thinking woman. So, whenever we found the time to play chess together, he would squeeze in as much knowledge as he could before I ran off with Adam Ardsley or rode into town with Renée. I remember one conversation my father and I had like I remember the day before yesterday. When we were playing a game of chess—he, of course, was kicking my butt as he usually did—he told me about one particular piece on the board. The knight. My father called the knight one of the most "effective" pieces on the board, even more effective than the bishop. I called the piece the horse, not the knight that moved in the shape of a letter L. As always, I would pick his brain and ask him as many questions as I could.

Once, I asked him how to utilize the knight efficiently.

Not in those exact words, but he understood what I was asking.

When I played, I had a habit of moving the knight closer to the opposite side of the board, away from the other pieces.

My father told me he wouldn't recommend that, certainly not the knight. He told me to think of the knight as. . . "as a knight."

He asked me, "What do you think of when you think of a knight?"

"The horse piece, of course," I said.

I always loved the sound of my father's laugh, deep and rich, even if the laugh was directed at me.

Next, he told me to think about a real knight, like the one from the Middle Ages.

My father said to me, "Tell me what you think about a 'real' knight."

I answered, "They wear metal armor."

Then, he said, "And they're tough, right?"

"Yes," I said. "They are."

"And they're always in the thick of the battle, close quarter combat," he told me, "which, in most cases, should be in the middle of the board. But not always. Sometimes, you have to blend in with the other pieces in order to survive. Nonetheless, you always want to keep the knight in a place where it can take advantage of its real power."

He moved the knight away from the group of pawns, three of them, and placed it on a square at the edge of the board.

"See. . ." my father told me, ". . . when you pull the knight away from battle and place it on the far end, you have minimized its full potential. It now has very little room to move. Just remember."

I nodded my head.

Lastly, he asked, "You always want to keep the knight where?"

Without missing a beat, I answered, "Close to the battle."

They stopped at a convenient store, Grier's Food Market, which was connected to a gas station called Red Rabbit.

Outside Grier's, two vagrants were hanging around a newspaper dispenser and begging for change. Henry was keeping his head down and trying not to make eye contact with the vagrants. As for T.J., he couldn't stop eyeing them and the track marks running down their forearms, preparing for them to poke the inevitable "can-you-spare-some-change" question.

Henry ignored the homeless men and held open the door for T.J.

"Ladies first," he said jokingly to T.J.

In return, T.J. jokingly winked at Henry and walked inside the convenient store.

The store had the basic necessities as well as nude magazines and, of course, junk food. It also had a small hot bar of all things fried (a favorite among the early morning construction workers). They had every part of the chicken, onion rings, burgers, and pizza. On Fridays, they served fried fish, mostly perch or flounder. The cook left about an hour ago. However, the food from earlier tonight was left under a heat lamp.

Henry tapped T.J. on the arm.

"Eat at your own risk," he whispered.

"You'd be surprised, Saint Henry," T.J. said, talking over his shoulder. "You'd pay double in one of them fancy restaurants."

"I seriously doubt a fancy restaurant has pepperoni pizza on the menu."

Henry squinted his eye at T.J.

"Have you ever been to a fancy restaurant, T.J.?"

"Once," he replied. "After my sister's wedding."

Henry couldn't help but chortle.

"I'm sure they were serving pizza."

"They had pizza," he said. "But not like this here. This had like vegetables and things you'd find in a salad. Pizza they called 'White Pizza.'" He mumbled, "Whatever the fuck that is." His voice then softened to a near whisper, "Fuckin' cracker pizza." He faced Henry. "If you gonna eat pizza you might as well do it right. You know?"

"Preaching to the choir," Henry said and fixed himself a hot dog. "This is what I like to call 'drunk food.'"

T.J. suspiciously glanced over at the wrinkled hot dog as if it was the only food to stay away from in the hot bar and yet Henry grabbed it without a second's hesitation. T.J. didn't say anything. He grabbed a slice of pizza with pepperoni and black olives from the hot bar.

"I mean," T.J. lifted up the slice of pizza to his face, "I want my pizza greasy. I want cheese to be drippin' from the crust. You can make pizza healthy or put things on it and stuff that you normally wouldn't, but let's face it. We talkin' 'bout pizza here, greasy fuckin' pizza. Not quiche."

"Do even know what quiche is?"

As he was known to do, T.J. smacked his gums and then tilted his head like a teapot.

The two of them laughed and paid for their food. The clerk made small talk. What are you two fellows up to tonight? That sort of thing. Henry and T.J. kept it plain Jane. They said their thank you's to the clerk and ate their food on the side of the curb. Halfway through their meal, a police cruiser pulled up to Grier's. First, a young police officer stepped out of the cruiser. He appeared new from the robotic movements and heavy surveillance around the rough neighborhood. Possibly his first week on the job. Next, his partner, who was driving, was slow to exit. He was a stern man, familiar and extremely arrogant. T.J. struggled to swallow his bite of food. He leaned closer to Henry and whispered in his ear, "I think that's the same police car."

Henry asked, "How do you know?"

"Jus play it cool," he uttered and recognized the one cop slowly making his way toward the curb. "This white dude has it in for me."

"What? What did you do, T.J.?"

"Not a damn thing," he uttered. "He always be messin' wit me."

"Maybe you should stop throwing rocks at buildings."

"You got my back."

Henry didn't answer.

"Henry?"

T.J.'s eyes were swollen.

"What are you going to do, T.J.?"

"You got my back. . . right?"

"Yeah," he said and nodded. "I got your back. But don't do anything stupid."

The hard cop—*Officer Ted Backer*, Henry noticed the name of the nametag—strolled up to the two. Partner remained at a distance. From where Henry was sitting, he couldn't read the name on his nametag. Officer Backer was staring long and hard at T.J. as if he knew him from somewhere. The officer recognized the damp, wringed collar around T.J.'s neck.

"Drop the food," Officer Backer demanded.

T.J. didn't know what to think.

"I'm not going to say it again," he said. "You drop the food or I'll drop it for you."

"You can't tell me what to do, cop." T.J. turned his shoulder and pointed to the security camera mounted at the corner of Grier's. "You gonna take the food from my hands in front of a camera? You haven't even given me a reason to drop my food."

"Vandalism," Officer Backer replied. "How's that?"

"We didn't vandalize nuttin."

The two officers took a couple of steps closer. Officer Backer was fingering the baton on his belt while his partner remained as stiff as a robot.

"You play me as a fool, T.J.?"

T.J. swallowed another dry lump down his throat.

"You mean to tell me you two weren't throwing rocks at the Post Office?"

T.J. smacked his gums.

"Nah!"

"Okay, tough guy," Officer Backer said and waved his fingers upward. "Get up."

"Must be a slow night. Huh, cop?"

"I said, 'get the fuck up!'"

His partner, who was standing quietly in the background, said, "Hey, Ted. Just leave the man alone. He said he wasn't the one."

"Man? He's no man. He's just a boy."

T.J. was shaking his head.

"You believe this fucking piece of shit," the officer fumed to his partner. "That's what these kids do nowadays. They destroy public property, steal, sling drugs, commit murder, and then they lie and give you some kind of sob story or they carry around some kind of resentment against you like their lives are so much harder than yours."

T.J. sprung to his feet.

"You think you might know me, but you don't. . . " he looked over his nametag, ". . . Ted. What good can you possibly be doin' for our city?"

"Our city? No," he said, shaking his head. His eyes flared madly. "This is *my* city."

"This is the same man who spends all night lookin' for fights to pick," T.J. interrupted. "You must be really bored, Ted? What's a matter? Your wife don't turn you on anymore? You ain't got a dick for yo wife to fuck anymore?"

His partner mistakenly giggled under his breath.

Officer Backer caught the end of the giggle and clinched his teeth in anger.

Henry tapped T.J. on the shoulder.

"Come on, T.J.," he said softly. "You're provoking him."

"You should listen to your friend here, T.J."

"Does this make you hard, cop? Go 'round harassin' folks like us," T.J. said amusedly. "You can't release any of that aggressive at home, so you go 'head and take it out on inno-cent people."

"That's it," Officer Backer said and pulled out a pair of handcuffs.

"What you doing?" T.J. asked, backing away.

Officer Backer seethed, "Your ass is going downtown."

"For what?"

"Resisting arrest."

"I ain't doing nuttin."

"Take it easy, sir," Henry said to the officer. "He's not resisting."

"Shut up!" He pointed at Henry. "You're next!"

T.J. was yanking away from the officer's grip.

"Don't fucking resist, you mother fucker," Officer Backer said and tried to grab T.J.'s wrist.

Again, T.J. yanked his hand away.

The officer pulled out the baton from his belt and rammed the end of it into T.J.'s abdomen, which forced him to his knees. The plate of pizza fell over the curb.

"Geez," the other officer said. "Take it easy on him, Teddy. Would you?"

Officer Backer applied handcuffs to T.J. After he was through, he pointed at Henry.

"Get that one," he said.

"But, Ted. . ."

"Now."

"Tedd. . ."

"DO IT NOW!"

T.J. grunted.

"I'm tired of this shit."

"Well, maybe you should've thought twice about the consequences before you broke the law."

Officer Backer kicked T.J. in the stomach.

The other officer slowly approached Henry.

He said anxiously, "Don't make this hard on me, son."

Henry shook his head and held out his hands, palm side up.

As the officer stood inches away from Henry, Henry got a closer look at the name on his nametag. The name read "Officer Tray Honeycutt."

As his partner did before him, he pulled out the pair of handcuffs and applied them to Henry.

Officer Honeycutt snapped the handcuffs over Henry's wrists and said closely, "Thanks."

After Henry and T.J. were both handcuffed, the two officers escorted them to the cruiser where they read them their Miranda rights.

TEN

THROUGHOUT his adolescence, Henry experienced many long nights: getting food poisoning after eating fried oysters at Jimmy's Fish Camp in Harrietsville; his backside falling victim to his mother's "shoe" after TP'ing Mr. and Mrs. Hamchild's house; in high school dropping two hits of acid and going to a back to school party and swearing he saw translucent spiders crawling all over his arms; snorting a line of cocaine and spending an entire night constructing a filter system that would fit over an automobile's exhaust pipe in order to help reduce the carbon dioxide emissions into the air (the next morning, the invention ended up looking like a extraterrestrial spaceship over the backside of his friend's Ford pickup truck); dragging from a roach that was laced with some foreign drug that Henry, till this day, didn't know exactly what it was. His friends assumed it was "angel dust" or "PCP." Then, there was that one Saturday night when he and his roommate, Afed, went to an Irish pub in downtown Lansford. The parking was free and drinks were only a dollar, which, to Henry, seemed strange, especially on a Saturday night. After he and Afed ordered their second drink, they noticed the scarcity of women around the bar (and the women who were there all had short, military style haircuts and were sitting with other girls, who couldn't pull themselves to look at the two handsome college students at the bar). Plus, an unusually large crowd was gathered around the karaoke machine. There, two fairly cut guys in Polo shirts were singing the song "The Sign" by Ace of Base. From that moment forward, the rest of the night was played out like a kill scene from a horror movie. Each frantic glance Henry took around the bar (the cute girl sliding her hand over her girlfriend's hand; her other friends playing footsy underneath the table; the two who were singing karaoke, one with a limp wrist, now dry humping each other on the dance floor; the masculine Calvin Klein model salaciously eyeing Afed through the mirror behind the bar; the cook with the curly mustache and striped zebra shirt, so tight that it looked as if it was painted on his body, winking at Henry; the middle aged bartender who, to Henry, could've easily passed as his third grade teacher, Ms. Carper, wiping the bead of sweat from her brow; the three men drinking blue margaritas with their pinkies slightly erected outward) was like listening to the screeching violins from Bernard Herrmann's score during the famous shower scene in Hitchcock's *Psycho*. Each glance. Each screech. Emasculating yet intriguing. Without taking another sip of his warm pilsner, Henry suddenly turned to Afed with little or no pride and whispered into his ear, "Dude, we're in a gay bar." Not like there was anything wrong with that. Both Henry and Afed preferred not to play for the *other* team. Somewhere, either in Henry's head or on that karaoke machine (Henry was too traumatized to tell), Boy George's "The Crying Game" was playing. It all made sense why that one burly guy with the shit-eating grin across his face kept holding out his palm in front of Afed—as if he was asking for something but didn't want to be so forthright with that matter.

None of those nights, including the night at the gay bar, compared to the night that he spent in jail. Time was like watching a cut scab over. The smells alone were enough to twist his stomach. The other prisoners in the holding cells next to him were like these strange dark beasts, snoring and growling and farting, throughout the darkness. Fortunately for Henry, he was able to get one phone call. He thought about calling his mother, but then again, she had her own troubles. So, he decided to call his roommate, Afed.

When morning came, the prison guard let Henry and T.J. out of their cell.

They shamefully gathered their belongings from checkout and exited the prison without saying a word to one another.

Once they left the prison, Henry took a brief moment to swallow up the bright sunlight. As for T.J., he cursed the sunlight and cloaked his face with his hands.

Henry said, "Never has freedom felt so damn intoxicating."

T.J. rubbed his crusty, red eyes.

"I think that's Sherman talkin'," he uttered.

Henry glanced over at T.J.

"Correct me if I'm wrong, but it looks like you actually got some sleep in the joint."

"I rather not talk about it, Henry."

"You didn't get butt raped. Did you?"

"Hells nah!" T.J. blurted out, his face squinting. "But it sure as hell wasn't as bad as that time we went to the Appalachian Mountains in fourth grade. Our bus broke down. You 'member?"

"I remember."

"We ended up spendin' the night in a cabin filled with all them daddy long legs."

"That wasn't so bad," Henry said, shrugging his shoulders. "Thought it was kind of fun actually."

"Fun?" he said, throwing his head back in bafflement. "Ain't nuttin fun 'bout being in a cramped cabin with a bunch of daddy long legs."

"That's not a bad idea for a song," Henry said. "It could be like a story... like... like ah... a Johnny Cash song or like that one Temptations' song, 'Papa Was A Rollin' Stone.'"

T.J. ran his fingers over his left eye.

"Not in the mood, Henry."

"Oh," he said and paused. "So, what did the lawyer say?"

"He said I got me a case," T.J. answered. "The camera caught that asshole kickin' me when I was down. He said the charges would probably be dropped by next week. Cop may be suspended for a month or two for 'cessive force."

"More like assault."

"Other than that, we straight, Henry."

"I know you don't want to talk about it, T.J." They made it halfway to the street. Henry stopped, faced T.J., and said, "But you can't be pulling that kind of shit again. If there was one thing my mom taught me, and I mean like singed it in my head, was not to mess with the police," exaggerating the *po* in police. "They got guns. Legally, they have the right to shoot you if you're acting up. And they don't hesitate to use them either!"

"They're a bunch of fuckin' bullies," T.J. said. "That's what they is. They probably didn't get laid in high school."

"Who knows, T.J.?" Henry shrugged his shoulders. "You can't explain what goes on in those kinds of people's heads. You can't. It's too complex."

"I know what you sayin'."

T.J. nodded at the white Mercedes parked on the curb.

"Is that your boy? In the Cedes!" He said under his breath, "Goddamn rich white boy."

"That's Afed," Henry said. "And yeah. He's kind of spoiled."

"Kind of?"

T.J. tried to hold back the laugh.

"So, he's the one we should thank or is it his parents?"

"He's the one," Henry said and then leaned in closer. "And watch with the cursing. He's a real sensitive bastard."

"Aight."

They made it to the Mercedes. Afed stepped out and greeted Henry. He was a slender man who was wearing an unbuttoned blue dress shirt over a pea green Club Flow tee shirt and the kind of shades Maverick and Goose wore in the movie *Top Gun*. He had thick brunette hair combed over one side of his head like an actor and skin like an underwear model. He removed the aviator shades and shook Henry's hand.

"I owe you one, Afed."

"Big time."

Afed cautiously glanced over at T.J.

"Oh yeah," Henry said surprisingly and pointed at T.J. "This is T.J. We go way back."

"Your friend from Reddington?"

"That's right." He pointed at Afed. "T.J. Afed. Afed. T.J., aka the Octopus."

T.J. smirked at the nickname.

"Ain't nobody call me that in years."

"Nice to meet you, Octopus."

"T.J.," he said. "Jus call me T.J."

Afed reached out his hand and warily shook T.J.'s hand.

"You're the one who's going to be staying with us?"

"I'm jus here wit my boy, Henry," he said. "Once we do our thing, I'll be out of your hair."

"You're not in my hair, yet."

T.J. didn't find the comment amusing.

"Listen, I wanted to thank you for bailin' me out," T.J. said. "I don't think anybody has eva dun anything like that for me."

"Well," Afed said hesitantly, "a friend of Henry is a friend of mine."

"Whatever," T.J. uttered. "Is it cool we stop at my place. I haf to pick up sum things."

"How do you think Screw is going to handle the news about you leaving?"

After T.J. picked up his things, he walked away from the complex. On the way to the car, he occasionally grabbed the side of his face.

"He didn't take it so well," he said, looking away from Henry.

He handed the saxophone case to Henry and placed his two black garbage bags of "things" into his trunk. Shirts and samplers were sticking out.

"Nice ride," Henry said and looked over T.J.'s hatchback parked behind the apartment complex. The back right tire was a spare. The back window was made up of a blue tarp from where the glass had been shattered from a brick.

"Lil' Red," he said, referring to his hatchback. "She may look ugly. But she's got a lil' fight in her." T.J. pointed at the saxophone. "I went through a lot of shit to get that thing back."

Henry witnessed the fresh bruise around T.J.'s eye. He walked over to Afed's car and placed Harry in the passenger seat. Henry and T.J. stood outside the Mercedes while Afed tapped his fingers over the steering wheel and frantically looked around the neighborhood in paranoia.

"So, I follow you," T.J. said.

Henry was too busy studying T.J.'s face.

"What happened in there, T.J.?"

"Nuttin."

"Then, where'd you get the shiner?"

T.J. didn't answer the question.

"So. . . "

"*So*," T.J. replied coldly.

Henry shrugged his shoulders in confusion and tried to read T.J.'s empty expression.

T.J. said quietly, "He pulled a gun on me, Henry. He held that fuckin' thing in my face! What was I supposed to do?"

"A gun? You're kidding?"

"No," T.J. said vacantly. "I ain't kiddin'. It's like I saw my. . . like I saw my life flash before my eyez."

"Why did he pull a gun on you?"

"I broke the deal, Henry," T.J. answered. "I promised him I sell the rest of his stash."

"But what about the demo?"

"We still gonna make our demo," he said. "Don't you worry. I threw that garbage in the trash on the way down here. I'm done being the bad guy's little henchman. For once, I wanna do sumtin good wit my life. You, Henry, you given me that chance. I realized that last night while we were in the pen."

Henry reached out his hand and shook T.J.'s hand.

"Then, you're with the right people," Henry said and tightened his grip around T.J.'s hand.

When they arrived at the house off campus, T.J. was as fidgety as a squirrel. Henry told T.J. to park Little Red on the street. So, he did. They got out of the cars (Afed's Mercedes taking up nearly the entire driveway) and met up with each other on the front lawn. T.J. was distracted by a voluptuous freshman strutting down the sidewalk with her hips swaying from side to side as if she was brushing flies away. Henry grabbed T.J. and told him to control himself and helped carry his bags to the house. T.J. didn't move an inch from where he was last standing. As Henry made it to the porch, he turned his shoulder and noticed T.J. looking around the street, but this time in great paranoia. Henry dropped the bags on the porch and walked back over to T.J.

"You have nothing worry about, T.J.," Henry said and tapped T.J. on the shoulder. "They won't find you here."

T.J. didn't respond. Yet, he looked into Henry's eyes and bobbed his head.

They made it into the house without bumping into the landlord, Montell, who lived across the street. T.J. was somewhat amazed by the size of the house and yet repulsed from its condition. Beer cans—some half full while others empty and folded like accordions—were scattered around the living room. Plates of leftover food, pizza boxes, and trays from microwavable meals were scattered about as well. Even the air carried the musty stench of cheap beer.

"I think I was better off wit Screw," T.J. said after seeing the pigsty around the living room.

"Good luck going back to the same guy who stuck a gun in your face." Henry shot a glance at Afed. "I thought you were going to straighten the place out."

"Something came up," Afed said hesitantly.

"Where's Ronnie or Lumen?"

"Where *you* should be?"

T.J. said from behind, "And where 'xactly is that?"

"Class." Afed turned to T.J. "Your 'boy' here has already missed like a week of class."

"Listen, Henry Man," T.J. said to Henry and dropped his bags on the floor. "I don't want you gettin' in troubles cuz of me."

"You're straight, T.J.," Henry said. "It's an art history class. What I like to call a cram class. It's one of those classes where you just show up for the test. You don't really have to go."

"I hope you don't approach our demo the same way you approach your edgacation."

"Is this coming from the same guy who dropped out of high school?"

T.J.'s face washed over with all seriousness.

"Man! Listen, Henry," T.J. whined. "All I'm sayin' is that if we gonna do this demo thing, then there ain't no fuckin' around."

"Like ten seconds ago you were talking about how much you wanted to get your dick wet."

"The demo comes first."

"Absolutely," Henry said.

"Then, the ladies."

T.J. grinned, picked up his bags, and followed Henry upstairs.

"Well, where do we start?" he asked as he arrived at the top of the landing.

"Here."

Henry pointed to the bedroom across the hallway.

T.J. poked his head inside the cluttered room.

"Kind of small for a studio. Don't you think?"

"We'll have to make it work."

Henry nodded at Afed.

"Is there any way you could sleep on the couch for the time being?"

Afed furrowed his brows.

"It's cool, Henry," T.J. said. "I don't want you rearrangin' your lifes ova me. I'll sleep on the couch. I hate to say it, but I've almost gotten use to sleepin' on the couch. Practically the only bed I've slept on for the past three years."

"Are you sure? Because Afed doesn't mind."

Behind T.J., Afed ran his straight hand, as sharp as a blade, across the jugular of his neck.

"Don't sweat over me," T.J. said and smiled. "Me, I'm low maintenance."

Afed blurted out, "You heard the man!"

"It's settled then," Henry said.

T.J. pulled out a Roland TR-909 and asked, "So, where should I put my equipment?"

ELEVEN

WITH Afed's help, Henry and T.J. consolidated most of the frivolous things in the bedroom. Half of the things they trashed. They crammed the others like the mini refrigerator, the sofa, the chairs, and the computer into the closet. They ended up turning the beds into bunk beds, which opened up more space in the room. Henry helped T.J. set up his equipment along the wall. Two Technics turntables were positioned at the center of the setup. On both sides of the Technics, he had four different Rolands: a TR-909, a MKS-80, a Jupiter-4, and an Octapad.

As they were tidying things along the wall, Henry couldn't take his eyes off one device in particular.

"This isn't what I think it is," he said with astonishment and hovered his hand over the device.

While T.J. was fishing out a couple of spools of instrument cable, Henry ran his finger over the microphone.

He said, "Vocoder."

"Korg VC-10," Henry read, his finger underlining the label of the model. "Get out of here. I've always wanted one of these. When I was younger, I remember I tried to save up lemonade money, not for this kind, but one similar to it."

"Well," T.J. said as he was plugging the last of the equipment into the eight-track recorder, which was connected to a pair of cheap speakers perched adjacent to one another. "What's mine is yours, homie."

Without blinking, Henry marveled at the vocoder.

T.J. slanted his body forward, poked his head in front of Henry's range of vision, and warned, "Jus don't fuck it up. You hear?"

Henry bobbed his head.

"I won't," he said.

"I'm glad we understand each otha."

"So, what's her name?"

"Name?"

"Yeah," Henry said and pulled his eyes from the VC-10. "Every instrument has to have a name?"

T.J. continued to map out the signal flow for each musical device.

He said under his breath, "Whatever."

Henry pulled out the last musical device from T.J.'s bag. It was an analog synthesizer. His eyes grazed across the name written over the interface.

"*Moog*," he uttered. "How the hell could you afford a Moog?"

"Technically, it's a Realistic Concertmate." He pointed at the label. "See. Right here. Realistic Concertmate MG-1."

"This thing must be worth a fortune." Henry drifted in thought. He traced his eyes back over T.J. with suspicion. "You didn't steal it. Did you?"

"Nah," T.J. said with a sudden frown. "But I can't say the same thing about the Roland."

"Which one?"

T.J.'s eyes innocently rolled up at Henry.

"All of them?" he said with his eyes swelling.

Henry sighed.

"Chills, Henry," he said. "It's all good. I know a guy. They was practically given to me. And the guy who owned the Moog, he must've grown out of it. Didn't really play it anymore. So, I told him that I would take it off his hands. So, that's what I did. Gave him fifty bones for it."

"That is a steal."

"That baby's probably worth maybe triple that price."

"This is what I'm talking about, T.J.," Henry said eagerly while studying the spread. Once more, he drifted momentarily in thought, an oblique appreciation glimmering over his face. He said in a trance, "The Moog has that trademark sound. You know?"

T.J. bobbed his head.

"Church," he said.

Henry continued, "I'm sure you've heard that trademark sound before." The excitement built in his voice. "Pink Floyd's *Dark Side of the Moon*, The Beatles' *Abbey Road*, any band that's made it big—and I'm talking mainstream, top of the billboards B.I.G., *BIG*—has to have at least one Moog in their collection!"

"Technically, it's a Moog," T.J. said, his voice gradually falling. "But, like I said, it's not like the ones you be talkin' 'bout."

Henry pointed directly at the label.

"It says 'Moog' right there."

"Ye. . . yeah, but the ones you hear on the radio, those costs like thousands of dollars." He tapped his finger over the Moog. "They sell these kinds of Moogs here at Radioshack. At least they used to. I don't know if they sell them there anymore. It's more of a vintage thing."

"Radioshack?"

"Hey, Henry," T.J. said, dropping his shoulders. "If you don't like it, then too bad."

Henry's jaw dropped a little.

"No," he corrected. "It's cool. This is a good start, T.J."

T.J. motioned toward Henry, "But we wanna be original."

"Absolutely," Henry replied.

Lounging over the top bunk bed, Afed was taking small, baby-like puffs from a tightly rolled joint and blowing out rings of smoke.

"So, what kind of sound you guys going for?" he asked casually as his eyes surveyed the layout. "I see the drum machines. The sampling thingamajigs. I see the old keyboards and all the electronic gadgets and whatnot. Then, I see the saxophone." His face tightened with perplexity. "Are we talking about some Glen Frey, Billy Ocean, Phil Collins, meets Kool and The Gang, Herbie Hancock kind of music? You two have to admit. Honestly, the saxophone," one side of his face squinted, "it is kind of cliché. After that whole eighties new wave invasion swept over America like a black plague."

T.J. said sarcastically, "Yeah, Afed. Lots of longhaired girls wearin' spandex, all them raunchy clubs, all the sex and the cocaine, and them big ass Afros. What's not to like?"

Henry chimed in, "Sounds like some real Dark Ages, Afed."

"You know what I mean," Afed said. "I'm talking about the music. It was pretty, you know, pretty cheesy."

"I take it you haven't heard my boy play then," T.J. said, glancing over at Henry. "I don't know how to say this without soundin' like a complete foo, but this man here is a *genius*."

"Henry doesn't strike me as a saxophonist," Afed said, taking another drag from the joint. His voice was deeper from holding the smoke in the lungs. "More like a clarinet kind of man."

"Clarinet?" Henry mumbled with a smirk. While helping out T.J. unroll another spool of wire, Henry directed his attention over at T.J. "Do me a favor, T.J., and smack this guy. Would you?"

T.J. never smacked Afed, although he did think twice about doing so.

Afed finally released the smoke with a chatter of coughing.

"We're not trying to copy anybody, Afed," Henry said with a straight face and stood upright. "We're just trying to create something that nobody's heard before, something a little updated."

"Sorry to burst your bubble, Henry," Afed said, "but there's no music that has never been done before by one artist or another. Nothing's new underneath the sun."

"That's sum deep shit right there," T.J. said and then repeated carefully, "*Nothing's new underneath the sun.* I like that shit."

"Whatever," Henry murmured.

Another thought suddenly came to mind.

"And by the way," he said to Afed, "Glenn Frey didn't play the saxophone."

"He did too," Afed said, sitting upright. "In that one song from. . . what's that show. . . "

"You talking about *Miami Vice?*"

"That's it!"

"No," Henry said. "You're thinking about Bill Bergman, not Glenn Frey."

"How much you want to bet?"

"What are you going to bet me with?" Afed asked. "You don't have any money."

"If I'm right, which, I know I am, you have to give me your pop's Mercedes."

Afed leaned back over the bed and said under his breath, "Get out of here."

"That's what I thought."

T.J. nodded at Afed.

"So, you used to listen to Herbie Hancock?"

"Why?"

Henry said to Afed, "Because this dude here was like obsessed with Herbie Hancock when we were growing up."

"True that." T.J. smiled with exaggeration. "I had all his tapes," he said. "'Member the time that old lady who used to live down the street from us took us to one of his concerts. Shoot! What was her name?"

"Dolores," Henry said mindfully.

"Yeah," T.J. exclaimed. "Dolores."

"So, are you going to be rapping?" Afed asked Henry, but Henry was caught in a temporary daze.

"Me? Rap?"

"Ever since I've known Henry, the kid ain't much of a rapper. Kid's got the shakes."

"The shakes?"

"Every time I used to rhyme in front of the other boys, I use to get all scared and start shaking."

"I wouldn't believe it," Afed said. "The other night when we got hammered, you were spitting some sick rhymes. But you weren't rapping, per se. You were, but it was done differently. More so, singing. Nothing like I've heard before. The guys were trying to figure what you sounded like. It was almost as if. . . as if James Brown had a son with. . . with Judy Garland. That son being you, of course. And then that kid was raised by werewolves, savage don't-give-a-shit kinds of wolves. And then that kid left his pack where Freddie Mercury found him on the side of the street. And then Freddie Mercury took him in as one of his own and taught him how to sing."

"Me?" Henry said, laughing. "I did this?"

"You don't remember?"

"No."

"You had these crazy Little Richard eyes," Afed said, widening his eyes.

"Maybe there is a singer trapped up in there, Henry," T.J. said calmly. "You jus don't know it. Not yet."

"So, what's your music going to sound like?" Afed asked, nodding at Henry.

"I honestly haven't figured that part out."

"I'm cool wit throwin' 'round sum ideas," T.J. said and used his hands to explain himself. "Sort of like. . . like play off each other. See where it takes us."

"You guys ever seen a John Carpenter movie?"

"You talkin' 'bout *Halloween*, that John Carpenter?"

"Yeah," Henry said. "He uses this ominous-sounding am-bience in all of his movies as well as these arpeggios like you might hear like in an Italo disco song or like a German pop song."

"Yeah!" T.J. exclaimed. "I know all 'bout sum arpeggios, not that other thing you be talkin' 'bout."

"Italo disco?"

"Yeah."

"Italian related."

"Italian music?"

"Yeah."

"What's Italian music supposed to sound like?"

Henry smacked his gums.

"Forget I said it," he said. "I was going for something like that, the John Carpenter vibe, subtle, though."

"I thought we was gonna be original, Henry. The last thing we wanna do is sound like a bunch of fuckin' posers."

"We're not," Henry said. "Trust me. But like it'd be cool to have that kind of mystery and suspense, like this kind of. . . this. . . this like darkness, like something really suspi-cious going on throughout the music, like an under layer on top of this massive wall of sound. For example: think about Michael Jackson's 'Thriller.'"

"I love that jam!" T.J. said excitedly. "Zombies dancing around and shit!"

"You get what I'm saying, though," Henry said enthusias-tically. "Then, I come in with Harry. It's more or less a statement from the time period we come from."

"I got the right equipment for that there, but. . . "

"But what?"

"But who in their right mind is gonna be jammin' out to like Halloween music in a club?" T.J. asked, scratching the backside of his head. "I mean it was cool and all when we was kids. But now. . . I don't know, Henry. People might find that shit kind of creepy if you ask me."

Afed said, "Not unless you're like stalking a fly girl at a club. . . "

"True that," T.J. said. "You want to dance wit her, not kill her."

Henry let out a sigh of frustration and said to himself, "I don't think I'm explaining myself clear enough."

After hours of hard work, the setup was complete. Now, all they had to do was make the room soundproof and then they could finally call it a "studio." This was where things got a little tricky. See, Henry, as well as Afed, wasn't too concerned about the neighbors. In fact, most of them were juniors and seniors and they could care less about the noise factor. However, they had to remember that they were still living in a house with two other people, two people who happened to be bookworms. Lumen, a sophomore, was a big fan of the classics: all of the Charles Dickens's masterpieces—one of them being the classic novel, *A Tale of Two Cities*—Steinbeck's *Of Mice and Men* (Lumen's favorite!), and then Hemmingway's *The Sun Also Rises*. Ronnie, on the other hand, a junior, enjoyed the authors who explored more of the darker sides of humanity: Lovecraft, Matheson, and King. Everybody around the house, including T.J., knew not to get Ronnie started on Stephen King. Ronnie's passion for Mr. King's stories was like a robust engine. If someone brought up the name *King* or one of King's stories, for instance, *Carrie*, that was Carrie with a C and not a K (on the second night at the house, T.J. learned the hard way when he and Henry's roommates were kicking back in the living room, bragging about their sweethearts or who they had sex with or who they had a crush on, and T.J. slipped his tongue and mentioned Henry's high school crush, Kerri, and instead of reminiscing about old times, he got an earful about another high school girl, a tormented protagonist name Carrie, spelled with a C, who was on the rag and, oh yeah, she had telekinetic powers and, oh yeah, she could move objects with her mind and set things on fire!), then Ronnie could go on for days, even weeks, babbling on and on about Mr. King without stripping a single thread. Besides the two bookworms,

Henry and T.J. (mostly Henry) were more concerned about the outside sound—most likely the street ambience—coming in and interfering with the recording process. Henry made Afed a laundry list of supplies and sent him to the closest Depot store. Afed came back to the house with a trunk load of hardware supplies: corkboards, fiberboards, foam, all cut to the proper length of the window frames and doorways, and not to mention, over six dozen cartons of eggs. The store manager, who was eyeballing Afed the entire time, even had to pull a couple of cartons from the back. When T.J. asked why egg cartons (the idea alone, he thought, seemed ridiculous), Henry told him that he once read in a DIY book on home recording that egg cartons help control and disperse the concentration of bounce waves or "*reflections*," thus creating a more easy listening environment.

After a lot of convincing, the three immediately got to work. They boarded up the window frames with fiberboard and drapes and old quilts, preventing any sound from escaping the studio, as well as keeping T.J. away from the girls who frequently passed by the house, and mounted a sheet of corkboard over the doorway, and filled in cracks with foam, tape, and anything they could get their hands on around the house like blankets or towels. All they had to do now was get rid of all the eggs, and they didn't want to waste them either. So, they used up half of them to make a breakfast for all of their friends. As for the rest of the eggs, they used them to egg a couple of sorority houses on their street. When the studio was finally complete, it turned out that Henry didn't know exactly what he was doing, especially about controlling the "reflections" part. However, the studio was definitely soundproof. Not a single peep heard from inside the house. Like the entire world around them had been completely shut off, done, finished, wiped away into oblivion. Now, all that remained of the world was maybe an early morning rumble from a marching band or a distant car horn. T.J. couldn't tell much of a difference about the sound. He thought it was just a fat waste of time, the acoustics part, but he never complained. Most of his equipment was digital and didn't need a microphone. Besides the saxophone, which was going into a SM57 microphone—"a popular and versatile mic," said the dealer at the local music store—most of what they were playing was going straight into an eight-track recorder. So, really, the whole setup was for Henry, as well as playback.

To begin the session, T.J. tested the levels on each device. He ran into a bit of a snag with the Roland TR-909. After making sure the jack was securely connected to the output, he ran yet another test. The troubleshooting was a success. While all of this was going on, Henry was standing with Harry and occasionally wiping the beads of sweat from his palms over his pants. At this point, Henry forgot most of what Ms. Craft had taught him. He assumed the skills would come back to him as soon as they started to create sound. If only there was a way he could play the same way he played at Hot Foxy. Till this day, Henry was still astonished by the performance—it was as if another person had taken over his body. When it finally came time for Henry to explain that beat in his head to T.J.—the one beat that had been eating away at him for some time now—he did so in a child-like manner, referencing various songs and movies. T.J. spent hours on the MG-1 and attempted to pinpoint that right sound through tweaking. Since Henry didn't know the correct music terminology—same with T.J.—it took them longer than usual. (*Square wave with pulse, detune up, sync out, octave up negative one*). . . T.J. grinned. . . (*Sounds like something from an old school Nintendo game*). . . The grin stretched even farther across T.J.'s face. . . (*very Mega Man*). . . Henry was frowning. . . (*I don't know, T.J.*). . . (*Hold on*). . . T.J. was now switching back and forth from saw wave to square wave, lowering and raising the pitch, or detuning, as it was called, on the MG-1, changing octave. . . (*Switch it back, minus two*). . . dropped an octave, now tweaked with the cutoff frequency in the filter section. . . (*I like that*). . . (*What's that slider right there do?*). . . T.J. slapped the top of Henry's hand. . . (*No touching*). . . T.J. now turned up the envelope attack. . . He kept searching for the right notes, right sound, so close. . . in the contour section, T.J. then switched over to continuous, not keyed. . . (*Let's raise fall time*). . . Henry listened very closely to the sound. . . (*Way too nasally*). . . (*Hold up*). . . switched over to sustain. . . (Mr. *John Carpenter, eat your fuckin' heart out*). . . Henry beamed. . . (*Sounds like something straight out of The Thing!*). . . T.J. was bobbing his head like a bobble head doll. . . (*You ain't heard nuttin yet*). . . In the mixer section, T.J. turned up Tone One and Tone Two to max level and tweaked from there. . . (*What's that there?*). . . Henry pointed at the bar graph-like symbol in the Tone Source Two section. . . (*That's the pulse right there*). . . He turned up Noise. . . (*Sounds weird, like a storm's coming*). . . Henry shrugged. . . (*Could be used as a cool effect*). . . T.J. was fiddling around with the modulation, pitch, and then oscillators. . . (*How about this?*). . . (*It needs to be fuller*). . . T.J. tweaked. . . (*No! There! You had it, T.J.*) . . .

Hours were exhausted on the MG-1, and no luck.

They came up with a couple of interesting ideas for a couple of songs—more or less—sound effects, but nothing they could develop into a hit.

So, they moved onto the Rolands.

(*Like Grandmaster Flash*)

Henry thought about the name of that one song in his head.

T.J. unpeeled the headphones from his neck.

"You're gonna haf to be mo specific than that, man," he said.

"White Lines!" Henry blurted out. "You know that one song 'White Lines'?"

"I know 'White Lines.'" T.J. hollered out, "Bass!" And then he sang in a high pitch voice, "*White Lines.*"

"Like ten seconds into the song there's this like throbbing beat. Right? Like an arpeggio. . . "

"I know."

"Before the bass drops. . . "

"Da-da-da-da-da-da-duh-da-da-da-da."

"Yeah!"

T.J. disconnected the headphone jack from the mixer.

"Right before 'Bass!'"

"It's like a bass line."

"No," he corrected. "Not the bass line."

"Jus that one beat?"

"Yeah," Henry said, bobbing his head. "It reminds me of something you'd hear in a raunchy club, slowly stalking through a sea of bodies, eyes like razors on the girl sitting alone at the bar."

Afed said, "You talking about killing a girl?"

"No, idiot," Henry replied with a loud grunt and explained to both Afed and T.J., who was too busy trying to find the right sound on the Roland. "You got it all wrong, my friend. I'm talking about finding the hottest girl in the club and showing her the best time of her life. Not killing her. You need to be surrounded by that beat, throbbing, driving you, giving you that extra bit of confidence to walk up to that girl. You could be the ugliest dude she's ever set eyes on and yet, somehow, that one beat, just that one, it makes you feel like nothing can stop you, not even an act of God."

T.J. shouted out, "There!"

"Deeper now, more throaty," Henry explained. "Like a. . . like a. . . like a frog being squeezed to death."

T.J. kept experimenting, more tweaking.

"There," he said, the air pouring from his lungs. "That's it."

Henry let in the beat, that beat, soaked the beat up like a sponge.

Next, T.J. played a choir pad underneath the beat, adding more depth to the sound.

The sound was extremely visceral, seductive!

After that, T.J. laid down a high hat from the TR-909.

Bass followed.

That beat rushed through Henry's head, collecting and sparking all thoughts and imagination.

"Keep it going, T.J.," Henry said, bobbing his head to the beat.

They recorded the beat and played it back through the headphones. Henry put on a pair of headphones and embraced the beat once more.

While Afed and T.J. listened to the track over the headphones, Henry joined in with Harry. He played a rough cut of what he played from Open Mike Night at the Hot Foxy over the beat. The melody altered to the beat, shifting in ways Henry never knew was possible.

After Henry finished, T.J. and Afed could only sum up the sound in one word. . . *magical*. They both went on like this for hours, days, catching little sleep. They would shoot out ideas and record them as quickly as they manifested.

Throughout the day, the two ate very little. Arguments flared. Tempers certainly ignited like small grease fires over a stove. Both Henry and T.J. weren't technically musicians by any stretch. They knew how to play, but they didn't know how to formulate their ideas. They played in a jazz-like scenario. At times, the two would improvise. Other times, Henry and T.J. wished they hadn't spent so much of Afed's money on all of that acoustic stuff for the home studio. Instead, they wished they had spent it on more important stuff like microphones. There was this saying in the music industry, one that Henry and T.J. would soon learn. The saying went something like "you can't polish a turd." Regardless, both Henry and T.J. were doing it. There was no question about it. They were making music, even though it sounded exactly like that, a stinky turd.

TWELVE

IT was getting late into the day.

Henry was stuck trying to keep up with a fast, industrial-like tempo that T.J. had created over hours of tweaking the night before. The song was tentatively called "Two Dollar Witch."

After hours of practicing were exhausted, Henry shouted out through the studio, "Damn it!"

"Would you guys like some advice?" Afed asked cautiously as Henry rubbed his sore throat. "I don't have one bit of musical talent. Making bubbles from Sherlock Holmes is about most of my music ability."

T.J. said angrily, "Makin' bubbly noises from yo bong ain't really considered music, Afed."

"*But,*" he exclaimed, "but I know a little thing or two about pop music."

Henry sighed and shifted his weight.

"Spit it out, Afed," he said.

"You guys have been playing for weeks now," he said. "Believe me when I say this. It sounds good. And I know where you guys are trying to go with the sound, which is really a cool idea, very unique."

Afed saw the glare over Henry's face.

"But it's thin," he said. "It doesn't have any. . . "

"Any what?"

"Any depth."

T.J said under his breath, "What does that even mean?"

"What I meant to say is that you guys need to expand."

"You mean forming a band?"

"Yes," Afed said with relief. "I was talking to this kid in my sociology class. He knows a guy who works at the record store. He plays the guitar. From what he said, he's really good. Plus, he's looking for a band to join. 'Something different,' he said. I told him you guys would be perfect."

"Afed is right," Henry said to T.J. "If we're going to do this thing right, we need a band. I'm talking guitarist, bassist, another person on keyboards, and a drummer."

"What a sec?" T.J. said earnestly. "What's the point of layin' all these beats down?"

"He doesn't mean it like that, T.J.," Afed butted in. "Drums are going to reinforce your beats. Your beats are sick. Don't get me wrong. You add a drummer. Those beats are going to explode like an atom bomb."

The next day, Afed got his classmate to contact the guitarist from the record shop. His real name was Deon Bellinger, but everyone who knew him called him D Finger. He was only a year younger than Henry, but he looked several years older than him. He had a patchy beard that he had been growing ever since his senior year in high school, eyes like the sun, bright and always squinting, and he dressed as if he had just gotten out of Nam.

Around two o'clock in the afternoon, they met Deon at the house. Afed was in class. So were the other roommates. The meeting went well. Henry and Deon instantly clicked and shared the same music tastes and interests. It turned out that Deon knew a couple of guys who were eager about putting a band together as well. One guy, William Darby (birth name Andrew Dorcas), played the bass. He was a fairly stout man with greased back hair and a five o'clock shadow on his face. Dressed as if he lived in the mountains. Willie or Darbs or Roller Darby or Darby, as most of his friends called him, was from the wealthy side of Boston. One would never tell from looking at him (same with the thick Boston accent, which had eventually flattened out from living a few years in Peregrine). Darby's parents, his father an immigrant from Greece and his mother a famous actress from Turkey, owned a chain of popular Greek/American restaurants called By Fireside across the entire East Coast. Four years ago, he moved to Madison on a college scholarship. Business grad. Now, he just bounced around from one minimum wage job to another while he played bass on the side. Another guy, a drummer named Geordie Roberts, AKA "Animal," had a degree in music. Tall. Slender. Wore lots of denim and walked around with a chip on his shoulder. The last guy played keys. His name was Socks, just Socks. Of all the guys, Socks was the strangest. Dark eyes. Long dark hair, bangs combed to one side of his pale face. Like Henry, he was a fan of the pop culture of the late 70's and early 80's. Went to art school. Art collector. Loved B-movies too! On his spare time, he painted old science fiction movie posters. When Henry told Deon about adding a saxophone into the sound, he was a bit skeptical. That was until Henry played "Captured by Light" for Deon, as well as the other guys. After the song, they were completely blown away. Deon was first to join the band and then the other guys after a second meeting the following day. The chemistry was there. They knew there was something special here. They couldn't quite understand how or why. They just did. The only bad thing now was that they had to move the bunk beds from the studio to the living room in order to make room for the other new band mates. When Henry broke the news to Afed about the bunk beds, he wasn't pleased at all. Eventually, he came around. What other choice did he have?

A minute into the song, Henry came in a fraction too early.

"Man!" he shouted out and removed Harry from his shoulder. "What am I doing wrong?" He perched the saxophone against the mount and paced around the studio.

Socks said, "It takes time, Henry."

"You're thinking about it too much," Deon followed. "Just play."

The band had been jamming hours into the night but weren't getting anywhere with the music. The sound was all muddled, chaotic, and structureless.

Fed up, Henry walked to the boarded up window and wildly ran his hand through his greasy, untidy, curly hair. A tiny gleam of moonlight was shining through a crack in the side panel and cutting across the middle of Henry's face.

"What's wrong with him," Geordie whispered to William.

In one movement, William clumsily shrugged his shoulders, rolled his eyes, and frowned.

T.J. said, "Talk to us, Henry Man."

"What's bothering you?"

"Is it from that phone call you got last night?"

One of Henry's still eyes was glistening with moonlight. The other one was tucked away in the shadows of the dusty quilt. He said consciously, "My entire life I've been running away from the shy boy, the stutterer in the corner of the room who no one would go near, the one who was always talked about behind his back, the one who was like this stranger walking around in limbo, the one who was treated like some kind. . . some kind of leper."

"Henry," T.J. said, sighing. "Don't be so damn hard on yourself. We'll get it right. It jus takes time. You know."

"And now. . . " Henry said, his voice picking up steam, ". . . now that I finally found my voice, my calling, nobody will listen to me. All my professors, the students on campus, they all think I'm throwing my life down the drain. What do they know about me? Nothing! It's like they saw what they expected from me and all of a sudden, I've let them down. Like they only saw one life for me. Now, they've already written me off." With the rage swelling in his eyes, Henry faced the rest of the band. "They like the basketball player better, the shy boy, the boy who didn't say a goddamn word, the boy who would just go along with whatever he was told to do, who never spoke his fucking mind. I'm not that boy anymore!" His voice grew raspy, vindictive. "I HAVE A VOICE! ME! I HAVE A GODDAMN VOICE!"

Astonished, Deon was bobbing his head as if his head was powered on a remote.

He said clearly, "You certainly do, Henry."

Socks finished, "And we're listening."

Deon and the others had taken a "five" minute break while Henry cooled off behind the sink in the bathroom.

Outside the studio, Deon whispered to the other band mates, "What do you guys think?"

Socks said closely, "He's the one."

THIRTEEN

ONE afternoon, T.J. and Socks were taking a break from a new song that they had been constantly working on. The working title of the song was called "The Big Bad Wolf." Socks was explaining the multiple algorithms of frequency modulation. Yet, T.J. couldn't understand a single word Socks was saying.

After the long discussion, Socks decided to take a break. He joined the others downstairs.

In the kitchen downstairs, Henry was fixing ham sandwiches for himself as well as the other band mates while T.J. stayed behind in the studio.

As T.J. went back over to his setup, he noticed a speckled composition book poking out from a backpack underneath the desk. He took out the notebook and saw crinkled pages filled with writing, lyrics. There was hardly any white space on the pages. Each page consisted of writing, years and years of writing perhaps.

T.J. read from a couple of songs, one called "Chickenshit."

Lines included: "*I see you walking, all talking, just prattling. You see me stalking, no talking, just rattling. I see your fangs, just your pretty fangs, from all your prattling. Then, you see mine, hewed smoothly, so fucking smoothly, from all the rattling.*"

Two more songs: "The Wind That Blows This Way" and "Blame It On The Rider."

T.J. read the songs to himself.

During the entire read, T.J. was wearing a long, sickening expression over his face.

Realizing that T.J. was nowhere around in the kitchen, Henry put lunch aside to check on the workhorse, only to find him reading from his notebook.

With a grimace forming over his face, Henry stood in the doorway.

"Where did you get that?" he seethed.

T.J. opened his mouth, but the words never came out.

"That's personal."

"Ah. . . sorry, Henry," he uttered. "It. . . it was jus—"

Henry interrupted, "What gives you the right, T.J.?"

T.J. raised his hands.

"Calm down, Henry," he said and held up the notebook. "There ain't nuttin to be ashamed of. This here is good work."

Henry marched through the studio and snatched the notebook from T.J.'s grip.

"My bad, man. Damn."

Once the emotions eased, Henry sat down on the chair next to T.J. and took several deep breaths.

In a surrendered state, he asked calmly and quietly, "How much did you read?"

"A couple pages maybe," T.J. answered. "That one song 'Blame It On The Rider.' Is that really true, Henry?"

"Nobody was ever supposed to find out," Henry said, hanging his head.

"Sorry."

In a sudden spurt of action, Henry (with glazed eyes) shot his head up at T.J.

"You can't tell them. You *can't* tell anybody."

"Ain't really none of their bizness if you ax me," T.J. said. "They ain't close like me and you. Personally, I think that's kind of cool, being the son of a legendary rock star." The excitement grew unexpectedly. "We practically grew up with Mr. Vortex! And you! You used to listen to all of his records!"

"It's not cool, T.J.," Henry exclaimed. "It's a burden, living in the shadows of a legend. I never had a father figure in my life like you did, T.J. The closest I got to a father was from a fucking song. You don't know what that's like, T.J. Wanting answers, advice, getting none."

"You know I ain't the closest wit my futhva, Henry," T.J. said. "I mean we used to be tight. I think when I hit sixteen it all changed. There's times when we hardly spoke. You 'member how he and my moms was. I know he loved us and all. But there's times when I wonder if he really cared." T.J. snorted. "'Bout anything. The only time I eva seen any emotion outta him was when he be yellin' at my moms. There was these nights when he couldn't take it anymore. He'd get in his car and leave. I 'member sittin' up in my room, wonderin' if he'd eva come back or not."

"But you still have a father, T.J.," Henry said, the ache resonating over his voice. "You still have a chance to make things right with your old man. I don't get that chance, T.J."

T.J. turned away and sighed.

Henry hung his head in a state of reflection.

"I've been running away from that name ever since I can remember," he said quietly. "I was born Henry McClintock, the Fifth. My mother even had the name legally changed. Went to the courts and everything."

"Damn," T.J. said, his voice drawn back. "That there is sum serious shit."

The leftover emotions were wearing on Henry. An ache that had been nagging at him all day made its presence known. In a brief grimace, Henry rubbed his throat.

He mumbled in deflation, "Tell me about it."

"I know you grew up and all listenin' to Mr. Vortex," T.J. said thoughtfully. "When did you finds out that he was your futhva?"

"Just before we moved from Reddington."

"Shit," T.J. said, chortling. "Your futhva must've loved the name so goddamn much that he named you afta himself. Guess he wanted you to pass on that legacy. You know."

"You can't say that, T.J.," Henry said angrily, shooting his head upright, eyes even more glazed. "I will never fill his shoes. Over these past years, I realized that I'm my own person. I may have the same name as my father, but I'm *not* my father."

"But you got his talent, Henry!" T.J. exclaimed. "We're talkin' 'bout the Vortex here. We used to sing to all of his songs! 'Member?" T.J. sat back and reminisced. "I wondered how you played the sax like that, man. Now, I know. It's like there's a piece of him in you. You may not think so. But I know. I believe in shit like that."

Henry tried to digest the comment.

"The whole jam session thing is over now, Henry," he said and tapped at the composition notebook in Henry's hand. "Now, it's time to lay down some lyrics from these here songs. Ever since we started playin', we wondered who was gonna sing for us. It's you, Henry. It's always been you. Deon and the others is right 'bout you. You have that presence. They listen to you."

"I can't."

"Somewhere in that there notebook, you got yourself a hit song. You may not know, but I do."

Henry exclaimed, "I can't, T.J."

"You can, Henry."

Henry sighed.

"There is a helluva singer in there, Henry," T.J. said and pointed at Henry. "You jus haf to find him." T.J. stood up and strolled over to the doorway. "You jus think it over. Aight."

As Henry pondered over the discussion in the quietude of the studio, T.J. went downstairs in the kitchen and joined the rest of the band.

Ever since Henry woke from Ms. Craft's voice (the words *what will your song be* deeply rooted in his mind), he had that one reoccurring dream with the strange futuristic prison facility, the prison cells, the unusual characters locked up inside, two of them being a younger version of himself sitting with Ms. Craft as she gave him lessons, the bloody Native American crawling to safety, the lively eye of an hologram, and then

the lanky stalker, as dark as a silhouette. On some nights—
usually the ones where Henry and T.J. had worked themselves to sleep—the dream had come and gone. Parts of the
dream had crept into other more uneventful dreams. On
some nights, Henry was so exhausted that he didn't dream at
all. Tonight, he had that same dream about the prison facility, only this time it was much more vivid:

In the same bright white hallway, Henry followed the
same dark blood trail smeared across the clean, glossy floor.
His stomach was twisted in knots. The tips of his fingers
were numb and cold. He cautiously followed the trail of
blood to the end of the hallway.

Once he rounded the corner, the blood trail stopped.

The Native American man whom he had once seen in this
exact same spot was no longer there.

There weren't even any footprints leaving the puddle of
blood. No handprints. That was exactly what it was: just a
puddle of blood. There wasn't any indication of the man
crawling or fleeing from the scene. It was almost as if the
man had vanished like a cloud of vapor into thin air.

Mindful of his surroundings, he pursued farther down the
hallway. He made it down another hallway, a new one and
yet still as white and brilliant as the previous one. He came
across another room—or cell, he realized. He didn't know
exactly what this place was. Such places only existed in science fiction movies, not in real life, he realized.

He glanced inside the room.

A flickering light was coming from inside.

Henry shielded his eyes, pressed his face to the cool glass,
and saw a familiar man strapped to a chair. He was wearing a
strange, helmet-like device over his head. A large monitor
was held inches away from his face. Rapid images were flooding across his eyes. Images of war, Henry saw, images of
death, carnage, brutality, violence, and manmade, as well as
environmental destruction. A camera, which was hooked up
to the television behind the man, was held close to his face.

A television screen was playing a close up of the man's disturbed facial expressions.

Dumbfounded, Henry pulled his face away from the glass, leaving behind a greasy print of his forehead. In a second glance, he noticed the reflection in the glass. His dark hair was cut differently and much shorter. Henry ran his hand over his forehead, across the fine lines. The sides of his head were shaved while the top part of his scalp was formed into the letter V.

Henry suddenly gasped.

In the reflection, he caught a shadow erecting behind him.

An old, liver spotted hand was slowly reaching to Henry's shoulder.

A gasp!

Then, a deathly murmur!

Henry spun around, only to find another cell across the hallway.

Whoever was behind him had vanished like the Native American from the blood puddle. Either they were never there to begin with, these strange people, he thought, or *I was*, in fact, *in a magical place*, a place where things could easily disappear.

"What's going on?" Henry asked himself.

Suddenly, he heard a sharp creak from the end of the hallway.

A shrill voice said, "Over here."

Henry turned to the creak, the voice.

"Where are you?" Henry asked, noticing the foreign smell in the air.

Someone had definitely been here, he concluded.

Henry tried to find the source of the voice, but couldn't.

As he rotated toward a glass pane on the side of the wall, he caught yet another reflection. The reflection was of a woman dressed in a black cloak. She moved quickly and swiftly like a ninja. Paranoia settled in. His stomach tightened like a fist. He found himself moving to every little creak and crack, hum and buzz.

"What do you want from me?" Henry asked, his voice growing with bitterness.

As he walked farther down the bright hallway, he heard the sound of a machine humming down another hallway.

"What the hell was that?" He slowly backed away from the sound. He backed his way to the end of the hallway until there was nowhere to go but back toward the sound. There was a vent near the base of the wall. A possible escape route, he thought. He thought of more escape routes, one being waking up. But for Henry, this didn't feel like a dream. It felt real. He tried to calm his breathing and listen closely to the mechanical noise. He could hardly hear anything over the heaviness of his breath, now building louder. Then. . . *Hiss!* The sound propelled Henry forward. The wall gave way, and a set of two doors automatically opened behind him. A tall figure, the stalker, Henry realized, was looming behind him. Henry eased himself around, only to find the stalker looming over him. His eyes trailed up the strange thing, mechanical in movement, as well as lanky with twig-like limbs as long as Henry's body. Henry's jaw fell downward in disbelief. With a gawking expression over his face, he backed away from the stalker. It was wearing an all black outfit, not a cloak, as he had seen or thought he had seen before in the hallway. The outfit was as tight as skin on its body, tailored to its joints and muscles. It could've, Henry thought, maybe, been very well the same thing previously pounding away at the door.

"If this is a dream," he mumbled to himself, "now would be a great time to wake up."

Before Henry could take another step, the stalker threw its lanky arm in front and grabbed Henry by the throat. Its hand was like metal. Its fingertips were like tiny rods digging into Henry's jugular. The stalker lifted Henry from his feet. It raised Henry at least three feet off the floor.

Squirming around, Henry desperately swung both of his arms around and tried to land a blow. Anything! Its arms were too long, too powerful.

The stalker brought Henry up to its eye level, which, by the way, was unrecognizable. It was wearing a tinted visor over its entire face. Henry couldn't tell exactly what it was, the thing behind the visor.

Not human, he assumed from the strong grasp around his neck.

The stalker squeezed its fingers tighter around Henry's throat, nearly crushing his larynx.

Henry hollered out in great agony.

"Wake up," he pleaded through his sharp, raspy voice. He pleaded again and again.

The hand *still* remained around his neck.

The stalker *still* remained in front of him.

Suddenly, the visor automatically opened and revealed the skeletal face of a corpse. Its greenish skin was in the late stages of decay. Its eyes were beady and black, glinting faintly in a beam of light.

With his eyes studying the rotten remains of the stalker, Henry squirmed around some more. The eyes, he witnessed, as black as the universe.

"Wake up. . ." he cried.

The stalker reached up with its other gloved hand and held its hand close to Henry's face. In return, Henry tried to pull away from the hand. *If I could only get my hands around its fingers*, he thought, *then I could set myself free.* He jerked and kicked and tugged away at the metallic fingers. But the grip around his neck was too powerful. Henry groaned while the stalker mechanically twirled its fingers (its first three fingers—the thumb, index, and middle fingers now facing upward in the shape of a L). The tips of the fingers automatically peeled open like tiny trapdoors. Henry's frantic eyes swelled greater, more fearful.

Without disregard, the stalker reached inside Henry's mouth. The fingers slithered around Henry's wiggling tongue and inched down his throat. A cold sensation suddenly ran down into Henry's chest, now burning. Henry coughed and gagged, the air closing from each breath. A sharply defined panic washed over his eyes, which slowly traced over the stalker's clutched hand and down his chest. He moved his eyes to his own hands. The skin around his own fingers and wrists darkened into the color of brass. He traced the shiny color, the brass, which was now spreading over his right arm, right shoulder, and now neck.

Before the breath closed from his chest, Henry quickly pulled himself from the dream.

Sweating profusely, he sprang from his bed.

As the dream faded from his thoughts, he could still feel those sharp, lanky fingers crawling down his throat. Henry frantically tried to regain the feeling in his dead right arm by throwing it around and banging it against the side of his leg.

When the tingly was gone, he rolled out of bed and hurried to the bathroom where he stood in front of the mirror for a couple of minutes. Eventually, he regained the feeling in his arm. His throat, however, was closing.

More panic washed over Henry, his eyes.

With one great push, Henry hawked up a black, slimy, resin-like piece of phlegm from his throat and spat it out into the sink. The black stuff splattered over the sink like a crime scene.

Relieved, Henry massaged the base of his throat. It was no longer congested, as it had been for the past few days, no longer tight like a straw.

Strangely enough, he felt much better and yet freaked out from the sight of the resin. He moved his eyes up at the mirror.

Over his shoulder, a shadow built over the hallway wall. Henry spun around and saw an empty space where a body (?) once stood.

He directed his attention to the mirror, no more shadows, only a dark hallway flickering from the light of a candle in the kitchen.

Henry looked over his shoulder once more.

Nothing.

He splashed his face with cold water and slapped each cheek until he was fully awake.

That night, Henry didn't get any sleep. Not even a wink.

FOURTEEN

Morning couldn't come soon enough.

The stark images from last night's dream, mainly that strange, affectionate, monstrous thing with its frisky fingers, were still fresh in Henry's mind.

The suit, he thought, *looked similar to a stillsuit.*

Being an avid reader as a child and, not to mention, a movie buff like Charles, Henry was aware of the controversial and critically receptive story *Dune*. During Christmas break of '84 (Henry around ten years old at the time), he and T.J. skipped choir practice to see the sci-fi flick, which did not live up to his expectations. Nonetheless, he found something good in it, even if it was minuscule, as he did with most popular culture. Henry remembered the Fremen, natives of the planet Arrakis, who wore these stillsuits. The ones from his dream were a bit altered, modernized. What if there was a connection?

Now focused on the song at hand, Henry approached the microphone as the dream eventually dissipated from his mind. The other band mates were somewhat pessimistic about Henry singing. They went over the lyrics of the song, practiced each shift and break, and knew that, in the back of their minds, if Henry could pull this off, then it would be one hell of a song.

Henry grabbed the microphone from the stand and cleared his throat. He directed his attention over at T.J., who was hunkered over the TR-909. With his head lowered and his sharp, pensive eyes rested under the rims of his upper eyelids, he nodded at Henry and mouthed the words, *"Find him."*

Henry cleared his throat yet again.

The song started out with that same pulsing, bloodcurdling appeggiator effect that T.J. had programmed on the MKS-80. The effect ran for about a minute and a half until Socks joined in a *"Thriller"*-like melody over the keyboard. In different parts, the rest of the band joined in on the song.

Bass, guitars, drums. . .

. . . And then Henry furiously sang the song "Mesaterrestrial."

When the song was finished, which ended with Henry playing a three and a half minute solo to fade out, Henry, shoulders slouched, breathing heavily, was holding Harry as if he was clinging onto a battleaxe covered in the blood of a dragon. The others rushed over to Henry and congratulated him. There, he received a round of high fives and pats on the back. Most of the band was at a loss of words from Henry's performance. His stern mien was finally lifted with a smirk. As if the band wasn't convinced from Henry's meltdown the other day, the band was confident enough to rightfully declare Henry as their new singer.

"The One," they called him.

From the interview "King of His Own Castle," (*Rolling Stone* magazine, Issue 740, August 1996, p. 32) by Daniel Murphy:

Daniel Murphy: *So, what exactly is a Mesaterrestrial?*
Henry the Fif: *It's whatever you want it to be. That's what I love about writing. I love having to put the interpretation in the listener's hands. For me, in my opinion, I like to think of the Mesaterrestrial as a special piece of land, like a mountain or a hill. It's a place where one must climb through obstacles and whatnot. Either it be through a new job or a new loved one. All figuratively speaking. In essence, we have to work hard for what we*

strive for or long for. We can't just walk a level path in life. We could, but that wouldn't be fun. We have to climb and we have to fight and we have to pursue these very things that we cherish deeply in our lives. And when we finally reach the top of our "Mesaterrestrial," that's (grinning) *that's where dreams come true. Like my mom always said, "Nothing in this world is for free. You have to work hard in order to get what you want." We have to keep climbing, keep fighting. Otherwise, who knows, you might find yourself stuck in a ditch somewhere. Figuratively speaking, of course.*

It took a couple of hours for Henry and the rest of the band to get down from the incredible buzz of recording their first song together, the same one that Henry had written so many years ago in his old bedroom after watching the movie *Close Encounters of The Third Kind*. During the singing of the song, the same feelings that he felt so many years ago, the anger, the sadness, the bitterness, the loneliness, the longing for the American dream and trying to define what it meant to him, resurfaced in the studio. When it was all said and done, he couldn't even remember what he had just done. He knew he had done extremely well from all of the celebratory around the studio. When he tried to describe it to the others, words couldn't quite explain what he was feeling. The best way he could put words on it was: "*An outer body experience.*"

"Outer body experience?" Deon replied as he kicked his feet over the porch railing. "That's one way of putting it."

As Henry sipped from the can of Diesel beer, a telephone rang from within the house. Afed sluggishly stumbled into the kitchen and picked up the telephone. He talked to the caller for at least a minute. From the serious and yet genuine tone in his voice, Henry knew it was an adult; and from the guilty expression over Afed's face, he knew it was someone whom he did not want to talk to right about now. Once Afed came walking outside onto the front porch with that peculiar look on his face, Henry knew exactly who was on the other end of the telephone. Afed held up the telephone and mouthed the words *it's your mom.*

Henry chugged from the can of Diesel and let out a loud burp as he stood from the chair.

"I'll be back, fellows," he said sharply to the others and made sure the door was all the way closed. He sauntered toward the kitchen where it was more quiet. Grabbed the telephone from the countertop. He waited until Afed was out of the room before he answered the telephone.

"Hello. . . " he answered with a sigh of frustration.

"Henry," Abbey said with a taunt uneasiness in her voice. "I was just calling to check up on you."

"I thought I told you, Mom," Henry said with a sharp pain rippling through his stomach. "You don't need to keep checking up on me. I'm fine."

"But I was worried."

"Well, you shouldn't be."

"It wouldn't hurt to call your mother every once and a while and see how I am doing, Henry."

"I've just been busy."

Her tone shifted, sharply.

"Busy doing what?"

"So, how are you doing?"

"Better," she said shortly. "Thanks for asking."

"Did you finish your treatment?"

"Just last week. I did."

"That's good to hear."

There was a moment of tense silence over the telephone.

"You didn't answer my question, Henry."

Henry pulled the telephone from his face and said to himself, "Tell her." He moved the telephone back to his face. "For once in my life," he said boldly over the telephone, "I finally found out what I'm supposed to do."

"You're still talking about the music thing. Aren't you?"

"I can't stop thinking about all of those years I wasted playing basketball," he said, his voice trembling. "I did it because of you, because you lost your job at the Depot and basketball was the only way I could support the both of us."

"Henry. . . don't. . ."

"No," he said and paced around the kitchen. "I'm through with readjusting my life for you."

"Sometimes you have to make sacrifices, Henry," she said, her voice growing. "That's all a part of life."

"It's my DREAM!" Henry's voice climaxed as he paced around the kitchen. The others were still and quiet from the muffled barking behind the closed window. "NOT YOURS! ALL YOU WERE WAS SOME GROUPIE WHO GOT KNOCKED UP BY A FAMOUS ROCK STAR! THIS IS WHAT YOU CREATED! YOU DID THIS! NOT ME! MY ENTIRE LIFE IS A LIE! UNCLE CHARLIE! YOU! MY FATHER! IT'S ALL A LIE!"

"Remember your father, Henry," she said, her voice held back. "Remember what happened to him."

Henry's eyes swelled with tears.

"I accepted who I am," he said, restraining his voice. "Now it's time you do the same."

"Henry. . . what did I do wrong?"

"You pushed me down a road that I didn't want to go down," he said, his voice held back. "You forced me here, right here in this position. And now, I'm paying the price." He pulled back the telephone and carefully calmed his breathing. "You know," he said curiously over the telephone. "I wonder where I would be if I didn't waste all that time playing basketball."

"But you're a natural, Henry," Abbey whined. "Even Charles said you were."

"Enough!" Henry seethed. "For once in my life, I understand my purpose. I'm meant to do something more, like I belong to something much greater. You may be right, same with Coach Boland. I may have talent to play basketball, but I don't have the heart. So, why don't you call Charles? He's better at listening to your problems than I am. After all, isn't that what he gets paid to do?"

Enraged, Henry slammed down the telephone against the mount.

Before Henry walked back outside, he reached into the freezer and grabbed a bottle of Jack Daniels. He took a swig and managed to hold down the liquor without throwing up. He breathed carefully and cleared his thoughts, just as Charles had taught him. The anger melted from his face.

"Better," he said to himself and walked back outside.

T.J. asked, "Is everything all right, Henry?"

Henry struggled to look at T.J.

"Henry," T.J. said. "You cool?"

"Yeah," he said and sipped from the beer. "I'm cool."

"Who was that on the phone?"

Henry sat back down in the chair and said, "Just a wrong number."

Only four had made it through the night without passing out: Henry, T.J., Deon, and Socks. The rest of the band, as well as Afed and the other roommates, had already passed out from the Diesel. The four survivors sat on the flat part of the roof and cycled around a joint that Deon had rolled. While enjoying the company of the other band mates, Henry took a long drag from the joint and held in the smoke until his lungs couldn't hold it any longer. He coughed out a bunch of smoke, which caused a couple of giggles around the rooftop.

"Damn, virgin lungs," Deon said in a high-pitched voice and then grabbed the joint from Henry's loose grip. "Spoken like a true champion."

The remaining clouds eventually parted ways and opened up the sky. The tranquil night sky cast its light over the four. They would watch an airplane fly overhead like a slowly moving shooting star. In wonder, T.J. gazed up at the brilliant stars, not on the airplanes or supposed "shooting stars."

"What a night!" T.J. said out loud and bumped shoulders with Henry. "Didn't think my boy here had it in him. He found it, though. Shore did."

Henry was bobbing his head and taking small sips of Diesel.

"Found what?" Deon asked curiously and poked his head across the other bodies.

T.J. answered, "His voice, o'course."

Deon glanced over at Socks, who was also gazing up at the stars.

"You've been awfully quiet over there, Socks," he said. "Whatchu thinking?"

"I'm thinking this might be it."

"It?"

"Yeah," he said. "*It.*"

"Really?"

"This group." Socks pulled away from the stars and looked around at the others. "Prior to this, I've been in three other bands, each and every one wound up with someone fighting with another band member or another not liking the direction another player was taking them." He shrugged his shoulders. "For once, I feel. . . I don't know. . . comfortable. How about you guys?"

"I'm pretty comfortable."

"T.J.?"

"I ain't complainin'."

"Deon?"

"Well," Deon said elegantly in his worst British accent and took another drag from the joint. "I hate to be the one to break the news to you, Socks. But we don't like the direction you're taking the band. The band mates and I have come to the conclusion that we don't need you anymore."

Deon giggled.

Henry and T.J. forced themselves to laugh.

As he continued to laugh from the awkward and untimely comment, Henry pointed at Socks and said, "By the way, where did you come up with a name like Socks?"

Socks shrugged one of his shoulders.

"I don't know," he said, his voice softened just a little. "People been callin' me Socks ever since I was a little dude. I guess it was because I am a nice guy. Hey!" He lit up briefly. "Who doesn't like a nice pair of socks?"

"Amen to that," T.J. said. "Shoot! I'd kill for a pair of new socks. I've been wearin' the same goddamn socks for two years now. Got holes all up in 'em and everything."

"Back it up," Deon said with a pause. "You mean to tell me that you got all of those Rolands and yet you can't afford a brand new pair of socks."

"Shit," T.J. said uncomfortably and wiped his sweaty palms over his knees. "I guess."

"I'm going to buy you a pair of socks, my brother."

T.J. waved off Deon and said, "Nah. . . you don't haf to do that."

"No," Deon said seriously. "Every man needs a pair of nice socks. Right, Socks?"

"Right," Socks said like a parrot and then chuckled.

Henry was still reminiscing over "Mesaterrestrial."

"That bridge leading up the chorus was pretty stellar, man," Henry said, his bloodshot eyes squinting. "I've never heard anything like that before, Socks. Just listening to it over the headphones, it's like, I swear, you traveled to this other world."

"Get outta here!"

T.J. gently shoved Henry.

"I'm serious, man," Henry replied, smiling. "Check this out. See, I got it all figured out. See, Socks here is our time traveler. He's our guy that's going to set down that warm, cozy blanket over the track."

Deon whispered in Socks's ear, "Someone's been smoking a little too much ganja."

"Seriously," Henry blurted out and pointed at T.J. "Then, T.J., he's our backbone, laying down the foundation of the song. '*That beat.*'" Next, he pointed at Deon. "Then, check this out. Deon here, he's like our lonesome princess confined in a. . . in a faraway tower, you see, his long, thick mane blowing in the wind, his guitar singing out over the highest landscape, crying out for her knight in shining armor."

Deon, who had his mouth closed and ballooned outward like a monkey, was doing his best to hold in his laughter.

"Geordie is the beast," Henry said smoothly. "Yeah! Our beast! He's like our dragon stomping around, creating all sorts of fucking carnage. He's that thing, that dragon, banging on the doors, trying to break his way in."

"How about Darby?" Socks said, chuckling. "Who's Darby?"

"Darby," Henry said, thinking. "Darby, he's our troll."

"Troll?"

Deon burst out laughing and rolled around on the rooftop.

"He kind of does look like a troll," he said over the diminishing laughter.

Socks shoved Deon.

"Play nice."

"I'm just being figuraaa. . . figarativ. . . lee. . . "

"Figuratively?"

"Yeah." Henry drawled, "*Figuratively*."

"Hey, Deon," T.J. said. "I wouldn't be sayin' that to the man's face."

Henry continued, "See, Darby, he's the one underneath the bridge, humming, creating a wicked groove for the. . . for the riders above."

"Riders? Now, I like that right there."

"How about you, Henry?" Socks said amusedly. "Let me take a guess. You're the knight in shining armor?"

"Save me, Knight," Deon cheered in a feminine voice as he leaned over Socks. "Before thee Geordie Dragon shall eat me with his delicious beats."

"Me?" Henry said, lounging back over the roof. He placed his hands behind his head and gazed up at the stars. "I'm King Panty Dropper."

The others cried out with laughter.

Tears, all of them good, were even shed from the remark.

"King Panty Dropper!" T.J. said, laughing. "Now, I like that!"

After a short while, the laughter slowly faded.

"If you think about it, King Panty Dropper," Deon said jokingly. "May I call you King Panty Dropper?"

Henry sat up and majestically rolled out his hand, "Be my guest."

"All the greats have that trademark sound to them," he said. "If you think about it, all of them played at least one instrument."

"The voice could be the most powerful instrument, my friend," Socks said. "Doesn't matter if you play guitar or whatever."

"True," Deon said continually. "The voice is the most powerful instrument. But," he exaggerated the word *but*, "if you can create a sound with another instrument that works with the voice, then you truly have something amazing. Think about it. Hendrix had his trademark wah-wah pedal." Sound effect included. "He could literally make his guitar speak. It's like the dude was speaking in tongues. And there was this. . . this. . . this marriage between the two, like pea-nut butter and jelly."

"Like peanut butter and jelly," Henry said coolly. "Nice."

"Then, you got Freddie Mercury and the piano. The an-guish in his voice soared over each cord."

"Amen."

Socks joined in, "Bob Dylan and the harmonica."

"And it worked in a weird way. Right?" Deon said and tried to do his best Bob Dylan impersonation. "You got *this kind of voice* followed by a bluesy harmonica. But it worked! Phil Collins and the drums. His voice sounded as if it was trapped inside a snare drum."

"With all that reverb," Henry said, giggling. "They should create a whole new reverb called the 'Phil Collins Reverb.' Yo, home skillet! I need a lil' mo 'Phil Collins' in my head-phones."

"My favorite," Socks said. "Geddy Lee on the keys."

"—The man's like a mad scientist back there—"

"—I know, right—"

"Kim Gordon from Sonic Youth with her throbbing bass."

"You're right," Socks said. "She did sound like a troll."

The comment sparked a couple of laughs from the others.

"And Sting," T.J. said. "Don't be forgettin' 'bout him."

Deon interrupted, "Fuck Sting."

"Hey, Man! I likes Sting," T.J. said, his voice drawn back. "That 'Every Breath You Take' song is the jam. When I was little, I was listenin' to that song before I went to bed like every night."

Deon said over T.J., "That was the Police, smart guy."

"Same thang."

"No, no, no," Deon said, this time louder and with more aggression. "Sting hadn't been the same ever since he left the Police."

Socks puffed from the joint, which was now burned down to a roach. He couldn't help but giggle to himself.

"How about the beefcake from *The Lost Boys*. You know who I'm talking about?"

Deon busted out laughing.

"That's who you need to be like, Henry."

Henry said seriously, "Get the fuck out of here. You talking about what's-his-name. . . "

"You know," Socks said. "The jacked dude at the carnival."

"The freak," Deon mumbled.

"Freak?" Henry uttered, pinching his face in confusion.

"What was his name?" Deon said. "Damn! It's at the tip of my tongue."

The name finally came to Henry.

"You're talking about Tim Cappello."

"That's him!"

Henry finished, "Dude was a *freak* on the saxophone."

"Yeah right" Deon said rudely. "I always thought he was like a vampire and he ate the real saxophonist on stage."

"Whatever," Henry said, shaking his head from Deon's wisecracks. "I like that song."

"And how's it go, Henry?"

"Something like," Henry was thinking. Pumping his fist, he was singing, "Something like. . . 'Still believe!'" And then, he was playing the air saxophone with the unlit cigarette in his hand.

Laughing, Deon uttered, "Sexy, man."

"But seriously," Socks said. "Henry's right. You look at saxophonists like the one from *Lost Boys*. Those guys, they were like trailblazers in the music industry."

"What about Charlie Parker, John Coltrane. . ." Henry said, ". . . they, my friend, they are real trailblazers."

"I'm talking about for us, our time," Socks said. "Yeah. Don't get me wrong. I go on for days talking about Coltrane and what he did on Love Supreme. I mean. . . back then. . . that was like historic. Now, I mean, it's different. We still pay homage to those guys. But now, we got to do our thing. Sort of map it out for the generations to come. I mean the game has changed, mainstream that is. You couldn't go anywhere without hearing a killer saxophone solo in a song. Not like jazz, though. It almost became like a staple in a song, especially in the early eighties. Tina Turner, Huey Lewis and The News, Billy Ocean, Elton John, Floyd, they all had 'em. . . "

"*Lost Boys* came out in the late 80's," Deon said seriously. "I'd say Mr. Cappello was a lil' late to the party."

Henry's cheeks washed over with red.

His voice turned defensive.

"What do you mean?"

"The saxophone was like HUGE throughout the entire 80's, not so much now."

Henry said, "Well, like '82 to '84 or 5. But still. . . the sax is coming back. Just watch and see."

"Honestly, I don't think it never left in the first place," Socks said. "Now, the saxophone is under assault."

"You can thank Kenny G for that."

More laughter spread over the rooftop.

"But now," Socks exclaimed. "Now, the music field is fertile. And it's ours for the taking."

"Amen."

"I really don't even care what year it is or *was*." Socks sat upright. "You're telling me when *Songs From the Big Chair* came out you weren't blown away! Like blown off your fucking socks!"

"Is that Tears For Fears?"

"Yep."

"I was like twelve or something," Deon said. "I was more into like Grateful Dead, Credence Clearwater Revival, CSN. . . you name it. . . practically anything from the 60's and 70's. . . "

T.J. said, "CNN?"

"CSN," Socks corrected.

"Who they?"

"Crosby, Stills, and Nash!"

T.J. smacked his gums.

"I ain't heard of them."

"My older brother was really into them," Deon said. "Whatever he listened to, I pretty much listened to."

"What's that one song where there's these like. . . like skeletons playin' on stage?"

"That's Grateful Dead's 'Touch of Grey.'"

"Cool song," T.J. said. "Very, how do I say, very. . . "

"I think I know where he's going."

"It's very white."

"Hey," Deon said. "I know some dark skin brothers who are Deadheads."

Henry nodded at Socks.

"Speaking of *Songs From the Big Chair*, the song 'The Working Hour'. . . I used to rock that song like everyday for like an entire year. It took me like months to learn how to play that song."

"Hell yah!" Socks said and slapped Henry's hand. "I don't know who played the sax on that song, but. . . " he blew out a sigh, ". . . goddamn! That shit was the bomb diggady! You want to talk about King Panty Dropper. You play 'The Working Hour' in a room full of smoking hot girls and they'll be *literally* throwing their panties at you. The song just oozes with sex. Seductive!"

"Aretha Franklin," T.J. said.

"'Freeway of Love,'" Henry said. "Great song. Great saxophone solo too."

"Don't forget Supertramp."

"And Kool and the Gang," Henry returned. "The song 'Cherish.' It had that kind of walking-on-the-beach-with-your-girl type of feel to it. Man! I remember those guys put out one hit after another. It's like they had a bunch secret elves somewhere writing songs day in, day out."

"Nice one, Henry."

T.J. cut through the laughter and asked, "What's that one song here wit the singin' animals in that big livin' room you'd see in them shows wit sum old dude readin' a book or sumtin by a campfire?"

The others were searching for the name.

"That one where that white dude be sittin' up in like a leather chair, strummin' his guitar, the livin' room starts comin' alive and shit. . . "

"That's ah. . . ah George Harrison from the Beatles," Henry said. "That's when he went solo."

"Didn't they all?"

"'I Got My Mind Set On You.'"

T.J. laughing: "Then Mr. George starts doin' sum *Dirty Dancing* type of shit, doin' all kinds of flips and twists and everything!"

"Great video."

The others joined in on the laughter.

"Hold up," T.J. paused, remembering what Henry said. "That guy played in the Beatles?"

"Yeah," Henry said in a high pitch voice. "And yet an-other great saxophone solo."

"And Queen," Socks said. "That one song from *High-lander.*"

"Yeah," Henry said. "I know which one you're talking about. Damn! I missed those fucking days. Nowadays, when people think about the saxophone, it's like. . . like they can't take it seriously anymore. It's like one big punch line."

Deon said, "Not after they hear you play."

"We still have a chance to change that, Henry," T.J. said. "I say 'Fuck all these haters who wanna make a mockery of the things we cherished as kids, like the sax.' Fuck 'em. In a year or two, they'll be irrelevant. So, really, there ain't no reason to worry 'bout 'em." T.J. shrugged his shoulders. "Fuck 'em. They all a bunch of nobodies."

"The saxophone," Henry said passionately, "it's supposed to represent so much more, T.J. It represents our generation, where we came from. You feel me? I mean, what happened to those days? I don't want to sound like a broken record here or like some cynical fuck, but it's time for people to wake the fuck up. Now, it's like nobody gives a shit about anything."

"It's called grunge, my friend," Deon said. "Grunge came along and ruined the party."

"—I like some grunge—"

"—Techno—"

"—I like some techno too—"

Henry said, "Or maybe it was because our generation was all coked out of their minds."

"You got a point there," Deon said, laughing.

"I wouldn't really say it was grunge," Socks said. "'Smells Like Teen Spirit!' Honestly, that might be one of the hardest hitting tracks I ever heard."

"That's your opinion."

"When I think about 'Smells Like Teen Spirit,' I think about Pizza Cave and that massive jukebox they got sitting up in the back," Henry said. "I remember first semester me and Afed would go to Pizza Cave and blast 'Smells Like Teen Spirit' over the jukebox. That guitar riff would start playing. All the parents in the restaurant covering their children's ears, glaring at us like we were monsters."

Next, Henry drawled the lyrics from the song "Smells Like Teen Spirit."

"*God*," Socks said breathily, "my parents, they never understood why we listened to that kind of music. Bands like Nirvana."

For a moment, Socks's eyes drifted in reflection.

"My father," he said and shook his head, "he hated it."

"What kind of music did your old man listen to?"

"Me," Socks said, pointing at his chest.

"Yeah you!"

"He wasn't a music man."

"But he had to listen to something! Anything! Right?"

"The only thing I've heard him listening to on the radio is *Wayne Cook*," the name Wayne Cook said with a poor Jersey accent, "the sports announcer for the New Jersey Hawks."

Deon reached around and patted Socks on the shoulder.

"I take it you and your old man never had that catch in the backyard."

"I know exactly where you're going with this, Doctor Bellinger," he said, tapping the side of his temple with his index finger. "But nice try."

"Mr. Mysterious?" Deon rolled his head back, chin in the air. "All right. . . "

Socks innocently shrugged his shoulders.

"What can I say?" he said with a smirk. "I'm unbreakable."

Henry accidentally let out a snort from the remark and said, "Because you were too busy listening to 'The Working Hour' in your room."

Socks slapped hands with Henry and then Deon interrupted the brief celebratory, "You say that now, Socks." He leaned forward into Socks's range of sight. "Wait till the right girl comes along. The kind of girl your ass can't stop thinking about all day long, the kind who's there when you wake up and there when you go to sleep. That's the girl I'm talking about." Eyes widened, he pointed directly at Socks. "And you know, Socks. The," emphasizing the word *the*, "one. Before you know what the hell hit you," he motioned to his head with his wormy fingers, "all those little nasty, little dirty secrets crawling around inside your head will all come gushing out."

Socks shrugged again.

"Whatever." Then, he directed his attention toward Deon and nodded. "How about you, D Finger?"

"My Old Man, he's a huge Fleetwood Mac fan."

Socks concealed a sudden chuckle before it could grow any louder.

"Ain't nuttin wrong wit Fleetwood Mac."

Deon motioned to T.J.

"You like Fleetwood Mac?"

"Yeah." T.J. paused. "They cool. Then," T.J. said abruptly before the unavoidable question came Henry's way, "there's Mr. Vortex. Can't forget 'bout that dude."

In return, Henry opened his eyes from their squinted position. A wave of seriousness washed over his face. He was suddenly shooting daggers at T.J.

"Honestly," T.J. said, pulled his calm eyes from Henry's, and looked at the others. "My boy Henry here is twice the saxophonist. He makes Mr. Vortex look like a fossil."

"I couldn't agree more," Deon said and toasted the Diesel in the air. "The way you play, it doesn't even compare to Mr. Vortex. I mean. . . Mr. Vortex, it seems like those kinds of players have an expiration date. Not you, Henry. They way you played, it was. . ." Deon was thinking, ". . . timeless," he said. "It was timeless."

"Yeah," Henry said, a glimpse of excitement shining from his grin. "You think so?"

"Damn straight," Deon said and toasted the Diesel once more.

He finished the cheap, skunky beer, crushed it, and then tossed it in the front lawn.

"I'm going to use the head," he excused himself.

"Don't fall in," Socks mumbled as Deon stumbled to his knees.

"Hardy fucking har har," Deon said and eased through the cracked bedroom window.

Socks said to the others, "It's time to eat. You guys want anything?"

"I'm good," Henry said.

"T.J.?"

"Uh," he uttered. "Yeah. Give me a minute. I'm gonna hang back here wit Henry fo a minute."

"Whatever."

Socks squeezed through the window.

While Henry and T.J. sat back and gazed up at the stars above, a relaxing silence grew over the two.

"Hey, Henry," T.J. said, "I never told 'em 'bout Mr. Vortex."

"I know you didn't."

"I'll only tell 'em if you want me to."

"Thanks, man."

"That's what friends are for."

Henry smirked, a warming one.

Another relaxing silence.

"So, that was your moms on the phone," T.J. said calmly. "Yeah?"

Henry glanced over at T.J.

"Yeah," he answered.

"How is she?"

"Better I guess," Henry answered. "Doctors said her cancer went into remission."

"That's good. Right?"

"Better than being out of remission," Henry said and sighed loudly. "I swear, though, sometimes she treats me like I'm still that little ten year old boy, always checking up on me. The way she talks to me sometimes, the way she treats me... it just makes me feel like I'm less than fucking zero... like... like I don't have a clue as to what goes on in the world."

"You mad?"

"Yeah, T.J.," Henry said. "I *am* mad. Not happy. If that's what you mean."

"But why?"

"I'm watching her slowly slip away, T.J.," he said. "And I can't do a damn thing about it. Times, she can't remember what she did the day before or what she said. I worry about her, T.J."

"'Bout what?"

Henry hung his head.

"That one day," he turned to T.J., eyes glazed, "I'm going to come home and she isn't going to even recognize me anymore."

"She old, Henry Man," T.J. said. "I've learned that you've gots to be patient with them older folks. The way I

see it, they almost like kids. I mean. . . if you ain't patient,
you probably go crazy and end up in one of them hospitals."
He smacked his gums. "My moms, you see, she was the same
ways with my nana. My nana drove my moms insane. Like
fuckin' INSANE! I 'member my moms crying at night. The
short tempers. All the yellin'. She even had a nervous breakdown at one point." He chortled unexpectedly. "Shit! One
time, my moms wanted to put my nana outta her misery. She
never did, though. She was jus messin'. I knew she was. I
knew she never do a thing like that. They only words. I
mean, Henry Man, if I ever get like that, seriously, where I
can't even take care of myself. . . " he placed his hand over his
chest, ". . . then you have my permission to— "

"—We all get old, T.J.," Henry interrupted.

"I guess so," he said quietly. "There's times I jus wanted
to tell my moms, 'Lemme go.' You know. I'm a grown man
now. I don't have to report to you like you is my probation
officer or something."

"Yeah," Henry said. "I know."

"It was like she wouldn't accept it anymore, like she ain't
have a choice in the matter." T.J. paused. "Eventually, I
guess I wore her down."

"When's the last time you talk to her, your mom?"

T.J. thought for a moment.

"Over a year," he said tentatively. "Last time I visited my
parents, they even still had that old baseball wallpaper hung
up in my room. You 'member?"

Henry laughed and bobbed his head.

"I remember."

"It's funny," T.J. said, pondering briefly.

"Not really if you think about it."

"I know right," T.J. said and pulled his eyes up at the
stars. "All you think 'bout when you is a kid is growin' up
and being that man you envision in ya head. Then, when you
do grow you wish you could've done things a lil' differently."

Like T.J., Henry gazed up at the stars and said over a sigh,
"I know exactly what you mean."

FIFTEEN

FINAL exams were right around the corner.

Ever since Henry started up the band, he hadn't even sat himself in front of a book in over two weeks. Soon, Henry realized, it was going to be summer. Soon, the semester would be over. And soon, a time of decision would be upon him: either stay for another semester and "wait it out," as his roommates had told him, or go where the music would take him. A part of him had his sights on Los Angeles, the City of Angels. Another part was ready and willing to open himself to the world. At this point in time, Henry honestly didn't know whether or not he was going to pass several of his core classes. He was hovering around a D in his geography class. The other classes were right in the ballpark (nothing higher than a C). Henry had missed so much class that he didn't know what was going on. During his time away, he hadn't kept in touch with his other classmates. He hadn't even picked up a basketball. In fact, the one he had, that old, coarse, raggedy one, was collecting dust in the closet and hadn't seen the light of day since he stashed it in there during the rearrangement. Most of his time was exhausted in the studio with the other band mates.

Every afternoon, they would hit up Frankie's Footlongs, a local favorite among the college students about four miles from Haddon University. The place drew quite a crowd every night, especially Thursday nights. Frankie's was known for its hot dogs (Peregrine style, of course, which was a slightly charred hotdog on a toasty buttery hot dog bun topped with maple syrup, fresh picked and sliced strawberries or, if a patron didn't like the strawberries, then he or she could also choose from diced pineapples or sliced bananas, and then finely chopped, crispy bacon, and finally a sprinkle of powdered sugar). One of the main highlights, besides the dogs, was the free refills on seasoned French fries. The waitresses, who wore these pink roller skates with pink cut off shirts and tight jean shorts—or daisy dukes, made well known by Southern belle Daisy Duke from the television show *Dukes of Hazard*—would bring out these mounds of greasy French fries, which always ignited the guys' arousal. Not the hot fries. But the daisy dukes, of course. The only green on the menu was from a leaf of iceberg lettuce on Frankie's Double, a double cheeseburger. It started to become a ritual for Henry and his new band mates, Frankie's Footlongs. There was just something about savory-sweet fast food that brought out the best in them. T.J. claimed it released the "creative juices." To some degree or another, he was right.

SIXTEEN

THREE weeks went by just like that; and there it was, almost glistening like a polished jewel in T.J.'s hand. He diligently placed the demo CD, which consisted of six tracks: "Captured By Light," "Mesaterrestrial," "The Carpenter," "Sleigh Bells," "Two Dollar Witch," and "Save The Last Dance Before The Zombie Apocalypse," inside the case.

With a smile stretched across his face, T.J. wagged the demo in the air.

"What do we do now?" Socks asked, standing over T.J. at the kitchen table.

T.J. looked up at Henry, who was nibbling on his fingernails and standing with his back leaned up against the counter.

Henry removed the fingernail from his mouth and said confidently, "Now we call Rockwell."

After they ate an early lunch, Henry gathered the rest of the band mates and sat them down at the kitchen table where they held a band meeting. They talked about who should call Mort. Since Henry had spoken with him before, they decided it was best that Henry be the one to make the phone call.

Henry, who was not particularly comfortable with making the phone call, picked up the telephone and breathed slowly, first through his nose and then out through his mouth.

As he dialed the first digit from the business card, there was a knock on the front door.

"Perfect timing," William said with annoyance, folded his arms, and leaned back in the chair.

"If that's that Afed kid I'm going to flip," Geordie mumbled and glared at Henry.

"What?" T.J. said confusedly. "You don't like Afed?"

Geordie rolled his eyes.

Henry placed Rockwell's business card on the table and said flatly, "I'll get it."

As he made his way toward the front door, he witnessed Coach Boland pacing around the front porch.

Henry suddenly froze and then backpedaled his way back to the kitchen.

"Shit," he whispered.

Even though he thought about doing exactly that, which was turning the other way and forgetting that he saw the coach on the porch, he accidentally caught Coach Boland's eyes crossing his path inside the house.

"*I know you're in there, Henry,*" Coach Boland said with his face pressed against the door window. "*Don't think I can't see you.*"

Henry shook his head and sighed.

With his shoulders deflated, he said to himself, "Time to face the music."

As Henry opened the door, he witnessed the tension throbbing in the coach's face.

Coach Boland was standing there with his hands on his hips.

"Did you forget?" the coach asked angrily.

"Sorry, Coach," he muttered and stepped outside before the coach shouldered his way into the house.

"What the hell is going on with you, Henry?"

Henry closed the door behind him and stepped onto the porch.

Coach Boland pointed inside the house.

"Who do you got in there?"

"Just some friends," he answered.

"So," the coach said, "what's the excuse for missing the annual meeting? The other players are starting to question your commitment to this team. They said you've been cooped up in this house for weeks."

Henry didn't know what to say. He did, actually. But he didn't know how to say it in front of the coach. He hadn't gone so far as to plan out a speech or anything. Not yet.

"You know we have a meeting every year before summer," Coach Boland said, folding his arms over his chest. "It's what keeps the team in check. By you not showing up, it sends a message to the other players."

Henry asked with a nod, "What message is that, Coach?"

"That you don't care about them," he said. "That you're better than them." He released a sigh, one that had been building in his chest all day. "Henry, I've been talking to some of your professors. They say you haven't been showing up to class. And when you do, your head is somewhere else. I'm worried about you, Henry. Tell me. What's going on with you?"

"Nothing," Henry answered.

"Is it drugs?"

"No," Henry said with a grimace. "I . . . I'm not on drugs."

"Then what is it?"

Henry thought long and hard.

"It's . . . it's you," he said both quietly and bitterly as he scowled at Coach Boland.

"What'd you say?"

"You heard me," Henry said louder. "It's you. It's my mother." His voice was growing, now intensely. It felt like he had an overloaded washing machine inside him, shaking and shifting off balance. Coach Boland observed the uplifting in Henry's eyes, the rebellion. "It's Randall. It's Jackson. It's Mansard. It's Lucky. It's Professor. . . Browning. Professor Clark. It's all the motherfuckers who look to me as if I have all the answers. Like I'm one of them. Well, I'm not."

"Settle down, Henry."

The coach eased his hands into the air.

"You're right, Coach." The frustration was releasing a bit of the throttle. A clear understanding swam through Henry. "Talent doesn't mean a damn thing when your heart is not working on the same page. Basketball, it's just another useless talent. Like brushing your teeth every fucking morning or tying your fucking shoelaces."

The coach said bitterly, "You can't make millions of dollars brushing your teeth, Henry."

"It's not about the money," he said. "Not anymore."

"What about Abbey?" he said, trying to wrap his head around what Henry was saying. "Everything she's done for you! You owe her that much!"

Henry didn't answer the question.

"I get it," Coach Boland said, bobbing his head. "It's this music nonsense. The kids have told me about it. At first, I thought they were playing a prank on me. Now, it makes sense." The coach peeked inside the house and then sharpened his eyes on Henry. "You're not a musician or whatever you think you are in your head. You're a basketball player, Henry. You will always be a basketball player."

"You don't know me. . ."

"I thought I did," the coach gave Henry a once over with his eyes. "But maybe I was wrong about you." He pulled his eyes away from Henry as if he was repulsed from the sight of him and said, "Just think about what Abbey would want you to do."

"It's not her life," Henry said, his eyes watering. "It's mine."

"Damn it, son," the coach said, throwing down his arms. "I wish you could see the talent you have. You could be playing in the pros next year! The pros, Henry! The NBA! You would be a fool to pass up an opportunity like that!"

Henry turned his back and walked toward the door.

Coach Boland pointed his finger at Henry just like his mother had done countless times during Henry's childhood and held it there like a blade.

"Don't turn your back on me!"

"I'm done," Henry said, his head held down.

"Excuse me."

Coach Boland made an attempt to block Henry from entering the house.

In return, Henry pulled away.

"I said 'I'm done,'" he said, his eyes sharpening. "I'm through playing basketball! Get that through your fucking head!"

Coach Boland stood frozenly now.

"So," he said, his face long and pale, "that's it?"

Henry drifted in thought and envisioned the path before his eyes, the demo, flying out to Los Angeles, signing with a big record label, the press release, all of the photo shoots, the debut album, the concerts, the stardom, the groupies, the fans, the screaming, the money. Henry pulled his eyes back to the wounded man before him and, without a sliver of a doubt, said, "I know what exactly I'm supposed to do now."

"You'll be living on the streets, Henry Burl!" the coach shouted. "Is that what you want?"

Henry remained calm, vigilant.

With his cheeks flaring red, muscles tightening in his face, the coach waved his hand away in great frustration.

"The hell with you," the coach said under his breath and marched down the steps. He turned back around before Henry walked back inside. "You know," he said, "it kills me, Henry. It kills me to watch God's gift being wasted. You don't even know how many other kids would kill to have your talent, Henry. I've seen so many kids come and go, Henry. Kids who knew they weren't cut out to play in the NBA. And yet, they gave it their all, blood, sweat, and tears. Why? It's because these kids played for the love of the game, Henry. Never, I mean, never have I seen a player like you. The way you move on the court. You're a natural, Henry. You can be standing shoulder to shoulder with legends. I wish. . . " the coach cleared his throat, ". . . take a real good look at yourself. . . throwing your life down the drain for a pipedream." The coach directed his attention behind him and stared down a long and empty street. "You know that road, Henry." He nodded at the road, the quiet one. "It's a lonely road. But if that's what you want, then so be it. You and me both know exactly where that road is going to take you." Coach Boland embraced a deep inhale without even opening his mouth. "Good luck, Henry," he said sharply. "You're going to need every bit of it."

The coach stormed away.

Henry grimaced and walked back inside the house. He went straight into the kitchen.

The others stood up from the table.

Geordie asked, "What the hell was that all about?"

T.J. noticed Henry's anger bubbling in his face.

"We don't have to call this guy, Henry."

"No," Henry said clearly. "Give me the card. I'll call him."

Socks hesitated, but then handed the business card to Henry.

For a moment, Henry gazed at the card.

Deon asked over Henry's gaze, "Do you want us to leave?"

He pulled his eyes toward Deon, at the rest of the band, and didn't even have to say anything.

Deon nodded at the others.

"Let's go smoke a fatty," he said.

"I'm right behind you," Socks said and followed Deon toward the back porch.

T.J. was last to leave.

On the way out, he stopped by Henry and held out his hand.

"He jus' another guy," he said and shook his hand. "He ain't God. You know."

Henry smirked.

"I know," he said, the tension falling from his voice.

T.J. patted Henry on the back.

"Good luck," he said and left the kitchen.

While Henry was on the telephone with Rockwell's secretary, Susan, the others anxiously waited on the porch.

They witnessed Henry, who was more alert, doing a lot of pacing around the kitchen. Henry paused. His tone was suddenly raised, eyes widened. He was bobbing his head a lot and keeping his answers as short as possible. The speed of his pace increased. Now, Henry was circling in various rhythms around the kitchen island.

"He's off," Geordie said and pulled his face from the kitchen window.

Seconds later, Henry ambled outside with a blank expression on his face and the telephone dangling from his hand.

"So," Deon said with his facial expression heightened. "What's the deal?"

"The deal is. . ." Henry said and paused, ". . . the deal is he wants us to send him the demo ASAP."

The rest of the band suddenly released their excitement with cheers and high-fives.

Socks exclaimed, "Fuck yeah!"

"He said if he's interested, he would give us a call back," Henry explained. "From what he heard at Hot Foxy, he said he shouldn't be disappointed."

"That's what I'm talkin' 'bout!"

"I can't believe it!"

"So, what do we do now?"

"We wait," Henry said. "I guess."

Deon was thinking.

He sprang forward from the porch railing and shouted out, "I got it!"

"What?"

"We throw a party," he said ecstatically. "What better way to top off this good news than to play a live show in front of hundreds of people?"

"I don't know about this, Deon," Socks said hesitantly. "Don't you think we should maybe ask, I don't know, the people who actually live here?"

"They won't mind."

"How do you know?"

"No."

"See," Socks said. "Henry said 'No.'"

"No," Henry said once more. "It's a great idea."

"But what about Afed?"

Henry callously shrugged his shoulders and said, "What about him?

SEVENTEEN

THE word had gotten around the campus: "Party at 32678 College Park Road!"

Everybody who attended Haddon University knew about the party except for one person: Afed.

After Afed finished his creative writing class, he drove two miles from campus where he stopped by KFS and picked up a steak biscuit and then a six-pack of pale ale from Holy Spirits, a local liquor store just across the street from the fast food restaurant.

While he was making his way down College Park Road and taking small bites from his steak biscuit and chasing each bite down with a sip of ale, he witnessed the cars on the side of the street. The closer he drove toward his house, the more cars he saw. He couldn't help but wonder where the party was being held (the cars were now lined across both sides of the street), or if it was the Pikes (they certainly knew how to throw a keg party!). Then, as he parked a couple of houses away from his house, he realized all the noise, the lights, and commotion was coming from his house. He accidentally dropped the bottle from his hand and spilled pale ale all over the leather upholstery. As he reached down to pick up the bottle, the foam erupted from the top like lava from a volcano. Afed caught most of the foamy ale with his mouth and placed the bottle underneath his Mercedes for the time being.

Lights, all ranging from reds and blues and greens, were flashing violently in the backyard, Afed noticed.

"What in the world..." he said and eventually exited from his car.

Afed meandered his way through the rowdy crowd on the front lawn. He passed an old hatchback with a spare in the driveway. Half of the tarnished car was parked in the grass. The inside was filled with thick smoke. Inside, three grungy hippies were passing around a roach. One of them, Afed noticed, was wearing a gas mask over his face. Besides that, all he could see was the tiny flare from the end of the roach igniting from inside the clouds of smoke.

Afed proceeded toward the house.

On the way, he spotted a freshman puking his guts out in the bushes.

Other students—sophomores, Afed guessed—had their shirts off and were wrestling around in the grass.

Once Afed arrived inside the house, he shouldered his way through the foyer and into the living room, which was packed to the gills with even more college students (if the ones on the front lawn weren't enough!).

With the music blaring throughout the house, he finally shouldered his way to the backyard where most of the noise was coming from. He acknowledged the band playing on the back porch. He was stunned to hear how good they were playing. Even sounded way better than that garbage one would hear on the radio, Afed judged over a minute of listening.

He bumped into his two other roommates, Ronnie and Lumen. They weren't the least upset. In fact, they were having the time of their lives.

Ronnie had his girlfriend, Jamie, hanging on his arm.

In complete intoxication, Lumen, the other roommate, was staggering back and forth, eyes swimming around his head, and screaming over the music, "THIS IS THE BEST FUCKING PARTY EVER!"

After "The Carpenter" came to an end, the band ended up playing three more songs, "Run Baby Run," a new one called "Fever Town," and then finally their most popular song, "Mesaterrestrial."

The crowd went absolutely wild for Mesaterrestrial. In fact, the entire following week the lyrics to Mesaterrestrial were being circulated and sung around the campus.

At the end of the show, Afed, who had already pounded down seven red cups from the keg of cheap domestic beer, three jägerbombs, and taken part in two keg stands—a first for him—squeezed his way through the house and hurried over to Henry.

He slurred, "You guys know how to put on one helluva show."

Henry grabbed Afed by the shoulder and shouted out over the stereo, "I thought you'd be mad!"

"Mad? I'm not mad!" Afed pulled his eyes away from Henry and gazed around at all the gorgeous girls in the room. "I'm on the fucking moon right now, Henry!"

"The moon, huh?"

Afed wrapped his arm around Henry, nodded at the two loose girls across the living room, and shouted into his ear, "Welcome to the life of a rock star, Henry!"

The girls were batting their eyelids and trying to conceal their childish smiles.

"Are those what I think they are?"

"Thas right, player," Afed slurred closely to Henry and patted him on the cheek. "You 'fficially have groupies."

Blushing, Henry asked, "What about Trilby?"

Afed waved off the comment.

"Fuck Trilby," he said angrily. "You d'serve better."

Henry shrugged his shoulder and chugged the rest of the beer in his cup.

"Maybe you're right, my friend."

"Hell, Henry!" Afed hollered out. "When am I ever wrong?"

Henry laughed and made his way through the crowd and introduced himself to the two groupies, who went by the names Sara and Amanda.

The very next morning Trilby cautiously stepped inside the smelly, messy house on College Park Road. Ronnie and Lumen were passed out on the couch. Over a dozen girls dressed in bikinis were sleeping on the floor. A garden hose had been brought in from the outside porch and was resting between the girls. The living room floor was covered with cigarette butts and Diesel beer cans. Trilby almost slipped over one of the many puddles on the hardwood floor. She regained her balance and slowly made her way up the stairs where Henry was sleeping.

When she arrived at the top of the landing, she found a Polaroid of Henry and the three other girls on the floor. And it didn't stop there. There was another Polaroid. And then another!

As the Polaroids slipped from her hand, she glanced towards Henry's bedroom and saw that the door was closed. Not only did she hear the sound of whispering and giggling coming from behind the door, but she also witnessed the three shadows scuttling like cockroaches underneath the doorway. She crumbled the last remaining Polaroid in her hand, wiped the racing tear from her cheek, and hurried from the nasty house as quickly as she could without tripping over a body.

EIGHTEEN

THREE days had passed since Henry mailed the demo first class to Los Angeles, California. Now the band was becoming a part of the daily discussions around campus.

On the fourth day, Henry received a telephone call from Mort. He put him on speaker so that the others could listen in on the conversation.

"Guys," Mort said over speakerphone, "Mort Rockwell here. Hey. Listen, guys. I absolutely loved what I heard on the demo. I want to fly you guys out to LA. How does that sound?"

Deon drawled, "Los Angeles?"

"That's right," he said over the speaker. "And who exactly am I speaking to?"

"Deon," he said and cleared his throat. "My name is Deon Bellinger, sir. Guitarist."

"Mort," he said. "Call me Mort. And by the way, great work on the fret. I love your style."

"Thanks!"

"Listen, you guys, I don't have a chance to meet all of you over the phone, but soon I will. I want you guys to take the rest of the day off to think it over and then call me back." His voice was inching closer to the speaker. "I look forward to hearing from you."

"Wait a second." Henry turned to the others gathered around the kitchen table. They were all bobbing their heads in agreement. Henry said with hesitation, "We'll do it."

"That was fast," Mort said, his voice drawn back. "It sounds like you guys know exactly what you want. I like that kind of attitude in a group. You'd be amazed how many prima donnas I deal with on a daily basis. It can drive a man up the wall."

"Well, you don't have to worry about us, sir," Henry said. "I mean, Mort."

The band mates could hardly control the smiles over their faces.

"You guys need to start packing because tomorrow you're going to California," he said gladly.

"We look forward to seeing you, Mort."

"I'll have Susan give you a call later today and inform you about all the details, flight arrangements, and so forth," Mort said. "In the meantime, you guys can take a breath. You've earned it."

"Yes, sir, Mort, sir."

"Have a safe trip, you guys."

Mort hung up the phone.

In shock, Henry's eyes scanned around the table.

"We made it," Socks said. "I can't fucking believe it."

"Did you hear what he said about my fret work?"

"Don't get a bighead about it!"

"Not so fast, Socks," Geordie said coldly. "We still haven't heard what the man's offering."

"Offering?"

"What if it's like millions of dollars?"

"What if he wants us to make a music video?"

Henry said, "Enough with the 'what ifs' guys."

Everyone was left in a state of shock.

Deon placed the glass of cranberry juice on the table and hollered out, "We're going to LA!"

He gave Henry a hug and lifted him up in the air.

Henry tried to catch his breath.

"All right already," he said and burst out laughing.

Deon shouted out hysterically, "We're going to be famous, motherfucka!"

Everyone around the kitchen table laughed at Deon's antics and rejoiced in triumph.

*   *   *

After Henry was packed for Los Angeles (two large duffel bags consisting mostly of eight or nine different outfits, all filled to the brim), he decided to pay his mother a visit in Queens Dive.

During the trip to Queens Dive, he was holding onto a mixture of emotions that, for the life of him, he couldn't shake. He was a bit nervous, a bit excited, a bit scared, a bit optimistic, a bit pessimistic, and a bit everything in between. As of now, he didn't know how his mother was going to react to the good news. Hopefully, Henry thought, surprised and, of course, proud.

Just before four o'clock in the afternoon, Henry pulled up to the driveway and caught his mother pacing around the front of the townhouse with a rusty watering can in her hand.

Ignorant of Henry, she scuttled back inside the townhouse, closed the door behind her, and peeked out the window.

As Henry parked the car and walked up to the front door, he could hardly control his nerves. Not only that, he wondered why his mother was acting so paranoid.

He rang the doorbell, only to receive the slam of a mini-van door behind him. Curious, Henry shot a glance over his shoulder and saw one of his mother's neighbors getting the mail from the mailbox. Holding her hand was a little girl. Henry waved at the neighbor and yet received a cold, icy glare in return.

Abbey finally answered the door.

"Henry," she said surprisingly.

"Hey, Mom."

Henry embraced Abbey in his arms.

"Well," she said over her son's shoulder, "this is a surprise."

"Yeah," he said. "I just wanted to see how my mother was doing."

"I'm doing just fine, Henry."

"That's good."

She pulled herself from her son.

"Is everything all right, Henry?"

"Yeah."

"Come in," Abbey said suspiciously and guided Henry into the warm house.

"I see you made some changes to the house," Henry said and noticed the floral curtains over the windows. "Where did you get the money?"

"A friend of mine, Jinnee," she said.

"The one at the hospital?"

"That's her," she replied. "She has her own interior design business on the side. She came in and put the curtains up for free. Wasn't that nice?"

"Yeah," Henry said and briefly eyed over the curtains once more. "Nice."

On the way to the kitchen, Abbey said bitterly, "So, why didn't you bring your little girlfriend over here?"

"Trilby?"

"You mean Trash?" she said under her breath. "Yeah. That one."

Henry clinched his teeth.

He took a deep breath and said collectively, "I'm no longer seeing her."

"Really?" Her voice grew gradually. "I see you finally came to your senses."

"Actually, Mom," Henry said loudly, "she was the one who dumped me."

As Abbey strolled away from her son, she said once more under her breath, "She was a whore anyways."

Henry only caught the *whore* part.

She said, "I told you about her, but you never listened."

As Henry tried to keep pace with his mother, he asked, "And who gave you the right to stick your nose in my business?"

"Because you're my son," she said. "That's why."

"How can you say something like that about her?" he said, his voice held with restraints. "You didn't even know her."

They arrived in the kitchen.

Abbey grabbed the knife on the counter and said, "I know her type."

"You were the one who ran her off," Henry exclaimed. "Not me. I still had a chance to make things right with her."

"Excuse me." Abbey faced Henry and then planted both hands over her hips. "By fooling around behind her back? Yeah, Henry!" she said with both resentment and ridicule. "That's one way of making things right with a girl." Abbey picked up the knife again and whispered, "I mean a *whore*."

Henry turned as red and angry as the devil.

"I don't want to hear it, Henry!"

"Please. . . " he said, cringing.

Abbey innocently held up her hands, the knife in one.

"I'm not in the mood to fight with you, Henry!"

He counted to ten and calmed his breathing like Charles had taught him after the murders in Sinclair Leprieur.

"I didn't come here to fight with you," he said over a deep breath.

"Then, why did you come here, Henry?" Abbey asked venomously and pointed at the kitchen window. "I see you saw Mrs. Chance. Did she ask how I was doing?"

"No," Henry said strangely. "She didn't. Was she supposed to?"

"Typical," she said sourly. "Nobody around here cares about anybody. It's like they have their own little cliques. Like they're too good to talk to you. They won't even acknowledge me." Abbey muttered to herself, "Arrogant. . . "

"You were the same way."

"What did you say?"

"When I was younger, you were busy taking care of me," Henry said. "Plus, you had two jobs. You had a lot going on. Listen. . . Mom. I didn't come here to talk about your neighbors. I came here to tell you something very important."

"You know what, Henry," she argued. "I was still courteous enough to say hello to my fellow neighbors. Those people over there won't even speak to me."

Henry bit his tongue and approached the counter.

Abbey snorted.

"I tell you what, Henry," she said, her voice still sour. "You can't be nice anymore in this world. If you do, people look at you funny like something is wrong with you or they ignore you or treat you as if you're invisible." Her voice turned gruffly. "I've about had it here—"

Henry interrupted, "Did you hear what I just said?"

"I heard you!"

Abbey fiercely cut the tops away from fresh strawberries as if it was a competition on the cutting board. She got through three more strawberries before she shot her eyes over at Henry as if she already knew what he was going to say.

Over a wave of tense silence, she stopped cutting and carefully placed the knife—blade side facing her—over the counter.

"Your upset about what I said over the phone," she said, the anger dissolving from her face. "It's your life, Henry. I'm not going to get in the way anymore. I'm not going to try and protect you. I'm not going to do anything, Henry. I'm going to leave you alone."

"Protect me?" Henry said, his eyes flaring. "Protect me from what?"

She sighed, which helped alleviate the tension in her chest.

"Your father was playing in Baton Rouge," she explained, her eyes pulling away from Henry in a state of reflection. Somewhere in her rigid expression, a smile was trying to creep through, just barely. "I went to most of his concerts. He used to put on quite a show. When the show was over, I met up with your father backstage. At the time, we were sort of a couple. . ."

"You told me this already," Henry said, the frustration easing back into his voice. "Don't you remember?"

"I did?"

"Do you remember when you picked me up from T.J.'s? You told me a story in the car, about my father, about Mr. Vortex, and his stepsister, Hannah."

"I don't remember telling you that?"

"Well, you did."

Abbey's eyes froze as she drifted farther into thought. The thought alone of the car ride seemed like an empty space. There was nothing there, only a dark abyss inside an ocean of disjointed thoughts.

"Don't you remember?"

Abbey didn't respond.

"Mom?"

"Yes, Henry."

"Is there something you're not telling me?" Henry asked and took a step closer to his mother. "What really happened between you two? If you loved him so much, then why did you leave him?"

"I tried to help him, Henry," she said sincerely. "I really did. How do you think I met Doctor Lowe?" Her dark eyes drifted away from Henry in another state of reflection. "He tried to hang himself, your father did. He said, 'It was the only way.' I didn't know what he meant at the time. Then, more stuff came out about his stepsister, Hannah. She wanted to destroy him, Henry."

"Because of the money. Right?"

"Money," she said and sighed. "And the jealously."

"Jealous from what? Fame?"

"No," she said. "She was also jealous of me, Henry."

"You? Why?"

Abbey sighed once more, but this time louder.

"She. . . she liked your father more than a stepbrother."

Henry was left in a state of complete repulsion.

"Are you telling me. . . "

Abbey nodded her head.

"And you see why he wanted nothing to do with her." She sighed yet again. "That's when Hannah met my mother, your grandmother, Claudia. At first, I didn't want to believe it, how she was involved in. . . "

Abbey struggled to look her son in the eye.

"Involved in what, Mom? You mean the witchcraft?"

She paused.

"Black magic."

Henry thought about the remark, *black magic.*

"I don't have to explain the rest of the story, Henry," she said. "You already know how the story ends. Just saying those words out loud sounds completely insane. Trust me. I know. But it's true, Henry." Her voice was sharpening. "Your father was cursed! I know it in my heart!"

Henry took a couple of steps back.

"When was the last time you talked to Charles?" Henry asked as he turned his back on Abbey.

Abbey said, "It doesn't matter, Henry. There was nothing we could do. The last time I saw your father, he was at the end of his rope. I couldn't let you see him like that. One day, you'll understand. Now, I don't expect you to."

"That wasn't your choi—"

"—Coach Boland called me this afternoon," Abbey interrupted, her voice overpowering Henry's.

"I didn't come here to talk about basketball."

Henry faced his mother, but struggled to look her in the eye.

"Why did you come here, Henry?"

"I came here. . . " he sighed, ". . . I came here to tell you that I'm leaving."

"Leaving? Leaving where?"

"I'm going to LA," he said.

Unresponsive, Abbey was gaping at Henry.

"During Open Mike Night, I met this producer," Henry explained. "He's flying me and my friends out to LA."

"Friends? What friends?"

Henry carefully thought about his next words, the ones that he recited in his head during the drive to Queens Dive. The thought of his father being cursed crossed over into his other thoughts. Black magic? How ridiculous? Maybe the loneliness had gotten to her. Was she really being serious? Fox was crazy. That Henry knew. But his mother. Was she right there with Fox on the crazy level? Henry focused. There was no other way of putting it. So Henry just did.

"My band."

"Your band?"

"We're going to LA and we're going to sign with a record label," he said. "It's happening, Mom, whether you like or not."

Abbey didn't say another word. Yet, she walked over to the kitchen window and peered at the neighborhood street outside.

Henry said over the silence, "Mom?"

"When I saw you play at that one club, I saw your father on stage," she said mindfully, still peering outside. "You play like him, your father." She snorted and faced Henry. "Even better." With her eyes never leaving Henry, Abbey walked over to him. "You grew up so fast on me, Henry, especially all that you've been through." She put each one of her frail hands on the front of Henry's shoulders and let out a sigh. "You're not that stuttering boy anymore," she said dolefully. "Look at you. You are finally a man." She made an attempt to place her hand over Henry's left cheek. Abbey never touched his cheek. Yet, she pulled back her hand and placed it back on his shoulder. "Now, you're old enough to make your own decisions. I just pray that you're making the right one."

Abbey hugged Henry.

"Just be careful," she said.

A blanket of relief covered Henry, overwhelming almost.

Henry chuckled.

"I'll keep an eye out for any bad omens."

Abbey tightened her grip around Henry.

"I'm sorry for what I said over the phone. I didn't—"

"It's all behind me, Henry."

Henry tried to pull himself away, but Abbey still had a bear hug around him.

"Mom. . ."

Abbey gripped tighter.

"Mom. . ."

Henry felt the compression in his chest.

Each breath grew fainter.

He grabbed a hold of his mother's arms and pried them from his body.

"Let go," he said.

His mother finally pulled away.

Henry asked, "Are you sure you're okay?"

Abbey wiped her tears and pulled herself away from her son.

"For so long, I wanted you to be someone who you're not," she said. "You must really resent me."

"No," he said vacantly. "I don't."

"You proved me wrong, Henry."

"Why the change in heart?"

"I've finally made my peace, Henry," she said resonantly. "Now, it's time to move on with my life."

When Abbey excused herself to the restroom, Henry found some papers underneath a folder on the kitchen table. He picked up the medical papers and skimmed over them. His face went long and expressionless: jaw dropped, eyes widened, skin turned pale. Henry slowly turned to the restroom, at the closed door, the light underneath, the thin shadow, and a ripple of shock raced through his body.

NINETEEN

EXCERPT from Starlet Rollinson's *Missing the Edges: A Memoir (New York: Tilted Hat Press, 2045)*, page 116:

When Henry first told me the story about his second—and last—encounter with Mort Rockwell, I responded with four words: "Been there, done that." However, through experience, I've learned how to choose my words a little more carefully, especially when it came to dealing with greedy producers.

Over breaks in the Den, which, there were a lot of during the *Rule or Be Ruled* recording sessions, Henry and I would catch up on our band's history. I shared Like Heroin's troubled beginning, me working two jobs, the rejections (I can't even count how many there were), and my short-lived addiction to heroin. The only difference between Like Heroin and Mona's Arch was that Like Heroin never split, whereas Mona's Arch did.

About a month into *Rule or Be Ruled* when the boys from Mona's Arch were laying down a couple of tracks at my lake front studio, I was one of the privileged few who got a chance to hear Mona's Arch first demo. The first time Henry described their sound to me he said (and I'm paraphrasing here): "*Mona's Arch is the soundtrack to the wildest night ever, a clash between old and new, 60's versus the 70's, 80's versus the 90's. Raw aggressiveness combed over melodic ambience. Imagine William Hart from the Delfonics* (Are you following me?) *on a coke binge playing with the Ramones at a raunchy underground club. I mean RAUNCHY! That be us. Then, you throw in the stage presence of Prince and Queen. The glamour of David Bowie. The high energy of the Stones. The unpredictability of James Brown. All crossing over into a more modern age of music, electronic and alternative. Then, you come in over all those dynamics* (that's me). *You're there to crawl inside the listeners' minds, keep them cozy, to lift them to faraway places beyond our minds, ones we've never reached before.*" Again, I'm paraphrasing here. Mona's Arch was the complete package all right, but they hadn't quite found "their" sound. Not until their sophomore album *Machine Mistress*. During the ROBR recordings, I fell in love with one track, which ended up making the final cut onto the album. That track was called "Fever Town" and it was one of the reasons why Henry's saxophone skills ranked at the very top. After we listened to the demo, including the one track "Fever Town," Henry was eager to tell me about his experience in Los Angeles, which he called "The LA Nightmare." "Everything happened so fast," he said, "the demo, the trip." Henry told me it felt like they were all crammed and trapped inside a spare tire rolling down a steep hill. Even if he tried, he couldn't stop the tire from rolling. So, I decided to poke fun at the situation, as we did with a lot of things around the studio. Henry and I did an interview together in order to pass time around the studio.

So, Henry, what was it like during your first trip out to LA?
(Henry, laughing from my hideous Barbara Walters accent, threw on his Wayfarer shades)
Henry the Fif': Please, Barbara. Call me the Fif'.
I like that name, the Fifth.
Henry the Fif': Nah, Baby. The Fif'. Spoken without the *t* and the *h*. Try it out. Fif'. Say it with me.
Fifth.
Henry the Fif': No. Fif'.
(I rolled my eyes)
Are we going to do this or not?
(Henry was laughing)
Serious.
Henry the Fif': Serious.
So, what was it like, your first trip to La La Land?
Henry the Fif': Well, Barbara, it was a fucking mess. (Henry shielded his mouth) Can I say fuck on national television?
(Eyes like daggers, I looked at Henry)
Henry the Fif': But seriously. (Henry cleared his throat and removed his shades) We were getting ready at the house. Next thing I know, we're boarding a private jet to Los Angeles. I've never been on a plane before. So, I was a little nervous. I had my two duffel bags jam-packed. The rest of the band mates were right there with me. You could see it in their eyes, the nerves. Their eyes were doing most of the talking. I remember the stewardess asking us if we wanted anything to drink. I was so fu. . . freaking nervous my stomach felt as if it was wielded shut. Couldn't eat or drink. Same went with T.J. Now, Deon, having grown up around two liberal parents whom he said frequently traveled across the world, he was the only one who didn't seem that nervous. I remember, (Henry smiling) Socks, I believe, mentioned something about Buddy Holly along with the words *plane crash*. That didn't sit too well with the other guys. From

what I've heard, though, they say flying is safer than riding in a car.

It's true.

Henry the Fif': Takeoff was the worst. But after that, it was a piece of cake.

You heard him ladies and gentlemen of the world. Famous rock star, Henry the Fif', was once afraid of flying. Can you believe that?

Henry the Fif': You told me to be serious.

What I do?

Henry the Fif': That's the thing. Once, Star. I was *once* afraid of flying, but I'm not anymore.

So, Henry the Fif', (accent now gone) how did the flight go?

Henry the Fif': Well, actually. It went really good. Better than I thought. Didn't even puke. Kept it all in like a good boy.

Impressive. What was LAX like?

Henry the Fif': Huge. When we arrived, we even had a limo there waiting on us.

Wow.

Henry the Fif': Throughout the trip, William warned us about signing our souls to the devil. The enticements, the private jet, the limo, were all nice. But it made me that more skeptical. I remained to myself for most of the trip to Phat Stacks' main headquarters. I haven't seen so many damn shops in my life.

Are you're talking about Sunset Boulevard?

Henry the Fif': You've been there. You know what it's like.

Trust me, Henry. I've been there many, many of times.

Henry the Fif': I know you have.

Too many.

Henry the Fif': Anyway, when we arrived at Phat Stacks it finally sunk in. "No turning back," I told myself. Everybody was about to jump out of their skin, even Deon. T.J. could hardly keep still even if his life depended on it. You know him. Paranoid as usual.

How about Socks? He was probably bouncing off the walls.

Henry the Fif': I swear I thought his head was going to explode all over the limo. We would have to blow off the meeting with Mort because we would be too busy scraping off all the brain matter from inside the limo.

So, how did the meeting go?

(A look of disgust over Henry's face)

Henry the Fif': A nightmare, one big ass nightmare. Mort wanted to "tweak" our sound. "Mesaterrestrial" was way too long for radio play, he told us. He wanted to trim at least five minutes from the song, especially the saxophone solo at the end. Said it was way too "cliché." When Mort started to talk about the figures, I completely zoned out. He was willing to offer each and every one of us seventy-five thousand dollars if we could sign with Phat Stacks that day. There was a catch, though. There always was.

Tell me about it.

Henry the Fif': All I could remember was Mort rambling on and on about the negatives of the song and not the positives. In the back of my mind, I fucking knew this would happen. I knew this piece of slime, Mort Rockwell, would try to turn us into his own hand puppets, just more whores in the industry. It wasn't about music with this guy. And I, especially, wasn't going to give in to his demands. Then, I heard a beat in my head like it was crying out for release, throbbing away in my head.

That beat, huh?

Henry the Fif': Yeah. That beat. This was our sound, Starlet, and this lowlife yuppie wasn't going to change our sound for more money, for the mainstream, for anybody! That beat got so loud that I couldn't even hear what Mort was rambling about anymore. The only thing I caught over that beat was Mort telling us how we needed to reshape our sound into Pink Floyd or something like that. I mean Pink Floyd is cool and all. But Pink Floyd is Pink Floyd and Mona's Arch is Mona's Arch, not Pink Floyd.

Amen.

Henry the Fif': I couldn't understand what this guy was saying anymore. Not a word. That beat was so strong in my head. Strongest it's ever been.

What kind of beat was it?

Henry the Fif': The song "Pretty Animals."

Absolutely.

Henry the Fif': Same exact one down to the tempo, the clap. Same beat.

That's crazy stuff.

Henry the Fif': Not as crazy as what happened next.

What happened?

Henry the Fif': Somewhere in my thoughts, believe it or not, I saw my mother's face like she was right there with me, resting inches away from my eyes. I saw the anguish in her eyes, the cancer slowly eating away at her. I know she wanted to tell me, but she didn't want to ruin my trip out to Los Angeles. That was when I stood up and yelled out, "Fuck this bullshit!" Mort thought I was joking at first. Then, Mort, the other guys included, saw the anger in my face. It was so thick you could cut it with a knife. Seriously. I don't even remember half of what Mort said next, something like how he was the one who controlled the music industry, how he knew what sells and what doesn't, and that musicians like me were like slaves to a master—Mort being the master. Then, I put it as simply as I could.

And how was that?

Henry the Fif': To go "fuck himself."

Are you serious?

Henry the Fif': As God as my witness.

I wish I could've seen the look on Mort's face.

Henry the Fif': Oh! The man was pissed off. All right. I could see a vein swelling in his forehead.

I take it he wasn't fond of the remark.

Henry the Fif': Not one bit. But I didn't care. I wasn't going to sit there any longer and let this asshole defile our sound and tell us what to do. I wasn't!

I would've done the same thing. Well, not entirely. I think I would've chosen my words a little more carefully. So, do you regret it, Henry? Do you regret flying out to Los Angeles?

Henry the Fif': That's a good question.

With a sudden pound at the door, Henry stormed out of Mort's office.

On the leather couch in the office, Geordie was shaking his head in hatred. Deon and Socks were shocked by what Henry had said to Mort, more so impressed than anything.

"You listen to me, you punk," Mort shouted as Henry stormed through the hallway. "You just destroyed any future you had in this fucking business. You hear me! After I get done with you, you're going to wish you never picked up a saxophone! I will ruin your life! Do you hear me? I will smear you fucking name across the gutter, you piece of shit!"

T.J. burst from his seat, dashed through the office, and followed Henry down the hallway.

Before Henry reached the elevator, he stepped in front of Henry.

He asked, "Is you fuckin' stupid?"

Henry was still jacked from the adrenaline. His hands were trembling. Eyes wired open. He could hardly look T.J. in the eye.

"That son of a bitch. . . " Henry bit his bottom lip as he paced around, ". . . he has no right."

"He has every bit of right, Henry," T.J. exclaimed and grabbed a hold of Henry's arm. "That's what he do for a livin'. He know the bizness."

"That man just wants money!" Henry cried out and removed his arm from T.J.'s grip. "I will NOT be a puppet, T.J! WE TALKED ABOUT THIS!"

"We talkin' seventy-five g's, Henry," T.J. argued as he maneuvered his head in front of Henry. "Think 'bout what you could do wit that kinds of money. You can buy your moms a new house. All her medical bills will be paid off. She won't haf to look for work eva again."

Henry turned away in frustration.

"What's your deal, Henry? This ain't like you, man."

He paused.

"It's. . ."

T.J. waited for a response.

"It's what?"

"It's. . ."

"Tell me, Henry," T.J. said. "You owe me that much, 'specially. . ."

"It's. . . it's my mother," Henry said. "The cancer came back."

"But. . . you said. . ."

"I know what I said, T.J.," he said and then looked T.J. in the eyes. "She lied to me. Again!"

The other band mates exited from Mort's office.

"What the hell was that all about?" Geordie seethed, glaring at T.J. and then Henry. He kept his eyes on Henry like a hungry predator would do with a prey. "Have you lost your fucking mind, Henry?"

T.J. held out his arms in front of Geordie.

"Back off, Geordie," he said, his eyes glued on Henry's.

"I won't back off," he said and pushed his way through. "Whatever future we had was ruined because of you."

"Chills, Geordie," T.J. said, sharpening his beady eyes. "I'm warning you."

Geordie moved his eyes over at T.J. and witnessed the thug breaking through his eyes.

He said closely to T.J., "You're going to stand here and defend this jerk?"

"His mother's sick."

"I don't give a flying shit about his goddamn mother!" Geordie made a move at Henry. "This band doesn't revolve around you, Henry."

T.J. warned, "Geordie. . ."

"You know what," Geordie said to T.J. "You can suck my dick." Then, he redirected his attention toward Henry. "You listen to me you piece of shhh—"

"Hey, Geordie," T.J. said from behind.

Once Geordie faced T.J., a fist was swinging at him at a breakneck speed. T.J. never broke Geordie's neck, but he would be lying if he said that he didn't wake up the next morning with a terrible crick in his neck. When T.J.'s fist collided with Geordie's jaw, Geordie went flying in the air. Once he hit the floor, T.J. straddled his legs over Geordie's body, leaving him with no room to defend himself. T.J. got in two really good licks across Geordie's face, one across the jaw and another directly in the nose and chin, before Henry jumped in and broke up the fight. Henry and T.J. scuffled briefly before the other band mates stepped in and pulled them apart.

Dazed and bloody, Geordie remained on the floor.

"I'm calling security," Susan said, standing behind the secretary desk.

Mort wandered into the hallway.

"What is this shit? Get these goddamn clowns out of here!"

"You see what you did, Henry," Geordie said, wiping the strings of blood from his chin. "Are you happy now?"

T.J. glared at Henry.

"T.J.—"

"Don't fuckin' talk to me eva again. . . "

T.J. shook the soreness from his hand as he stepped into the elevator.

"T.J.—"

Henry reached out to T.J., but the elevator doors were already closing. The last image Henry remembered of T.J. was a partial scowl over his face.

He would never forget *that* a look.

Never.

For the remainder of the trip in Los Angeles, Henry didn't say a single word to the other band mates.

The whole time, he was mentally going over the confrontation with Mort Rockwell as well as the fight that ensued. Geordie and T.J. ended up taking separate taxis to LAX and then separate flights—each a one-way ticket—back home to Lansford, which, at this point, was best for everyone.

Since Deon, Socks, and William had gotten along with Henry so well throughout the demo recording and knew that he was a great saxophonist as well as a singer who really wanted to make an impact on the industry—"to shake things up," he preached—they took a flight with him back home.

When Henry made it back to Haddon, T.J. was already gone.

After hours and hours of contemplating, Henry decided to drive to Parker Square. Screw hadn't seen T.J., as well, but he told Henry the next time he ran into T.J. to tell him that he was "a dead man." Henry was fortunate enough that he made it out of Parker Square with only a couple of bruised rips and a nice shiner to show the other students on campus. T.J. hadn't fully enlightened him about this Screw guy and how he was a man who carried around grudges. Apparently for Screw, the past didn't remain in the past. Instead, Screw embraced it. There were so many of them. Like three or four of them (and about twice Henry's size too), Henry counted, all standing over top of him. The only thing Henry could remember was the backside of their knuckles coming at him. The rest was ancient history.

PART FIVE

A SHADOW CAST OVER FAMILIAR LAND

WHEN the semester was over, Henry went back home to Queens Dive where Abbey revealed the news about her deteriorating health. She said that the doctors had only given her four to six months to live and even that seemed like an exaggeration considering her rapid decline. But the doctors didn't know Abbey, not like Henry did. Sure enough, she ended up surprising them all, her doctors—most of them. However, over the long eight months, Henry watched the transformation in his mother. He didn't know how much longer his mother could fight off the cancer. The medication that she was taking was helping a little. Abbey was on this one drug called *Xenophine*. Being a fairly new drug on the market, it hadn't been approved yet by the FDA. The side effects—an entire list of them—were even worse than the benefits themselves. Things went on like this for eight long months. They tried the cancer treatment centers, holistic doctors, folk remedies, shrinks (besides Doctor Charles Lowe), and even a hypnotherapist, but the money eventually fell short. Henry decided to take off a semester and work in order to support his mother's treatments as well as hospital bills. He ended up working two jobs, one during the day as a cashier at the Depot and the other at night as a pharmacy technician. The last time he spoke with his former roommate, Afed, Afed told Henry that William Darby joined a local thrash band called In Cold Blood. They recorded an EP that spread like a common cold throughout the underground music scene during the fall of '94. When winter came, In Cold Blood was a thing of the past. Most, if not all, of the band mates, including William (who found a decent job at Irony's Emporium), worked on the side while doing local gigs around Lansford. Geordie ended up replacing Leech Stevenson from Stella's Harbor because of Leech's bad coke problem. The band was riding high from the single "Into the Blue" off their *Anthology* album, which dropped Madonna's beloved "Secret" to a number 4 spot, leaving Stella's Harbor steady at number three on the billboards for two weeks straight. The band never made it to that number one spot, which was held tightly by Boyz II Men and their single "I'll Make Love to You." Nonetheless, Stella's Harbor's hit single became a high school anthem. . . but only for a couple of months. Henry hadn't heard anything about the other guys, Socks or Deon or T.J. During the breaks between both jobs, Henry found himself thinking a lot about T.J. Of all the band mates, he was the one whom he thought about the most. He wondered what he was up to, if he had reverted to his bad habits.

Every year winter showed its teeth right around Henry's birthday. Last year it snowed. The basketball team threw a party for Henry at the Pike's house. The drink of choice for the special night was bourbon snow cones. That night, Henry ended up throwing back twenty shots of Jim Bean. Later that night, Henry ended up throwing up twenty shots of Jim Bean, as well as two cans of Chef Boyardee's ravioli. Henry didn't remember a thing about that night, just the massacre that erupted from his body. All he remembered was waking up from his hangover with a sylphlike woman sketched horizontally across his face: her face underneath his ear with a cartoon bubble extending from her mouth, saying, "*EAT MY CUNT, SEXY*"; a pair of ample breasts over his left cheek; a patch of pubic hair shaped like a landing strip next to the corner of his lips; and then two skinny legs trailing over his right cheek and across the side of his neck. Henry remembered the humiliation, the giggling behind his back, the finger pointing, and then spending hours in the shower trying to rub away the purple ink and lipstick from his face. The year before that it was ice. Henry spent his nineteenth birthday blowing out the candles of a chocolate naked lady cake in the dark.

Almost every year, Mother Nature had done something: snow, ice, or rain. This year it was snowing.

As the pharmacy was minutes away from closing, Henry secretly slid the six hydrocodones from the tray into his pocket while the store manager was checking out one of the last remaining customers.

Once the drug store was closed, Henry made his way through the entrance. The cold was like a thousand needles pressed against his face. He tightened up the collar of his heavy coat and threw the backpack on his shoulder. As he stepped into the salted sidewalk, the burly manager walked up behind Henry.

"Henry," the manager said from behind.

Henry paused, a sneaking suspicion crawling into his stomach.

"You think it's best to wait till the storm passes?"

Henry slowly turned around and said, "I've driven in worse conditions. This," he looked around at all the snow, "this is nothing."

"I wish I was like that," he said and rubbed his chest. "I hate driving in this crap. Gives me severe heartburn."

"I was the same way, Guss," Henry said with casual composure. "I guess you just get used to it."

"Not me," the manager said and waved at Henry. "Anyway, drive safe."

"Always do, Guss."

Henry tightened up his coat once more as he trudged through the blizzard. The backpack was clinking, drawing even more suspicion. Henry glanced over his shoulder and spotted Guss standing there, eyeing him down, lighting the end of a cigarette. Henry made it to the Jelly Bean. He had a difficult time finding the lock over the door from all the snow. Once he did, he jerked the squeaky door open and sat shivering in the car. He turned the key in the ignition. The heat came on momentarily, but then finally died. Frustrated, Henry punched the controls and nearly ripped them from the panel.

On the way home, he grabbed a bite to eat at Momma Demeter.

Two nights ago, Henry made the mistake of drinking on an empty stomach. For the rest of the night, he ended up with his face inside the toilet. While he was vomiting up a storm, he tried his best to keep the explosions of coughing to a minimum and hit the sides of the toilet bowl, not the water. One of the many girls that Henry was seeing spent the night nursing Henry to sleep. Her name was Michelle. Then, there was Aileen, Naomi, Patrice, and Brooke, none of whom Abbey would "approve" of. He was never steady with these girls. In fact, Abbey wasn't even aware that her son was seeing these girls. And Henry planned on keeping it that way too. Almost every night, he would smuggle one of them into his bedroom like a member of the cartel smuggling drugs across the border. The sex was simply there to take his mind off things and, of course, to fulfill the urges of any young man with hormones. For months, he had done this: sneak one of his girls inside the house either through the backdoor or through the window. And it was getting worse, the urges. Even the sex was getting rougher, more experimental. On some mornings, Henry would wake up with cuts and scratches and red marks over different parts of his body—mostly back—and he didn't have the slightest clue as to how he had gotten them. On others, he couldn't remember anything about the night before. Over the entire fall season and into winter, Henry fell into a much darker state of self-indulgence.

Each time Henry fulfilled the urges, the drinking and the sex, it made him that more dead inside.

After he ate his food in the freezing cold car (Momma Demeter had closed two hours ago and left the drive thru open all night), Henry arrived at his house, which was now located in a much smaller neighborhood, south of East Haven, about ten minutes away from Queens Dive. All of the houses were ranch style houses—single-story.

As Henry trekked his way through the foot of snow and finally made it to the front door, his mother's aide, Odyssey, was there to greet Henry.

"Hello there, Henry," she said as she gracefully stepped aside.

"Hey," Henry mumbled with his head down.

Odyssey's eyes were mistakenly drawn to Henry's weary eyes.

"You look like you could use some sleep, Henry."

"Tell me about it," he said, now looking the other way. He placed the bag of leftover food on the counter, removed his backpack, and placed the clinking thing on top of the chair, this time more carefully than the bag of food. "Sorry I'm late," he said to Odyssey. "So, how did she do today?"

"It wasn't one of her good days."

"What else is new?"

His weary eyes crossed the cake on the table.

Intrigued, he stopped what he was doing, trivial things like biting his fingernails or checking the time on the microwave or fiddling with loose knobs around the stovetop, and read the cake. It read: "Happy 21st Birthday, Henry!"

He smiled and said to himself, "I completely forgot."

"I hope you like it," Odyssey said as she cracked a smile on her round face. "Your mother, she told me your birthday was today. Happy Birthday, Henry."

"Thank you," he said, gazing over the cake.

"You're very welcome," she said and smiled once more. "It's chocolate. Your mother said that was your favorite."

"Yeah. . ." he trailed off and looked at Odyssey. "It is. Thank you."

There was a silent pause.

"I better get going," Odyssey said, letting out an uncomfortable sigh as she grabbed her purse from the table.

Before the aide made her way to the front door, Henry hugged her and said into her shoulder, "I don't know what I would do without you."

Odyssey embraced Henry and displayed a warm, beaming smile across her face.

"You get some rest," she said closely. "You hear."

"I'll try," he said and walked her to the door.

"Don't try," she said motherly. "You do."

"Be careful out there," Henry said and opened the door for Odyssey. "The roads are kind of slick."

"I will." She held open the door. "Thank you, Henry." She wrapped a red scarf around her neck, bundled up from the cold, and said, "Good night, Henry."

Henry waved goodbye to Odyssey and checked on his mother.

When he arrived at her bedroom, which was just down the hallway from his bedroom, Abbey was sleeping. Henry decided it was best to let her sleep. So, he carefully eased into the room, placed a comforter over her puny body, and tiptoed away.

On the way out, he heard a rustling over the bed.

"I seeeee how it is," a weak, resonant voice slurred from behind. "Yoooou. . . you talk to Odyssey more so than you talk to your poor. . ." a phlegmy cough, ". . . your poor ole mother. . ."

Henry stopped at the lit doorway.

He walked back into the dark bedroom and said sternly, "Go back to sleep."

Her eyes grew with panic.

"The raft is too small," she said, her eyes racing around the ceiling. "It won't hold the three of us. Faaather? He's coming. . . coming down the hill. No. He isn't. Yes it is, Margaret. Where?"

Frightened from his mother's sudden blathering, Henry inched over to the bed, stood over his mother, and studied her with confusion.

"Mom. . ."

Henry tapped his mother on the shoulder.

She murmured, "He's coming, Margaret."

Another tap.

"Mom. . . you're dreaming. . ."

Henry carefully shook his mother's shoulder.

Abbey finally snapped from her trance. A gasp! It took her a couple of seconds to gather her surroundings, her son. She saw his two eyes above, looming there like tiny moons in the dark.

Delighted from her son's presence, she reached out and touched the side of his face. To Henry, her hand was like bones wrapped in worn plastic.

Henry pulled his eyes toward her darkened, sunken eyes and said quietly, "You need to sleep."

"I can't, Henry," she said weakly.

"But you need to."

Abbey pulled her frail hand away from Henry's face and turned to the moonlit window.

She groaned, "I. . . I don't want to beeee a burden anymore, Henry."

As Abbey swallowed the lump down her throat, her face shivered and grimaced in excruciating pain.

Henry said, "Don't talk like that."

"Do you remember when I told you about your grandmother?"

"Don't do this to yourself," Henry said and then let out a sigh. "You did what you had to do. You protected me."

"The year before she was diagnosed," she explained, her voice still weak and faint, "I was planning a trip out West. At the time, you were only three years old. I had over ten thousand dollars in my life savings, Henry. That was our ticket out of here. I was going to take you far away from that place where they would never find us."

"Mom. . ."

"We were going to move out West, Henry, where your grandfather lived," she said as Henry sat down in the chair next to the bed. "I was only a little girl when I met your grandfather for the first time. Eleven, I believe. While she was away, he visited me at the house." Abbey cleared her throat, the phlegm. "I. . . I remember. . . I remember I saw this man, this strange white man standing outside my window, standing there looking up at the house with his hands in his pockets, not a. . . care in the world. I went outside." Another phlegmy cough. Henry handed his mother a tissue from the nightstand. "Even though I was told not to leave the house. I did, anyway. Something about him. He was a nice man, charming. . . nothing like what she had told me about. He claimed to be my legal father. He told me all about what she had done to him and how they were only allegations and that they weren't true and that. . . that new evidence had come forward after all these years." She took a moment to catch her breath. "Later," Abbey breathed, steady now, "I found out that he did prove his innocence in court and that he tried to gain custody of me. Ten years he spent in prison, Henry. All those years wasted. For what?" Abbey paused for a moment, steady. "I. . . I remember he came back over to the house with the police. But she was there." That word, *she*, turned her face sour. "I could hear the arguing from my room. I went to the window. Something happened, something I can't explain. It's. . . it's like they. . . they died and yet they were still standing there in the driveway. Finally, they turned around and walked away the same way they came. . . even the police officers. No expression. Like dolls."

Henry said curiously, "Dolls?"

"Like dolls, Henry," she said, wiping away the phlegm from the corner of her mouth. "That was the last time I saw him, my real father, your grandfather. Last I heard, he was living in Sedona and starting a family of his own."

Henry asked, "Have you talked to Doctor Lowe today?"

Her eyes flickered over at Henry.

She said, "I'm talking to you, Henry."

Henry innocently held up his hands and leaned back in the chair.

"What if your grandfather really was innocent, Henry?" The tears formed around Abbey's eyes. "If he never spent all that time in jail for being accused of raping your grandmother, he could've saved me. . . especially from her."

"But you never would've met Mr. Vortex."

Abbey sighed and rolled her head to the other side of the pillow.

"I thought we got past this," Henry said and grabbed his mother's frail hand. "I thought we moved on."

Abbey wept into the pillow.

"I can't, Henry," she cried. "I can't move on."

The crying calmed after a couple of deep breaths.

Sniffling, Abbey said, "I wish. . . I wish you could've met your grandfather." Suddenly, her eyes wandered. "What is it, Margaret?"

Henry studied his mother yet again, this time in greater confusion.

"Mom. . . "

"She was sick," Abbey drawled, her eyes drifting back to Henry's. "Harvey, you know he couldn't take care of her on his own. He couldn't."

"I know," Henry said softly and caressed the top of his mother's hand. "You told me."

"I had to stay, Henry. I had to make sure that she was dead." Her head rolled toward Henry. She peered into his eyes. "Leave while you still can, Henry. Don't sacrifice the one dream you had because of me. When I'm gone, what will you do? Where will you go?"

"What are you trying to say?" Henry said, the anger in his voice rising. "That I. . . I should abandon you? That I should stick you in a home?" He sat up from the chair and paced around the dark room. He pointed his finger at the lit hallway. "I'm out there working my ass off for you!"

"I don't know how much longer I can do this, Henry," she begged. "Six months, six years."

"I'll talk to Doctor Cowen tomorrow," Henry said and walked over to his mother. Once more, he placed his hand on top of her frail hand. "We can get through this. This is nothing compared to what we've been through."

"No," Abbey cried out, her voice stretched out in agony. "I'm so tired, Henry. I'm tired of. . . feeling like this. Not having control of myself."

She was trying to catch her breath.

"Easy," Henry said, stroking the top of her hand. "Just like we practiced."

Abbey did as Henry commanded, cleared her thoughts, and carefully inhaled.

"I'm right here," Henry said calmly. "And I'm not going anywhere." He briefly lit up with joy. "I almost forgot." He reached into his pocket and pulled out a small music box. Inside, there was a tiny ballerina dressed in a pink leotard underneath a white tutu. Both of the ballerina's arms, which were in an en haut position, and feet were in the fifth position. Henry cranked the switch on the side of the box. The ballerina mechanically twirled around like a carousel over an unsteady melody.

Abbey smiled, the loose skin stretching over her skeletal structure.

She asked, "Where did you get that?"

"I found this in my closet the other day," Henry said as he handed Abbey the music box. "It must've gotten misplaced during the move."

"Harvey bought this for me when I was a little girl," she said in reflection. The pain in her face momentarily melted away. "She took it away from me." The second she mentioned the word *she*, Abbey's face washed over with resentment. "But Harvey, he found it stashed away in her room and gave it back to me." She carefully ran her fingers over the music box. "Every night, Patsy would put me to sleep."

"Patsy?"

"Huh?"

"Patsy?" Henry asked. "Who's Patsy?"

Abbey held up the music box.

"Patsy," she said, grinning. "This is Patsy."

"After Patsy Cline?"

Abbey's grin slowly widened. A couple of her teeth were exposed in the pale moonlight.

"How'd you know?"

Henry smiled and shrugged his shoulders.

"Lucky guess," he said.

Abbey pulled her eyes toward the music box, on Patsy.

TWENTY-ONE

It was in the middle of the night when a strange whispering woke up Henry from his drunken sleep. The line, "*Soon, the whole world will be watching. . .*" faded over the buzzing in his head.

He gasped and surveyed the eerie, quiet bedroom.

After he cleared the blur from his eyes, he glanced at the time on the nightstand.

The time read: 3:37.

Henry stood up from the chair, stretched the soreness from his back, and went over to his mother, who was sleeping in the same exact position as the last time he left her.

As he stumbled away, he noticed something else about his mother, an object in her hand. He turned back around, reached around her body, and gently pulled a CD case from her weak grip.

He peered down at the CD.

The demo, he thought.

Henry opened the case and saw that the CD was missing.

Without waking his mother, Henry searched around the bed but couldn't find the CD anywhere. Next, he came across the stereo perched on top of his mother's dresser. At first, he didn't notice the stereo from the darkness of the bedroom. Abbey must've gotten Odyssey to hook up the stereo. The thought alone of Odyssey, who was technically challenged like his mother, hooking up a stereo system seemed farfetched. Maybe they had gotten the neighbor.

No way Abbey and Odyssey could've done it all by themselves, Henry thought and walked over to the stereo.

There, he found the CD inside, his CD.

Surprised from the discovery, he let out a quiet *hmm*.

A stirring of bed sheets!

"She's coming," Abbey said frantically from behind. Her voice was sharp and raspy. "She's coming for you, Henry."

Startled, Henry spun around and saw his mother's glistening eyes frozen on him.

Henry asked, "Who's coming?"

As he slowly made his way toward the bed, he grabbed the pillow from the chair. His eyes moved down at the pillow. For a moment, Henry studied the pillow closely before his mother could see his interest in the pillow. What if I let him kill her? Then, there would be no suffering. His mother's latest words—not what she had mumbled about someone coming for Henry, but what she had said to him prior to his sleep about being sick and tired of feeling like this and then the sheer agony in her face when she spoke it, the same agony that Henry had watched for the past three months—ran through his mind.

It would be painless, he thought. *It would only take a couple of seconds.*

With the pillow down by his side, he strolled over to the bed.

Abbey set her stiff eyes on the pillow, the one in Henry's hand. She moved them back up to Henry and forced herself to smile.

She said in a flat tone, "I have never seen mountains like these, Henry. Reds, oranges trapped in the sunlight. Did you see the mountains? They call them cathedrals." Henry moved the pillow to his mother's face, closer now, inches. "Cathedrals, Henry." After second thought, he placed the pillow underneath Abbey's head and propped up her head. "Around them, the desert is vast and lovely and stretches to the horizon like an endless ocean. I want you to come with me. Would you like to go to Sedona with me?"

Henry stood over Abbey and gently shook her on the shoulder.

"Mom," he whispered.

"There's a river that runs through the canyon," she went on to say, as her eyes slowly rolled toward Henry. "We can sail across the desert and into the light."

"Mom?"

Abbey's eyes froze.

"Mom. . ."

Suddenly, her eyelids flickered.

Her eyes widened.

"What happened?" she said to Henry.

"You were dreaming again."

"I was?"

"Yes," he said. "Go back to sleep."

Her eyes jerked to the left, on Patsy.

"Can you?" she asked jubilantly.

Henry wound up the music box for his mother, placed it over the dresser, and went into the kitchen where he paged Doctor Cowen. It didn't take long for Abbey's doctor to return the page. Henry got up from the kitchen table and answered the phone before it had a chance to ring twice.

Henry said tearfully, "Doctor Cowen. It's me, Henry. There's a problem."

The doctor asked, "How's Abbey?"

"Not good," he said. "Not good."

TWENTY-TWO

THE next day was Sunday, January 22, 1995. Henry was scheduled to close at the pharmacy, but he took off work a couple of hours earlier after explaining to his manager, Guss, the condition of his mother. On the way home, Henry picked up some groceries. The basics: bread, milk, apples, and eggs. He was planning on fixing his mother a nice dinner: lasagna (this being *Stouffer's*, not the homemade kind).

When Henry returned home from the grocery store, he went to check on his mother upstairs. Halfway up the stairs, he heard the sound of somebody sniffling over the delicate music from the music box. His first thought: she was having another bad day. From there, his thoughts grew. He saw himself eating lasagna at the kitchen table all by himself; winding up that music box every time his mother fussed or demanded; cleaning up the excrement; lighting up a dozen scented candles in order to mask the awful smell; drinking alone (he didn't know exactly how much he was going to drink, but surely enough to put him to sleep); and then, finally, sitting by her beside, watching the minutes pass before him. Henry made it to the bedroom where the sniffling and the music were playing together. As he stood at the doorway, Odyssey was sitting with her head held downward next to his mother's bedside. The first thing he saw was the wet Kleenex in her hand and then the mascara smudged across the upper part of her cheeks.

"Mom. . ." Henry uttered as he stood at the doorway.

Odyssey pulled her hands from her face and wiped the tears away with the tissue. Henry couldn't help but notice the window and how it was cracked open. His mother couldn't stand the cold. Yet, there it was. . . open. A cold draft was blowing into the bedroom. The curtains were gracefully blowing around the room like a mane of white hair. Henry pulled his eyes away from the bedroom window and witnessed the expression on Odyssey's face. He felt his stomach shoot up into his chest. He ambled over to the bed, leaned over his mother, who lay motionlessly on the bed—on her back with her eyes closed—and gave her a gentle nudge on the arm.

"Mom," he said, this time more loudly.

She didn't respond.

"She's gone, Henry," Odyssey said, wiping the phlegm from the tip of her nose.

Abbey's face was pale and ghostly, skeletal.

Henry shook her once more.

"Gone? What do you mean 'gone'?"

"I mean she. . . she passed away."

"Passed away?"

Once more, Henry nudged his mother on the arm.

"Mom. . ." he said and burst into tears, ". . . Please. Please wake up."

His head fell against her chest.

He tried to hear a heartbeat.

He heard none.

So, he just sat there.

Ten minutes expired until Henry finally realized that his mother was not coming back.

She was, as Odyssey said, gone.

The funeral service went smoothly. Due to the condition of Abbey's body, there was no visitation the night prior to the funeral. Minister Clark gave the eulogy at the Saint John Baptist Church, according to his mother's will. After the service was over, family and friends drove in a convoy to the burial site, Lansford Memorial Park, where they buried Abbey. All of her friends from Lansford Medical and Saint John were there to pay their final respects. Charles was there as well, along with his staff and their families. So too were Abbey's former coworkers from the Depot, as well as their friends and families. Only two of Henry's girlfriends showed. Naomi and Aileen. The night before, Naomi told Henry that she was going to straighten out her life and finish up college. "No more partying," she said and then later told Henry that she was thinking about becoming a nurse. She was a very nurturing woman, Naomi was. She helped Henry through a lot of troubled times, and Henry wasn't the least upset. In fact, he encouraged her to go to college. He said it would be a good thing "for the both of us." Then, there was Aileen. Henry had never spoken to her since his mother's death. During the entire service, she was flirting with one of Abbey's former nurses at Lansford Medical, a young man with a face shaped like an alien. Guss, his boss at the pharmacy, was there too. He said his condolences and then went on his way. And for Henry, that was about it until he went to embrace Charles.

As Henry hugged Charles, he glanced over his shoulder and noticed a familiar face behind the convoy. *T.J.?* Baffled, Henry gave the face another study. *No way.* Henry excused himself from Charles and walked over to T.J., who was standing with his hands held down by his side on the edge of the street. Henry shouldered his way through the remaining friends and family leftover from the service.

"Hey, Henry?" T.J. said as Henry approached the street.

They stood about three feet away from one another. T.J. witnessed the weariness on Henry's face, what his mother had done to him, the stress, the pain, the misery, all indented over his face, as well as the added weight (at least twenty pounds of fat). On the other side, Henry witnessed the change in T.J.'s eyes. He was more confident. He appeared more mature, straight.

T.J. said, "I'm sorry to hear 'bout your moms."

"Thanks," Henry mumbled and gazed around the cemetery, as well as the thick blanket of gray cast over the sky.

"I missed you at the church," T.J. said. "Man! There was so many people there."

"My mother knew a lot of people, more than I imagined."

"Listen, Henry—"

"How did you know?" Henry interrupted.

"Obituaries," he said over thought.

"Little too young to be reading the obituaries," Henry said. "Don't you think?"

"Well, never know when you might see sumone you knows," T.J. said and stepped closer. "I tried callin' you, Henry. I even drove by your house in Queens Dive."

"We moved," Henry said sternly.

"It didn't take me too long to figure that part out." T.J. gazed around the cemetery as Henry had been doing throughout the conversation. "Geordie was wrong 'bout you, Henry. He shouldn't haf said them things 'bout you and your moms."

"It's all in the past, T.J.," Henry said. "I've moved on."

"But I haven't," T.J. said, grabbing Henry's attention.

"What are you trying to say?"

"I'm sayin'. . . I want give this thing another shot," he said clearly. "It took me sum time to take it all in when we got back from LA. You was right. Rockwell. Phat Stacks. Them greedy bastards were jus gonna use us. I never seen it at first. But now I do. I. . . should've been on your side, Henry."

"My mother just died, T.J.!"

"I know that, Henry," T.J. said tenderly. "And I'm sorry. I truly am."

"I thought you had my back."

"You needed your space, Henry. You know."

"When things like this come along, you find out who your true friends are."

"It's hard to find your friend when he's gone up and changed his phones and, most importantly, moved away. I'm here now, Henry. Aren't I, man?"

Henry didn't answer.

"Listen, man," T.J. said. "There ain't a day that goes by that I haven't thought 'bout you."

Henry grimaced, his eyes glazed over.

"What do you want from me, T.J.?"

"A chance," he replied.

"It's too late," Henry fumed. "I'm stuck here. This is my doing. . . my fault."

T.J.'s natural reaction would be to smack his gums. He never did, though. Instead, he shook his head in disagreement and placed his hands in his pockets.

"When you're ready," he said and made his way toward the navy blue Oldsmobile parked at the back of the convoy, "I'll be waitin'."

"Don't get your hopes up, T.J.," Henry said as T.J. walked away.

"*Well,*" T.J. turned his shoulder, "if you decide to change your minds, I'm stayin' in a loft above Chessman's."

Slightly intrigued, Henry said, "The music store?"

"Yeah," T.J. said as a grin flashed over his face. "The music store."

Henry asked curiously, "What are you doing back in Reddington?"

"I don't know," he said. "I guess I wanted to start over from scratch." T.J. nodded at Henry. "Maybe that's sumtin you should do as well."

It was four o'clock in the afternoon.

While Abbey's friends were in the kitchen preparing a roast in the oven, Henry was locked in his bedroom. The whole time, Henry remained in his thoughts as he sat on the edge of his bed. The only action in the room was coming from the daytime show, Judge X, on the television set. The volume, however, was muted. In the corner of Henry's eye, he saw the judge, as he was known to do, springing from the bench with a wooden gavel in hand and animatedly striking it down against the sounding block. Any avid fan of the show was known for calling the judge the X-Man, mainly for two reasons: one, the judge was a white man, as white as they come; and two, the judge had a bald head that looked as if he waxed it daily with a car buffer. Henry didn't exactly know why they called him the X-Man, despite the two reasons. He figured it had something to do with Professor X, maybe? Henry turned off the television and focused his attention elsewhere. His leg started to twitch, slowly at first and then rapidly. That beat was coming back, violently throbbing in his head. He couldn't keep his leg from twitching now. That beat was different, altered a bit, even taking over his bodily functions. As the one before, the one that he heard during the meeting with Mort Rockwell, the beat was raw, untouched like a relic. The surrounding sounds of the bedroom reinforced that beat in his head: the slow hum of the air conditioner, the steady clicking of the sleet tapping over the windowpane, the muddled dialogue from the kitchen below. Suddenly, a gust of wind whistled from outside. The sleet picked up speed and hit harder, louder against the glass. The wind caused branches, which were like long fingers, to slide across the windowpane. Next, the bedroom door violently trembled and nearly loosened from the hinges.

"Who's there?" Henry asked as the door quickly stilled.

He walked over to the door. Opened it. He checked each direction of the hallway, but nobody was there. As before, his mother's friends were downstairs in the kitchen talking, laughing, drinking, and stuffing their faces with hors d'oeuvres.

As Henry walked back into the bedroom and closed the door behind him, his eyes fell upon the closet doors, two of them both closed. He carefully opened the closet doors and pulled out the dusty case from the top shelf. He noticed the handle was broken. The lock was broken too.

"What in the. . . " Henry trailed off and placed the case on the floor.

Harry was revealed before his eyes, slightly larger, polished, brand new. The setting sun cut through the gray and cast a beam through the blinds and shined over the saxophone. He checked the initials just to make sure it was the same alto saxophone.

There, at the bottom, Henry saw the initials *H.M.*

TWENTY-THREE

THE next morning, Henry called out sick from work and drove to Reddington.

All Henry ate for breakfast was a piece of buttered toast and a ripe banana—nearly black—which was washed down with a few sips of orange juice. The temperature outside was extremely frigid. Forecasters said in the low twenties, but the wind chill was much lower than that. Therefore, he wore a black scarf, which was wrapped twice around his neck, and a long black wool coat that belonged to a friend of his mother's. Henry didn't bother driving down his old street, as he would normally do whenever he found himself on the old block. Yet, he went straight to Chessman's, the music store where he and T.J. used to hang out as kids.

After Henry, who was still bundled up from the cold, parked the Jelly Bean on the side of the curb and stepped onto the sidewalk, he heard music coming from across the street. Twice, he shot a glance toward either side of the desolate street. There wasn't a single person in sight, only the crows perched on the buzzing electricity wires above. The air was still too. No gusts or breezes. Things around him were still, as well. Even the crows. No doors shaking either. Nothing of that nature.

Interested, Henry said under his voice, "Music."

For about a minute, he searched around the street with his eyes and finally located the origin of music. The sound was coming from the loft above Chessman's. Possibly T.J.'s place? He dodged the cold by lifting the collar alongside his neck and strolled inside the grungy building through the side door. The vague odor of freshly dried paint was hovering like a fart in the air. The panels around the door were still glossy from the paint. There was even a piece of paper warning guests about the wet paint. But the wet paint was the least of Henry's concerns. He was more enthralled by the sound of music. Couldn't be from T.J. No way. The music was now louder, muffled, but much louder than outside.

Doing his best not to touch the fresh paint on the walls, Henry made his way up the creaking stairs.

The beat, which was throbbing like the heart of a man who suffered from an irregular heartbeat, grew louder, now engulfing his ears. *It couldn't have been coming from T.J.,* he thought again as he arrived at the top of the landing.

Finally, he came across the origin of the sound behind a partially cracked door.

A colorful light was glowing from inside the loft, enticing.

Both cautiously and curiously, Henry nudged open the door with his foot and peeked inside the brilliant loft.

The only windows were located near the high ceilings, shining very little light. The light was different, however, not natural. The song that was playing was unlike anything he had heard before: like a song heard at a rave, a blend of electronic, slightly experiential, slightly alternative, slightly ambient, slightly shoegaze, slightly new wave, slightly disco, slightly trance, slightly dark. Definitely had sort of a Euro flare, music inspired from the 1970's and 80's. Two players, maybe three or four, Henry determined as he inched through the loft, one on the piano, another using a synthesizer, a sampler perhaps, and then, finally, one not playing the drums but one *wailing on the drums!* The beat from the drums was incredible, Henry collected, booming inside his head—Boom dah ba boom boom dah! Boom dah ba boom boom dah! He rounded a corner where the loft opened up in a wide space. Besides a bed, an old leather couch that looked as if it was pulled right off the streets, and a couple of lounge chairs, the loft was nearly deserted. He rounded yet another corner. A wall of thin bed sheets was revealed before him. The music was coming from behind the sheets, highlighted from a purple spotlight faintly shining through. There, Henry witnessed three silhouettes behind a wall of sheets, all three playing the same instruments: piano, synthesizer, and drums.

Henry eased his head inside the lit sheets and found T.J. playing with precision behind the massive drum set. Socks was hard at work on a brand new Moog, modulating the sound, stellar. The owner of Chessman's, Chuck, a long-haired man in his fifties who always wore a black baseball cap, was playing from an old Beckwith piano.

As he listened to the incredible jam session, he couldn't help but smile. From what he could gather, they had been practicing a lot. And the equipment, Henry saw, there was so much of it scattered around the studio! The first thing Henry witnessed: a Mellotron.

Once the three musicians spotted Henry standing at the edge of the curtain, they stopped playing.

"You guys have been busy," Henry said, smiling.

"I knew you show," T.J. said, trying to catch his breath. He pointed the drumstick at Chuck. "Henry, you remember Chuck."

Henry stepped forward and shook Chuck's hand.

"How could I forget?"

"Nice to see you, my friend," Chuck said genuinely and firmed his grip around Henry's hand.

Henry returned, "Nice to see you, Chuck." He turned to Socks. "Socks! I like the new sound."

"It ain't the same without you, Henry." Socks smirked. "Hey, Henry. Sorry to hear about your mother," he said seriously and stepped forward. "I was going to come to the funeral, but I didn't know if you wanted me there or not."

"No sweat," he said, waved off the comment, and shook Socks's hand. "It's good to see you."

Henry couldn't help but pull his eyes back to the setup around the studio.

Another smile.

T.J. asked, "What you think?"

"I like it." He pulled his eyes away from the setup and looked at T.J., who was anxiously waiting behind the drum set. "So," Henry said, "looks like we don't need a drummer anymore."

T.J. and Socks burst out in laughter.

After the nerves had settled, Henry finally joined in on the laughter.

After they got caught up on the last eight months of their lives (what they had been up to, how they were doing, if they were in any relationships or not, that sort of thing), Socks didn't waste any time getting on the telephone and making a couple of calls, the first one to Deon and the next to Darby. He had no luck with William, who had changed his number twice.

After making three more calls, Socks finally got a hold of William.

At Chessman's, the two remaining band mates, William and Deon, reunited with Henry. They both expressed their condolences for Henry's recent loss. None of them were pleased with how their lives were going. Not one of them could actually say that they were happy.

After the band split, things weren't the same.

So, when they picked up their instruments and jammed together, it was as if they picked up exactly where they left off, only Geordie wasn't in the band anymore. Instead, T.J. had taken over on the drums. Everybody was more focused and determined. Henry shed the twenty pounds of fat and was now lean and mean. Every morning, he did a hundred push-ups and sit-ups and ran two miles down Main Street (occasionally, running through the old neighborhood). He kept most of his diet to fruits and vegetables and lean meats and grains like oatmeal. No bread. Before they even knew it, a year had passed, and they had ten brand new tracks to add onto the demo. "Steaming At The Fronts" was one track, a staccato-like joint that literally blew out one of the amplifiers in the loft (Good thing they not only had a music store at their disposal, but also one of the finest engineers in the city. His nickname was Twi'lek for the massive goiter underneath his neck as if his chin had its own little beer belly). And then there was "The Dead Beats," a fast paced joint with shades of old electronica. Then, "I Hear American Singing" was a song taken from Walt Whitman's poem. Henry memorized the poem from high school. Loved the poem so much that he decided to turn it into a song. The song was simple, "minimal," and yet one of the most power-fully gripping songs on the demo. The lyrics were sung over a couple of spoons playing over T.J.'s leg. Finally, the fourth track was called "Pretty Animals," which was one of the most intense songs to date. William's bass lines "killed over the track!" The song—just shy over seven and a half minutes long—ended up being one of the band's favorite songs on the demo, especially for T.J. The song was pretty much about their previous drummer, Geordie. One of the lines went as followed: *"When pretty animals step out of line, they get slapped in the mouth. Keep on teaching 'em your dirty tricks. Mort's got a couple of 'em up his sleeve. I say the hell with 'em. Give 'em both another lick. Show 'em who's running this bitch."*

At the start of February, Henry and the others managed to rehearse each song from the entire album, which now consisted of sixteen tracks. Now, the goal was to cut down the album to twelve tracks, which turned out being one of the hardest tasks. It was hard to cut one song when that one had grown on a particular band mate like a child. That went for other songs. Some they liked. Others they didn't. One thing was for sure. "Mesaterrestrial" was a keeper—a "definite." Now, they just had eleven more to go to make a full LP. From the pace of their playing, it didn't seem too far from reach.

TWENTY-FOUR

FOR about three months prior to Abbey's passing, Deon had been hanging out in Nashville with his older brother, Duncan. Duncan was a guitarist as well. He played in a cover band called The Corpses From Garcia's Closet. Being an official Deadhead, Duncan and the CFGC covered Grateful Dead songs. Most of the members had other jobs. They played mostly in small clubs and bars and whatnot. Duncan himself was, in fact, an attorney. He usually received the classic line "Get out of here!" or "Shut up!" whenever he was asked what he did for a living. Over the telephone, Deon told his brother about the band, their unique sound, the nearly finished album they had, and how they were looking for a record label, especially one that focused primarily on the music and less on the "image." Duncan told him about this one cat, a woman actually.

"Like Heroin?" Henry said hazily and gazed over the CD cover from Like Heroin's latest album *Take What You Can.*

The front cover was of a hand, withered and beaten. Part of the ring finger was missing, severed just below the knuckle with dark blood caked around the wound.

"I figure if we're interested in joining their record label, you might as well know what they sound like."

Henry said vacantly, "Never heard of them before."

"I wouldn't have bought the CD for you if they weren't any good."

"Have you met this woman, Starlet?"

"No," Deon answered. "But my brother has. He actually went to school with her. Every year or so, they catch up on what's going on in their lives. Usually, it doesn't go farther than a phone call."

Socks said disappointedly from the chapped leather couch, "Sounds like a long shot, if you ask me."

"So far, she only has three other bands under her label."

Henry searched for the record label on the back of the CD.

"*Night Owl*," he finally read.

"Says she's one cool ass chick." Deon sat down next to Socks on the couch. "Plus, she's not in it for the money, Henry. And she's always looking for new bands to sign to her label. And, most importantly, she's not some fucking dick in a suit sitting behind a desk."

"Hey," Socks said, "you know what they call her?"

"What?"

"They call her the 'Hummingbird.'"

"Hummingbird? Why Hummingbird?"

"Woman's a workaholic," he said. "Like a hummingbird, always moving in order to survive."

"Sounds like my kind of woman," Henry said. "But if she has firsthand knowledge on how the industry works, then how come I haven't heard about. . . " Henry glanced over the CD cover once more, ". . . Like Heroin?"

"That's the thing about the biz, Henry," Socks whined. "Sometimes you have to go the extra mile and find new music. New music isn't always going to find you."

And Deon finished, "They have a concert coming up at Lime N' Light."

"Lime N' Light? I thought they tore that place down."

"They redid the whole place," Deon said. "I went by there the other day. It's very. . . how do I say. . . intimate."

Henry turned to the other band mates around the loft.

"So what's it going to be, fellows?"

T.J. said from the stool, "I'm down for whateva."

"Darby?"

"Yeah," he said. "I'm down."

"Socks?"

"Of course, I'm in," he said rapturously. "You're talking to one of their biggest fans. Got like all their LPs. And from what I've heard, Starlet's one crazy girl on stage. I mean, like, CRAZY!"

"No shit," Henry said in surprise.

"Let's just say," Deon said closely, "she knows how to draw a crowd."

"Night Owls is where it's at, Henry," Socks exclaimed. "If there was one label you wanted to be on, it's them. But like I said, it's still a long shot."

Henry returned, "I guess it's better than no shot. Right, Socks?"

"Right," he parroted.

On the way back from lunch, Henry listened to *Take What You Can* on full blast in the car. He was captivated from Starlet's sultry voice, similar to the R&B artist, Sade. Starlet's voice oozed from the speakers like fresh honey and seeped inside Henry's head and soothed and nurtured each and every thought. The feeling was indescribable.

Like Heroin, he thought.

Although he had never done the drug, he could only imagine that this was what it felt like.

An hour later, Deon got off the telephone with Duncan.

"Okay," he said and turned to the others gathered around the loft. "We have a five minute window."

William asked, "What should we wear?"

"Whateva you want, Willie Man," T.J. said confidently. "We go as ourselves. No façade."

"T.J. is right," Henry said and stood up from the couch. "This time, we make our own rules."

Henry held up the new demo in his hand and slid it toward T.J. across the old, marked up table.

T.J. grabbed the CD case before it fell off the ledge.

"Now," Henry said sharply, "it's our time."

"For damn sho'. "

TWENTY-FIVE

CHUCK had closed up Chessman's for the night. He said goodnight to Henry and left the light on for him while the other band mates went back to Socks's apartment where they were currently sleeping on a pull out couch while recording the additional songs for the demo. T.J., who, like Henry, went outside to grab fresh air, discovered Henry sitting by himself on the bench in front of the music store.

"Tomorrow's the big day," T.J. said quietly from behind and sat down next to Henry on the bench.

Henry mechanically turned toward T.J. and then gazed at the sky.

"I didn't see you," he said vacantly.

T.J. noticed the cigarette in Henry's hand, as well as the long stick of ash from where he had let the cigarette burn.

"You nervous?"

"A little," he said peacefully, flicked the long ash from the cigarette without getting any on his clothes, and pulled his attention away from the sky.

T.J. nodded at the cigarette.

"How 'bout you be a pal and hook up a brotha wit one of them coffin nails?"

"When did you start smoking?"

"I don't," T.J. answered and chortled.

Henry pulled out a cigarette from the squished pack of Camels and handed it to T.J.

"Hey, T.J."

"Yeah, Henry."

"You sure you don't mind me staying here with you?"

"No sweat, brotha," he said and waved his hand. "The way I see it. . . after this whole thing wit Starlet, we'll haf nuff money to move up to the hills of Madison Grove and say adios to this shit hole."

"You think so?"

"Hells yeah!"

"And live with the same rich folks who used to roll their eyes at us when we were kids? Remember when your mom drove us up there that one time." T.J. kept to himself. "I mean what's so bad about this place, T.J.? Reddington, it's where the music's at. Reddington is home."

"I jus wanna live in a place where I belong."

"Belong?" Henry said confusedly. "People like us don't belong in Madison Grove. That's for sure."

"Whateva," he said flatly and waved Henry off. "We all haf a fantasy home. I guess livin' in a nice house in Madison Grove would be mine or. . . or like. . . like one of them houses wit them stilts on the side of the hills."

"You and that POS."

"Shit," T.J. uttered. "I ain't never gonna get rid of Lil' Red. We been through some serious shit."

"One day you're going wish you had," Henry said, grinning. "Besides, you roll up in Madison Grove with Little Red. . . talk about 'belonging.'"

T.J. laughed.

"Nah," he said and then sighed. "It won't be like that. I don't know. I jus got a good feelin' 'bout this, Henry."

"You said that last time—"

Henry paused.

The expression over T.J.'s face sharpened.

"Listen, Henry Man," he said solemnly. "I never got a chance to thank you for gettin' me outta Parker Square. If you hadn't," another sigh, "I probably wouldn't be talkin' to you right 'bout now. Thank you."

"No problem," Henry said. "That's what friends are for. Right?"

"Right."

Henry smiled at T.J.

T.J. smiled back.

Thinking, T.J. pulled his eyes from Henry and said quietly, "There was this one cop, though, Officer Ted Backer was his name. . . "

"How could I forget," Henry said and put out the cigarette in the ashtray before it could burn his fingers. "He must've really had it in for you."

"When. . . if we get famous. . . I mean, what if he. . . "

"Really? Don't talk like that, T.J."

T.J. shrugged his shoulders.

"Maybe I shouldn't haf broughten it up."

"You're speaking to a friend here."

T.J. sighed.

"I seen him before at that place I used to stay at."

"So?"

"I don't think he was there arrestin' folks."

"What was he doing?"

T.J. sighed once more, but this time with greater frustration.

"Maybe I was fucked up, seein' things," T.J. uttered. "I don't know."

"What did you see, T.J.?"

"Things," he answered. "I don't know." T.J. thought carefully. "I saw him takin' money from the tenants. And it wasn't jus that one time."

"Have you told anyone about this?"

"Jus you."

"Is that why I always see you looking over your shoulder? It's because of him, this Backer guy?"

T.J. hung his head.

"You can't. . . don't start talking like this, T.J.," Henry said closely. "You have to put this out of your head."

"I haf," T.J. said. "It's jus. . . it's jus sumtimes I think 'bout it."

"Well don't," Henry exclaimed. "You're safe. That's all in the past."

T.J. was tentative to bob his head in agreement.

"Your turn," he said abruptly, a glint of excitement shining through his face. "What's your fantasy home?"

"I haven't really thought of one."

"You gotta haf a fantasy home, Henry Man!"

"I don't know," Henry said, thinking. "I guess I want a family first."

"Really?"

"Yeah," he said seriously. "I'm just. . . I'm tired of playing games with these other girls. I just want a woman who loves me for who I am, a woman. . . a woman who knows what she wants and goes after it, a woman who can, I don't know, roll up her sleeves and not be afraid to get her hands dirty. Beautiful. Down-to-earth. Maybe retire somewhere out West."

T.J. said quietly, "Sounds too good to be true."

"By the way, I've been meaning to ask you," Henry said and pulled out another cigarette. "How the hell did Chuck hook you up with the place upstairs?"

"Ahh! I see how it is." Grinning, T.J. bobbed his head. "Change the subject."

"I'm serious," Henry said, his voice raised louder. "The last time I remember Chuck couldn't stand your ass. . . and mine! Remember when we were kids and he used to beat us away with his broom. Remember that?"

"He came 'round I guess," T.J. said, laughing.

"Obviously," Henry joined in and lit another cigarette. "He really had it in for you. Not so much me. Sometimes, I guess. I just annoyed the hell out of him."

T.J.'s laugh eased like a heavy-footed teen hitting the brakes for the very first time.

"Well, when we make it big, Henry Man, I'll make sure to pay him back for all them cables I used to steal from him."

"But seriously. . ."

T.J. eyed Henry carefully.

Then, he pulled his attention toward the street ahead of him.

"He hooked me up wit this place after we got back from LA," T.J. explained, occasionally glancing over at Henry. "I help him 'round the store. Keeps food on the table. He says the more music we make upstairs, the more customers it draws in. Chuck, he even sent sum of his customers up here to jam out wit us. They all curious as to how to play. The customers, that is. I ain't really the man to teach 'em. But I show 'em a thing or two and let 'em go to town."

"No shit," Henry said and finally lit the cigarette for T.J.

At first inhale, T.J. coughed a little.

Henry laughed.

"First time?"

"Yeah, actually," T.J. answered and grimaced. "It's like smokin' a damn chicken bone."

"I've been thinking," Henry said, drifting in thought. "If this thing with Starlet doesn't work out tomorrow night, then. . ."

"Then we go to the next label," T.J. interrupted. "And if that doesn't work out, then we hit the road wit these songs."

Henry took a long drag from the cigarette and blew the smoke from his nostrils.

"All I'm saying is that if Starlet doesn't like what we have to offer, then I don't know who will. I mean this has to work. Right? I just. . ." Henry trailed off, ". . . I don't know."

"Me, I ain't never heard anything like what we've been playin' upstairs, Henry," T.J. exclaimed. "Even if it don't work out wit Starlet, there'll be other opportunities. Trust me."

"What? You know this business now?"

"I ain't sayin' that, Henry," T.J. said, his voice growing louder. "What we have goin' on is special. Don't overlook that. When the time comes will you rise to the occasion or will you fall? Will you be up to the challenge, Henry? If not," T.J. shrugged his shoulders, "maybe you can stay here and help out Chuck. You know Christmas time gets a little hectic 'round here."

Henry sighed and sat back on the bench.

Before he could get comfortable on the bench, he leaned back over to T.J. and said mindfully, "You're either a starving artist doing what you can to survive or a puppet sitting pretty in a mansion."

"And which one does you wanna be, Henry?"

"Neither, T.J.," Henry said passionately and sat upright again and faced T.J. "I don't want to be neither. If we do get famous, then so be it. I'll never change who I am. Not for anybody."

"Yeah," T.J. moaned. "You won't be sayin' that when sum suit offers you millions of dollars."

"Right," he said with a loud snort. "And we saw how that turned out."

"Well, we certainly did."

Henry glanced across the street at the hydrant and drifted back into thought.

"When we were kids, do you remember we used to bust open that hydrant across the street?"

"On them hot summer days," T.J. said, a smile hooking across his face. "We even wrote that song about it. 'Member?"

"I completely forgot," Henry said. "How did it go?"

"God dog!" T.J. blurted out and leaned back against the bench. "I don't *even* know."

"I'd like to listen to it just to see how stupid we used to be."

"I think I got sum at my parents' house," T.J. said, a partial smile fading. "I hafn't heard them tapes in years!"

"Remember that one time Danny ran across the stream and got tossed like five feet in the air," Henry said, laughing. "His trunks came flying off."

T.J. laughed as well.

"And he is runnin' 'round butt naked, tryin' to chase 'em down, and all of them girls 'round was laughin' at his doughy, fat ass."

"I wonder what Danny's up to nowadays," Henry said, thinking.

"Knowing him, he probably workin' at a restaurant or sumtin that involves food," T.J. said, another thought coming back to him.

"Ain't that right?"

"Then, you 'member Abbey found out and all hell broke loose."

Henry suddenly turned serious like a switch in his face had been turned off.

"Tell me about it," he uttered. "Grounded me for a month."

T.J. noticed the difference in his friend's demeanor.

"I didn't mean to—"

"No," Henry said, hanging his head. "It's cool."

Silence surrounded the conversation.

"Do you miss her?"

"Everyday, T.J.," he said and looked up at T.J. "Everyday."

"You know you done a good thing, goin' back home and takin' good care of her," T.J. said. "Most people our age wouldn't do what you done."

"Maybe that's why I have my doubts, T.J.," Henry said. "Seems like every time something good happens, there's always something that comes along and just fucks everything up."

"That's life, Henry," T.J. said and smothered the cigarette in the ashtray. He tapped Henry on the shoulder. "Sumtimes you jus haf to roll wit the punches." He motioned inside. "'Member. We got a big day tomorrow."

T.J. made his way to the door.

Henry said, "Go on. I won't be too long."

From *Missing the Edges,* page 83:

When I first laid my eyes on Henry, I knew there was something special about him. He was about nine years younger than me and incredibly mysterious. As usual, it was raining. Unseasonably warm too. I saw him from a distance. So, I honestly didn't know what to think of him at first. Thought he was kind of cute from where I was standing. Plus, there was a patron in the front row yelling out all kinds of obscenities that would make a nun see red. I never looked down at the patron.

On any other night, the patron would've been treated to the darkness.

On that night, I was too distracted by the mysterious man sitting across the club. He was quiet, very reserved in nature, and yet he looked as if he had absolutely nothing to lose.

Like Heroin was playing at the club, Lime N' Light, outside Reddington. We had a decent turnout. Our fan base, "The Junkies," was down in the front as always while the skeptics, the drinkers, and first timers hung out in the back.

Two days prior to the show, our bass player, Ricky, had caught the flu. One of the roadies filled in for him.

After the show, our manager, Kurt Tater, introduced me to these two strung out individuals. They looked as if they hadn't slept in weeks. One of them, the mysterious one from the back of the club, was smoking one cigarette after another while the other one kept rambling on about how good the show was. I remember my eyes settling on him, the chain smoker, several times throughout the show. He was wearing a black duster and was perched at the bar like a raven. His eyes locked with mine. Something about him caught my eye. The fireworks were there, flashing over his eyes. I admit, though, he definitely did have that "It's better to burn out than fade away" type of aura about him. Your typical rock star. In my Like Heroin days, I've met lots of people who shared that same quality—maybe too many than I could count. Henry was different, though.

I remember the conversation went something like: "My name's Starlet, but my friend's call me Hummingbird."

The mysterious man smiled and said smoothly, "Please to meet you, Hummingbird."

I smiled back at him and spotted a twinkle in that tiger's eye, a firework.

He said his name was Henry, but his friends called him the "Fif."

I didn't know if he had taken off the *t* and the *h* because it sounded cool or what, or if he was just plain illiterate, or if he had a speech impediment.

Henry played it real cool, though, as if he didn't care what I thought about him. I liked to call it his swagger. And boy! Did he have a lot of it! It wasn't like an arrogant swagger, the kind that made you sick. His swagger was one of confidence. Henry knew exactly who he was. No gimmicks. No façade.

I remember the two of them were like these two superheroes on recruit, searching for the right piece to fit in their puzzle.

After the introduction, we got a table and had a couple of drinks.

Over the third drink (Bloody Mary, I think), Henry told me why he and his friend, Deon, were here. And I knew it wasn't for Lime N' Light's famous Buffalo wings. He said they needed a singer and that I was exactly what they were looking for.

"Perfect," Henry said.

From the expression on the other man's face, he acted as if he had a different agenda in mind.

Then, I asked about their band.

Henry said they were called "Mona's Arch."

Again, Deon acted as if he didn't know what Henry was talking about.

Immediately, I was intrigued and still smitten as well.

TWENTY-SIX

FOR hours, the young man, who was dressed in a raggedy smiley face Nirvana tee shirt underneath a thick hooded jacket, listened to Mona's Arch debut album, *Rule or Be Ruled*. Twice now, he had gotten through the CD without little pause or interruption. During each pass, he would remove his headphones for a couple of seconds and give his ears a chance to relax and then get up from the plastic tub that he had been sitting on and stretch his legs.

"Listen. . . ah. . . " the clerk said finally as he peeked his head over the front counter, ". . . Dennis. . . "

"It's Deco," the young man mumbled into his lap as he peeled the headphones from his ear.

". . . Whatever, kid."

The young man, Deco, placed the headphones over his ears.

Every morning, most New Yorkers who lived around Manhattan had become accustomed to the name, *Babe*—not like the baseball player, but the name of the clerk. Babe, whose parents had named him after the famous baseball player Babe Ruth, lived up to his name, not the baseball part, but the look and it wasn't far off from the real Bambino. He had a portly frame, which sat over a pair of chicken legs. His face was round and doughy, especially around the eyes, like an aged baby. He was wearing a purple dress shirt, black slacks, and a gray flat cap over his head. Most admired Babe, not for his looks, but for his personality. He was the type of fellow who told it how it was. No front. No bullshit. My way or the highway. "A man's man," was what most said about Babe or, "Don't let the looks fool you."

After Babe observed the two men, both of them dressed in really nice suits, move their weary eyes away from their newspaper before them and toward the tormented young man seated at the corner of the newsstand, Babe finally decided to approach Deco. Upon leaving the newsstand, he passed several New Yorkers, "local customers," he would say, who, like the two men before them, were growing apprehensive in front of Deco.

With a soggy *New York Times* shielding his face from the rain, Babe hovered over Deco.

"You mind waiting somewhere else, kid," Babe said, acknowledging the distance among the locals. "You're scaring off my customers."

Deco removed the headphones from his ear and settled them around his neck.

As the song "Steaming At The Fronts" kept playing over the headphones, he aimed his sharp eyes up at Babe who, unlike the two businessmen, wasn't the least apprehensive.

"He might come later this afternoon," Babe said over the rain. The sides of his chubby face flexed in anger. "Hell! Maybe even tomorrow."

Right before Deco made an attempt to leave, a brown Toyota truck pulled next to the curb.

"Well, I'll be..." Babe snorted, "...you're in luck, Dennis."

"Deco."

"Whatever."

The carrier got out of the truck and slammed the stack of *Rolling Stone* magazines on the wet sidewalk. The front cover of the magazine read: EXCLUSIVE. Below that: The *Secret Life* of Jerry Garcia. And below that: *Mona's Arch* To The Top.

"You're a life savior, Manny," Babe said to the carrier as he cut away the string from the stack of magazines.

Next, Babe handed Deco the copy underneath the top soggy one.

"Here you go 'Deco,'" he said sarcastically. "That will be thirteen bones."

Deco reached in his pocket and handed the clerk the money, the "thirteen bones," and walked down the sidewalk with his eyes glued to the magazine.

From the review "Mona's Arch: Rule or Be Ruled," (*Rolling Stone* magazine, Issue 740, August 1996, p.63-64) by Daniel Murphy:

"Take off the makeup and let 'em see the scars," croons Mona's Arch's frontman, Henry the Fif', over a statically charged beat on the opening track "Steaming At The Fronts," which instantly hits the listener across the face with a sledge-hammer and continues its brutal assault well into the next track, "Fever Town." *Rule or Be Ruled* is a tour de force, lasting shy over seventy minutes long. Starlet Rollinson, best known from her fame in Like Heroin, is featured on the Portishead-influence, "Fever Town," one of the darkest tracks on the album. "The first time I met the boys in Mona's Arch," Starlet said during an interview at The Flags Festival, "it was like we finished each other's sentences. Never have I been around a group of talented musicians who had so much energy and tenacity. They knew what they wanted. And I knew they weren't going anywhere anytime soon." Listening to *ROBR* is like carrying around Hunter S. Thompson's briefcase from the movie *Fear and Loathing in Las Vegas* for a night: every drug known to man, uppers and downers, depressants and stimulants, hallucinogens and narcotics. "Leave me be and let me bleed here. . ." pleads Henry the Fif' on the track, "Wax Sculpture." All together, *ROBR* manages to muster rock, alternative, electronica, trip hop, soundtrack (yes, that's right, there's an interlude called "Behind the Mask," a homage to the lead singer's admiration for director John Carpenter), R&B, bluegrass ("I Hear America Singing," a song taken from Walt Whitman's poem tediously bites like a trash compactor with keyboardist Socks laying down a industrial-like effect that would even make Trent Reznor dustrial-like effect that would even make Trent Reznor cringe over a pair of clinking spoons) shades of 80's nu wave, shoe gaze, and post punk ("I'll Meet You Half Way," which cautiously ventures into the familiar territory of Joy Division's "Atmosphere"), and then finely molds the genres into something disturbingly beautiful; but, might I say, it works. Each track is meticulously infused like a flick shown in a grungy grindhouse theater, always keeping the listener on his or her toes. On the final track "Mesaterrestrial," which is right up there with the great saxophone solos like The Stones' "Brown Sugar" or Springsteen's "Murder Incorporated," Mona's Arch does something that no other band has done prior: the track abruptly ends halfway through the chorus. "Pretty Animals" was written after former drummer, Geordie Roberts' (current drummer of Stella's Harbor) departure before the recording of the album. Original member and percussionist, T.J. Livingston, took over Geordie's role behind the skins after a brawl that temporarily pushed the band into hiatus for eight months. Henry the Fif' drones, "There's a mutiny among the colony. A tick burying in the hide. Pulling the strings. Teaching us how to hide." Somewhere, Geordie is listening to the track "Pretty Animals" with a scowl over his face, repeatedly smashing the stereo with a baseball bat. At least one would think so. 5/5 stars

The "visions," not dreams, as Henry was now calling them, were happening more frequently. And they were getting worse every time.

The apartment door trembled violently over the muddled ambience of traffic.

Henry stirred in bed as the morning light poured like a pitcher over his face, warming.

With a drawn-out gasp, Henry suddenly woke from his unconscious state and located the direction of the trembling, the door. He finally found the door, still, not trembling or pounding. Gradually, he absorbed the ambience of traffic in his ears. He lifted his scored face from the cold pillow, ran his hand over the top of his scalp, which was shaved into a Roman Numeral 5, not V (although, the design could easily pass as a V), and gazed around the strange apartment.

For a moment, he didn't know where he was.

What city?

What apartment?

What time?

What year?

Then, his eyes came across a picture frame on top of the dresser.

I didn't, he thought as his memory slowly came back to him.

Did I?

Henry reached underneath the rumpled sheets, wiped his hand over his damp crotch, and then ran his fingers by his nose. The odor over his fingers was pungent, same with his lips and chin. . .

. . . *impossible*, he thought.

In a sudden uproar, Henry rolled from the bed and sat on the edge of the bed. With a couple of flexes and grips of his hands, he heedlessly worked the blood back in his fingers. While doing so, he found a note, as well as a Granny Smith apple, on the pillow next to his. He picked up the note.

"Lock the door on your way out," he read.

Lastly, Henry recognized the initial at the bottom of the note.

"*K*," it read.

Just K.

He crumbled up the note and shot it at the closest trash-can. The ball of paper hit the side of the rim and fell to the floor.

"Brick. . . " Henry uttered amusedly.

He didn't bother placing the trash in the trashcan.

Instead, he picked up the apple.

"What the fuck?" he said to himself. "Is she trying to kill me?"

With a full body stretch, Henry stood on his feet with his arms climbing to the ceiling. He wiggled his toes over the hardwood—the floor being somewhat cold and unpleasant.

After the abbreviated moment of relaxation, he strolled over to the bare window that stretched over the entire span of the living room wall and gazed out into the cityscape of New York City. The sun broke free from the dark clouds above and shone over half of the vast cityscape. Henry spotted the Empire State Building tucked away from a distance. Other buildings were foreign to him, although he had seen them before on television as well as magazines. Never in person, though. Henry pulled his attention away from the cityscape and noticed the size of the apartment. She must've made *good money*, he thought. She had to in order *to afford a place like this.* That's always a plus.

Still dazed from last night, Henry floated his way around the apartment and checked out the picture frames perched throughout, each one different from the other. One was of her in a red and white cheerleader uniform (high school?). Another posed with a spiky-haired man wearing a pink polo shirt (college perhaps?). Henry picked up one frame in particular. This girl, K, was standing in middle of four friends, all girls, displaying the sweet dimples in her face. The photograph was taken at an exclusive bar, Henry could tell.

For years, Henry would take a second from his busy day and imagine what she had looked like prior to last night. The only pictures he had of this girl, K, were from Hailey Chapel Elementary yearbooks, '84-'85, '85-'86, and '86-'87. And those pictures alone were beyond recognition after the big move from Reddington to Lansford. Each one had been diligently altered with a black Sharpie. Facial features were drawn with exaggerated proportions, which bled into the surrounding pictures of students. Her fourth grade picture was monstrous: warped tongue slithering from her cankerous lips, bulging eyes, fangs, and a nose like a toucan with a massive pimple bursting over the entire page. Her fifth grade picture was marked up with cuts and stitches and bruises and black eyes and missing teeth. Her sixth grade picture: a drawing of a giant penis, which was in the shape of a shitake mushroom, spread across her chin, giving her a messy facial (again, like the pimple on her nose, bursting over her face as well as the entire page). In the back of his mind, Henry wished he hadn't done such an immature act like doodling over her yearbook pictures.

Throughout the years, she had grown. She went to college (matured?). Got a job as a fashion designer for a well-established brand, Dee Donovan, or *DD* (the two Ds being back to back). Her face was longer now and not as globular. Her cheekbones were higher and prominent. Her eyes were still the same color and yet they carried a little bit of wear in them. Her breasts were larger as well. He thought they might have been implants from the way they were perfectly shaped. And they didn't have much bounce to them when Henry was gazing up at them last night. The thought alone of Kerri and her breasts (real or fake?) sent a rush of blood through Henry's body. A stark image suddenly came to Henry: K straddling over his naked body, her perfectly shaped tits slightly bobbing above. Henry shook the image from his mind and concentrated on the pictures before him. Years of memories (not of last night but of younger days) had been brought back to his thoughts. He had never forgotten about her, about K. Whenever Henry found himself alone, he would think about her, what she was doing with her life, her interests, weekends, what she looked like, especially her face, and then his face next to hers. Over time, the image had deteriorated, mostly in tiny fragments, which made it tougher for him to conjure up her face in his mind. So when Henry saw her last night, the face that he had so desperately tried to revive was brought back into his mind.

As Henry studied the photograph, the other girls inside the picture, the bar behind them, the drunk making some orgasmic face behind them, the bartender, he caught half of the lit green sign in the background. It read "... use Tavern."

For a moment, Henry carefully thought back. He remembered this bar called the Tree House just two blocks from here.

After Henry gathered the rest of his clothes scattered around the bedroom, he left the apartment without locking the door. He took the elevator downstairs and stumbled into Deon, who was pacing around on the sidewalk.

"About damn time," he said and breathed a sigh of relief. "I. . . we were starting to worry about you."

"Relax, Deon," he said and tossed the apple to Deon. "Here. Catch!"

Deon caught the apple and gave it a once over with his eyes.

Henry said, "Breakfast."

Deon's eyes were drawn back to the apple.

"I don't get it," he said.

Henry responded with a simple and yet gracious smirk.

They made their way to the curb where a taxi was parked.

"Where is he?" Henry asked, walking away from Deon.

Deon caught up with Henry and guided him over to the parked taxi.

"He," Deon emphasizing the word *He*, "is right here."

"I want to see."

"You don't trust me?"

Henry stopped and glared at Deon.

"Fine," Deon said and rolled his eyes.

He popped open the trunk and showed Henry the saxophone case on top of the other luggage. Henry opened the case and made sure Harry was inside. He was, of course.

In a trance, Henry ran his hand over the glistening saxophone and smiled.

"So," Deon said over Henry's shoulder, "did you bang that girl from last night?"

"Girl?" he closed the case and then the trunk. "What girl?"

"The one you were hanging around with at the bar? *That* girl?"

Henry shook his head and walked around the taxi.

"Does Starlet know?" Deon said without trying to draw too much attention and shot a glance at Starlet as well as the rest of the band exiting from the lavish hotel, The Montgomery, across the street.

"Starlet doesn't have to know," Henry said seriously and glared into Deon's eyes. "Besides, it's not like we're a couple, Deon."

"Yeah, but. . . "

"But what?"

Deon changed his thought.

"It's not my place to talk."

"You're right," Henry said bitterly. "It's not."

Before Henry got into the taxi, he couldn't help but notice Starlet and T.J. flirting with one another. Starlet did the old "What's that on your shirt?" jape. Once T.J. fell for the line, T.J. glanced downward and caught Starlet's finger against the bottom of his chin. Meanwhile, William and Socks were hailing the next taxi.

Deon asked around Henry's shoulder, "Do you want to tell them we're leaving?"

"Nah," Henry responded casually. "We'll just meet 'em there."

"Suit yourself."

Deon stepped into the taxi.

Then, Henry.

The taxi driver was a husky man who smelled like aftershave. His tired, bloodshot eyes trailed across the rear view mirror and landed over the two in the backseat.

"Where to, gentlemen?"

"JFK Airport," Deon said to the taxi driver.

"You got it," he said and drove off.

An awkward silence built inside the taxi.

Occasionally, Deon glanced over at Henry.

"You know you're going to have to tell me about her," he said finally.

Henry snorted and kept his focus on the streets before him, the pedestrians, the vendors, the tourists, the eccentric street performers, and whatnot.

"Don't hold out on me," Deon begged. "Come on. I promise I won't tell Starlet. Cross my heart and hope to die."

"Enough, Deon."

"Come on, Henry. . ."

"Really?" he said, his voice drawn out. "Are we in sixth grade now?"

"What was she like?" he asked girlishly. "A woman as fine as that." Deon puckered his face. "She must've been something in bed."

Henry reflected back on last night's encounter.

"She was aight," Henry uttered as another stark image came to him: his naked body over hers, relentlessly pounding away.

Deon said, "I'm sure you've had better. Right, playboy? So, tell me. What was her name?"

"*Kerri*," Henry said with clarity. "Her name was Kerri."

"Cute name," Deon said with a grin worn over his face. He opened the flap of his jacket and displayed the new bag of marijuana in his pocket. It wasn't like that stuff he used to smoke before. This stuff was bright green with these red hairs, sticky, and extremely heady too. A fruity fragrance wafted toward Henry. "Rhymes with my favorite lady."

Henry sniffed, briskly glanced ahead at the taxi driver, and whispered angrily to Deon, "Are you out of your mind? You can't sneak that shit onto the plane. . ."

"Relax, Brother," Deon said smoothly. "I'm going to do the ole shampoo bottle trick." He winked Henry. Then, he made a loud clicking noise with the corner of his mouth. "They'll never know. Trust me. I've done it like hundreds of times."

Henry leaned back and sighed.

"So, anyway, about this Kerri girl," Deon said haughtily. "What made her just 'aight'?"

Henry sighed once more, greater.

"After the second drink, we took the party back to her place," he said, looking back. He eased into the seat and said to himself, "I can't believe she actually recognized me."

"Now, you're a famous rock star, Henry the Fif'," Deon said and slapped Henry on the shoulder. "Now, there's no place to hide."

"I guess so," Henry said, thinking about whether or not to tell Deon the whole truth about this Kerri girl and how she wasn't just another groupie. Yet, this girl was someone much more. "Once we arrived at her place," he said, "we didn't waste any time."

Deon interrupted, "I bet."

"Before we got there," Henry explained, "I was quarterbacking the rest of the night in my head. I figured we play it nice and slow and, you know, get to know each other a little better that way when we had sex it wasn't just any ordinary sex. Put on a little Delfonics. Something nice and slow. Bust out some ice cubes perhaps, maybe some toys. Hey! Maybe some chocolate. Do a little exploring. You dig."I dig, Christopher Columbus," Deon said with a grin. "You wanted to be inside her thoughts. That's a dangerous place, especially for a one night stand."

"Well, we never got there."

"So it was just another wham-bam-thank-you-ma'am?"

"More like a wham-bam," Henry mumbled and shook his head. "It was like a race to the finish line."

"No thank you ma'am? No green eggs and ham?"

"Not even green eggs and ham," he said, pulling his attention toward the passenger window. "Woke up to a note and an apple."

"Ouch." Deon grimaced. "So that's where you got the apple," he said with a sort of ah-ha expression over his face. "Did she not know you were allergic?"

"Either that or the sex was so damn bad that she wanted to put me out of my misery."

"I planned on cooking her a nice breakfast in the morning."

"I bet your were."

"Really."

Without Henry looking, Deon rolled his eyes.

Henry said to himself, "Didn't know the woman was a fucking lark."

"Welcome to New York City, my friend."

Henry drifted in thought and the words just slipped from his tongue. . . *I was so obsessed with her when I was a kid, carving her name into the desk, waiting for her at my locker, missing class, altering my routes to school just so I could get a glance at her, imagining a future together with her. Every night, I drove myself sick thinking about her. Couldn't sleep. There were times when I didn't eat for weeks, months. Most of the time, I had to force myself to eat.*

Henry paused for a moment.

"There was a catch."

"There always is, my friend."

"She didn't even like me," Henry confessed. "I felt as if I had gotten played by the best scam artist in town. She led me on. Played games with me. So, I would play them back. Then, I saw her true colors."

"What color was that?" Deon asked.

After a pause, Henry said, "Black ice."

"Easy to miss," Deon said, bobbing his head.

"I didn't know exactly how I missed it." Henry shook his head in disappointment. "I guess I was blinded by love or the idea of love. She was fake, Deon, not nurturing, not caring as she claimed she was, phony, all talk, Santa Clause, smoke and mirrors, a one-trick pony. I remember I would get all excited like it was Christmas morning, ready to open presents, new toys, ready to play with them. I felt like that with Kerri, not like a toy, but it was something new, something special, like I was ready to open up to her and share a life with her, to protect her, fight for her, to make sure she never got hurt or damaged. I was oblivious, Deon. Fucking *oblivious*." Henry turned to Deon, who was now solemn. "At times, I wish she never existed at all."

"It makes sense, Henry," he said cautiously. "It really does."

"You know I tried to find every little excuse not to like her just because she was my neighbor," Henry said clearly.

"Even tried imagining her as this. . . this. . . this monstrous girl when she was the most beautiful thing I'd ever laid my eyes on."

"Hold up, Henry!" Deon blurted out. "You never told me she was your neighbor."

Henry chuckled to himself.

"Lived like two houses down from me," he said after the chuckle died out.

"That would've been cool as hell, living next to a good looking girl, you know, the girl next door!" Deon retraced his thoughts. "But then again, I don't know, it might feel like you guys are married. Always there. Always checking up on one another."

"It wasn't like that, Deon."

Deon returned, "How so?"

"I was only ten years old, Deon," Henry said annoyingly. "Besides, we never went out. In fact, she thought I was a creep."

"You are a creep, Henry," Deon said teasingly.

"Don't put me in that same category," he said, his voice filled with discontent. "Thomas Yorke, now that dude is a creep."

"Tom Yorke is cool in my book," Deon said. "He's got some brother in him."

Henry laughed.

"Shit," Deon said, now leaning closer to Henry. "You'd be surprised how many girls like dudes like that. . . "

"I'm not a creep, Deon," he said, his voice raised louder.

"Just joking, Henry. Damn."

"I was just an ordinary boy with ordinary problems."

"Weren't we all?" Deon mumbled.

Like Henry before, he momentarily drifted in thought.

"Are you telling me, Henry, that all this time she never approached you? Never talked to you?"

"I approached her. . . once or twice."

Amazed, Deon asked, "And how'd that turn out?"

"With her running away with a bloody nose."

"Get out of here!" Deon exclaimed. "You smacked that bitch? Please tell me you didn't smack that bitch."

"No!" Henry said abruptly. "I didn't smack her. I. . . I tossed her a basketball. She was supposed to catch it."

"And I take it she didn't."

"Then, she's running away with a bloody nose," Henry said. "I even wrote her a letter once."

"How'd that go?"

"With her father burning it."

"Really?"

"Can you believe that?"

"He must've hated you."

Henry let out a nasally snort.

"And now that I'm in a band, she acts as if it never happened," he said mindfully. "Something like that stays with you. Kerri. . . " Henry was drawn to a sigh, ". . . she was probably the worst and best thing that ever happened to me."

Deon smirked.

"It all makes sense now," he said and chortled. "When I saw you last night with her—this Kerri girl I mean—I saw a man who was in love or was once in love. The only time I've seen you like that is when you're with Starlet. I mean, when you get like that, the love, man, it's practically pouring from your eyes. You got to learn how to control that shit or else it will drive you fucking insane. Girls, Henry, they're like your kryptonite."

"Kryptonite," Henry said, forcing a smile. "Nice."

"I know you, Henry," Deon said convincingly. "You're my friend. I'm just looking out for you."

"What do you know about love, Deon?"

"A lot," Deon said. "I've had my fair share." Then, he tapped the side of his jacket. "Now, I found a brand new love. She doesn't judge. She doesn't treat me bad."

Shaking his head, Henry let out another snort.

"If you knew anything about love, you would know that it's something you can't control, can't reason. It just happens."

"Whatever, Romeo. . . "

"You have those feelings now," Henry drawled. "Wait twenty years, thirty years. You won't have the same feelings when you're sixty years old with liver spots on your hands and clinging onto scraps of hair and alone."

"Get out of here," Deon said, thinking. "You know. I bet Kerri's bragging about you to her friends right now."

"Well, like I said, the sex wasn't great. Nothing worth bragging about."

"I wasn't talking about the sex, my friend."

Henry remained in thought.

Throughout the conversation, the taxi driver was occasionally aiming his eyes into the rear view mirror.

"I've seen you guys before," he said finally, nodding into the overhead mirror. "Are you guys famous?"

"Depends on your definition of *famous*."

"No," the taxi driver returned. "I've seen you guys on TV." His eyes lit up. "The song about the alien thingy! Now I remember. Mesa. . . mesaterrest. . . "

"Mesaterrestrial," Henry said, staring out the window.

"That's the one!" the taxi driver blurted out. "Mesaterrestrial. My kid loves that song."

Deon asked, "And how old is your kid?"

"Zachary's twelve."

"Twelve?" Henry mumbled and then snorted.

"I know what you guys are thinking," he said. "But my Zachary, he's mature for his age. He's even starting to ask if he can borrow his Old Man's ties. Ties!" he blurted out. "I tell him, 'You're too young to be wearing a tie. A boy your age should be rocking the jeans and the tee shirts like the other kids do.' That's what I wore when I was his age. But the kids nowadays, they change like chameleons."

Deon said, "You got that right."

The taxi driver said, "You never know what kind of fad they're going to go through. If you know what I mean."

Deon agreed, not so much Henry.

"One day," the taxi driver said, "it could be old flannel shirts like the grunge kids. The next, it's all black like the Goth kids. Then, they bring back the bellbottoms like the hippies. So, as I was saying, I ask him why he wants the tie. You know. Then, he tells he wants to wear the tie around his head like a headband. He says he saw in a Mona's Arch music video. That's something. Huh?"

Deon tapped Henry on the shoulder.

"Hey, Henry," he said. "I think you just starting a new fad."

Henry said, "Didn't know me being hot and sweaty on the day of the shoot would end up having kids wearing ties over their heads. I even did it as a joke. Remember?"

"A dare, actually," he said and suddenly tossed his finger in the air. "I almost forgot."

Deon reached to his side.

Next thing Henry knew, a magazine was on his lap.

His eyes fell below.

Jerry Garcia was on the cover of the latest *Rolling Stone* magazine.

Henry flipped to the album review section toward the back of the magazine.

"Have the others read it yet?" Henry asked Deon.

"They have indeed," he said, trying to hide the smile on his face.

Eager, Henry read the review. He read as quickly as he could. "*Somewhere, Geordie is listening to Pretty Animals with a scowl over his face, repeatedly smashing the stereo with a baseball bat.*" Henry couldn't help but laugh. He turned to Deon with a mischievous grin pulling like a tightrope across his face. "That's the whole point. Right?"

From *Missing the Edges,* page 127:

Before I "officially," a term that I always held loosely throughout my career, joined Mona's Arch in '97, I was asked to play a couple of shows on their summer tour before the release of their debut album, *Rule or Be Ruled.*

Mona's Arch's manager, James Drexel (the boys ended up calling him "Kermit," a nickname that he rightfully earned in

Tampa after an incident involving a half gallon of Smirnoff and a bottle of Chi-Chi's Hot Sauce), introduced us to a man named Endo Reify, who would later become Mona's Arch's new road manager on the first headlining tour, The Bound and Dangerous Tour. We had no nicknames for Endo. He was the size of a Porta Potti and could kill a man with his pinkie (at least that was what he told the other boys). Endo ran a tight ship. I reckon the military had something to do with that aspect of his personality. The boys, including me, didn't blame him. Each night on the road that summer, he was like a rancher trying to ring in the wild cattle. In all good fun, the boys, but mainly Socks, joked around behind Endo's back (this was, of course, always done at a safe distance). Socks thought he came from the Planet Eternia. I swear some nights you could've fried an egg over his head. Till this day, I still remember our first conversation with Endo in New York: "A tour will make or break a band." Endo was right about the first part. Mona's Arch's first tour was a complete disaster. Stagehands were a no-show half the time. There were problems with lighting almost every night. One time the pyrotechnics went awry and nearly scorched off Henry's face. Luckily, it happened while Henry was running around stage—doing that trademark gesture where he jokingly pounded his fists against his chest like a silverback gorilla. The flame caught him by surprise and sent him literally five feet in the air. The crowd didn't think anything of it. They thought it was all a part of the show. But what they didn't realize was that the flame had completely singed Henry's eyebrows. For the next couple of weeks, the boys had branded Henry with the name *Android*. Whenever Henry would speak, he would quickly be interrupted, "What Android?" or "Shut up, Android" or "Grab me a cup of coffee, Android." Henry never fetched coffee nor did he ever do any of the strange demands. When his eyebrows finally grew back, he was more than pleased to say the least. This was one of many mishaps on the road. Luckily, no one was hurt. In a way, the diversity of issues made the band. It brought us that much closer together.

We were excited to hit the road with the new batch of songs that we had recorded in the Den a week before the tour. A couple of shows down, we still weren't believers. We hadn't figured out what Endo was talking about yet. The boys in Mona's Arch were still getting the feel for how I performed on stage since I was a newcomer. Other than Deon, who occasionally hovered toward the crowd or smashed his Les Paul at the end of a show or threw water on the fans, the boys were pretty easy to play around. However, Henry was a different story. He didn't have a nightly routine. He was like a puppet master out there, controlling the crowd, absorbing their energy. Some nights, I wondered what he had in store for the crowd: Was he going to stage dive? Was he going to bring young women onto the stage with him? Was he going to run out into the crowd? It was like a spinning wheel with him. You didn't know what you were going to get that night. The rest of the boys and I just sat back, watched, and enjoyed the show.

When Henry and Deon arrived at JFK International Airport, they met up with James, as well as the other band mates, who were unloading their luggage from the back of the taxi.

Once Henry stepped outside, two cold hands secretly slipped around the sides of his face and covered his eyes.

"Guess who?" the bubbly woman said in a manly voice.

"Gee. . . lemme see. . . The Cookie Monster?"

Starlet removed her hands from his eyes.

Henry spun around.

"Very funny," he said, smiling wearily.

"Looks like someone was burning the candle at both ends," she said suspiciously as if she knew something that Henry didn't know. "I was wondering where you ran off to last night. Surely, it wasn't with that pretty young girl at the bar."

"We went to school together."

"Is that so?"

Henry's face cocked back with his tongue rolling under-neath his bottom lip.

"I'm afraid she couldn't resist my charm."

Starlet said bluntly, "So, did you fuck her?"

Exasperated from the remark, Henry glanced around at the other band mates. His cheeks were red with both anger and embarrassment. They were just as baffled as Henry from the remark. Deon shrugged his shoulders, innocently gave him that "Don't look at me" expression, grabbed his things from the trunk, and hurried away from the taxi.

Starlet slapped Henry on the shoulder.

"I'm just messing with you."

"Right," Henry said, struggling to smile.

The taxi driver approached Henry.

"Excuse me. . . Henry. . . right?"

"Yeah."

The taxi driver handed Henry a piece of paper.

"How about an autograph for the little one."

"Sure," he said and grabbed the pen. "Zachary?"

"That's the one," he said, expressing with his hands. "He's a big, BIG fan."

With her eyes shriveling, Starlet shook her head and fol-lowed with a turn of her shoulder.

While Henry was signing his autograph on the piece of paper, he glanced through the corner of his eye at Starlet, who was now walking away from him. She wrapped her arm around T.J. The two of them strolled gleefully into the air-port like a couple. Henry's eyes shriveled into these tiny, en-vious slits. Henry pushed through and finally finished signing the autograph.

"Thank you, Henry," the taxi driver said and held up the piece of paper. "And the best of luck to you!"

"You bet," Henry mumbled and gazed back to the airport entranceway.

With her arm around T.J., Starlet walked through the automatic doors. She turned her shoulder toward Henry and immediately turned away without saying a word.

*   *   *

From *Missing the Edges,* page 187:

I was honored to be included in the photo shoot in New York. I knew that Mona's Arch had a great future ahead of them. I was thrilled to be a part of that future. The boys had a week off before they finished the remainder of the Bound and Dangerous Tour. During that time, Henry and I became even closer. I didn't know what we were, boyfriend/girlfriend, partners, dating, or what. All I knew was that we were having the best time of our lives. The boys were fully aware of what was going on, including T.J. They never warned me, though. A part of me wishes they had warned me not to get involved with another band mate. Another part was too madly in love to listen.

TWENTY-SEVEN

MONA'S Arch had a couple of days off until they finished the rest of the tour on the West Coast.

Over the short break, Deon drove to Nashville and paid a visit to his older brother, Duncan. Since Socks hadn't seen his folks in over two years (the last time he had seen them wasn't on good terms; in fact, the last time he saw them he ended up getting into a huge argument with his father, which resulted in Socks moving out of the house), he went back home to the small town of Clever where he and his father reunited. His father, who was a minister at Dorsey Plains Baptist Church, had heard about his son's success. After the two, father and son, put their differences aside, they refurbished a 1957 Plymouth Fury, which had been rusting in the garage. William and T.J. went back to their new homes in Lansford. T.J. did exactly what he had told Henry before their success and moved to the valley of Madison Grove where he bought a two-story house with a white picket fence. As for Henry, he bought a condo in The Vistas, which was located on the hills around the luxurious million dollar homes of Madison Grove. The first day of the break, Henry spent most of his time pacing around the condo (packing and then unpacking and then packing once more). Once he finally made up his mind, he took a late night flight to New York City—on a whim, of course. The flight was one of the worst flights he had ever been on. Rough. During most of the flight the plane flew through bad turbulence. He sat next to a nervous man who didn't wear any deodorant and had breath that smelled as if he had ripped gas. The nervous, smelly man was familiar with Henry's music, the band, Mona's Arch. Wasn't a fan, though. Throughout the whole flight, he wouldn't stop talking about the music he listened to as a kid or what he did on his spare time and how he once was in the marching band and how he always dreamed about being in a ska band or something like that, but he didn't have the time. Not only that, the captain told all stewardesses to hold alcoholic beverages. When Henry wasn't having his ears filled with what Tom the Tooter liked to spread on his toast in the morning or how tomatoes gave him heartburn or how the Hogs should've traded Gibson in the first round, he never thought about whether or not the plane was going to go down. Although, at one point, he wished it had. He thought mostly about Kerri, Henry did. He wondered what she was doing, what her reaction might be once she saw him, was she alone, or was she with her friends and if she was with her friends, what would her friends think of him. Would they be surprised? Infatuated? And Kerri. Would she be turned off? Afraid? Or would she be impressed, more so happy, that Henry had gone out of his way to visit her?

Still nauseous from the flight, Henry hailed a cab outside La Guardia Airport. Even though Manhattan was only twenty minutes from La Guardia, it took him over an hour due to traffic. Once he finally arrived in Manhattan, he paid a visit to the tavern, the Tree House. Henry found no luck there.

So, he went to Kerri's apartment complex and took the elevator up to her level. The thoughts were back, the questions. So many questions there were. Each one without an answer, only assumptions. The walk toward her apartment was like walking down death row—at least that was what he imagined. The walk felt so long and yet it was so close. Thoughts were running into another thoughts: Was Kerri going to be afraid of me now? Horrified? Was she going to call the police? Would Kerri think of me as a stalker? Are these feelings too intense for one person? Would Kerri feel the same? He made it to her apartment without vomiting. There, he paced back and forth in front of her apartment door for about fifteen minutes. It was like an invisible force field surrounded the door.

Henry finally said, "Fuck it," and knocked on the apartment door.

He waited there for about two minutes until he finally heard a person behind the door.

Over faint whispering, he heard the clinking sound of belt buckle.

He moved his eyes to the floor and saw a shadow growing underneath the doorway.

Then, she cracked the door.

The chain was still attached to the lock.

"Henry?" Kerri said, half of her face visible through the narrow crack.

"Listen, Kerri," Henry said, his voice shaking. "I didn't want to show up uninvited like this, but. . . I'm sorry. . . " he glanced around the hallway, ". . . can we talk? I know a place not far from here. We can grab a drink if you like."

Confused, she asked, "What is there to talk about?"

Henry tried to hide the grimace over his face.

"Can you just open the door," he said, his jaw slightly flexing. "I can't see your face."

"Henry," she said, "you shouldn't be here."

"I. . . I couldn't stop thinking about you. . . about the other night."

(Who the fuck is it?)

A dark figure slowly rose from behind Kerri.

Henry curled his hand into a fist.

"Henry," Kerri said considerately, "you have to leave."

He could hear heavy footsteps behind the door.

Kerri quickly spun around and closed the door behind her.

As Henry stood in shock—his heart nearly touching his feet—he could only make out bits and pieces of the conversation behind the door.

All he could hear was Kerri's voice over a man's.

There was cursing, lots of it, most of it directed toward Kerri.

She was saying something like "Don't you dare, Brian" and "Just go."

After the confrontation subsided and the large man went storming off, the door cautiously opened.

Kerri tied her silk pink robe and warily stepped out into the hallway.

She gazed around the hallway, but Henry was nowhere in sight.

From *Missing the Edges*, page 210:

When the Bound and Dangerous Tour was coming to an end, I was asked to join Mona's Arch for the last three shows: San Jose, Mesa, and Albuquerque.

Throughout the remainder of the tour, I could tell that Henry's head was somewhere else.

Two weeks after the tour was over, Mona's Arch began their international tour, Europe, Asia, Australia, and then South America. The boys loved the way the tour ended so much that they decided to ask me to tag along.

So, I did.

Before the concert in Hyde Park, Henry and Starlet spent the entire day traveling around parts of London. They ate fish and chips at a pub called The Raleigh Point, which was named after Sir Walter Raleigh. Everybody around London was well aware of the history of the pub. At lunch, the line would be wrapped around the building for two reasons: one, the fish and chips; and two, the possibility of bumping into a celebrity. Inside, the walls were filled with celebrity photographs, including a photograph of John Lennon from the Beatles, as well as other famous musicians. The ebullient owners, Sir Philip Wilmer and Fran Vignes, had heard that Mona's Arch was in town and invited them to the pub. Since the rest of the band was off doing their own thing, Henry and Starlet decided to take up the offer and pay a visit to the famous pub.

When they got there, Philip and Fran asked them if they could take a picture and hang it up on the wall next to the other celebrities.

Honored from the opportunity, the two gladly had their picture taken.

After Henry and Starlet left the pub with their bellies full of fish and rich ale and their clothes reeking of cigarette smoke, they listlessly traveled to Wellington Barracks next to Buckingham Palace.

In one of the many photograph sessions, Henry posed with one of the Queen's foot guards (something he always wanted to do) and slipped bunny ears behind the guard's tall bearskin hat. Starlet got a kick out of Henry's antics, the guard not so much. Other tourists were looking at the two as if they had completely lost their minds. Henry and Starlet didn't care what other people thought, though.

To cap off the day, they followed James's advice and visited Camden Town and wandered through the markets and ate more food. Starlet bought Henry a painted miniature that looked identical to Henry at a bric-á-brac shop.

After the concert in Hype Park, it took Henry longer than usual to decompress.

When he finally went to sleep, the night was screaming at him. The faces, he saw, so many faces, so much detail, so

many different expressions, all flashing over the darkness behind his closed eyelids.

"No. . ." Henry moaned as he rolled around in the bed,
". . . no. . . no. . . NO!"

He suddenly bolted from the smashed pillow.

Starlet woke, rolled to her side, and switched on a lamp.

"What happened?" she asked as she sat upright in bed.
The sheets around Henry were doused with sweat. She ran
the backside of her hand across Henry's perspired forehead.
"Oh my God! You're soaking wet."

Henry's chest rapidly pumped.

The sweat from his forehead ran down his face and neck
and around the contours of his chest.

"Breathe, Henry. . . " Starlet said as she carefully massaged
Henry's shoulder.

Henry pulled away and slid over to the edge of the bed.

"It was another nightmare," she said softly from behind.
"Wasn't it?"

With his back turned to Starlet, he bobbed his head.

"Another vision," Henry said, trying to catch his breath.
"Yeah."

"Henry, they're just nightmares."

Henry cleared his throat.

"I hope so," he uttered and ran his hands over his sweaty
face. "God. . . I hope so."

From *Missing the Edges*, page 218:

We just finished doing a show in Hamburg, Germany,
when the chaos began.

As the band was making their way to the bus, Henry had a
confrontation with one of the locals. Ever since we got back
from New York, I noticed a gradual change in Henry. At
times, he seemed way more irritable, which, in my case, made
me love him even more. For once in my life, I found a man
who actually cared about something. That was what I truly
admired about Henry. He would defend the band at all

costs, even if it meant spending a night in jail. The fan made a harsh comment about his outfit (the trademark black blazer with chain mail underneath, which I liked to call very "Modern Medieval"). I'm not too sure what the fan said to him—certainly nothing along the lines of Modern Medieval. Surely, it wasn't something far worse.

Whatever it was, it didn't sit well with Henry.

Before T.J. could step in front of the two, Henry swung. I remember watching the fan leap backward into another fan. He was grabbing his broken nose, cupping the blood in his hands. The fan pressed charges against Henry. James did all he could to reason with the polizei, but his German wasn't up to par—at least not enough to talk his way out of the mess.

Both Henry and James ended up spending a night in jail.

But the chaos didn't end there.

Then, there was the show in Tokyo, Japan.

The song "Dead Beats" came to an end.

As Henry grabbed the towel from the speaker and wiped the sweat from his face, an empty water bottle struck him on the side of the head.

Enraged, Henry handed Harry to one of the engineers close by, walked to the end of the stage, and peered into the sea of bodies. Somehow, he spotted two Japanese men pointing at Henry, laughing hysterically. One of them was jokingly stumbling forward and motioning to his forehead, imitating Henry's previous movements. Henry cringed his teeth. His eyes flared with madness.

Before the rest of the band could gather what had taken place, Henry took a couple of steps back from the edge, sprinted from the stage, and dove headfirst into the crowd. He tackled the two drunken fans. Broke one of their arms in two places. Security swooped in and pulled Henry from the fans before things got out of hand.

They wrestled around a bit.

Finally, security took control of the situation and kicked out the two fans from the venue.

Toward the end of the concert, T.J. stormed into Henry's dressing room and made sure to close the door behind him.

Concerned, T.J. asked, "What the fuck is goin' on wit you, Henry? You hadn't been the same eva since you came back from New York."

Quiet, Henry was sitting in front of the mirror.

He couldn't even bring himself to look at T.J.

T.J. walked up to Henry.

"It's that Kerri girl," T.J. said. "Ain't it?"

Henry suddenly chortled.

"Kerri?"

"Yeah," T.J. said. "The girl from Reddington."

"That girl is dead to me."

"Is she?"

"Yeah."

"I hope so."

"Do you, T.J.?"

"Yeah, Henry," he said suddenly, his voice rising in volume. "That girl don't give a fuckin' shit 'bout you, Henry! She jus playin' games wit ya head! Don't you see, Henry Man? That girl, she ain't nuttin but poison in your goddamn veins! If you let her, she will destroy you like cancer! So, you best quit wastin' time on that girl! Let her go!"

Henry shouted back, "I can't damn it!"

"Yes!" T.J. shouted over Henry. "You can! CUT HER OUT OF YOUR LIFE! AND MOVE ON, GODDAMN IT!"

"I CAN'T, T.J.!"

"Why, Henry?"

"I just. . . I just. . . I just want to belong, T.J."

"You *do* belong. . . here wit your family. . . we your family. . . us. . . and then the fans. We all family, Henry."

"It's different," Henry said quietly, his head held downward.

"How is it different, Henry? Tell me," he returned, the frustration building inside his voice. "You think them people like Kerri and her friends give a damn 'bout you? Huh? Do you, Henry? Those people, they are them same fuckin' arrogant assholes who ignore us or made fun of you in front of otha people or talk garbage behind our backs our entire stinkin' lives, same goddamn fools who thought our music was a joke. That girl. . . Kerri," T.J. paused, "she couldn't even stand you. And now, *what*, all of sudden, her and all her friends are your friends now cuz, what, you're famous or you make more money than them?"

Henry seethed, "You're jealous."

T.J. responded with a shrug, "Jealous? Why in the fuck would I be jealous, Henry?" He smacked his gums, loudly. "I don't need toxic people like that in my life, fair-weather friends. One minute they there for you and the next minute they ain't. That's why we got the band, Henry Man. We here for you no matter what!"

Henry struggled to look T.J. in the eye.

In the back of his mind, he knew T.J. was right. He always was. No matter what the case. He was *always* right.

T.J. stepped forward into Henry's range of vision.

In return, Henry forced himself to look at T.J.

"I would've done the same goddamn thing," T.J. said to Henry. "But, Henry Man, you gots to realize that there's a right and wrong place. If you lose your cool over a couple of drunk fans, who knows what you're capable of doin'. I mean. . . you pull off a stunt like that you not jus affectin' yourself, Henry, but you be affectin' the entire band."

Henry remained quiet, still trying to decompress after the incident off stage.

"Forget this," T.J. muttered and stormed to the dressing room door.

Before T.J. exited, Henry said with his breath pulsing, "You want to fuck her?"

T.J. paused at the doorway.

"Kerri?"

"No."

"Then what is you talkin' 'bout?"

"You know what I'm talking about," Henry said as T.J. slowly spun around. "You want to fuck my girl?"

"Henry. . . I. . ."

"Starlet," he said, his eyes staring crazily at T.J. "You want to fuck her? Don't you?"

"Henry," T.J. said unsteadily and held out his hands. "I think you need to get sum sleep, man."

"Who made you a fucking doctor?" Henry said bitterly before T.J. had a chance to answer Henry's question. "You didn't answer my question, T.J."

"Henry," T.J. said, his voice still unsteady and his hands held outward. "Don't do me like this. We friends."

"We were," Henry said sharply. "You think I didn't see you two out there—"

"You know Starlet, Henry. She was jus entertainin' the crowd."

Henry said it nicely and slowly and clearly now.

"Do. . . you. . . want. . . to. . . fuck. . . her?"

T.J. scowled at Henry.

"Don't do me like this."

"DO YOU WANT TO FUCK HER?"

T.J. shouted out, "It ain't like that, Henry!"

Henry replied, sharper now, "Then what's the deal with you two? You think I'm an idiot, T.J. Come on. I know you."

"After all these years, Henry. . . "

Henry snorted.

"If you really knew me, you would know I would never do such a thing to my friend," T.J. said. "She's like a big sister, Henry. You know this."

The dressing room door suddenly opened.

Starlet was standing at the doorway with one hand resting over her hip and a vacant expression on her face.

She asked confusedly, "What's going on in here?"

T.J. turned to Starlet.

"Henry's jus tired. That's all."

"No," Henry fumed and hurried from the dressing room. "Henry's just getting warmed up!"

"Where are you goin', Henry?"

Henry strolled away saying, "This show isn't over yet."

From *Missing the Edges*, page 229:

Till this day people still talk about the show in Tokyo.

When Henry went back on stage after the confrontation with T.J., he sang and played as if he had the Holy Spirit driving him. That night in Tokyo, Henry was a god. . .

As the final song to the encore came to a conclusion with Henry on the saxophone, he saw a familiar woman shouldering her way through the crowd. He moved Harry down to his side and stared out into the audience.

"Mom. . . " he said under his heavy breath.

Before Henry could make out the face in its entirety, the haggard woman turned away and then shouldered her way through the crowd.

Henry desperately tried to find his mother's face again among the never-ending field of faces basking over the pink spotlights.

Yet, she faded into the darkness.

And Henry lost her.

From *Missing the Edges*, page 248:

We were most definitely living the American Dream, but it didn't make the coldest day in December any less cold.

Once the international tour ended, Christmas was right around the corner. I took a hiatus from Like Heroin and went to Amsterdam for about a week to chill out. When I got back, I hooked up with André, who told me about his two friends from high school and how they were interested in starting up an experimental band. André played me an instrumental EP that they had created. After listening to their stuff, I was immediately interested. Before I knew it, André and I started up a side project called Like Sex. We recorded a batch of songs at Leo's home studio in Hollywood and then mixed the album at the Den. The album, *Bullets for Daisy*, was by far the quickest album I had ever produced and funniest. It was a concept album about a woman's unexpected journey to find a mythical "unicorn." Those who have heard the album need no more explanation. Plug: those who haven't should go buy the album. Anyway, when I visited New York with Mona's Arch during their photo shoot for their debut album, I fell in love with New York City, the energy, the grind, how there was another artist just like me who was working twice as hard and staying up half as late as me. These admirable qualities of New York had made me stronger and more dedicated to my work and inspired me creatively as an artist. From the success of Like Sex and Mona's Arch, it had certainly paid off. I bought a loft in the Upper East Side of Manhattan. Nice place on the outside. Half the time, though, the water didn't work. And when the water did work, it had this rusty color and smelled like the inside of a sewer. The tenant, Dewey, told me it was a newer building and that it was "working out the kinks." After about a month, the water issue was finally fixed. But then, of course, something else would happen. The water heater wouldn't work or the toilet wouldn't flush or the sink would leak.

After two months of living in New York City, Dewey and I saw each other more often than I wanted to. I'm just thankful that I was on his good side and not his bad.

Once I finished laying vocals on the album *Mount Everest* in the spring of '97 with Like Heroin, I got a phone call from Mona's Arch. They finally wanted to make it official. Having enjoyed making the two tracks from *Rule or Be Ruled*, I agreed to join the band. I took about two months off after I did a thirty day tour with Like Heroin to promote our new album and reconvene with Mona's Arch the following February to record Mona's Arch's sophomore album, which was planned to be released in the last quarter of '98. Plus, I had two up and coming bands, one from Oregon and the other from Memphis, that I was about to recruit onto Night Owl. So, the pressure was on.

Before I hooked up with Mona's Arch, I had some free time on my hands, which, in my world, almost never happens. I decided to invite Henry out to the Big Apple and show him around the city. He stayed with me for a week. Thankfully, there weren't any issues with the loft. Everything was pretty much smooth sailing. From the first day I met Henry at Lime N' Light, I knew it wouldn't be the last time I would see him. There was a connection there. Even my manager at the time, Stewart, couldn't understand a single word that came out of my mouth after Henry and I met. It took me the next day to finally retrace the scene in my head. You can picture this whole romantic scene in your head—the scene playing out like a scene in a James Bond movie. Then, there are particular lines you want to use. Each line retraces over in your head until it is just right. When you finally do confront that special one, the words just fall short like a game of Scrabble. Stewart said he could see the glint in my eyes, the intoxication oozing throughout my words. He called it the *I'm-so-deeply-in-love* buzz. Stewart was good when it came to reading women. I never quite understood how he did it. He called it a gift. As for the week in the Big Apple, it went by too fast. Henry and I went to the museums, the Statue of Liberty, and the Broadway shows. Since he didn't have the time to experience these things during his first visit to New York, we took full advantage. I even showed Henry what authentic, greasy New York pizza tasted like. He claimed that there was a place in his hometown that made good New York style pizza. But I told him, "It wasn't authentic New York pizza." So, I took him to Lorengeonie's Pizzeria. The owners were stepbrothers who clashed heads on about everything. They couldn't come up with a proper pizzeria name. Lorenzo wanted to call it Lorenzo's. And Geonie wanted to call it Geonie's. So, they decided to call it Lorengeonie's. Some of the loyal patrons would come to the pizzeria just to see the two argue and, of course, taste the special pie. At first, Henry was skeptical. He was fairly particular when it came to his pizza. It had to be two things: greasy and cheesy. Lorenzo and Geonie made Henry a believer. It wasn't the last time Henry visited the pizzeria. Every time Henry was in the Big Apple, he paid a visit to the pizzeria. We had some great times, Henry and I. They will stay with me until the day I die. But, as you know, all real love stories aren't made from fairy tales.

TWENTY-EIGHT

WHILE Henry was home sleeping in his own bed (something he hadn't done in over a month), a gentle breeze blew open the door and ran across the backside of Henry's neck and caused Henry to stir.

Standing at the lit doorway, the silhouette of a man was revealed.

The dark silhouette was the same height as Henry, slender and graceful too with its subtle, almost robotic movements. The living room light that shined over the outline of its body faintly glistened. In three keen movements, its head mechanically tilted like a confused dog trying to listen closer to its master's foolish demands.

Unaware of the opened door, Henry rolled from his side and found a more comforting position on the bed.

As Henry fell back asleep on his back, the strange figure inched through the light cast from the doorway and crept farther into the dark bedroom. The light was shining over the backside of its evenly shaped body, glistening brightly. The figure was smooth and featureless like a manikin. Its skin wasn't made of flesh or plastic, but made from brass. Its head was also covered in brass, featureless as well.

As Henry slept, the brass figure loomed over the bed and studied Henry's body with both fascination and great eagerness.

Again, the figure tilted its head like a dog.

With its brass hand, it reached out toward Henry.

Slowly, the hand moved closer toward Henry's face, his mouth.

The air around Henry suddenly grew more frigid.

Suddenly, the hand firmly cupped over Henry's mouth.

As a cold rush of pain ran over Henry's cheeks, his eyes shot open like blinds.

He let out a loud gasp and rose from bed.

The brass figure was gone. Gone like the pain.

However, the door was still open.

Little light was creeping in.

For years, Henry had always slept with the door closed. *Always.* So, he was a bit confused. More so curious now as to why the door was open, he rolled out of bed and ambled over to the door. During the trip over, he picked up on the light in the living room and how it was pale blue and not yellow. The air was much colder too, so cold that he could see his own breath in the air.

He made it to the doorway.

Behind Henry, the same brass figure crept through the shadows. Henry kept walking, though, rubbing the sides of his arms and occasionally breathing into his cupped hands. He grabbed a white tee shirt from the arm of a chair and put it on.

Dressed now, Henry cautiously exited the bedroom.

The living room was no longer there. Gone. He found himself standing inside a cave of ice. The walls were bright and glossy. The ceiling overhead was covered with icicles, some as long as swords while others as tiny as knives. The prodigious cave ran as far as Henry could see. There were many cavities in the cave, some shaped like the inside of a human throat.

Henry strolled farther into the cave.

He got about ten feet into the cave when the bedroom door suddenly closed behind him. Henry flinched from the sudden *thud* and turned his shoulder.

The door was gone.

No outline.

Only a wall of ice.

He ventured farther into the cave.

Two passages were revealed, both forked in either direction. One ran into darkness while the other one ran into a soft, enticing light.

Henry decided to travel down the lit one.

During his journey through the lit tunnel, his reflection altered over the ice, morphing into something much taller, much slender, much darker.

As he walked, the corner of his eyes followed his reflection.

Occasionally, the reflection shifted and distorted. And whenever Henry faced the reflection, it returned back to normal.

He proceeded farther down the tunnel until he reached the light, which was beaming down from a narrow orifice in the ceiling overhead.

In the center of the cave sat a brass object mounted on a perfect cylinder of ice.

He crept over to the brass object and picked it up from the cut of ice. He studied it closely. An arm guard of some kind, Henry concluded, artfully crafted to fit his right forearm. A floral design was engraved over the frontal plate—one side was lined with rods similar to the ones on Harry's body.

Over careful thought (like what exactly it was, what did it do, was it a weapon), Henry slipped his hand inside the guard, pulled it up his forearm until it fit nice and snug, and marveled at the guard's unique design. The feel alone of the cool brass on his skin sent warm and vibrant waves of ecstasy throughout his body.

Roused now, the atmosphere around him turned thick and humid. The coolness gradually fell from the air, which caused Henry to flush. His body temperature spiked. The clothes dampened over his entire body, especially his boxers, like a weight continually tugging them downward until he was stripped bare.

The ecstasy heightened.

In his highest state of arousal, he heard a sharp noise like a bone cracking from above.

Henry spun around to the noise and witnessed the tiny crack in the wall of ice.

Slowly, the crack spread over the ceiling of ice, pulling the cave in two halves.

As the warm light splashed over Henry's face, his breath grew more labored as if the invisible weight—once tugging at his clothes—was now pressed against his chest.

Harder now!

He had trouble breathing.

Each breath narrowed, tightened.

He cleared his throat. . .

Gasp!

With a sudden jolt upright, Henry woke in a cold sweat. The weight was lifted from his pumping chest. The sheets around him had been stripped from the bed. A comforter was lying on the floor along with a couple of smashed pillows. He glanced down at his twisted boxers and found a damp stain over his genitals, as well as a viscous substance scattered over the lower part of his abdomen.

As he caught his breath, his eyes crossed the bedroom door.

The door was the same way as he last left it before he fell asleep: closed.

From *Missing the Edges*, page 262:

The first signs that things were going south began at the "Run and Hide" video shoot in November of '98. It was only a matter of time before Henry developed lead singer syndrome, or LSS. When I first started out in Like Heroin, I too had LSS. I can't tell you how many times I fought with the guys in Like Heroin. Eventually, I grew up and realized that the world didn't revolve around me.

When we first met with the director, Mitch Theodore, for the idea of our first video shoot, we were extremely leery about the direction Henry was taking the band. Never have I been involved in such a massive production before. It was like a movie, literally. They had these sets that were the size of an airplane hanger. Henry said they looked like something you'd see in an *Alien* movie. At first, the band didn't want to do the video. It seemed way too commercial, sort of defeated the purpose of why Mona's Arch started playing music in the first place. Our managers and friends in PR told us that we needed to make a music video. Once it got to the point where people were telling us, especially Henry, what to do ("You *need* to this" or "You *need* to do that"), then that was when you saw Henry's dark side. It was fair to say that Henry made some enemies real fast. We ended up making the video anyway. And to really stick it to James, we made the most profound, most over the top video to date. *Entertainment Weekly* ranked it as the best music video since Michael Jackson's "Thriller." The inception of the video had come from Henry. He claimed these vivid images and scenes in his head were all from his "visions," as he called them. Since the sophomore album was a conceptual album, we decided to make the music video as cinematic as possible. I figured if music videos had Academy Awards, then Mona's Arch would've easily been walking home with an Oscar. No question. The song was called "Run and Hide," about a heist that takes place in the distant future. I remember during the entire shoot Socks was complaining about his costume and how it was cutting off his circulation. During the chase scene into space (after Henry and Socks stole this so-called "artifact" from a highly secured underground facility), Henry and Socks were the lucky ones who got to ride the beautiful spacecraft that Gabe Nightingale had designed. The spacecraft was powered by all these hydraulics. Just watching Henry and Socks being jerked around in the spacecraft made me queasy to my stomach. During the first shoot, Socks ended up getting sick from all the shaking. Except for the scenes that took place in the facility set, most of the video was done behind a green screen, which, till this day, is beyond my head. At the end of the shoot, things came to a head. Throughout the entire shoot, Henry and Mitch were at each other's throat. Those who knew Mitch knew that he could be hard on his actors. Those who knew Henry knew that he could be hard on the boys. At times, it was hard to watch two great artists like Henry and Mitch clash in such a negative light. Deep down inside, I knew something was bothering Henry. Like Mitch, he wanted the video to be perfect. Maybe too perfect.

Once the video shoot for "Run and Hide" finally wrapped, the band mates went their separate ways without saying much to one another. Henry, who was mentally and physically exhausted from the shoot and looking forward to the flight back home to Peregrine, caught T.J. getting into Starlet's white Suburban and then leaving Warner Brothers Studio.

On a whim, Henry hurried to his black Porsche 911 without drawing much attention from the production crew and followed Starlet through Burbank and toward Universal City, the opposite direction of Bob Hope Airport. He mostly kept his distance from Starlet and eased back several cars during stoplights. She kept driving, making several more turns, once running a yellow light. Henry gunned the Porsche around two other cars in order to make the light. She took Cahuenga Boulevard West, drove past the Hollywood Bowl, and hopped onto North Highland Avenue. For a couple of minutes, she cruised through Hollywood. *Maybe they missed the turn*, he thought as he grinded his teeth together. *Sight seeing. Or maybe they're lost. It's an easy town to get lost in.* Then, she kept driving, now into West Hollywood. Swerving at times. He wondered what was going on inside the SUV. Was T.J. making moves on her? Was there an argument? Henry did all he could (like counting to ten or taking in deep, slow belly breaths) to prevent himself from tearing off the steering wheel. Henry tailed the two into the parking lot of a bar called The Lou Lounge. Starlet parked in the back of the parking lot and remained in the SUV for some time while Henry parked across the street in a deserted lot. From the tinted windows in the back, Henry couldn't exactly see what was going on inside. After five minutes expired, they finally exited and went inside The Lou Lounge.

Outside, Henry waited in the car for about two hours. Throughout the entire stakeout, his mind was racing. For a moment, he thought about marching inside, catching the two together, smashing a beer bottle over T.J.'s head, and then stabbing him to death with the jagged remains of the bottle. He decided not to. Yet, he kept it all in, the anger and sadness, like an insect in a bottle. No perforations. The thought alone of Starlet cheating on him was as if he had been hit by a freight train.

Two hours had expired now.

As Henry stepped from the Porsche to stretch his legs, he heard the sound of laughing from afar. He directed his attention across the quiet street and found the two stumbling from the entrance of the bar. T.J.'s arm was around Starlet's shoulder. They were giggling and whispering into one another's ear.

When they got back into the car, T.J. leaned over and kissed Starlet.

Henry cautiously walked across the street where he got an even better look inside the Suburban.

Without the two noticing, Henry witnessed the entire events unfold. Both of his hands gripped tightly into fists. He grimaced in a quaking rage.

Ignorant of the traffic around him, Henry staggered back to the Porsche. Somehow, he made it back to Burbank in one piece. However, he didn't even remember the drive back.

For the rest of the night, Henry sat outside the airport and relived the recent events in his head.

ELLIS KROSS

*　　*　　*

From *Missing the Edges*, page 256:

It all started with a simple and innocent touch across the hand. It happened at the Den where we were recording the song "The Deadliest One" from our sophomore album, *Machine Mistress*. While Henry was in the booth, my hand accidentally grazed over T.J.'s hands as I was reaching for the volume knob on the console. I was singing along to Henry's lyrics, "Wooh"ing to the bridge of the song, my eyes rolling over to T.J. It was like time had stopped. We both stared at each other. He had a look on his face as if he wanted to leap at me right then and there while Henry was singing. As much as I yearned for such actions (over the years, T.J. and I had become extremely close), I couldn't do that to Henry. Such a move would destroy him. This was the first of many connections that T.J. and I shared, all secretive—of course. Whenever Henry asked about us, I lied. Everyone knows that lying just makes it worse. But all of that would be trivial after the night of July 27, 1999, the second to last show before we finished the Buick Crossover Tour on the West Coast. The day following the 27th was one of the hardest days of my life.

In one way or another, I like to think that we all carry around a specific date with us if it is a birth date, an anniversary date, or even the date of a tragic event. We all have certain days, scarred or unscarred, that will stay in a place where no one can reach. It is there for us, and the loved ones who surround us, to access in times of remembrance. Mine was July 28, 1999. Not once did I ever blame Henry. Mostly, I blame myself. Ever since Henry ditched Harry while making the record, things. . . well, things just fell apart.

The first time Starlet met James, he warned her, as well as the band, about success. He said, "If you let it, it will go to your head." That was exactly what happened. It just happened all so fast.

A couple of months into promoting their new album, James was informing them on the new music video "Last Ride Home," which followed and tied into the track "Run and Hide." The two tracks combined formed a short film that lasted over twenty-three minutes, which was recorded as the longest video of all time. The climax of the song featured a choir of children, which in Mona's Arch case, was definitely pushing the envelope and taking them to realms where they had never explored before. Critics said the song was one of Starlet's best sounding records.

"Last Ride Home" was nominated for a MTV Award.

They band was over the moon, except for Henry.

"An award?" Henry seethed as he paced around the hotel room.

The shattered glass from a vase, as well as a lamp without a shade, was scattered over the carpet floor.

James was holding out his hands, trying to calm down Henry.

He whined, "It's great exposure, Henry."

"When the hell did awarding art become the norm in this fucking country?"

"Don't think about it that way," he said.

"Then how should I think about it, James?"

"Think of it as a compliment for all the hard work we've done."

Henry screamed, "Goddamn it!"

He grabbed the chair from the desk.

"Henry!" James cried out. "Wait!"

"You tell MTV to take their award and shove it up their fucking ass!"

In two fluid movements, Henry flung the chair at the mirror. The glass from the mirror shattered everywhere. Parts of the mirror fell at his feet. James could hardly force himself to look at Henry. He was standing, shoulders deflated, with a look of defeat on his face.

"The hell with this," James said under his breath as he left the hotel room.

While taking in deep breaths, Henry glanced down at the jagged pieces of glass over the floor and witnessed his many warped reflections. He didn't like what he saw. In fact, he was terrified from what he had become.

Levine, Eric A. "Bloody Fantastic" <u>The Commercial Appeal</u> 22 July 1999, late ed., G8:

The concert ended with Henry the Fif' drenched from head to toe in pig's blood and holding up the classic Vulcan salute hand gesture to the crowd. The entire city of Jackson was buzzing after the show was over. My head was still ringing. And boy! What a show it was!

Worst coughing spell yet.

Henry stood underneath the shower faucet and diligently caressed the back of his neck with a bar of soap. He didn't know if it was from all that pig's blood; and surely, there was quite a bit of it. In the back of his mind, he wished it was only that, a cough brought on from the pig's blood, and nothing else.

The pig that Henry and the rest of the band (except for Starlet, who wanted no part in the killing, even after Henry had gotten down on his knees and begged her to come) had gutted was called Napoleon, whose owner Randy had named after the tyrannous one from George Orwell's *Animal Farm*, not the "lil' French fella." Napoleon wasn't a Berkshire boar, nor was it a mean one like the fictional character in Orwell's novel. Randy liked the way the name Napoleon rolled off his tongue. Napoleon was actually a domestic pig, a moderately large one weighing in over two hundred pounds with a birthmark in the shape of West Virginia on its left leg. On the morning of the concert in Jackson, Mississippi, Henry and the band drove to the Thomason's pig farm, which was located deep in the countryside. When they first got there, Henry picked out the fattest pig to cook. Henry had claimed it would be a good bonding experience for the band, especially with all of the tension building among the band, mainly the two band mates in particular. Plus, it was a way of giving back to the rest of the road crew, who had been working their tails off these past couple of days. When they arrived at the pig farm, Mr. and Mrs. Thomason introduced them to a slippery man named Randy Horton, Napoleon's caretaker. Randy wasn't a man of many words. He wasn't easy on the eyes, either. He had a nose that looked like a root, disproportionate to his face. Large bone structure and yet skinny frame. He didn't have many teeth. In fact, he was down to no more than a dozen or so. Randy skipped the foreplay and went over the steps of how to properly gut a pig. Most of the band couldn't understand a single word Randy had to say. He mostly mumbled. And when he did raise his voice, he spoke incredibly fast like a Mexican with a thick southern accent and a slight whistle whenever he said the letter s. So, when he pulled out the Smith and Wesson pistol from his back pocket and mumbled something like "shootin' (*whistle*) one of yous (*whistle*)," the band didn't know whether or not he was going to kill them or take their money or both! Randy reiterated, "Which one of yous fine folks (*whistle*) liked to shoots (*whistle*) here Napoleon?" Since none of them had ever fired a pistol before, except for T.J., who vowed never to pick up a gun ever again, Endo, their manager on tour as well as the one who was going to be cooking the pig back at the coliseum (the entire bus ride he had been bragging about his famous rub, said it was "to die for"), stepped forward and decided to take the rap. The kill was quick and painless—at least that was what Randy had said to the other band mates. Single gunshot between the eyes. Napoleon flopped over like a flimsy hurdle after it had been swept over. This was the part where things were done with urgency or else the meat would spoil. After Randy hosed away the dirt from the carcass, Endo gave the others a hand and hoisted the carcass over the table where they soaked the carcass in scolding hot water and scrubbed away its bristly hair with a steel wool pad. For the hair that was hard to remove, Randy scorched it away using a small hand torch. Next, they strung up the carcass by its feet. Placed a bucket underneath. In the first couple of seconds of the gutting (when that honed blade came sliding down the carcass's underbelly), Henry and Darby were the only two survivors who kept their breakfast all together. T.J. was actually the first one to gracefully bow out. Then Deon. The sound alone of organs, all spilling out over the tarp underneath the carcass (blood splashing over their shoes and shins), had sent Socks running back to the bus. Henry and Darby had never cut through a dead animal before. Randy ended up doing most of the butchering for them. He saved the swine's organs, including the liver, facial features like the ears and snout, as well as the intestines for blood sausage. He kept other parts of the pig, mostly the butt, shoulder, and ribs, to barbeque. Lastly, the band, especially T.J., was wondering why Henry decided on keeping the blood that Randy had drained from the carcass. His reason: "You never know when it might come in handy."

In the back of T.J.'s mind, he had an idea of what Henry was up to, but he didn't dare express what that idea might be to the other band mates.

When the concert was about to start, all four members of Mona's Arch were on stage, expect for Henry and Starlet. The audience wasn't aware of what Henry was doing backstage nor were the other band mates. Henry was stripped down to his undies, a pair of white briefs. Except for Henry, Starlet was last to take the stage.

As she anticipated the arrival of the Fif', she witnessed him carefully reaching for a metal bucket in a cooler of ice behind the monitor. That was when her earliest suspicions had come true. At that moment, Starlet knew Henry was about to do something really bizarre.

When the stage lights came on and Henry the Fif' strutted out on stage, all covered from head to toe in Napoleon's blood, the audience, as well as the rest of the band, was shocked to say the least. Later, when the other band mates asked him what in the hell was he thinking, he simply told them that it was his "rebirth."

Whatever that meant.

Throughout the rising steam in the empty locker room, Henry slouched farther against the wall with his head held down in distress.

The leftover pig's blood—Napoleon's blood—streamed down his back like hot lava sliding down Mauna Loa. One hand was keeping him balanced while the other hand was repeatedly running across the backside of his aching neck.

Henry raised his head, embraced several deep breaths, and let the hot water from the shower faucet pour down his face.

As the steam rose into his sinuses, he violently coughed up a tarry substance from his throat, not Napoleon's blood but a different kind of blood, darker than ordinary blood, a new blood. Parts of the dark liquid were coagulated, dripping from his nostrils and lips and splashing into the drain below, circling around the spiraling water.

After about a minute, the coughs finally subsided.

Then, another string of dark blood poured from his nose and mouth and trickled down his chin, body, legs, and into the drain below.

As the congestion cleared, Henry raised his head upward.

He embraced yet another deep breath, this time with great relief.

PART SIX

THE THINGS THAT SURVIVED THE FIRE

TWENTY-NINE

WHILE the members of Mona's Arch eagerly prepared for the upcoming show in the band's dressing room, Henry waited in his own separate room.

In front of the mirror, he was rapidly tapping his foot against the floor. The vanity lights shined above and highlighted each bead of sweat dripping from his forehead.

A door quickly opened from behind.

The door didn't even stay open long enough for Henry to make out who exactly opened the door. All he heard was a monotone voice, *Endo's voice*, he thought; and that voice was telling him that he was on in "three minutes."

Henry didn't pay much attention to the stage director. His lifeless eyes were focused ahead on his reflection in the mirror. He methodically tightened up the three-fingered, customized leather gloves over his hands. He was wearing a well-crafted brass guard over his right hand and forearm. A black acute angle was painted over his left eye. He was wearing his trademark blazer too. Underneath the blazer, he was wearing a top made of chain mail. His scalp was finely trimmed into that trademark letter V, or in Henry's case, the Roman numeral 5, not V as in Victor.

Throughout the hype behind the door, the roars of the crowd above, he remained focused with his eyes aimed directly ahead.

Three minutes hadn't seemed so long.

*　　*　　*

Halfway into the show, the other band mates could see the irritability in Henry.

So far the show was going great, lots of high energy from each band mate. However, they knew something was surfacing with Henry. They just didn't expect to see it played out on stage.

The track "Everybody's Frankenstein" from Mona's Arch's debut album came to a sudden halt.

The crowd erupted in an uproar.

"This next song, St. Louis," Henry said over the microphone, his breath labored. Occasionally shooting glances over at Starlet and wiping the sweat from his brow, he paced around the front of the stage. He walked around a prop of rock on the elaborate stage, which was designed to look like an alien planet—of course, Henry's idea. A bed of rock was scattered around the drum set and monitors. Green and blue mountainous props stretched high above the line arrays. In between the mountains was a gigantic television set. Rapid images of war—Vietnam and the Gulf War—were streaming over the screen. "This next song is going to be on our next album," he said to the audience in the sold out coliseum. "It's called 'Bermuda's Triangle.'" The smile dissolved from Starlet's face. "The song is dedicated. . . " he glanced over at Starlet once more, ". . . to a very special friend of mine."

The other band mates looked at each other in confusion.

Henry threw a nod at Deon and said with the mike tucked in his armpit, "Do the crazy jam."

"*The crazy jam*," Deon mouthed and leaned closer to Henry, "I thought you said we weren't going to do that one."

"Just play the goddamn song," Henry whispered, his eyes filled with something else. Deon couldn't tell if it was madness or sickness. This foreign entity that was throbbing through Henry's beady eyes had completely taken over him.

Deon cautiously took a step back from Henry.

In return, Henry leaned even closer.

Inches now.

Henry fumed, "I said '*Play it*.'"

Deon shook his head in annoyance and nodded to the others. He plucked a couple of strings on the guitar, which gave the cue to the others on what song Henry was fuming about. William shook his head, like Deon, as if Henry was about to step on a landmine. Behind the drum set, T.J. was grimacing in rage. Socks was just as confused as the others. As for Starlet, she could hardly look Henry in the eye.

The song started with a whirling effect that Socks created with a synthesizer. Starlet inched her way closer to Henry and said closely, "Don't do this. I beg you, Henry."

Henry peered into Starlet's eyes.

"No," he said sharply away from the microphone. "You made me do this."

"Bermuda's Triangle" was a far cry from their original sound. It was much darker. The song had shades of The Cure's "Lullaby," with William plucking the bass like Stewart Gallup.

Henry sang over an effect, *"How does it feel to lose yourself in the water? Ten thousand miles deep in the dark and now you're swimming with the sharks. . ."*

A quarter way into the song while Henry was crooning about Starlet's "Bermuda Triangle" and how it was a place where one could easily get lost, T.J. threw the drumsticks in Henry's vicinity and flounced his way backstage. The engineer filled in on the remaining drum parts before the crowd could make sense of what was happening. The rest of the band eventually quit playing as well, while the crowd now stood dumbfounded.

The tears filled Starlet's eyes.

Sniffling, she said to Henry, "You're an asshole. You know that."

Then, she dropped the microphone onto the stage and ran after T.J.

After the meltdown on stage, Henry marched into T.J.'s dressing room.

As soon as Henry swung open the door, T.J. clobbered him with a right hook. Henry staggered backward and tripped over his own foot. With his nose gushing blood, Henry made an attempt to stand on his feet. Before he had a chance to retaliate, T.J. was already on top of him. Starlet hurried inside and tried to pull T.J. off Henry. T.J. pushed Starlet away. The shove caused Starlet to stumble over a stool and fall headfirst into a full clothing rack. The purple wig that she was wearing on stage flew off. But she didn't bother picking it up. Once Henry saw that Starlet wasn't injured, he reached upward and tried to strangle T.J. to death. Henry was no match for T.J.'s toughness. T.J. pinned down Henry's shoulders with his knees and pummeled his face. T.J. got off a couple more blows before the other band mates finally rushed into the dressing room and yanked T.J. off Henry.

"What the fuck is going on in here?" Deon yelled out and did his best to separate the two.

William did all he could to help Deon restrain T.J. Socks rushed in and gave William and Deon a hand. Even the three of them had difficulty trying to keep T.J. from rushing toward Henry, who suffered a cut over his eye and another one on the corner of his lip. Trails of blood were streaming down the sides of his face as well as both nostrils. His eyes struggled to keep focus. He staggered, which forced him to brace himself against a chair.

As the fight settled and T.J. was pulled to the opposite side of the room, Deon tended to Starlet and helped her up.

"Are you okay?" he asked.

"Let me go," Starlet said angrily, jerked her arm away from Deon, and held onto the small gash on the top of her head.

William and Socks pulled T.J. from the dressing room and took him outside into the hallway to cool off.

"Leave us, Deon," Starlet said to Deon as she removed her hand from her head.

With his arms folded, Deon appeared as if he wasn't going anywhere.

"Deon," Starlet said, her eyes swelling.

Deon unfolded his arms and raised his hands in surrender.

"Whatever," he whined and shot a glare toward Henry's direction. "This is really getting fucking old."

Deon marched from the dressing room and slammed the door behind him while Henry was struggling to the seat in front of a mirror. His hands were shaking. He propped himself upward, grabbed a washcloth from the drawer, and began to wipe the blood from his face.

"I'm sorry, Henry," she said, her shoulders deflated.

Henry cried, but not from the pain.

"You love him," he said, sniffling. "Don't you?"

"You and I. . . " she was crying too, ". . . we can never be a couple, Henry." She inched her way toward Henry and stood behind him in the chair. "It would never work out."

"What does he have that I don't?"

"T.J.'s a good guy, Henry," she said. "He's like my opposite."

"I get it," he said. "And I'm the bad guy. The bad guy never gets the girl. Right? The bad guy is the one who gets fucked in the end and then left behind like road kill. Is that right?"

"Don't. . . "

Henry threw the washcloth against the counter and bolted from the chair. In a burst of rage, he spun around and faced Starlet.

"You can't tell me that you love me and then go behind my back with another man!" he cried. "I thought we really had something special, Starlet!"

"We did," she pleaded with some relief pouring from her voice. "But we're too much alike, Henry. T.J. is nothing like you. He makes me feel good about myself."

"And I don't!"

"You do, Henry," Starlet bawled. "It's just sometimes you can be a little overbearing. You're just going to have to accept that."

Henry fumed, "So, you want a man who slaps you around! Pushes you away when he's beating the shit out of his best friend! Is that the kind of man you want?"

Starlet slapped Henry across the face.

Henry carelessly grabbed his jaw and tongued the side of his bloody lip.

"You're right," he said solemnly. "You two are meant for each other."

Henry shook his head in both disgust and amusement. He rushed from the dressing room. William and Socks were still trying to cool off T.J. while Deon was pacing around and biting his nails.

Deon shouted out, "Henry!"

Henry kept on walking.

Deon followed.

"Where are you going?"

"Just leave me alone, Deon."

"Henry," Deon grabbed Henry by the arm. "Come on."

"Get your fucking hand off me!"

"All right," Deon said and raised his hands, again in surrender. "Chill."

Henry marched down the hallway.

Deon said from behind, "I'm just trying to help. . . "

"I don't need your help!"

Deon whined, "Please, Henry. . . "

From *Missing the Edges*, page 278:

With severe highs come severe lows.

As the crowd roared above, I was standing backstage in the dressing room and wiping the lines of mascara from my face. I couldn't believe that this was how it was going to end: with me in the middle of two best friends. With all that had taken place over the last couple of days, the lies, the irritability, the acts of betrayal, the demise of Mona's Arch was imminent. For the first time in my music career, my foolish heart had gotten the best of me, as well as the worst.

*　　*　　*

They arrived in a city called Pennytown, not too far from Lansford.

Once the band stepped off the bus and gathered their belongings and luggage from storage, Henry and T.J., who had sat at the opposite ends of the bus during the ride home, went their separate ways. There was a small crowd of fans lingering behind a secure barricade in the high school parking lot.

Once Henry saw the fans outside, he pulled aside their manager, James.

"What the hell is this?" Henry asked, his eyes flaring. "I thought we told you no autographs."

"I got a couple demands," James said innocently. "I thought it'd be good for you, Henry, especially after, you know. . . "

Henry stormed away from James.

Among those fans, a young boy was waiting with one particular photograph and a pen in hand. The boy sought out T.J.

Surprised from the boy's engagement, T.J. sighed and said, "Sure, kid. Why not?"

T.J. signed the boy's photograph while most of the other fans hovered around Henry.

Just as T.J. finished the signature, he noticed something really strange about the photograph.

He looked more closely at the two people in the photograph.

What the. . . The photograph was taken when T.J. was around twelve years old. He and Henry were standing next to one another. Henry was dressed in a white LA Lakers tee shirt and holding that same nasty basketball in his hand. T.J. was wearing a black RUN DMC shirt and jokingly giving Henry bunny ears from behind.

Upset from the photograph, T.J. grabbed the boy's arm.

He asked, "Where'd you get this?"

The boy shrugged his shoulders.

"Answer me!"

The boy jerked T.J.'s hand away and ran off.

T.J. suspiciously looked around the deserted parking lot.

Meanwhile, Socks, Deon, and William hung back and stood quietly next to the bus while Henry quietly signed autographs.

"It was inevitable," Socks said to Deon.

"Just give them some time," Deon said optimistically. "They just need some space to clear their heads."

Starlet was last to exit the bus.

Deon took a drag from the cigarette and nodded at Starlet.

"What?" she said innocently.

"You know," Deon said. "This is all your fault."

"Don't even start with me, Deon."

"I'm just saying—"

"No," she said shortly. "You're bored and just trying to start another fight."

Deon raised the peace sign, not the bunny ears.

William blurted out, "Would everybody just fucking relax! Jesus!"

"I think we need to settle this with a fat ass joint," Deon said. "Everybody's wound up like a clock."

"Amen to that," Socks said and grabbed the cigarette from Deon and took a drag.

He nodded at Henry and asked, "What are we going to do about them?"

"It ain't like they haven't fought before," William said from the side. "They'll work out their issues. They always do. And it makes us better as a band."

"Let's just hope so," Socks said. "Otherwise, this could very well be the end of Mona's Arch."

"Don't talk like that, Socks."

Socks shrugged his shoulders.

"I'm just saying. . . "

Across the street, a beat up chocolate brown Coupe Deville was parked on the side of the curb. The headlights were cut off and yet the engine was running. The boy with the autograph ran up to the passenger side of the car.

The boy said, "I did like you asked, sir."

A throaty voice said from inside, "Are you sure it was him?"

"Yes, sir," the boy replied and handed the photograph to Screw, who was sitting in the passenger seat. Three black men sat in the car. In the driver seat sat a heavier set man with a finely trimmed beard. His name was Orlando, but most people around Parker Square called him Big T (aka Teardrop) due to his plump frame. In the back sat two thin men. Both of their combined weights equaled Big T's weight. The one with the gold teeth and the black bandana wrapped around his neck was named Detric. The other one with the Mohawk was Cedric, aka Shank.

Screw pulled out a twenty-dollar bill from his pocket and handed it to the boy.

"Now beat it," he said to the boy.

The boy looked down at the bill.

"You said fifty dollars," he whined.

"I did?"

"I want fifty dollars!"

"Would you like it to be no dollars?"

The boy sighed.

"You punk," he said.

From the backseat window, Cedric pulled out a switch-blade and displayed it in front of the boy.

"Who's the punk now?" he slurred.

The boy suddenly scurried away.

Cedric smirked.

"That's what I thought," he said under his breath.

Orlando patted Screw on the arm and said, "You gonna teach that lil' fool some manners?"

Screw giggled from the remark and made a call on his cell phone.

"Backer," Screw said over the phone. "It's Screw. We found him. He's just getting off the bus as we speak."

(*That son of a bitch thought he could steal from us and not face the consequences*)

"What do you want us to do?"

(*Follow him*)
"As you wish."

When T.J. arrived at his house in Madison Grove, which was about a twenty-minute drive from the city of Lansford, he unpacked his things and then checked his messages on the answering machine. Two were from his mother, one from his cousin up North. T.J. had a hard time listening to the messages. His mind was wandering. He was still a bit jacked from the previous fight with Henry. Not only that, he was left with a strange feeling in his gut from the encounter with the fan, that one boy. The entire ride home T.J. tried to make sense of how the boy acquired the personal photograph. He checked the locks, the closets, the drawers, and everything was just the way he left it before he went on tour. *Henry*, T.J. thought, maybe the boy knew Henry. . . maybe he was. . . a friend of a friend. . . maybe he lived in Reddington. . . maybe his mother gave the boy the photograph. . . maybe the photograph belonged to Henry. What if they went to Henry's place and stole the photograph from him? T.J. tried to remember who the photograph belonged to. It was either T.J. or Henry. T.J. remembered seeing the photograph at his old house in Reddington.

"I don't know," he murmured in thought, "it could've been there."

The boy could've acquired the picture from his mother. Why would she give him that one in particular? Recently, T.J.'s mother, Mrs. Livingston, cleared out the entire guest room and turned it into a Mona's Arch memorabilia room. Most of the neighbors on Davie Morris, even the new ones, frequently paid visits to the room. Most, if not all of the neighbors, didn't think much of the room. They just thought that Mrs. Livingston was a mother who was incredibly proud of her son and all of his success and accomplishments and wanted to showcase him and his band and all of their merchandise on the walls. She had every Mona's Arch album in every format (vinyl, cassette, CD), posters, tee shirts, sneakers, and even bobble head dolls. Others, including Mr. Clydesdale, looked at the room in a more negative light as if it was a shrine or something that fanatics got off on. But that wasn't the case at all.

Over some more thought, T.J. finally decided to check the window. For a second, he thought he saw a Cadillac, the Coupe Deville, parked two blocks down. He pulled his eyes from the window (making sure they weren't fooling him), scratched his bloodshot eyes, and sharpened his peer. The heavyset man in the driver seat looked familiar. The other man in the passenger seat—the one who caught T.J.'s attention—was hiding in the shadows. T.J. couldn't quite tell if his mind was seeing that man or what or if, in fact, his eyes were really fooling him. He peered once more and the same man was sitting there in the driver's seat.

Is they here for me?

T.J. hurried into the kitchen. Picked up the telephone from the mount. He only got through the two digits—the 9 and the 1—before he decided to hang up the telephone.

"Get a grip, T.J." T.J. said to himself.

Tomorrow was going to be a big night.

So, he decided to go to bed early.

Before T.J. turned off the lights, he checked the locks once more and made sure they were locked.

THIRTY

THE day had gone by so fast.

Henry and the other band mates, including T.J., spent most their time apart from each other, which, over the several years of being in a band together, turned out to be the best solution in fixing a broken marriage.

When two o'clock came, Henry drove to Central Reserve Coliseum where he met up with the other band mates on the bus, except for T.J. He had hardly eaten anything that day but a wedge of grilled ham and cheese sandwich and a handful of painkillers that he had washed down with a bottle of water. His body was extremely sore, especially the side of his face. Earlier, when he had awakened on the floor with an empty bottle of Jack Daniels hanging from his hand and an overturned bed next to him, it felt as if a house (a Colonial style house built by callused hands, not like the jerry-built houses that get thrown up in a couple of weeks) was sitting directly on the side of his head. Both the alcohol and the pills helped mask the pain, but only for a short while.

Before Henry entered the bus, he paced around outside and thought about what to say. He had nothing inside, no inspirational speech or pep talk, no explanation for his recent—might they say, erratic—behavior, only apologies.

Henry finally stepped foot inside the noisy bus, only to hear a slightly intense conversation about Starlet's upcoming band, Screwdriver, come to a sudden halt. Heads suddenly turned toward Henry, who was standing at the front of the bus. At first, there was a long standoff between the lead singer and the other band mates. The silence, as thick as pollution, was wearing on their elongated faces.

James suddenly cut through the other band mates and stared down Henry.

The other band mates remained in silence, waiting for their lead singer to say something. Most of their attention was drawn to Henry's bruised face, his swollen eye.

"I'm sorry for what I put you guys through," Henry said finally and drew his eyes on Starlet. "I. . . I. . . "

Henry, teary eyed, was at a loss for words.

Socks stood up from his seat, walked up to Henry, and hugged him.

"You don't have to explain, Henry," Socks said, kissed Henry on the cheek, and turned to the others. "Come on, everyone. Bring it in for a group hug."

Except for Starlet, William and Deon got up from their seats.

"That includes you, Star," Socks said and stirred up an awkward tension between her and Henry.

Starlet was slow to get up.

With her head held down in her chest, she sauntered over to the group and joined in on the hug.

William brought Starlet close to him while Henry kept a modest distance from her.

Henry asked, "Anybody talk to T.J.?"

"Haven't seen the man all day," Deon said. "You know him. It takes him a little longer to cool off."

With his face wounded, Henry rolled his eyes toward Starlet's direction.

He said softly, "Star?"

"I haven't seen him," she said, her voice soft as well.

"Well, he better cool off soon," William said. "We got an hour before rehearsal."

Exactly one hour passed and T.J. was still a no show.

Henry and the other band mates, except for their guitarist, Deon, stood on the stage while the army of stagehands prepped the stage and set up line arrays. Pyrotechnics set up rigs over the very front of the stage, and the engineers and mixers went over sound check.

Deon strolled onto the stage.

"So," Henry said, anticipating the good news.

"He didn't pick up," he answered and threw his hands down by his side.

William shifted his weight to one side of his body and asked, "What do we do? WHAT DO WE DO?"

Henry acknowledged Starlet, who was quietly sitting in front of T.J.'s drum set, and then said to the other band mates, "We'll start without him."

As the parking lot gradually filled with fans, the sun set over the Central Reserve Coliseum. Hooting and hollering and singing their favorite Mona's Arch's songs, the fans anxiously made their way toward the coliseum. Before too long, the entire coliseum was packed with giddy fans.

Meanwhile, Henry glanced over the strange prop on the stage and noticed the rowdy fans gathering around the front of the stage. He hurried back to the dressing room where the rest of the band was staying.

Starlet was the first one whom Henry bumped into. She was expecting something like "He's here," or "He's on the way," but, instead, she received Henry shaking his head.

In return, Starlet let out a sigh of frustration.

William exclaimed, "For God's sake! Where the hell is he?"

Henry stopped his pacing and drifted in thought.

"I. . . I think I know where he is," he said with sudden awareness.

The car, he thought, *from last night.*

While signing autographs last night, Henry remembered, he saw a suspicious car parked across the street.

Henry's face turned slightly pale.

His eyes filled with horror.

Suddenly, he hurried toward the door.

Starlet followed Henry.

"I'm coming with you."

"No," he said to Starlet. "You stay here."

She recognized a peculiar expression over Henry's face, almost one of guilt.

"Where are you going?" Starlet cried out. "We're on in thirty minutes."

Henry breathed slowly and said to Starlet and then the others, "If I'm not back in time, start without me."

Socks bolted upright from his seat.

"What? Are you crazy?"

Henry glared at Socks.

Starlet asked, "Did something happen to T.J.?"

Henry ignored the question.

"Start with the song you and I worked on," he said to Starlet.

"We weren't going to play that track till the end of the show."

"I don't care," Henry said and brushed off her concern. "Just start with 'Happy Trails.' And by the time you jump into 'The Dead Beats,' T.J. and I will be back and ready to rock."

Deon said, "But who's going to fill in your parts?"

"Just get Omar."

"Omar?"

"How about T.J.?"

"We'll get Big Ray."

"Ray is going to flip."

Deon shouted out, "Just hold up, Henry! Omar's never played Harry before!"

"Well," Henry said, glancing at the saxophone case on the table as he made his way to the door, "he's just going to have to."

In the parking lot of Frankie's Footlongs, T.J. was sitting on top of Little Red and wondering whether or not the band was missing him or who was going to fill in for him. He made sure to park in the back, way back—outside the floodlights— therefore nobody could recognize him or his car. It didn't matter much, really.

The parking lot was completely deserted. The majority of the city was at the coliseum or at the bars surrounding the coliseum.

A couple of stragglers, who were both wearing Mona's Arch tee shirts (one tee with a silver origami unicorn on the front and another with a portrait of Mona Lisa who had a green smile spray painted over her face and a list of concert dates on the back), were buying footlongs before the big show, which had started about ten minutes ago. The opening band, an electronic band called Double Barrel, was currently playing and had about twenty or so minutes left into their show.

When the stragglers left, so too did T.J.

On his way to the driver's side door, he spotted a mysterious car pulling up to the front of Frankie's.

After a second glance, he realized it was the same exact one camped outside his house last night!

Suddenly, T.J.'s attention was pulled upward at the dark sky above. A couple of raindrops grazed the side of his face.

"Shit," he said and wiped the rain from his forehead.

Without making any sudden movements—mainly head movements—he casually gazed around, checked his watch, and then got back into Little Red as if he was minding his own business.

As T.J. sat in the driver's seat, he subtly traced his eyes over at the suspicious Cadillac parked across the street. At first, he couldn't find the car. Then, he peered closer. The Cadillac had cut off its headlights!

T.J. quickly put the car key into the ignition and turned it over. That was the last thing T.J. wanted to hear right about now. He tried once more to start up the car. Again, he heard the dreadful sounds of an engine choking.

"Damn it," T.J. said under his voice as he slammed his palm against the steering wheel.

The rain was coming down harder now. He couldn't see a thing. He tried hitting the wipers. They didn't work either. The battery was completely dead. He went over his options and thought about an escape route. After all, he did know the area like the backside of his hand.

It was the only way, he thought.

"Lord help me," he said and opened the door.

Casually, T.J. stepped out of Little Red, popped his collar, curled his shoulders into his chest, and strolled toward Frankie's through the heavy rain.

Once T.J. passed one of the ordering parking spaces, he made a run for it.

Screw, who was sitting in the parked Cadillac across the street, lost T.J. in the rain.

"I can't find him," he said to the driver, Orlando.

"There. . . " Cedric said from the backseat and pointed at the back of Frankie's.

As he sprinted behind Frankie's, another car—a Crown Vic, T.J. realized—switched on its headlights just feet away from him.

"Oh shit!"

T.J. briskly cut into an alleyway.

The strange man behind the wheel gunned the Crown Vic at T.J., fishtailed, and knocked over several trashcans behind the restaurant.

Orlando followed the Crown Vic into the alleyway.

They couldn't keep up with T.J. through the tight turns and a maze of shortcuts. He cut through two other alleyways (much narrower than the ones before) until the two cars were out of sight.

"Should've taken Henry's advice," he said and breathed a sigh of relief.

After T.J. caught his breath, he crossed four other alleyways until he found himself a block away from Frankie's. Last thing they'd expect, T.J. figured as he paced down the sidewalk. He found the sign for Frankie's Footlongs just ahead. He glanced over his shoulder in intervals. One car passed, a white and blue one.

T.J. ducked into another alleyway.

After second glance, he realized the car wasn't just some ordinary car. It turned out to be a police cruiser. T.J. tried to flag down the cruiser (screaming out, "OVER HERE!"), but it was too late.

The cruiser took a right onto Main Street and kept driving, not braking the slightest. So, after some thought, T.J. took yet another alleyway back to Frankie's. In fact, it was the same alleyway from before.

On the way to Frankie's, Henry didn't bother to keep to the speed limit.

If a cop was to pull him over right now, they would easily throw him in jail for going at least thirty miles over the speed limit. He entered a school zone, but still that didn't stop him from slowing down.

*   *   *

The dressing room door opened.

Endo poked his head inside and said, "Let's do it, guys."

"Any sign?" Starlet asked cheerfully.

Their manager shook his head, which left Starlet and the rest of the band in a state of desolation.

"Like it or not, the show must go on," he said to her as well as the others.

In the hallway outside, the engineer, Omar, paced back and forth as he went over the notes to "Happy Trials" in his mind.

Next to Omar, James stood with his arms crossed and his head held downward. The pep talk hadn't done the least amount of good, clearly.

Deon was last to exit the dressing room. He strolled up to Omar and patted him on the back.

"Don't worry, Omar," he said arrogantly. "Just think. If you mess this up, then you'll never find a job in this business ever again."

Socks quickly followed, "Don't mind him. You're going to be fine."

"You think?"

"Of course."

"Thanks."

Socks looked down at Omar's hands.

They were both trembling.

"Just breathe," he said to Omar.

Omar did as Socks said and breathed, slowly this time.

While making his way down the alleyway, T.J. thought he saw Little Red in the back of the parking lot. So far, T.J. didn't see the two cars from earlier. Ever since he tried to flag down the police cruiser, he hadn't seen another car in sight. Not the Coupe Deville or the Crown Vic.

The closer T.J. reached the end of the alley, the clearer Little Red became. Part of the streetlight cast an eerie amber light over Little Red. Still, T.J. didn't have the slightest clue as to how he was going to drive to Central Reserve. Make it to the car, he concluded, and then I go from there. At this point in time, the concert was the last thing on his mind. Just make it to *Lil' Red*, T.J. thought. There was a bus stop not far from Frankie's.

Suddenly, T.J. heard a foot splash over a puddle of water!

A rush of blood raced across the backside of his head.

The sudden blow sent him stumbling forward.

Grabbing the backside of his head in agony, T.J. fell to the wet asphalt. A stream of blood trickled down the sides of cheeks and across his mouth. T.J. staggered to his feet, but a sudden dizzy spell sent him back to the asphalt.

Two blurry men stepped from behind the corner of the building and revealed themselves. One of the men was Officer Wheaten. The other was Officer Marson. They were both dressed in casual clothes. The one man was wearing a black nylon bomber jacket and the other one was wearing a blue windbreaker with LANSFORD POLICE DEPARTMENT on the front breast pocket.

Another man, scrawnier, made himself known.

Then, three more stepped from the shadows. One was a heavyset man while the other two were slender and fairly built.

T.J. cleared away the blur from his eyes and recognized Screw's face, as well as the three other guys whom T.J. had only heard about. *OCD?* The sight alone of Screw's gauntly face struck T.J. with ravenous anger. The sound of his teeth grinding together sounded like coarse leather being twisted and tightened. The two officers, as well as OCD, didn't personally know T.J. and T.J. himself didn't know OCD or the officers, which left him even more confused from their appearance. However, T.J. knew Screw, maybe even too well.

"There's how you fuck a nigga up right there, Screw," Cedric slurred to the others.

Swaying from side to side in his awkward strut, Screw tightened his grip over the baton. T.J.'s blood was dripping from the tip of the weapon. Most of the blood was gushing from the backside of T.J.'s head.

"Surprised, muthafucka," Screw sang, which caused several laughs from the other two officers.

Screw took yet another swing at T.J., but T.J. caught Screw's wrist and knocked the baton from his grip.

T.J. grabbed Screw by the collar and flung him against the wall and threw one right hook after another at Screw's kidneys. The beating provoked several laughs from OCD. T.J. was like a machine. He switched it up and threw in a couple of left jabs and then a combination, right hook, left jab, and then a right uppercut catching Screw in the jaw.

"Damn, Screw," Orlando said surprisingly from behind. "You're gonna let that nigga fuck you up like that."

T.J., the scrapper, was relentless. He continued his tireless assault on Screw.

An emotionless Officer Wheaten nodded at Cedric.

In return, Cedric glared at both Orlando and Detric, the smiles now removed from their faces.

Before T.J. could throw another punch, the members of OCD, including Screw—who was still recovering from his injuries—were on top of T.J., kicking and punching him. T.J. was thrown to the ground. He gazed up through the mass of bodies and saw yet another familiar man, Donnie's brother, Ted, at the end of the alleyway.

The stern man stood there with arms crossed and a sinister grin on his face, not dressed in his uniform. Like the other officers, he was dressed in casual clothes.

T.J. made an attempt to crawl away from the brutal assault, but he was quickly thrown back to the asphalt from a swift kick in the face.

At Central Reserve, the audience was buzzing from the recent performance.

As before, Omar paced around backstage and went over the song "Happy Trails" in his mind.

The stage director nodded at Starlet, who, like Omar, was equally nervous about the upcoming performance.

The band huddled together, said a prayer, and walked onto stage, while Omar waited in his position behind a thin four-foot wide transparent screen that stretched all the way up into the rafters.

Omar cleared the sweat from his brow, breathed deeply like Socks had told him recently, and said to himself, "You can do this, Omar. Just like we practiced at home."

Approaching T.J., Officer Wheaten said, "Where you running off to, tough guy?"

Officer Marson followed with a chuckle, "Not so tough anymore."

Screw, OCD, and the other two officers continued to wail on T.J.

"Enough," Ted said from behind the other men and approached T.J., bloody and curled in a fetal position. "Look at him." He kneeled down next to T.J. and studied his injuries. "Poor thing."

The others laughed.

Ted nodded at Screw.

"Nice work," he said and focused on T.J. The right side of T.J.'s face was battered. Thick streams of blood were oozing from his mouth. The faster T.J.'s heart raced, the faster the blood came gushing from his nose and mouth. A long gash over his face was oozing blood too. He coughed, tongued the upper part of his gums, and spat out a couple of teeth.

"Hello, T.J.," Ted said casually from above.

T.J. murmured and groaned a couple of words that were completely incoherent. He managed to spit out two more words, more distinguishable.

"Fffahhhekkk. . . youuuuu. . . "

"That's no way to speak to an old friend, T.J.," Ted said superiorly. "Say! Why aren't you running that big mouth of yours? No more dick jokes, T.J." Ted leaned in closer and tapped T.J. on the temple with his index finger. He said softly, "That's right because your jaw is probably broken right about now. But don't you worry. That's not the only thing we're going to break, my friend."

A *zoom!* And then a *zap!*

The screen suddenly lit up with a blinding light and revealed Omar's stark silhouette at stage level. The audience cheered from the sight of the mysterious saxophonist.

From the audience's viewpoint, the screen appeared like one continuous beam gleaming down from the heavens.

The song "Happy Trails" started with a brief solo on the saxophone.

So far, Omar hit all the right notes.

Then, Starlet joined in. . .

Ted stood from his kneeled position and paced around T.J.

"All of that fame must've really gone to your head," Ted sermonized. "The groupies," he eyeballed Screw, who was still recovering from his injuries, broken nose, possible broken ribs, "all the women constantly throwing themselves at you. For what? For money? For attention? For bragging rights? Or is it because their deadbeat daddies never loved them," and then Ted eyeballed Orlando, "or is it because, T.J., they can't find a decent man. All the money, the new house, the jewelry, all of that must've been really nice, T.J." He glanced down the alleyway toward Little Red parked behind Frankie's. "Surprised you didn't buy a new car with all of that money." Ted clapped his tongue against the roof on his mouth, which made him sound like a woodpecker. "That's a real shame, T.J. Think about what you could've done with all of that money." Ted thought carefully. "For starters, you could've bought yourself a new car. I mean," he shrugged his shoulders, "I would've." He pointed at Cedric. "Shank?" And then he pointed at Detric and said, "How about you?"

"Damn straight," Detric said with hesitation.

Ted directed his attention back to T.J.

"Otherwise, you probably wouldn't be lying here," Ted said, his voice finely molding with sarcasm. "Then, you could've given it back to your community. Right, T.J.? All of that money you made from pounding your little sticks against a drum. Isn't that what a brother should do? Help out another brother in need or those less fortunate. Help rebuild old schools and start charities. Nah, T.J. You're like the rest of them, these savages, these filthy degenerates. All you care about is yourself. And all you. . . you degenerates will keep on doing what you do, killing each other, tearing apart families. You're little boys. That's what you are. You a little boy afraid to become man." Ted kneeled down once more. "You think killing another man makes you a man?"

T.J. moaned, "I. . . I ain. . . ainnnn. . . "

"Shhh," Ted said jokingly to the other two officers, "the degenerate wants to say something."

"I ainnin't. . . killlll. . . nobodeee. . . "

"Sure you haven't, T.J.," he said. "But you will. I know you, T.J. It's only inevitable." Ted stood to his feet and paced around T.J. "You idolize and dress like these rappers and actors who glamorize violence and then you go out and kill one another. Ask Orlando. He knows what I'm talking about." Ted glared at OCD and spat in their direction. "By the rate you people keep killing yourself, I'd say sooner or later you'll be extinct." With his foot, Ted flipped over T.J. and looked him directly in the eyes. "We were born in violence, T.J. Brought up in violence. On the television. In the movies. In our music. It's what we are." He flicked T.J. on the shoulder. "It's in our blood. Am I right, T.J.? Us men, T.J., we're savage creatures. All we think about is fucking and killing. Right, T.J.?" Yet again, Ted kneeled over T.J. "What we had, it was *special*, T.J." Closer now. Close enough as to where T.J. could smell the alcohol on Ted's breath. "You didn't think you could walk off with all my dope without any consequences."

In a state of shock, T.J.'s eyes trailed upward and landed on Ted.

With a frown over his face, Ted glanced over at Screw.

"He didn't know, Screw," Ted said amusedly to Screw with a high pitch "ha-ha" erupting from his mouth. "But of course he didn't. 'He's like the rest of them,' I told you. You see, T.J." Ted loomed over T.J.'s helpless body and said, "In this town, *I* control the streets." Ted's eyes flared. "In this town," he said, "*I'm* god."

Starlet crooned: "*You left me all alone without saying good-bye. . .*"

In one last attempt, T.J. reached out to strangle Ted.

Before T.J. could grab Ted by the throat, Officer Marson kicked T.J. in the face.

"Stay the fuck down," he said from above.

A deep moan spilled from T.J.'s closed mouth.

Ted snorted with amusement.

"You see, T.J.," he said and paced around T.J. "In this town, I control the drug dealers and all the nasty criminals out there that you only hear about on the news. There's a price. It's called 'commission,' T.J. See Screw and OCD here sell the drugs that we pull off the streets to the same filthy degenerates and then we get a percentage of the sale. You see, T.J. It's a cycle of drugs and money that keeps going and going and going, round and round." Ted madly circled his hand around in the air. He paused in thought. "It's like that one commercial."

"The Energizer Bunny," Officer Marson said and smiled.

The others giggled.

"That's it," Ted said in awe. "The Energizer Bunny."

A crescendo in "Happy Trails."

Starlet's voice now soared: "*You left me here on the dusty trail, all alone, broken, and confused. . .*"

As Omar played another solo three and a half minutes into the song, his eyes flickered with great panic. A strange sensation crept into the base of his throat, which caused his esophagus to tighten and his tongue to swell. Omar hit a couple of wrong notes.

Suddenly, he violently gagged.

A tingling sensation built inside his chest. Then, it felt as if a hand reached into his throat. His eyes billowed in alarm now.

The audience observed Henry—or what they thought was Henry—fall to his knees behind the screen. However, most of the audience thought it was all a part of the show. Then, the audience saw Henry clutching his throat. Then, they knew something wasn't quite right.

Half of the audience fell silent.

In desperation, Omar tried to yank the saxophone from his mouth, but the reed tightly pinched over his tongue.

He moaned in agony.

The mouthpiece opened and clamped tighter over his tongue.

Omar screamed in horror.

"*Help. . .*" he garbled through his raspy throat.

Once more, he tried to pull Harry from his face.

The mouthpiece was so tight around his tongue that it drew blood from the corners of his mouth.

In a state of panic, he yanked as hard as he could over Harry's bow. The release was relieving and yet devastating at the same time.

Omar's swollen eyes crossed the stage below.

He frantically reached up to his gaping, drooling mouth.

The blood was now squirting from his mouth like a fissure in a water hose.

As soon as Omar witnessed it there, peculiarly squiggling in the mouthpiece, his eyes rolled in the back of his head. One of the mixers witnessed the horror and motioned to the other engineers. They ran over to Omar.

"Son of a bitch," one of the engineers uttered in disbelief. "He bit off his fucking tongue."

The mixer clutched his stomach in repulsion from the sight of Omar.

"I think I'm going to be sick," he said and briskly turned away and puked up his previous dinner over the speaker.

Once everyone realized what had happened, they called the paramedics, who were on standby not too far away.

Deon and Socks saw the commotion behind the screen. They quit playing and hurried over to Omar, who was now sprawled out over the stage. One engineer plugged Omar's mouth with a towel as well as a tee shirt. The blood just kept coming out. In a matter of seconds, a puddle of blood formed underneath Omar's head.

William quit playing, as well, and checked on the other band mates.

As far as Starlet, she kept singing.

Her eyes were mad and flared, possessed.

While the paramedics tended to Omar, Starlet continued to viciously sing.

"*. . . All alone! All broken! All confused!*"

As Ted paced around T.J., he sermonized, "You see, T.J. The great thing about doing what I do is that almost everybody at the station knows what the hell is going on. But do they say anything? No. The answer is no. And do you know why, T.J.?" T.J. didn't respond, couldn't. The pain settled over his body and left him clinging to consciousness. His eyes paddled around his head. The things around him became blurry and distorted. Not Ted's face, though. It most certainly remained clear. "I take that as a no. Then, I'll tell you. It's because nobody gives a shit. I got Screw here playing them all. And these degenerates are too fucking stupid to realize that they're getting played. A junkie gets caught once and learns a lesson. Gets clean, job. I say 'good for him, her, whatever.' I'll personally pat 'em on the back and send their merry self on his or her way. But when it happens twice, three times, four, then that just tells you something right there. These people, they're pretty much saying that they DON'T GIVE A SHIT about society, that they don't care about the *rules*. So, what better way than to teach them a lesson? That's when we come in. It's the *rules* that keep society from crumbling apart. It's the *rules* that keep things in order. You can't help people like that. The junkies, the degenerates or the homeless. . . " his eyes sharpened over T.J., ". . . the musicians, the ones who inspire disorder."

Officer Marson said, "Just like that one asshole. Remember?"

"What did they call him?"

"Right?" Ted said. "Mr. Vortex? How could I forget?"

"We fucked him up pretty good. Didn't we?"

T.J.'s eyes swelled in shock, greater this time.

His big eyes traced Ted's body in the coldest angle.

"Just like what we're going to do with our drummer boy here," Ted said, his voice rising. "Me, I say step on you people like roaches! That's what you are! The junkies, the degenerates, the homeless and the musicians, you're fucking cockroaches, always taking up space, making it more difficult for people to go on with their daily lives, contributing nothing to society! Are you listening to me, T.J.!"

T.J.'s spat a mouthful of blood at Ted. His jaw was so weak and numb that the spit dribbled from his mouth like warm molasses and didn't come close to hitting Ted.

In return, Ted grunted, wiped his own saliva from his lip, and nodded at Screw as well as the three in OCD.

"Break this drummer boy's arms. . . "

"With pleasure," Screw said, a small smile curling over his dark face as he strolled over to T.J.

Along the way, he patted the baton against his palm.

T.J. mercifully glanced through the downpour and up at Screw.

Officer Marson and Wheaten held out T.J.'s arms while Orlando stepped from behind him, wrapped his thick arm around T.J.'s neck, and kept his head stable. Screw reared back the baton and struck down on both of T.J.'s arms and elbows.

T.J. moaned loudly.

He squirmed and tried to free his arm from the officer's grip.

With another whack, his forearm split in two halves.
The second arm didn't break as easily.
Screw struck down repeatedly until the bone shattered.
Armless now, T.J. struggled to crawl away.
Along the way, the blood slowly seeped from each orifice of his face. T.J. was moving painfully slow, snail-like. He used his right shoulder to push himself forward but didn't get anywhere—maybe a few feet. A couple of fingernails dug in the asphalt and then broke off from where he made an attempt to pull himself to safety.
"So sad," Ted uttered, unfolding his collar. He solemnly looked at the two officers and said, "Kill this piece of shit and then throw it in the trash," and then he strolled away.

When Henry finally arrived at Frankie's, the rain had let up a bit. He parked in the front, near the ordering lane, and, on foot, tracked down Little Red parked in the back of the parking lot. The keys were still inside. In fact, they were dangling from the ignition. Henry scoured the parking lot, but he didn't find any sign of T.J.
As Henry inched around the front of the drive-thru, he swore he heard a person groaning from the back.
Henry rushed toward the direction of the groan.
Trashcans were toppled over the steamy ground.
He darted toward the trashcans.
In a state of frenzy, Henry scoured the area and found fresh tire tracks. Despite the previous rain, the smell of an engine was still fresh in the humid air. Then, Henry saw a trail of blood flowing over a stream of rainwater. The trail led to yet another trashcan, the only one standing. Henry's heart pounded like a kick drum, beating harder and faster. The shock rippled through his body.
Without doubt, he knew his friend was inside the trashcan even though the black man inside was completely unrecognizable—only the leftover remains of a man scrapped from the streets and thrown away like trash.

Henry looked twice. Again, the face was unrecognizable from all the blood, cuts, bruises, and welts.

Crying now, he darted over to the trashcan and studied the man's face. Mentally, he shaved away the damage, the carnage, and saw his friend, T.J.

Henry was shrieking out, "No. . . no. . . no. . ."

Next, he grabbed T.J.'s neck and checked for a pulse.

He barely found one.

"Oh God," he cried, which sounded more like a baby's cackle. "Oh God! T.J.!"

T.J. was unresponsive.

Henry fell to his knees and reached up to T.J.

"T.J.," he cried. "No. . ."

Moments later, Henry arrived at Lansford Medical Center in his Porsche.

Henry sped up the Emergency Room ramp and skidded directly in front of the entrance.

All covered in blood, he yelled to the top of his lungs, "HELP! PLEASE! HELP!"

A team of nurses and paramedics sprinted from the entrance. Henry was in the process of carrying T.J. from the passenger seat when a team of nurses grabbed a hold of T.J. before he fell to the ground.

Henry cried out, "Watch his arms!"

The nurses carefully placed T.J. onto a gurney and immediately wheeled him into the emergency room.

Disoriented, Henry tried his best to keep up with the nurses. One of them was asking him all kinds of questions (*What happened to him? Are you two related? Is he allergic to any medication?*), which were going in one ear and out the other. The lead nurse held out her hand and blocked off Henry before he could follow them into the ICU.

"I'm sorry, sir," she informed. "You can't be here."

Another nurse stepped in front of Henry and guided him to the waiting room.

THIRTY-ONE

AFTER the excitement died out, Henry managed to make a couple of telephone calls in the waiting room, one to his manager James and the other to T.J.'s mother, which turned out to be one of the hardest telephone conversations that he had ever made in his life.

While Henry waited for word on T.J.'s condition, he sat on the hallway floor with his back against the wall and his hands cupped around his knees.

Next to him, the automatic doors from the ICU would periodically swing open with a team of nurses and doctors or a gurney scampering by, but Henry didn't pay any attention to them. His focus remained forward on the parallel wall. His mind was like a padded cell. The rage was like a foreign being causing bedlam in his mind.

With slow and steady breaths, the great rage would take on other forms, sharp and precise, strategic. Another was mountainous, like a nurturing beast, eyes crimson and flaring over an ocean of darkness, cradling a baby in its arms.

Henry's thoughts were racing uncontrollably, the rage. Thoughts of T.J. and the path he had chosen with Henry, now the horror, the blood, his skull crushed, the skin swollen, the smell of urine on his face, the two broken arms, and then the people responsible for committing such inhumane, horrendous acts. Henry deliberately banged the back of his head against the wall until there was a knot. The rage was like fire running in his veins. His eyes flared over the endless darkness. Gnawing! Cursing God! How could you let this happen? Why? What's the reason? Why T.J.? Why not me? If anybody, it should be me! Not my T.J.! Why couldn't you stop them? Each muscle in his body flexed to the point of tearing. Henry kept banging the backside of his head until his head hurt. One side of Henry yearned for the thoughts to go away. How persistent they were. Flashing violently over his mind's eye, the blood, the horror, the smell. Tormenting. Feeding the rage! Maybe if he banged hard enough they would flee far away from his thoughts and never return. Another side of him yearned for the punishment. Then, after the banging stopped, the emotion vanished from his body, his face. And he just sat there, quiet and shaking.

About ten minutes later (Henry was so distraught he lost track of time), the rest of the band arrived at Lansford Medical Center.

With the black mascara smeared around the sides of her cheeks, Starlet hurried down the hallway and shouted out, "Where is he? Where's T.J.?"

Henry quickly stood to his feet and embraced Starlet in his arms.

"He's in surgery," he said softly over her shoulder.

"What happened?"

She pulled herself away and faced Henry.

"He was beat up," he said.

The tears fell from her bloodshot eyes and traced like ink down the center of her cheeks.

"How bad?"

Henry didn't respond.

"How bad, Henry?"

Henry rolled his tearful eyes upward at Starlet and answered, "Bad."

He sobbed uncontrollably.

Emotions like the rage and the sadness and the thoughts of what had recently happened to his friend were unable to control. The vase, which held all these emotions together, had shattered inside Henry. Now, all Henry had to do was pick up the pieces and put them back together. Even that seemed like a job not worth handling. His breath vibrated like the tail of a rattlesnake. Starlet's hands balled into fists like two steely hammers pressed against Henry's kidneys. She squeezed the sides of the blazer tighter, leaving deep wrinkles behind.

Then, Henry pulled Starlet closer to his body, held onto her as tightly as he could, and cried into her ear, "Oh my God."

The rest of the band was speechless. They too were just as distraught about everything that had happened. Henry ended up pulling the other band mates into a group hug.

After four painful hours expired in the waiting room, Deon decided to fetch some sodas and junk food from the vending machine. He brought a couple of bags of Oreo cookies and Doritos over to the band. Last but not least, he offered a grape soda and a bag of pretzels to Henry. As before, with that same vague expression over his face, Henry shook his head no.

Deon suggested the Oreos.

Still, he accepted nothing.

"Come on, Henry," he urged. "You have to eat something."

Starlet, who was sitting next to Henry, slid her hand over Henry's hand. She caressed the top of his hand.

Henry glared at Deon and drawled, "I said, 'I'm not hungry.'"

The malicious look left Deon temporarily speechless. It was as if he witnessed firsthand a singular entity, as rare as a mythical sighting. Deon took a couple of steps backward and distanced himself from the eyes of a man who only had blood on his mind. Since Deon didn't have a mean bone in his body, he didn't have any knowledge of what it meant to have that kind of hankering for blood, for vengeance, for absolute destruction, to hunt down each and every person responsible for such a crime toward his friend and do things to them that the authorities could never do. Throughout his brief existence, Deon had never experienced such darkness. The only tragedy he had experienced was when The Doors' frontman, Jim Morrison, or drummer, John Bonham, from Led Zeppelin, both passed at an early age. And Deon wasn't even aware of their deaths at the time. Deon was only five years old when Bonham passed. Morrison passed before he was even born. When he discovered the two bands in the sixth grade, his brother, Duncan, broke the news about their deaths. Dark times. So, when Deon witnessed Henry's primitive eyes, he was left frightened and more cautious.

"When you are," Deon said gingerly and threw down his arms, "you let me know. Okay?"

William leaned over to look at Henry.

"Hey, Henry," he whispered. "I was going to grab some smokes. I can stop by the house and grab some clothes."

In a trance, Henry glanced down at his clothes, at all the blood. He ran his pruned hands over his shirt and pants in fascination. Then, his hands gripped the damp clothes. He moved his eyes up at William.

Another glare.

"I'll go grab you some clothes," William said cautiously. "Straight?"

"Yeah," Henry said in a trance.

William and Socks left the waiting room and stood outside in the hallway.

"What's wrong with him?"

"He's in shock."

"Right now, Willie," Socks said and glanced at Henry in the waiting room, "I think we all are."

After another painful hour passed, Mr. and Mrs. Livingston finally showed up at the hospital.

As soon as Henry told them what had happened to their son, the two parents both broke down and cried into each other's arms. Mrs. Livingston took the news about her son the hardest.

Not too long after, William and Socks returned with a new pair of clothes: a gray hooded jacket, a plain white tee shirt, and a pair of black jeans. Henry went into the restroom to change. As he removed the wet, cold, sticky shirt and blazer from his body, he bit down on the bottom of his lip and tried to seal the scream that was climbing through the pit of his chest. The hankering, that gnawing was back. Stronger! For some time, the gnawing had sat there in his chest, waiting for the shock to clear away. Now, it showed its ugly head.

Henry reared back and punched the mirror with his fist.

Sharp blades of glass fell into the sink.

A couple of blood drops trickled down his knuckles and splashed over the blades of glass in the sink.

In a daze, his vengeful eyes fell upon the multiple reflections, the drops of blood. Each one was unlike the other, distorted.

The door behind Henry suddenly shook.

"Henry," Deon was calling out from behind the door. "You okay in there?"

"Fine," he said, his voice trembling.

Deon sat against the wall and waited for Henry to exit.

"Mr. and Mrs. Livingston?" a voice said from the opening of the waiting room.

Optimistic, T.J.'s parents stood up from their chairs.

Deon knocked on the restroom door.

"Go away, Deon. . . "

"Henry," he said over Henry's mumble. "It's the doctor."

Henry threw on the shirt and jacket, scrambled over to the toilet, and wrapped toilet paper around his hand. As he quickly exited the restroom, he bumped into Deon. They rushed over to the doctor. The other band mates gathered around T.J.'s parents.

"We finally stopped the internal bleeding," the doctor informed. "T.J. suffered a great deal of injuries: collapsed lung, several broken ribs, broken jaw, both of his arms are broken, and. . . " then, his face went long, ". . . there was also severe trauma to the brain. Whoever did this to T.J., well. . . you get the picture."

Henry asked, "When can we see him?"

"He's stable at the moment," the doctor said. "But I'm afraid he's going to have to go back into surgery. We are talking heavy reconstructive surgery here. If he does manage to survive this ordeal then," the doctor sighed, "then most likely he'll be eating from a feeding tube for the rest of his life."

Henry asked, "Can he talk?"

"Listen, young man," the doctor said grimly, "there was severe damage to your friend's brain. Just imagine holding a plate of jello and then throwing that plate of jello against the wall. That's what T.J.'s brain looks like. So right now, it would take a miracle for your friend to speak. We'll do all we can for T.J." His eyes crossed T.J.'s parents. "We have some of the best doctors around the world working on T.J. But if I were you, I would start praying."

Once more, Starlet broke down into Henry's arms. As before, her hands switched over into fists. After it all sank in, especially the doctor's grim remarks, she pulled herself from Henry and ran out of the waiting room.

THIRTY-TWO

AT dawn, the rest of the band mates, William, Socks, and Deon, went home to get a little shuteye while Henry and Starlet stayed behind at the hospital. T.J.'s parents were still there as well. The whole time, the two resilient warriors, Mr. and Mrs. Livingston, were wide-awake. For about an hour or so, they asked Henry the basic questions: *What had he been up to? What was it like to be a rock star? Did he get treated any different when he was in public?* Mrs. Livingston did most of the talking. Like her husband, she, too, was still left in awe from how much Henry had grown, how he had "shot up like Jack and his beanstalk," and how he was no longer the little "shrimp," as he was known around Reddington. Then, the laughing and catching up stopped. Moods turned serious, so did the questions. For another hour, Mr. and Mrs. Livingston both grilled Henry about who may have done this to their son. Henry had an idea of who was responsible from a previous conversation he and T.J. shared outside a music store, Chessman's, but he never told them. Instead, he dodged every question that came his way and kept it all to himself.

Later that morning, the weary doctor came into the waiting room.

"Mr. and Mrs. Livingston. . ."

Mr. Livingston shook his sleeping wife on the shoulder.

They both glimmered with anticipation.

". . . Your son's surgery was a success," he informed and smiled through his closed mouth.

T.J.'s mother cupped her hand over her mouth and concealed the excitement.

"Can we see him?" she asked.

The doctor nodded his head.

"But only two of you," he said.

T.J.'s mother grabbed Henry by the hand.

"It should be you, Henry."

"But you're his mother."

"And you're his brother," she said and urged Henry to visit T.J. "Go. You and Starlet go see my T.J."

Both Henry and Starlet walked through the intensive care unit, or ICU, and stood at the edge of T.J.'s room.

When Starlet witnessed his condition, she broke down yet again. She couldn't even recognize him from all of the bandages and the tubes, which were attached to a breathing machine. Henry pulled her close and tightly held her in his arms. Together, they both shuffled their way into the room and got a closer look. Each one of his arms had metal rods in them in order to keep them from bending. On each side of his arms there were long slits to reduce the swelling and pressure caused by compartment syndrome. He had white bandages wrapped around his face—one side of his face being as big and round as a grapefruit.

They both stood over T.J.

"I love you, T.J.," Henry said, sniffling the phlegm from his nose. He didn't bother wiping the tears from his eyes. Yet, he let them run wild, same with the phlegm now. "I'm going to find out who did this to you. Okay, brother? I'm going to find out who did this to you. . . even if it takes my entire life. Okay, T.J.? I'm going to find the people who did this to you."

Starlet didn't know what to think of Henry's comments. One side embraced the comments, the promises that were extremely heavy and heartfelt. The other side was frightened to death. She slid herself from Henry's arms, leaned over the bed, and kissed T.J. over the sliver of warm, unmarked flesh that was showing on his forehead. Right now words couldn't explain how she felt.

Starlet's eyes were red from all the crying and rubbing.

As Starlet patiently stood in front of Henry, a tiny glint lifted in her eyes.

"I'll call you if anything changes," she said carefully, with her voice still cracking from the wear as she gradually oozed her weakened body inside Henry's arms. Henry breathed in deeply and massaged the backside of Starlet's neck. The touch of her body alone, especially after witnessing T.J.'s critical condition, temporarily nurtured that gnawing sensation in the pit of his stomach, the vengeance, and replaced it with one of great warmth and delight. Henry didn't pay any attention to the hospital surroundings, the nurses rushing around them to other patients, or family members tending to other loved ones. The embrace was like two drained energy sources reconnecting, now sharing equal strength. Before he pulled himself from the hug, Starlet readjusted her grip around his waist and said, "I love you," and pecked Henry on the cheek. The secretion left from the kiss was half phlegm, half tears, half saliva. The wet smudge over his cheek didn't bother Henry. Not the least. Those words, though, so catalytic, cut through him like a lightning bolt.

With his senses heightened, Henry barely cracked open his mouth.

"I. . ."

Starlet squeezed Henry's hand from below.

"You don't have to say it back."

"But. . ."

She tightened her grip around Henry's hand.

"I'll call you."

"Call me," he said softly as he stared into her sore eyes.

Once more, Starlet wiped the tears from her eyes and bobbed her head.

She said somberly, "Goodbye, Henry."

The kiss stayed warm on Henry's cheek. That wasn't what stayed with him the most. It was what she said. Not her "I love you," but her "goodbye." Starlet said the word as if this was the last time she was ever going to see Henry. What did she mean by that? Did she know Henry's intentions?

As Henry reached the end of the hallway, he turned his shoulder and witnessed Starlet with her hands cupped over her face. She couldn't bring herself to look back at Henry. The temptation was there, to run to her, to embrace her once more, to absorb her, the strength, and to tell her that things were going to be all right and that they were going to get through this.

These urges came and went.

Right now, the blood was back.

The vengeance.

After he exited the ICU floor, two men in trench coats approached Henry from behind. One was older. Another was at least twenty to thirty years younger with hair gelled to the side.

"Mr. Burl?" the older one said.

"Yeah. . . "

Henry slowed down his walk, thinking about the recent conversation with Starlet.

"I'm Detective Corpus," the older man said, pulled out his wallet, and showed Henry the badge inside. The other detective pulled out his badge as well and displayed it close for Henry to see. "This here is my partner, Detective Devon Merrotti." The young detective greeted Henry with a flick of the head, a kind of arrogant nod. "Listen, I know you've been through a lot these past couple of days. So, I'll make this as quick as possible."

"Whatever," Henry said with frustration and then kept on walking.

"Can I ask you a couple of questions?"

Henry said, "You're going ask anyway. Right?"

Corpus followed Henry.

With both hands in his pockets, the other detective, the younger one, eased back and kept his distance.

"Are you aware of any enemies T.J. might've had?"

Henry was slow to answer.

"Not to my knowledge."

"None?" Corpus asked.

"No," Henry said again. "None."

"Okay," the detective drawled. "Have you ever heard of the name Johnnie Farrow?"

"I don't know anybody by that name."

"On the street, the kids call him Screw."

Henry tilted his head in curiosity.

"I take it you've heard of him."

"T.J. may have mentioned his name once before," Henry said and glanced over at the detective. "You think he did this to T.J.?"

"We don't know yet, Mr. Burl," he said. "We're going to find out who did this to your friend."

"Then, why are you wasting time talking to me."

"If you don't mind me asking," Corpus said, pointing to the fresh bruises on Henry's face. "Where exactly did you get those marks?"

Henry suddenly grimaced.

"I'm sure you already know, Detective," Henry seethed. "You wouldn't be talking to me if you didn't. Right?"

"I'm just trying to help."

"How dare you?"

The anger tightened over Henry's face like a hand shaping a baseball glove. Wrinkles formed around the sides of his eyes. Jaw clinched. Before he stormed to the hospital exit, he glared at the two detectives before him.

As Henry was about to exit, Detective Corpus hollered out, "You don't remember. Do you?"

Henry stopped at the entranceway.

"Detective Corpus," the older detective said, grinning and holding out his arms.

Henry shook his head, spun around, and faced the old detective.

"So. . . "

"I was the one who worked on your father's case," Corpus said casually. "I spoke to your mother, Abbey I believe, while you were playing basketball with your friends."

"Oh yeah," Henry said sternly. "And how did that work out?"

Henry hurried from the hospital.

Merrotti strolled up to Corpus.

Hands still in pockets.

He said imperiously, "That didn't go so well, Al."

Corpus glared at Merrotti and said, "Like you could've done any better," and then strolled down the hallway without his partner.

THIRTY-THREE

WHEN Henry finally returned home to his high-rise condo on the hills of Madison, he went straight to his bedroom and closed the door behind him. He hadn't thought about what he was going to do to Harry the moment he wrapped his hands around him.

In a state of frenzy, he searched for Harry under the bed, in the closet, and on the dresser; but he couldn't find the saxophone anywhere. He hurried back into the living room and then moved his search to the kitchen.

There, he saw the saxophone case lying on the kitchen table.

"You. . . " he said, his voice trembling in rage, ". . . You did this to me. How could you?"

He dashed toward the worn case, opened it, and pulled out the saxophone.

With his eyes wide and menacing, he gazed over Harry from neck to bow. His hands were shaking, slowly at first and then violently. He paced back into his bedroom with the saxophone gripped tightly in hand. Henry did two laps around the room from closet to dresser, dresser to closet, before he fell to his knees and let out a piercing wail from his chest. The wail exploded from his mouth like the roar of a lion.

Outside, a couple of surrounding condo lights flickered on.

Back in the bedroom, Henry was smashing Harry over the floor.

"YOU MO. . . MOTHERFUCKER!" Henry shouted out as he flung the saxophone against the wall. He picked up the dented saxophone and struck it against the corner of the dresser, which caused a couple of keys to break loose. Next, he stomped the saxophone with the base of his heel until it was completely inoperable. "FUCKIN' PIECE OF SH. . . PEICE OF SHIT! HOW DO YOU LIKE THAT NOW! HUH? DIE, MOTHERFUCKER! DIE! DIE!"

Parts, keys and rods mostly, were flying all around his head.

But Henry didn't stop there.

Once the saxophone was destroyed, he stomped some more until he was finally out of breath.

THIRTY-FOUR

FOR the rest of the day, Henry dragged himself around the condo. He spent most of the time waiting next to the telephone wondering if it was going to be Star or Mrs. Livingston who would tell him that T.J. was dead.

For hours, he was plumped in the same exact position on the floor of his living room: his back against the front of the couch, head hung downward, glassy expression over his face, eyes gazing over the photographs from Abbey's photo albums. The only time Henry got up from the floor was to fetch another bottle of wine. So far, he had gone through a bottle of Cabernet Sauvignon.

Now, he was working on the second bottle.

On the coffee table, a knife rested next to the half empty bottle of wine.

A look of contentment suddenly glistened over Henry's face as he looked over the old photographs. His lips were stained the color purple from all the wine he had drunk. Tongue purple too like a Gila monster. He would take gulps from the glass of wine, not polite sips, and then flip through past photos: Henry and T.J. as teenagers, his mother (there was one that her aide, Odyssey, had taken of him standing next to his mother's bedside when she became ill), Henry holding the soprano, Adrian, in Ms. Craft's private studio (the edges were crumbled from where Abbey had thought about trashing the photo), Henry playing basketball (AAU as well as around the blacktops on Davie Morris), and then a photograph of two little girls standing in front of an old cabin in the desert. A double take: two brown-eyed girls, nine or ten perhaps (Henry didn't know), complexion sallow from the desert sun, were dressed in all white dresses, which were both stained with smudges of dirt and mud. *Sedona*, Henry remembered the conversation he had with his mother on her deathbed. She talked about Sedona, the vast beauty of the desert, the mountains and how they were shaped like cathedrals and then. . . that mysterious light. Then, his mother talked about her father, her real one. A white man who always wore a suit and tie. Henry remembered his mother said he came to visit her in Sinclair Leprieur. Left a different man.

Intrigued, Henry placed this one particular photo, the one of Sedona and the strange cabin, at the edge of the coffee table.

Next, he came across one photograph that he had never seen before. The photograph was taken on Henry's second birthday. A black man had taken the photo in front of a bedside mirror. In the mirror, he was holding a bulky camera and smiling from ear to ear. His teeth were clean and bright. He was older, he realized, familiar. Henry studied the black man in the photograph with his weary, bloodshot eyes. For a second, he thought he could see a face behind the bright flash in the mirror. Then, once the strain cleared from his eyes, Henry saw him, his father, Henry the Fourth. He looked so happy, his father did. Then, he came across yet another photograph. Henry (The Fifth) was two and a half. His mother had taken the picture in the master bedroom. The same man, his father, was standing in the reflection of the mirror, only this time he didn't look so happy. He looked almost depressed.   Henry reached into the box and pulled out yet another photo album.   The front read "The McClintock Family Tree."   Henry placed the photo album aside and found a couple of worn hardbacks in the box.   He pulled out the hardbacks, one called *The Winds of Eastback* and the other called *Mimi's Bluff*, which were both written by the author, Julius Hampton.   The name didn't ring a bell.   Henry couldn't remember how many times his mother had talked about one man in particular, his grandfather, a writer, who lived in Sedona, while on her deathbed.   His name, however, was William Wright, WW.   "He was the salt of the earth, Mr. Wright was," she once said.   "Blamed for a crime he did not commit."   Henry retraced the conversation with his mother in his head.   "I wish you could've met your grandfather, Henry," Abbey told Henry.   Whenever Abbey talked about her father, she always did so with a smile on her face. Never had Henry seen his mother smile like that before. Henry flipped over the hardback of *Mimi's Bluff* and read the biography in the back.

J. HAMPTON is the author of The Fire Dance, which won an Edgar Allen Poe award, and The Winds of Eastback. He lives with his cat, Achilles, in Sedona, Arizona.

"Sedona," Henry slurred and placed the photograph of the two girls inside the hardback, *The Winds of Eastback*.

After he skimmed through soiled folders and worn books (a couple of them being *occult* paperbacks that he collected when he went through what he liked to call a "Goth phase" at the latter stages of the age of seventeen), he placed them aside, mainly the one hardback, *The Winds of Eastback*, and riffled through the other belongings inside the box.

His next discovery was one of confusion.   Buried deep in the box was a One Step camera, which reeked of cigarette smoke, as well as a Nike shoebox full of Polaroids that he and T.J. had taken when they were younger: the two on the courts or messing around with that Casio in Henry's bedroom.   Like the basketball, he took that camera with him everywhere.   The other items to the right of the One Step were a mystery.   He closely studied the two items, a Chinon

Whisper Dual 8 projector, as well as a Chinon 723 XL, both of which Henry had never seen before. Then, as he pulled the spool of film, a memory came to him. One afternoon, when he was a senior in high school, he accidentally walked in on his mother watching old reels of himself when he was around two or three years old. At the time, Henry didn't have the time to reminisce with his mother or even ask her what she was doing. He remembered that he was in a hurry. He forgot his basketball shorts. When he got back from basketball practice, he had a history test to study for that night. Henry *didn't* have the time. But he would be lying if he didn't say that accidentally walking in on his mother watching old movies of her son when he was younger never lingered with him throughout practice. After he finished basketball practice and his studying, he searched the house for the Super 8. Henry even checked the attic of the house. He never found the film that Abbey was watching on the bedroom wall. And he never asked his mother about the film either. Not that night or the next morning. Maybe she threw it away, Henry wondered, or. . . The next school day came and went, but Henry didn't have the time to search for the film. And then, the next day came and the film disappeared from Henry's thoughts like a two-day-old smudge of ink on his finger.

He pushed the video equipment aside and came across an old newspaper article, which dated back to March of 1989, and like the others, was soiled and worn. He carefully unfolded the delicate newspaper and found an article on his father—Henry the Fourth—on the second page. He read the name *Timothy Snead* in his head over and over and over again until the name brought forth the pain as well as the mystery of his father's death. Unlike most of the artifacts inside the boxes, Henry was well aware of the article, in fact, too aware. When Abbey had finally showed Henry the article after their return from Sinclair Leprieur (several months prior to the trip, that one name, Timothy Snead, had been living there inside his head), he was left in a state of confusion—mainly, as to why his father, who was once a famous musician known domestically and internationally as the legendary saxophonist, Mr. Vortex, was living on the streets of Lansford without any food or money. For years, such a name, Timothy Snead, was like a thumbtack against his mind. Over time (in fact, after his freshman year of college), the thumbtack had loosened and fallen into his other thoughts. Now, that one name, *Snead, Timothy* Snead was back. Sharp. Sturdy. Pinned up like a tack on a wall.

Not going anywhere. Not anytime soon, he realized.

Like the photograph from Sedona, he slipped the newspaper inside *The Winds of Eastback* book and then placed them aside.

Next, he picked up the photo album from the coffee table. Inside, there were old photos of his father, his grandfather, Henry the Third, a devoted Catholic who worked as a salesman at Rooney Hills and played the saxophone on the weekends whenever he wasn't traveling from city to city selling cookies and crackers (four years prior to Henry the Fifth's birth, the Third passed away from a massive stroke), his great grandfather, the Second, a well-known street performer, and even his great great grandfather, the First, all of whom resembled Henry the Fifth from either the eyes, the brow, or the chin. They were *all* musicians. Every last one of them. Each photo Henry came across he could see these very men, his late ancestors, who were nothing more than strangers to him, in his head, performing either on a stage or on the side of Bourbon Street like the Second, who was, in fact, a legend around Louisiana.

He placed the photo album aside and found more photographs of his father in the bottom of the box, ones that were meant to stay buried for Henry's sake. This time Abbey had taken the photographs. There were photos taken at concerts, more photos of Henry and his father, ones of the two shooting hoops together. Henry was around the age of two. He wiped the dust from them and did his best to avoid smudging them with greasy fingerprints.

One photograph in particular drew tears from his eyes. Henry cleared the tears before they could fall onto the photograph of his father lounging on a burgundy recliner with his son's head held peacefully against his chest. The Fourth was kissing the top of his son's forehead, Henry's forehead.

"*You bitch. . .*" he seethed, the tears now flowing from his eyes. "You fucking bitch! How could you?"

As Henry flipped through even more photographs in the box, his eyes accidentally crossed the glistening blade on the coffee table. Henry reached to grab the bottle of wine, which was resting just over the edge of the table. The bottle suddenly slipped from his greasy fingertips and crashed against the side of the table. For three or four cycles, the bottle spun around the table until it fell to the floor. Red wine came gushing out over the table and then the carpet. Some of the red wine splashed over the photos, ruining the childhood ones, the ones of T.J., leaving them stained with the color red.

Henry hissed, "Shit!"

As he moved backward away from the puddle, he keenly watched the remaining drops of wine dribble from the bottle. The puddle of wine provoked something inside Henry. In his mind's eye, he saw a flash of his friend's face, T.J.'s face, all bloody and pleading for help. T.J., who remained helplessly inside the trashcan, called out, "Help me. . . help me, Henry. . ."

Henry forced the stark image from his head, salvaged the other photo albums, and placed them on the coffee table.

As he moved the wet photographs from the puddle, he came across another item from his past. This wasn't a photograph. Not the slightest. It was his mother's music box. He carefully picked up the music box and cradled the thing in his hands. The music skipped at first. Then, steadied. The ballerina inside twirled round and round.

"You bitch. . ." Henry cried and gasped, ". . . you dumb fucking bitch. . ."

Screaming until the veins swelled in his forehead, Henry chucked the music box against the wall as hard as he could. The box shattered into pieces. The toy ballerina inside the box broke apart, mostly at the limbs. The remaining pieces scattered over the floor, parts underneath the couch.

Henry was forced to his knees where he finally caught his breath.

Once more, his eyes—accidentally or not—crossed the blade on the coffee table.

He picked up the knife and marveled at the blade.

As Henry carefully traced his finger across the blade, he felt the sharpness. The blade made a painless slit over his skin. A drop of blood blossomed over the slit.

It's the coward's way out.

Yet, the blade felt so right, so good against his flesh.

Suddenly, there was a knock at the door.

Startled, Henry stood to his feet and shouted out, "Just a second!"

He frantically gazed around the room and searched for something, anything to cover up the mess. Henry found a pillow from the couch, threw the pillow over the puddle of wine, grabbed the knife, and cautiously walked over to the door. Starlet was standing behind the peephole, her face twice the size as her body. Henry gradually eased the knife behind his back, took in a deep breath, cleared away the tears from his face, and answered the door.

"Starlet," he said surprisingly.

"Is everything all right?" she asked suddenly. "I heard a loud noise."

"It's fine," Henry said. "Did anything happen to T.J.? You didn't call."

She didn't even bother to wait for Henry to invite her inside. She stepped right inside the condo and didn't say a word.

Confused, Henry said, "Star?"

She said flatly, "T.J.'s stable, Henry."

"Then why are you here?"

Starlet unbuttoned the collar from her silk blouse and presented one of her breasts for Henry.

With her breast exposed, Starlet took one step toward Henry and kissed him on the lips.

Henry pulled away.

"I can't do this right now," Henry said, closing his watery eyes. "I'm too vulnerable."

Starlet replied, "Aren't we all."

Henry's eyes traced over Starlet's lips.

"I need you," she said, her eyes honing in on Henry's.

"What about T.J.?"

"Shut up," she said unevenly, her eyes filling with tears.

Starlet reached out and grabbed the backside of Henry's head. She thrust her plump lips into Henry's. Her tongue plunged into his mouth and swirled around his tongue.

While madly kissing one another from different angles, they stumbled into the bedroom and didn't even bother to turn off the light.

THIRTY-FIVE

AFTER Henry and Starlet finished having sex, they smoked cigarettes in bed.

In a strange silence, they both lay with their pillows folded behind their heads. The sweat was rolling down their warm bodies. A full ashtray was lying over Henry's chest. After each drag Starlet took from the cigarette, she would carefully flick the ash into the ashtray. Henry wasn't so vigilant. He smoked the cigarette down to the filter and flicked away the ash only once after the second drag. In the meantime, Starlet noticed the round punctures in the wall that were the size and shape of fists, as well as the flattened saxophone pieces on the floor, but she never quite asked Henry as to why there were holes in the walls or pieces of Harry scattered on the floor—at least not directly.

"Looks like a hurricane swept through this place," she said, blowing the remaining smoke from her mouth. One of her legs was resting over Henry's legs, kind of like holding hands but with legs.

Henry said simply, "Yeah."

He took a slow drag from the cigarette.

Over another wave of silence, Starlet said, "Tell me what happened."

Henry remained cool as he had been doing after the sex.

"Don't want to talk about it," he said.

Starlet directed her attention toward Henry.

"Don't shut me out, Henry," Starlet said. "Please don't. . ."

Henry sighed and answered, "I got mad."

"Yeah," she said sarcastically. "Obviously."

Starlet waited for more.

Henry glanced into Starlet's eyes and witnessed the anticipation swelling inside them.

"I. . . I. . . I'm turning. . ." Henry said and sighed once more, ". . . I'm turning into my father right before my eyes and it scares the living hell out of me."

"Who was your father, Henry?"

"He was a saxophonist," Henry answered without any hesitation. "But that's not what bothers me. I've never even met the man and yet I know everything about him through his music . . . and photographs."

"You never met him?"

"No," Henry mumbled. "My mother kicked him out on the streets when I was little. All he is to me is a forgotten memory."

"Was your father famous?"

Henry paused, unsure whether or not to tell the truth.

"Not really," he said clearly. "He and my mother split when I was two or three. I don't even remember. I'm a bastard, Starlet. Plain and simple." He shook his head with amazement, not disgust. "From what I've been told, he had other children with other women."

"Well, I'm on the pill," Starlet said with a grin on her face. "If that's what you're concerned about."

"No," he said as he barely cracked a smile. "It's not that."

Starlet moved closer.

She asked, "Then what is it, Henry?"

"From what I've seen and heard, my father was never a happy man," he said. "I always wondered if he ever did find happiness. When I look at old photographs, I see those shades of happiness there in his eyes when he was with me. But my mother said he always walked around with this, this black cloud over his head. Maybe he did. I don't know. It's just. . ." Henry cleared his throat, ". . . when I look at these pictures, I don't see that at all. I see a man who was trying to do the best he could with all he had, even if it was nothing."

"I would like to see those photographs whenever you have the time."

"Sure," he said, smiling. "I got a whole stack of them in the closet."

He reached over and gently stroked Starlet's shaved scalp. As he was stroking her scalp, the question nearly spilled from his lips. *Do you believe in black magic?* Unaware of what Starlet's reaction might be, Henry was mindful enough to correct the abrupt start in question with a sigh.

"What is it, Henry?"

Henry puffed from his cigarette.

"A hiccup," he said.

"These past days have been crazy," Starlet said, her eyes widening. "T.J., Omar. . ."

Henry shook his head and said, "Omar?"

"You know," she said, "what happened at the concert. . ."

"What do you mean?"

Henry placed the ashtray on the nightstand and sat upright.

"What happened at the concert?"

"I don't know," she said, sitting upright as well. "Something terrible. I don't know the whole story. But they said Omar's tongue was severed. You should've seen it. There was blood everywhere, Henry."

"Severed?"

"They said they think he bit off his tongue," Starlet said. "They're not sure. It all happened during 'Happy Trails.'"

"Who else knows about this?"

"Just the band and the crew."

"Nobody else?"

"And the paramedics," she said thoughtfully. "They rushed Omar to the hospital. Last I heard he was starting to come to. Lost a lot of blood. They couldn't attach the tongue. I know this is probably the last thing you want to hear right about now." Her eyes sharpened over Henry's. "You mean nobody told you?"

"Yeah. . . " Henry trailed off. "Now that you mention it. James. Yeah. James told me about it. I must've forgot."

"He must've gotten someone to bring Harry by the condo after the show."

"Yeah. . . " Henry said, his voice trailing off once more. "He did." Henry pulled his eyes back to Starlet. "Pepe dropped off the saxophone last night."

It finally hit Henry and nearly knocked the wind out of him. When it did, he tried not to look at Starlet. Otherwise, the gig would be up.

Harry. . . His eyes moved forward and fell upon the remaining brass pieces on the floor. He rose from his elbow, eased backward, and rested himself against the headboard. As he sat in a daze, Starlet leisurely mimicked Henry's previous movements and sat next to him with her body squared, shoulder pressed against the headboard. Once more, her eyes honed in on Henry's eyes, which were both drawn forward. . . *It's happening again.*

THIRTY-SIX

THICK lines of blood slowly trickled down Henry's forehead and washed over his open eyes.

The blood eventually faded from red to white, revealing a stale hospital room before him. It took Henry a couple of minutes to finally come to. Then, there were sounds, all precisely shaped. A neglected machine was humming to the right of him. A cylinder-like canister with a strange pump inside was making breathing noises. On top of that, there were clicking noises, faint beeping noises coming from various medical devices. Next to the empty bed, a heart monitor chirped like a finch over the other mechanical ambience. The activity outside the room was another story. It was dead silent. No nurses. No doctors. No patients. No visitors. A ghost town, Henry realized. He peeled his hand from the side of his face and checked the empty hallways. Even the hospital rooms across the hallway were deserted. Each room appeared as if it had been rummaged through by a pack of ravenous wolves. Medical equipment was overturned. Some instruments broken. Tubes from the feeding machines had been yanked from the patients. The liquid food from the bags was spilled over the floor—same with the saline solution and medicine. There were bright red stains shaped like continents over the beds. The loose bed sheets were resting over the cold tile floor, not on the beds.

Henry directed his attention back to the hospital, now T.J., who was resting inches away from him. The atmosphere darkened. The fluorescent lights overhead dimmed. Something suddenly changed. Something terrible. . .

"T.J.?" Henry said quietly and slowly stood to his feet.

He observed the carnage. This time, T.J. wasn't wearing any bandages over his face. Now, he could see the full extent of the injuries. The blood was trapped underneath the skin, turning it black and blue. The lines from the baton had been tattooed over his forehead. One wound, infected, he could tell, appeared like a volcano ready to erupt with gobs of blood and puss. The skin was alive in its own way, pulsing vaguely. The sight alone of T.J. made Henry's skin crawl.

Grabbing his aching stomach, Henry was drawn back to the seat.

T.J. robotically rotated his head toward Henry.

Henry gasped and struggled to look at his friend.

"Avenge us, Henry," T.J. said through the corner of his mouth. "Avenge us."

Henry violently jerked from the chair.

Then: the bed.

The words *avenge us* were echoing throughout his head. Sweat was dripping down his face and chest.

The sudden wakening stirred Starlet, who was sleeping next to him in the bed.

Scratching the corner of her eyes, she uttered, "Is everything all right, Henry?"

"It's just. . ." He grabbed the top of his perspired forehead, ". . . I'm fine."

"Are you sure?"

"Yeah," he said.

He slipped from the damp sheets and sat on the edge of the bed.

Starlet rolled toward Henry, curled her arms around his warm loins, and rested her cheek over the soft flesh of his shoulder.

"It's not your fault, baby," she whispered in Henry's ear.

Henry tried to fight back the tears.

He couldn't fight any longer.

"If I'd only gotten there sooner. . . "

"Don't say that, Henry," Starlet said, massaging Henry's shoulders. "Don't you say that. You heard what the cops said. There were others involved."

". . . I don't care." He sniffled up the loose phlegm back into his nose. "I would've. . . would've taken on every single one of them. . . I would've taken on a fucking army. . . "

"I know you would, Henry," she said calmly. "I know you would."

Starlet gave a little peck over Henry's neck.

Two more now.

In return, Henry rotated his body around and kissed her on the cheek, the nose, and then the lips.

Starlet kissed him back, softly.

Then, Henry eased Starlet back into the damp sheets.

This time, they made love and it lasted for hours.

THIRTY-SEVEN

SIX hours until daybreak, Henry was out of bed.

While Starlet slept, Henry calmly stood behind the bedroom window and watched the dying night lay over the cityscape. The pale moonlight washed over both the window and Henry's forbidding face (contours of his skeletal structure were now as dark as shadows). For about ten minutes, he drank in the pale light, letting it fill his body. Behind his beady eyes, a battle was taking place—the greatest war ever fought by man, the battle of self. His mind was racing, occupied with the ones who may have been involved in T.J.'s beating. Who were they? How many? Who else involved? The only thing Henry could wrap his mind around was the conversation he and T.J. had outside Chessman's that one night. How could he forget? The two of them, Henry and T.J., had shared great memories that night—mostly good— while smoking cigarettes and enjoying each other's company underneath the stars. The bad memories, especially the ones where T.J. had spoken of two specific individuals, had buried deep inside like a splinter, but now they were slowly surfacing. The more he thought about that night, the more it stung. One of them, he remembered, happened to be a cop. And the other one, Henry assumed, was working with the cop. He had met both of them before, once at T.J.'s former residence in Parker Square and the other during a fun night in town with T.J.

After Henry thoroughly mapped out the timeline in his head, he pulled himself from the window and watched Starlet sleep soundlessly on her side of the bed. The sheet was covering her naked body. One of her legs was spread across the side of the bed where Henry once lay, which, as of now, was a wrinkled depression.

Quietly, he ambled over to her resting body and gently kissed her on the forehead. He grabbed a night outfit from the closet (a black leather jacket, a black long-sleeved tee shirt, and a pair of blue jeans) and exited the condo.

After Henry left Madison, he planned to drive to the nearest bars in Lansford. Two of the bars were somewhat close, one he had been to before and the other one he had always thought about going to but never did.

On the way to Lansford, there was hardly anyone on the road. There was a DUI stop just outside uptown Lansford. Other than that, he passed maybe one or two cars.

While driving, his eyes occasionally glanced into the rear view mirror.

During one glance, he suddenly caught a shadowy figure sitting in the backseat. A woman? Her face and body was a void of darkness, except for the eyes, which were like two glistening pearls. Her hair was white and wavy. She sat calmly and gracefully with her eyes aimed dead ahead. Below the shadow, there was the same knife as before, the one rest-ing on the coffee table. The passing streetlights brought out the sparkle in the blade, which, after a couple of passes, turned out to be a seat buckle. Henry briskly spun around and saw nothing. No shadow. No knife.

The Porsche gradually steered across the white line.

The ride suddenly became bumpier.

Aware, he pulled his attention to the dark road ahead and jerked the car from the dirt and back onto the road.

Once more, he looked into the rear view mirror.

Again, there was no shadow or knife.

This couldn't be happening, he thought. Could it? How could a person appear and disappear like that, like the ones from his dreams?

Henry feverishly rubbed his eyes and slapped himself in the face a couple of times.

"I need a drink," he said to himself and concentrated on the road.

Roughly three hours later, Henry's Porsche 911 pulled up to Screw's apartment complex in Parker Square. The Porsche found a parking space in the back of the parking lot and parked in the shadows away from the streetlights. The profile was the same as Henry: thin with broad shoulders. Other than that, the person was a complete mystery: wearing a slightly frayed green flannel shirt underneath a varsity jacket—black chest, gray sleeves—with the gray letter H (standing for *Hawks*) over the front breast pocket, a pair of tight black jeans, green surgical gloves, and an old werewolf mask; in fact, the same exact salt and pepper mask with the singed snout that Henry used to wear for Halloween as a teenager. The eyes behind the tiny holes of the mask were much darker and sharper than the eyes of an ordinary human being. Contacts? From the darkness of the car (only a distant floodlight lit up half of the parking lot), it was hard for any civilian to distinguish with the naked eye. Perhaps that was the whole point: for the face to stay hidden in the dark shadows and never reveal itself to its enemies like any masked vigilante. Henry once heard from a movie: "Keep your friends close and your enemies closer." The line had, in a way, become like a staple in movies, mostly Hollywood movies. This insight never made sense to a young boy who had grown up idolizing actors and their lines and trademarks and the clothes that they wore, not until he was fifteen years old when a disturbed man named Fox try to kill him and his mother in the small town of Sinclair Leprieur. At the time, Abbey did all she could for her and her son—even if it meant killing another. In their case, murder was the only option or as Abbey put it, self defense. Five years had passed when this insight was finally handed down from one person to another. Names, however, were unspoken. Henry had told T.J. about the incident in Sinclair Leprieur; however, he did so as if he was a novel journalist standing in a dark room with only a flashlight. Occasionally, Henry would shine the flashlight on the details (the abduction, the plantation home in Sinclair Leprieur, the skeletal remains in the backyard, the basement, and the chains) but still, the room was dark and the light couldn't capture everything in one passing. The story was told like a campfire story. T.J. never took the story too seriously. He just thought it was a good story. Not once did Henry ever reveal the true identity of the suspect and/or the victims, only profiles. Now, after the recent incident with T.J., such insight—*keep your friends close and your enemies closer*—was nothing more than a code now, a way of keeping one's body and soul coupled together. How could the Werewolf forget such words?

The Werewolf killed the front headlights and exited the Porsche.

Once the parking lot was clear (there were only a dozen or so cars parked in the lot), the Werewolf made sure to close the door delicately, not loudly.

During the long stroll toward the complex, the Werewolf checked the bleak surroundings and made sure everything was in its proper place. Nobody was in sight, which, to the Werewolf, wasn't too odd. Nights around here, the Werewolf remembered what T.J. had said during a cruise through the old hood, were pretty dangerous. Then, T.J. said, "You haf to halves eyez in the back of ya head."

With T.J.'s advice in mind, the Werewolf scoured the empty playground next to the complex. A swing was gently swaying back and forth. There was a soft *squeak* from the metal chain. The Werewolf sharpened its dark eyes only to find a sickly looking tabby strutting around a swing set. Its body bent up against the monkey bar post. In repetitive motions, it rubbed each side of its chin on the metal post. Then, the tabby drew its glowing eyes to the Werewolf and skittishly scurried away into the dark night.

Once inside the complex, the Werewolf stalked its way up the seven flights of stairs.

On the way up, the Werewolf passed a grumpy old man sitting in a chair at the top of the seventh floor. The old man was snoring out loud. Calvin the Crank was his name, but he acted more like Calvin the Constable. The slap of the surgical gloves against the Werewolf's skin suddenly woke Calvin from his partial sleep.

"What in the. . ."

With a sudden flinch, the old man gasped from the eerie presence of the Werewolf. His face was long and stupid. His jaw bobbed in intervals (his tongue searching for saliva), but he could only utter a couple of disjointed groans.

As Calvin slowly repositioned himself in the chair, the Werewolf placed its index finger over the singed snout of the mask and warned the old man to be quiet, very quiet.

Calvin frantically bobbed his head in agreement.

Sitting there, stupid and all, Calvin watched the Werewolf stroll down the hallway until it arrived at 7B.

In one subtle move, the Werewolf turned its shoulder toward Calvin. His eyes never left the strange masked person nor did his eyelids ever blink from the moment he set his eyes on the Werewolf, who was now reaching down and gently twisting the doorknob. The door was locked, the Werewolf discovered, so it searched for another way inside by surveying the dim hallway.

After a thorough survey (its vision partially obstructed from the tiny eyeholes in the costume mask), the Werewolf found another flight of stairs at the end of the hallway, as well as the sign ROOF ACCESS.

On the way toward the staircase, the Werewolf counted each apartment.

Eight, it counted.

The Werewolf kept this number, the number 8, in mind and quietly walked up five flights of stairs while those two numbers, the 8 and the 5, ran through its mind like a grid.

On the roof, the Werewolf walked eight apartments down from the roof access door.

Once the Werewolf found the correct position, it stood over the ledge of the building and peered at the ground below.

Five down, it mentally said to itself.

With the breeze gently blowing around the Werewolf, it took in a deep breath of fresh air and looked up to the sky. The clouds slowly parted. The moon was big and bright, full. The pale light danced over the Werewolf's glossy eyes. Its chest was pumping, shoulders bobbing. The Werewolf suddenly dropped to one knee and hung its furry head into its gloved hands, which were now trembling, both of them, gradually and then uncontrollably. The Werewolf was crying too, breathing with quick explosions.

"I can't do this. . ." it murmured underneath the mask.

In its mind's eye, the Werewolf suddenly witnessed T.J. lying there in the hospital bed. His face was hardly recognizable, damaged and all. The person behind the mask observed all the blood, the wounds, so many there were over T.J.'s face. For a moment, the Werewolf struggled to catch its rapid breath from the dampness inside, almost suffocating. Then, after several long deep breaths, the Werewolf finally caught its breath and directed its attention to the brilliant moon once more. It grabbed its gloved hands and massaged away the trembling. The Werewolf's hands were ready, now steady. Its eyes suddenly went dead, now ready. Everything about the Werewolf was cold and murderous.

Not wasting any more time, the Werewolf stepped onto the wobbly fire escape ladder and carefully tiptoed down five flights of stairs. Each apartment the masked vigilante passed spoke of different stories, mostly of struggling families trying to make ends meet: a single mother taking care of three other children, two of whom weren't her own; an abused wife who carried around bruises and felt as if she was a hostage in her own home; an elderly couple madly in love and yet still working day jobs at warehouse stores in order to pay the bills; a lonely prostitute who was at the end of her rope; and then a drug dealer and soon to be victim.

Cautiously and quietly, the Werewolf pressed the mask against the window, scanned the apartment inside, and finally discovered Screw sound asleep on the couch.

The Werewolf placed its rubbery palms on the window and carefully lifted it upward. The window opened with a tiny *squeak*, which caused the Werewolf to freeze momentarily. Yet, Screw remained asleep on the couch. Once the window was fully opened now (no more squeaking), the Werewolf crouched downward and stepped inside the dark apartment. On the way down, its foot stepped on a television remote. The television switched on. The show, *Yo!*—previously name *Yo! MTV Raps*—was airing on television. The song "Fuck tha Police" by N.W.A was playing. Again, Screw remained asleep. From what the Werewolf gathered (after carefully studying the beer cans—seven of them, all empty—and cold roaches in the ashtray), Screw was apparently passed out. Somewhat relieved from Screw's current state, the Werewolf inched its way toward the couch. The light from the television highlighted its glistening, furious eyes underneath the mask.

During its prowl, it spotted the revolver sitting on the table.

With its gloved hand, the Werewolf picked up the revolver, the barrel end and not the grip.

As it carefully placed the revolver in its pocket, Screw drifted in and out of sleep. The Werewolf acted as if a cop suddenly walked up behind and froze with its gloved hands curled into fists. Meanwhile, Screw was moistening his dry mouth and rolling his head around on the pillow. He sniffled and caught a musty odor in the air. Slowly, his eyelids peeled open. At first, he didn't think anything of it—just some idiot dressed up for Halloween. Must've been some crazy dream. Then, his eyes grew wide and worried. They tried to focus over the dark sketchy body looming in front of him.

On impulse, the Werewolf suddenly slammed its gloved hand over Screw's mouth and pummeled him in the face. Screw kicked and jerked around a bit. The Werewolf, the dominant one, kept him there on the couch. Screw didn't put up much of a fight. The Werewolf pounded away on Screw's vulnerable face until he was choking on his own blood. "*Take that,*" the masked vigilante was mouthing underneath the snout as its fist clobbered the poor man across the weary face. AND THAT! The Werewolf punched until it could hear the bones crack. Strings of blood squirted over the partially burnt werewolf mask. For a second, the Werewolf caught its breath. Gave the knuckles a break. Then, it went on like this for at least twenty more punches, despite the crushed bones. Even his jaw shifted around a bit. Probably broken or maybe dislocated, the Werewolf imagined. But it didn't care! The beast kept at it. *That's for T.J.!* And that! *That's for his mother!* And that! *That's for his father! His band! His family!* TAKE THAT, YOU LOWLIFE PIECE OF SHIT! Screw's eyes finally rolled in the back of his head from the barrage of blows to his face.

As the blood streamed down the couch, the Werewolf rose up from its hunkered stance, its gloved fist still curled but now bloody. Its heart—if it even had one—was racing at what felt like a thousand beats per minute. Its right fist especially was throbbing from the adrenaline.

After the pummel was over, the Werewolf ended up exiting the apartment the same way it came in, which was through the living room window. Instead of walking back into the apartment, it climbed down the fire escape. The Werewolf safely made it to the Porsche 911 without getting spotted. The hardest part: removing the bloody surgical gloves from its hands. Once the Werewolf removed its gloves from its trembling hands and quickly placed them inside a weed baggie that it had stolen from Screw's apartment, it put on a pair of brand new ones.

After that, the Werewolf reached down into its pocket and pulled out Screw's pistol. The Werewolf held the provocative thing in front of its beastly face and studied it more closely underneath the brilliant night. The whimsical moonlight glimmered over the Smith and Wesson double-action revolver, a Model 29 with a four-inch barrel. Worn strips of duck tape were wrapped around the handle. The edges of the tape were peeled with traces of grease and grime underneath.

After two failed attempts, the Werewolf finally opened the chamber. *Six shots*, it counted and then carefully closed the chamber.

The Werewolf had never held a gun or pistol before in its life. On that note, never fired one before. Shot at once, but never fired one. Besides that, the closest the Werewolf had ever come to touching a gun was on a television screen. When it came to firearms, holding them, shooting them, disassembling them, posing with them, the Werewolf was like a virgin on prom night. The Werewolf had seen them on television, the firearms, the weapons, guns just like this one in its hand, and these fictional characters, like the ones in the movies, the Paul Kerseys and the Harry Callahans and such, using them to eliminate the dregs of society. At such a young age, the Werewolf had learned to separate the two distinguishable worlds, the television world and, of course, the real world. Later in life, the worlds, especially the television world that the Werewolf had forgotten all about, were reinforced by another similar creature and yet opposite of its kind. One, the Werewolf learned, was merely an exaggerated hue, more or less, of the other and such worlds were strictly meant to stay far apart. But at that point in time as the Werewolf sat behind the steering wheel of the Porsche 911, Smith and Wesson gripped tightly in hand, the two worlds were beginning to merge.

And the Werewolf knew what had to be done.

THIRTY-EIGHT

Two hours now before daybreak.

In the Porsche 911, the Werewolf pulled up to a white-collar neighborhood, Oaklyn Springs.

As the Werewolf cruised down the neighborhood street, it unfolded the piece of paper that it had torn from the city phonebook and held it closely as its finger traced down the wrinkled paper until it came across Theodore Backer and the address next to the name. The Werewolf followed the addresses on the side of the mailboxes, 17896, 17894. There, 17892 Oaklyn Springs Drive. The Werewolf never stopped at the correct address. Instead, it kept driving until it reached the third house down (the house that was all dark, no lights) and parked the car on the side of the street.

The Werewolf grabbed Screw's revolver from the glove compartment and then, as before, checked the chamber.

Meanwhile, in the living room of his house, Ted was kicked back on a leather recliner with several crushed beer cans beside him. The lights were off inside the living room, except for the television.

From behind the living room, the Werewolf heard the song "*Bad Boys*" by reggae band Inner Circle playing over the television. On the television screen, one cop was chasing down a suspect through the woods. The cops shined the light on the bushes, which caused the suspect to slither out like a snake. Before the suspect had a chance to run away, the cop tackled him and threw him to the ground.

Next door a dog suddenly barked, which woke Ted from his sleep.

Startled, he got up from the recliner and stumbled over to the living room window and peered outside. He didn't see anything out of the ordinary. So, he went back to his recliner, sat down, and turned up the volume a couple more decibels.

Once Ted was back in the recliner, the Werewolf sneaked away from the bushes.

As the Werewolf adjusted the surgical gloves around its hands, a light from above suddenly switched on.

The Werewolf briskly ducked back into another row of bushes.

While doing so, a pointy twig scratched the sides of its partially exposed neck underneath the mask and left these long red lines over its skin.

The scratches swelled with blood, but didn't swell enough to draw any substantial blood drops.

The Werewolf ran its left hand across the exposed flesh of its neck underneath the mask and pulled it back to its face. A small trace of blood was smeared across the palm of the glove.

"*Damn it*," the Werewolf whispered.

Making sure not to touch the blood with the other hand, the Werewolf delicately wiped the blood over its shirt underneath the jacket. The Werewolf rooted around its pocket for another glove, but couldn't find one.

"*Great*," the Werewolf said to itself as yet another light suddenly switched on from above.

Curious from the light, the Werewolf directed its attention upward and witnessed Ted's wife, Liz, in the master bedroom's bathroom. From the obstruction of the windowsill and dresser, the Werewolf could only see part of her face. She was staring at her reflection in the mirror, especially the swollen black eye on her face. She turned to her obnoxious husband who was yelling out all kinds of obscenities downstairs. The Werewolf watched the poor woman's face pucker up, not with anger, but with sadness. Her shoulders were rapidly bobbing. She reached over, grabbed a piece of toilet paper, and wiped the tears from her cheeks. In return, the Werewolf's eyes sharpened. The Werewolf already knew what had happened to the poor woman. "A monster," just as T.J. had told the Werewolf.

Suddenly, another *bark* cut through the night darkness!

The Werewolf's attention was directed toward the curious black Labrador strutting around the neighbor's house.

Over the commercial break, just as he was about to doze off, Ted thought he heard yet another bark. Same dog. At first, he thought it might have been the television. But then another commercial came on. And yet, he heard the sound of barking. He turned down the volume on the television.

Outside, the dog, Darwin, was barking at the stranger looming near.

"That damn mutt," Ted garbled and sprang from the open recliner.

Halfway toward the backdoor, the dog's bark was suddenly silenced.

Ted stopped at the kitchen and listened closer now.

Then, Ted proceeded toward the backdoor. He opened the door and saw Darwin, as well as the leftover piece of fat from an overcooked steak that he was chewing on. His neighbor, Scott, who was dressed in a burgundy bathrobe, strolled from the backdoor. He acknowledged Ted stepping from his house. Scott waved at Ted and then tended to Darwin.

"What's a matter, boy?" Scott said and petted Darwin underneath the neck.

Ted approached his neighbor.

"Do you know what time it is, Scott?"

"Didn't mean to wake you, Ted," Scott said and kneeled down to Darwin.

"Is everything all right over there?"

"Darwin must've heard something in the woods," Scott answered, his eyes away from Ted. "Must've been those critters again."

"Must've," Ted said suspiciously and stared down his neighbor who was too busy petting his dog. "Have a good night."

"You too, Ted," Scott said anxiously and came across a piece of meat on the ground.

In a childish manner, he asked Darwin, "Where did you get that, boy?"

While Ted walked back to his house, Scott picked up the piece of meat and tossed it back in the trashcan. He wondered how the lid came off. Certainly, Darwin didn't know how to remove the lid. And most certainly, his wife, Lauren, wasn't teaching her dog any tricks behind his back. The only thing Darwin was good at was rolling over for treats. That or sitting on command, if that was considered a trick.

"Come on, boy," he said warily and walked Darwin back inside the house.

As Scott and Darwin went back inside, Ted locked the door behind him. He strutted back into the living room, plumped himself on the recliner, and turned up the volume on the television.

Before Ted could get comfortable, the doorbell chirped throughout the house!

Ted muted the television.

Moments later, Ted was rushing into the master bedroom. His wife, Liz, was hobbling from the bathroom. Her injuries were more severe than the Werewolf had witnessed from below in the bushes. The left side of her hip was bruised. She could hardly put weight on the one side of her body.

"What I do this time?" she asked, brushing the wet, curled bangs from her face.

"Shut your mouth, woman," Ted mumbled and went to the drawer.

He pulled out a Beretta semi-automatic pistol, standard police edition, and checked the clip. He turned off the safety and rushed back downstairs.

When he opened the front door, Ted didn't see anyone around.

The atmosphere was eerily quiet.

Frantic, Ted checked the walkway, the sidewalk, the bushes (the ones in the front of the house, not the back where the Werewolf was once residing), the driveway, and then Scott's front lawn.

Moments later the backdoor crept open.

Ted readjusted the grip around the Beretta and looked twice at the walkway. With pistol held securely in hand, he inched from the front porch and found a pile of debris at the end of the walkway. Two trashcans were toppled over. Trash bags were ripped in half. The smelly contents inside were dumped and scattered all over the driveway.

"Damn coons," he seethed.

When Ted walked back inside, he picked up a strange smell in the air. He lifted up one of his armpits and took a whiff.

After a couple of seconds went by, he callously shrugged his shoulders.

Ted closed the door and slipped the chain over the lock.

As he proceeded back to the living room, the doorbell rang once more!

Eyes squinted, jaw line raised, Ted spun around toward the door and held the pistol close to his body.

Behind Ted, a shadow was lurking near the doorbell box mounted on the side of the hallway wall.

Once more, Ted readjusted his sweaty grip around the gun and walked toward the door as if he was walking through a minefield. Each step was meticulous. This time, he was slower to answer the door. Again, no one was there! He darted outside and checked each direction.

Ted yelled out, "Show yourself, you fucking coward!"

The notion finally hit him once he stepped outside on the front lawn. The doorbell wasn't being rung from the outside, he realized over a moment of thought. The doorbell was being rung from the inside!

Cooper, he thought, *fooling around with the goddamn doorbell again.*

What Ted didn't realize, not yet, was that the Werewolf was directly behind him. The Werewolf stalked from the inside of Ted's house, removed the Smith and Wesson from its waist side, and aimed the revolver at Ted's back.

As soon as Ted heard the sound of the hammer being cocked from behind, he froze and snorted with both surprise and failure.

Before he could rotate around and witness the Werewolf stalking behind him, the Werewolf honed in on its target. Like before, its mind's eye visualized a flash of horror, a still frame of T.J.'s mutilated face. There were more flashes of images running more frequently into sequences: Officer Backer looming over T.J. after vandalizing an old abandoned postal office and asking him to drop the food from his lap;

T.J. refusing; Officer Backer kicking him in the stomach and then arresting him in front of the convenient store; Screw sitting in the back seat of a police car; Officer Backer exchanging bags of narcotics for Screw's money; the struggle that the Werewolf had witnessed in Parker Square during a drive through the "old hood" with T.J.; Officer Backer and Screw beating T.J. to near death in an alleyway behind Frankie's; the rain washing away the blood and piss; now standing in front of Ted's bedroom dresser (grabbing the candle from the mantle and dropping the flame over the dresser and watching the police badge, the police plaque, the ribbon, the uniform, the police hat, the framed photographs of him and his police buddies, all situated over the dresser like a memorial, ignite into flames); the great flames stretching and slinking like phantoms over the bedroom walls; and then finally, another flash of T.J.'s face crying out for help. Keeping the face close, T.J.'s face, the Werewolf squeezed its finger over the trigger. The grip was so tight over the Werewolf's hand that the revolver barely recoiled. The gunshot sent Ted stumbling forward through the front lawn. In a kind of stupefied expression, Ted gazed down at the blood spreading over his white tank top as he staggered through the dewy grass. He fingered the bullet hole in his chest and flopped over.

The Werewolf prowled over to Ted and flipped him over with its black sneaker.

With its gloved hand, the Werewolf removed the mask from its face and revealed itself to Ted.

As soon as Ted witnessed the glossy-eyed shooter, he gasped in utter shock.

"I. . ." he uttered, ". . . you. . ."

The shadowy person aimed the revolver at Ted's face.

As the shooter was about to pull the trigger, a gurgle bubbled from Ted's chest. His eyes froze, death. The rage was gone, the fire extinguished. But then. . .

. . . The shooter suddenly heard a couple of tiny footsteps shuffling over the pavement.

Then, the footsteps gradually changed volume.

Now, they were moving through the grass.

The shooter slowly turned its shoulder.

In the lawn, a little boy was standing feet away.

"What did you do to my father?" the boy asked quietly.

A sickening feeling splintered the pit of the shooter's stomach.

The shooter couldn't even answer the simple question that the boy had asked.

Shocked, more so than Ted Backer before he died, the shooter made an attempt toward the street.

On the way, the shooter tripped over Ted's lifeless body.

"Ted!" a woman's voice screamed from inside the house as the shooter sprinted toward the Porsche on the side of the street. "Where's Cooper?"

The woman's voice moved closer.

The shooter ran as fast as its legs could manage.

"Cooper!" the woman hollered out.

As the shooter made it two houses down (one more house to go and the shooter was back at the Porsche 911), screams of horror pierced from behind.

The shooter didn't bother to turn around to acknowledge the screams.

Instead, the shooter kept running.

"Ted. . . Ted!"

As Liz grabbed the boy and tended to her husband, the shooter got in the car and sped away.

THIRTY-NINE

CORPUS was the first detective called to the crime scene.

When he arrived, a swarm of police cruisers were parked in front of Ted's house. A couple of police officers were questioning Ted's neighbor, Scott. Investigators were taking photographs of the crime scene. A couple of them were taking pictures near the backdoor. The coroners were there ready to carry Ted's body away in a body bag.

One officer raised the caution tape for the detective.

"Does Donnie know yet?" Corpus asked the officer at the scene.

"Officer Horton gave him a call," the officer replied. "He should be here any second."

"Great," Corpus muttered and arrived at Ted's body.

"Shot in the back," the officer said. "The wife said that she thinks the shooter broke into their house. She said the backdoor was wide open."

Corpus looked toward the house and then drew his eyes toward Ted.

"Looks like your past finally caught with you, Teddy," he said so quietly that the officer couldn't hear as he turned his shoulder to Liz and Cooper who had their heads held together and were praying on the front steps of the porch. Corpus directed his attention to Ted's body. His head was slightly tilted. Intrigued, he kneeled down and pulled out a glove from his pocket. He picked up the strange gray hair with the glove from the grass and placed it inside a plastic bag.

After the Werewolf left Ted's house in Oaklyn Springs, it stopped by Lansford Medical Center and paid a visit to T.J.

Since visiting hours were over, the Werewolf was careful about not getting caught. As before, it was wearing a pair of surgical gloves that it had found stashed away in the glove compartment. The Werewolf managed to sneak past the nurses' station in the ICU. It finally made it to T.J.'s room. Inside, T.J. was sleeping. No progress. He was about the same as the Werewolf had left him earlier that day. The Werewolf quietly walked inside the room, partially closed the curtain around T.J.'s bed, and stood at the end of the bed. Once more, the Werewolf peeked around the curtain, through the holes of the mask, and scanned the desolate hallways of the ICU. As before, it was quiet, dead quiet. The only activity was coming from one nurse, who was checking another patient. *They wouldn't hear it from all the machines running*, the Werewolf thought as it pulled out the Smith and Wesson from its pocket, *and if they did, I would already be gone.*

The Werewolf aimed the revolver at T.J.'s face.

They would never know, it thought. *T.J. wouldn't suffer anymore.*

The Werewolf thought about placing a pillow over his head and shooting him that way. It wouldn't be messy that way. The bullet would go in and out. Quick and painless. The Werewolf placed its gloved finger over the trigger.

As its gloved finger tightened over the trigger, the Werewolf swore it saw T.J.'s lips moving. A closer look: T.J. saying something like "Help me." But then, after a second glance, the Werewolf realized what T.J. had said. "Kill me," he said to the masked vigilante before him. T.J.'s eyes slowly cracked open. He kept mouthing the words *kill me.* And again, *kill me.* Then, T.J. moaned, which sounded something like "kill me," but the Werewolf couldn't quite make it out. The Werewolf shook its head and rubbed its tired eyes, repositioning the mask a little on its face. T.J. wasn't mouthing or moaning any words. He was the same as he was when the Werewolf entered the room. He was asleep. Not conscious. Both of his eyes were closed too. Not opened.

As the Werewolf lowered the revolver from T.J.'s face, a stern voice said from behind, "Excuse me, sir!"

The Werewolf darted behind the curtains and hid underneath the hospital bed as the nurse entered the room. The nurse on duty, Sue was her name, quickened her pace. She quickly slid the curtains back. T.J. was revealed in the bed. As before, he was asleep. The Werewolf, however, was nowhere around. Sue checked the bathroom, behind the door, and then closed the window, which was left cracked. Next, she took a couple of steps back and carefully surveyed the quiet room. *The bed*, she thought as her eyes fell below the hospital bed. It was the only hiding place left. Sue cautiously inched her way to the bed and kneeled down, only to find a dusty floor before her. No Werewolf. The nurse sighed, stood to her feet, and wiped her knees clean.

"I need a cup of coffee," Sue said as she exited the hospital room.

After barely escaping from the nurse, the Werewolf made it to a desolate alleyway off Main Street where it found a rusty oil drum behind a dumpster. There, the Werewolf finally peeled off its face, which, like the gloves before the mask, was like trying to remove a strip of tape from skin (the sweat acting like glue), and placed it on top of a couple of scraps of plywood inside the oil drum. Following the ordeal, the intoxicating coolness of the night pressed tightly against the shooter's stern face and sent a wave of arousal through its body. The shooter struck the match against a box of bar matches, tossed the lit match into the drum, and watched the werewolf mask, its face, as well as the bag of bloody gloves, burn to a crisp.

After Donnie left his brother's house, the sun was already out.

He drove to Parker Square and went straight to Screw's apartment, 7B.

"Open the fucking door, Johnnie!" Donnie shouted out as he pounded on Screw's door, 7B.

No answer.

"Screw!" he shouted. "I know you're in there!"

Again, there was no answer.

"SCREW!"

Donnie pounded his fist against the door.

Now, he did so with repetition.

"This is your last chance! I'm warning you!"

Nothing.

Donnie pulled out two hair clips from his pocket and picked the lock. He shoved the door open and rushed inside the apartment only to find Screw lying in his own blood on the stained couch. Donnie ran up to Screw and grabbed him by the jaw.

Ugh. . .

Frustrated now, Donnie kneeled down to the couch and squeezed Screw's two cheeks together, which released more blood from Screw's mouth.

Eventually, Screw's eyes opened.

He moaned, "Wha. . . what happened. . . "

"I was hoping you tell me," Donnie seethed, his eyes studying Screw's wounds. "Who did this to you?"

"Don't know. . . " Screw murmured.

Donnie shouted out, "My brother is dead, asshole! Who did this to you?"

Screw struggled to sit upright.

Donnie helped him up.

As Screw grabbed the side of his jaw and grimaced from the pain, he mumbled, "Summ fuckin' aszzzhole. . . dressed up as a wolf."

"Wolf?"

"Ye. . . "

"You're not making any sense."

"It's the god's honest truth," Screw said to Donnie. "I swear. . . was wearin' a were. . . wolf masss ova his face."

Donnie stood to his feet.

With his hands rested over his hips, he strolled over to the living room window, which was barely cracked open. His eyes traced the small smudges of blood across the panel of the window.

"So, wha da fuck we do now?" Screw asked, grabbed a shirt from the table, and wiped away the blood.

"We find this wolf character," Donnie said strictly.

"I need. . . go to the fuckinn hossppital. . . "

"You'll live," Donnie mumbled.

"Pleaseeee, Donnieeee."

"First, we find the person who killed my brother."

"And then wha?"

"Then we kill him," Donnie said clearly.

As Screw carefully readjusted his jaw with his fingers and wiped away the blood from his swollen face with a raggedy tee shirt, Donnie glared through the greasy window and watched two kids shooting basketball through the chained net on the court below.

The air was still and soundless save for the beat of the basketball against the blacktop.

Unlike his brother, Donnie wasn't familiar with a place like Parker Square or the struggle that these very people, like the two kids playing basketball, go through on a daily basis. He had only been to Parker Square once when he was a detective. Most of what he had heard of this place came from his brother. So, Donnie wondered if there was hope for Parker Square and if it was really worth saving. "Everybody deserves a chance," he once preached to his brother. But then again, blood was thicker than water. Donnie was absolutely certain of this, regardless of who had killed his brother or what his brother had done to deserve such a death.

BOOK THREE

FALL TO ARMS

At 2:16 AM, Henry arrived at his condo in Madison only to find two police cruisers parked in front of his neighbor's building.

Henry suddenly slammed on the brakes.

A *screech* of tires over asphalt!

What. . . they couldn't be here for me?

Could they?

But. . .

Trying not to draw too much suspicion, Henry pulled into the side parking lot—away from the two cruisers. The blue lights, silently pulsing over the roofs of the cruisers, were scattered across the full parking lot from Building A to Building I. To Henry, it was nothing more than a turbulent sea of iridescent jellyfish.

. . . Could they really?

Next, Henry trained his eyes to focus on the two cruisers parked in front of Building E—not the twelve cruisers and their strange sirens as his eyes had fooled him the first time around—by occasionally blinking and flexing the strained muscles around both of his eye sockets. The lights grew brighter and wider now. Eventually, the lights dwindled over their means of origin after Henry rubbed the backside of his eyelids and closed one eye and focused with the other. Three aged faces manifested over the pulsing lights, still shrinking. Henry's neighbor, Miles, he noticed, was outside arguing with two Madison County police officers—whose faces were completely unrecognizable from where Henry was idled.

Miles was hunched forward like an elderly man with his hands planted over his hips and his head cocked to the side. He would occasionally move his hands from his hips and motion to his parked car in repeated karate chops.

Were they really here for me, for what I did to that guy? But Miles. . . he would never. . . to me. . . just a week ago, I helped him with his grill. . . we hit it off. . . we talked for hours about music. . . The thought suddenly fired at Henry before he had a chance to make out exactly what happened outside his condo. If I get caught, he realized, they'll throw me in jail. . .

As one of the officers glanced over his shoulder at the approaching Porsche 911, Henry quickly cut off the headlights and made a swift turn into a parking space behind an evergreen. The front right tire mounted over the side of the curb while the other three remained on the concrete.

The officer, not thinking too much of the erratic driver from across the parking lot, directed his attention towards Miles's complaints.

Meanwhile, Henry's hands were shaking over the steering wheel. His knuckles were throbbing. Even the bones in his hands (mainly the right hand that had done most of the punching) ached.

As Henry waited in a humming silence, the shock eventually went away. Then, the shock was replaced with the torment of more questions. Can they see me from here, the cops? The questions never let up. In fact, they charged at Henry like an infantry storming a fort. Did the bartender at The Crawl Bar *warn* them about me? What about the barfly who kept talking to me at the bar? Did he call the police after I smashed his face in with my fist? To Henry, the barfly didn't appear too harmless—at least not after he smashed his face in with his fist. The barfly was in his late forties and had a clear weight advantage over Henry. The barfly was about five inches taller than Henry and weighed around fifty pounds more. However, when the man drank, he was aggressive, incredibly emotional, sloppy, and overbearing. Throughout the night, Henry kept a keen eye on the barfly who had been circulating from one pretty girl to another, only to taste the bitterness of rejection. When the barfly (this was after he had been rejected over four times) stumbled to the loner sitting at the very end of the bar, he got more than he bargained for. Henry didn't remember exactly what the barfly had said to him. First, the conversation started with "You think you're better than me?" From there, his words were all a blur to Henry. All he remembered was the snarl on the barfly's scruffy face, him getting close to Henry's face, and then the gobs of spit projecting from his mouth when he degraded Henry. Where was the respect? Next, like two savage creatures fighting over territory, they took it "outside" like real respectable men do, not at the bar, especially in the company of a group of women who were enjoying a nightcap. When it was all said and done, the two brawlers, Henry and the rude barfly, left on good terms: a simple handshake and then two apologies, one from the barfly who apologized for getting in Henry's grill (this was, of course, after he spat out a couple of teeth on the ground) and the other from Henry about breaking the barfly's nose and, of course, his teeth.

Once the two parted ways, Henry paid his tab, kindly tipped the bartender, and stopped at the nearest convenient store to buy a drink for the road. The questions kept coming, more disjointed now. He didn't know how much longer he could hold it in. The stuff was right there at the cusp of his throat, ready to jet from his mouth like a busted fire hydrant. He turned off the ignition of the car, grabbed the bottle of Muds, which was concealed in a brown paper bag, and sneaked about halfway toward his building when he quickly ducked his head between two oleander bushes and vomited. Most, if not all of it, was a combination of bourbon and some fruity blue cocktail that a sweet cougar had bought for Henry at the bar. After Henry vomited, his empty stomach was doing push-ups against his chest. The rest of the ordeal was spent hurling up a ghost—dry heaves and trapped saliva. Henry wiped his mouth clean with the sleeve of his jacket.

The argument that ensued behind Henry picked up even more steam.

He listened closer.

When he realized that the two officers weren't there for him (in fact, the two cops were there for an infamous vandal who was apparently tossing cinder blocks through windows, mainly the back of car windows—he had heard his neighbor, Miles, yell out something like, "I've about had it with these goddamn kids, Officer! They have no fucking respect for other people's property. . . NONE WHATSO-FUCKING-EVER! I WANT YOU TO FIND THESE LITTLE SHITS AND ARREST THEIR SORRY ASSES! IF YOU DON'T, I WILL!" Then, the patient officer said, "I'm going to have to ask you to calm down, sir." After, Miles returned: "DO YOUR FUCKING JOB, OFFICER! THEN, I MIGHT CALM DOWN!"), a weight was lifted from Henry's chest.

Just kids, he thought as he breathed a sigh of relief.

Keeping low to the ground without falling over, Henry stumbled around the parked vehicles—six of them smashed by the infamous vandal, Pinhead, also known as the "little shit" from Madison County—and into his building, Building F, without being spotted by the two officers.

The blue police sirens flashed behind the closed blinds and flooded the living room of the condo.

Without switching on a light, he gently placed the set of keys, as well as the Muds, on the granite countertop in the kitchen and stumbled over to the window where he peeked through the blinds at the officers trying to calm down his neighbor. As before, Miles was still arguing with the police officers. His movements, though, were less abrupt. Henry shut the blinds, went straight to the master bathroom, and scrubbed away the traces of blood from his trembling hands until they were nearly raw.

After he washed his hands, he hopped into the steaming hot shower, repeatedly ran a bar of soap over his clammy skin (mostly the cracks of his fingers and fingernails), and sham-pooed his hair. Lastly, after he cut off the water, he used the damp white towel on the floor to dry himself.

Once Henry stepped out of the shower (his skin pruned now), he saw in the mirror the backside of a svelte body lying on the bed. A sharp beam of light cast from the bathroom settled over the two shoulder blades across her back. He threw on a pair of black boxers, stepped from the bathroom, and ambled over to the bed where Starlet was lying. She shot open her left eye as Henry, as dark as a silhouette in front of the lit doorway, prowled away from the bed. He thought it was best not to wake her, and Starlet thought it was best not to turn and acknowledge Henry.

Quietly, Henry inched away from Starlet and closed the bedroom door behind him.

In the living room the flashing of police sirens over the windows was replaced with the steady glow from a distant floodlight. Henry peeked outside and made sure the police were gone. They were, as predicted.

On the way to the couch, he grabbed the twenty-two-ounce bottle of beer from the kitchen counter and generously sipped from the bottle. He picked up a blanket, the golden one that his mother had sewn for him as a young child, and wore it like a cloak over his bare body. The blood was moving from his eyes and working its way toward his extremities. That gnawing sensation in his gut for vengeance was still there, however, unwinding. But still, it was there for access. The barfly helped satisfy the gnawing for the time being. But still, that gnawing sensation was there. How much longer would it last? Would it ever go away? He rubbed his burning eyes and thought of something else besides the vengeance. He thought about what tomorrow was going to be like. To-morrow was going to be a really good day. He focused his thoughts on what was in store for him: the sun was going to be out, the birds, the airplanes would be flying overhead. He was going to catch a solid eight hours, uninterrupted. Then, after he ate a big breakfast, he was going to visit Lansford Medical Center where his friend was hopefully going to wake up. T.J.'s parents were going to be there. The band was go-ing to be there too. Then, there was going to be a heartfelt reunion. Emotions high. Tears would be shed. It was going to be a good time. Over the positive thoughts, the blood suddenly ran through his mind. All the red inside. The barfly's face, all bruised and caved in (more exaggerated than before), lay below Henry on the pavement. He was starring vacantly at Henry, who was now towering above him with his hands curled into fists. The barfly had a cut, which was more grotesque and infected, across the brow above his right eye. The veins in his eye had burst open and left the white of his eye dark red. The blood tediously creeping down the side of his face from that nasty cut, as well as his nostrils and around the corners of his lips, washed over his mind entirely, soaking his thoughts in crimson red. Now, the blood oozed from each of the barfly's orifices, even his ears. All that was left in Henry's mind was a wall of dripping blood. Why take it out on another, he thought, when it should've been taken out on the real culprit? Then, *maybe*, the need for vengeance would go away. That gnawing. He pulled his fingers away from his eyes, now glazed with tears. He was drawn to an object in the corner of the room: a dusty projection reel protruding from one of the many boxes that he had unearthed from storage after the incident with T.J.

Gingerly sipping from the bottle of Muds, he shuffled over to the dusty box and pulled out the reel, THE GALLERY OF STARS.

Henry dug around until he finally found a projector. He snapped the reel into the projector and dropped onto the couch.

As soon as Henry hit the couch, he sank down into the cushions, sniffled up the phlegm from his nose, and released a moan that carried across the living room.

Shortly after, the reel started to play and projected the Doves of Saturn's performance over the blank wall.

Henry rested his head against the back of the couch; and his eyes, which were focused on the glowing ceiling above, slowly closed.

Suddenly, he heard a loud *squeak* from the bedroom!

He pulled himself from the cool, enticing darkness.

His eyes flickered open before he could make sense of the noise.

His head snapped forward.

There, he witnessed Starlet's face, pale and shadowy from the pulsing glow of the projector.

She was standing behind a closed bedroom door with an expressionless face. Long shadows were cast under her dark, glossy eyes, as well as the curves around her cheeks, from where the pale light hit her face.

Apprehensive from Starlet's empty state, he placed the bottle of Muds near the foot of the couch and sat upright while Starlet mechanically approached him.

Henry said innocently, "Starlet?"

Starlet didn't respond from Henry's comment. Instead, she walked closer to him with both of her arms held down by her side.

"Star?"

Again, she didn't respond to Henry's voice.

She kept walking, almost gliding like a ghost.

Henry said cautiously, "Didn't mean to wake you. . . "

With her vacant expression, she said, "I couldn't sleep."

She smelled the air around Henry.

He asked, "What is it?"

"You smell nice," she said softly, a grin breaking through her icy stare. "Smell like a new man."

"I feel like a new man," Henry said quietly with a smile.

Starlet struggled to smile back.

"That's the first time I've seen you smile in a long time, Henry."

Her naked black body slipped into Henry's arms inside the blanket.

They both drew their eyes to the projection on the wall.

"What are you watching?"

Henry paused.

Then, he sighed.

"When I was a young boy, I lived a couple of houses down from this older lady," he said calmly to Starlet as he watched the evocative performance. "You remember?"

"What was her name?" Starlet thought out loud. "Ms. Craft? Right? Your mentor?"

"That's right," Henry said weakly and then corrected himself. "Well, Dolores. The kids on the street called her bad names, horrible names. Thought she was this kind of evil monster when she wasn't. If she hadn't hit me with her car that one day, I would've never gathered enough nerve to talk to her."

"Wait a minute," Starlet said, her voice raised slightly. She glanced over her shoulder—her face inches away from Henry's. He felt her breath, which was like ice, on the side of his cheek. "You never told me she hit you with her car. I thought you said. . ."

"What I meant to say was. . . she accidentally hit me."

"What were you doing?"

"She was backing up," Henry said. "I was running. . ."

"Running from what?"

Henry barely cracked open his mouth to answer. However, the words never came out clean.

"I. . . I don't remember," Henry said with hesitation and then threw his head in a nod. "Anyway, Dolores took care of me. Bandaged me up. Later that night, I went to thank her. She let me inside her house. We got to know each other. Before I knew it, we were. . ."

"You were what, Henry?"

". . . friends," he said. "And then, one day she showed me something that would change my life. . . forever." Once more, Henry threw his head into a weak nod, this time at the projection on the wall. "She showed me this performance. Then, I found out she went by another name, Gloria Silk."

Starlet took a moment to listen closely to her voice.

"She has a wonderful voice," she said.

In a state of reflection, Henry said, "She taught me everything about music. I mean everything. We became really close." The thought brought another warming smile onto his face. "Even after school, I would make up some excuse to tell my friends and go behind their backs and hang out with Dolores. I didn't care how old she was, the wrinkles on her face. She never acted like an old woman. She was like. . . like me in a way, only much older." He mistakenly chortled. "We talked about all kinds of music, played music. She even taught me how to dance."

"You were lucky, Henry."

"How so?"

"You lived next to a legend."

"I wouldn't go so far as to call her legend."

"But she was, Henry."

"Maybe," he said with a shrug. "I guess so. Dolores had brief success. First time I met her, she was like this broken down woman, worn down by life." He smiled once more. "After we got to know one another, she was a completely different person, as I was. It sounds kind of lame, I know, but it was like we were connected to one another and yet we were at the opposite ends of life."

Starlet said, "You never told me what happened to her."

"My mother found out I was hanging around Ms. Craft. She didn't like it." Henry sighed as the performance came to an end. "During my sophomore year of college, I saw her again. She was teaching, giving piano lessons I believe. That was the last time I saw her. Honestly, I don't know what happened to Dolores after that. But," Henry sighed, "every once and a while, I find myself thinking about her."

Starlet rolled her eyes up at Henry.

She said softly, "She sounds like a great woman."

"She was, Starlet," Henry said and ran his hand across Starlet's cold arm. "She was."

Starlet shivered slightly.

"Your hand. . ." Starlet said as she touched the top of Henry's trembling hand.

In the pale light, she peered closer at the hand before her and saw the different shades of purple over his swollen knuckles.

Henry struggled to look Starlet in the eyes.

"It's nothing. . . "

"Nothing?"

"Yeah," Henry said quietly. "Nothing."

Starlet briefly fell into thought.

"So," she said mindfully and moved her harmless gaze toward Henry's red eyes, "is it over?"

She traced her hand over Henry's and curled her fingers between the cracks of his.

Henry's eyes followed Starlet's fingers.

Then, the trembling finally ceased.

Henry glanced at Starlet's narrow eyes and then set his eyes on their two hands entwined together like yarn and said finally, "It's over."

While Henry lay awake on the couch, Starlet rested her head against Henry's chest, closed her eyes, and fell asleep in his arms.

It didn't take long for the barfly's bruised face to ease back into his mind and then the blood.

So much.

A single drop of it turned into a wave washing over everything that was once good.

Now, all that remained behind his steely eyes was a wall of crimson red.

PART SEVEN

HENRY SEEING RED

ONE

A heart monitor faintly beeped over the washing machine steadily running in the laundry room across the hallway.

More noises: the clinking and clanking from dishes being moved around both in the sink and stacked in the cabinets above the stovetop and then the clacking from the buttons of a jacket rattling inside the dryer.

Two more beeps, each one throatier.

Over the sounds, the darkness behind Henry's eyelids brightened with a soft red light.

"*Rise and shine,*" the piercing voice of his mother pulled Henry from his sleep.

The pain slowly surfaced behind his eyes.

With both of his arms crossed like a cold stiff in a coffin, Henry opened his sore eyes.

A burst of light, which brought upon pain in his head, basked over his eyes and forced Henry to squint over the morning sunlight shooting through the open blinds.

At first glance, he witnessed a younger Abbey (late thirties?) standing with a spatula in her hand and a beam across her face in the kitchen.

Over several rotations, he cleared the blur from his red eyes.

"How you doing over there?" a voice said, but this time differently.

Henry shook his head, wiped away the crust caked between the corners of his eyes, and witnessed Starlet, not Abbey, standing in the kitchen. She was dressed in a pair of purple panties from the night before (one of her legs slightly

667

arched upward) and an unbuttoned powder-blue dress shirt that she had borrowed from the closet in Henry's bedroom. The sleeves, frayed and crinkled, were loosely rolled to her forearms. The collar of the shirt was unfolded—popped—upright against her neck. In one hand, Starlet was holding a spatula while in the other she was holding the handle of a skillet over the stovetop.

On one of the skillets she had several strips of crispy bacon.

On the other she had pancakes.

When the batter bubbled on one side, she flipped over the pancakes on the skillet, revealing a nice golden brown side. She cooked the other side on the skillet. Then, she carefully placed the warm pancakes on a serving plate.

Starlet did the same for the bacon. Only the plate was much smaller with a napkin covering the top.

"What time is it?" Henry drawled.

"Just after eleven o'clock," Starlet said from the kitchen. "Must've had a long night. You were sleeping like a rock over there."

Henry rotated toward his right. The projector from last night was gone, so too was the reel and the box of miscellaneous stuff. However, the boxes of photo albums were still there, but the reel, gone.

He murmured, "Yeah. . . "

"I made you breakfast," Starlet said gleefully. "Well," she corrected, "more like brunch."

Henry removed the blanket from his bare legs and rolled from the couch. The bottle of Muds that he had bought last night at the convenient store was gone, as well. But Henry had no recollection of the misplaced bottle. He was wearing the same black boxers that he had slipped on after the shower, but, like the Muds, he had no recollection of the boxers.

"Making brunch," Henry turned to the laundry room as he curled his toes into the carpet, "doing laundry. You're a real Stepford housewife."

"I am," Starlet said, grinning. "Aren't I?" She pointed at Henry, who was slipping on a white tee shirt. "I found your clothes in the bathroom. They reeked of something awful, Henry."

"Yeah. . . " Henry mumbled.

Curious, Starlet asked, "So, where'd you go last night?"

He answered, "Out."

Then, Starlet: "Out where?"

"A drink."

"Just a drink?"

"Yeah," Henry said and rolled his eyes at Starlet. "Just a drink."

In a sudden rush of panic, he searched around the living room for the projector. Maybe Henry moved it behind the couch before he dozed off. Or maybe he even stuck it back into the box.

"Hey, Star," he said curiously and searched the couch and then the boxes. The reel was nowhere to be found.

With her cleavage partially exposed, Starlet faced Henry and said, "What's wrong?"

"Did you move the projector?"

"Projector?"

"Yeah."

Starlet carelessly shrugged her shoulders and then proceeded to flip more pancakes.

She said, "I haven't seen any projector."

"The projector, my projector," Henry exclaimed and then pointed to the center of the living room. "It was right here."

"I didn't touch any projector, Henry," Starlet said as she removed the rest of the pancakes from the skillet. "Are you going to complain about projectors all morning or are you going to eat something?"

Henry tilted his head in confusion.

"I must've stuck it back in the closet last night."

"Right," she said slowly as she studied Henry in the corner of her eye.

Henry paused as he drifted off into a trance.

"Say," he said loosely. "Did you talk to anyone from the hospital?"

"I just got off the phone with Mrs. Livingston. She said he's still stable."

"Good," Henry said and wandered into the kitchen.

On the way, he passed the trashcan in the pantry, which was packed to the brim with empty bottles of beer, flasks of liquor, plastic water bottles, and trays of TV dinners.

"Thanks for cleaning up," he said to Starlet.

"No problem," she said with a sigh. "So, are you hungry?"

Henry walked up behind Starlet, slid both of his arms around her narrow waist, and kissed her on the cheek.

"I'm starving," he said softly into her ear.

Uncomfortable from the touch of Henry's lips, Starlet spun around, faced Henry, and smiled awkwardly

"Good," she said and patted him on the chest. "That's good."

They spent the entire breakfast reminiscing over past events on tour.

Henry and Starlet could hardly contain their laughter. The thought alone of T.J. getting wasted and pretending his name was Zoloft from the planet Ecadoria and strutting around backstage with a giant alien head that one of the roadies had bought at a local costume store in Birmingham, Alabama, and pulling pranks on the other crew members, provoked more laughter around the kitchen table.

"Do you remember that one time in Newark?" Henry said, his strung-out voice trying to recover from the laughter. "Where he and William almost got into—"

"—With that one fan," Starlet completed Henry's sentence and laughed wildly. "I think you started to rub off on them, Henry."

"The fan threw like. . . like a beer cup at T.J.," Henry said, still laughing. "Then. . . then, T.J., he got so mad that he stormed through the crowd and tackled the guy." Several bursts of laughs trickled from his mouth as he tried to explain the story. "William pinned down the guy. . . while T.J. lifted up the man's shirt. . . and. . . and then he started to play the drums over his stomach."

Henry leaned back in his chair and tried to tame his hearty laugh.

"I remember that thing was like a conga."

"I know," Henry said, the laugh fading a little. "Right? T.J. wailing over that man's big ass belly."

"Didn't the guy start to laugh as well?"

"I think so." Henry shook his head and said, "I haven't laughed so hard in my life."

"Surprised the fan didn't file a lawsuit."

"I think he did, actually," Henry said and struggled to swallow his next bite of pancakes. "He looked more embarrassed. . . than hurt."

"You okay over there, cowboy?"

Henry cleared his throat.

"My stomach," he said and took a sip from the glass of orange juice. "It's been acting up lately."

"I'm sure it's in knots from everything that's going on."

Starlet's eyes traced downward on the cuts and bruises over Henry's swollen knuckles.

"Your hand, Henry," she exclaimed and pulled the fork from her mouth.

"This," Henry said casually and moved his hand underneath the table. His thoughts retraced back to last night, the conversation he had with Starlet on the couch. He was about to speak when suddenly the thought of him waking up in the middle of the night with his head against the back of the couch and his eyes staring at the ceiling left him in a state of disbelief. No projector in the living room. His hair was still wet from the previous shower. He also remembered the ache in his neck and then repositioning himself over the couch.

Starlet finished chewing the scrambled eggs.

"Is there something you're not telling me, Henry?"

Henry stayed hidden in his trance.

"Henry?"

The voice pulled his attention toward Starlet.

His head moved almost robotically.

"Henry?"

"What?"

"Is there something you're not telling me?"

"What are you talking about?"

"Like why your hand looks like it was chewed up by a pit bull," Starlet said, growing upset. "You didn't get that from the holes in the walls. You didn't have those marks on your hands last night. So, where did you get them?"

Henry stared at Starlet mischievously.

"Henry? Are you going talk to me?"

He cleared his throat and said, "I am talking to you."

"Then, answer my question."

As before, Henry dodged the question.

Starlet asked yet again, "Where did you get these marks, Henry?"

"If you weren't too busy blowing me," Henry said as his eyes narrowed, "then maybe you would've noticed them."

Starlet's eyes fell into a state of shock.

Once the comment sunk in, *way* deep, she grimaced and threw down the fork against the glass plate.

"Star. . . "

Starlet sprang from her chair and ran toward the bathroom.

"Star. . . " Henry stood up from the kitchen table, ". . . I didn't mean. . . "

Starlet slammed the bathroom door behind her. Henry didn't have to travel too far. He could hear her crying from behind the door.

In a sudden burst of rage, he grabbed the plate of pancakes from the kitchen table and flung the plate against the wall, which caused a louder sob from Starlet. Pancakes and shards of broken glass covered the kitchen floor.

With his eyes drawn like pistols, he shouted, "FUCK!"

Inside the bathroom, as Starlet sat against the lip of the bathtub with her hands curled around her knees, she heard more disturbance from the kitchen, more plates being shattered against the cabinets and the walls around them, and then more shrieks coming from Henry. The rampage finally let up a little, less shattering, less screaming. The last thing she heard before Henry stormed toward the hallway closet was a *thud* of the kitchen table being overturned on its side. More plates and now silverware fell to the floor, which sent more panic through her veins.

With her eyes, she followed Henry through the hallway until she heard him swinging open the closet door.

Henry ripped off the light jacket from the clothes hanger and slipped one arm into the sleeve.

On the second sleeve, he paused and caught his breath. He glanced over at the closed bathroom door. The pulse in his furious eyes calmed a little as he heard Starlet crying from the inside of the bathroom.

I always do this, he thought. *I'm sick and tired of running. That's all I do now. I run from the problem, instead of facing it head on.*

He sighed greatly and threw the jacket inside the closet instead of hanging it up on the clothes hanger. He strolled over to the bathroom and sat down on the floor next to the closed door.

The light from underneath the doorway cast a warped reflection of Starlet, who was still sobbing, against the tile floor.

"Star," Henry said from outside, "I'm sorry."

Starlet wiped the phlegm from her nose.

She cried, "Go away, Henry. . . "

"Starlet," Henry said, this time louder, "I'm sorry for what I said to you. You know I didn't mean it. Please. . . "

Sniffling, she said, "Then why did you say it, Henry?"

Henry leaned closer to the doorway.

"I. . . " Henry said and hung his head, ". . . I. . . I don't know. I don't know what I'm doing anymore, Starlet. It's like. . . like I'm watching my own world before me slowly crumble apart and I can't do a damn thing to stop it from destroying itself. The band, my family, has lost faith in me. You're all that's left, Starlet. I need you. . . Starlet, I need you more than you'll ever know. Please. . . " he begged as his lips trembled, ". . . don't. . . please don't abandon me now." He was now crying too, Starlet not so much. "Not you. If T.J. doesn't make it, then you're all I have."

The reflection below him suddenly rose from the curled position and stood upright.

"Star. . . "

Henry pressed his forehead against the door.

The reflection grew larger in scale.

"Star. . . please don't do this to me. . . not now. . . "

The bathroom door opened.

Henry jerked back his head, sprung to his feet, and faced Starlet, who was standing there without any expression on her face. The black mascara was smeared underneath her pink eyes. One of her plump breasts was partially exposed underneath the loose dress shirt.

She stepped forward and hugged Henry.

"I'm so sorry, Starlet," Henry cried into her shoulder, leaving smudges and wet stains over the pale blue shirt.

Starlet said, "The only way we get through this is together, Henry. . . "

Henry peeled his head from Starlet's shoulder and kissed her on the lips.

Starlet quickly removed her lips from Henry's.

"Henry. . . " she said as she eased away.

"What?"

Starlet didn't respond.

"Star?"

Again, no response.

"Please. . . "

She looked into Henry's eyes and finally said, "Henry, I need you to do me a favor."

Topshell River was known for two things: its scenery during sunset and its incredible population of turtles.

On the east side of Lansford (not too far from the hospital where T.J. was currently staying), Henry was standing on the edge of an old pier with a flask of Jack Daniels in his hand and staring down into the murky water.

As the sun sat highest in the sky, he watched his own reflection in the glistening water below. The stark reflection occasionally shifted or distorted from a curious turtle that came paddling by. He thought about the next move as his eyes traced over the flask of Tennessee whiskey. Police were already at Ted's house. Talking to neighbors. Witnesses. Dusting for fingerprints. Tracing the bullet back to the revolver. Doing whatever they could to find the scumbag responsible for the death of one of their own. The task alone was going to be a challenging one, Henry realized as, once more, his dull eyes traced across the half empty bottle, especially for a cop killer. Million-dollar reward? Bounty? *If I don't quit now*, he thought, *how much longer do I have?*

Then, the idea came to Henry!

When it did, his heart suddenly fluttered.

His skin turned warm.

His breath escaped from his chest.

His mouth let out a weak gasp.

While they were recording their debut album, *Rule or Be Ruled*, Henry and T.J. had a long conversation about their childhoods, the memories. Somewhere in the conversation, T.J. had shown Henry an apartment key that he had kept in his pocket like a rabbit's foot. Henry remembered asking T.J. why he kept the key. He answered, "It reminded me of the awful place I used to live at."

Minutes later, Henry was rushing through the corridors of Lansford Medical Center.

When he reached the ICU, he marched directly toward the waiting room where T.J.'s parents greeted Henry in the hallway.

"Henry!" Mrs. Livingston said and hugged Henry.

"What happened?"

"It's T.J.," she said gladly. "Doctor said he responded to a couple of commands."

"Is he awake?"

"Sort of," she answered with slight hesitation and sat Henry down on the nearest bench. "He's still in and out of consciousness."

"That's good news," Henry said, thinking. "Right?"

"Yes," she replied with uncertainty. "I think so."

"When can we see him?"

"We're waiting on the nurse as we speak."

Henry briefly pulled himself away in thought.

He turned back around and faced Mrs. Livingston.

"I was meaning to ask you," he said. "T.J.'s belongings. Do you know where they are?"

"Why do you ask?"

Henry hesitated.

"His car key," he said plainly. "I left some things in his car."

"All the nurse gave me were his clothes and wallet," she answered. "The keys must've fallen out. I don't know." She acknowledged her husband who was standing next to the bench with his arms crossed over his chest, not saying much at all. "Greg used the spare and drove that beat up thing back to the house." Frustrated from T.J.'s stubbornness, she mumbled to herself, "I don't know why he even drives that piece of garbage anymore. He has the money to buy a house in Madison Grove, but he can't buy a decent car." With a frown, Mrs. Livingston directed her attention toward Henry. "Look at me," she said to Henry. "Going on another rant." She reached out and grabbed Henry by the hand. "You are more than welcome to swing by the house and gather your things, if you like."

"It's fine," Henry said, waving his hand. "I can get them later. I just thought I'd ask."

Henry stood up from the bench and paced around the hallway. Like Mr. Livingston, he wasn't saying much at all. He didn't even know that he had done it until Mrs. Livingston called out his name.

She said sharply, "Henry Burl! Do you know what kind of germs you're putting in your mouth?"

Henry pulled his fingernails from his mouth and mumbled, "Right."

Mrs. Livingston walked over to Henry and grabbed his attention by easing her head into his range of vision. His eyes, which were mostly held down to the floor in thought, drifted upward into Mrs. Livingston's worried eyes.

"If you need anything," she said, "we're always here to help."

"Yeah," he said quietly. "Sure. I know."

Mrs. Livingston stood up and hugged Henry once more.

Over her shoulder, Henry drew his eyes to the television suspended in the corner of the waiting room.

The news reporter was standing outside Ted Backer's house along with several reporters from other news channels.

Henry couldn't make out what the reporter was saying. However, he read part of the caption on the bottom of the screen.

The caption read:

SO FAR, NO SUSPECTS ARE LINKED TO LAST NIGHT'S SHOOTING. HOWEVER, THE LANSFORD POLICE DEPARTMENT IS TELLING US THAT THERE WERE SEVERAL WITNESSES WHO CLAIMED THEY SAW THE

SHOOTER, ONE OF THEM BEING OFFICER BACKER'S
FOUR YEAR OLD SON. . .

Three doctors, including Doctor Yung, who had been frequently updating T.J.'s condition, came into the waiting room and told T.J.'s loved ones that they successfully reduced the swelling in T.J.'s brain with the shunt they had implanted and that he was now stable and able to have visitors, however, only one at a time.

After Mr. and Mrs. Livingston left the room, Henry entered next.

He stood over T.J.'s bed and grabbed his swollen fingers.

"He's dead, T.J.," Henry said carefully into T.J.'s ear.

The thought alone of the person responsible for putting T.J. in the hospital made Henry grimace with rage. In the back of his mind, he knew that Ted Backer wasn't the only one involved in the crime. Henry understood that one man wasn't capable of doing such a heinous act to one person.

There were others.

Two or three, he guessed.

Maybe even four.

With his voice sharper now, he whispered, "That son of a bitch who did this to you got what was coming to him. Same thing goes for every last motherfucker who did this to you. . ."

T.J.'s eyelids twitched a little.

"I know you're in there somewhere," Henry said, tightening his grip over T.J.'s hand. "I need you to stay strong. You hear me. Stay strong. Please, T.J. Give me some kind of sign."

T.J.'s fingers, index and ring finger, slowly pulled apart and revealed the letter V.

Henry's eyes grew with excitement.

He rushed outside the hospital room and flagged down Sue, the nurse.

"Is something wrong, Henry?" she asked and then followed Henry into the hospital room.

"He just moved his fingers for me," Henry said, the excitement collecting in his voice.

Sue pulled a flashlight from her pocket and scanned it across T.J.'s eyes several times.

After she was done with the eyes, she checked his vitals.

"So. . ."

Henry waited.

Sue grabbed Henry's shoulder and said tenderly, "Keep talking to him, Henry."

"What does this mean?"

"It means he's trying to come back to us."

"How long will it take?"

"I honestly can't answer that question," she said bluntly. "I wish I had better news. These things just take time."

"Right," Henry said with deflation in his voice.

"Keep talking to him, Henry," Sue encouraged. "The more stimulation, the better."

The nurse exited the room while Henry stood over the hospital bed and waited for T.J. to wake up.

While Henry was sleeping in his bed (the last three nights he had only caught around nine hours combined), he witnessed the barfly's bruised face over a sea of darkness. He focused on the face, the wandering stained eyes, the cut above his eye, and then the blood caked around his nostrils. Behind the bloody face, the darkness was gradually brought to light. Now, a flat slab of pavement with a blood puddle forming below the disfigured face was brought forth. The barfly's face had changed unexpectedly. The bone structure of his face reshaped, cheekbones higher and jaw narrower. The eyes were now blue, not hazel. The face, Henry saw, was familiar. The blood cleared from the man's clean face, Ted's face. The pavement was gone too and replaced with something else entirely. Wet grass. Ted was lying on the front lawn of his house and staring up at Henry with wide eyes. The eyes, he saw, were laced with great panic. The eyes suddenly froze into a lifeless state. The face of death, he realized as he stood above Ted's lifeless body. Henry followed the string of blood streaming from his chest and across his jugular. From over his shoulder, the sharp *ring* of a telephone suddenly pierced throughout the vacant house. The door was cracked open. Inside, the glow of a television was sporadically flashing throughout the living room. The porch light was on, as well.

Another telephone ring!

Henry turned his shoulder toward Ted's house and suddenly woke from his sleep, only to hear the same telephone ring piercing next to the bed.

With his head rolled to the side of the damp pillow, he pulled his eyes to the telephone on the nightstand.

The telephone rang once more, a fourth time now!

"This better be fucking good," he groaned as he made two attempts to pick up the telephone. The first attempt was a whiff and ended up with Henry smacking his numb wrist against the corner of the nightstand. The result: an empty flask of Jack Daniels was knocked to the floor. The second attempt was right on target.

With the telephone pressed against his ear, Henry rolled back into bed.

He muttered, "Hello. . . "

Once Henry heard the sound of Mrs. Livingston's voice, a sense of worry churned in the pit of his stomach.

Her voice was unsteady at first.

Then, the frantic set in.

"Take it easy," Henry said patiently and sat upright in bed. "What's going on?"

Henry's face dropped in shock.

"I'm on my way," he said and hung up the telephone.

Henry gathered the clothes scattered around the bedroom and rushed to Lansford Medical Center.

When Henry arrived at LMC reeking of Jack Daniels and Cherry cigarettes from several hours before he passed out, a team of doctors had stabilized T.J. His fever had spiked to a hundred and five. His heart rate had jumped in the two hundreds. The doctors had to stop T.J.'s heart and then use the paddles on T.J. His parents, both extremely upset, were there to stop Henry before entering the room. Henry caught a glimpse of the team of nurses and doctors circled around the bed. A priest had also been called to the room. Henry could only see T.J.'s two feet, both curled up at the end. Henry tried to get a closer look by craning his head around their shoulders, but three nurses stepped aside and escorted him away from the room.

In the hallway, Mrs. Livingston embraced Henry.

"He almost didn't make it, Henry," she said, holding tightly to Henry as if he was her own. She could smell the liquor on his breath and the cigarette smoke on his clothes, which forced her to ease away from Henry. Mrs. Livingston never voiced a complaint about Henry's personal hygiene. Right now, his condition was the least of her problems.

Henry pulled his eyes away from Mrs. Livingston's and glanced over at Mr. Livingston, who, as he had been doing throughout each visit in the hospital, stood quietly with his arms crossed over his chest. He was standing there, alone, wearing the face of anger: eyes sharp, teeth adhered together, jaw line swollen. Mr. Livingston unfolded his arms and smeared his hand across his face and did his best to wipe away the tears without anyone looking. For the first time throughout this whole experience at the hospital, the tears fell from his eyes. Mr. Livingston cleared them away before they could roll down his cheek. That face of anger slowly began to crack. The strings that were once holding all the sadness inside eventually snapped. Mr. Livingston wasn't an emotional man, obviously. He hardly carried any emotion at all. Ever since Henry had known him, he had never seen much emotion from him. Maybe kicking a lawn mower after it broke down or ran out of gasoline or yelling at T.J. to quit horsing around or get down from there or some kind of strict command. Mr. Livingston was a rather quiet man, Henry knew. If something was bothering him, he kept it inside. But this had gotten to him, this moment right here with his son coming that close to death. Now, it was real. Henry witnessed the anger melting over his eyes, now taking a much better, more stable shape. He had seen such a look before. It was the same one that was looking back at him in the mirror the other day. Not only was it both anger and sadness, Henry knew, but also an incredible thirst for justice.

THREE

FOR the remainder of the night, Henry didn't venture too far from the ICU. He spent hours lounging around the waiting room, sipping lots of coffee. Then, when his legs grew tired and numb and the headache returned, he would down another aspirin with a sip of coffee and pace around the quiet—almost eerie—hallways. At times, Henry would walk alone through the corridors of the hospital without any sense of direction. Other times, Mrs. Livingston would take walks with Henry and keep him company. During one walk, she decided to ask Henry how he was doing. She told him about the alcohol and how she could smell the liquor on his breath earlier that day. As for the cigarette smoke ("The Devil's Breath," as Mrs. Livingston called it), she didn't care too much about that. But the liquor, however, was a real problem. Since her father had been an alcoholic for twenty-three years, she never touched a drink in her life. She told Henry a story about her father, one that she had never told anyone about, including T.J.'s father, Greg. The story was about her father and how one night he came home from the mill reeking of booze. At the time, before they relocated to Reddington, they were living in an apartment complex. Her father got into a heated argument with her mother just outside their apartment. Usually, the fights were verbal, never physical. The verbal altercation ensued farther down the hallway. Mrs. Livingston's mother accidentally tripped over her heel and fell down a flight of stairs. The fall ended up breaking her hip.

From that day forward, she was never the same person. She could only sit for a short time before the pain hit her. The accident had broken up her father so much that he finally quit the bottle and made a vow to his wife that he would never touch a drink ever again. Mrs. Livingston called it "sacrifice." Ten years later, when Mrs. Livingston was around twenty years old, her mother passed away. Not too long after, her father passed. Till this day, she knew her mother passed from the injuries of the accident. She just never told anybody—at least not until now.

Around nine o'clock in the evening, the team of doctors and nurses finally stabilized T.J. Since he was unable to have any visitors, Henry decided to go downstairs to the cafeteria and grab a bite to eat. Mrs. Livingston, who had been eating most of her three daily meals in the hospital, raved about their tuna salad sandwich and how it was to die for.

In line, one of the cooks was eyeing Henry throughout his shuffle. He drew his eyes forward and caught the cook whispering into another cook's ear. The woman blushed and giggled like a schoolgirl. Henry did his best to ignore the cooks and grabbed a tray from the stack of other trays and slid the tray across the counter and shuffled closer to the fidgety cook. He grabbed two tuna salad sandwiches, one for Mrs. Livingston and the other for himself, and placed them on the tray.

In the corner of his eye, he caught a large presence behind the foggy glass window in front of the hot vegetables.

Henry glanced up and found the same cook from before standing there with her head slightly held downward and her sweaty hands anxiously rubbing against one another.

Batting her eyelashes and struggling to look Henry in the eye, the cook discreetly waved at Henry.

"Excuse me," she murmured with her head held downward.

Henry already knew what she was going to ask him.

"Sure," he said confidently. "Do you have a pen?"

The giddy cook bobbed her head.

"I know it's not the right place or time. . . "

"No problem."

"You sure?"

"Sure."

"I heard about T.J.," she said, her voice pulsing with nervousness. With her shaky hand, she handed Henry both a pen and a napkin. "This. . . I'm afraid this is all I have."

"I've signed worse," Henry said calmly and then smiled. "One time, a fan got me to sign her dog."

"No way," the cook said blissfully, the nerves releasing from her erratic giggle.

"Like I've said, I've signed worse."

"Totally!" The cook's face suddenly straightened like a soldier's. "I just want to say. . . Henry the. . . I mean. . ."

"Call me Henry," he said to the cook.

"Yes," the cook said. Again, she wiped the sweat on her palms over her pants. "I wanted to say that I'm truly sorry about what happened to T.J. Every night," she glanced at the other cooks wandering around the kitchen, "we've been praying for him."

"Thank you," Henry said sincerely. "That means a lot." Henry was about to finish the autograph. He paused and glanced up at the cook. "And who should I make it out to?"

"Kimberly," the cook said gladly.

Henry finished the autograph and handed the napkin to the cook.

He said smoothly, "Here you go, Kimberly."

"Thank you *so* much, Henry the Fif'," she said, unable to control her beaming smile. "I mean. . . Henry."

"It's okay."

"I'm going to frame this."

Deflation eased into Henry's voice.

"You do that," he uttered.

As Henry was about to slide the tray down the line, he felt a tug on his coat. He looked down and saw a strange boy tugging away at his coat.

"You want an autograph too, little man," he said and smiled up at Kimberly.

Kimberly smiled back and assisted the next person in line.

The famished boy didn't respond from Henry's comment. He appeared incredibly exhausted. He had dark bags underneath his lazy eyes. His posture was weak and slouched too. Mainly, Henry was drawn to the strange scar on the boy's neck. The scar was the shape of a sun, round with tentacle-like lines running outward. The inside of the strange scar was pale and glossy. The farther the sun lines extended outward, the redder they got.

It took all the strength in the boy's body to hold up the pair of keys.

"What's this?" he asked and grabbed the keys from the sickly boy's hand.

He held up the keys to his face.

T.J.'s keys, he thought. *Screw's apartment key!*

Henry zoned out for a minute.

Once more, he moved his eyes down at the boy.

"Where did you get these?"

"Your. . ." he said faintly with his eyes falling to his feet, ". . . your friend dropped them."

"I've been looking all over for these keys," Henry said and smirked. "Thanks, kid."

A woman in her fifties was calling the boy's name from across the cafeteria. Henry couldn't exactly make out the name because of the chatter from three nurses behind him. All he could hear was an *S* at the beginning of the name. The rest was faded out. Samuel perhaps? Saul? Henry was too baffled to ask.

The boy started to walk away.

Before he got too far, he turned back around and said to Henry, "I hope your friend gets better."

"Me too, kid," Henry said and then eyed the keys in his palm. He tossed the keys in the air like a baseball, caught them, and said to himself, "Me too."

FOUR

THE next morning Henry drove to Parker Square.

For about three hours, he waited outside Screw's apartment complex in his Porsche 911. He passed the time by killing half of a pint of Jack Daniels that he had bought from the Spirits store the night before. When he finished the Jack, he worked his way through the six-pack of Muds beer. After Henry broke the seal, he stumbled from the car every thirty minutes or so and pissed in the nearest bush next to the parking lot. Despite how much alcohol he had already drunk (by noon, Henry was considered to be legally drunk), the nerves were still there. First, Henry thought, he was going to plant the Smith and Wesson like they do in the movies. Somewhere *conspicuous*. Hopefully, the revolver was registered and not illegally owned. More than likely, it was illegal or registered to another person other than Screw. Nonetheless, Henry didn't want to get caught with the weapon (obviously, not part of the plan), and he couldn't just toss it in a dumpster. He thought about doing what the Werewolf couldn't do, which was to murder Screw by walking up to his apartment, knocking on the door, and then shooting the weaselly fuck directly in the face. Then, he thought more about the plan and why the Werewolf used Screw's Smith and Wesson to shoot Ted to begin with. The bullet from Ted's body, Henry concluded, would lead back to Screw's apartment address—that was if the Smith and Wesson was registered under Screw's legal name, Jonathan Farrow.

*   *   *

At one o'clock in the afternoon, Screw finally stepped foot outside the apartment. He was wearing a pair of thick black shades that looked like the ones found in an optometrist's office in order to cover up the bruises over his face. The shades didn't help one bit. Some of the neighborhood kids mocked Screw as he made his way to the burly black man who was dressed in a blue jumpsuit with white lines running down the side. Screw slapped hands with the man and got into the Coupe Deville.

Once the two drove away, Henry grabbed Screw's revolver, which was wrapped in a rag on the passenger seat, and exited the car with the apartment key in his pocket.

Halfway there, he paused in his tracks.

"Damn it. . . " he slurred, walked back to the car, and placed the rag on the hood of the Porsche.

He opened the driver's side door, reached into the glove compartment, and grabbed the green surgical gloves that were stolen from the ICU.

Once he acquired the gloves (and the Smith and Wesson), Henry entered the complex and walked up the seven flights of stairs. He passed a couple of kids and a single mother who looked as if she had her own troubles—Henry being the very least of them.

As soon as Henry arrived at the seventh floor, he secretly pulled out the apartment key from T.J.'s set of keys; and without wasting anytime, he unlocked the door to apartment 7B.

Meanwhile, Corpus casually stepped from the Crown Vic, which was parked across the parking lot, and strolled toward Henry's black Porsche 911.

At the driver side of the car, he pulled out a flat bar that was shaped like a ruler with a hook at the end. He called the piece his "Slim Jim," dirty cop's best friend. He pushed the head down into the window until he heard a click.

The door unlocked.

Corpus, who was wearing plastic gloves, gazed around the neighborhood and then nudged open the car door. He rummaged through the inside of the car, but he didn't find anything that would pin the murder on the lead singer for Mona's Arch. He could've nabbed him for a DUI. However, he decided not to. Instead, he moved his search toward the glove compartment. Inside, he found a folded up newspaper from March 1989. The paper was badly discolored, brownish, and not that normal newspaper gray. He pulled out the old newspaper and unfolded the paper. He wondered what he was doing with a newspaper from 1989. Then, he came across the article on Henry's father, Henry McClintock, and how two kids came across his dead body in Josette Park and how Timothy Snead was charged for the crime. Corpus kept reading, even though he could recite the entire article, word for word. Time and memories had faded. But one had remained intact, that one name *Timothy Snead*.

As the detective skimmed through the article, the words slowly came back to him. The memories. *How could I forget?* He foreshadowed reading that one name, the arresting officer. One afternoon, a half of dozen cruisers arrived at Mr. Snead's house off Lemon Avenue. There was a saying in the force that went something like, "All guilty men run." But Mr. Snead's crimes were the kind that usually went unnoticed. Somehow, during the arrest, Mr. Snead managed to escape the band of officers. Mr. Snead fled through the backdoor and hoped to lose the officers in the woods. That one arresting officer, though, a former all-conference tailback for West Lansford High, chased down Mr. Snead and made the arrest. The name was right there. Easy access. Corpus was even hesitant to utter the name out loud. After all, he had been gazing over crime scene photographs of the man's face from the previous night.

As Corpus placed the newspaper back inside the glove compartment in the exact same position he found it and then pulled himself from the Porsche, he made a discovery. He let out a grunt as he stretched his body over the center console and toward the passenger seat. That same unique gray hair was lying in the crevasse of the seat. Corpus knew it couldn't be a coincidence.

With his gloved hand, Corpus picked up the gray hair and placed it in a bag.

Then, as he leaned away, he came across an empty water bottle in the cup holder.

He would never know, he thought carefully.

With everything going on, it would be easy enough to misplace a bottle of water, especially for a lush.

Henry closed the apartment door behind him and made his way into the living room. He heard a rap song playing behind the closed bedroom door. However, he couldn't hear anyone in the room.

Not wasting any time, he crept toward the couch, pulled out the surgical gloves from his pockets, and slipped them on his hands. Next, he pulled the rag from his pocket and carefully slid the revolver underneath the cushion without touching any part of the revolver.

Out of curiosity, he shot a glance over at the window, which was locked. In fact, Screw had one of those thingamajigs that one would use over his or her steering wheel against the window to keep it from opening.

Strange. . .

As Henry was about to stumble from the apartment, a sassy voice called out from behind him, "Who the hell are you?"

Startled, Henry eased forward.

A naked woman, as pale and thin as a corpse, was standing at the bedroom doorway. She had a short blonde haircut like a teenage boy. A long tattoo of black flames ran over the side of her hip and down her right leg. Her ribcage was exposed under her blotchy, bruised skin, possibly from where she had tripped. Like Henry, she was doing all she could to keep herself from tipping over as she braced herself against the doorway.

After a strenuous gaze, Henry noticed a couple of track marks on her forearms. The right corner of her mouth was bright red either from where Screw smacked her around, he thought, or something blunt was forcibly stuck inside her mouth.

"I'm..." Henry uttered, "...I'm...I'm just a friend of Screw's."

"You," she slurred, "you're kind of cute, boy."

Henry didn't say anything.

With one side of her lip slanted, the woman nodded at Henry.

"Johnnie didn't say anything to me 'bout you."

"That's because I just talked with him, John...Johnnie I mean," Henry trailed off and pointed outside. "I forgot my..." Henry frantically scanned around the apartment, "...my hat." He carefully walked over to the coffee table and picked up the red ball cap. "Johnnie said I could pick it up. He also told me not to wake the 'beautiful diva' who was sleeping in the bedroom."

"Are you drunk or something?"

"Me..." Henry said in a high pitch voice, "...Nah. A little buzzed."

"Beautiful diva?"

"That's what he said."

Her face momentarily lit with joy.

"Johnnie didn't say that. Did he?"

"Just a messenger."

The wobbly woman gazed at Henry strangely.

"Do I know you from somewhere?" she asked, squinting one eye.

Henry remembered: When he walked inside the apartment, he spotted a *WMU* tee shirt hanging on a chair.

He asked, "Did you go to West Madison University?"

"Two years ago," she said. "Then I dropped out."

"That's probably where you've seen me."

"No kidding," she said with a grin. "You went to West Madison?"

"All four years," he said and made his way toward the door.

"Hey!" the woman suddenly called out.

She staggered toward Henry. Her eyes were moving all over the place.

"I never got your name," she slurred.

"Ah. . . " Henry said abruptly, ". . . Jack. Name's Jack."

"Where you running off to, Jack?"

"I gotta go," Henry said unsteadily and made an attempt toward the doorway.

"Go where?"

"Things. . . " he said, thinking. ". . . I got things to do. Busy day."

The woman stepped in front of Henry and flicked her eyes toward the bedroom. He got a closer look at that red mark, which turned out being a perfect red circle, around her lip. Then, he realized it wasn't from a smack or blow or whatever.

"So, Jack." She ran her cold fingers over Henry's collar. "Before you go do what you got to do, how 'bout you follow me back to the bedroom so we get to know each other a lil' better?"

Once more, his eyes came across that red circle on the corner of her lip.

"I'd love to," he said and quivered, "but I gotta split."

He pulled the woman's hand from his shirt and quickly exited the apartment.

As Henry went to open the door to his Porsche, he came across a tiny scratch over the driver's side window.

"I can't fucking believe it. . . " he said under his breath.

While he licked the tip of his finger and tried to wipe away the scratch, which, after a couple of attempts, wasn't coming off, Corpus approached him from behind.

"Mr. Burl," Corpus said austerely, "you must be lost."

Henry ignored the detective, ignored the scratch, and got into the car.

With a loud sigh, he rolled down the window.

"What do you want, Detective?" Henry asked annoyingly.

"Did you hear about Officer Ted Backer?"

"I don't know who that is," Henry said snappishly and turned away from the detective. "Don't care either."

"He was gunned down two nights ago, Henry."

"Like I care."

"Well, Officer Backer was the same cop who used excessive force on your friend, T.J., back in the spring of '94," Corpus informed. "Backer was suspended for a couple of months without pay, only making his reputation that much worse. I think Ted Backer had a score to settle with T.J. That's my opinion. Let's just say that he's known to carry around grudges."

"Then, why the fuck is he a cop?" The anger reformed like a mask over Henry's face. "You tell me."

"Now that's a great question, Henry."

"Wait a second," he said, thinking. "Are you suggesting to me that T.J. shot this. . . this Officer Backer guy?"

"That's not what I'm saying, Henry."

Henry said angrily, "Then, what are you saying, Cop?"

"Easy, Henry," the detective said and innocently raised his hands. "I'm just trying to help here."

"If you want to help, then leave me alone."

"I'm afraid you're not going to get rid of me that easily, Henry."

Henry sighed, pulled out a cigarette, and lit one up in front of the detective. After each drag, he blew the smoke through the driver's side window, which forced the detective away from the Porsche.

Annoyed from Henry's defiance, Corpus leaned back on his heels and stuck his hands in his pockets.

"Before the incident did T.J. mention anything about Officer Backer? I mean anything."

"No," he answered shortly and dragged from the cigarette. "Not that I'm aware."

"I'm going ask you again, Henry," Corpus said and shot a quick glance at the beer cans on the floor mat. "Are you telling me you never heard the name Ted Backer?"

"Hey, Corpse," Henry exclaimed and squared himself toward the detective. "T.J. wasn't like that."

"It's Corpus," he corrected.

Henry snorted.

"If T.J. had a beef, he squashed it. Immediately." Corpus couldn't help but notice the faded scars over Henry's face. "He never carried around grudges like your friend."

"Or like you, Henry. Right?"

"What the hell is that supposed to mean?" Henry said sharply and pulled the keys from the ignition.

"What exactly are you doing here, Henry?"

Henry hesitated.

"Uh. . . just seeing an old friend. . . "

"You and I both know you don't have any friends in this neck of the woods."

"Oh yeah! And what makes you so sure?"

"Because I know you, at least I thought I did," he said calmly. "I know you're a good person, Henry."

"You don't know me. . . " Henry snarled, the tears glazing over his eyes, ". . . You. . . you don't know what it's like to lose someone close to you, to have them ripped from your life without having any say in the matter. You don't, Detective. . . "

"—I do, Henry," Corpus interrupted. "More than you ever know. When I was twenty-four, I lost my son."

Henry curbed his emotions before they could take over him. Calm now, he turned away from the detective, took another drag from the cigarette, and said under his breath, "Sorry."

"I was out of college working a dead end job," Corpus explained. "My wife ended up finding a part time job near the school. My son, Sam, was starting preschool. It was his first day. When Marie went to pick up Sam, he wasn't there. When she went inside, Sam's teachers told her that his father had picked him up. What they didn't know was that I was at work." Corpus placed his hands over his hips and shook his head with bitterness. "For years, we looked for my son. Marie drove herself sick. The truth was that my boy was gone. . . for good." Corpus cleared his throat and scrubbed away the growing tear around his eye. "After my wife and I accepted our loss, we thought about having another. Marie could no longer cope. So, we ended it."

"Did they ever find his body?"

"No," Corpus answered. "But we knew he was gone. There were times," he said, a smile tracing over his face, "when I would find myself thinking that someday he's just going to show up out of the blue. Maybe I'll spot him in a crowd or pass him in the grocery store. Hell! Maybe he even has kids of his own. Maybe I'll see him with a family. You keep the pictures around, the baby pictures, and you imagine what he might look like now. But. . . " his face went steely, ". . . after a while you give up and you realize he's never coming back. So, I know what it's like to lose someone close to you. Then, when they're gone, you feel that much more alone in the world." Corpus leaned over the window. "I know you're looking for blood, as would I. I'm telling you, Henry. Just let us handle it."

"I'm sorry for your loss, Detective. . . I am. . . " Henry's eyes narrowed, ". . . But I don't need a dirty cop telling me what to do."

"I'm just like you, Henry," Corpus said passionately and leaned closer to the car, only to receive a whiff of alcohol on Henry's breath. "My entire life, I have swum with the current and done what I was asked. Now, I'm the only one who is swimming against the current."

Henry shook his head.

He sniffled and said quietly, "That doesn't mean a thing to me."

"Listen, pal," Corpus's glossy eyes were flaring brightly, "my hands are clean now. I've paid my dues. I've done shit that I didn't want to do. I've done what I was told to do. I rolled over and bit my tongue, even when I didn't want to.

Those days are over." He leaned closer to Henry. "I want to nail these guys, Henry! Can you help me or not?"

Henry thought about the comment and then the newspaper lying in the glove compartment.

"I'm not like them, Henry," Corpus said over the tense silence. "If you help me, I'll help you. Deal?"

Henry thought more about the detective's comments.

"I'll start right now, Henry, by not having you arrested," he said and leaned away from car.

"Arrested? For what?"

"Driving while intoxicated," he said sternly and planted his hands over his hips.

"I don't know what you're talking about."

Corpus sighed.

"I've been doing this for over thirty years," he said. "I know you want to get back at Farrow for what you think he did to T.J. Screw, he isn't worth it. So, let it go."

Henry pulled himself from his thoughts.

"Curious, Detective," he said vaguely. "How did you get over the loss of your son?"

Corpus said, "Well, about three years later, I became a cop. When I first strapped on the badge, I realized that this is what I wanted to do for the rest of my life. I'm not trying to tell you to become a cop or anything, Henry. Just find something you love doing, like your music, and work your ass off at it."

"Can't argue with that," he said and once more drifted in thought.

"Go be with your friend," Corpus said. "He needs you now more than ever." He eyed Henry carefully. "You can start helping by cleaning yourself up. You look like shit."

Henry turned on the ignition.

"Goodbye, Detective. . ."

"Not so fast," Corpus said abruptly and extended his hand. "Are you forgetting something?"

Henry returned with a glare.

"Hand it over, Henry," he said as he aimed his eyes on the passenger side floor mat.

Henry sighed, grabbed the four beers from the floor mat, and handed them to Corpus.

"You're going straight home?"

He shrugged one of his shoulders and said, "Yeah. . . "

"If you get pulled over, I won't be able to help you out."

"Whoever said I was going to get pulled over?" Henry said annoyingly and drove away.

Corpus strolled back to his Crown Vic.

As Henry reached for the water bottle in the cup holder, he found none. Henry searched around the car, the floor mats, and couldn't find the bottle. With so much on his mind, T.J. in the hospital, Officer Backer now, the recent conversation with Corpus, he thought that he easily misplaced the bottle.

On second thought, Henry stopped the car and drove back toward the detective who was strolling through the parking lot with his hands in his pockets. Henry pulled up beside him and stuck his head out the window.

"You won't find him there. . . "

Corpus asked, "Find who?"

"You know. . . Screw. . . " he replied. "So, when. . . to be honest. . . this conversation is only between me and you. Right?"

"You have my word, Henry."

"Back at the hospital, when you asked me if T.J. had any enemies. . . I wasn't being totally honest with you." Henry glanced around the neighborhood in paranoia. "That Ted Backer guy. T.J. mentioned his name before. To be honest, he talked about him a lot. Said he had it in for him.'"

"That's it."

"There's more," Henry said. "T.J. told me that Officer Backer was stealing from the people who lived in there. He told me he was as dirty as they come."

With a nod, Corpus asked, "So, what else do you know about Screw?"

"I know Screw and T.J. used to share an apartment together," Henry explained. "He was hustling."

The detective said under his breath, "Tell me something I don't know."

"Screw asked T.J. to sling some drugs him," Henry informed. "T.J. trashed the drugs, got his life back in order, and joined the band. Screw wasn't pleased. He threatened T.J. Showed me the bruises and everything. I'd say he had it in for T.J. So, that makes two. If you were looking for a place to start," he gazed up at the apartment complex before him, "I'd say you found the right place."

"There's also a gang, well, three of them," Corpus said. "They call themselves OCD? Ever heard of them?"

"OCD?"

"They're a real nasty crew," Corpus said. "You probably couldn't walk a block around here without hearing their name."

Henry shook his head no.

"Never heard of them."

"Are you sure?"

"If I had, I'd tell you, Detective," Henry said. "Why? Do you think they were involved?"

"We don't know yet," Corpus said and placed his hand on top of Henry's car. "But we're going to find the people who did this to your friend." He ended the conversation with a bob of his head and a slap over the roof of the car. "Drive safe, Henry."

"Yeah," Henry said suspiciously. "See ya around, Detective."

"And Henry," Corpus said before Henry drove away, "I don't want to see your face in Parker Square ever again. Is that understood?"

Henry didn't respond.

"Understood?"

"Yeah, Detective," he said. "I hear you."

FIVE

BACK at the precinct, Corpus was sitting with Liz and her son, Coop, better known as Cooper or Little Coopy. Merrotti, who had been sitting behind the three and not doing much at all but chewing sunflower seeds, made himself useful and fetched a carton of milk and a box of chicken nuggets for Coop as Corpus went through mug shots of suspects on the computer screen.

When Corpus finally came across Jonathan Farrow's image, Coop's eyes blistered open. He stopped chewing the chicken nugget in his mouth, which left one side of his face ballooned into a little ball.

Corpus noticed the kid's reaction and paused.

He asked, "Is that the man who shot your father?"

With his glossy eyes innocently looking up at the detective, Coop slowly bobbed his head.

"Uh ah," Coop answered as he recognized the strange tattoos around Mr. Farrow's neck, the claws.

"Are you sure?"

Coop's mother leaned her head over his shoulder.

"Listen to me carefully, Coop," Liz said urgently. "Is this the same man you saw at our house?"

Coop observed his mother closely and then bobbed his head once more.

Detective Merrotti was given the go ahead from Corpus.

With urgency, he grabbed his coat from the chair and hurried from the office.

Corpus wasn't too far behind.

*　　*　　*

After the two detectives received the warrant from Judge Roanoke, the SWAT team was at Screw's apartment complex later that afternoon. The SWAT led the way into the complex while the two detectives hung safely in the back. Any residents or persons who were in the vicinity of the apartment complex scattered like skittish nocturnal creatures into their apartments or anywhere far away from the seventh floor. The SWAT moved through the apartment like a quiet gust, breezing around any obstruction ahead of them. They arrived at Screw's apartment, 7B. One of the agents, Pick, who was as short and wide as a tree stump, shouldered his way in front of the team and stood in front of the apartment door. Before Pick smashed in the door, he gave three practice swings with the sledgehammer—not exactly hitting the door, though, but only signaling to the other agents to get ready. On the fourth signal, Pick reared back like a batter and broke open the door with the sledgehammer. Now, with the door open, the remaining agents darted inside the apartment. They checked each and every room, starting with the living room and then the bathroom and then the bedroom.

"Clear!" the agent shouted.

Several more *Clears* traveled throughout the apartment.

After the apartment was all clear, Detective Corpus and Merrotti were last to enter.

The agent grabbed a smoking butt from the ashtray and walked up to the two detectives.

"Still warm," the agent said and displayed the cigarette, which had a hot pink lip smudge around the filter. "Either he knew we were coming or we just missed him."

"Or Johnnie Farrow likes wearing lipstick on his spare time," Corpus sneered and pulled his attention toward the cracked window.

On the floor was one of those thingamajigs.

*   *   *

While the SWAT hung back, the investigators flipped the apartment inside out. Hours of searching had gone by and still they hadn't found a weapon.

While Corpus was talking to Calvin from apartment 7F (during the entire questioning, he was spouting out about a giant wolf with fangs as long as his fingers, eyes as dark as the night, walking upright on two human legs), one of the investigators checked the couch. The investigator lifted up the cushions and found the handle of a revolver protruding from the crevasse of the couch. He lifted the wedged revolver from the couch and held the weapon in the air.

"Got a weapon here!" he shouted out.

One of the cops rushed to the hallway.

"Corpus," he said. "Eland's found something."

Corpus excused himself from the old man.

"You believe me!" Calvin cried out as Corpus marched down the hallway. "Don't you! It was the full moon I tell ya. It was standing right there, right in front of Johnnie's apartment!"

Corpus ignored the rambling old man and entered 7B.

The investigator, Eland, showed Corpus the Smith and Wesson revolver, the one with the handle wrapped in duck tape.

"Just what we were looking for."

"All we need now is to find Screw. . . " Corpus said as he gazed over the revolver.

Another cop darted inside the apartment.

"A black and white just spotted Screw entering a house off Fairsight and Parker," the cop said, out of breath.

"How far away?"

"Ten minutes tops."

"Tell them to stay put," Corpus said. "We're on our way."

*   *   *

Twelve minutes later, the SWAT agents were creeping with their shotguns and assault rifles drawn around the side of the ranch house.

Inside the living room, Screw was watching television.

Every single light was off.

The only light came from the flickering glow of the television.

As Screw flipped through the many cable channels, one being the news channel with Officer Backer's face blown up on the screen, tiny shadows moved robotically underneath the doorway.

Screw caught the shadows in the corner of his eye.

He went still and muted the television.

"Oh fuck. . . " Screw droned, his face slack.

Before he could stand from the couch, Pick had already knocked down the door with the sledgehammer. A beam of sunlight shone inside the house and revealed the clouds of dust throughout the living room. The remaining agents flooded inside the house, shining lights on a stunned Screw. He dropped to the couch and threw up his hands in surrender.

With his Glock 17 drawn and held upright against his shoulder, Corpus strutted through the dusty doorway and approached the couch. Next, he holstered the pistol in the leather shoulder holster and said, "You can't hide from the law, Screw."

The agent, who was perched behind the detective, got on the radio.

"All right, fellows," the agent said over the radio. "We got him."

SIX

IN his dark bedroom, Henry sat on the edge of his ruffled bed and stared down at the half empty bottle of Wild Turkey in his hand. So far, he had been sober for twelve hours. Twelve hours hadn't seemed so long. What better way to pass the time than having one drink, just one sip? One sip, he knew, turned into two sips and then a drink and then two drinks. Three drinks! The cycle would never end.

Honed beams of sunlight glinted through the tiny cracks of the closed blinds and brought out the narrow strips of dust floating around inside the room. A beam of light even glistened through the glass bottle before him.

As he sat motionlessly, a gentle brewing crackled inside his mind.

He pulled his attention around the calm room.

That beat was slowly coming back now, throbbing like a heart!

The blinds slightly nudged forward from the window as if a breeze had crept through the crack of the windowsill.

Henry stood from the bed and confidently paced toward the bathroom. He switched on the light and went directly toward the sink.

The beat, Henry thought. That beat was stomping like a foot solider inside the recesses of his mind, leaving very little headroom.

Slowly, that beat was breaking through. . .

. . . Distorting now!

Before Henry could think about the repercussions of the sip (just one little sip!), he was pouring the liquor into the sink until the bottle was completely empty.

Next, he tossed the bottle into the trashcan. Henry did the same exact thing with every alcoholic beverage he had in the condo. Wine. Beer—he had at least three cases of beer in the fridge. A fifth of Absolut that he had forgotten about in the freezer.

Then, after all the alcohol was emptied and tossed in the trashcans, he grabbed a bottle of Valium from the medicine cabinet, as well as his mother's many expired prescriptions, including her Thorazine, an antipsychotic. He flushed the pills, including the Thorazine and the antidepressants and the painkillers, down the toilet.

Last but not least, Henry walked back into the bedroom and opened up the blinds. The sunlight spread over his face and gloriously lit up the bedroom. He embraced it all, the sun, that intoxicating light of rebirth.

For once in a long time, Henry wasn't a prisoner inside his own skin.

Now, he could finally breathe.

SEVEN

A loud *smack* rang out inside the interrogation room!

Screw flinched and glanced down at the file on the metal table—his "rap sheet." Mostly drug charges, possessions with the intent to sell.

"Why so jumpy, Cool Whip," Corpus said closely.

Screw, whose hands were still shaking from withdrawal, pushed the file across the table.

His attorney, David Minter, who was seated to the left of Screw, wasn't so pleased from the scare tactic. He casually removed the clear-framed glasses from his face, wiped the smug look from his face, and then cleaned the lenses of his glasses with the bottom part of his red tie.

As Corpus walked laps around Screw, Screw kept his beady eyes on the seasoned detective.

"I'm going to cut to the chase," Corpus said. "Our investigators matched the same .44 Magnum that was pulled from a dead cop's body to your revolver, the same revolver we found in your apartment. So, Johnnie, do you want to tell me where you were two nights ago?"

"You don't have to answer the question, Mr. Farrow," David whispered in Screw's ear.

"I was talking to you, Johnnie," Corpus said as he glared at the attorney. Now, his eyes on Screw: "That means you answer. That's how this thing works. I ask questions. You answer. So, where were you two nights ago?"

"I'll answer," Screw said coldly and sipped from the cup of cold coffee.

His attorney leaned closer to Screw.

"Mr. Farrow, I would advise. . . "

Screw gave the attorney the hand.

"I was sleeping on the couch." Screw showcased the bruises scattered over his discolored face. "Why don't you take a good look at my face? These are what the son of a bitch who broke into my apartment left behind. That was before he stole my piece." Screw waved his trembling hand around his face. "He was wearing some kind of werewolf mask. It was dark. Couldn't make it out."

"Then, how do you know it was a werewolf mask?"

"I just do," he said, this time loudly. He reached across his jaw and grimaced from the sudden outburst. "That fool must've broken into my apartment when I wasn't there and planted that gun. Either that or you fucking porkies set up a nigger."

"You watch too many movies, Mr. Farrow," Merrotti said, hanging back. "Do you have anybody to verify that you were sleeping in your apartment?"

Screw smacked his gums.

"No," he answered. "I was alone. Are you not listening to a fucking word I've said? Damn!" He grimaced once more. "I'm telling you. I was asleep. A strange dude dressed up like Halloween broke into my apartment. . . "

"We heard you, Johnnie," Corpus said. "What else can you explain about this so-called 'werewolf'?"

"I don't know," Screw said annoyingly. "Like I said, it was dark. I remember the teeth. It had like fangs."

"Could've been a vampire. . . "

"No," Screw suddenly returned, his bruised eyes narrowing. "Like a wolf, a fucking werewolf."

"So, you're certain it was a werewolf mask?"

"Probably," Screw whined. "I'm telling you. . . I didn't shoot that dirty fucking cop!" He stood from his chair and revolted. "AND THAT'S THE GODDAMN TRUTH!"

"That's enough," David said calmly and eased his client back into the chair before getting hauled away.

Corpus sat over the edge of the table.

"Are we calm?"

Screw rolled his sharp eyes up at the detective.

"We calm."

Then, Corpus said calmly, "I got a four year old kid who says you were at Ted Backer's house the same night he was gunned down."

"Come on!" Screw blurted out and leaned over the table. "You're going to believe a little fucking kid. . . that's ridiculous!"

Screw's attention was drawn to Detective Merrotti, who was perched against the wall and eating sunflower seeds and making quite a mess on the floor. Screw was most interested in what Merrotti was eating than Merrotti himself.

"Okay, Johnnie," Corpus said and sat down across from Screw. "I don't care about the drugs or paraphernalia we found in your apartment. I don't care about your lowlife friends. Right now, that's the least of my concerns. What I do care about is what this was doing in your apartment." Merrotti handed Corpus the evidence bag. Corpus placed the bag on the table, close enough for Screw to see. Inside the bag was a broken baton, still bloody. "To me," Corpus turned to Merrotti, "I don't know. It looks like. . . I don't know. . . a souvenir?"

Merrotti said with a mouthful of sunflower seeds, "That looks about right, Detective."

"You motherfuckers planted that shit!"

"And when we run the blood I'm sure it's going come back as a match to T.J. Livingston," he said. Once more, Screw smacked his gums together and made every effort not to look the detective in the eyes. "This is called evidence, Johnnie. And with this evidence you will be convicted in a court of law. Do you understand me, Johnnie? Do you?"

Screw was speechless.

Corpus eased away from Screw.

"I just want to know, Johnnie," he said. "Why'd you do it?"

David said sternly, "You don't have to answer him, Mr. Farrow."

"I know you weren't the only one. Am I right? There were others. Who were they, Johnnie?"

Screw crossed his arms, sat back in the chair, kept his eyes positioned mostly at the floor, and muttered, "I ain't saying shit."

"If you tell me the names of the people who were involved, then your charges will be reduced." Corpus leaned closer to Screw. "Face it, Johnnie. You're alone. And will die alone behind bars. If you cooperate with us, Johnnie, then there still might be a chance for you. Sure. By the time you get out, your junkie girlfriend will either have another lowlife boyfriend to cling onto or she'll be six feet under. I have odds on her being six feet under. Nonetheless, Johnnie, you still might have a chance to do something good with your life."

Thinking about being alone, especially dying alone in a cell, Screw grimaced.

"If not," Corpus said, closer now, "you better hope T.J. Livingston makes it out alive because if that poor man dies, then you'll be facing murder, Johnnie, which means you'll be living out the rest of your days in a jail cell. Just you and four walls, Johnnie."

Screw unfolded his arms, looked Corpus directly in his eyes, and seethed into the tape recorder, "That piece of shit deserved everything he had coming his way."

Screw's attorney bolted from the chair.

"That's enough," he blurted out and removed the glasses from his face. "We're done here, Detectives."

Corpus got up from the chair as well and said to Screw, "I'll see you on the other side, Johnnie."

While Screw was given a chance to think things over in his holding cell, Corpus and Merrotti were back at their desks. As always, Merrotti was sitting on top of his desk and still eating those same Salt Farm sunflower seeds. Corpus was replaying the recent exchange in the interrogation room.

"Screw and some other cops beat up the drummer for Mona's Arch out of retaliation," Merrotti said, the chewed up seed shells falling over his shirt. "Right? So, if Screw worked with Backer, then why in the world would he want to kill him?"

"Money," Corpus mumbled, his eyes falling in a trance. "You put two ticking time bombs together it's only a matter of time before one of them goes off."

"How about OCD?"

"We'll bring them in for questioning, starting with the big one."

"You mean Orlando Covington."

"I hear he goes by another name."

"And what's that?"

"Teardrop," Corpus said as he skimmed over Mr. Farrow's file on his desk. "Apparently, he's got a soft spot for murder. The word on the streets is that he doesn't go anywhere without those other two homeboys."

"Cedric Johnson, aka Shank, and Detric Walker," Merrotti said. "I hear they're like Siamese twins."

"Siamese twins are two, not three."

"Then, they're like a three headed monster." Merrotti grabbed Corpus's attention by holding out the bag of seeds and said, "Sunflower seed?"

"No thanks," he said mindfully. "Doctor says I have to watch my blood pressure." In curiosity, he nodded at the bag in his partner's hand. "Meaning to ask you. When did you start eating sunflower seeds?"

"Wheaten got me hooked on them," Merrotti answered.

"Wheaten, huh?"

"I tell you, Al. You can't eat just one."

"Corpus," Lieutenant Reed said from the doorway and pointed his finger at Corpus. "I need to have a word with you."

Merrotti stood up from the desk and placed the bag of seeds aside.

"Not you, Merrotti."

"Thanks for fucking including me," Merrotti mumbled and went back to eating his sunflower seeds.

Before Corpus exited the office, Lieutenant Reed was already marching down the hallway.

Once he caught up with the lieutenant, they ran into District Attorney Ellie Kolinsky.

"He's going to agree to the plea bargain," the DA told both Corpus and Lieutenant Reed.

"I fucking knew it."

Corpus asked, "How many were there?"

The DA worked her bony hands underneath her jacket, placed them both over her hips, and faced the two cops.

"He said, including Office Backer, there were five others," she said and moved her eyes toward Reed. "He said he's willing to give us two of them. It gets better, Lieutenant. He said they're both cops in your department. He's not giving any names until we fulfill his needs."

"Goddamn it," Reed said under his breath as he ran his hand over the side of his coarse face.

Corpus said, "He can rot in that cell for all I care."

Reed glared at Corpus and returned, "Take a step back, Al."

"All he wants is immunity, Detective."

"Once the press finds out about this, it'll turn into one giant fiasco." Reed sighed loudly. "In the meantime, we keep a lid on this," he said to Ellie. "I'll have a talk with Captain Laverne." Then, he nodded at Corpus. "Mr. and Mrs. Livingston are going to want justice for their son. I think it'd be better if it came from you. You're good at these kinds of things." He reinforced, "And keep it as short as possible. I don't want this thing leaking out to the public."

"How about Backer's death?"

Ellie said to Corpus, "He keeps saying that he wasn't the one who shot Officer Backer. His testimony won't hold up in court. Unless a witness steps forward, all the evidence points to Mr. Farrow."

Reed pointed at Corpus.

"You said there was a crazy man going on. . . " Reed said, thinking, ". . . something about a. . . a guy dressed as a wolf."

"That's right," he said. "A werewolf. But the man was nuts, if you ask me."

"I doubt the jury is going to believe a man like that."

Ellie returned, "Nonetheless, we can't overlook it."

Before Corpus walked away, he said, "I'm on it."

As Corpus made his way back to the office, a thin man with a nose like a bird, clothes two sizes too large, approached him from the side. The man was lead forensic investigator, Christian Van Dyer.

"If it isn't my good friend, Mr. Van Dyer," Corpus said emotionlessly.

"Got some good news and some bad news, depends on how you look at it."

Corpus said bluntly, "What's the good news?"

"Well, the good news, Al, is that I pulled Mr. Farrow's print from the Smith and Wesson."

"And the bad news. . . "

"Well," Christian said with distress, "turns out I have a lot of bad news, Al." He widened his eyes. "For starters, we found traces of dirt on the doorbell box."

"Did you find a print?"

"No," he said hesitantly. "Couldn't find any fingerprints. It was possible that the shooter rang the doorbell from inside in order to draw Backer away from the house. Also," he exclaimed, "we managed to pull a shoe print from the hallway where Mrs. Backer claimed the shooter entered. Kersey also found this jammed in the side panel of the door, the strike plate."

Christian held up a baggie.

"A rock?" Corpus said and examined the small pebble in the bag.

"The shooter must've placed the rock inside the strike plate that way the dead bolt wouldn't close all the way."

"Pretty amateur."

"You know, from what I read, Ted's neighbor heard a noise just before the shooting," Christian said. "Maybe it was a diversion. Maybe to draw Ted from the house."

"Maybe."

"As far as the shoe, we narrowed it down to four tennis shoes, but. . . "

Corpus mumbled, "But. . . "

Christian finished, "But the shoe print in Backer's house doesn't match Screw's shoe size."

"What else?"

"I found another print on the Smith and Wesson, a partial."

"You did?" Corpus's eyes widened. "And?"

"I had the print run through the database. . . "

"And?"

"Nothing."

"Shit," Corpus whispered and ran his fingers across his puffy eyes. "Who else knows about this?"

"Just you," he said and held up a file. "It's all in the report."

"Thanks, Christian," he said and glanced over the file in Christian's hand. "May I?"

"I need it back, though."

"Of course."

Christian handed Corpus the file.

Corpus walked away.

"Where you headed?"

"I got to go to Lansford Medical."

As Corpus was walking down the hallway, Christian said from behind, "I almost forgot. I ran that hair you found at the crime scene. It's in the report as well, but I thought I'd tell you in person anyway. . ."

Corpus turned his shoulder.

"It was faux fur," Christian informed. "It's mostly found in women's clothing, jackets. Get this. It's also used for Halloween masks."

Corpus said, "Like a werewolf mask. . ."

And then Christian followed, ". . . Just like a werewolf mask."

EIGHT

AROUND four o'clock in the afternoon, a lanky, homeless man named Demetrius Brown left the corner of Town and Seventh Street where he panhandled daily with a cardboard sign: "WIL WERK 4 FOOD."

Every afternoon before the rush hour, Demetrius hit up two popular routes, one between Seventh and Jefferson Street for some shut-eye and then the other from Third to Court Street for a little extra dough to take back to the shelter. Court Street was always teeming with lawyers and bankers with substantially deep pockets, especially after five o'clock. Mornings were fairly decent, depending on the traffic. Demetrius usually targeted the strollers, the gazers, and the slow coffee sippers. Fridays, however, were the worst days. Same went for Saturdays. Over the five long years of living on the streets, mainly around the business district in uptown Lansford, he had learned who to avoid and who not to avoid. Roughly eighty percent of the time spent panhandling on the street, Demetrius learned that the women were the most generous and sympathetic. The other twenty percent of women (the white businesswomen in their thirties, maybe forties, Rolex, no ring on their fingers, stern face—almost never smiled—cell phone clung to their ear like an earring, and a hair cut from the 1970's) were a hard sell, the "proceed with caution" type, the uptight and conservative, or what Demetrius called in high spirits "Miss Ratched." Demetrius, of course, had learned the hard way about approaching a Miss Ratched, especially after he was accused of trying to grope one when, in fact, he was preventing one from walking out into moving traffic when she was jabbering on her cell phone and not paying attention to what she was doing. The act of kindness resulted in Demetrius spending a night in jail. Working the men was a little trickier. Most of the time with the men (*but* not all the time), it came down to the classic lines: "Why don't you get a job!" or "Quit taking up space and do something productive!" or "Scram, you goddamn bum!" As much as Demetrius didn't appreciate hearing the hostility, mainly from his own gender, he surprisingly welcomed the curt responses and took it—more or less—as a sign of progress. The one thing he dreaded throughout the day was being ignored. Sure. Demetrius had a thick hide, a lot thicker than most homeless men his age. For years, Demetrius had been living with one swift rejection after another. After five years of rejection, Demetrius had almost become numb. At times, he longed for responses: "Get a job" or "Get lost." But the neglect, he dreaded, was something he still couldn't handle. Panhandling aside, the one joy of his day (besides a smile or a handshake or a simple act of acknowledgment from another patron) was dumpster diving. Sort of became a daily ritual for Demetrius. After he lost his job at the shoe factory, he never thought he would resort to bottom feeder behavior. Prior to being homeless, he had bought everything, including food and clothes, with his own money that he earned at the factory. These customs were soon cast aside once Demetrius went broke. The game was different now. He was a shrimp living among sharks. Out here, it was survival of the fittest. Five years had gone on like this: panhandling, dumpster diving, panhandling, more dumpster diving, and then, finally, getting in line early at the shelter for a cozy bed. For Demetrius, he had never grown comfortable to this way of life. As long as he had been homeless, he had run into some pretty strange people, especially other homeless men like himself at the shelter. But never, in all his days of living on the streets, had he ever run into a person dressed up as a werewolf.

Suspicious of the Porsche 911 parked in the shadows on the side of the alley between Seventh and Jefferson, which so happened to be his favorite resting spot during the late afternoon hours, Demetrius looked twice at the person behind the wheel.

"What in the. . . "

As Demetrius crept closer to the black car for a closer look, his eyes suddenly bulged with fear.

The driver's side window was rolled down.

"*Hey there,*" the Werewolf said from inside the car. The Werewolf was wearing the same outfit as before—the black and gray varsity jacket with a gray letter H on the front breast pocket, green flannel, and green surgical gloves. The only difference was the mask. Unlike the previous mask that the Werewolf had burned on the night of the shooting, the hair wasn't salt and pepper. This particular werewolf mask, which was bought at the Attic's sister store, the Cellar, was dark brown with crimson red eyes and black gums around its fangs. The tiny pupils of the eyes were made up of holes where the person could see. The range of vision was exceptionally limited, more so than the last mask.

Demetrius took a couple of steps away from the car.

The Werewolf said, "*I promise I won't bite.*"

"Excuse, Mister, he said, "but why in God's name are you dressed up like a wolf?"

"*Werewolf.*"

"Oh. . . okay. . ."

"*It's called disguise.*"

"Disguise from what?"

"*From bad people,*" the Werewolf said and pulled out a wad of cash, mostly hundreds, from its pocket. "*Would you like to make some money?*"

"Ahhhhh. . . depends on what you want me to do. . ."

"*There's a group called OCD. Ever heard of them?*"

The homeless man couldn't help but notice the cash in the Werewolf's hand.

"Ma. . . maybe," he stuttered.

"*So, how much do you know about them?*" the Werewolf asked and held out the hundred dollar bill.

Demetrius hesitated at first.

Once more, his eyes fell upon the crisp bill.

He grabbed the hundred from the Werewolf's hand and pocketed it.

"Hhhhhhhhh. . . how much do you want to know about them?"

"*All there is. . .*"

"Well," Demetrius said through his trembling voice and looked around the drab alleyway in paranoia, "you ain't a cop. Are you?"

The Werewolf shook its head.

"You see," Demetrius said and stepped closer and marveled at the Porsche 911, "I don't exactly know the folks you speak of, but I can take you to some people who might know a thing or two about them."

"*Can you take me to these people?*"

"Ahhhhh. . . yeah. . . sure. . ."

"*Then hop in, my friend,*" the Werewolf said and opened the passenger side door for Demetrius.

"What. . . what's exactly in it for me?"

"*You'll be doing your city a favor,*" the Werewolf said. "*In return, you'll be rewarded. . .*"

The Werewolf counted five hundred dollars. Then, the Werewolf displayed the crisp bills in front of the homeless man, who hadn't blinked his eyes from the moment he ran his fingers over the hundred-dollar bill.

"*. . . I'll make it worth your while.*"

Demetrius reached his fingerless gloved hand toward the cash, but the Werewolf briskly pulled back the cash.

"*First, you find out all there is to know about OCD, then you get your money. Is that a deal?*"

"Who are you?"

"*Is it a deal?*"

Demetrius nodded.

"Yes, sir," he drawled.

"*Now, get in.*"

After the Werewolf dropped him off in Parker Square with a pen and a piece of paper, Demetrius, who wasn't quite familiar with OCD, only heard about them through word of mouth on the streets, found a couple of elementary school kids playing a game of P.I.G. on an old basketball court behind Screw's apartment complex. The two boys, Antwaine, also known as the "Ant," and Craig (despite how young they were) were the eyes and ears of Parker Square. The two knew everything about everyone, especially Ant. Most people around Parker Square knew him as another name: the Little Gossip Queen. If someone needed the scoop on somebody, they were the ones to turn to, especially the Little Gossip Queen. Demetrius (who was going over the questions the Werewolf had listed in his head) stumbled upon the two boys and asked them if they could help him out with a little information about a certain group of people who called themselves OCD. The boys, who, at first, were somewhat skeptical about helping out the homeless man and even more so eager as to why a homeless man wanted to know the lowdown on one of the deadliest groups of people in Lansford, decided to help with any questions Demetrius had, but only for a fee. After some convincing from the two, Demetrius ended up forking out a hundred dollar bill, or a "Benjamin" as they asked for, that the Werewolf had given him in the alleyway.

Demetrius's questions were straightforward: Who is OCD? A: *Three rough niggas: Orlando, Cedric, and Detric.* So, what's their game? A: *Easy* (Ant shrugged). *They what I call the don't-fuck-wit crew. Yep.* Watch your mouth, lil' man. *That's what they is, though. When there's heat on these streets. . . well, you get what I'm sayin'. They act like they own these streets, but they don't. They just a bunch of niggas up to no good.* Then, start with Orlando. What's his deal? A: *People call him Teardrop.* Teardrop? And why do they call him Teardrop? A: *Because he's a Pillsbury Doughboy nigga. . . . Because he shaped like a teardrop. Get it.* I get it. So, what else? A: *He got a baby and a baby momma and a baby's momma momma. He ain't never wit them, though.* And how about this Cedric guy? *Shank.* Shank? *Yeah. Shank. Meaning you fuck wit him, then your ass is gettin' shanked.* What can you tell me about him? A: *He and Screw hustle these streets here.* (Craig joined in) *And his girls too. His 'Hoes.' They be slingin' most of their smack for them.*

Demetrius asked more questions about OCD and jotted down the answers on the piece of paper that the Werewolf gave him. In return, the boys told Demetrius all he needed to know about OCD, including the stocky one, Orlando, the "alpha" of the pack, where he lived; they even walked Demetrius over to Orlando's car, the Cadillac Coupe Deville, which was parked outside a housing complex. While Demetrius walked the boys back to the basketball courts, they also told him about this one cop they had frequently seen in the neighborhood. His name was Ted Backer, but the Werewolf knew him best as Officer Backer, or better yet the late Officer Backer.

When Demetrius left with a clear understanding about OCD and enough information to bring back to the Werewolf, what OCD was up to, the players involved, their connection with Screw and Officer Backer, Demetrius told Ant and Craig that they didn't see him and like the movies, did so with a wink.

By sundown, the Werewolf, who was now well informed about OCD, found another candidate, a prostitute named

Victoria Wise, better known as her working girl name, Vick Licky, walking the streets outside Chinatown in uptown Lansford. The Werewolf pulled up beside Ms. Licky, whose first reaction was one of amusement. Ms. Licky's laughter soon came to a halt. All seriousness washed over her heavily painted face. The Werewolf asked Ms. Licky if she wanted to make some money, in fact, five hundred dollars as the Werewolf had paid Demetrius. "You a freak, boy," she said, sliding her slippery tongue between the massive gap between her front two incisors. When the Werewolf displayed the wad of cash in its hand, Ms. Licky, who was extremely leery about getting in the car, especially after witnessing the surgical gloves, finally agreed to the proposal. For Ms. Licky, a werewolf fantasy wouldn't have been the first time. She had blown stranger men. There was that one freak, she remembered, who had a bag full of outfits in the backseat of his car. One of the outfits was a French maid outfit. Then, there was that one guy with a bag of skimpy clothes that he had stolen from his sister. How could she forget about him? The Werewolf and Ms. Licky drove ten minutes from Lansford to a hardware store called O'Riley's Home Improvement located just outside Madison. The entire car ride Ms. Licky had her hand gripped tightly against the can of Mace in her pocketbook. If he made the slightest move, then she was going to unload the entire can into his eyes. The Werewolf sent Ms. Licky in the hardware store where she bought a set of auto jiggler keys, which consisted of ten keys, a universal lock pick, binoculars, and a box of Kill-A-Rat (most potent poison on the market). As with Demetrius, Ms. Licky was rewarded for her services with five hundred dollars and the words "*you never saw me*" spoken to her as she exited the car.

Next, the Werewolf drove across town to a Radioshack where a cockeyed man named Jake the Snake informed the twelve year old boy, Kenny, short for Kenneth, about a friend of a friend's brother who he thought would be able to take care of the Werewolf's so-called "dilemma." Kenny never walked out with what the Werewolf was looking for, the special eavesdropping device. However, Kenny told the Werewolf about Jack the Snake's friend's brother and gave the Werewolf a torn sheet of paper with a phone number and the name "Van Man." Even though Kenny didn't do much but ask the clerk about a certain device, he was still rewarded—like the two other candidates, Demetrius, the homeless man, and Ms. Licky, the prostitute—with the five hundred dollars.

After leaving Radioshack, the Werewolf met up with Jake the Snake's nameless friend, the Van Man (a sketchy-looking individual from Ukraine), behind a dark brown unmarked van parked in the back of a grocery store where he showed the Werewolf the "goods" from a briefcase. The entire time, the Werewolf was waiting for cops to spring out from the back of the store or repel down buildings or helicopters to come zooming overhead or, even worse, for Jake the Snake's nameless Ukrainian friend, the Van Man, to brandish a gun. Luckily, that wasn't the case at all. The transition went smoothly, the Werewolf suspected, maybe even too smoothly. The Werewolf ended up buying a two-way GSM audio listening device, which was about the size of a box of matches, as well as a SMI card that could be inserted in a disposable cell phone, or a "burner" as the Van Man called the phone. The scoop: place the SMI card in the back of the burner and then dial in the special number on the GSM. Next: once the GSM is securely planted, then any audio signal closest to the device would send a call to the Werewolf's burner. The Van Man strictly informed the Werewolf that the stuff came from New Delhi and that if the Werewolf just so happened to get caught with such devices (most importantly by the "authorities"), then the Werewolf didn't know him or even meet him for that matter. "This little meeting here never took place," the Van Man said and then the Werewolf strolled away, in essence, like a ghost.

With the set of auto jiggler keys, the Werewolf broke into Orlando's Coupe Deville while he was being interrogating downtown and planted the two-way GSM device behind the vent of the dashboard and then parked a safe distance away. An hour passed during the stakeout when Orlando finally arrived at his complex. His girlfriend, Sissy, a petite woman who had dyed gold hair, parked next to the Coupe Deville in her beat up Pinto. The Werewolf didn't have to listen in on the conversation from the burner. The masked vigilante could hear the whole conversation quite well from where it was parked. In fact, the entire neighborhood could hear the conversation from their living quarters.

Orlando quickly stormed out of the car and slammed the door behind him.

Sissy was tailing him to his Coupe Deville and shouting at him, "Are you gonna come in and take care of your baby or are you gonna run off to that skinny bitch like you always do?"

Orlando didn't respond from the remark.

Instead, he waved his hand away.

Sissy's mother, a sixty-eight year old woman named Beverly Riggs, who was best known around the neighborhood as Sister Beverly for her work at the church, hurried from the complex with Orlando's three-year-old daughter in her arms.

She asked, "What's going on out here, Sissy?"

"I don't know!" Sissy shouted out. "Why don't you ask Orlando here!"

Orlando backed away from the Coupe Deville.

"You know what!" he seethed with a grimace. "I'm sick and tired of your mouth, girl!"

He suddenly stepped forward and raised his right hand at Sissy.

"Go on, then!" Sissy shouted back as she took another step forward—now inches away from Orlando. "Go 'head and hit me for the whole neighborhood to see! They already know what you are!"

Orlando stepped even closer, a breath away from Sissy.

"And what is that. . . "

"A coward," she said, the tears falling from her eyes.

"Orlando," Beverly said sternly from behind, "you lay one finger on my daughter and I'm calling the police. You hear me?"

Orlando snorted and walked back to the Coupe Deville.

"The hell wit you people," he said under his breath, got inside the Coupe Deville, and drove away.

The Werewolf started up the ignition and made sure to keep a distance from Orlando.

For about a half an hour, Orlando cruised around the city of Lansford. He stopped twice, once at a convenient store to pick up a pack of Phillies Blunts and a forty-ounce of Sherman's malt liquor concealed in a brown bag and another time on the side of Roseberry Lane to dump out the tobacco inside the Phillies cigar. After Orlando was done cruising around, he stopped in front of Screw's apartment complex where Cedric and Detric were waiting for Orlando outside. The two got inside Orlando's Coupe Deville. As before, the Werewolf parked at a safe distance from the Couple Deville.

Two car doors slammed.

A man shouting!

Suddenly, the Werewolf's cell phone rang.

"*We're in business,*" the Werewolf said, switched on the speaker, and placed the burner on top of the dashboard.

The Werewolf reached to the passenger seat, grabbed a composition notebook, as well as a pen, and flipped to an empty page in the back. The Werewolf listened closely to the conversation inside the Coupe Deville:

What took you so long, fool?
Man! My girl be trippin'. She's all up in my face all the god-damn time.
I don't blame that girl. You gotta kid now, Orlando. You need to settle that shit before they get your ass in troubles.
Settle it? Settle it how, Shank?
(Cedric sniffled)
First, you can start wit her nosy fuckin' mother.
What? You fuckin' junkie. I ain't doing that shit.
(Leather cracked)

From where the Werewolf was parked, he witnessed Orlando's portly silhouette rotating around in the driver's seat toward Cedric in the backseat. In the composition notebook, the Werewolf wrote down the word *junkie* in perfect cursive next to Cedric's name.

If Screw finds out that you pinched from his shit, he's gonna flip.
(A snort)
How he gonna know when he's in jail? Besides, I got a personal stash. No sweat, nigga.
So, how'd it go wit the cops?
They found the baton. Had Screw's prints all over that shit.
Bullshit.
You say anything?
Not a goddamn word. That's the truf.
You sure?
(Orlando smacked his gums)
I ain't say shit. I swear.
(Another sniff, this time from Orlando)
The shit ain't right, man. Sooner or later, Screw's gonna talk. I know that fool is. They even said they know there was two other cops involved.
You know Wheaten or Marson ain't gonna nark us out. If they do, then they dead men. THAT'S THE TRUF!

The Werewolf wrote down two more names, *Wheaten* and *Marson*, both with the word *cop* and *question mark* written down beside both of their names.

It ain't them I'm worried 'bout. It's Screw. You know that piece of shit. Dude be always looking out for himself.
If you were in his position, would you?
What the fuck we do now?
We lay low.
How'd they know we wit Screw to begin with?
I don't even know. They said a witness saw us with him that night, but it don't sound right.
Witness?
That's what they said.
There ain't no witness. They just fuckin' wit us.

(Static)
I say we jus kill that muthafucka. . .
We ain't killin' nobody.
(More static and interference)
What if he talks, Orlando? Then your flabby ass is going back to jail. Same for the rest of us.
I can't go back. You know I can't handle the slammer again. I'll die by my own hand before I let them pigs take me in again.

Next to Orlando's name, the Werewolf wrote down the word *frightened.*

The connection broke up over the cheap burner and drifted into a steady wave of static.

After a minute of loss signal, the Werewolf pressed the END button on the burner, tossed it on the passenger seat, and directed its attention back to those three names, Orlando, Cedric, and Detric, in the composition notebook.

The Werewolf knew nothing about Wheaten or Marson (at least nothing that it had gathered from Demetrius earlier that day in the alleyway), only that these two individuals were possible cops working for the Lansford Police Department. The Werewolf certainly couldn't go after two more cops, it realized after careful consideration, especially with all the heat that Henry was getting from Ted Backer's murder. As far as Detric, the Werewolf didn't have much to go by other than he was a stone cold killer. "Heartless," some would say.

After careful consideration, the Werewolf wrote down a giant *question mark* next to his name.

NINE

AT high noon the next day, the Werewolf cruised around the outskirts of Parker Square in search for the next candidate.

Only five minutes into the drive, the Werewolf spotted a tweaker twitching on the side of the road. The tweaker was acting as if she had ants in her pants, scratching various parts of her body. Her teeth, the Werewolf noticed as the Porsche pulled up to the curb, were brown and decayed—"meth mouth," was what the locals called it.

As with the other chosen candidates, the homeless man, the prostitute, and the young boy, the Werewolf promised the tweaker, Jasmine was her name, five hundred dollars for her services. Showed Jasmine the money. Even let Jasmine touch it just to show her that it was, in fact, "real" and not a figment of her imagination. The job wasn't as easy as the Werewolf had planned, especially working with a tweaker. The job: buy one gram of dope from Cedric's "Hoes," who were doing their daily rounds on the corner of Grover and Thirty-second Street. The job seemed easy enough; however, the Werewolf was dealing with a tweaker.

When the Werewolf found them, the three women, they were in the process of slinging a bag of dope to a couple of high school kids who were skipping class. As the Werewolf kept its distance behind a hearse parked outside Kersey's Funeral Home, which received plenty of business around here, especially during the holidays, Jasmine carefully observed the exchange between drugs and money. From what the Werewolf gathered, the transition was hardly noticeable. *"You see,"* the Werewolf pointed out to Jasmine, *"if they asked where you got the money, just tell them you stole it from a friend."* If one blinked, one would've missed it, the exchange. It was that good. Surprising too, coming from a bunch of high school kids. The whole process went down with a simple handshake. There, drugs and money were passed along from the connection of hands, one hand grabbing a folded up bill while the other one grabbing a bag of drugs. One of the women, the butch who was doing the slinging of the dope, was wearing black leather gloves over her hands. Over the palm, she had a slit where she stuffed the money inside with her fingers. So, when the exchange was complete, she never did anything sudden like cram the money inside her pocket or stuff it down her cleavage or, even worse, count it on the sidewalk for the entire neighborhood to see. Instead, the butch gave a nod and said her goodbyes to the customer and joined her fellow girls on the post. After the Werewolf watched Jasmine do a couple of mock trials and practice the exchange several times with a folded dollar bill, she was released from the Porsche to buy a gram of heroin. The exchange was sloppy, amateur at best. Jasmine was a jitterbug. She kept glancing around the street in paranoia with her bug eyes. Her legs were like wobbly stilts, about to bend and crack. The whole time she appeared as if she really had to go—as if a number two was poking out and she didn't know how much longer she could hold it in before it slid down the side of her thigh. When the deal was over (during the exchange hardly any words were spoken), Jasmine dropped the bag of dope on the ground. The Hoes, the butch mainly, didn't think too much about the awkward deal. She just thought the customer was new to this sort of thing—most definitely not a cop and if she was working with the cops, then black and white would be on them right about now. Occasionally, but not always, the Hoes dealt with Jasmine's type, the first time buyers or the ones looking for a quick alternative from crystal meth or just something to settle them down. Jasmine left Thirty-second Street and walked back to Kersey's Funeral Home where the Werewolf was waiting. As promised, the Werewolf gave Jasmine the five hundred dollars (the Werewolf, of course, grabbed the bag of dope first and then handed Jasmine her money).

Two hours later, the Porsche was parked three houses down from a ranch style house in a suburb called Meadow's End off Baker Road (about five minutes away from Screw's apartment complex) where Detric and his mother, Jacqueline, best known as Ms. Walker to her students, resided. Two individuals were camped inside the Porsche, one being Ashley Sparks or Ash, a freshman who recently transferred from Green Acres, a reputable prep school in North Madison, to South Lansford High School, who was seated in the passenger seat and then the other being the Werewolf who was seated in the driver's seat. The Werewolf discovered Ash sitting alone on top of the Space Rock, a famous hangout in the woods outside Parker Square where high schoolers (mostly from South Lansford) went to smoke weed and drink beers and play truth or dare or as in Ash's case, to cut themselves with a razor blade. Ash, whose parents had recently downsized after his father got laid off from his job at the Company, always wore long sleeves in order to cover up the scars on his arms. For about a year, Ash had been cutting himself, never deep enough to penetrate a main artery but deep enough to draw blood. The Space Rock used to be the perfect place to get away from parents, especially for Ash. As of lately, though, the massive boulder, which was as tall as a two-story house, had been known to attract another kind: the junkies, tweakers, homosexuals, and even homeless people. Before, the giant rock was a paradise for high schoolers, a place where high schoolers could act like high schoolers without any repercussions. Now, it was a dirty place, disease ridden with used needles or condoms.

"*So,*" the Werewolf said as he handed a hundred dollar bill to Ash, "*what'd she have to say?*"

"Her name is Kasha," Ash said casually, glancing over to the Werewolf seated next to him in the Porsche. "Kasha has two kids. Seems like a nice woman."

"I don't care about her. . . just tell me about Detric's mother."

"Ms. Walker?"

The Werewolf slowly bobbed its head.

Ash focused on how the recent conversation went down: Kasha answering the door with one hand on her hip and carefully eyeing Ash, starting from the red and black Vans on his feet. Then, Kasha saying with an attitude, "We don't want any of your magazines you be selling." Ash: "I'm actually looking for Detric." Kasha: "That fool next door?" Ash: "He didn't answer." In the background, Kasha's two children were laughing at Bugs Bunny on a television as small as a textbook. Then, Ash: "I was wondering if you knew where he was." Kasha, as she had been doing ever since she laid her eyes on Ash, smacked her gums. She said, "Tell me. Do I look like his mother?" Ash: "Sorry. I don't mean to disturb you." The conversation came back, details, facial expressions, and whatnot.

"She said Ms. Walker's son is a lowlife," Ash said to the Werewolf.

"*What else?*"

The Werewolf unpeeled the bill from the wad of cash and handed Ash another hundred dollars.

Ash remembered: Before Ms. Walker's neighbor shut the door in his face, Ash suddenly extended his hand in the way and nearly got his fingers smashed in the process. He said, "I'm new to the neighborhood!" Kasha cracked open the door, cautiously; half of her body was now concealed behind the panel. She noticed a couple of fresh cuts over Ash's wrists. Ash continued: "I actually met Detric a couple of nights ago. I was just wondering if you knew anything about him." Kasha: "You a cop? You know, like one of them undercover ones." Ash: "No." He chortled, causing Kasha to roll her eyes. *What's up, Doc?* He heard the sound of Bugs Bunny chewing a carrot in the background. The details blurred a little. Kasha was saying something like "That fool ain't nuttin but trouble." Her lips puckered on one side of her face. Then: "You look like a good person, at least from what. . . from what I can see. But that don't mean a thing, especially nowadays. If I was you, boy, I wouldn't be hanging 'round fools like that, like Detric." Ash: "So, you do know Detric?" Kasha smacked her gums and said, "I know his kind if you feel me. He be blasting music at all hours of the night, waking up my kids. Cops practically live over there. And I've seen with my own eyes the marks on her face, Detric's mother. She tried covering them up once, but I seen them. Uh. Shoot!" Kasha shook her head in repulsion. "That poor woman, Jacqueline." She went on to say: "Still can't believe Jacqueline keeps that fool around. Ain't like Jacqueline got a choice in the matter. Detric, he don't give a darn 'bout anyone 'round here! You should hear the way he be talkin' to poor Jacqueline. And that one kid he be hangin' out wit. Cedric! He just as worse." Ash: "What more can you tell me about Jacqueline? What does she do for a living?" Kasha: "Ms. Walker, she a special ed teacher at the East Ridge Academy. She been teaching for forty-three years, I believe so. Now, she be constantly living in fear because of her deadbeat (*lowlife*), loser son of hers." Kasha cleared her throat. "You sure you ain't a cop?" Ash: "No. I'm no cop." Kasha: "You sure do be actin' like a cop, coming up here with your questions and all." Ash: "I promise." The neighbor ran her eyes down Ash's body and then looked around the street. "Jacqueline, she's a good woman. She has a good heart, unlike her son. All Detric cares about is himself. At times, I seen him come home late at night, three o'clock in the morning, with a gun in his hand. Then, the next day you hear all 'bout these shootings and killings in Parker Square. And cops ain't doing a damn thing about it!"

Then, the Werewolf gave Ash another hundred.
Ash informed, "She said the guy's a killer."
"*A killer, huh?*"
"That's what she said," Ash said and innocently lifted up his hands in the air. "If you don't believe me than the hell with you, Wolf Man."
Ash opened the passenger seat.
"*Wait,*" the Werewolf suddenly said and unpeeled another hundred from the wad of cash.

The conversation went blurry.
Ash focused: Kasha was saying, "His kind (*Detric's kind?*) don't belong here anymore. This is a society. And we're good people here. If you wanna to go live like that, like an animal, then you can go 'head and live in a jungle. Not in here!" Her lips, Ash could see in his mind. They slanted to the side. Then, her eyebrows. One of her brows was furrowed downward as if it was grinning at him. "It's only a matter of time for that fool ends up behind bars. Me, I'm

just counting down the days." Ash: "That bad?" Kasha rolled her eyes and smacked her gums. She said, "Sure is," and gave Ash another once over. "It's that bad. Me, I just don't see how can a good-looking person such as yourself be associated with someone like Detric. To me, it don't make any sense."

"*Is that it?*"
"No," Ash said. "There's one more thing. . . "
The Werewolf mechanically rotated its head around.
"Am I dead?"
"*No,*" the Werewolf said to Ash. "*You're not dead.*"

After the Werewolf left Meadow's End and as with the other candidates, paid Ash the five hundred dollars and sent him on his way as if this conversation never took place, the Werewolf tailed Orlando's girlfriend, Sissy. The Werewolf followed her to her two jobs, one where she worked as a cashier at the local Choice Food in Parker Square and the other where she worked as a clerk at a Xpress Mart at the opposite side of town (all done, of course, from a safe distance). Just after ten o'clock at night, she came back home where her retired mother, Beverly, was waiting on her with her daughter. The next morning, Sissy woke up, fixed her daughter breakfast—a bowl of *Kool Kelly* Flakes—and did the same routine over again.

On the next night of the stakeout, the Werewolf stalked closer to Orlando's apartment. Like the days before, the Werewolf followed Sissy to work, to her two jobs, and then back to her home. The Werewolf used a pair of binoculars that Ms. Licky had bought from the hardware store and kept an eye on the three inside. Before they were about to go to sleep and tuck Melanie into bed, Orlando, reeking of booze and cigarettes, stumbled inside. The Werewolf witnessed the entire events unfold: Orlando yelling at Sissy, Orlando tossing a beer bottle against the wall, Sissy then yelling back at Orlando ("Where the hell have you been?") and then Orlando slapping Sissy across the face. Beverly came between the two and did all she could to break up the fight. In return, she was struck in the face as well and sent to the floor where she twisted her ankle. Next, Sissy scurried over to Melanie, who was crying. The Werewolf was tempted to act like a vigilant guardian and break down the door and rescue the two from harm's way. Taking into account what the Werewolf was planning so far (these past couple of days, the stakeouts, the supplies that it had gathered, the questionings, using the citizens of Lansford to its advantage), the Werewolf decided to let things play out. . . Orlando went on a tirade about how he was treated around here on a daily basis, how he wasn't respected anymore, by anyone, how he was forced to take action. The Werewolf desperately wanted to kick down that door and show Orlando what respect really looked like. Not in front of the girl, *not in front of Melanie*, the masked vigilante thought, anything but in front of Melanie. She would be affected for the rest of her life, traumatized. The Werewolf specifically told itself, "Leave it alone." So, the Werewolf did exactly that, left Sissy and her family alone, and forced itself to watch through the binoculars. Ten minutes had gone by. The yelling and the crying finally died out. Eventually, Orlando passed out in the living room (arms and legs spilled over the couch like a grizzly bear in hibernation) while the other three slept in the bedroom next to the living room. Melanie didn't have too much of a problem sleeping in her queen sized bed with her pink Kool Kelly blanket and her stuffed Kool Kelly doll in her arms. However, for Sissy and her mother, Beverly, they didn't sleep at all that night.

TEN

WHILE Cedric was grabbing a bite to eat with his Hoes at KFS, the Werewolf started the campaign.

"Every junkie keeps a stash close by," the Werewolf said as it surveyed the empty apartment.

In case their memories fall short, which, in most cases, they always do, the Werewolf knew from experience they had that stash for extra support like a crutch or a life preserver. Somewhere close by, a place that received a lot of traffic, such as a nightstand or dresser.

While wandering into the bedroom (used tank tops and holey and tattered FUBU jeans scattered across the stained shag carpet like the average college dorm room, naked lady posters on the walls—one of them of Darine Stern on the iconic cover from the1971 *Playboy* magazine—the stench of must and stale booze in the air, bags of marijuana, mostly broken stems and seeds, as well as a pack of rolling papers and a box of Black and Mild on a wobbly poker table, and a stack of burned CD's on top of a gutted subwoofer), the Werewolf came across a nightstand.

The Werewolf kneeled down beside the nightstand and with its gloved hand, opened the top drawer. There, the masked vigilante found several baggies that Cedric used for slinging. However, the baggies were empty. Next to the baggies was an electronic scale and then hand scales. Next to that were twisties for the baggies. The Werewolf fished through the junk and drug paraphernalia, mostly glass and metal pipes, lighters and bullet casings, a poorly sculpted clay turtle painted blue—which the Werewolf thought was strange—until it came across a Holy Bible.

A King James Version, the Werewolf read, New Testament.

"Hmmm. . ."

Curiously, the Werewolf picked up the Bible from the pile of junk and opened it up. A balled up gram of heroin, which was wedged inside the Gospel of Matthew, slipped from the worn pages and landed next to the Werewolf's black Chucky T's. The Werewolf reached into its pocket, pulled out a baggie of its own, and compared the two bags in its hands: its "special" bag of heroin that it had made last night with a stolen medicine crusher from Lansford Medical Center and then Cedric's personal stash.

The two stashes looked almost identical.

"He'll never know. . ." the Werewolf said to itself and replaced Cedric's secret stash with the other stash, the special one.

The Werewolf closed the New Testament and placed it back in the drawer in the exact same position as before.

ELEVEN

THE next few days were like watching a tiny crack steadily stretch across a pane of glass.

Soon, the glass was going to shatter (this was inevitable) and then all the pieces would fall to the ground.

The first piece to fall: Cedric Johnson, aka Shank.

The morning after the Werewolf planted that "special" stash in Cedric's apartment, the police were called to the scene.

Cedric's Hoes discovered Cedric's body on the bed with a needle in his vein, a rubber tie around his elbow, and his personal stash, which had been cut through with a razor, as well as a warped spoon and a butane lighter on the nightstand.

Shortly after, the paramedics were called to the scene and then the coroners.

When the two detectives, Corpus and Merrotti, finally arrived at Cedric's apartment, Cedric's Hoes were huddled in the corner like an ant colony, talking to several LPD police officers.

Merrotti identified Cedric's body.

"Shank," he said. "Looks like an overdose."

Then, Corpus said it best to Merrotti: "This is only the beginning."

*   *   *

Every Thursday for the past eight years now, Jacqueline left the East Ridge Academy and took a bus to Beatty Road where she volunteered at Smith & Roger homeless shelter. Every week, she would bring her famous cranbrosia that she had kept refrigerated throughout the day and serve the cool dish to the homeless people of Lansford.

After Jacqueline left Smith & Roger, she took the nine o'clock bus back to Grier Springs where she walked three blocks down Baker Road. In all of the eight years she had been taking the bus home, she never expected to run into a person dressed up as a werewolf.

Halfway toward her house, Jacqueline was yanked into a dark alley between Valentine's Bakery and a vacant building, which used to be a jewelry store, where a sharp blade was placed gently over the pulse on her neck.

A gloved hand firmly slipped over her mouth.

"*Don't even think about it, bitch*," the muffled voice of the Werewolf said sharply from behind. The shadowy face, Jacqueline witnessed through the corner of her right eye, was beastly, not human. The eyes too, she observed before the Werewolf jerked her head forward, were as red as two distant brake lights glistening in the overhead streetlight. "*I'm going to slowly remove my hand. If you scream, I will run this blade across your fucking throat. Is that understood?*"

With her eyes opened widely, Jacqueline quickly bobbed her head.

The gloved hand peeled away.

"Please. . . " Jacqueline murmured as she extended the purse from over her shoulder, ". . . take the purse."

The Werewolf pushed the purse aside.

"*I don't want your money.*"

"Then, what do you want," Jacqueline cried as she made an attempt to turn her head.

The gloved hand grabbed her cheek and redirected her head toward the street.

Jacqueline flinched and wailed out.

"*Hushhhhhh,*" the Werewolf said calmly.

The blade moved from the pulse of her neck and slightly pressed against Jacqueline's jugular.

A taunt silence built over the two.

Jacqueline heard the person breathing behind her, which was much deeper and hollower than her rapid breath.

The Werewolf said, "*There's still a chance you can make it out of this thing alive.*"

"What do you want from me?" Her voice was shivering, hands too. "I. . . I don't have much—"

"*—It's not you I want,*" the Werewolf interrupted.

Her eyes shriveled.

She sighed greatly.

"Oh dear. . . "

The Werewolf readjusted its grip around the handle of the blade.

Jacqueline's face went long, expressionless.

She said vacantly, "What has he done now?"

"*He's been a bad boy, Ms. Walker.*"

"Please. . . " she begged, the muscles protruding slightly from her neck, ". . . whatever it is you're about to do, don't do it. PLEASE DON—"

"*—Face it, Ms. Walker,*" the Werewolf said louder, its voice more raspy now. "*Your son, Detric, is a killer.*"

"I. . . I don't know what happened to him," she whined and stood there like a pole as her eyes glazed over. "He was never like this. Whatever he's done to you and your family, I swear it's not who he is. He was a good boy. It's those losers he hangs out with. They've turned my flesh and blood against me."

"*That's no excuse.*"

"I know it isn't," she said and struggled to breath.

"*Easy. . .*"

Jacqueline breathed slowly and deeply and then easy as the Werewolf had told her.

"After his father left us," she said, "he just wasn't the same." The crying then stopped. Her face washed over with seriousness. "My Detric died a long time ago."

Jacqueline made yet another attempt to face the strange creature behind her.

Again, a swift hand was there to redirect her attention.

"I don't think so."

The blade drew a drop of blood over her neck.

Jacqueline hissed and shut her eyes with all the muscles in her body tensing up. She embraced herself for what was to come next: murder. She waited three seconds now, four. The blade never ran across her throat, as she had expected. Yet, it remained there tightly pressed against her throat.

With her eyes closed, she said, "What are you going to do to him?"

"I'm going to make sure he doesn't harm another person ever again."

"Are you going to kill him?"

"Yes."

Without sobbing, the tears escaped from Jacqueline's closed eyelids and slid down her cheeks.

"Tonight, you stay at your sister's house in Freemont and wait for further instructions. Otherwise, you will share the same fate as your son." The blade pressed harder against her neck. *"And if you so dare tell the cops about our conversation, then I won't stop with you, Ms. Walker. I'll kill your sister, your two nephews, Jordan and Blake, and then I'll kill your mother. Is that understood?"*

Jacqueline frantically bobbed her head.

"Now, you hold their lives in your hands," the Werewolf said from behind. *"The choice is yours, Ms. Walker."*

The Werewolf released the blade from Jacqueline's neck and stepped back into the shadows of the alleyway.

Shaking, Jacqueline slowly rotated around and peered into the dark alley and witnessed the glint of the blade from below and then two red eyes hidden behind a hairy, beastly face drifting back into the darkness.

Jacqueline fell to her knees and cried, not inward like before, but loud and relieving.

*   *   *

Detric was rapping, "I said fuck you, you fuckin' little trick! Get your ass up on that pole and ride it until you feel fuckin' sick!"

While blasting the song "Pole Licka, Booty Shapeshifta" by Young Millionaire, formerly known as the underground prodigy, Dice, in his bedroom, Detric was weighing several grams of china white on an electronic scale that Cedric had loaned him. He immediately stopped what he was doing, including the rapping, and smelled something burning from the other room.

As the song blasted throughout the house, Detric got up from the chair and hurried from the bedroom, only to find the curtains alongside the living room wall up in flames.

"What the. . ." Detric said under his breath and rushed into the living room, only to find a wall of flames ripping through the plastic covers on the wool couch and spreading across the living room carpet. The black smoke was filling the room, making it nearly impossible to breath or see for that matter. Detric placed his sleeve over his mouth and dashed toward the front door.

Halfway toward the door, he saw two blood red eyes behind the door window. A wave of terror raced through his veins. He didn't know what to think of the eyes, red and menacing. His pace slowed. Then, a face manifested itself over the darkness of night. The face didn't turn out to be the angel of death or the devil himself, as Detric suggested at first glance, but rather yet, a person wearing a Halloween mask over its head.

Detric flipped on the porch light for a closer look, only to witness the Werewolf standing behind the front door.

With his face frozen in shock, Detric slowly backpedaled.

The flames suddenly climbed behind him in the living room.

Regardless of the person or thing standing on the porch, Detric had no other choice but to hurry to the door and open it.

The door didn't budge.

Now, he tugged and kicked.

He shouted out in desperation, "LET ME OUT!"

The Werewolf mechanically shook its head no.

Once more, Detric tried to kick open the door.

The galvanized chain that was wrapped around the door handle and locked around the barred windows prevented the door from opening.

"YOU MUTHAFUCKA!"

The smoke now overwhelmed Detric's body.

"YOU DEAD, BITCH!"

With his arm shielded over his nose and mouth, Detric rushed toward the back door, but the door was chained shut like the front door. Detric didn't have enough time to take a crowbar to the steel bars from the windows. So, he stumbled to his bedroom, which, like the living room, was filled with smoke, and grabbed the .45 from his desk. He loaded the gun and staggered from the bedroom.

During the trip toward the front door, he fell several times from the smoke inhalation. His vision was blurred. The flames covered most of the living room as well as the kitchen. Parts of the ceiling had collapsed from the flames.

In one last attempt of desperation, he shuffled toward the front door and fired a couple of rounds but didn't come close to hitting the masked vigilante, who, as before, remained like a stalker behind the front door.

Eventually, Detric's eyes rolled in the back of his head.

As Detric fell to the floor, the Werewolf took a drag from the cigarette and blew the smoke from the snout of the mask and stepped away from the burning house.

As soon as the Werewolf realized Detric was out cold, it removed the galvanized chains from both doors—the ones tied around the front and the ones tied around the back— with its gloved hands and stood on the front lawn where it marveled at the rising flames with Jacqueline's dog, Toto.

The strung out woman named Clementine placed her hand over one side of her hip and said in her sassy voice from the dark bedroom, "Are you gunna come back to bed or what, fool?"

"Shut your goddamn mouth, woman," Orlando said sternly from the couch as he watched the breaking news report on the television.

On the TV, Jacqueline's neighbor, Kasha, was talking to Jessica Veil, a Channel 6 news reporter, on the street as the fire blazed behind the two (reds and blues from cruisers and fire trucks flashing all around them). Kasha was holding Jacqueline's trembling cairn terrier, Toto, in her arms and jabbering about a strange creature—"this wolf-like thing," Kasha said in a state of disorientation—and then how this wolf-like thing was standing outside on the lawn while Ms. Jackie's house was up in flames.

In awe, Orlando slowly stood from the couch.

Clementine stumbled from the room and was revealed in the dim light of the living room. She appeared slightly anorexic, a quarter of the size of Orlando. She had dark circles underneath her unsteady, droopy eyes. Her ruffled weave was jacked to the side of her scalp as if it had been flattened by the wheels of a car.

She moaned, "What is you doing, Orlando? Ain't you gunna lay wit me?"

"It's Detric," he uttered, his face elongated, eyes never leaving the screen. "Some dude dressed up as a werewolf killed him."

"Wolf?"

"Werewolf," Orlando corrected.

"Whatcha mean 'werewolf'?"

Orlando pulled his eyes from the television and glared at Clementine.

Then, he said sharply, "That's what I just said, bitch."

"Aight," Clementine said harmlessly and gradually eased back into the bedroom. "Didn't mean anything by it."

"*Gunshots fired in The Cloves, apartment 532,*" the Werewolf said over the payphone.

Instead of hanging up, the Werewolf dropped the phone from its grip.

While the phone dangled below, the 911 operator on the other end of the line continued to ask the Werewolf about the recent emergency, but all she received was the sound of footsteps walking away through gravel.

As the swarm of police cruisers came speeding down the windy streets of The Cloves, the Werewolf stood vigilantly below the apartment complex and gazed up at the glowing window of Orlando's apartment.

The sirens came closer now.

Louder now!

Brighter!

The television suddenly switched off from the inside of the apartment.

Orlando rushed toward the window where he saw the flashing sirens from a distance.

"Oh hell nah. . ." he mumbled as his eyes traced to the vacant field below.

His eyes came across a shadowy figure, the Werewolf.

The Werewolf was gazing up at Orlando.

Infuriated, he pounded his fist against the pane of glass and shouted, "WHAT DO YOU WANT FROM ME?"

The Werewolf remained still, like a stalker.

As the police cruisers entered the Cloves, Orlando finally stormed away from the window and grabbed a semi-automatic pistol from his pant's pocket over the couch.

"I ain't going back. . ." Orlando cried out as he paced around the messy apartment, ". . . Fuck that. I ain't going back, man. . ."

Once more, he hurried to the window and watched the cruisers park in the parking lot outside the complex.

At least a dozen cops were rushing inside.

Guns drawn.

". . . I ain't going back. . ."

With his hand tightening around the grip of the pistol, Orlando paced around the living room.

"What the hell is going on, Orlando?" Clementine said from behind.

She crept from the bedroom when Orlando placed the pistol against his temple.

"Orlando!"

From below, the Werewolf heard the bang and then saw the flash from the pistol blast flicker over the apartment window.

The Werewolf strolled away, in essence, like a ghost into the darkness of night.

PART EIGHT

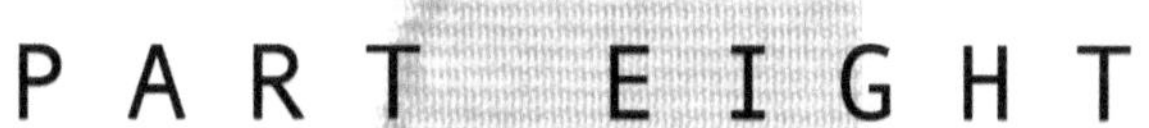

BRITTLE

TWELVE

AT 5:13 AM, Henry rolled his head to the other side of a glazed ceramic pillow, only to witness the Werewolf standing motionlessly before him in the bedroom.

The moonlight cast from the bedroom windows highlighted the outline of its slender frame, the tousled salt and pepper hair around its head, its primordial black eyes, and its claws, as long as knives, below its waist side.

Henry suddenly woke from his dormant state with his heart nearly leaping from his chest.

The pain brought on from a combination of alcohol and drugs and now a light from the vanity now rippled throughout his entire body, mainly behind his eyes.

"You can't be serious. . ." he whispered over a grumble as he pulled his face from the bathroom floor.

In the process, he pulled a long string of reddish drool from the tile and up into his mouth.

After Henry wiped his face clean with his sleeve and embraced several deep breaths through his nose, his heart finally beat into a more comfortable rhythm. He barely mustered enough saliva in his parched mouth to clear his throat. Then, he cracked his other eye. The bathroom? *But. . .* Henry soon realized the drool over his sleeve wasn't drool at all but leftover vomit from last night. This had soon become evident once he checked the toilet bowl and witnessed the carnage splattered over the sides of the toilet. *When did I. . .* Even the smell emitting from his body was gagging. His drenching wet clothes reeked of cigarette smoke. Several lines of blood had traced down his face, which left his damp white undershirt stained with brownish spots. His throat burned and ached from the entire pack of cowboy killers that he sucked down. He eventually gathered more saliva from the corners of his mouth, but the pain was still there in his throat, in his head, in fact, all over his body now. One side of his face, Henry realized after he managed to lift himself up to the mirror, was scarred with finely drawn lines from sleeping on the tile. He identified the deep cut over his chin as well. Henry didn't exactly know how he ended up with a cut on his chin. The stains on his shirt, he supposed, were from the cut. But the cut itself was unexplainable. He braced both hands around the sink, leaned forward, and sipped from the faucet without falling over. Before he could take another sip of water, the blood ran into his head and caused him to stagger from a sudden dizzy spell. He breathed slowly and braced himself against the sink. Eventually, the spell went away. He reached inside the medicine cabinet, grabbed the bottle of aspirin from the shelf, and downed three pills with a sip of water from his cupped hand. Next, he wiped the traces of cocaine from his nostrils, splashed his face with cold water, and then dried his face with his shirt. The cool water helped a little with the pain in his head, as well as the burn in his eyes.

Once he was all settled, he sat down on the toilet seat where he tried to remember how he ended up in the bathroom. He remembered driving home from where. . . Henry didn't exactly know where. Next, the sounds of police sirens were all around him, blaring. Then, he heard the *ding* of a cowbell overhead. Did it really happen? He focused his thoughts on the sharp ding and then the events that unfolded afterwards: strolling into a dirty convenient store off East Jester Avenue, grabbing a bottle of Mountain Spring water from the back, and then standing behind three other people in line. One of them was a middle-aged man, he remembered, arguing with the clerk about ringing up the wrong price. Then, a young man in his early twenties with a diamond in his left ear, Henry remembered, was standing in front of him with a forty ounce of Sherman's in his hand. All it took was one whiff of the man's jacket to send Henry to the edge. The young man had already been drinking earlier that night, even though he wasn't drunk. From what Henry observed, he was working his way through another forty ounce, maybe even two or three.

Six beers later, Henry found himself in a rundown bar with strange people doing one shot after another. Country music was playing overhead. The singer was singing something about losing his dog during a thunderstorm or something like that. Henry couldn't remember the details. He remembered, however, going to the lady's room with another woman, who was at least twenty years older than himself and wearing enough makeup on her face to pass as the Joker, and doing at least three pencil length lines of cocaine on the seat cover of the toilet. Next, he remembered breaking one of the hinges on the stall from where he accidentally slammed the woman's back into the door. Lozenges, he remembered as he picked up the strange odor on the very back of his tongue. The woman tasted like throat lozenges. Her breasts smelled like coconut and yet tasted nothing like that. They left together. They stopped near a dumpster in the back of a grungy alleyway where the older woman made yet another pass at Henry. While the woman was going down on Henry, a man dressed in all black was attacking a man (or woman?) not too far from them. The man (or woman?) was making all sorts of sounds with his (or her?) throat. The woman below acted as if she didn't hear the sounds or the screams for help. Whenever Henry had brought it up, about the helpless person screaming, she told him to be quiet and stand still. The man in black was straddled on top of the man (or woman?) and smothering him (or her?) with a pillow. Both of his (or her?) arms were erected outward. One hand was trying to grasp the man's dark hair while the other one was trying to gouge out his eyes. Did it really happen? Did I really witness a person being murdered? If I did, then why didn't I do something to stop the man in black from killing the man (or woman?)? From that point forward in the night, Henry didn't exactly remember what time he left the alleyway or how he made it back to his condo in one piece. The rest of the night, including what went down in the bathroom stall as well as in the alleyway, was a complete mystery.

THIRTEEN

THE clock just struck 9:18 AM.

On the way to the precinct from Clementine's apartment in The Cloves, Corpus was going over the timeline in his head. Things became a little hazy when he came across Henry's name and where exactly he was during the early morning hours of Ted's murder, mainly from 2:06 AM to 7:32 AM. Not only that, the detective was running on no sleep.

While driving, Corpus passed the record store, *Ezee Peez's Discs*. He caught a glimpse of the store in the corner of his eye. On a sudden impulse, he slammed on the brakes and made an abrupt right turn into the strip mall. A burly employee greeted Corpus at the entrance. The employee had a bushy white beard and hair down to his shoulders with an overly tanned and wrinkled face as if he had spent his younger years in the desert. He had bright blue eyes. When he smiled, his teeth sparkled like white marbles. The sight of the teeth caught the detective off guard. Everything about the man appeared old and weathered. Yet, those teeth were like brand new, straight out of a package.

"Welcome to Ezee Peez's," the employee said through his gravelly voice. "How can I help you, brother?"

The merry employee spotted the leather holster, as well as the Glock's handle protruding from Corpus's armpit. Then, the bright smile faded a little.

"I'm not sure," Corpus returned.

"Are you looking for anything in particular. . . Officer?"

"Well," he said, realizing the pistol was exposed. He peeled his coat around his body and concealed the pistol. He retraced his previous thoughts. "There's a band called Mona's Arch," he said. "Ever heard of them?"

"Righteous!" the employee exclaimed. "I love those guys." He waved to Corpus. "Right this way, brother. . . I mean, Officer."

The employee guided Corpus into the ROCK section of the store. Along the way, Corpus passed a diversity of people, spanning from all races and creeds and even the ones living on the streets (mainly tweakers) acting as if they were browsing when, in fact, they were just enjoying the free air conditioning and, of course, the free music. Most of the crowd was burn-outs. Others were college students or high schoolers skipping class. Corpus could tell from the eyes, so red and squinted and strung out they were. Plus, they smelled like marijuana.

They finally arrived at the M's.

"Here she is," the employee said gladly and pointed at the column of CD cases. "Mona's Arch."

"Thanks for your help," Corpus replied.

"Not a problem, Officer," he said and patted Corpus on the shoulder. "If you need any help, just give me a holler."

"I will. Thank you."

Corpus flipped through the CD cases, two LP's—*Rule or Be Ruled* and *Machine Mistress*—and a couple of EP's, singles, and B-Sides including the songs: "Pineapple Queen," "Bermuda's Triangle," "The Last Ferry Home," "Playin' it Softly," "Easter Egg," "Slink," "Whatever Could Have Been Never Was Ever Going To Be," "The Ponders of the Night," "The Things They Say About You When You're Not Around," and "Cookie Monster (a Mr. Vortex Cover Song)."

Corpus came across their sophomore album, *Machine Mistress.*

The track list was as follows:

1. Run and Hide
2. They're Here
3. Find A Way

4. Lexicon
5. To The Hills of Oy
6. New Weapons
7. Taking Over
8. Gone With The Wind
9. The Ghost In The Machine
10. Last Ride Home
11. Thirteen O'Clock

Corpus, who was, strangely enough, both intrigued and disconcerted from the front cover of the album (a grainy, distorted pale face of a gaunt woman over television darkness), inserted the CD case back inside the shelf and continued flipping through the other CDs. He was interested in one CD in particular, Mona's Arch debut LP called *Rule or Be Ruled*. The cover, which was done in black and white, had to do with a controversial subject matter. . . BDSM.

In July of 1996, a couple of weeks after doing the final mix of the record, Henry and Starlet came up with the concept of the title. Since they could go on for days talking about the music industry, as well as the gradual shift from CD to digital downloading over the Internet and how, if major record labels kept bullying around their artists and treating them like "puppets," as quoted by The Fif', they were going to be a thing of the past, words scribbled on pages, old gossip passed down from one generation to another, Henry and Starlet centered the title around the act of submission, the ruler versus the ruled. That was when Henry came up with the title, *Ruled or Be Ruled*. Starlet, who, like most of the people who watched the show, was afraid to admit that she did, in fact, watch the show, mentioned a trend—if that was what one called it—which, as of lately, had been growing in numbers. The trend had started about a year prior to the record when a popular series aired on HBO called *Bad Daddy*, about a married man struggling with a midlife crisis. In dealing with a failed marriage and a daughter who despises everything about him, claim adjuster, Stewart Dougherty, decides to open up his own sex club. But it's not just any ordinary sex club. The club specializes in BDSM. The B and D stood for Bondage and Discipline. The D and S: Domination and Submission. The S and M: Sadism and Masochism. After the first season, *Bad Daddy's* followers were talking about whether or not local pimp, BLT (Big Lip Tony), was going to come after Stew and his family after taking most of BLT's business, or if Stew was going to make amends with his daughter behind closed doors, in long lines at the DMV, in coffee rooms, which was all done, of course, at a minimal volume like a taboo. From there, the ball started to roll; and when it did, it was hard to stop. There were going to be two people in the photograph, Henry discussed over a group meeting, one representing one party and the other representing another. Henry and Starlet liked highlighting the role of record labels. In a way (Starlet owning her own record label as an independent artist), it was like turning the tables on them, the labels, flicking their fingers underneath their chin, saying, "Take that, Industry!" The concept was mostly aimed at one of the largest record labels on the West Coast, Phat Stacks, and how they cornered their artists into submission, "tweaked" their sound, and left them very little wiggle room to express themselves artistically. The photo shoot took two days, the first for the front and back cover and the second for the band members' inserts inside the CD booklet. On the first day, Henry was the only one in the shoot. The shoot was done in a Manhattan loft, which was about as large as a high school gymnasium. Beer cans were scattered over the floor. Bed sheets. Needles. A toppled over ashtray of cigarette butts. Several lines of blood were sprayed along the plain white wall. Underneath the bed lay a woman's body. The only exposed part of her body was her bare legs and feet. For nine straight hours, Henry, who was only wearing a pair of old tighty-whities, lay in the same exact pose on the blood stained bed: eyes sharp like a model, both wrists tied over the headrest with a piece of rope and a leather dog collar wrapped around his neck, and then bed sheets scattered about his feet. In front of the bed stood the six foot, four inch Russian model, Innochka, who was decked out in a full body black leather suit and a whip in hand. With all that had been happening for the past several months, finishing the record, doing the countless interviews and radio shows, the shoot was well worth it—even if he had cameras and lights and crew and a dominatrix stuck in his face for nine hours. As to why the photo of the album was shot in black and white and not color, Henry loved the murkiness and grittiness of the photograph and the many questions surrounding it, mainly the body underneath the bed. Who was that person? Was it even a person at all? Why were only her feet sticking out? And why were her feet so gnarly? How about the tall dominatrix? Who was she supposed to represent? And what was the deal with the blood on both the walls and bed? Where did all that blood come from? Was it possibly from the dead body underneath the bed? It could've been. Henry didn't have one mark on his body. Henry asked: When do we, the artists, the musicians, the writers, draw that line in the sand? Was there a line at all? What was black or white? What was right or wrong? For Henry, he liked the middle, the gray part where things hovered in either direction.

Corpus, with the CD cover before him, was more or less intrigued from the front cover of the album. He flipped over the CD's case and took a gander at the track list.

The first song that caught the detective's attention was the song, "The Lonely Wolf." He let out a subtle "Hmm," and wagged the case in his hand.

Suddenly, he pulled himself back into thought.

Faux fur, Corpus thought and remembered what Jacqueline's neighbor, Kasha, had explained to him last night, as well as the old man in Screw's apartment. They both had similar stories, ones about a man dressed up as a werewolf.

He read the songs on the rest of the track list:

1. Steaming At The Fronts
2. Fever Town
3. The Dead Beats
4. I'll Meet You Halfway
5. The False Prophet

In the car ride home, Corpus listened to the track "The Lonely Wolf" from the *Rule or Be Ruled* album. He didn't find anything that would pin the shooting or the other murders to Henry. The song was exactly that, about this lonely lost wolf in the wild that was searching for a place of refuge. That was until the wolf stumbled upon a faraway house. Over an industrial beat, Henry rumbled: *"Keeping the sheep in order seemed so easy. Yet, it turned out to be a lot tougher than you thought. Outnumbered, your back is now against the wall. Every breath you take brings you closer to God. Who's going to take the blame when you're not around? Lucky you. You found a new face, cold, calculated, crimson, corrupted."* Corpus switched to another track, a slow ballad. The song: "Everybody's Frankenstein." Corpus felt somewhat inspired from the lyrics: *"The monster won't stop chasing you until you cut off its head. Now, take a good look into its eyes and tell me what you see. You were right all along. The monster you've been running from turned out to be yourself."* The detective listened carefully as the rest of the band joined in. The song turned heavier, more aggressive. *"It turned out to be yourself. YOURSELF!"* Deon was one of the main highlights on the song. He used this pedal effect that sounded as if the guitar was being played underwater (this was after he spent days in the Den mastering the melody). *"You talked about your place of refuge. You talked about the glory days all ahead of you. You even carried around the picture in your pocket. To remind you of what was to come.*

But when it came time to walk, you ran back to your cave where all the other dead monsters roam. . ."

FOURTEEN

IT was 3: 36 AM.

Corpus was dreaming of Henry: The night was calling out to Corpus with the crackling of wood. The heat was pressed against his face, so close that he could feel its pinch along his skin. The smell of char was thick in the air. Henry was standing on Jacqueline Walker's front lawn and watching the flames rip through her house. Next to Henry perched a wolf—not like the ones he had seen in the horror movies—but an actual wolf. Henry turned away from the fire and walked toward Corpus, who was standing at his car, and like Henry, watching the flames, only he was doing so from the street. Henry strolled through the front lawn. Yet, it was like he was walking in slow motion. Years, it felt, before Henry reached Corpus. He glared into the detective's eyes and said coldly, "You're next."

Rolling around in his bed, Corpus sprang from the strange dream. He wiped away the cold sweat from his face with the backside of his hand and sat on the edge of the bed. He kept thinking about that one song in particular, "The Lonely Wolf," that he had listened to twice, once back at the station and the other time on his way home. In the dream, he imagined Henry standing with a wolf in front of a burning house. The two of them, man and wolf, acted as if they were untouchable.

After Corpus finally caught his breath, he rolled out of bed, and went into the kitchen where he fixed himself a cup of coffee, Columbia's finest, Joe Black.

Next, after the coffee was brewed and his LPD mug was filled to the brim with Joe Black, he switched on the lamp on the desk, which was covered in clutter, files and crime scene photographs, mostly taken from Ted Backer's house, and put on Mona's Arch debut album, *Rule or Be Ruled*. On the wall above, Corpus had hundreds of photographs from Henry, who remained at the top of the pyramid, to the band, Mona's Arch, to the LPD police officers, all tacked on the wall with pieces of red string stretching from one suspect to another. He grabbed a pen, as well as a pair of reading glasses from the drawer and then a piece of paper, and wrote down the lyrics to each song on the album. He did this until he finished listening to the CD from start to finish. Then, after the last song finished, Corpus listened to the album yet again.

Three hours later Corpus was back at the precinct.

There was a knock on Christian's laboratory door.

Christian answered.

"Just in time."

"Hey, Christian," Corpus said and handed Christian a cup of freshly brewed coffee with two creams and two sugars.

"What are you doing here so bright and early, Detective?"

"I need you to do me a favor."

Christian shrugged his shoulders.

"That's why the coffee," he said and grabbed the coffee from the detective's grip.

Corpus pulled out a plastic bag containing a water bottle and handed the bag to Christian.

As Christian pulled the bag closer to his body, Corpus kept a firm grip over the bag.

"You can let go now," he said, his fish eyes moving upward.

"This is off the record, Christian," Corpus said seriously.

Christian finally let go of the bag.

"What exactly am I getting myself into, Al?"

"I just need you to run this print on the bottle with the partial on the Smith and Wesson."

"That's it," Christian said hesitantly. "I'm not going to have Reed busting my balls over this. Am I? I'm already up to my knees in this Backer case."

"You owe me one, Christian."

Christian glared at Corpus.

"Fine."

"Remember."

"Yeah, yeah, yeah," Christian said and twisted an invisible key around his mouth. "My lips are sealed. So, while we're exchanging Christmas presents, I'll give you mine." He reached around the desk and handed Corpus a file. "The toxicology report on Cedric Johnson came back. You won't believe this, but I found traces of potassium cyanide in Mr. Johnson's system."

"Potassium cyanide? Isn't that found in. . . "

"Household products," Christian finished, "pesticides, and even some over the counter rat poisons like one in particular, the kind that kills a rat instantaneously. The product is called Kill-A-Rat."

"You're serious?" Corpus said in confusion.

"I ran it twice just to be certain."

"Potassium cyanide?"

"Yep."

Corpus fell into thought.

Then, a distant voice: "Al?"

"Yeah. . . " he said as he snapped from his trance. "Listen, Christian. I got some things I have to take care of. I'm going to need that print ASAP."

Christian said, "I'm on it, Detective."

"Remember. . . "

"Of course, Detective," he said. "This is between you and me."

In a parking lot outside a dilapidated textile factory off Howard Street in uptown Lansford, a police cruiser pulled up to a white unmarked police car.

Office Wheaten, who was dressed in his LPD uniform, stepped out and approached Officer Marson, who was dressed in casual clothes: a black leather jacket, blue jeans, and white sneakers.

"He's going to give us up," Officer Wheaten said to Officer Marson. "That fucking junkie kept the baton. They found it in his apartment."

"I knew I couldn't trust that piece of shit," Officer Marson seethed, pacing around the unmarked car. "What the fuck do we do now?"

"There's only one thing left to do," Officer Wheaten said to Officer Marson.

"Which is?"

"You know. . . "

FIFTEEN

HENRY mumbling in his sleep: "*What do. . .* "

He groaned and repositioned himself on the couch.

"*. . . What. . . What do you. . .* "

The black, glossy eyes penetrated through his dreams.

A cryptic body manifested.

With his body covered in sweat, Henry tossed and turned on the couch. The pillows underneath his body fell to the living room floor.

He said louder now, "I said, 'What do you want from me?'"

He suddenly gasped.

Abbey's brusque voice: *Look at what you've become, you loser!*

"WHAT DO YOU WANT?"

The voice was relentlessly pounding away at him, smothering now.

Abbey: *YOU LOSER!*

"QUIT LOOKING AT ME!"

LOSER!

Henry suddenly grunted as he heaved the upper part of his body upward.

"LEAVE ME THE FUCK ALONE!"

While Henry sat upright on the couch and tried to catch his breath, he grimaced from the weight pressed against the left side of his face. Not a weight, he concluded as he reached up and touched the side of his face, the blood.

He let out a sharp hiss.

Gently, he ran his fingers across the swelling once more.

Another hiss, more subdued now.

With his clothes scattered around the living room, Henry rolled from the couch and stumbled into the closest bathroom. There, in the mirror, he witnessed the fresh shiner on the side of his face. The swollen socket around his eye was dark purple. The eye itself was completely red, no white at all. As before with the cut on his chin, he couldn't comprehend as to where he received the injuries. Henry strolled back into the living room where empty beer cans were scattered around the couch. Unlike the time before, Henry didn't remember a thing about last night—at least nothing after his fifth drink. He remembered Starlet coming over around five o'clock in the evening with carry out. Mexican food from the restaurant Don Juan, Henry remembered, as he sat himself down on the couch. Starlet had a salad and Henry had three tacos with carne asade—cooked dangerously rare, not medium as he normally ordered—and a side of rice and refried beans. Henry knew Don Juan portions were big enough to feed at *least* three or four people and yet he still placed the order. At dinner, he only had a couple of bites from a taco before he began to feel nauseous from the sight of the blood dripping from the tortilla. More red oozed from the tacos. The rice: red. The beans: red. The plate: red. The napkins: red. His fingertips: now red. So much red, he witnessed, only from a single drop of blood from the rare meat. Henry decided to push aside the food. So, he had a drink: a Crown and Coke. He slurped the drink down as if he had just finished running a marathon.

After dinner was over, they fooled around for a little while. Henry had yet another drink. Something happened while in bed with Starlet, he vaguely remembered. He and Starlet smoked cigarettes and talked in bed. She mentioned something about Henry's condition and how he was taking a downward spiral. "Slipping," was the word she used to describe his current state. Then, he remembered he said something ugly to Starlet, which caused her to roll out of bed, throw on her clothes in a hurry, and storm out of the condo. Henry didn't exactly remember the entire argument that followed after the vile remark in bed. When Starlet was finally gone (and made it clear for him by slamming the front door— that, Henry knew), he had another drink, which led to a fourth drink. As before, the events that unfolded after the fifth drink were a complete mystery.

During morning visiting hours, Henry, who was now working his way through the splitting headache with his second cup of coffee that he had picked up at a convenient store called Q and E, decided to give Mr. and Mrs. Livingston a break and send them home to sleep, clean the house, feed the dog, take out the trash, get the mail, check the answering machine, or whatever it was that they needed to do (for the past sixteen hours they had been taking shifts at the hospital). On the way to the ICU, he passed the rest of the band, excluding Starlet. They informed Henry on T.J.'s progress and thought it was in their best interest to let Henry spend some time alone with T.J., especially with all that had been going on between the band and Henry.

The other band mates walked back to the waiting room while Henry stood alone in the hallway.

Five minutes passed until he finally walked into T.J.'s room. He made his way to T.J.'s bedside.

"Do you remember when I ran away to Louisiana?" he asked T.J.

In return, T.J. didn't say a word. He remained, as he had been for the past ten hours, sound asleep.

"I told you that I went to New Orleans because I've never been there before and I wanted to see what it was like, but my mother would never take me," he said and sat down on the edge of the cushioned chair next to the hospital bed. "Then, I told you that story about that boy who was abducted." He let out a sigh and hung his head in sorrow. "I lied to you, T.J.," he said into his lap. "I never went to New Orleans."

A sudden movement in T.J.: his hand slightly inched closer to the remote dangling over the side rail of the bed.

Henry moved his head upward from his lap.

T.J.'s hand remained still, however, much closer to Henry than before.

"That boy in the story was me," he said. "And that woman in the story was my mother." He leaned closer to T.J.; the story, of course, being for T.J.'s ears only. "I took a bus to Baton Rouge and then walked to a small town called Sinclair Leprieur, which was only a few miles out," Henry explained, his voice softening from a nurse walking past the room. "I went there, T.J., to find answers about what really happened to my father." Henry's head was mostly held downward as he told the story. "Instead," he said, "I was abducted on the side of the road by a man who called himself Fox. He lured me into thinking he had a flat tire." He momentarily shot his head up at T.J., who remained asleep. A smile flashed over Henry's face. "You remember how our mothers told us never to trust strangers, to never get in a car with them or accept candy from them. I wonder if we had listened to half of what our parents said, then maybe we would've turned out differently." The smile vanished from Henry's face before it could grow any further. "This man," his head held downward again, "Fox, he was a murderer, a killer of innocent children. I don't remember much after the abduction. I remember waking up in a basement, in the darkness, alone. . . scared that I might not make it out alive." Henry sighed, shaking his head. "I didn't know what to do,

T.J. I thought that this was it. I was going to be some sad face in the morning newspaper. Another victim. Turns out Fox knew my grandmother. He told me her name was Claudia and said that she. . . she did things to people, bad things." T.J.'s eyelids suddenly flickered a bit, but the reaction went unnoticed. "Then, I found out that one of those children was my mother. But she wasn't murdered like the other ones. No. She was Claudia's daughter. When she was little, she ran away from Claudia. This man, Fox, ended up finding her. Didn't kill her. He was the caretaker of the house. He knew my mother too. Fox and Claudia," Henry intertwined both his index and middle finger together and showed T.J., "they were like this," he said. "The story goes that Claudia was a woman possessed by demons." Henry shrugged his shoulders from a sudden inward laugh. "They called her a witch, if such a thing exists. They even said that she could raise the dead. . . like zombies in *Night of the Living Dead*. That's why my mother wanted to escape from Sinclair Leprieur. 'Not because of Fox,' she told me, but to get away from her mother. Then, my mother got older. Ran away again. But this time she was successful. That's when she met him, my father. He was playing in a show not too far from Sinclair Leprieur. When I was much younger, my mother went back to that house, the same house that Fox had me trapped in. She said Claudia was knocking on death's door. I only remember bits and pieces of what she looked like. . . " the sudden image of the haggard woman was back in his mind, staggering through his mother's old bedroom and reaching out her frail hand. Her eyes were dark and menacing. He could see her bones and the outlines of her skull over her glossy skin. Henry closed his eyes and cleared the memory from his mind before it could take hold of him. ". . . But, after my mother told me the truth about my grandmother, Claudia, and what she did to her as a child, how she locked her in her bedroom and how she sheltered her from the world and treated her like an animal, I knew she didn't go there to take care of her mother. She was there for another reason." His eyes glazed over as he looked up at T.J., who, as before, was sound asleep. "I was just five years old when it happened. I watched her, T.J.," Henry said closely. "I watched my mother kill Claudia with my own eyes. My grandmother, T.J. Not a witch. Not a monster. But a human being." The face of death flashed before his eyes, Ted Backer's face, not the barfly's. A stream of blood was carefully flowing down the center of his chest and settling over the trachea of his neck. Both of his eyes stilled in terror. Then, the eyes washed over with guilt. Ted's face eventually faded from his thoughts. He leaned closer to T.J., "There isn't a day that goes by that I don't think about that one day. . . "

In the corner of his eye, Henry saw Starlet standing motionlessly at the edge of the doorway.

Henry suddenly cleared his throat and wiped the tear from his eye.

"Hey," he mumbled and quickly stood up from the chair. "How long have you been there?"

"I just got here," she said flatly with both of her arms folded over her chest. She nodded to T.J. "What were you talking about?"

Henry shook his head and stuttered, "I. . . I. . . I was just telling T.J. a story."

"What kind of a story?"

"It's nothing," he said quietly and stood over T.J.

With her arms still crossed, Starlet walked toward the bed.

"How's he doing?"

"About the same," Henry said without acknowledging Starlet.

"Can I talk to you outside for a minute," she said, her voice unsteady.

"When we were kids. . . " Henry smirked as he nodded at all tubes running through T.J.'s body, ". . . we use to call him Octo, short for Octopus. . . "

"I can't do this right now, Henry," Starlet said sternly, fighting back the tears. "Please."

Henry said coldly, "Whatever you have to say, you can say it in front of T.J."

"This isn't about us, Henry, or what we did," she said, her voice slightly raised. "I need to talk to you in private."

Henry could sense the tension in her voice. He decided to step outside in the hallway with Starlet.

"I'm sorry for whatever I did or said that made you so upset last night," Starlet said. "I really am, Henry."

Henry gave Starlet the silent treatment when, through Henry's perception, it should've been the other way around.

Starlet sighed.

"Listen, Henry," she said. "I just had a conversation with Drexel over the phone. He said he needed to have an answer."

Anger built in Henry's voice: "What planet is that man living on? Does he not know that our drummer is lying in the hospital with two broken arms? Not only that, he's fighting for his fucking life!"

"He said he found a replacement."

Henry paused in curiosity.

"Replacement?"

"Yes."

"Who?"

"Geordie."

His long face tightened into a grimace.

He shouted through the hallway, "Give me a fucking break!"

Two nurses, who were both fans of Mona's Arch, directed their attention toward Henry and went along with their business, but, in secret, were listening closely to the conversation between Henry and Starlet.

"I know you two got into it a long time ago, but he said Geordie always admired you."

"Ah!" Henry groaned. "That's bullshit, Star!"

"He said he feels torn up about what happened to T.J. He wants to help out the band and finish the tou—"

"Without T.J., it won't be Mona's Arch," Henry interrupted. "T.J. is our backbone. Without him, it'll never be the same."

"I know that, Henry," Starlet said, patiently holding out her hands. "Drexel is going to reschedule the West Coast Tour three months from now. That's *more* than enough time for Geordie to learn the songs and. . . and. . . "

Henry quit pacing back and forth in the hallway and faced Starlet.

He said sharply, "And what?"

"And for you to clean yourself up," she said over a tense silence. "He's not going to do it unless you're ready."

Henry strolled back to the hospital room.

"I can't go back on stage," he muttered and peeked into the room. "Not without him. Not without T.J."

Starlet said candidly from behind, "You should've heard yourself last night, Henry. You need help."

Henry's shoulders swelled violently. The sides of his face turned red. His eyes flared like a predator ready to strike at its prey.

"Help?" He snapped his body around and snarled, "I don't need your fucking help!"

"Please, Henry." Her voice was weak and tired. Starlet furrowed her brows and carefully stepped closer to Henry. "Don't do this here," she said softly. "I'm begging you, Henry. Please. . . "

Henry turned away and embraced a deep breath, as Charles had once taught him. Deep through the nostrils, Henry remembered, and out through the mouth. The breathing technique helped calm him down a little.

"It wouldn't be right to our fans, Henry," she pleaded and crept even closer to Henry. "Do it for them. Most importantly, do it for T.J."

Starlet's calm composure, as well as her gentle voice, helped alleviate the anger brewing inside Henry.

"I can't leave him," he said over the long—not so tense— silence and faced Starlet once more. "Not like this."

"What would T.J. want you to do?"

Henry carefully thought about the question.

He turned his shoulder to the room and gazed at T.J., the Octopus.

"I. . . I. . ." Henry stuttered as he swallowed a dry lump down his throat.

Starlet slipped her hand into Henry's grip and squeezed tightly.

"Just think about it," she said sincerely.

She leaned her body forward and kissed Henry on the cheek.

Henry didn't know what to say from the kiss. Yet, he stood there and gazed into Starlet's mournful eyes.

"When you have an answer, you know where to find me." Starlet walked away. As she made it halfway down the hallway, she stopped in her tracks and turned her shoulder. Her eyes narrowed like a blade. "I almost forgot," she said to herself as she reached in her pocket and tossed Henry the spare key to the Porsche. Henry caught the spare, opened up his palm, and looked down at the key. Starlet said, "By the way, that detective, Corpus, he came by here earlier and asked me a whole bunch of questions about you like where you were the night T.J. ended up in the hospital."

With a nod, Henry said suspiciously, "And what did you say?"

"I told him that you were with me all night," she said casually and walked away without looking over her shoulder.

As Henry pulled his attention away from Starlet, who was now exiting the ICU, he caught a strange woman standing in the middle of the hallway. Horrified from the appearance of the woman, he paused in his tracks and looked closer now. His skin suddenly turned bloodless. Henry dropped his jaw slightly. His mother, Abbey, was standing among a group of nurses and doctors and visitors, some loitering while others moving throughout the hallway. Abbey's skin was a dark gray, almost corpse-like. She had little to no muscle mass or fat on her bony body, mostly skin and bones. She was wearing a black dress, frayed. *Mom?* Abbey robotically turned her shoulder toward her son's direction and then proceeded to walk down another hallway. Henry quickly followed. He made it to another hallway where Abbey led him down yet another hallway. Henry pushed his way through a couple of nurses and did his best to keep up with his mother. He passed a chaplain who was walking with a young woman (sixteen or seventeen years old?), who was crying. Finally, Abbey entered a hospital room at the end of the hallway. Henry, now cautious, slowed down his pace and inched toward the hospital room. There, he witnessed Abbey standing over a patient in the bed. A couple of nurses were changing the medicine bags over the patient's IV. The patient's limbs, Henry witnessed, were severely swollen and his skin was yellow in color, nearly glowing from where Henry stood.

"Excuse me," a fragile voice said from behind. "May I help you?"

Henry suddenly turned his shoulder and found the same scrawny woman with glasses who was walking with the chaplain in the hallway now standing in front of him with a balled up tissue in her hand.

The young woman waited patiently for a response from Henry.

Instead, Henry turned toward the room.

Abbey was nowhere around.

"I. . . I was. . . "

"Yes?"

The young woman's glazed eyes swelled with anticipation.

"I. . . "

"You were. . . "

"I was just passing by."

The young woman closely studied Henry's confused face.

"Do I know you from somewhere?"

"I don't think so."

The young woman's eyes drifted away from Henry in careful thought.

With one eye squinted, she asked in a slightly upbeat tone, "Is your name Henry?"

"*Yeah*," Henry said strangely.

"The nurses told me all about you," she said and then corrected, "but like in a good way." The sniffling young woman patted the phlegm from her nose and blushed. She shrugged her shoulders and uttered, "Sorry."

Henry said, "It's okay."

"They also told me about your friend. I'm sorry to hear about what happened. T.J., right?"

"That's right," Henry said solemnly. "He's not doing too good." A sigh. "He's. . ." Then, he cleared his throat, ". . . he's got a long road ahead of him."

The young woman touched Henry on the side of the arm.

"Hang in there, Henry," she said tenderly.

Henry smiled from the young woman's remark.

"Thanks," he said, a tear tracing across his eye.

As he turned to the unconscious patient in the bed, he tried not to let the young woman see him wipe the tear from his eye.

The young woman extended out her hand.

"Name's Dottie. . . "

Henry looked down at Dottie's hand and then shook it.

"Henry the. . . Henry Burl."

"It's a pleasure to meet you, Henry Burl."

Smitten from Henry's appearance, Dottie smirked and puckered up her shoulders.

Henry pulled his attention back to the room.

"Do you know the man in this room?"

Dottie said, "He's my father."

"How is he doing?"

As Dottie held back the tears, she shook her head.

"Right now, they. . . they say it's only a matter of time," she said and cleared her throat. "Right now, his liver is failing. The doctors just took him off the ventilator."

"I'm so sorry."

Once more, Dottie shook her head.

"It's okay," she said with a crack in her voice. "I knew this day would come." Her voice rose slightly with optimism. "My father sure did love his Scotch on the rocks." She said under her breath, "More than my stepmother. She left my father three years ago. I wasn't around when she left him. By the time he quit drinking, it was already too late. His liver was already shot. I could never do what my stepmother did and give up on him like that. We had some good times, though. The stories he would tell." A smile lifted over Dottie's face. "He could go on for days telling all kinds of stories. He is. . . was a special person."

Henry asked, "Where is your real mother?"

"I lived in Bangladesh with my mother until she passed when I was twelve years old," Dottie said. "Then, I moved to the States where I first met my real father."

"How was that?"

"At first, it was like living with a stranger," she said. "But then we became close friends. He and my stepmother didn't get along at all."

"Really?"

Dottie said, "Yeah. They hated each other."

"When things happen to you, bad things," Henry said, "you find out who really has your back. Sometimes the people who you think are your friends aren't really your friends at all. When bad things happen, the people who love each other *always* stick together."

Dottie was nodding her head in agreement.

Henry looked around the hallway and asked, "Is it just you?"

The tears fell down Dottie's cheeks.

Once more, she shook her head and said with her head held downward, "It's just me."

"I see." Henry took a final glance in the room and then faced Dottie. He said to her, "Take care of him. Anything he needs."

Dottie wiped the tears from her eyes.

"I will."

"It was very nice to meet you, Dottie," Henry said and hugged Dottie.

Dottie kissed Henry on the cheek.

"Nice to meet you, Henry," she said and then Henry walked away.

As Henry got about two rooms down from Dottie, he suddenly paused and turned back around.

"Hey, Dottie. . . "

Dottie took two steps into the room before she walked back into the hallway.

Her face was bright, eyes glowing.

"Yes, Henry."

"Is there anything I can do for you?" he said, his eyes watering. "Coffee? Ice cream? You name it."

"Really?" Dottie said surprisingly. "That's nice of you."

Then, she paused in thought.

"I. . . I'm fine," she said hesitantly. "But thanks."

Henry returned, "Anything, Dottie."

She paused once more.

"Can you. . ." Dottie said, nibbling on the inner part of her lip, ". . . can you just stay with me for awhile. Tell me a story."

Henry cleared the tears from his eyes.

"Yeah," he said and cracked a smile. "I got a couple of stories that you might like."

SIXTEEN

ON the way to Screw's holding cell, Corpus nodded to Officer Marson, who was walking down the hallway with a little extra pep in his step. Corpus didn't think too much about the officer's hastening from the holding cells. . . at first. Then, he thought about the one face he had been looking at for the past couple of nights. Marson and Teddy were tight, maybe too tight. Whenever Corpus saw Officer Backer, Officer Marson wasn't too far behind.

Corpus suddenly stopped walking and tried to make sense as to why Officer Marson was down here.

Then, the guard at the station said from behind, "Can I help you, Detective?"

In a daze, Corpus faced the guard's station.

"Came to ask Mr. Farrow a couple of questions," Corpus said vaguely and looked back at Officer Marson, who had already fled from the hallway.

"No visits during lunch hour, Detective," the guard said and then observed the blank expression on the detective's face. "But let me go check if he's done."

The guard sighed annoyingly, got up from his seat, and walked over to Screw's cell. As the guard strolled to the cell, he didn't hear Screw eating. He didn't hear anything at all for that matter. Screw was sitting motionlessly on the bed. His body was arched forward. His face was planted on his plate.

"Mr. Farrow," the guard said cautiously and banged on the bars, "the food ain't that bad, son."

Screw didn't move an inch.

The guard inched closer and noticed the foam bubbling from the corner of Screw's mouth.

"DETECTIVE! COME QUICK!"

The guard opened the cell and tended to a lifeless Screw. He touched Screw on the shoulder, which caused his body to flop to the side. The tray fell from his lap. The plastic plate of food, as well as the plastic utensils, scattered over the floor.

Corpus arrived at the cell.

He asked, "What the hell happened in here?"

The guard grabbed Screw's face. More foam spilled from the mouth. The side of his face was covered with blobs of mashed potatoes. Next, he checked Screw's pulse on the side of his neck.

"The son of a bitch isn't breathing. . ."

Out of breath, Corpus stood in a daze. He didn't see a single mark on Screw's face or body.

No blood either.

SEVENTEEN

AT the Hit Box Studios, which was officially going to be Mona's Arch's new studio for the remainder of the Buick Crossover Tour, and also known for spitting out one hit record after another, including Rocket Jimmy's smash "Switch," The Golden Triplets' one hit wonder, "See You In Hell, Sunshine," which held down the number one slot on the billboards for four straight weeks, and then every single released from Coral Rising's debut album, *The Butterfly Effect*, including "Mr. Paper Man" (hence why they called the place the "Hit Box"), the band anxiously waited for Henry to show in the rehearsal studio while Starlet was in the bathroom.

"Maybe you should go check on Star," Deon, who was sitting on the edge of the stage, said to Socks. "She's been in there for a long time."

"Hey, you guys," Socks said quietly to the other band mates, including Deon. "You've noticed she's put on a little weight."

William, who was sipping from a cup of warm tea, said calmly, "I was about to say something, but you know. . . "

"You didn't want to start some shit."

"Exactly."

Geordie said from behind, "Did you ever think that maybe she's pregnant."

"Pregnant?" Deon turned his shoulder. "Get the fuck out of here."

"Hey," he said and leaned forward over the drum set, "it's possible."

"It could be from depression," Socks suggested. "You know I've heard you tend to put on extra weight when you're depressed. You know with everything that's happened with T.J."

William said flatly, "Starlet's not depressed. Trust me. The woman's a rock."

In the dingy restroom next to Stage B, the walls, including the stalls, were covered with handwritten messages, signatures, or doodles (some graphic in nature) left behind by musicians. "*Jace was here*," Starlet read the message written in lipstick over the backside of the seat cover as she pulled herself from the toilet and then flushed. Jace, Starlet knew, was the lead singer for Coral Rising. But Jace, of course, was the last thing Starlet wanted to think about right now.

"Later, Jace," she muttered as she wiped her mouth clean with the backside of her hand. She sauntered over to the mirror, which, like the walls, had doodles drawn over the glass, and primped for about a minute. In her primping (mostly her shirt), she rotated to her side. Carefully, she lifted up her purple tank top and studied her stomach. From what she could see, there wasn't a pouch over her abdomen. She put on at least ten pounds. Starlet wondered if it was from all the hotel food she had been eating as of lately or the "other." The box said they were 99% accurate. What about that one percent? If the test was right (so far she had taken two of them and they both turned out reading the same plus sign), then she knew it would take a couple of months before she started to show. The big question: When was she going to tell the other band mates?

So far, an hour had passed and still there was no sign of Henry.

"He's not going to come, Star," Socks finally said and ran his hand over his parched mouth.

"Yes," Starlet said confidently, her eyes never leaving the door. "He will. I know he will."

"I should leave," Geordie said as he sat behind the massive drum set. His right foot was rapidly bouncing over the floor. The nerves were high and not just with Geordie. He sighed greatly, making it known to the other band mates. "I knew this was a dumb idea," he said. "I feel like I'm stirring up the hornet's nest."

"No," Starlet said sternly and shot a glance at Geordie. "You're staying, Geordie. That's final."

He returned, "I think my face is the last thing Henry wants to see right about now."

Socks swigged from the bottle of water.

"So," Socks said. "Have we decided who's going to talk first? I've never really done this kind of thing before. Well, I mean, once, my uncle and aunt did one with my cousins. They had the whole family there and everything."

"How do you think he's going to react?"

"He's not going to like it one bit," Deon said sternly with his arms crossed. "That's for sure."

James, who was dressed in his everyday black, removed the lime green Aviator shades from his eyes and said reassuringly to the entire band, "Well, he has to get his head clean before we hit the road again. We will *all* talk to him." James nodded at Geordie. "That includes you, G. We'll tell him what the deal is. Then, if all goes according to plan, he'll go to rehab for a month and then he'll come back a brand new man."

"It's not going to be that easy, Jam—"

Suddenly, the metal door *squeaked* open! A ray of sunlight filled half of the studio. A couple of seconds expired before Henry stepped through the hazy light and entered the studio. A few steps into the studio, he paused and looked around at the other band mates in bafflement. No Harry in hand. Just himself.

"Henry," Starlet said and stepped forward, "we need to talk."

Henry said clearly, "What is there to talk about?"

Starlet glanced at Socks.

Her eyes flashed at him as if she was giving him a cue to speak first.

"Socks," she said after Socks didn't say a word, "do you want to start?"

"Why aren't you guys practicing?" Henry asked, drawing several relieving sighs from the band.

"Well, we were waiting on you, Henry," Geordie said arrogantly from the drum set and strolled up to Henry.

The studio became dead quiet.

Once Henry spoke clearly and confidently, the thought of intervention wasn't even in the front of their minds.

Face to face, both Henry and Geordie stood in silence.

James inched closer, ready to leap in the middle of the two.

Geordie made the first move by stepping forward and hugging Henry.

"I'm sorry to hear about T.J., man," he said into Henry's shoulder. He pulled himself from Henry and looked him in the eyes. "Listen, Henry. What I said. . . "

"It's done, Geordie," Henry interrupted Geordie's train of thought and grabbed him by the shoulder. "Now, let's play some music. What do you say?"

The other band mates breathed another sigh of relief.

So much for the intervention.

In the rehearsal studio, they practiced a handful of new songs, all done without Harry. On one song, tentatively titled "Roots," Geordie played from a set of conga drums that he had brought with him from his home studio in Nashville, Tennessee. Then, there was "The Dampening," which was in the vein of Smashing Pumpkins' "Zero," and another called, "Lady Black," where Henry played the piano, and then "V for Vulcan," and "Burn Your Throne," which the other band mates called "the best Mona's Arch songs to date." Out of the handful of songs they wrote, about three or four of them were instant hits and favorites among the band. Henry expressed to the band that three of the twelve songs (all from their previous albums) on the set list were way too personal. "Sacred," he claimed. The three of the songs also happened to be played with Harry. Since T.J. wasn't going to be joining them for the rest of the tour and Henry wasn't going to be playing Harry, Henry didn't want to play the songs on tour.

"That's the whole reason why half the fans come to the show, Henry!" Deon expressed over a five-minute break.

"Let's give them something different," Henry explained while seated behind the piano. "And after the show, they'll get a copy of our brand new CD."

Dumbfounded from the comment, Socks said, "Brand new CD?"

William chimed in, "Pretty ballsy, Henry."

"Wait a second!" Deon blurted out from the side. "Are you talking about recording an entire new record in the matter of two months?"

"That's what I said."

"That's impossible!"

"It's time we rattle the cages again," Henry said, stood from the seat, and directed his attention behind the drum set. "Right, Geordie?"

"Hey, Henry," he said. "You're the boss."

They went ahead and wrote and practiced more new songs. Then, after they finished, they went to the Den and recorded an entire new album.

From *Missing the Edges*, page 340:

I can't believe we were back in the Den. It seemed as if yesterday we were sharing laughs and stories during the *Machine Mistress* recordings. Even during those times, as great and memorable as they were, there was something growing like a tumor beneath the band. When we went back to the Den after writing eleven songs at the Hit Box, a new spark was ignited throughout the band. However, it wasn't the same. With T.J. not around, the entire session felt like a 9 to

5 job. The tensions were extremely high. The creativity was coming from every direction. The incident with T.J. had certainly brought out a current of emotions. Geordie was something else behind the drums. In all my years of playing music, I have never seen a man pour his heart and soul into an instrument like Geordie did with the drums. Thankfully, Deon was there to help fill in T.J.'s shoes and provide the comic relief when it was due. But still, it wasn't the same. Regardless, our third album was, by far, the darkest and yet most uplifting material that we had ever recorded.

EIGHTEEN

AFTER lunch, Jacqueline's younger sister, Pamela, got off early from her job as a filing clerk at the hospital and went home to make sure her big sis, Jackie, was doing all right, especially after everything she had been through.

As Pamela arrived at her two-story brick house located in a white-collar neighborhood, Maple View, she stopped by the mailbox as she had done each and every afternoon when she arrived home from work and dug out a handful of mail and then parked the Chrysler minivan in the driveway.

On the way to the house, she sorted through the mail (which mainly consisted of junk mail, flyers, advertisements, and credit card promotions that went directly to the paper shedder). Then, she came across an envelope addressed to Jacqueline Walker. The return address was from Lansford. She held up the envelope to the bright sun above and stared closely as if she had the trained ability to look through paper. All she saw was the outline of a letter, no paraphernalia or anything of that nature. Just a letter. Once more, Pamela looked over the front of the envelope. There was no name written on the envelope. Just an address: 138 Almond's Court.

Pamela walked inside her house and checked on the kids, Jordan and Blake, who were both playing Nintendo in the playroom, and then went to the guest room, or the "Big Bird Room" as the kids called it, where Jackie was currently staying.

Before entering, Pamela knocked twice on the door.

"May I come in?" she asked quietly.

With a tissue balled in her hand, Jacqueline finally answered the door. Her eyes were bloodshot from all the crying. She was still wearing makeup from the night before when she ate dinner with the kids. Most of the makeup was from leftover eye shadow that had been smeared across her temples. In two days, she hadn't changed her clothes. She hadn't even taken a shower. Her hair was still flat and greasy too. Jacqueline left the door open and walked back over to the bed where she sat down next to her cairn terrier that Kasha had brought over the following morning after the fire.

Pamela sat down next to her sister and wrapped her arm around her shoulder.

"You can't keep doing this to yourself, Jackie," she said and stroked the side of her sister's hair. "You need to eat something." She tightened her grip around Jacqueline's shoulder. "Please, big sis." She leaned forward and looked into her big sis's lifeless eyes. "Pretty please... do it for me..."

She kissed Jacqueline on the top of her forehead.

"I let him die, Pamela," Jacqueline said vacantly as she stared at the blank yellow wall. "I could've gone to the police and had them arrest him. But I let him die."

"This is ridiculous, Jackie," she said and reinforced her grip around Jacqueline's shoulder. "You got to stop blaming yourself. You did all you could."

Pamela held Jacqueline closer to her body. Then, after a sudden thought, she reached in her back pocket and pulled out a folded up envelope.

"Here," she said sharply over the crinkle over the envelope. "You got this in the mail."

Jacqueline's eyes widened.

She cautiously grabbed the envelope from Pamela's hand and opened it.

"What does it say?" Pamela asked curiously as she witnessed Jacqueline's eyes skimming over the letter.

After she finished reading the letter, she turned to Pamela without any expression on her face.

"We have to go," she said urgently.

"Go where?"

Jacqueline darted past Pamela and exited the bedroom.

"Jackie. . . " Pamela uttered and followed her big sis into the hallway, ". . . what's gotten into you? Where are we going?"

"Madison," she replied while walking.

"Madison?" Pamela paused. "What's in Madison?"

From *Missing the Edges: A Memoir,* page 345:

I knew Henry was up to something, but I didn't know what.

Not just yet.

While we were having California rolls off Central Street (The Slanted Eye, a favorite of ours while rehearsing at the Hit Box), Henry hardly spoke a word to me or the other band mates. He sat mostly at the bar with his head in his plate. He hardly ate any sushi, which, after I took him out a couple of times in New York, turned out being one of his favorites things to eat besides pizza, of course. I couldn't count how times he excused himself to use the phone. At least a dozen times that phone of his rang in his pocket. I couldn't help but overhear one conversation while I was going to the lady's restroom. On the phone, he was talking about a spotlight. I didn't know exactly what he meant. But soon, I would. So would the entire city of Lansford.

As Sissy headed toward the door in a quickening pace, Beverly stumbled across a black gym bag on the living room floor.

"Wait!" Beverly called out and picked up the heavy bag, which caused her to grimace from the weight. Somehow, she managed to pull the bag up to the kitchen counter.

"Sissy!" she exclaimed before Sissy exited the apartment.

"I got to go, Mom. . ." she swung open the door and turned around ". . . I'm going to be late for work!"

Beverly said quietly, "This must be Orlando's bag. . ."

Sissy grunted, rolled her eyes, closed the door, and walked over to her mother who was zipping open the gym bag.

"We got everything, Mom," she whined.

Beverly said under her voice, "Apparently not."

Sissy gazed at the bag in suspicion as she walked over to the bag.

"That's not his," she said, her voice drawn back. "That's not Orlando's."

"Are you sure?"

"I'm sure," Sissy said, loudly this time. "That's not Orlando's, Mom."

Beverly opened the bag entirely and staggered backward.

"Mom. . ." Sissy uttered and rushed over to the counter.

Beverly was speechless.

She asked, "What is it?"

Beverly braced the counter behind her. Her face was now expressionless. Her eyes were wandering around like a toddler. Sissy eased her head over the bag and carefully reached inside. She pulled out the wad of cash, all hundreds, bound by a rubberband. There were at least fifty more wads like this, all bound by rubberbands, inside the gym bag. There was a note on top of the stack of cash.

In a state of disbelief, Sissy picked up the note and read it out loud for her mother, "Dear Sissy, I hope this money will give you and your family peace of mind."

After a twenty-minute drive from Freemont to Madison, Pamela arrived at the address in the letter. The mansion, which sat on the edge of Lake Darlington, was twice the size of Jacqueline's old house in Parker Square. The front lawn and shrubbery were well manicured. The neighbors were friendly and smiling and waving at one another. There were even a couple of palm trees in the front of the house. The two sisters walked up to the house while Jordan and Blake hung out inside the minivan and played the game *Tetris* on their Game Boys. A note was attached to the front door. The note read, "Open." So, after a brief survey across the neighborhood, Jacqueline did as the note instructed and opened the door.

"What are you doing, Jackie?" Pamela whispered frantic-ally.

Jacqueline didn't respond to Pamela's obvious question. Instead, she walked right inside the empty mansion. She walked through the foyer, which was about the size of her old living room, and gazed in awe at the sparkling chandelier above. Marble floors. On the wall hung a large mirror with a golden frame. They passed the living room, which was fur-nished with leather furniture and an entertainment system. Even the smell of the mansion almost reminded Jacqueline of the inside of a brand new tennis shoe.

After they passed the living room, Jacqueline finally made it to the kitchen.

Pamela was slow to enter. She too was so amazed from the pristine condition of the place, the marble floors, and the chandelier. She didn't even want to touch anything, not even her own two feet against the hardwood floor in the kitchen.

As Jacqueline stepped inside the kitchen—her sister not too far behind—she came across a house key with another note on the granite countertop.

She picked up the note and read it to Pamela out loud, "It's never too late to start over."

Pamela asked suspiciously, "What exactly is going on here, Jackie?"

Jacqueline gazed down at the house key.

"Jackie?"

"Someone's looking out after us," Jacqueline said, her eyes never leaving the key.

*   *   *

From *Missing the Edges: A Memoir,* page 353:

It certainly felt like the end, and the beginning of something new and exciting. Deep in my heart, I knew Henry just didn't do it for T.J. He did it for the entire city. His message was a universal one: bring all races and creeds together through the power of music, most importantly, to love one another despite our differences. After awhile, it started to make sense. . .

NINETEEN

IN a dimly lit office, Corpus was staring down at the GSM device that was found by investigators inside Orlando's Coupe Deville the day after his suicide, as well as three manila folders on his desk, two on them containing the toxicology reports from both Cedric Johnson and Jonathan Farrow and the other one being a file on Henry Uriah Burl.

The weary detective moved his unsteady eyes from the files on his desk to the office window where the other police officers were loitering around. *Do they know the truth about Johnnie? How he was working with several officers in the LPD. How many more were there? Two? Three?* Corpus got up from his desk to stretch his legs and walked over to the office window. *Did they know the person who killed Johnnie in his cell while he was eating his meatloaf?* Poor bastard. What a way to go out? One minute you're stuffing your face with food. The next, you're dead. For the first time in his career, Corpus knew; and he never felt more alone than now. He couldn't trust any of them, even Merrotti.

After lunch, the word had gotten out about Detective Corpus and lead forensic investigator, Christian Van Dyer, and what the two were doing behind Reed's back. Apparently, Christian wasn't good at keeping secrets, especially when he found himself in the presence of an incredibly beautiful woman, the new ballistics examiner who worked downstairs.

At exactly 4:38 PM, Ted's brother, Donnie Backer, sneaked inside Corpus's office while he was relieving himself in the restroom and rummaged through the files on his desk until he found one folder in particular. He opened up the file and read over the name, *"Henry Uriah Burl,"* as well as his personal information, including his home address in Madison. Donnie took the other folders, the two containing Jonathan Farrow and Cedric Johnson's toxicology reports, and sneaked out the same way he came in, which so happened to be through the front door.

By the time Corpus came back from the restroom (the last two days had been wrecking havoc on his digestive system), the folders on his desk were nowhere to be found. Same with that GSM device he had been gazing at all morning. *How could I be so careless?* With all that was going on, the Backer case, mainly the pressure he was receiving from the lieutenant, he completely forgot to take the folders with him to the restroom. Has it really come down to this, Corpus wondered, for a detective to cling onto important files and evidence and protect them from the traitors within the department? Even go so far as to take evidence into the shitter with you? Has it *really* come down to this? Corpus was the one who checked out the GSM device from the evidence locker. Now, the device was gone. The only person to blame: himself. Then, the questions came and went like the police officers inside the precinct.

"Who was it?" Corpus asked himself as he stood behind the office window and watched the other officers wandering around the precinct as if nothing had happened.

Was it Merrotti, he thought, or *has Reed gotten to Christian?*

TWENTY

WHEN the inception first came to Henry in the middle of the night, he never expected this many people to actually show up at the vacant Clark Building directly across the street from Lansford Medical Center.

At *least* five thousand people, Henry counted from the ledge of the rooftop after spending the entire day stapling flyers to telephone poles and taping flyers to street posts and once the tape and staples ran out, handing out flyers to pedestrians around Lansford, including Parker Square where he spent most of his day, as well as going on air at 106.7 The Wedge radio station and promoting a so called "little gathering" in front of the Clark Building at sundown.

While thousands of Mona's Arch fans and patrons alike gathered below the Clark Building, Henry stepped down from the ledge and paced around the rooftop as the other band mates stood back in disbelief. At the same time, Deon curiously inched closer to the ledge and gazed at the sea of bodies below.

"Jesus. . . " he mumbled.

Socks patted Deon on the back, leaned over his shoulder, and said into his ear, "Jesus doesn't have anything to do with tonight, buddy."

Deon turned his shoulder.

"If you say so. . . "

From behind, the roof access door swung open with a loud *squeak*!

Henry stopped his nervous pacing and marched directly toward Starlet, who was standing still by the doorway in a state of confusion from both the amount of people who showed for the gathering, as well as Henry's unyielding charge at her.

"What took you so long?" he said, his shoulders inflating with anger.

In return, Starlet callously shrugged her shoulders.

"I. . . I had to get some gas in my car," she said, her voice slighter higher than usual. "I've been running on fumes for the past two days."

Henry returned, "That's no excuse."

"Plus," Starlet said over Henry's voice, "it took me some time trying to find the right outfit for this thing."

The band, including Socks, acknowledged Starlet's outfit: a black biker jacket worn over a glittery tank top; a pair of tight black jeans, which were faded with tattered holes at the knees and thighs; at least ten bracelets, all ranging from tiger eye stone to silver, over her left wrist; and finally, a pair of black pirate boots that ran up to the bottom part of her shin. Except for the black eyeliner and mascara, which was always applied heavily, the rest of the makeup on her face was subtle: a shade of purple eye shadow matching the lipstick and then a sprinkle of glitter on the sides of her cheeks.

"You look gorgeous, Star," Socks said as he strolled up to Starlet.

"Thanks, Socks," she said with relief and then directed her narrow eyes toward Henry. "At least someone around here appreciates me being here."

"I'm not going to fight with you, Starlet," Henry said closely. "Not now—"

Geordie interrupted, "Are you two finished. . . "

"Yeah," Henry eyed Starlet closely, "we're finished."

"Arrr. . . arrrrrrr. . . are you sure you still want to do this, Henry?" William said with a tremor in his throat as he and Geordie stood next to the two giant spotlights. "Th. . . think about all the trouble we can get into."

"No backing out now, Darby!" Henry shouted out as the crowd chanted the three-syllabled words, two from *Mona's* and the other from *Arch*. As the chanting rumbled from below, Henry walked away from Starlet, who, as before, stood in a state of confusion. "These people need us more than ever," he said, walking toward the ledge. "If it's Mona's Arch they want, then Mona's Arch we will give them!"

Parallel to the Clark Building, a steely-eyed man named Felix Harding gently eased over the ledge of Lansford Medical Center, placed a handful of Big League Chew into his mouth, and rotated the curved bill of his LPD baseball cap until it was facing backwards. He turned up the level of the walkie-talkie and placed it on the ledge next to him.

"I'm in position, sir," Felix said over the walkie-talkie.

"*Wait until my command*," Donnie said over the other end.

"Roger," Felix said as he adjusted the scope of the Heckler and Koch PSG1 in his arms.

On the Clark Building, Henry pointed at Geordie from behind and yelled out, "Light it up!"

"You're the boss," Geordie said under his breath and hit the switch next to the spotlight, which made a loud *clonk*.

Next, William hit the switch on the other spotlight.

The two spotlights shot up into the dark sky above.

Ews and *ahs* and gasps of wonder lifted from the gaping faces of the crowd below.

Meanwhile, Corpus, who was still working out a headache with a to-go cup of coffee from the café next to the precinct, spotted a strange light shining in the sky. The detective placed the cup aside in the cup holder and leaned forward over the steering wheel for a better look. The building tops on the Main Strip obstructed most of the view.

Corpus drawled, "What in the world is going on. . . "

The light, he wondered and leaned back in the seat, *it's coming from LMC.*

His hands gripped tighter over the steering wheel. He suddenly slammed his foot on the gas pedal, cut across idled traffic, and then made a quick detour through Lansford. He finally made it to Madison where he parked on Overlook Hill and scanned the valley below. The light was perfectly clear from here. Best seat in the house. Corpus stepped out of the Crown Vic and observed two brilliant spotlights shooting upward like lasers into the cloudy sky, revealing the giant letter V over the city of Lansford.

"Henry," he said to himself, "what are you up to now?"

The crowd below the Clark Building cheered in great triumph from the sight of the V in the sky. Henry paced over to another set of lights between the row of monitors and flipped on a switch, which displayed pink flashing lights—certainly not as dominate as the two spotlights—and then turned on a smoke machine.

"Really," Deon whined as he pointed at the smoke oozing from the smoke machine. "Is the smoke machine really necessary?"

Socks said, "Special effect, Deon."

"If I knew you were going to use a smoke machine, then I would've saved you the trouble and brought Bubble Bobble."

The comment sparked a couple of laughs from the other band mates, except for Henry.

As Henry paced toward the ledge of the roof (the pink light faintly grazing across his unsmiling face), he nodded at Deon.

"I have a clean shot, sir," Felix said, peering through the reticle of the scope. "Do you want me to take it?"

"*No. . .*"

"Sir?"

"*Wait, Felix. . .*"

Parked in the 1998 silver Lincoln Continental inside the third level of the parking deck, Donnie pulled the walkie-talkie from his face and observed the bright V shining behind the pillar of the deck. In his other hand was a red flyer: "JOIN THE VIGIL IN FRONT OF CLARK BUILDING WITH LANSFORD'S OWN, MONA'S ARCH!"

After receiving the cue from Henry, Deon pressed the PLAY button over the stereo.

The track was an instrumental track without any vocals or saxophone. Henry had called the track a "teaser" to the rest of the band. For Henry, as well as Socks, the track was nostalgic and played out more like a score for a soundtrack, gripping, provocative, ambitious. . . visceral.

During the recording session, Henry had compared the track to a montage at the end of an 80's movie. He said he wanted it to be like a "modern John Hughes movie." As with the spotlight, the inception of the song came from a girl whom he once had a crush on a long time ago and then, out of a twist of fate, reentered his life when he first made it big as a famous rock star. That girl's name was Kerri Coleridge (Henry's first "real" crush other than Kelly LeBrock from the 1985 movie, *Weird Science*,), most notably known as The Girl Who Lived Across The Street or The Cheerleader Who Wanted Nothing To Do With Him; then, after peeling back the layers over time and seeing Kerri for who she really was, she had become no other than The Pretentious Neighbor. While making the song, he couldn't help but think about Kerri waiting alone on a street corner in the pouring ran. Why she was waiting on a street corner was beyond Henry. He wondered if it was he who left her there alone, waiting. Waiting for what? Henry found her, though. In the song, Henry found Kerri throughout the haze. He ran to her— that seductive beat from the track fueling each stride he took. He kissed her in the pouring rain, held her tightly in his arms, and told her that he was always going to be there for her. After Henry completed the track, he realized it was never going to happen between him and Kerri, as hard as he worked at it or as much as he wanted it to. Even if Henry gave her everything, it still wouldn't be enough for her. It would never work out, he understood. For years, he had imagined her as a more mature woman, a nurturing woman who didn't judge people and loved him for who he was and would stand by his side through thick and thin. The woman in New York wasn't the woman whom he conjured up in his mind. She was exactly the same woman, or better yet, the girl whom he had known back in Reddington—only more physically enhanced and a bit more cynical. And a *bit* was saying a lot. For Henry, spending a bright future together with Kerri had turned out to be exactly that: a fantasy. Sharing a life with Kerri, creating a life with her, waking up next to her, and telling her those three rousing words that always went unspoken, only rehearsed in his mind, weren't going to be. The thought alone left him with mixed emotions. Happy in knowing that it was finally over and that he could move on with his life. Sad in knowing that he *could've* lived a wonderful life with her. Henry didn't know which side he gravitated to the most. He was more or less confused as to how things went south before they even had a chance to go in the right direction. And then there was one more emotion, the one buried inside. . . way deep.

Suddenly, the bridge of the song turned aggressive like a rally song, mutinous!

As the track soared over the rooftop, Henry snatched the megaphone from Deon's hand and stood on the ledge.

Intimidated from his belligerent attitude, Starlet eased away from the ledge while, with his ravenous eyes, Henry peered down at the many faces from black to white and every complexion in between below him.

Henry shouted into the megaphone, "I CAN'T HEAR YOU, LANSFORD!"

The crowd cheered, louder this time.

"*Mona's Arch! Mona's Arch! Mona's Arch. . .* "

Henry pulled the megaphone away from his face and cupped his hand over his ear.

"I still can't hear you, Lansford!"

"MONA'S ARCH! MONA'S ARCH. . . "

A grin pulled across Henry's face.
"THAT'S MORE LIKE IT!"

"Sir, I have a shot," Felix said. "Do I take it?"
"*No.*"
"Sir?"
"*That's a negative, Harding.*"

The crowd cheered from below. Some of the fans were dancing in their own way to the repetitive beat of the track. Others were holding up the Spok (Henry the Fif') sign, others the peace sign, while others were holding up lighters for T.J.
"TONIGHT IS NOT A CELEBRATION BUT A RECKONING! LET T.J. KNOW THAT YOU HAVE HIS BACK! T.J., T.J., T.J. . . ."
The crowd followed along with Henry's chanting.
"*T.J.! T.J.! T.J. . . .*"

From inside T.J.'s room in the ICU, Mr. Livingston was drawn to the spotlight beaming into the sky.
As he ambled over to the window beside T.J.'s bed, his face fell momentarily and then rose with excitement.
"Where's all that noise coming from?" Mrs. Livingston said from behind and listened closely. "It's sounds like stomping."
"Honey," Mr. Livingston trailed off as he gazed out the window at the crowd below. "You might want to take a look a this."
Mrs. Livingston got up from the chair and hurried over to the window where her husband was standing. They both gazed outside and witnessed not only the spotlight in the sky, but also the thousands of fans and patrons below the hospital, lighting the parking lot with lighters and candles. Not too far from the hospital at least twenty cruisers were racing down

the streets, all following one another in a single file line. The fans below were shouting out T.J.'s name. "T.J.! T.J.! T.J.!"

"LOUDER!" Henry shouted. "HE CAN'T HEAR YOU!"

The crowd chanted louder.

"ON THIS NIGHT," the crowd settled and listened closely to Henry's speech as the song was turned down in the background, "PEOPLE OF LANSFORD, WE ALSO PAY TRIBUTE TO THE ONES WHO HAVE FALLEN VICTIM TO THE *CORRUPTION* OF LANSFORD!"

The crowd suddenly roared from below.

"ON THE NIGHT OF JULY 28, 1999. . . "

As before, the crowd settled.

Henry paused for a moment and removed the megaphone from his face. His eyes shifted over to Starlet.

With both of her arms folded over her chest, Starlet was shaking her head as if she was warning him not to go there.

". . . ON THE NIGHT OF JULY 28, 1999," Henry said, "I DISCOVERED T.J., A MAN WHO IS A DEAR FRIEND TO ALL OF US, CLINGING TO LIFE! T.J. WAS BEATEN WITHIN AN INCH OF HIS LIFE! FACE SMASHED BEYOND RECOGNITION! AND THEN HE WAS THROWN AWAY LIKE SOME PIECE OF TRASH!"

The repulsed fans and patrons below were shaking their heads. Others were booing from Henry's remarks, not about T.J., but what had happened to T.J. and how he was, in fact, beaten within an inch of his life.

"T.J. . . . " Henry said, ". . . AS LONG AS I'VE KNOWN T.J., HE'S BEEN A FIGHTER! AND I KNOW THAT HE WILL *FIGHT* AS LONG AS HIS BODY IS WILLING TO FIGHT! AND HE *WILL* CONTINUE TO FIGHT UNTIL THE PEOPLE WHO DID THIS TO HIM ARE BROUGHT TO JUSTICE!"

*   *   *

While the cheers rang out from below, Felix readjusted the grip around the PSG1.

"I'm through listening to this big mouth," he said to Donnie. "This son of a bitch is going down."

"I said 'wait until my command' goddamn it!"

"THE FACT. . . " Henry said as he paced back and forth on the ledge of the rooftop, ". . . THE FACT: T.J. WILL NEVER BE THE SAME EVER AGAIN! ONE DAY, HE MIGHT BE ABLE TO FEEL WHAT IT'S LIKE TO WALK AGAIN, TO TALK AGAIN, TO *LAUGH* AGAIN, OR EXPERIENCE THE SIMPLE THINGS IN LIFE THAT YOU AND I TAKE FOR GRANTED! THOSE THINGS WON'T BE SO SIMPLE ANYMORE!"

The crowd turned somewhat silent from Henry's hopelessness.

Henry said, "I'M NOT GOING TO STAND HERE TONIGHT AND TELL YOU, MY FRIENDS, THAT T.J. WILL BE OKAY OR THAT HE WILL RETURN TO PLAYING MUSIC WITH MONA'S ARCH OR THAT WE WILL RIDE OFF INTO THE SUNSET! IF I SAID THOSE THINGS, I WOULD BE LYING TO YOU!"

As Henry held the megaphone down by his side and caught his breath, he turned to the rest of the band mates and motioned them away from the shadows and to join him on the ledge. Deon was hesitant about joining Henry on the ledge. Socks was the first one to make a move toward the ledge. Then, William, who was afraid of heights, cautiously walked over to the ledge and stood next to Henry. Finally, the rest of the band, including Geordie, followed. Starlet was the only one who stayed back. Once more, Henry turned around and waved her over.

He said sharply, "Join us, Star."

Starlet, who still had her arms folded over her chest, finally joined the rest of the band on the ledge.

The crowd cheered from the sight of the band.

"THOSE OF YOU OUT THERE WHO KNEW T.J. LIKE WE DID," Henry said, motioning to the other band mates, "KNOW THAT T.J., HE HAD HIS OWN PROBLEMS! WE ALL HAVE PROBLEMS! NOT ONE OF US HERE TONIGHT IS PERFECT! BUT THAT IS WHAT MAKES US HUMAN, TO BE IMPERFECT, NOT NORMAL, TO MAKE MISTAKES AND THEN, AS IN-DIVIDUALS OF A SOCIETY, TO LEARN FROM THOSE MISTAKES WHEN THE OPPORTUNITY KNOCKS AT OUR DOOR!"

"Donnie, what the fuck are you waiting for? I have a clean shot!"
Donnie switched over channels on the walkie-talkie.
"Wheaten," he said over the walkie-talkie, "Marson. You there?"
No response.
"Marson?"
"Here, Donnie," Marson said as he stood guard in his po-lice uniform by the staircase doorway.
"Keep your eyes peeled."
"Yes, sir."

"T.J.," Henry said, "HE, MY FRIENDS, WAS AN IMPER-FECT MAN LIVING IN AN IMPERFECT WORLD! HE MADE HIS MISTAKES AS WE ALL DO. BUT WHAT MADE T.J. SPECIAL, WHAT MADE HIM AN INDI-VIDUAL OF A SOCIETY, IS THAT HE OVERCAME HIS PROBLEMS AND HE LEARNED FROM HIS MIS-TAKES AND CHANGED HIS LIFE FOR THE GREATER GOOD! UNLIKE THE CHALLENGES THAT ARE AHEAD OF T.J., HIS MESSAGE WAS SIMPLE: TO LOVE ONE ANOTHER DESPITE OUR DIFFERENCES! T.J. UNDERSTOOD THE CRISIS THAT WE ARE NOW FACING AS A CITY *AND* AS A NATION. NOW, MY FRIENDS, IT'S TIME FOR US TO PUT ASIDE THE

BULLSHIT AND THE FUCKING POLITICS AND COME TOGETHER AS ONE!"

In her stern demeanor, Starlet glanced across the street and saw a tiny glare coming from the hospital's rooftop. Intrigued from the peculiar light, she peered closely. The pink lights flashing on top of the Clark Building momentarily shined away from her eyes. She peered closer, clearly now. In that brief moment of clarity, Starlet witnessed the silhouette of a sniper perched on top of Lansford Medical Center. Both of her arms slowly unfolded from her chest. Her eyes honed carefully now. Then, she glanced over at Henry, who was giving his speech: *"IT'S TIME TO STOP CRITIQUING HOW THE WORLD IS RUN AND FOCUS ON THE SOLUTIONS ON HOW TO MAKE IT A BETTER ONE!"*

The crowd cheered. . .

Felix: "Donnie!"

"I said, 'wait'! That is a fucking order! Do you hear me?"

Felix placed the PSG1 aside and switched off the walkie-talkie.

"Now," he said, "back to business."

"IF YOU HAVE A PROBLEM WITH THE WAY SOME-ONE DRESSES OR THE WAY THAT PERSON CARRIES HIMSELF OR HERSELF," Henry shouted out into the megaphone as he flailed his arm in the air, "THEN YOU, MY FRIEND, NEED TO TAKE A GOOD LOOK AT YOURSELF IN THE MIRROR BEFORE YOU POINT THE FINGER AT SOMEBODY ELSE! IT'S TIME TO PUT ASIDE THE BULLSHIT! I'M SICK OF IT! AND I KNOW I'M NOT THE ONLY ONE HERE WHO FEELS THE SAME!" More cheers. "ALL THE HATERS OUT THERE, ALL THE NAYSAYERS, ALL THE *CRITICS*, ALL THE HYPOCRITES AND CYNICS, ALL THE ONES WHO CAST YOU FROM SOCIETY BY THE WAY YOU LOOK OR THE WAY YOU TALK,

THEIR TIME IS UP! DO YOU HEAR ME! YOUR TIME IS UP! NOW, IT'S OUR TIME! AND *THEY* WILL NOT SHUT US UP!"

"Harding? Do you copy?"

Donnie switched through channels on the walkie-talkie.

"Harding?"

Nothing.

Donnie switched over to another channel.

"Marson?"

"*Go ahead, sir,*" Marson said.

"It's Harding," Donnie said over the walkie-talkie. "I lost communication with him."

Donnie waited for a response.

As with Felix, he received no response.

"Marson? Wheaten?"

"*What the. . . what the hell is that thing. . .*"

"Marson?"

"*Did you see that, Wheaten? Or was it just me?*"

A creature darted across the hallway.

"*No,*" Wheaten said carefully. "*I saw it. It's him.*"

"Him who? Marson? Wheaten?"

Screaming over the walkie-talkie!

Gargling. . .

The speaker of the walkie-talkie distorted from the sudden gunshot.

"*Marson. . . Wheaten. . .*"

As Officer Marson and Wheaten were unconscious on the floor, the stairwell door swung open.

Henry pleaded, "IF YOU EVER FEEL THE URGE, PEOPLE OF LANSFORD, TO DO SOMETHING THAT ISN'T RIGHT IN YOUR GUT OR TO DO HARM AGAINST ONE OF YOUR FELLOW BROTHERS OR SISTERS, THEN THINK ABOUT THIS ONE NIGHT! THIS NIGHT HERE, THE NIGHT WE SAID 'NO

MORE!' WE..." Henry said, the tears rolling down his cheeks, "...PEOPLE OF LANSFORD, WE ARE HERE TO STAY...THIS IS OUR HOME! THERE IS NO MORE TERRITORIES! NO MORE TURFS! IF YOU LIVE HERE, THEN YOU HAVE THE RESPONSIBILITY TO LOOK OUT FOR ONE ANOTHER!"

The crowd cheered, quaking this time.

As Henry grinned from the sudden uproar from the crowd, he rotated his shoulder over to Starlet, who wasn't standing with the band on the ledge. In fact, she was nowhere on the rooftop. He pulled the megaphone from his face and whispered into William's ear, "Where's Star?"

William shrugged his shoulders.

"She was just standing right here," he said to Henry. "Maybe she wasn't feeling too good."

He carefully looked around the street and then pulled the megaphone back to his face.

"BUT..." Henry said, "...BUT IF THERE'S ONE THING THAT WE, THE PEOPLE OF LANSFORD, WILL NOT IGNORE, IT'S THE ONES RESPONSIBLE FOR THIS ACT OF BRUTALITY! THEY ARE STILL OUT THERE, MY FRIENDS, SOME OF THEM WEARING BADGES AND UNIFORMS AND POSING AS POLICE OFFICERS, THE SAME PEOPLE WHO WATCH OVER US WHILE WE SLEEP!"

Donnie heard the crowd booing from where he was parked.

"Harding," he said and stepped out of the Lincoln, "if you're there answer me goddamn it! He's coming! Did you hear me? He's coming for you!" Donnie tried once more to reach Felix. "Harding?"

No response.

"Shit," Donnie whispered as he peered across the parking lot and at the crowd below the Clark Building. He said over the walkie-talkie, "It's not Burl, Harding...I repeat...it's not Henry..."

*   *   *

Back to Henry: "TONIGHT, I BRING A MESSAGE OF MY OWN, LANSFORD! IF THE ONES WHO DID THIS TO T.J. ARE OUT THERE LISTENING, MY MESSAGE IS CLEAR: MAKE IT EASY FOR YOURSELF AND TURN YOURSELF IN! JUST DO THE RIGHT THING! WE, THE PEOPLE OF LANSFORD, HAVE HAD ENOUGH! DO YOU HEAR ME! WE'VE HAD ENOUGH OF THE *CORRUPTION*, THE *VIOLENCE*, AND THE *BLOODSHED*! IT'S TIME WE TAKE A STAND AND MAKE A CHANGE. THAT CHANGE, MY FRIENDS, STARTS TONIGHT!   RIGHT HERE! RIGHT NOW. . . "

As the crowd cheered, nearly shaking the Clark Building, Felix placed his finger over the trigger.

"All right, big mouth," he said through the corner of his mouth. "Say cheese and smile for the fucking cam. . . "

As his finger lightly squeezed over the trigger, he heard a sudden rustling of gravel from behind.

"Huh. . . "

"TONIGHT IS FOR YOU, LANSFORD," Henry said as he pointed to the crowd below, "AS WELL AS THE MOTH-ERS AND THE FATHERS WHO HAVE LOST THEIR SONS OR DAUGHTERS OR BROTHERS OR SISTERS FROM POLICE BRUTALITY! YOU WILL NOT BE FORGOTTEN!"

The dark shadow of a creature grew over Felix's shoulder.

He suddenly turned his shoulder, only to witness the let-ter *H* over the breast pocket of a gray and black varsity jacket and then the beastly thing lurking behind him on the rooftop.

As the wad of bubblegum slipped from his gaping mouth, Felix quickly sprang to his feet.

Before he could reach for the handgun holstered over his waist, the Werewolf was on top of him.

With its gloved hands, the Werewolf clobbered Felix over the jaw and dazed him.

A gunshot rang out!

The bullet, however, struck the roof below.

The Werewolf grabbed Felix by the collar and hoisted him upward over the ledge.

JOIN US, LANSFORD, AS WE WELCOME IN A NEW ERA!

Felix seethed, "What the fuck are you?"

The Werewolf's dark, glossy eyes narrowed through the tiny red holes of the mask.

"I'm your reckoning. . ."

TONIGHT, WE TAKE A STAND!

"You can't kill a cop. . ." Felix begged. His heart was pounding against his chest once he glanced over his shoulder at the twelve-story drop underneath him. He looked back at the creature before him. "You're going to kill me in front of all these people! THERE ARE RULES!"

NO MORE VIOLENCE!

"I only have one rule," the Werewolf said, closer. *"Don't get caught."*

NO MORE CORRUPTION!

"Please," Felix cried, "Don't kill me! I have a child! I have a family!"

"You should've thought about them before you decided to take the law into your own hands. . ."

"PLEASE. . ."

From below, the crowd was chanting out T.J.'s name.

"Looks like the people have spoken."

"NO! NOOOOO. . ."

The Werewolf released Felix from its grip.

The fans and patrons among the crowd, who were unaware of the sniper plummeting twelve stories to his death, chanted, "NO MORE! NO MORE! NO MORE!"

Henry pointed at the crowd.

Over the megaphone, his voice grew louder, raspier. . .

"YOU, LANSFORD," Henry shouted out, "YOU HAVE THE POWER TO MAKE A DIFFERENCE! SO, LET T.J. KNOW THAT YOU, THE PEOPLE OF LANSFORD, HAVE HIS BACK!   LET YOUR VOICE BE HEARD NOW AND FOREVER!"

As the track marched like a drum beat, Henry pumped his fist. "T.J.!"   He yelled over the megaphone.   "T.J.! T.J.! T.J.!"

The crowd followed along, pumping their fists in the air and shouting out T.J.'s name as loud as they could.

The name T.J. softly chirped through his ears.

As T.J. embraced a deep breath, he opened his eyes—fully this time. Mr. Livingston turned away from the window and found his son opening his eyes.

T.J. slowly rotated his head toward his parents.

"I don't believe it!" Mr. Livingston said ecstatically and rushed over to T.J.'s bedside. "Honey! Come quick!"

Mrs. Livingston hurried over to the bed as well and kissed T.J. on the forehead. Tears were running down her cheeks. She never wiped them away. She let them run wild. In one stroke, she ran her hand over the side of his face and said, "Can you hear me, T.J.?"

T.J. blinked his eyes.

"I think that was a yes. . . "

"We're here, baby," Mrs. Livingston cried. "We're here."

In a sudden rush of excitement, Mr. Livingston found a passing nurse in the hallway.

"My son opened both eyes," he said to the nurse.

The nurse entered the room and shined the light into T.J.'s eyes. T.J. followed the light with his eyes, both of them.

"T.J.," the nurse said clearly. "Can you hear me?"

T.J. blinked his eyes.

The nurse turned to T.J.'s parents.

"He's responding to my commands, quicker than before."

"Why isn't he saying anything?"

"There was a lot of damage to his brain, Mrs. Livingston," the nurse said and placed the light back into her breast pocket. "Give him time."

"But T.J. has to see this," Mr. Livingston said mindfully and pointed at the window.

"See what?"

Mr. Livingston guided the nurse to the window.

"That!"

Mrs. Livingston suggested, "Why don't we move the bed?"

Meanwhile, the nurse was gazing at all of the fans and patrons below.

As the nurse fell witness to the commotion below, Mr. Livingston was trying to detach the heart monitor from the wall.

The nurse's face sharpened as she spun around.

"I wouldn't advise that, sir," she said suddenly.

"I don't give a damn what you say, lady." Mr. Livingston ignored the nurse and unlocked the wheels of the bed and said to himself, "My son, he has to see this." The nurse grabbed Mr. Livingston on the arm. In return, Mr. Livingston turned and looked the nurse in the eyes. He exclaimed, "There isn't a damn thing you can do that's going to stop me. Understood?"

The nurse tried to stop Mr. Livingston once more, but he didn't listen to her.

"Sir! You can't do that!"

"I'll do it myself then," he said and tried to push the bed, as well as the monitors, from the room without pulling out the intravenous line in T.J.'s arm.

Frustrated, the nurse finally helped Mr. Livingston with the bed. Four more nurses joined in and helped wheel the machines that were attached to T.J. from the room. The group made it to the end of the hallway in front of a larger window where they could see the crowd and the spotlight clearly.

"Raise him up," Mr. Livingston said urgently.

The nurse raised T.J.'s bed. T.J.'s eyes were wandering around in both wonder and confusion. His eyes fell downward, toward the crowd below and the fans cheering for him.

"You see, T.J.," Mrs. Livingston said closely to her son. "It's *all* for you."

Donnie finally arrived at the other two cops, Marson and Wheaten, who were slowly coming to.

"What the hell happened here?" he asked.

"He came out of the blue," Officer Marson said, holding the cut over the side of his head.

"Who?"

"That fucking werewolf."

"Come on," Donnie said and helped up Marson. "Let's get the hell out of here."

Out of breath, Henry finally arrived at T.J.'s room where Mr. and Mrs. Livingston were talking to their son.

"Henry!" Mrs. Livingston said surprisingly and hugged Henry. "You should've seen it, Henry. We rolled T.J. to the window. You should've seen the smile on his face."

Henry walked over to T.J. who was sleeping after the whole ordeal.

"T.J.," he said closely and T.J. cracked open his eyes. Henry's eyes turned glossy and wet. "What'd you think? That was something else. Huh?"

T.J. smiled enough to draw the tears from Henry's eyes. As he closed his eyes and fell back into a deep sleep, he gave Henry a thumbs up. Henry reached down and grabbed T.J.'s hand. Then, a hand fell upon Henry's shoulder.

"I hear you're a wanted man, Henry," Mr. Livingston said from behind.

Henry rotated around.

"I doubt they'll release the hounds on me for shining a little ole light in the sky and telling the people of this city the truth about what really happened."

Mr. Livingston finally smiled. For as long as Henry had known T.J.'s father, he had never seen him smile—at least not like this. Henry couldn't help but smile as well.

"Nice job, Henry," Mr. Livingston said as he extended his hand. "Have you ever thought about going into politics?"

Henry shook his hand.

Silence built.

Then, Henry laughed.

Eventually, Mr. Livingston laughed as well.

"At first, I never understood why you kids got into the music and all," he said, still laughing. "Now, it all makes sense."

Henry was drawn to the flashing sirens below and the police officers shouldering their way through the crowd. He walked over to the window and peeked outside. A group of police officers was storming inside the hospital.

"I better get going," Henry said to T.J.'s parents.

One last time, he grabbed a hold of T.J.'s hand.

"I'll be seeing you soon, Octo."

Henry directed his attention toward Mrs. Livingston and hugged her.

"You didn't see me," he said into her shoulder.

"We got you covered, Henry," Mr. Livingston said and patted Henry on the back. "Now get out of here."

As Henry made an attempt to exit, Mrs. Livingston exclaimed, "Henry! I forgot to tell you." Henry heard the voice, but didn't quite make out what she said. The voice was somewhat distorted from all of the adrenaline.

Henry stopped in his tracks and spun around only to find Mrs. Livingston staring at Henry with a blank expression.

"*Yeah*," he mumbled.

"There was a girl who came by here earlier," she said, her lips barely moving. "She said she knew T.J. from Reddington."

"What was her name?"

"Shoot! I forget."

A *ring* in Henry's ears!

Mr. Livingston said, "She said her name was Kerri."

"Kerri?"

Kerri who?

"That's the one," Mrs. Livingston said gladly and pointed at Henry. "Kerri Coleridge is her name. Beautiful girl. She asked about you. That's right. She told me that if you dropped by to tell you that she was going to be downstairs in the cafeteria."

Henry asked, "How long ago was this?"

How long was what, Henry?

"Well, about ten minutes before we rolled T.J. in the hallway," Mrs. Livingston replied. "She was a very nice girl, Henry."

"I gotta run," Henry said urgently and rushed from the ICU.

Dumbfounded, Mr. Livingston turned to his wife.

"Did you catch what he just said?"

Mrs. Livingston chuckled.

She said, "I think he's so overwhelmed from everything that's going on. Aren't we all, honey?"

Mr. Livingston shook his head.

"Kids these days," he said under his breath. "They're something else."

After Henry rode the elevator down ten stories to the first floor, he dodged a couple of police officers prowling around the main lobby area, as well as a dozen or so police officers camped in front of the entrance of the hospital, and slipped into the cafeteria without being detected.

Except for a couple of grieving families, most of the cafeteria (mainly the dining area) was empty. Henry carefully scanned the quiet cafeteria until his eyes landed on one person, a woman with brunette hair sitting in the back of the cafeteria. His heart nearly skipped a beat from the sight of the woman. Yet, the woman could've been just any ordinary woman. A stranger perhaps? Or Kerri, Henry wondered as the blood rushed from his face, it *could've* been her. After all, she did have the same profile. She was sitting with her back facing Henry. Her shoulders were deflated. Henry noticed that she kept moving her right hand up to her face and then down into her lap. She did the movement twice more. On the second time, Henry spotted the wet tissue in her curled hand. He breathed carefully—deep breaths through the nose and out through the mouth, as Charles had showed him—faced the stark reflection in the cafeteria window, and primped his hair before walking over to the brunette who, as before, was still sitting with her back facing him. Halfway through the dining room, the brunette finally turned her shoulder. Once her glossy eyes connected with Henry's, she stood up and faced Henry. She was wearing a long expression on her face. Her eyes remained as before, glossy and innocent. Despite the youthfulness in her eyes, her face appeared much older than Henry had imagined in his mind and nothing like he remembered from New York. However, the face was still attractive.

"Hey," Kerri said shortly.

Henry swallowed the lump down his tightening throat.

"Hey," he returned, wiping the sweat from his fidgety hands onto the sides of his pants.

"I'm sorry to hear about T.J.," she said, her glossy eyes never leaving Henry's.

"I know," Henry said, his voice slightly quivering. "These past couple of days have been really. . . crazy."

"All those people outside," she said and mistakenly chuckled. "They're all for T.J."

"Yeah," Henry said. "Crazy. Huh?"

"Totally," Kerri returned.

"It's really good to—"

"So, do you want to get out of here?"

"Ah," Henry said. "Sure."

"Okay."

"Where do you want to go?"

With a frown on her face, Kerri shrugged her shoulders.

She asked, "How about your place?"

Once more, Henry cleared his throat and then asked, "What about that one guy you were seeing?"

"I'm through with him," she answered expressionlessly. "So, do you want to get out of here or not?"

"Yeah," Henry said gladly after a moment of thought.

They dodged the police in the main hallway and exited through the kitchen of the cafeteria where they slipped past the crowd of fans and patrons. They got inside Henry's Porsche 911, which was parked on the very top level of the parking deck. While inside the car, Kerri couldn't help but look over the inside of the car with astonishment. Her hand ran across the leather dashboard.

"Nice car," she said, eased back into the seat, and smirked.

Henry glared at Kerri and replied, "You should see my other ones."

"I would like that," she said, her seductive eyes now tracing over Henry's lips.

"You might want to buckle up," Henry said casually, started the ignition, and then revved the engine.

A couple miles from Lansford Medical Center, Henry took the Porsche onto the open interstate where he flexed the muscle of the car. They didn't say much at all in the car. Surprisingly, Kerri enjoyed the silence inside the car and was somewhat impressed from the speed of the car. However, she never showed the emotion in front of Henry. About ten minutes into the drive (Henry still hadn't said much to her, especially as to why she was back in Lansford), Kerri unbuckled her seatbelt, slithered over the center console, and ran her hand across Henry's crotch.

"Are you sure?" he said, furrowing his brows.

"*Yeah,*" she said seductively while she bit down on her bottom lip.

Henry carefully readjusted himself in the seat as Kerri leaned over the driver's seat. Her innocent eyes weren't so innocent anymore, he observed. Now, they were as sharp as a reptile's. Even the sight of her eyes aroused him to the point of readjusting himself in the seat yet again. She carefully eased her head underneath Henry's hands—one hand positioned on the steering wheel and the other on the gear stick—and then unzipped the zipper on his pants.

As Kerri placed her head into Henry's lap, Henry suddenly hit the clutch below and then reached around Kerri's bobbing body and slammed the stick into fifth gear.

From *Missing the Edges: A Memoir,* page 354:

Till this day, I will never forget the vigil we had in front of Lansford Medical Center. Over a hundred people were arrested, including the band. The news said it was the most people the Lansford Police Department had ever arrested before. Apparently, we made some kind of history. Whatever that meant? The only person who managed to get away was the provoker himself. Jail wasn't so bad, not as bad as I thought. We only spent a night in jail and then we were released the next morning. Besides, it was for a good cause. I just wish Henry had lived up to his word.

TWENTY-ONE

BY the time Henry and Kerri arrived in Madison without wrecking on I-36, they were all over each other the second Henry opened the door to his condo.

The next three days bled into one another. Throughout the days and long into the nights, Henry and Kerri had sex in every position throughout the condo: in the bedroom, in the shower, in the living room, on the balcony of the porch, and even on the kitchen counter. Whenever they took a break from having sex, they would ride through the hills of Madison in one of the many sports cars that Henry collected in a garage not too far from his condo. When the sun was out, they would take the Red Rocket (a Chevrolet Corvette C5) and ride with the top down. On other days, they would take GEEK (a green Lamborghini Countach LP400). During their frequent excursions, they would catch up on their lives, what their dreams and aspirations were. Kerri asked about Henry's mother and how she was doing. Since Henry never got a chance to inform Kerri about his mother during their first reunion, he told her that she passed after his sophomore year at Haddon. Kerri asked more questions about Henry's life, mainly about what it was like to be a famous rock star and have pretty girls constantly throw themselves at him. Henry answered as honestly as he could, which, after an exchange of harmless blows on the arm and shoulder with her fist, made Kerri like him even more. Nonetheless, Henry was still a bit shocked from being with Kerri—especially after all she had put him through as a child, as a teenager, and as a young man. And she didn't leave either. Not after the sex. Not after dinner. She hung around. Never intruding. Never interfering with Henry's life. Two more days passed, and Kerri was still with Henry. One afternoon, after they ate turkey sandwiches together on the porch (Kerri, in fact, making the sandwiches, which completely caught Henry off guard), Kerri gave Henry a tiny figurine of a ballerina and told him that it was a "gift" when, in fact, it was Henry's to begin with. The figurine was the same ballerina that went inside his mother's music box, which was now broken to bits inside a cardboard box somewhere in his closet. Kerri had taken the liberty of fixing the ballerina after she found the broken figurine with the limbs broken off underneath the living room couch. She managed to superglue the parts back onto the torso of the ballerina, making it look as good as new. Henry didn't know what to think of the ballerina, about his whole experience with Kerri. When Henry finally asked, mainly why Kerri was here to begin with, she told him about her job and how she was taking a vacation in order to clear her head from the grind of New York City. In the back of Henry's mind, he knew it was a lie. Why would she come here for a vacation? She could've gone to the beach or the Hamptons (she certainly had the money) or somewhere overseas like

Paris. But here? In Madison? With Henry? He couldn't make sense as to why she would fly all the way from New York City to spend time with him in Madison, when, in fact, she was the one who wanted nothing to do with him. Why the change of heart? Of course, Henry never asked her. One day when Kerri was rummaging through Henry's closet, she came across a dusty print of Mona Lisa, framed too. Starlet bought Henry the painting during their tour over in Europe (a little shop in Naples was where she actually bought the painting). With all that was going on with the band, Henry never got a chance to hang the painting up on the wall. Kerri thought the painting was one of the ugliest paintings that she had ever seen—an "*eyesore*" was what she said to Henry. She told Henry to do himself a favor and burn the painting. After a couple of hours of convincing, Henry did exactly that. While Kerri was upstairs sleeping, he went to the backyard and burned the Mona Lisa painting in a rusty oil drum.

TWENTY-TWO

A whisper cut through the night darkness: "Sedona. . . "

In a cold sweat, Henry jolted upright from his bed with the word *Sedona* drifting from the bedroom.

He rolled out of bed, which caused Kerri to elbow Henry in the side.

"Go to sleep already," she groaned and then fell back to sleep.

Henry threw on his clothes, went to the kitchen, and searched for a liquor bottle, anything with alcohol. He spent several minutes searching. Each time he came up empty, the search turned more aggressive. Louder noises such as Henry slamming cabinets and stomping through the kitchen.

In great frustration, Henry grabbed the nearest object, which happened to be a flower vase that he had bought in

Japan, and chucked it against the wall. The glass shattered over the wall and rained over the floor.

The bedroom door swung open.

Kerri stormed outside.

She asked sharply, "What the fuck is going on out here?"

"I just dropped a piece of glass."

Her facial expression widened, eyes and brows.

"What are you doing?"

"Just getting some water."

Kerri rolled her eyes and then shook her head.

"You're so weird," she mumbled and went back to bed.

Exhausted from the lack of sleep, Henry ended up kicking back on the couch. He stirred around and tried to find the right position to sleep.

For hours, he tossed and turned on the couch.

Somehow, in his tossing and turning, he slowly fell into a deep sleep.

As the darkness flooded his eyes (images of faces from the crowd at Clark Building manifesting behind his eyelids), Henry suddenly woke from a piece of glass sliding across the floor.

He bolted upright and peered into the dark kitchen.

After a brief scour, he saw nothing out of the ordinary.

Just as he went back to sleep, he heard the door suddenly shake.

His eyes shot open!

Once more, Henry peered into the darkness toward the front door and saw nothing out of the ordinary.

The door was still, not shaking.

With a sigh, he curled back into the couch and covered his head with a pillow and tried to sleep.

As Henry drifted asleep, that pounding was back. The pounding was faint like a pulse against the pillow.

Increasing now, louder!

As the pounding became deafening, Henry suddenly woke from his sleep. He found himself lying on the couch.

The pounding was gone.

The door was still.

Frustrated from the lack of sleep, he rolled from the couch and stumbled toward the door where he checked the peephole. Of course, nobody was at the door.

TWENTY-THREE

THIRTEEN days remained until the New Year's Eve concert in Los Angeles.

While Henry was scrambling around the bedroom in a frenzy state, Kerri was in the living room quietly packing her bags and making sure she had everything she needed for the trip. The past couple of days with Kerri were like a cloudy mess. Henry never had any alone time to carefully dissect the whole situation. She was always there. In the morning, she would always be there next to him when he woke up. During the day, she would always be there to play with him around the condo. In the evening, she would always be there to have sex with him. When Henry set his body in motion (like gathering up his things in the bedroom), he had a way of putting things into perspective. In Henry's case, he put more stock into this "Kerri Situation." He gathered shirts and pants and outfits that he could take with him and tossed them in the luggage. *How did she know T.J. was in the hospital? The news,* he thought carefully. *She could've heard it on the news.* Henry crossed the nightstand and came across the hardback, *The Winds of Eastback*. He reached down and picked up the book and cracked it open. The photograph of Sedona, the one with the two girls, as well as the address written on back, fell from the book and landed next to Henry's feet. He kneeled down and picked up the photograph and studied it closely. *More questions*, he thought. More answers. Answers led to more questions. More roads.

More doors. More stories. Henry had known about such discoveries as a young adolescent. *If I hadn't run away,* he thought about the swamps, the plantation house, Fox, the pit of skulls and bones, I would've never known about my mother's history, *her condition.* Was it best to leave it alone? After long deliberation, Henry pocketed the photograph. As he continued to pack and think about Kerri (every now and then, he would glance her way), he couldn't help but acknowledge the saxophone case perched against the corner of the wall. For days, it had sat there—*he* had, Harry—all smashed to pieces and crammed inside the case. Once or twice, Henry thought about opening the case and checking on Harry's condition. . . *Would he look brand new?* Or *would it finally be over?*

As Henry fished out another pair of jeans from the bottom drawer, he came across a business card in one of his jeans pockets. While he was doing laundry the other day, he completely forgot to empty out the pockets. He completely forgot that he had grabbed the card from his box of "HENRY'S THINGS." He remembered hauling the boxes into the living room and going through them, the photo albums and old toys and comic books (he even had the #1 Batman from 1940 protected in a plastic sleeve). When he came across his box of "*things*" from his past, he remembered coming across the werewolf costume from Halloween of '89 (the salt and pepper one), picking up the suit, and wondering what happened to the original werewolf mask and if he threw it away or not, or if Starlet did something with it when she was helping him move the boxes back into the closet. Then, he remembered grabbing the card from underneath the werewolf suit. The card was intact, crinkled a bit. Some of the ink was washed off, but it was still readable, especially the address and that name, *Witch For Hire.*

Suddenly, he heard two knocks at the front door.

Henry pulled himself from his thoughts.

"Who could that be?" he asked himself and then tossed the worn business card in the trashcan in the bathroom.

"Are you expecting anybody?" Kerri asked from the living room.

"Not that I'm aware of," he said as he cautiously approached the front door.

Once Henry recognized the person behind the peephole, he turned right back around.

"Who is it?"

Henry squared himself in front of the door and blocked the peephole as if Kerri had incredible vision.

With his voice softened, he said, "Will you excuse me?"

Kerri sighed, rolled her eyes, and walked out onto the porch where she lit up a menthol cigarette.

Henry opened the door wide enough to slip his body through the crack.

Before Starlet could make an attempt to step inside, Henry stepped into the hallway and closed the door behind him.

Starlet squinted her eyes in confusion.

"Did I catch you at a bad time?"

"No," he said and exhaled sharply. "I just sprayed a whole bunch of chemicals inside. I could use the fresh air."

"Chemicals?"

"*Yeah*," Henry said with hesitation. "I'm. . . I'm doing some cleaning."

"Cleaning?"

"It's a pigsty in there."

Starlet folded her arms.

"I haven't seen you in a few days," she said. "How've you been?"

"Good."

"Are you sure?"

"Yeah."

A strange tension built over the conversation.

"Listen, Henry," Starlet said and hung her head, "Deon told me about the trip."

"If you're here to convince me to stay, then it's not going to work."

"Are you sure you want to go through with this?" Starlet said and grabbed Henry's hand. "We go to Los Angeles together, like a real band."

"If I don't do this, Star," Henry slipped his hand from Starlet's and paced around the hallway, "then there's no way I'm performing. I need this more than anything. Surely, you can understand after all we've been through. I just need to get away before I step into the spotlight again."

Henry paused and thought about his words, especially the word *spotlight*. He nearly asked the question: Where did you go the other night at the vigil?

Before Henry could muster enough courage to ask the question, Starlet asked a question herself: "Where will you go?"

Henry sighed.

"I actually don't know yet," he said.

"You're just going to take a random flight?"

"Something like that," he said. "Yeah. Maybe somewhere exotic." Henry thinking: *Maybe the desert.* "Maybe a place with a lot of. . . *mountains*. Who knows?"

Starlet grinned.

"Any room for two?"

Henry inched closer to Starlet.

"I wish," he said and gave Starlet a once over with his eyes. "But I need to do this alone, Starlet."

Starlet said seriously, "I know things between us have been a little difficult. . ."

Henry grabbed the side of Starlet's face. He leaned over and kissed her on the lips. He held his lips there on Starlet's and kept them there until she returned the kiss. For minutes, they kissed while the tears ran down her face.

"I love you, Starlet," he said, holding onto the sides of her glazed face. "I love you so much. But you were right about us. We can't be together."

She said, "But you said it back to me."

"I know I did, Star," he said passionately. "And I meant every word of it. But just because I love you doesn't mean we have to be together."

"But what if T.J. never. . ."

"Don't," he interrupted. "Don't say that."

Starlet was sniffling.

"We'll get through this," he said. "I promise."

"You promise?"

"Cross my heart and hope to die."

Starlet flexed the sides of her face.

She quickly pulled her face from Henry's grip.

"I have to go." She sniffled and then briefly glanced into Henry's jittery eyes. Her head was held down toward the floor when she uttered "I'll see you in Los Angeles."

"Star," he said clearly as Starlet walked away from Henry, "we still haven't finished our conversation from the other night."

Starlet turned her shoulder.

She said, "Some other time, Henry," and walked away.

As she made it to the end of the hallway, Henry said from the doorway, "I know it was you, Starlet. . ."

Starlet paused, but never turned around to face Henry.

"I know. . ."

Before Henry could finish his sentence, Starlet proceeded down the hallway and exited the building without turning around.

From *Missing the Edges: A Memoir,* page 356:

After I left Henry's place and drove back to the studio, I knew that things would never be the same between us. Now, it was only a matter of time before things went bad. I just wish I could've done more to stop what was about to happen next. . .

TWENTY-FOUR

As an excellent problem solver who enjoyed putting together puzzles or Rubik's Cubes and knew—at such a young age—what he was destined to do with his life, which was to fight crime and solve puzzles on a much larger platform, Corpus could never understand why the job turned a detective's mind into putty. The question would come and go, but never with a reasonable answer. Perhaps it was from witnessing these violent images throughout the day or wondering how a person could commit violent acts on one another. After awhile, he quit asking the questions (mainly about what went on inside a person's head) and focused on the evidence, motives, and facts. The only thing that was clear to him now was that he knew he should've retired two years ago when he had the chance. But he needed the money. Needed the pension. For the first time in his life, he was *not* in control of his life. Of course, the cases were there to help keep that one thought at bay. He thought if he kept his mind busy enough, then the thought would never find him. At times, he would go to the shooting range and fire off a couple of rounds or talk to a grieving widow or two to help ignite a passion to fight crime again. The numbness was back, that dreadful apathy. Now, the one thought was back skulking around the murkiness of his mind.

How cliché for such a thought to enter a seasoned detective's mind!

Is this what happens to us, the jaded dogs? Is this what the job turns us into, a shell of what used to be a man?

From the moment he woke till the time he arrived back home in Cityside, a gated community outside uptown Lansford, he thought about how he was going to do it. Quick and painless, of course. The pain, however, wasn't the real issue. For his entire life, he had experienced many degrees of pain. None, of course, would ever top the pain of losing the one joy in his life, the whole reason he got started as a detective. Was it going to be with a knife? Recently, he was given a set of new knives for Christmas. On many occasions, he had accidentally cut his fingers on the blade while cooking. If it was going to be with a knife, he thought, then he was going to do it in the bathtub. Somewhere easy to clean. Then they wouldn't have too much trouble selling the house. However, they would never find him until days later. By then, Corpus wondered, the body would've already started to decompose. The odor would have already seeped into the walls, ruining the entire house. They would never miss him. Merrotti maybe, he thought, would probably be the one to discover the body. But how long? In a matter of days? Weeks? Surely not months? Next, he thought about hanging himself. Quicker than the blade, Corpus imagined. Very old fashioned. On the other hand, it would take too much planning, too much time, too much diligence. He would have to buy a rope at the home improvement store. Sturdy enough to support a two hundred pound man. The thought alone of standing in the checkout line with other people who were as equally miserable as him could maybe make him reconsider. Perhaps that was the solution: be around people who were worse off than himself. The man standing behind him in line gave him an interesting idea: a chainsaw. *Way* too messy. Corpus came back to a rope. How about the support? Where would he tie the rope? The pole from the closet? The beam above the kitchen? Too much work. Then, there was the other, much easier way: eating a bullet. He already had a gun. Already had a bullet. The neighbors next door would definitely hear the gunshot. That is if they weren't blasting their television at all hours of the night. If they did hear the gunshot, they would call it in. And by the time the boys in blue finished their cup of Joe Black, they'd be getting word about that old dog from the precinct and how he had finally grown a pair. Had it really come down to this? Had they become so cynical? Corpus thought as he sat motionlessly in the running parked car. He turned his attention away from the steering wheel and toward the dark house to the right of him. Such a big house, Corpus thought, for a single man. She gets the boot while the old dog keeps the house.

As Corpus dragged himself through the front door, he had already made up his mind on what he was going to do. He switched on the lamp inside the bedroom, tossed the handful of mail (mostly junk) on top of the desk, and then neatly folded the coat over the edge of the bed. Next, he loosened the black tie around his neck, removed the holster from his shoulders, and hooked the strap around the backside of the chair. *The last eyes I want to see*, he thought as he carefully placed the Glock on the desk and settled the picture frame of his wife and child, Sam, in front of him.

Corpus plumped down in the chair.

"I'm so sorry," he whispered, the tears running from his eyes.

He kissed his wife and child goodbye, leaving a wet smudge of phlegm and saliva on the glass of the frame.

After Corpus centered the picture frame in front of him, he picked up the Glock from the desk and turned off the safety.

"Fuck it. . . " he said bitterly and without wasting anymore time, he stuck the barrel of the Glock into his mouth.

As he was about the squeeze the trigger, a blank envelope slipped from the stack of mail and fell from the desk.

Corpus removed the Glock from his mouth and pulled his watery eyes toward the floor where he discovered the blank envelope.

He placed the pistol aside, reached down, and picked up the envelope.

No address, Corpus noticed. No return address. No name. No nothing.

He looked around the bedroom in paranoia and didn't see anything out of the ordinary—the bedroom was the exact same as he had last left it before he went to the precinct. He opened the envelope, pulled out an old newspaper article from March of 1989, and held the article underneath the lamp. The article was about the murder of the famous musician, Henry McClintock. The name *Timothy Snead* was highlighted with a yellow highlighter. Attached to the article was a note. Corpus peeled away the note and read it to himself, "Are you sure you're on the right side, Detective?"

It was raining that night, Corpus thought as he frantically searched for any details that he might have missed at Frankie's Footlongs.

Corpus followed the pair of tire marks to the back of Frankie's drive in.

He marched over to nearest sewage drain.

With his flashlight, he scanned the drain.

He kneeled closer and came across sunflower seeds, all chewed up and spat out, inside the cracks and crevasses of the drain.

With a glove, he fingered a cracked sunflower shell from the drain with his glove and held it up to his face.

He pointed the flashlight on the sunflower seed.

Yes, he thought. *It was raining. The seeds washed into the drain.*

Then, Corpus aimed the flashlight down into the drain and saw more sunflower seeds, all chewed up as the ones before.

He pointed the flashlight over the parking lot and mentally mapped out the stream in his head. He found the origin, a pile of seeds not too far from those tire tracks.

"You were *watching* him," he said angrily to himself. "That's it. You were watching him. Weren't you? You like to watch. Don't you, you sick son of a bitch. You followed him here as you were ordered and you watched him. How long were you watching him? How long, you son of a bitch?"

Corpus stood exactly where the onlookers were parked and aimed the flashlight where Little Red was parked next to Frankie's Footlongs. "He saw you watching." Corpus's facial expression went blank, eyes sharpened. "So, he ran away." He pointed the flashlight toward the alleyway, tire tracks following. "Then, you came after him. He didn't stand a chance. He was outnumbered. You joined in along with the rest of them. Isn't that right, YOU SON OF A BITCH!"

An image of Officer Marson walking down the hallway from a holding cell flashed over his mind's eye. Then, Merrotti talking about the sunflower seeds, how Wheaten got him hooked on them.

Then, Corpus uttered in disbelief, "No. . ."

TWENTY-FIVE

WHEN Henry and Kerri arrived at Conway International Airport outside Lansford, Corpus was already waiting for him.

"Ms. Rollinson said I might find you here," Corpus said over Henry's shoulder.

Caught off guard from the detective's sudden appearance, Henry turned around toward the voice. He glanced over at the detective and then directed his attention toward Kerri.

"Give me a minute," he said vaguely to Kerri.

She asked, "Is there a problem?"

Henry shook his head and said, "No problem."

"Am I interrupting something, Henry?" Corpus said over Henry's muttering.

Kerri left her luggage with Henry and sat down in the nearest waiting area.

Corpus noticed the several bags of luggage on the floor.

"Lot of luggage, Henry," he said, moving his eyes upward at Henry. "Plan on going away for a while?"

"Maybe."

"I had a little chat with Ms. Walker before I came over here," Corpus said suspiciously. "She told me that the house she is currently residing in is under the name, Henry McClintock. Showed me the deed and everything. Now, Ms. Walker might not know who Henry McClintock is nor will she ever know; but you and I, Henry, know exactly who Mr. McClintock is."

Henry didn't respond to Corpus's remark.

"Pretty nice gesture, Henry," Corpus said, "to buy a house for a complete stranger."

"After all she has been through, it was the least I could do," Henry answered calmly. "Is it a crime to buy a house for a woman whose son was a criminal?"

"No, Henry," the detective said sternly. "But murder is."

Henry sharpened his eyes.

Corpus stepped closer and said closely, "I know you were at Backer's house that night."

Henry didn't respond.

"I have to bring you in for questioning, but. . ." Corpus said and then glanced over his shoulder at the parked mustard-yellow Mercedes outside the airport. He saw four faces, but only recognized three. They were the same four faces that had been following him from the time he left Frankie's. ". . . But you have a plane to catch. So, I'm not going to get in your way, Henry."

"Thank you. . ."

"You're welcome," Corpus said and threw his head in a nod. "But remember when you get back, we're going to have a serious conversation."

"And what makes you think I'm ever coming back?"

"Your band needs you, Henry," he said. "Most importantly, the people of Lansford need you."

While Henry stood in a daze and thought about the detective's comments, especially about Lansford and the people of the city needing him, Corpus exited from the airport. During his walk from the main entrance, he glanced over at the parked Mercedes and made sure it was still there. The Mercedes was still there, but two of the four faces weren't. He saw the one behind the steering wheel and then the one in the passenger seat. He knew who the man was in the passenger seat, but he couldn't make out the one in the driver's seat. The other two who were sitting in the back of the car were nowhere around.

Officer Marson and Wheaten, who were both dressed casually and not in their LPD uniforms, followed Henry through the airport. They made sure to keep their distance as Henry roamed through a crowd of foreigners. Unaware of the two undercover police officers on his tail, Henry shouldered his way through the crowd and stopped in front of a massive flight board. He checked each departure on the board. He finally found a flight to Sedona.

Henry read the board.

Flight: *337C* (Courtesy Airlines).

Gate: *C14*.

Scheduled departure: *2100* (9:00 PM).

He checked the time at the bottom of the board.

The time read: 7:45 PM.

Meanwhile, Corpus hurried back to his car and grabbed the Glock from the glove compartment.

Out of breath, he checked the magazine and made sure he had a bullet inside.

Once he slid the magazine back inside the Glock and directed his attention toward the back of the carpool line, the Mercedes was gone.

"Damn it," he seethed and looked around the carpool lane.

Once he realized the Mercedes was nowhere around, he got back inside the car and checked the rear view mirror.

Moments later, Officer Marson and Officer Wheaten stepped inside the Mercedes parked in parking lot C. They both entered via the backdoor. Officer Marson reached over the passenger seat headrest and waggled the three tickets in his hand while Officer Wheaten slid over the saxophone case to the middle of the backseat and sat down.

"So," Donnie said from the passenger seat, "what's the deal?"

Officer Marson said, "Three tickets to Sedona."

"I hate the desert."

"Tell me about it."

"Donnie, we can't keep chasing him around like this," Officer Wheaten said. "I say we just end this once and for all." "Patience, Wheaten," Donnie said. "Soon, this will all be over."

Officer Marson asked, "And Corpus? What the hell do we do with him?"

"Al won't be a threat," Donnie said casually as he watched the airplanes take off from the runway. "When we leave," he turned to the driver's seat and nudged Merrotti on the arm, "Merrotti will take good care of him. Isn't that right, Merrotti?"

"Yeah," he said, his voice trembling. "I'll take care of him."

"What to do you mean 'take care of him'?"

"He means, Marson, that he'll handle it," Donnie said and glared at Officer Marson. "Do you got a problem with that?"

The officer shook his head.

"No problem," he said.

Fifteen minutes of driving in circles around the Conway International Airport and still no sign of the Mercedes.

As Corpus made another right into the first terminal, he spotted the Mercedes pulling out of a row of taxis in the car-pool lane.

"Gotcha," he said and closely tailed the Mercedes.

Eventually, the traffic thinned out the farther they drove from the airport, which, for Corpus, was the perfect opportunity to do the unthinkable.

As soon as they reached the open two-lane road next to the airstrip, Corpus floored the gas pedal and sped around the Mercedes.

Corpus clinched his teeth: "Time to turn the tables, you mother fuckers. . . "

As he pulled directly in front of the Mercedes and gently eased off the gas pedal a bit, he suddenly slammed on the brakes. The sudden move forced the mysterious driver in the Mercedes behind Corpus to slam on the brakes as well, which, by doing so, caused the Mercedes to skid off the road and crash fender first into a small trench.

While Corpus drew his Glock, he glanced into the rear view mirror and saw the front two wheels of the Mercedes spinning in place over the wet mud. The mysterious driver in the driver's seat was slamming his hand against the steering wheel as if hitting the steering wheel would make the Mercedes move from its stuck position.

A couple of tense minutes expired before Corpus finally decided to take advantage of the Mercedes' immobility. He stormed from the Crown Vic and cautiously approached the Mercedes only to find Merrotti sitting calmly behind the steering wheel.

"Merrotti?" Corpus said, lowering the Glock down by his side.

"Sorry, Al," Merrotti said flatly from inside the Mercedes.

While Corpus carefully studied his partner's face (his eyes!), Merrotti snapped his eyes downward at the pistol held in his lap and then back up at Corpus. They shared a long stare, Corpus wondering which way to avoid the bullet and Merrotti aiming directly for the heart, the kill shot.

As Merrotti fired the pistol from inside the car (the bullet coming inches away from Corpus's head), Corpus simultaneously lowered his left shoulder and rolled out of the way and shot Merrotti precisely in the shoulder.

"There's still a few tricks left in this old dog. . . " Corpus said as Merrotti wailed out in agony.

With both of his hands wrapped tightly around the Glock, Corpus rose to his feet, hurried over to the Mercedes, swung open the driver's side door, and ripped an injured Merrotti from the driver's seat.

The pistol slipped from his bloody hand and dropped to the road.

Corpus kicked the pistol away from Merrotti's reach, even though Merrotti was in no condition to retaliate.

His hand was pressed over his shoulder while he cried out like a child, "YOU SHOT ME, YOU SON OF A BITCH!"

"You'll live. . ." Corpus seethed as he holstered the Glock.

As Corpus reared back his fist, Merrotti cried, "I DIDN'T MEAN TO. . ."

"Too late," Corpus said while in wind up.

Merrotti's head whipped backward from Corpus's fist.

"Where are your friends?"

Merrotti was too dazed from the punch to answer.

In return, Corpus punched Merrotti across the face yet again.

A string of blood was drawn from the young detective's nose.

Corpus: "Where are they?"

Another punch.

Then, he threw another one across Merrotti's chin.

"Sa. . . Sedona. . ." Merrotti whined, ". . . They. . . they said something about Sedona. . . "

"Arizona?"

"YES!"

Corpus sighed and threw the young detective to the road.

As Henry's airplane took off beside the two detectives, Merrotti said from below, "They. . . they said they were going to kill me, Al. I SWEAR!" In a loud hawk, Merrotti spat out a mouthful of blood as well as a couple of teeth from his mouth. "If I didn't do what they had asked me to do. . . " the blood ran down his chin, covering the collar of his shirt, ". . . they. . . they were going to kill me. . . "

"Shut the fuck up," Corpus said snappishly as he watched Henry's plane, Courtesy Airlines, lift off from the airstrip. With his eyes, he followed the airplane until it was nothing more than a speck of light among the stars above. A sudden realization came over Corpus, along with a wave of anger. Then, he slowly pulled his narrow eyes down at the young detective, who was both crying and wiping the blood from his face. *The line in the sand has finally been crossed,* Corpus thought as he acknowledged his partner's helpless state. For a brief moment, the detective witnessed a younger version of himself sitting there before him, obedient. If he was a good dog and did as he was told, he was going to receive a treat. How much were they paying him? Or was Merrotti right? Were these guys actually going to kill him? Or were they just empty threats? Sooner or later, the thought would come to him. The question: Would he have the guts to pull the trigger? If he pulled the trigger on one of his own, then he would have no problem pulling the trigger on himself. This was personal, to put down an old dog. How much longer would the corruption go on like this? Now, he finally realized, there was only one more thing left to do.

"Al," Merrotti reached up to Corpus, "I'm sorry."

Corpus grimaced, teeth clinched.

"You were supposed to be my partner."

"I know. . . " he begged, ". . . I'm. . . I'm sorry. . . "

"And Reed? Does he know?"

Merrotti shook his head.

"I. . . I don't think so. . . "

"You're lying."

"I swear, Al!"

Corpus kneeled down to Merrotti and said closely, "You should be ashamed of yourself."

TWENTY-SIX

THE pain was like a beacon lost somewhere in a sea of darkness: each pulse, so distant and yet so bright, filling his body.

So many of these beacons, these strange burnished light-houses, he discovered, each one now routinely passing before him. Eventually, the beacons equally broke apart from one another. Now, they came in twos.

As the pain doubled, he crawled closer to the building lights, so close he could touch them with his own hand. Another pair of lights whizzed by and left him against a cold dark wall of silence, terrorizing. The pain surfaced once more, growing ever so brightly. A thunderous sound of waves crashing all around him seized all command and brought forth silence once more. He pulled himself from the momentary cessation and ran far away from the silence, a dark place where the pain was subtle, and followed the crashing waves. The light built again and again and then the pain, the noise.

A bright light suddenly overwhelmed him. . .

. . . Then, a car horn blared out!

As Henry embraced the pain, he pulled the side of his face from the warm asphalt. His eyes reached up to the blue sky above him. The pain doubled as the scorching light beat down on the side of his face. The bright light, a much different one, coursed through his eyes and into his body, filling it with no pain, but with satisfying warmth. Soon, the pain would be back. Henry knew all too well about the pain from the trials. Until then, he absorbed the warmth, the purity of the air. Those once soothing waves—like the ones in the dark—lacked any kind of naturalism. Now, they were smelly and motorized. He pulled his eyes away from the sunlight, pulled himself from the warmth, and glared through the blurry horizon. An object materialized across the vast sea. A car, he realized. The car sped by without stopping. The sea suddenly ran dry and barren, a land untouched by man. With his weary eyes, Henry followed the car down the long, desolate desert road. Baffled, Henry tried to make sense of how he ended up in such a parched, spectral land, which carried no sound—only the cars that came and went. His ears were still ringing from the night before. There was also nothing there in his head, like a blank canvas. Even the name *Henry* was dead to him. He moved his fingers across his perspired forehead until they crossed a knot and depression. The wound on his scalp was deep, tender to the touch. Areas around the wound, where they blood had dried, scabbed over from the night before. He pulled his eyes toward the Africa-shaped bloodstain near the breast pocket of his white dress shirt, which wasn't so white anymore. In fact, the shirt was the color of the desert. Same with the ripped sports coat, which was once black but now covered in blood and dirt. He extended his worn, callused hands before him. Each one was covered in blood as well. Pieces of flesh were poking out from a couple of his fingernails. All Henry could remember was scratching a man's neck and then the high pitch scream. That was it. Everything else was empty, a blank canvas. The distant memory had come and gone like the pain. Nothing was attached to the image, only pain.

For miles, Henry dragged himself along the desert road. He could hardly feel his legs beneath him. Each step over the hard asphalt sent sharp, stabbing pains through his knees. His right arm was sore and heavy, hard to move. His breath was labored. Chest extremely sore. He did all he could to lift his arm into his shirt where he made a temporary sling with his left arm, his good arm, in order to ease the pain. He wandered, making sure to keep close to the road. At least four cars passed. Not one had slowed down for Henry. Finally, after he could no longer stand on his own two feet, he fell to the ground and rested a bit. Even though the enticement was there throughout each sudden flicker of his eyelid, Henry never ventured into the silence. Instead, he blocked it out and focused on the road ahead. The sunlight was still coursing through his weary eyes. The vacant sounds of the desert were still there too. Every now and then, the sounds of life (hawks and vultures running racetracks overhead) would penetrate his ears. The sounds, however, sounded no louder than a distant echo.

As time expired, Henry kept close to the light, the surrounding naturalistic sounds. He never closed his eyes, at least no longer than a couple of seconds. Any longer and there was a possibility that he could venture back into the darkness. So, Henry embraced the unlikely sounds. One in particular, a small shuffling sound, was so close to his ear that he could feel it pecking away at his eardrum. He moved his lazy eyes toward his right and found the two beady black eyes of a tortoise staring at him. The tortoise didn't do much at all. Occasionally, it would robotically jerk its head or move its jaw up and down and taste the pungent odor emitting from Henry.

As Henry shook away the numbness from his arms, the sound of a girl's voice cried out from across the road.

"We're safe here, Margaret," the girl said and tended to another girl who was curled up in a fetal position.

Henry pulled his attention away from the tortoise and listened closer now.

The name *Margaret* was distorted and bubbly and sounded as if it was being spoken underneath water.

"How do you know," the Margaret girl said, sniffling.

Henry stumbled to his feet.

"Girls," he uttered.

The two little white girls traced Henry, who was teetering across the desert road.

"Where are your parents?"

The traumatized girls didn't answer the question.

"It's okay," Henry slurred. "I'm not going to hurt you."

Still the girls didn't answer.

Henry said desperately, "I'm lost."

"Go away," the Margaret girl whined. Her hands were cupping her face, leaving her voice muffled. "You're not supposed to be here!"

"I don't mean any harm," Henry cried and held out his hand. "Is she hurt?"

"My sister," the other one said, "she's just scared." Her eyes sharpened over Henry's. "You should be too."

Henry heard the sound of one of those motorized waves again.

From a distance, a red thing appeared from the blur hovering over the scorching road. Henry scratched his eyes and squinted his eyes.

A truck wasn't slowing down!

"Girls," Henry uttered, holding out his left arm.

The girls acted as if they didn't hear or see the truck.

"Girls!" Henry shouted out and stumbled farther across the desert road. "Watch out!"

As Henry had trouble catching his breath, he waved down the truck and then hurried to the girls. Exhausted, he tripped over his own feet and fell to the road. As soon as he crawled forward in agony (the impact of the fall had temporarily knocked the wind out of him), Henry realized there were no girls.

Drifting in and out of consciousness, he managed to lift his head to the parked truck before him. A puddle of blood was growing underneath his body, soaking his clothes. The slam of a door forced Henry to open his wandering eyes.

"Are you okay, young man?" a soft-spoken voice said.

The figure of a tall man with tan brown spotted skin and deep, cavernous wrinkles on the sides of his face towered over Henry's body.

Henry tried to speak, but the words fell short.

His ears were drawn to the desert. The sound of music gently reverberated over the distant mountaintops, some flat and others spiked and jagged and capped with snow. The music sounded so familiar and yet so strange and unobtainable—a high note from a synthesizer playing over an ominous sounding piano. Before Henry could distinguish the music, only a scrambling of notes, a voice called out to him.

"*Young man. . .*"

The red truck was the last thing Henry's eyes came across before he collapsed and drifted off into the silence. That red truck. . . so familiar. . .

. . . Blades of sunlight cut over Henry's eyelids. Three bodies, all as dark as silhouettes, were gathering in formation around Henry's body. One of them reached down and tried to keep him steady. The coolness of the bedroom was sending violent chills through his trembling bones, body. Suddenly, a sword cut through his right side, leaving him in a state of trauma. A clinking sound pierced and then faded through his right ear and forced him back to the darkness. . .

. . . A burst of warm light, like nothing he had witnessed before, swept over Henry's eyelids. The pain and trembling was gone. Yet, they were both defeated by tranquility and remedy, two means working together in partnership. For a brief moment, Henry cracked his eyelids. A beautiful ivory face in front of a calming wall of burning fire loomed over his body.

"*Mister. . .*" the woman said fluently. Her voice was soft and sweet, tangible, as if Henry could hold it in his palms. He kept close to the voice, the warmness of it, and drifted back into the darkness. . .

. . . Another burst of light swept over Henry's eyelids. He opened his eyes, completely this time, only to be greeted by a sandy brown face with a smile as sweet as butterscotch.

Henry said faintly, "Dolores?"

With her dark brown eyes, she was looking down at Henry with a calming smile marked across her face. She ran a damp towel across Henry's forehead. She patted away the perspiration from his temples.

"Hush now," she said, smiling.

The voice wasn't Ms. Craft's, yet it was that same soft, sweet voice, the tangible one.

Once more, Henry drifted back into the darkness. . .

. . . Another voice, this time coming from the same tall man who discovered Henry on the side of the road. Henry cracked open his eyes. The brilliant sun shone over his body. The walls around him (he couldn't quite make out the wallpaper) were revealed behind two still standing silhouettes. His eyes crawled to the walls and a ceiling above, not the sun as he witnessed the first time around. Then, he discovered the sound of another voice, more familiar in tone. There, he witnessed the tall man standing next to a woman who was around his own age. The woman handed something to the tall man.

"I found this in his pocket," she said cautiously.

The tall man replied, "That's Mr. Hampton's girls."

"Do you think they're related?"

"I don't know." He ran his hand across the stubble on his face and directed his attention toward Henry. "Something doesn't seem right," he said. "Don't let him out of your sight. You hear?"

"It's not like he's going anywhere, Tad. . . "

"I know." The tall man handed the woman the photograph and then the rifle, which Henry thought was a long stick. "Just as a precaution," he said quietly.

PART NINE

ADENIUM OBESUM

TWENTY-SEVEN

Several days passed like the cars on SR (Scenic Route) 179.

A hazy light washed over the savory darkness. The familiar sounds of pots and pans rhythmically beating in the kitchen downstairs pulled Henry from his deep sleep. The sound was distracting and yet it reminded him of home. A couple of childhood memories surfaced: eating breakfast with a middle-aged woman, his mother perhaps, and then shooting hoops with another kid, a black kid. The soothing sunlight washed over Henry's face and gave him that needed strength to roll out of bed. Henry struggled a bit as he sat upright. He ran his hands over the stained dressings over his chest. Then, he moved his hand over the dressings on his arm. Unlike the dressings over his chest, the dressings on his arm were clean and unblemished. He braced himself against the drawer until he could stand properly on his own two feet and ambled through the small guest room, as plain as vanilla, toward the window, and gazed outside. There, a desert was stretching out for miles. There were strange mountains, some as red as clay, which etched the brilliant blue horizon. He had seen these mountains before, he realized, but in a smaller form. A hawk was gracefully gliding overhead and observing the dinner land below.

A door carefully opened behind Henry, which forced Henry to rotate his sore body toward the other side of the room. He found an older woman standing at the doorway. Her hair, rich and full and yet going gray, was like a loaf of bread knotted in the back. She had shared the same characteristics as the tall man from the desert road, slightly tan with wrinkles. In her hands, the old woman carried a plate of food. Besides the hint of cinnamon, Henry could smell the savory bacon in the still air. Both of his rested eyes fell over the steam rising from the scrambled eggs, which was floating upward into the old woman's unsure face.

"I see you're finally up," the strange woman said tentatively. "Your color looks much better than it did yesterday. For a second," she sighed, "we thought we were going to lose you."

"Wh. . . wh. . . wa. . . wheeeeee. . . where am I?" Henry asked, looking around the old room. The words projected differently on his tongue. They were harder to deliver. He moved his eyes around the room. The only pieces of furniture were a bed, an armoire, and a dresser. The walls were covered with floral wallpaper. A tall grandfather clock sat just outside the doorway. Picture frames were scattered on top of the dressers, all containing faces that he had never seen before.

"We're about twenty miles from West Sedona. . ." the old woman said, ". . . in the middle of the desert."

Sedona, Henry thought clearly, *the desert*.

"My name is Rebecca Blakeney," she said. "You can call me Becca or Becky, if you like. I'm afraid we couldn't find any identification in your pockets."

Henry studied the clothes, a flannel shirt and a pair of blue jeans, folded on the chair in the corner of the room.

"I washed your clothes," she said. "Took time getting all that darn blood out. I can go get them for you, if you like."

She pointed at Henry's clothes hanging on the laundry wire outside.

"Nnnnno," Henry said carefully.

Rebecca nodded at the clothes on the chair.

"Those were my father's clothes," she said. "They might be uncomfortable on you."

"I. . ."

Henry stood in a daze.

Rebecca's eyes fell over Henry's chest.

"Here," she said and nodded at Henry's chest. "I need to change your bandages, if you don't mind."

Rebecca placed the food on the dresser and tended to Henry's dressings over his chest. She eased him back onto the bed where she changed his dressings and replaced them with new ones.

"There you go," she said kindly and waltzed back to the doorway.

"I. . . ca. . . ca. . . caa. . . can't   reme. . . mem. . . member any. . ."

"It's all right, dear," Rebecca said patiently. "It will come back to you, hopefully sooner than later." She nodded at the food. "Try to eat something. You'd be amazed how quickly the body can recover after a hot breakfast."

"There was a wo. . . woman. . ."

"Yes," Rebecca said, stopping at the edge of the doorway. "You must mean Sheila."

"Sheeeila?"

"You must've seen her plenty while you were drifting in and out of consciousness. She was the one who saved your life." She pointed at Henry's forehead and then his arm and then his chest. "She stitched up your wounds there: the one on your head and the hole in your chest. Removed the bullet from your arm." She pointed outside the room. "Whenever you feel able, she's doing some chores outside if you like to thank her."

As Rebecca stepped outside the doorway, she suddenly paused and walked back into the room.

"I almost forgot," she said as she strolled over to Henry. She pulled out a photograph from her pocket and handed it to Henry. While carefully keeping her eyes on Henry, she said suspiciously, "I found this in your pocket."

Henry studied the photograph of the two girls. One girl was standing with her younger sister next to a giant boulder in the desert. Behind them was an old cabin. While Henry was gazing over the photograph, Rebecca kept a keen eye on him. She gathered nothing from his gestures or his demeanor, just a blank expression. The only thing he could remember

was the two little girls and how he saw them on the side of
the road before he collapsed. He believed one of them went
by the name, Margaret.

Henry flipped the photograph around and came across an
address written on the back.

Morganson Road NA-173, Sedona, Arizona.

Once more, Henry flipped the photograph around and
tried to identify the two girls in the photograph.

Again, blank canvas.

TWENTY-EIGHT

AFTER Henry managed to hold down a few bites of food, Rebecca gave him a quick tour around the house.

They passed the upstairs bedroom, which was right next
to the guest room (the one that Henry had woken up in).
He only caught part of the room due to the cracked door.
From a quick glance, Henry thought he saw a record player as
well as a stack of records on the side of the wall. A large win-
dow, which was cracked open as well, rested behind the bed.
Beige curtains were carelessly blowing over the headboard.
The smell of the room was familiar too, and sweet.

Before Henry had a chance to walk inside the bedroom,
Rebecca slipped her body between him and the doorway and
closed the door.

"That there is Sheila's room," Rebecca said carelessly and
showed Henry to the stairs.

Along the way, they passed another room.

The door was closed all the way.

Henry stopped in front of the closed door and picked up
an awfully cold vibe.

The lights were off inside.

The only light was coming from a natural outdoor light.

An elusive shadow drifted underneath the sunlit doorway.

Henry asked suspiciously, "Who's ro. . . ro. . . room is this?"

"I'm afraid that room is off limits," Rebecca said dourly, which made Henry even more intrigued as to who or what waited behind that mysterious door.

Rebecca walked Henry downstairs into the living room.

On the way to the kitchen, they passed an upright piano made up from maple wood. Several picture frames, mostly of Rebecca, her husband, and a handsome man, younger and much more athletic with a shaved head, perched on top of the piano.

Henry paused, looked over the picture frames, and then the piano.

He lifted up the fallboard, which revealed the dusty keys inside.

When his eyes fell upon the keys, the whites keys and then the black ones, he visualized a pair of frail, liver spotted hands—fingers like long spider legs—gracefully skipping over the keys. The stark image of the hands erected goosebumps over his flesh. Chills suddenly ran up his back like a snake, bending every which way around his spine.

Rebecca tilted her body forward, in front of Henry.

Henry gasped.

"My father bought that piano for me when I was seven years old," she said, which caused Henry to snap from his trance. "Do you know how to play?"

Henry briskly closed the piano and turned to Rebecca with a strange expression on his face.

Throughout his empty thoughts, an aged and yet soothing voice called out to him, "*What will your song be. . .*"

"Is everything all right?"

Henry pinched the top of his nose and tightly shut his eyes.

He drawled, "Ye. . . yeah."

"Come," Rebecca said, her eyes squinting in curiosity.

She guided Henry outside the house and walked him around the ranch.

"Nice place you ga. . . ga. . . got here," Henry said, gazing around the open ranch.

Two horses, one big and black and the other one white, were chasing each other around as if they were kids playing a game of tag.

There was a circular corral that was keeping a couple of other horses inside. Some of the horses were drinking from a wooden tub of water. Others were standing in statue-like postures and observing the tranquil environments around them.

"Thank you," she said, smiling. "My husband, Tad, the man who found you on the side of the road, his grandfather built this place back in 1883. He handed it down to Tad's father, Hubert, and then Hubert handed it down to Tad when he passed." Her peaceful eyes trailed upward at the blue sky above. "God rest his soul."

Rebecca walked Henry farther along.

The two stopped at a sturdy fence, which was wrapped around the entire ranch. A small section of the fence—no longer than four feet—had been completely destroyed from a bad storm. However, Henry was still left a bit curious and slightly flustered from the sight of the contorted fence. Must've been *really* bad. To the left of them, he heard the sound of rustling followed by a couple of metallic objects being thrown around. The noises got louder, clinking and clacking over the barn walls. They eventually stopped, the noises.

A woman suddenly came tottering from the barn with a scorpion in her hand.

Curious from the young woman's presence, Henry said, "Tha. . . tha. . . that must be Sheila."

Rebecca smirked at Henry.

She said, "She's a pistol all right."

Rebecca and Henry strolled over to the barn.

Henry tried to keep up with Rebecca.

"Is she yrr. . . yrrr. . . your daughter?" he said from behind Rebecca.

"Like a daughter," she answered and slowed down and waited for Henry to catch up. "She's been through a lot. Her parents were killed in a plane crash about six years ago. We adopted her. She helps out around the ranch."

They met up with Sheila halfway. The light from the sun was glaring off the copper roof, which created a blinding glare. Sheila sauntered in front of that glare, covering her face. At first, Henry couldn't quite make out the young woman's face from the glare. He shielded his eyes and then caught a glimpse of her white face. Then, her face pulled from the light. A sudden pain surged through his heart. The blood rushed through his body like a train.

Once he witnessed Sheila's face in its entirety, he slowly came to a stop while Rebecca kept on walking. Eventually, she stopped as well, turned to Henry, and, for a moment, wondered why he had stopped.

As Rebecca stood in the middle of the two, she could literally feel the gravity pulling them together, two beings opposite in polarity. Henry continued to check out Sheila, her face, her frame, her movement, her. . . way. Her hair was the color of fire, thick and lively and tied in a ponytail. Her eyes were chocolate brown, calm and quiet. She carried herself sternly and independently, divine in nature, mature, playful, and yet, at the core, was a worthy understanding of the land, a sequestrable tenderness and appreciation. From her appearance, the young woman was much younger than Henry. Five, six, *maybe* seven or eight, years younger than him, Henry guessed, and yet, from the way she carried herself, she acted as if she was much older than him, five or six years, maybe even seven or eight. He honestly couldn't tell her age nor did he even care. Both of her sleeves from her blue flannel shirt were rolled up to her elbows. Her hands were dirty, scratched, and coarse.

"I see you found a new friend," Rebecca said to Sheila.

Sheila held up the scorpion by its stinger and displayed it like a trophy to Henry.

"Wha. . . wha. . . what is that?" he asked, leaning back with fright.

"This is a hairy scorpion, silly," Sheila answered with a chuckle as she approached Henry.

"Scorpion?"

His skin crawled from the sight of the deadly creature. He had seen scorpions before, the big black ones. But not like this one, which was as tawny as the desert and much smaller too.

"Of course," she said. "You've never seen a scorpion before?"

Henry stepped backward and pulled his eyes from the scorpion.

"Sheila, this here is. . ." Rebecca pointed at Henry, ". . . well, he can't remember his name just yet."

"Man Without a Name," she said heedfully and shook Henry's hand.

She showcased a tiny glimpse of a bewitching smile. As quick and partial as the smile was, Henry was well aware that it could have been so much more. Just the thought of her smile and what it could have been drew him closer to her. He couldn't take his eyes off Sheila.

"Tha. . . tha. . . thank you for ta. . . taking care of me."

Even with the deadly creature dangling just inches away, his starry eyes were left in a state of fascination. The crawling sensation he had was no longer there. Other sensations intensified, smells and, of course, sights. Now, a different sensation swelled inside Henry, a seemingly foreign sensation that he hadn't felt since he was an adolescent.

"You're very welcome," Sheila replied gladly and placed the hairy scorpion in a jar. She sealed a perforated lid over top. "So," she turned to Henry, "you can't remember anything?"

"I remember wa. . . waaaa. . . waking uh. . . uh. . . up on the sa. . . side of the roooad," he said, the stutter gradually fading from his speech. "Other thaaaaan that, that, that, that. . . that's about it."

"Wow," she said seductively. "A real cowboy."

"Sheila," Rebecca said, smiling from the instant connection between the two. "Why don't you show our guest around?"

"My pleasure," she answered and nodded to the barn. "Come, Man Without a Name."

Throughout the walk, Sheila did most of the talking while Henry listened with a kind of wobbly excitement. She talked mostly about the ranch, the owners, Tad and Rebecca, or Becca, and the chores she handled on a daily basis like flowering the plants in the greenhouse or cleaning out the stalls or feeding the horses, "the kids" as she called them, or keeping coyotes or other predators like wolves from the chicken coop as well as the livestock. Then, Sheila went through the list of basic get-to-know-you type of questions: *Where are you from? Where did you grow up? Do you have any siblings?* Since Henry couldn't remember much of anything at all, the questions weren't as easy to answer as Sheila expected. Most of the time, Henry drew awkward blanks. Henry answered mostly with shrugs or frowns or looks of disappointment. The conversation was a bit strained and unpleasant. Sheila kept at it, as did Henry. Each time Sheila thought up new questions like *what kind music he listened to* or *what he did for a living*, she reminded herself of Henry's condition. More intervals, each one being longer, built between questions. After that, Sheila gave up and kept mostly to herself. Occasionally, though, she would turn toward Henry in an eager, youthful demeanor as if Henry would remember something from his past. As Henry focused ahead, she would study him, his features. Whenever Henry would turn toward Sheila, she would instantly turn away. They played this game of cat and mouse for two more times, going back and forth, until they caught each other studying one another as Sheila showed Henry the botanical garden. When Sheila and Henry both went to touch a cactus plant, their hands mistakenly grazed one another. They both studied each other, longer this time around.

*   *   *

"So," Sheila said, walking alongside a hobbling Henry, "this is where we feed the kids." They arrived at the barn. She showed him the stalls on both sides of the barn and where to place the horse feed. "This here is my favorite." Sheila nodded as she reached inside the stall to pet the gray Andalusian horse. "Say hello to She Runs With Horns." As her hand crept closer to the horse, the horse quickly pulled away and ducked back into the dusty shadows. "She's just being shy. Aren't you, girl?"

Henry lightly chortled.

"Where di. . . id you get a na. . . na. . . aaa. . . name like that?"

"If you weren't so banged up, I would take you out and let you see for yourself," she said. "I'm just teasing. She Runs With Horns doesn't like anybody riding her. I tried once. I still have the marks to show." She peeled back her shirt and showed Henry the two long scars over her collarbone. "There's others," she said, her eyes lecherously moving up into Henry's. "Maybe I'll show you sometime."

Henry's eyes became more aware. His pupils swelled.

"Yeah," Henry said softly and breathed a sigh of relief. "Maybe." He cleared his throat. "Even if I. . . di. . . didn't get shot, I don't know if I could ride a horse anyway. It looks ha. . . hard."

"Really? You've never ridden a horse?"

He shamefully pointed to the side of his temple.

"Not that I remember."

"You don't know what you're missing."

"When I get be. . . be. . . be. . . better, ma. . . maybe you can take me out on wha. . . one."

Sheila smiled, this time bright and wide.

"I would like that," she said, staring into Henry's healing eyes.

They shared a long stare.

Before the stare could last any longer, a masculine voice hollered from behind, "I see you're finally awake."

Henry spun around and noticed the tall man, whom he presumed was Tad, approaching him.

"Tad?"

"Rebecca must've told you all about me."

"Yeah," he said. "Sa. . . sa. . . sort of."

"How's that head of yours?"

"All right. I guess."

"Can't remember what happened to you?"

Henry shook his head and then slightly hung his head.

"It'll come back, son," he said and carefully eyed Henry. "In the meantime, you're welcome to stay at my ranch. I'm not going to let you sit around and feel sorry for yourself. If you stay here, you're going to have to work."

"Wh. . . wha. . . what kind of work are we ta. . . talking about?"

Tad patted Sheila on the shoulder.

"Sheila, she'll show you," he said conceitedly and then smirked.

TWENTY-NINE

THE first task of the day included scooping the horse feces and putting them into a wheelbarrow.

As Henry stood at a standstill, he was trying to make sense as to what Sheila had told him.

Sheila shrugged her shoulders.

"Is that a problem?" she asked as Henry placed the shovel against the side of the fence.

Henry said, "You want me to shovel shha. . . shhhit?"

"This is nothing compared to the others."

"Count me ah. . . out," he said and folded his arms over his chest.

"Would you rather step in it?"

"The horses can scoop up their own sh. . . shit."

"You're a city boy," Sheila said with surprise. "Makes sense."

"I don't know who I am," Henry replied, this time more clearly and angrily. "But I know it didn't. . . include shoveling horse shit!"

"You know, for a handsome man you sure do whine a lot," Sheila said as she rolled her eyes and shook her head at the same time. Like Henry, she folded her arms over her chest and then nodded to the desert. "Would you rather be out there? Out on your own? You best be thankful you have a place to stay. Tad usually doesn't take in strangers. He could've dropped you off at the nearest hospital, which, by the way, is, well. . . let's just say if Tad didn't bring you in when he did, then you'd be a dead man."

"Then wh. . . wh. . . why didn't he?"

Once more, Sheila shrugged her shoulders.

"That's a good question."

Henry snorted.

Sheila said, "He said, 'You were different.'"

"Different?"

"Maybe you should ask him," she said, studying Henry's face.

Henry pulled his eyes away from Sheila and glanced over at the shovel. He finally decided to pick up the shovel, but, of course, he did so with a loud sigh.

With a squint of his eye, he curiously gazed at Sheila.

Dumbfounded from his strange expression, Sheila said safely, "What?"

"I'm going to keep my eye on you," Henry said, motioning to his right eye, the fully open one.

Sheila replied, "Are you now?"

"That's right," Henry said.

He wasn't doing much with the shovel. He was more or less pushing around rocks with the edge of the shovel. In one fluent stab downward, he drove the tip of the shovel into the hard dirt.

"Are you just going to stand there?"

Henry was thinking to himself.

"Anybody home. . . "

"When I was out of it," Henry carried one side of his weight against the shovel and soaked in the beauty of the desert, "I swear. . . "

He suddenly paused and concealed a closed smile.

"You swear what?"

"Never mind," Henry said, released the shovel from the dirt, and childishly pushed around the rocks on the ground. "You. . . you'll think I'm crazy. . . "

"Go ahead," she said and shifted her weight to one side of her body. "You start something. Then, you best finish it. That's sort of the saying around here."

"I thought I saw a. . . a. . . an angel like I died or something."

"That's not supposed to be like a pickup line," Sheila said. "Is it?" She couldn't help but roll her eyes. "If it is, it's kind of lame. But nice try."

"No," he said sincerely. "I swear. You had the whole like. . . angel thing go. . . going on. . . though. You were wearing this halo around the top of your head. You were dressed in wha. . . wha. . . white. It was a nice touch."

Sheila chuckled and glanced to the blue sky above.

"You're ridiculous," she said as she shoveled up a piece of horse feces and chucked it into the wheelbarrow.

"I'm serious. . . "

"Hey," Sheila said and stopped shoveling, "you didn't escape from a mental hospital. Did you?"

Henry laughed as well.

"I sure ho. . . hope not," he said, pulling his eyes back to the surrounding desert. "I don't know. It's weird. It's like the lil. . . lil. . . li. . . lilll. . . little things come natural: walking, talking. . . "

"I was meaning to ask you, about the stutter." Sheila quickly interrupted her own thoughts. "I'm sorry. I didn't mean to judge." She innocently shrugged her shoulders. "Me, I have flaws too."

"Wha. . . wha. . . what stutter?"

"Well. . . I . . . I've noticed you have. . . this stutter that comes and goes."

"Oh?"

Henry drifted back into thought.

I didn't even notice it.

Slightly deflated, Henry went back to shuffling around rocks.

"I really didn't mean to. . . "

"I re. . . re. . . mem. . . member when I was a kid, others would make fun of me. . . and my stutter."

"It's not so bad," she said and then pointed at Henry's chest. "You could be worse off. I mean you did get shot directly in the chest. Most people wouldn't have survived."

"But I did."

"You sure did." Sheila scanned over Henry's body. "If I didn't know any better, I'd say you had a guardian angel looking after you."

"Basketball. . . " he said suddenly and slowly froze. A sudden glimpse of himself playing basketball with another kid from his neighborhood surfaced and then vanished from his mind. Henry could only make out the race of the kid and what he was wearing. He was the same black kid from before. His face was more distinguishable. He had a lightning bolt shaved on the side of his head. Dark eyes. He was wearing white sneakers. *Pumps*, Henry remembered. ". . . I played basketball. . . " he uttered. "I think."

Sheila shoveled another pile of feces into the wheelbarrow and then paused as well. She placed her hand over her hip and, as she had a tendency to do from time to time, shifted her weight to one side of her body.

"Basketball, huh?"

Henry noticed Sheila's perplexity.

"Wha. . . what'd I say?"

"Nothing," she said flatly and got back to work.

"Hey," Henry exclaimed. "You start something. Then, you *best* finish it. Isn't that how things work around here."

"Get to work," she said bossily.

Henry observed the sternness over her face and got back to work.

THIRTY

In the cool darkness, Henry heard a woman's voice saying, "What will your song be, Hen. . . "

Then, Henry woke up in a cold sweat before the entire name could be complete.

Hen, he thought.

Grimacing from the soreness, he rolled out of bed and hobbled over to the cracked window. Beyond the horizon, the first shades of light were showing over the vast desert. He stood there for several minutes and took in the view. Half of the sky was lit with dark reds and pinks while the other half was still night. A glorious light birthed behind the red rocks, which left them as dark as silhouettes.

"What is this place," he whispered to himself.

Henry was suddenly pulled from the postcard snapshot with two gentle knocks at the door.

At the doorway, Sheila was standing with a fresh pair of jeans neatly folded in her arms.

"I see you're up early," she said. "Did you sleep?"

Henry shook his head.

"Not really," he mumbled.

Sheila crept inside, placed the blue jeans on the edge of the bed, and said to Henry, "There's breakfast downstairs when you're ready. We have a long day ahead of us."

After the hearty breakfast, Henry joined Sheila on the next task, which was to break down the section of broken fence (the section that was apparently destroyed from a "storm," as Rebecca had told Henry on the first day of his awakening).

Once they cleared away the debris—mostly the jagged parts—they place the remains, the wire and the posts, on a trailer. Two hours of chopping away with an axe and lifting the remains into the trailer, Henry was drawn to the thick clouds darkening overhead.

"I knew it," Sheila said, following Henry's tired eyes and looking above as well. "Looks like it's going to rain."

"How much longer do we. . . we have?"

"We're almost through."

While Henry struggled to lift up the wooden post from the fence, he felt a couple of raindrops on the back of his neck. Sheila briskly stepped in and gave him an extra push. They both lifted up the post with a grunt—Henry having the loudest grunt—and tossed the post into the trailer.

"Nice team work," Sheila said, wiping her hands clean.

Henry's back suddenly gave out, which caused him to slip over the mud and fall on his back. On the way down, he banged the back of his head against the ground.

Henry cried out, "Goddamn it!"

"Are you okay?"

"Fine," he said as he grabbed the side of his ribcage.

"Let me help."

Henry waved off Sheila, grabbed the side of the tractor, and pulled himself onto his feet.

"Did you strain yourself?"

"I'm fine," he said, grimacing.

He ran his hand over the backside of his head and felt a tiny knot surfacing.

"By the way, a little advice," Sheila said as Henry wiped the mud from his jeans. "Tad, he isn't too tolerant when it comes to using the Lord's name in vain. Just a heads up."

"My bad," he said even clearer now. "Won't happen again."

Sheila nodded at Henry's injuries.

The rain came down harder now. It was a slow and steady rain, not a drizzle and not a downpour.

"You know whoever did this to you must've really had it in for you."

"You think," Henry returned coldly and shot daggers at Sheila.

Sheila couldn't tell if Henry was being sarcastic or not, especially from the sharpness of his eyes.

As Henry finished wiping the mud from his jeans, which turned out making it even worse (spreading the mud farther down his pant leg), he heard the same familiar music from earlier playing over the tapping of the rain. A piano playing, he heard. However, he couldn't make out what notes or chords or scales were playing over the rain. C sharp minor was the first thing to come to his mind. Henry had never taken piano lessons before—at least this was what he thought—but C sharp minor was the first thing that came to him when he heard the piano playing from across the desert. He stopped what he was doing and listened closely to the piano. Then, he heard a synthesizer underneath the piano. The sound of the two instruments, piano and keyboard, was more constructed now, not muddled or scrambled around.

Meanwhile, Sheila embraced the steady rain. She rolled her head back, eyes now facing the gloomy sky, and felt the raindrops splash over her ivory face. In a sort of youthful manner, Sheila closed both of her eyes, opened her mouth, and let the raindrops bounce over her tongue. She closed her mouth and swallowed a couple of raindrops. A smile bloomed over her face, nearly stretching across her entire face. She directed her attention back to Henry, who was still left in a state of severe concentration.

She asked, "Who's Dolores?"

Henry snapped from his trance.

"Who?"

With the backside of his hand, he wiped the rain from his brow, which left a line of mud across his forehead.

"You mentioned her name when you were out of it."

"I did?"

"Becca and I were trying to figure out what you said," Sheila said. "I'm pretty sure you said the name *Dolores*."

Henry said solemnly, "I don't remember."

Sheila carelessly shrugged her shoulders.

"Maybe she was a girl that you once loved."

Henry exclaimed, "I said 'I DON'T REMEMBER!'"

"Easy now, cowboy," Sheila replied with a surrendering tone as she held her hands in front of her. The voice, not Sheila's voice, but another one came from her mouth. The word *cowboy* came from Sheila's lips and yet, to Henry, it sounded different. When the word was spoken to him, it was done so in a sultrier voice rather than Sheila's laid back voice. The smell of savory bacon wafted over Henry, which made him nauseous. The black face of an attractive woman with a shaved head appeared in his mind. She was thin and elegant and stern with broad shoulders and had a smile that could light up a room. Henry rubbed away the ache from behind his eyes, then the image of the face from his mind, and took in several slow, steady breaths. "It's lunchtime," Sheila said curiously with her voice back to normal. As she proceeded to remove the gloves from her hands, she nodded at the distant house. "Let's get out of the rain and dry off." Next, Sheila tossed the gloves on the tractor's seat. "Come on," she said. "I'll make you some lunch."

"You cook too," Henry uttered.

"You don't see a McVille's around here. Do you?"

"Right," Henry mumbled and then followed Sheila back inside the house where Rebecca was waiting for them with clean towels.

Before they ate lunch, Sheila hooked up Henry with a dry pair of clothes: a pair of corduroy pants, a navy blue sweatshirt that was two sizes *too* big, and a pair of socks. Sheila too had changed. She was wearing an orange blouse and a pair of blue jeans that was two sizes *too* small.

Once they were all dry, both changed, they sat on the floor of the screen porch, ate pimento cheese sandwiches, and listened to the beating rain. Sheila was sitting with her legs crossed. Henry was lounging on his hand. The other hand was holding the last bite of the sandwich. Henry had never eaten a pimento cheese sandwich before. Somehow, he had a feeling that this wouldn't be the last time either.

"So," Sheila said, taking a small bite from the sandwich. She ate slowly and carefully unlike Henry, who had scarfed down the entire sandwich in the matter of minutes. "What do you think?"

"It's delicious," Henry said simply and pounded down the last bite. "You're like a Renaissance woman."

"A Renaissance woman, huh?" Another smile stretched across her face. "Why do you say that?"

"Well, you cook, you do work that normally men would do, you clean up horse shit, and plus," his eyes traced over Sheila's intoxicating smile, her shapely lips, her lonely eyes, "you're..." a pause, "...say," Henry changed his thought, "...how come a woman like yourself doesn't have a boyfriend? You're very attractive."

"Thanks," Sheila said with yet another smile, closed this time, not opened.

Then, she shrugged her shoulders.

"Just never really happened," she said quietly. "I guess."

"Do you ever go into town?"

"Sometimes," she answered, "when Tad lets me borrow the truck. Sort of slim pickings, if you know what I mean."

"I see," Henry said quietly. Then, his voice rose slightly. "So, you mean to tell me that you never sneak any young country boys into your bedroom at night?"

Sheila rolled her eyes.

"Please." She groaned. "I'm not that type of girl." The tone of her voice lifted to a near shout. "Hey!" Sheila said, the upper part of her cheeks washing over with pink. "If I didn't know any better..." she tilted her head in thought, "...I'd say you were a comedian in your past life."

"Clearly it didn't work out for me," Henry said, showing his wounds.

They shared a laugh.

Before the conversation fell into silence, Henry pointed at the chicken coop in the backyard.

"So, I take it you take care of the chickens."

Sheila turned toward the chicken coop.

"No," she said shortly. "Becca takes care of the chickens. She kills them, plucks them. The whole works."

Henry smirked and then shook his head.

"What?"

"It's nothing," Henry said, "I mean. . . I don't know if I could do all that."

Again, Sheila shrugged her shoulders.

"Somebody has to do it."

"If it came down to survival and I had to kill a chicken in order to survive, I guess I'd do it. But. . ."

"But you wouldn't do it if you didn't have to."

"Exactly."

"But if you had to?"

"Had to what?"

"You know, kill a chicken? Would you?"

Like Sheila, Henry shrugged his shoulders too.

"Yeah," he said.

"Me," Sheila said, "I tried once. Becca even walked me through it and everything. I just couldn't go through with it."

"Why not?"

"I don't know," Sheila said and turned to the chicken coop in a state of reflection. "When I was girl, my father and I used to drive down to Mexico and stay the weekend with his friend, Raul. They knew each other from business."

Henry asked, "What kind of business?"

"Exporter," she answered. "My father exported computers."

"Computers?"

"You would never tell by looking at him," Sheila said. "Usually, when you think about someone who loves computers as much as my father, you think that he might look like the nerdy type. You know. Glasses and pocket protectors and that sort of thing."

"Well. . ."

"He was not like that at all," Sheila said and looked into Henry's eyes. "You would've liked him."

"Yeah?"

Henry was tempted to ask more about her father, but he didn't know if it was the right time or place.

"Anyway," Sheila said over a sigh, "Raul's home was very much like this place. He had a lot of land and a chicken coop like the one Tad and Becca have. In the mornings, he would take me out to the chicken coop and we would feed the chickens. There was this one chicken. Raul called him Pepé after the American cartoon character, Pepé Le Pew, who, if you don't know this, was a part of this series called the Looney Tunes."

"Doesn't ring a bell," Henry said blandly.

"Well, Pepé is this skunk with a French accent," Sheila explained. "And in the cartoon, Pepé is always chasing after this other skunk, a female skunk, who, in actuality, is a black cat with white stripes. But Pepé doesn't know this. Pepé is blinded by love. I don't know why exactly Raul called this one lonely chicken Pepé. He didn't really smell like a skunk. Maybe he did to the other chickens. That's why they didn't go near him." Sheila shrugged her shoulders. "I don't know. What I did know was that Pepé was the smallest chicken in the flock. The runt. *And* he certainly wasn't chasing after any other chickens or animals pretending to be chickens. Every time I saw Pepé, he was always alone in the corner of the coop. The other chickens kept their distance from him until one day another chicken, twice as big as Pepé, who Raul called Franklin after the former president, Franklin Delano Roosevelt, well, Franklin decided to venture away from the flock and approach Pepé. Pepé wanted nothing to do with Franklin. But Franklin, he kept antagonizing Pepé. Then, out of nowhere, Pepé went all Rambo on Franklin."

"Rambo?"

"Like the movie?"

Henry didn't respond.

"Never mind," Sheila said. "He went absolutely nuts. Next thing you know, there was a chicken fight. It wasn't much of a fight. Pepé ended up breaking both of Franklin's legs. I remember Raul said there wasn't any point keeping

Franklin around anymore, especially with both of his legs broken and all. So, he did what he had to do."

Henry said, "And I'm sure Franklin. . . Delano Roosevelt tasted pretty good that night."

"Best chicken I've ever had," Sheila said amusedly. "Seriously! Raul slow cooked the chicken in all these Mexican spices. Talk about delicious."

"That's some story," Henry said, laughing as well. "I bet no other chicken messed with Pepé after that one day."

"Not one," Sheila said intensely. "In fact, Raul didn't even kill Pepé. He loved Pepé so much that he kept him as a pet."

"Really?"

"God as my witness."

"That's amazing."

Their laughter slowed.

"Well, I guess sometimes the loneliest one of the flock is the deadliest," Sheila said, a smile dwindling from her face. "You never really know what's going on inside that head of theirs."

While gazing into Sheila's eyes, Henry said softly, "Is that right?"

"Your stutter," she said unexpectedly. "It's gone."

Henry was caught in a momentary haze.

"I didn't even realize," he trailed off.

Henry shrugged his shoulders and chortled.

"Maybe I have you to thank for that."

There was silence, uncomfortable and yet enticing.

Instead of laughing, they shared a long, vulnerable stare. Sheila's eyes sharpened, lecherously. Henry's heart skipped a beat, like his heart moved directly up into his eyes. Sheila witnessed the pulsing now in his lustful gaze. Her left hand slowly slid across the floor and traced over Henry's hand.

As Sheila inched closer to Henry, closer now, Rebecca walked onto the porch and spoiled the mood.

"I see you two are getting along well," she said from the doorway. "Would you care for some more lemonade?"

"No thank you, Becca," Henry said, cleared his throat, and then backed away from Sheila.

The upper parts of Sheila's cheeks suddenly washed over with bright red. She widened her furious eyes at Rebecca. The jaw muscles on the sides of her face flexed into these tiny protrusions. Henry caught a glimpse of the agitated look over Sheila's face and felt somewhat relieved. Aware of Henry's involvement, she immediately removed the look from her face before it had a chance to grow into something ugly. Throughout lunch, while anxiously working his way through the pimento cheese sandwich, Henry wondered numerous times if Sheila had feelings for him. The look alone on her face finally put things into perspective. Henry couldn't help but smile at Sheila's youthful annoyance. In return, Rebecca remorsefully held out her hands as if she had done something truly horrendous.

"I'll leave you two alone," Rebecca said quietly. "So sorry." She hurried back inside the house and closed the door behind her.

They both kept their awkward laughter hidden behind closed smiles.

"We got to work on that name of yours," Sheila said as she studied Henry's eyes. "How about Sam? I always liked the name Sam."

"Too plain," Henry said as he shifted closer to Sheila. "Sounds like a pet's name."

"Then Samuel," she suggested. "It's Biblical."

"I'm thinking maybe something with some spice to it. Some jazz."

"Okay then." She hung her head in thought. Her eyes lit. She said cheerfully, "How about José?"

"*José*," he said jokingly. "Good try. How about. . . I don't know maybe. . . Ricardo?"

"Really? Ricardo?"

"Manuel?"

Sheila rolled her eyes.

"John?"

"No."

"David?"

"Nah."

"Michael?"

Henry heard the sound of a man's voice in his mind, stretched like elastic.

Keifer?

"Mason?"

"Come on. Really?"

"Scott."

"Mmmm," Henry thought. "How about no?"

Sheila groaned.

"Bob."

Henry shook his head.

"Bill. . . Eric. . . Mathew. . . Brad. . . Andrew. . . Richard. . . Ryan. . . Bryan. . . Larry. . . Luke. . . Mark. . . Harry. . . Henry. . . William. . . "

"Wait. . . "

Henry drifted into thought.

"No," he said finally and shook his head.

"I'm running out of names here," Sheila said and took a bite of her sandwich.

"How about. . . " Henry tapped his fingers over his chin, ". . . Elvis?"

"Elvis?" Sheila said confusedly and rocked back in her seated position. "You mean the King?"

"The King?"

"Whoa, whoa, whoa!" Sheila blurted out. "You're stepping on sacred land here, buddy."

Buddy?

"What do you mean?"

"Yeah," Sheila said seriously. "You and me both know there can only be one king." She suddenly paused. "Wait just a minute. You didn't sneak into my room. Did you?"

"No," he said, his voice strained. "Why?"

Sheila observed the sheer bafflement over Henry's face.

"You don't know who I'm talking about? Do you?"

Henry innocently shook his head no.

"Can't say that I do."

"*Elvis*," Sheila said. "Elvis Presley, the King of Rock n' Roll."

"Never heard of him."

The truth was there in Henry's face, his eyes. Either he had a great poker face or he really didn't know who "The King" was.

Sheila carefully eyed Henry and said, "You don't know what you're missing out."

"Really?"

"Really," she said. "Come on." She stood up and held out her hand. "Let me show you."

Henry grabbed Sheila's hand and stood up.

They were both due back to work in a couple of minutes.

In the meantime, Sheila took Henry upstairs to her bedroom and showed him a fairly extensive record collection, mostly of the King himself, the King she had spoken of earlier, Elvis Presley. She had other records too, mainly from the 50's through the 80's. But Henry couldn't count how many times he saw that one name, Elvis Presley.

Stupefied, Henry slouched over the record collection.

"So, your name, Sheila," Henry said. "Where did your parents come up with that name? Was it a family name?"

"Believe it or not, but the name came from a song."

"A song? Really? What song?"

"The song is called 'Sheila.'"

Sheila reached around Henry's body, her breasts grazing his shoulder, and pulled out the vinyl record, Tommy Roe's *Greatest Hits*.

More closely now, Henry asked, "Who is Tommy Roe?"

"He's from fifties, I believe."

"Fifties, huh?"

"My parents were fond of music."

Henry placed the record aside and marveled at Sheila's vast collection.

"I can tell."

"The name means 'heaven' in Irish."

"Really? Were your parents Irish?"

"Father was."

"Red hair," Henry said, both of his glossy eyes falling over Sheila's thick mane. "How about your mother?"

"She was an ABC."

"ABC?"

Henry thought: *Academics, Basketball. . .*

". . . Chinese. . . " Sheila said abruptly and pulled Henry from his thoughts. "American Born Chinese."

"Chinese. . . " Henry said quietly to himself.

Once more, he thought more about those letters, ABC, not the ones standing for American Born Chinese, but the other ABCs, the ABCs from his childhood.

While deep in thought, Henry's eyes mistakenly fell upon Sheila's.

In a sort of foreign attentiveness, he carefully examined her brown eyes.

"You don't. . . "

"Don't what?" Sheila leaned back from Henry. "Why are you looking at me like that?"

"You don't look Chinese."

"I know. Right?" She slapped Henry on the shoulder. "Because I have my father's eyes. . . and my mother's smile, of course."

"They sound like good people," Henry said and pulled his eyes down at the many Elvis Presley records before he could share yet another long, lecherous stare with Sheila.

Sheila leaned in even closer to Henry and said solemnly, "They were."

"So, I see you like Elvis Presley."

She said in Henry's ear, "I'm his number one fan."

"I see."

"But not in a creepy way."

"Yeah," Henry said sarcastically. "Right." He turned to Sheila and said with great esteem, "You can open up a record store with all of these records."

"I know right," she replied with jubilation and placed a record on the player and lowered the needle and placed it over the record. She played the song "Unchained Melody" from *Moody Blue*.

"This is the last record before the King passed away," Sheila said mournfully as she turned up the volume a little. "You want to talk about an angel. This here, this is what an angel sounds like."

As the song began to play, the two drifted into the song.

Henry leaned closer to Sheila.

"Where have I heard this song before?" he asked softly and tried to put an image to the song. The thought alone melted away as he stared into Sheila's brown eyes.

"I think it's a remake," Sheila said as she moved closer to Henry.

"A remake?"

Sheila bobbed her head.

Her eyes, Henry saw, were both lonely and hungry.

As the two embraced the song together, the lyrics, the melody, the air, a small white thing suddenly moved across Henry's range of vision. The tiny thing made a *squeak* and darted from the edge of the table.

"Whoa!" he blurted out, stretching his arms in the air. "What was that?"

Sheila reached behind the record player and grabbed the little white mouse. She carefully cupped the mouse in her hands.

"It's just Mrs. Frisby."

"Mrs. Frisby?"

"My pet mouse."

"You have a pet mouse?"

"Of course I do, silly."

She pointed to the many jars and glass tanks on the bookshelf.

"And a pet tortoise and a pet tarantula and a pet lizard," she said and then pointed at the hairy scorpion in the jar. "And now a pet scorpion."

At first, Henry was frightened of the mouse.

"It's only a little ole mouse," she said reassuringly. "You never had a pet before?"

Henry hesitated.

"I forgot," she mumbled. "Your memory."

Sheila held out the mouse.

"Go on," she said eagerly. "You can pet her. She won't bite."

"Really?"

"Go on, silly," she insisted.

Henry reached out and gently petted the top of Mrs. Frisby's head with the tip of his index finger.

"I think she likes you."

"You think?"

"Of course."

A smile crept over Henry's face.

They both paused and shared yet another long, open stare.

Suddenly, a throaty voice said from behind, "Sheila."

Tad approached the doorway.

Next, he said the name *Henry*.

The name sounded like a distant echo in Henry's mind. The closer Henry listened, the name traveled farther into a muddled state.

Before he could make sense of the name, the name became distorted and fell into silence.

"Yes, Tad," Sheila said and slid the needle from the record.

Tad removed the hat from his head.

"Sorry to interrupt you two," he said. "I'm afraid playtime is over. It's stop raining. So, that means it's time to get back to work."

"Right."

Sheila rolled her eyes over at Henry.

As Tad exited the room, Sheila hollered out, "Elvis."

Tad spun around.

"I am quite aware."

"No," she said and pointed at Henry. "Man Without a Name. His name is Elvis."

"You know there can only be one king."

Sheila said jovially, "That's exactly what I said!"

"Well, I like the name," Henry said, crossing both of his arms against his chest. "And I'm sticking to it."

"Whatever," Tad mumbled. As he walked away down the hallway, his voice grew louder and louder, "When you and the King are done messing around, we have some work to do outside!"

The two made it through the rest of the day without letting their most basic temptations take over.

When that fine line was crossed on the porch (and now, they both had a heightened understanding of how they felt for one another), they didn't get anything done in the labor department. They were supposed to clear away the rest of the debris from the chewed up fence, as promised to Tad. Both Henry and Sheila were too busy flirting with one another to fulfill the promises that they had made to Tad. Whenever they weren't chasing each other around, Sheila would help Henry with his memory loss by showing Henry around the desert lands or explaining to Henry the history of the ranch, Tad's father and his father before him, and hoping that, while doing so, it would trigger a lost memory. At sunset, they decided to call it quits on the fence. During dinner, they hardly ate a thing on their plates. Instead, the two spent most of the time playing footsy underneath the table and exchanging quiet giggles like two children in love. Tad and Rebecca didn't know exactly what was going on between the two, Henry and Sheila.

Rebecca sort of did.

THIRTY-ONE

THE following day, they moved on to another task, which was an irrigation problem that both Tad and Sheila had been tirelessly working on for the past two weeks.

When Sheila first informed Henry about the task over breakfast, Henry started to question the whole "You start something around here, you finish it" thing in the back of his mind. To Henry, it seemed as if there was always something to do around the ranch. Lunch was about an hour away. All Henry could think about was food, mainly those delicious pimento cheese sandwiches that Sheila made for him yesterday. For the past ten minutes, his stomach was growling up a storm—loud enough to be heard by Sheila. Both his arms and legs were depleted of any strength. His mouth was parched like the desert before him.

As Henry made another attempt at lifting the drainage pipe from the muddy trench, his knees suddenly buckled. Next thing he knew, he was moaning from the blunt impact of the ground. His face, as well as his clothes, was soaked with dirty water. A tiny, jagged rock was burrowed into his back.

Henry slapped the water beneath him and hissed, "That's the second fuahh. . . "

"I don't think you're cut out for life on a ranch, Elvis."

Exhausted, Henry wiped the muddy water from his face and glared at Sheila.

"I think you're about right," he said.

As soon as Sheila became aware of Henry's fragile condition and that he wasn't injured, only his pride, she chuckled quietly at first and then loudly. Henry chuckled too, only shamefully. Sheila's chuckle gained velocity and suddenly switched over into a full-bodied laugh. Henry's state alone drew more laughs, more tears, the friendly kind. In return, Henry reared back his hand and struck the muddy water beside him. A couple droplets of water splashed into Sheila's mouth, which caused her to let out a nasty "Yuck!" The laughter came to a halt. Her eyes suddenly billowed in deranged excitement. She kicked the water below her and splashed Henry. One thing led to another. Before Henry could wrap his mind around the situation, he found himself wrestling around with Sheila. Even the little strength he had overpowered Sheila. In two graceful movements (a roll and a pin), Henry was on top of her body. His knees were rested beside her abdomen, leaving her no room to struggle. Both of his hands were pressed against her shoulders. She squirmed a little and let out a grunt while doing so. After wearing herself out, she finally surrendered to Henry. The sun poked from the clouds above and glistened off the water, which appeared as if it was sparsely covered with diamonds. With a lunge forward, Sheila kissed Henry on his dirty lips. She pulled her head back and with her lustful eyes, innocently gazed up at Henry. The kiss sent a warm wave of excitement through Henry's body. He released his hands from her shoulders and gave her more room to move. She remained in the same position, vulnerable. Her eyes softened, begged. Henry slowly traced his hand around the contours of Sheila's gritty face. He leaned forward and kissed her back. His tongue slid and twirled around hers.

As he kissed Sheila, faster now, the taste over his tongue turned sweet like honey. Her breath was more potent. Lips different, more full and talented.

As Henry removed his lips, he ran his hands over Sheila's hair. The entire mane of hair came off from the scalp! Suddenly, Henry found himself face to face with a strange dark skinned woman lying underneath him. She wasn't Sheila. She was, in fact, Starlet. She was lying there in one of her stage outfits that she often wore during the Bound and Dangerous Tour: a silver glittered top with frayed ends, which was untouched from the dirty water. Her head was shaved like the savory image before. Henry traced his eyes over the wig in his hand.

As he slowly pulled himself from the familiar woman, the sunlight was gradually revealed over his shoulder. Each ray struck Starlet's top, which caused the shirt to majestically glimmer and sparkle in Henry's diamond eyes. The peculiar woman's features were much different than Sheila's. Her eyes were as green as emeralds, not brown. Her lips were big and painted with bright red lipstick, not plain and slender. She also had small, perky breasts, not as plump as Sheila's.

Henry sat in a trance and tried to remember who exactly the woman was.

I know her, he thought, *but from where.*

Before the name came charging at him (the first letter *S*, the second letter *T*, and then the third letter *A*), he violently shook his head and forced away the memory.

"What is it?"

Henry's eyes wandered around the surrounding desert.

He slowly stood to his feet.

His eyes settled on the young woman underneath him.

Shocked, he gaped at Sheila's beautiful brown eyes.

"Elvis?"

"Who the hell is Elvis?"

Henry snapped from the daze.

"It's me, Sheila."

As Sheila sat upright, she reached out her hand.

"I'm sorry," Henry cried. "It's my fault. I shouldn't have."

"No," she said sullenly. "It's. . . it's my fault."

Henry's face went slack.

"I have to go," he said despairingly.

He climbed his way out of the trench and ran through the open field.

"Wait!" Sheila shouted out as she crawled out of the muddy trench. "Elvis! I'm sorry!"

THIRTY-TWO

ON the kitchen table, the chicken, which Rebecca had personally killed, plucked, seasoned, and cooked all on her own, as well as the potatoes and the greens from the garden, were all getting cold.

Both Henry and Sheila weren't seated at the table. Sheila was up in her bedroom. Henry was still outside, alone with his thoughts. Somewhere in his thoughts, he could hear a song playing, slowly at first and then eventually gaining momentum. The song was called "Falling" from Mona's Arch debut album Rule or Be Ruled. As Henry concentrated on the song, he still couldn't put his finger on exactly where he had heard the song. The beat, the melody, the harmony, everything about the song was there inside him and yet he had no idea where the song had come from. A dream? A memory? The lyrics were right there within his grasp. Something like *"Falling from the sky. . . passing another. . ."* The words petered out, leaving behind the same emotions that he once felt when he wrote the song in his bedroom and then revised it in the Den (something about falling in love and finally meeting the right one, "Ms. Right," as he called her).

Frustrated from Henry and Sheila's distant behavior, Rebecca let out a sigh and got up from her chair. She strolled over to the kitchen window and searched for Henry. From a distance, he was sitting on a rock and staring out into the pink sunset before him. From the angle Rebecca was standing, the dull red sun appeared just inches away from his face and yet it was so much farther away. The sun lost its shine and remained easy on the eyes.

"He said he wasn't hungry," Tad said from behind and placed a spoonful of mashed potatoes on his plate.

With her hands held over her hips, she said worriedly, "I should go talk to him. Shouldn't I?"

"Will you just leave him be, Becca," Tad said. "He's a grown man. He'll eat when he's ready."

Rebecca moved her hand to her chest, over her heart.

"I feel so bad," she said.

"Would you sit down and eat," Tad said, his voice turning upset. "We know nothing about the man. For all we know, he could be a criminal. You saw the picture he had in his pocket."

Rebecca turned her shoulder.

"Don't talk like that," she said bitterly.

Tad scooped larger amounts of mashed potatoes onto his plate. He didn't realize how much mashed potatoes were on his plate until he drew his eyes downward.

"Oh dear," he uttered and then scooped half of the portion back into the bowl of mashed potatoes. "There are only two types of people who get shot, Becca. You and I know exactly who they are, victims and criminals. I'm still not quite sure which one he is."

Sheila stepped from the shadows of the hallway and ambled into the kitchen.

"He's not a criminal," she said from the edge of the doorway.

"I didn't see you, Sheila. . . "

"Forget it," she seethed and stormed back upstairs.

"Sheila?" Rebecca said and chased after Sheila. She got to the edge of the hallway and, with her eyes, followed Sheila into her bedroom. Sheila slammed the door behind her. Rebecca hurried back over to the kitchen table and stood there until Tad drew his eyes on her.

Tad glanced up at Rebecca with his eyes wide and guilty.

"What'd I say?" he said in a high pitched voice and naively shrugged his shoulders.

Her hands rested upon her hips.

"Can't you see, Tad?"

"What is that supposed to mean?"

Rebecca sighed once more and made her way around the kitchen table.

"She likes him."

"She doesn't like him," he said and grabbed the bowl of greens. "She's. . . she's just lonely, Becca. She hardly sees any people, men especially, her own age 'round here. So, of course, she's going to be drawn to them. Who wouldn't? He's a handsome man. But that doesn't mean she *likes* him." He stopped scooping from the bowl and dropped the serving fork back onto the table. "She doesn't really like him. Does she? I mean. . . bu. . . he's not even. . . you know. . . "

Rebecca said bluntly, "White?"

"Well. . ."

"He looks like he has some white in him, but. . . you know. . . he's not really white, Becca. He's not really a person of color either. You've seen his nose. He doesn't have a black nose."

"I didn't know people of 'color' had the same nose."

"Most of 'em do."

"What if he wasn't white, Tad? Huh?"

"Well," Tad stuttered, "she should be with someone of her own race."

"Sheila will be with whoever she wants to be with. Besides, we're not living in the 1950's, honey."

"I know that," Tad said loudly. "It's just. . . "

"Just what?"

Tad sighed and quit talking.

"Times have changed, Tad," Rebecca said sternly. "If he makes her happy, then so be it. Black, white, green. . . whatever. It's her choice. Not yours."

"Green?"

Rebecca rolled her eyes and cut a slice of meat from the whole chicken.

When Henry returned to the house, it was already night. Rebecca and Tad finished dinner early. Tad ended up taking his dessert—a bowl of peach cobbler—with him to the living room where he read one of his nightly Western novels while Rebecca did the dishes. After the kitchen was cleaned, she decided to put the leftovers in the refrigerator and relax outside with a glass of iced tea.

An hour passed before Henry ambled up the stairs and found Rebecca sitting in one of the several rocking chairs on the front porch and sipping from her nightly glass of iced tea.

"Have a seat?" she said, rocking back and forth in the chair.

Instead of acknowledging Henry, she was gazing at the bright night sky.

Henry shuffled toward the rocking chair and sat down next to Rebecca.

"I know it may seem as if you're alone in the world right now," she said in a motherly way. "Like the world has completely forgotten about you. I want you to know, Elvis or whatever your name may be, that you're not, I repeat, *not* alone. There are people here who care about you."

With his head hung, Henry replied, "But you don't even know me."

"Yes," she said and finally acknowledged Henry. "I do. From the second I laid eyes on you, I knew who you were."

"You did?"

"Of course," Rebecca said and stopped rocking in her chair. "You're a man who just lost his way and who wants to start over again." She reached over and grabbed Henry's hand. "I don't care what you did in the past. There's a reason they call it the past because that's where the past remains, behind us. I know you're a good person. I've seen it with my own eyes." Her voice stretched out. "And my eyes *don't* fool me." She eyed Henry closely. "I've seen the way you look at her, at Sheila. It's the same look Tad had in his eyes when he first met me." Rebecca placed her glass of iced tea on the table beside her and leaned in closer to Henry. "You must understand that we have to learn from the past in order to move on, on the right path."

"Hard to move on with your life when you can't remember a single thing from your past."

Rebecca said earnestly, "If it doesn't come back to you, then it wasn't meant to be."

"You believe in stuff like that."

"Sure." She smiled at Henry. "We all deserve a second chance at life, that is if we are willing to move on with our lives. We have to make the best from what we got. And if what we got isn't good enough, then we make it better and we keep trying. You understand." With her thumb, Rebecca pointed inside the house. "She's waiting for you. Go to her."

After a second thought, Henry stood up from the rocking chair.

He faced the door and then turned back around.

"What do I say?" he asked.

"I've been with Tad for thirty-eight years, going on thirty-nine this March," Rebecca explained. "The secret in a lasting relationship is to be honest. Don't hold anything back. Honesty will bring out the best in both of you. Trust me."

"Nice talking to you," Henry said quietly and walked back inside.

"Any time," Rebecca said casually and sipped from her glass of iced tea.

Each step felt long and heavy.

By the time he finally reached the top of the landing, he hadn't prepared a single thing to say. And if he did, the words were all jumbled up in his head and lacked structure and clarity. He cleared away the racing thoughts and approached Sheila's bedroom. She was playing the song "Can't Help Falling In Love" by none other than the King himself.

Henry waited at Sheila's doorway. The door was cracked, of course. He reached up to knock on the door and immediately pulled his hand away. He walked away from the door and paced around the hallway until he finally found the nerve to enter the room. As the song was coming to an end, he knocked on the door. He heard two people whispering behind the door. Curious, Henry nudged open the door and was greeted by yet another face, familiar and yet totally opposite from the one he witnessed in the trench. She had a guilty expression over her face. Her skin was pallid like Sheila. However, her hair was dark, not red. The name came to him without any extra thought. *Kerri*, he thought as he stood at the doorway in a daze. A woman sniffled. The sharp, airy sound pulled him from his thoughts, from this Kerri woman, and toward the bed before him. On the other side of the bed, Sheila sat with her head hanging down into her chest.

With her back turned to Henry, Sheila said solemnly toward the floor, "Who is she? Her name is Dolores. Isn't it?"

"No," Henry said softly and inched farther into the room.

"I could see it in your eyes, you know," she said with her back facing Henry. "She must've been something else. Do you love her?"

"Yes," he said, thinking of Kerri, not Starlet. "I did love her, at least I thought I did. When we kissed, all those emotions I felt when I was with her all came rushing back to me. For the first time in my life, I finally know what I want. I guess that was what scared me, knowing that I'm falling." Henry stood next to the bed and studied Sheila, the tears racing down the side of her face. "I'm not scared anymore."

Sheila made an attempt to look at Henry.

Before she could see him squarely with her eyes, she held her head back down into her lap.

She asked, "What do you want? You— "

The words suddenly closed inside her throat. With her lips puckered downward in a frown, Sheila lifted her clutched hand, the one with the balled-up tissue inside, and threw it back down in her lap.

"—You loved this woman," she whimpered, "but you don't even know her name?"

She snorted, sniffled, and shook her head.

"*Kerri*," he said out loud. "Kerri was her name."

Sheila let out a nearly undetectable sigh.

"When we kissed, I saw these fragments of my childhood," he explained and eased himself next to Sheila on the bed. "In those fragments, you were there. It's like you've always been there, waiting patiently for me. It just took me all this time to finally find you."

Henry inched closer to Sheila.

She made an attempt to turn toward Henry. Then, at the last second, she pulled her head downward and focused on the floor.

"I want you, Sheila," Henry said directly to Sheila.

Sniffling, Sheila slowly gazed up at Henry.

Henry said closely now, "Every inch of you."

Her eyes were wounded, red and glossy. The tears fell from the corners of her eyes and curled around her nostrils and trickled down over her lips.

Henry crept even closer to her, wiped the tears from her face, and gently kissed her on her salty lips.

She kissed him back, much more weakly.

The kiss became more aggressive, harder and faster. The lips moved in rhythm.

Henry tilted his head back and forth, kissing her at different angles.

Sheila's breath became heavier, more labored.

From there, the two eased into the bed sheets and removed each other's clothes from their bodies (Sheila helping Henry with his clothes and then Henry helping Sheila with hers).

For the rest of the night, they made love until the sun rose the next morning.

THIRTY-THREE

A *tap* over the door!

In a sudden lunge forward from his sore position, Henry opened his eyes and peered through the hazy bedroom.

A rectangular light filled the darkness. The light grew brighter and brighter and shined light over Henry's body.

Slowly, Henry pulled himself upright and heard the faint sound of an audience behind the lit door.

The audience was cheering, louder now, screaming!

Words manifested.

Now clearly!

"T.J.!" the crowd yelled repeatedly.

Henry listened closer.

The light behind the door grew so bright that Henry was forced to shield his aching eyes.

Then, the pounding was back!

The door was shaking. . . rattling.

The hinges of the door loosened and fell from the doorway panel.

Then, the door suddenly burst open.

A gust of wind exploded like a buckshot into the bedroom. The wind was so strong that it caused the bed to move across the room. The jars of creatures on the shelves shattered. Shards of glass came flying across the room.

Before the glass could blind Henry, he quickly sought cover behind a pillow.

The brilliant light from the door warmed over Henry's body, his face. . . the morning sunrays splashed over his eyelids. The brilliant light dampened into a soft red.

As Henry cracked open his refreshed eyes, he gasped— quietly though. He rolled his tongue around his mouth in a quest for saliva. His lips were parched. The corners of his mouth were about as dry as a bone. It took him a couple of seconds to recognize his surroundings. The bedroom was lit, not dark or ruined. A gentle breeze was blowing over his cool shoulders. He suddenly felt a rumble over the side of the bed, which, after the loud *clink* of a bedspring, shifted and dropped. He turned, only to find Sheila strutting toward the restroom. Henry lay there, using his right palm to keep his head upright, and admired Sheila's slender, natural, curvy body. A smile eased over his face, satisfied. His eyes lifted with immense joy.

As Sheila stepped inside the bathroom, Henry mistakenly paid closer attention.

In the reflection of the mirror, Kerri, *not* Sheila, was brushing her teeth. The smile vanished from his face. The joy plummeted from his eyes. She carelessly scrubbed away on her teeth, reaching the wisdom teeth in the back. Startled from the reflection, Henry bolted upright against the barred headboard and scratched his eyes. He looked back at the mirror and witnessed Kerri yet again. In the corner of her eye, she noticed Henry in the mirror's reflection. She grinned and spat the foamy paste from her mouth and followed with a sip of water. She turned and faced Henry.

"You have that look again," Sheila said, tilting her head to the side.

After she patted her mouth dry with a bath towel, she walked back into the bedroom.

Henry said, "What look?"

"The same one you had yesterday," she said and slithered herself back underneath the bed sheets.

"It's nothing. I just. . . "

"It's another memory. Isn't it?"

Henry slid over and made room for Sheila on the bed. The sun beat down on his cool shoulders, slowly warming them.

"I think so," he said. "Maybe. . . maybe I guess I'm still in a state of shock."

"Shock?" Sheila said, smiling greatly.

With her hand curled into a fist, she hit Henry on the arm.

Henry suddenly grimaced and grabbed his sore arm.

A burst of laughter projected from Sheila's lips.

"I'm so sorry," she said and clinched her teeth together. The hair spilt over her eyes, only showing one side of her face "I totally forgot." Sheila eased her body closer to Henry. "So, you're still in a state of shock." While kissing Henry, she said, "I would never tell."

"Well, for starters," Henry said, going back to his cool composure, "waking up next to such a gorgeous woman as yourself. I really must be the luckiest guy in the world right now. I mean, seriously, meeting a girl like you just goes to show that someone really special can come into your world and change it forever." He ran his hands through Sheila's silky red hair. "Even when you least expect it."

"Aw," Sheila said, puckering her face. "That so sweet." She rolled over, planted her crotch over Henry's, and straddled him. "Hey! You want to see something gross?"

Sheila extended out her arm and popped her elbow joint inward.

"Whoa!" Henry shouted out. "How'd you do that?"

"I broke my arm when I was eight years old," Sheila explained, playfully moving her elbow like a lever. "That's what I get for showing off on the monkey bars."

"You could work for the circus with a trick like that." Henry balled his hand into a microphone and held it to his mouth. "Ladies and gentlemen, boys and girls of all ages, step right up and feast your eyes on the 'Amazing Rubberband Girl.'"

"Hey! Rubberband Girl! That's not very nice."

Her eyes suddenly flared.

Then, Henry laughed.

"It's a compliment," he said, still laughing.

Sheila wasn't laughing.

Instead, she had a strange grin on her face.

The laugh slowly ceased.

"I wouldn't change a thing about you," he said seriously and ran his hands around Sheila's hips. "I like you just the way you are. You and your. . . freak elbow."

"Thanks," Sheila said.

Then, she bit the bottom of her lip, pounced on Henry, grinded away on his pelvis, and kissed him over the lips.

While kissing Henry repeatedly on the lips, she said, "I had a wonderful time last night."

"What can I say," Henry said, maneuvering his lips to speak. "I love to please the ladies."

"Shut up!"

She hit him once more in the arm, the good one, while kissing him. Another hit on Henry's arm. This one was softer and pricklier. Henry moved his eyes downward and caught Mrs. Frisby crawling on his arm.

"Looks like we have a visitor."

"Mrs. Frisby!"

Sheila carefully cupped the mouse in her hands.

"When I was kid, I remember my mother would never let me have a pet."

"You remember?"

"Yeah," he said with confidence. "I do."

"What was your mother's name?"

Henry thought long and hard about the name.

It suddenly came to him.

"Abbey," he said. "Her name was Abbey."

"That's a beautiful name," she said. "Like Abigail."

Sheila placed Mrs. Frisby on the drawer next to the bed and kissed Henry again.

After they kissed, Henry sprang out of bed and stumbled over to Sheila's incredible music collection.

"I swear I've never seen so many records," he said, marveling at the shelves of records.

"They belonged to my parents," she said with the tone shifting in her voice.

Henry stopped flipping through the records and turned to Sheila, who was repositioning herself against the headboard. She used one of the pillows as if it was a Teddy and squeezed it tightly.

"Rebecca," Henry said and paused, "she told me they died in a plane crash."

"They were on their way home from Portugal," she said. "For three years, they had planned this trip across Europe. They flew to France, Germany, London."

"London?"

"That's right," she said. A smile crept on her face, one of reminiscence. "I remember they would call me like every five minutes to check up on me. I think my mother spent the entire trip on the phone talking to me. She absolutely hated that I didn't go with them."

Henry asked, "Then why didn't you?"

"I was afraid of flying," she replied and looked at Henry with guilty eyes. "One time, they tried to get me on a plane. And this was to New York, which was only a couple of hours in the plane. I had a severe panic attack. Can you believe that? I just wonder if I went with them if they would still be here today."

"Huh," he said under his breath, thinking about the city name New York. *The Big Apple*, he thought. An image of a face suddenly flashed over his mind's eye, the same face that was looking at him in the reflection of the bathroom mirror, *Kerri's face*. Her eyes were as sharp and sinister as a reptile's eyes. She was easing through a lavish Manhattan loft and closing the door behind her, saying something like "Have a nice day, rock star," and then taking a bite from a green apple.

Henry pulled his attention back toward Sheila.

"I just think about them sometimes, think about what they would be doing right about now," Sheila said soberly. "My father would be downstairs working on the house. My mother would be coming up with a new recipe to fix for dinner. I wish you would've met my parents."

Henry said, "Me too."

"You said I was like a Renaissance woman," Sheila said, smiling. "My father, he was 'The Renaissance Man.'"

"Like father, like daughter."

"Absolutely," Sheila said. "It's like he knew everything. If there was something broken in the house and it needed to be repaired, he was the person who would fix it, and not just the electronics.   And whenever you asked him a question about. . . I don't know. . . like how to build a fire, he would go on for hours. Or if you asked him who. . . the thirty-fifth President was, he would tell you. It was like he always had an answer for everything."

Henry said, "John Fitzgerald Kennedy."

Sheila burst out laughing.

"JFK!" she said amusedly. "How did you know that?"

Henry bobbed his shoulders.

"Good guess."

"Nice."

"So, who watched over you while they were gone?"

"My aunt and uncle," Sheila answered. "Two years later my uncle passed from a stroke. Then, not too long after, my aunt passed. That was when Rebecca and Tad took me in. They were good friends of my uncle."

"I see," Henry trailed off. "I mean, I'm sorry."

The tears brimmed over Sheila's eyes.

"Look at me." She pouted and then patted the corner of her eyes. "I'm going on about my parents when you've practically lost everyone in your life. I can't imagine what that must feel like."

"It's hard," Henry admitted and directed his attention to the records, "not knowing whether the memory of your loved ones will come back to you. But there's no reason to sit around and dwell about it. Like Rebecca said, the past will remain in the past."

Sheila slid out of bed and held onto Henry from behind.

"How about we make some new memories," she said and nibbled on Henry's neck.

He kissed Sheila and said, "I think last night was a great place to start."

"It was indeed," she said, kissing Henry.

Henry pulled his lips from Sheila's and focused on the pile of records. He flipped and flipped until he came across one record in particular. The record was called *Hard Rider*. The artist on the cover was a tall black man who was wearing a strange biker-like outfit, red with these metallic spikes over shoulder pads. The man had a sparse beard, penetrating eyes, white gloves. . .

In a daze, Henry ran his fingers over the familiar man's face.

"Do you know that one?"

Henry hesitated to answer.

"I don't," he said finally. "Who is he?"

"Mr. Vortex," Sheila answered. "He was big in the sixties and seventies."

Henry never gave the name any thought.

Instead, he continued to flip through the records.

THIRTY-FOUR

CHRISTMAS was on a Saturday.

Tad and Rebecca didn't do much decorating around the house. The most they had done in the living room (mainly Rebecca) was stick up a skinny silver artificial Christmas tree from 1973 that they had kept in the attic all year, dress up the stairwell with a few strings of garland, and hang mistletoe near the kitchen doorway where Tad would occasionally swoop in at the perfect moment and plant a wet one on Rebecca when she passed through the kitchen.

After a feast of a lunch, Tad and Rebecca spent a romantic weekend in Sedona while Sheila and Henry had the entire ranch to themselves. Sheila suggested horseback riding to Henry. At first, Henry was apprehensive and a bit skeptical. Every time he walked by the stalls in the barn, he kept an eye on one horse in particular, the gray Andalusian horse, She Runs With Horns. Sheila warned Henry not to go near She Runs With Horns. Otherwise, he would find out the hard way. Henry wasn't much of a listener. Hardheaded, some would say. A sign of the old Henry finally coming back. Over thorough consideration (*I mean,* Henry thought, *what else was there to do in the middle of nowhere*), Henry agreed. Sheila decided to bring out She Runs With Horns's sister, Casper's Locket. Henry refused and said he'd prefer the bashful one, that "big son of a bitch, She Runs With Horns." Sheila didn't exactly understand the meaning behind Henry's motivation. She thought it maybe could've been a macho thing, Henry wanting to ride the meanest, toughest horse in the barn. In a way, Henry's determination—*and* ignorance—drew Sheila much closer to him. Out of good fun, she dared Henry. In fact, she made a bet with Henry that he wouldn't be able to even strap on the saddle. Henry made an attempt to strap on the saddle but failed miserably. The gray Andalusian ended up throwing Henry from the stall as if he was nothing more than a tiny insect. He tried again, two more times, three! On the fourth attempt, Henry was left with a bruised hip and sore belly. Henry soon found out that not only was She Runs With Horns a mean son of a bitch, or better yet, just a "mean ole bitch," but also a kicker. Later that night, he fulfilled the arrangements of the bet and gave Sheila a full body massage. Of course, the massage led to the two of them making love. At the very end of the day, there were no losers or winners, only two lovers.

After Henry recovered, he decided to go with Sheila's pick, Casper's Locket. During the first trial, Henry fell off Casper's Locket a couple of times. She was much smaller than She Runs With Horns and not as wild. Eventually, Henry got the hang of her. Sheila picked one of her favorites, a Mustang named Sophia, a mare with a chestnut body and mane. For the rest of the afternoon, the two of them rode through the open desert and explored the canyons and the secluded rivers running between them. In the early evening, they set up a picnic in a cave called Cinder's Mouth and made love. Monday came around. They did the daily chores around the ranch. They ended up clearing out the fence and building a new one. Every now and then, Henry and Sheila would sneak off somewhere like the barn or the garden or behind the house to make love. Out of respect, they tried not to show their affection for one another in front of Tad or Rebecca. Since Henry and Sheila were madly in love, it was a task all by itself. They could hardly keep their hands off one another. Wednesday morning after Henry and Sheila finished up their chores earlier than expected, they packed a lunch and rode horses into the desert. Last night, while resting in bed with Sheila, Henry finally confessed about Kerri, not just that he was once in love with her but that he wasn't alone before Tad found his body on the road. As best as he could, he explained to Sheila that he was with Kerri and that something terrible happened, something that he couldn't explain even if he tried. There might have been an accident, he told her. All Henry could remember were several other faces, none of whom he could identify. So, after a night of serious contemplation, Sheila agreed to ride out with Henry in search of Kerri. They traveled back to the same road where Tad discovered Henry and rode about ten miles west into the desert. They ended up taking a couple of breaks during the trip, once to eat and another time to relieve themselves. Once they arrived at their destination (just over a steep gorge Henry remembered), they searched for Kerri but all they could find was a dried up puddle of blood in the sand. Henry found a series of footprints and tracked them to another set of prints. By any stretch, Henry wasn't the outdoorsman and he didn't have much skills or advantages when it came to tracking. However, a dumb eye could spot what went down here, in this one spot in the desert. Henry found the blood splatter and then the blood puddle stained over the parched land, a crime scene. Then, Sheila came across a bullet casing and showed it to Henry, which confirmed that this was the location where he was shot either in the chest or in the arm. But, as before, there was no sign of Kerri. While Henry searched for her body in the desert (a hand possibly protruding from the dirt or fingers or leftover bones from where the vultures had picked her clean), he found nothing but yet another memory flashing through his mind. The vivid memory was of Donnie aiming a gun at him, not Kerri. Henry was raising his arms in the air and screaming out, "NO!" He fell to the ground, to the parched land, alone. That was all Henry could remember: the face of the shooter, a gunshot, and then the blood oozing from underneath. After they ended the search, Henry didn't say much to Sheila for the remainder of the trip back to the ranch.

So far, the dinner was fairly quiet.

Tad and Rebecca ate mostly in peace, whereas Sheila and Henry, as usual, couldn't keep their eyes off one another.

Once Sheila was finished with the meal (the meatloaf and vegetables mostly pushed around her plate), she took a sip from the glass of water and excused herself from the table. Without Tad or Rebecca watching, Sheila carefully rolled her eyes toward the bathroom, modestly patted the corners of her mouth with a napkin, and winked at Henry.

Trying not to draw too much suspicion, Henry, in return, waited around for a minute or so and then finally excused himself from the kitchen table. He wasn't so subtle as Sheila. Yet, he took a swig from the glass of iced tea and rushed from the kitchen, which left Tad and Rebecca as disconcerted as lip readers trying to read an auctioneer.

As soon as Sheila stepped out of the hallway bathroom, Henry grabbed her, cradled her in his arms, and carried her upstairs. Sheila tried to cover up the surprising cackle with her hand.

From the kitchen, Tad heard the exclamation from across the hallway.

"Those two have been acting strange for the past week."

"Are you blind, Tad?" Rebecca said foolishly and placed her fork over the plate. "They're in love. It's written all over their faces."

"Please," Tad uttered with a sigh. "How many times have we gone over this? It's getting a little old. Don't you think?"

Rebecca rolled her eyes at Tad across the table.

"We were once that age too," she said. "Just remember that."

"Well, he can't stay here forever," Tad said closely to Rebecca. "He's starting to get way too comfortable 'round here."

"He seems to be helping out around the ranch," she said and wiped her mouth clean with a napkin. "Those two managed to put up the fence just in a matter of days. That would've taken you and Sheila at least two more solid weeks of hard work to complete."

"You're right about that," Tad said and shrugged his shoulders. "He is a hard worker."

"Give him time to find his feet again, honey," Rebecca said and caressed the top of Tad's hand. "Besides, it's always nice to see a new face around here."

After they made love, Henry and Sheila lay in bed with the cool desert breeze gently blowing through the cracked bedroom window.

Sheila rolled over Henry's naked body, her warm leg easing around his. Her plump breasts spilled over his chest. She maneuvered her arm around Henry's neck and grabbed the crinkled photograph of the two girls from the nightstand. As she rested her head over Henry's breast, over his heart, she held the photograph above.

"Did you know them?" Sheila asked over the sound of Henry's steady heartbeat.

Henry glanced at the moonlit photograph above him and said softly, "I. . . I think they were my mother's sisters. . . well, stepsisters."

"Really?"

Sheila's eyes lit up.

"Yeah."

Henry anchored his arm around Sheila's shoulder and played with her hair around the backside of her head, mostly curling it between his fingertips. He acknowledged the bafflement over Sheila's face. Her eyes were moving to each thought in her head.

He asked, "What's wrong?"

She answered mindfully, "Tad told me that he knew them, the two girls in the photograph. He said they were Mr. Hampton's girls."

An outcast, he thought, *a man shunned from society*.

"Mr. Hampton?"

"Do you know him?"

The Chiameca Tribe.

Henry could almost feel the coarse binding of a hardback over the ridges of his palm, as well as smell the sour scent of the insides of an old book.

The name *Julius Hampton* was right there stretching out like a wilted hand, along with the vivid characters within a novel that he wrote after he was released from prison for serving a ten-year sentence.

"Vaguely," he finally answered.

"Tad said Mr. Hampton's two girls passed away a long time ago," Sheila said as she handed the photograph to Henry. "However, they never found their bodies."

"What do you mean?"

"One day, they went missing," she explained and ran her fingers through Henry's chest hair. "After they had given up on the girls, Mr. Hampton became a recluse. Tad hadn't seen or spoken to him since."

Henry flipped over the photograph.

"I know this address," she said curiously and pointed at the address above. "It's not too far from here. Have you been there before?"

"No," Henry answered. "Maybe there's a part of me that doesn't want to know."

Sheila rolled her head up Henry's chest and said, "Maybe."

She moved her eyes away from the photograph and settled them over Henry's calming eyes.

"Or maybe you do know," she said as she gazed into his eyes. "You just choose to forget."

"Maybe." Henry kissed Sheila on the forehead. "Maybe."

Sheila ran her finger over the fresh scar on Henry's chest.

"Elvis. . ."

"Yeah."

"What is love?"

The question seeped deeply into Henry's thoughts like a seed into soil. Henry thought more about the question: What is love? A sequence of images flashed through his mind. *It was raining. Henry was sprinting toward a trashcan in an alleyway. A bloody, beaten man was curled inside and clinging to life.* Another sequence: *It was dark. Henry was stepping into the path of a bullet. With his arms raised, he was screaming out,* *"No!"* The images eventually fell into silence. Henry did all he could to bring them back to life, the images, but the faces among them were as dark as shadows.

"This," Henry said sincerely and stared into Sheila's eyes, "this right here. This is love."

She rested her head over Henry's chest.

"Is this what happens when you're in love?" she said against his chest.

Once more, she ran her finger across Henry's pale scar.

"No," Henry said softly. "It's the ones you can't see."

Sheila's eyes fell into thought. Ever since they returned home from the search for Kerri in the desert, Sheila wondered about what really happened to his friend, this Kerri woman, or if she would ever return to Henry and if she did, and she showed up at the ranch, would he choose Kerri over her and abandon her. The thought alone of losing Henry put knots in her stomach.

With her glossy eyes, Sheila pulled herself from thought and once more, gazed up at Henry.

"I don't want to lose you," she said.

Henry kissed Sheila on the forehead and said, "I'm not going anywhere."

"You promise?"

"Yeah." He interlocked his hand with Sheila's hand. Again, he kissed Sheila on the forehead, kissed the top of her hand, and whispered into her ear, "I promise."

THIRTY-FIVE

ON a Friday morning, Henry and Sheila finished work early around the ranch and brought a picnic to Cinder's Mouth where they ate lunch, which consisted of a leftover casserole from last night. Then they rode their ambling horses down a small bank into the cool shade alongside a winding river that ran in between a canyon. Henry spent most of his ride gaping at the sandstone walls around him, jagged at parts, whereas smooth and curved at others, as if a set of almighty hands slipped their way inside the rugged earth and punctiliously shaped each recess and fissure the same way a sculptor would shape wet clay. Throughout their tranquil ride, the sun would find the four of them, both man and horse, ambling below and cast a brilliant light over the sandstone and bring out the many layers and contours around each groove and bend.

Sheila finally said to Henry, "You've been pretty quiet ever since we left Cinder's Mouth."

Henry slowed down Casper's Locket to a near standstill.

"I've been thinking. . . "

"Oh yeah?"

Henry thought about whether or not to tell Sheila about Mr. Hampton's novel, *The Fire Dance*, the story about a man and a tribe.

He directed his attention to Sheila.

"I remember a story, a novel."

"What kind of novel?"

"One about Mr. Hampton, well, one that he once wrote," Henry said as a dark shadow cast over his face. "Can't remember the name of the novel. But I remember the story as clearly as I see you right now."

"Is that right?" Sheila moved her eyes downward in thought as they carefully rode into the dark shadows together underneath a looming bluff. "I remember Tad mentioning to me the other day that Mr. Hampton was once a famous mystery writer." She moved her eyes upward and studied Henry's face, which, like hers, was masked with dark shadows. "I'm not much of a bookworm, nothing like Tad. The man reads like two books a week." She carefully threw her head into a nod. She asked, "How about you? You like to read?"

"Yeah," he returned with a shrug. "I like to read here and there."

Sheila asked, "So, Elvis, what's this story about?"

Henry didn't answer the question. Instead, he smiled and pulled his head down toward his chest as if he was embarrassed to tell the story.

"Hey," Sheila said and cracked a smile, "you start something around here—"

"I know, I know," Henry said as he glanced up at Sheila, who had her head tilted to the side. "It must've been another memory that came back to me last night."

"That's good. Right?"

Henry mumbled, "I guess."

He ambled even closer to Sheila, closer to the shadows.

"Anyway, this story," he said, "it's about a man who is accused of murdering his girlfriend in his sleep."

Sheila frowned.

"A murder mystery?" Her eyes sharpened now, more so flirtatiously than angrily. "I like it already."

Henry said, "The story revolves around this one character, John Wheeler's his name. He's a college English professor who is head over hills in love with a postgrad named Emily Hurley. Every morning while Emily is asleep, John slips out of bed and goes over to a small alcove in the baseboard, hidden to the eye. In this alcove he pulls out a wedding ring and just gazes at it."

"Gazes at it," Sheila said. "Why?"

"Because I guess he's not ready to, you know, pop the question."

"He's just waiting for the perfect time."

"Yeah," he said. "I guess so. Anyway, only John knows about the alcove, so his girlfriend will never stumble upon it."

"Of course. . . " Sheila said quietly and then to herself, ". . . clever."

"So," Henry explained, "one morning, John wakes up, like the morning before, and does the same routine. However, this morning is unlike any other morning. John notices something strange. He has blood covered all over his hands and shirt. John thinks he's trapped in a nightmare that he can't wake up from. Then, he turns to the other side of the bed where Emily is sleeping and finds her not sleeping. She's dead and the blood on his hands is from her. He panics. He can't even recognize her from the injuries. All he sees is red. And it's everywhere: on the bed sheets, on the walls, on the curtains, on the ceilings. . . "

Sheila drawled, "Geez. . . "

"During the trial," Henry said, "the prosecutor explains to the people of the jury the graphic details of the murder. He says that Emily Hurley was stabbed over sixty-three times in the chest and abdomen."

"Wow! Sixty three times?"

"No joke." Henry rose up his finger in the air as if he had a moment of eureka. "The catch: They never find a murder weapon in the house. The investigators check all of the knives in the kitchen's drawers and cabinets and compare them to the stab wounds on Emily's body, but none of them match."

"Get out of here!"

"No signs of breaking and entering," Henry explained. "No trail marks of John leaving the bedroom. With all that blood, he would've left a trail."

Sheila said, "Of course."

"The bedroom was the exact same way as it was the night before he went to sleep," he said seriously. "Then, John wakes up like he would every morning in his bed right next to his girlfriend, except his girlfriend, Emily Hurley, was dead, brutally murdered by a monster. John was a hundred percent certain that he did *not* kill his girlfriend, that he was framed and that someone else was responsible."

"So, did the jury believe his testimony?"

"They did," Henry said, his eyes widening. "And John never went to prison, but he wished he had."

"Guilty conscience?"

"No," Henry said abruptly. "Worse. For three months, the trial was televised everywhere. In those three months, the trial had the highest ratings on TV. Turns out that it was the most viewed trial in the entire history of TV. John ended up being found 'not guilty.' Everywhere John goes if it's to the grocery store or the movies or to, I don't know, the dentist, he's known as a killer who got away with murdering his girlfriend. In fact, he can't go anywhere without being spotted. For those three months, you couldn't flip a channel without seeing John Wheeler's face on a television. People fear him. Some walk in the other direction if they see John approaching them. And John wasn't what people thought of him. He was the kind of man who would hold the door open for people or say thank you or. . . I don't know. . . or always start off a conversation with asking how that someone was doing. He was that kind of guy and yet now his world was all warped. One day, John goes from a gentleman. The next, a complete monster."

Sheila said quietly, "That's a shame."

"Later in the story," Henry said, "John does a little investigation of his own. He finds out that his girlfriend's name wasn't even Emily Hurley and that she wasn't even an American citizen. She was a part of a satanic cult called The Devil's Little Spawns. They said Emily was a 'vessel' and that she, along with this cult, was working with Satan himself and that John was one of the 'chosen ones.'"

"Okay," Sheila said carefully. "The story was really getting good until you lost me at satanic cul—"

"—Wait," Henry interrupted. "It's get better, though."

"So, John actually talked to these people in this cult?"

"Yeah," Henry said, "but they didn't kill him. They said that the devil wasn't done with him."

"So, what does John do?"

"Get this: John buys a sailboat."

"A sailboat?"

"He has no other choice," Henry said and then cleared his throat. "He isn't safe anymore, especially after knowing that a cult is after him for what reasons John doesn't know. In a way, John may have been crazy and he could've killed his supposed girlfriend."

"Maybe he was a sleepwalker?"

"Who knows?" Henry shrugged his shoulders. "John did what he thought was best and he sailed across the Atlantic."

"That's one way of getting away from the world."

"Then, another world finds John Wheeler," Henry explained. "An island. And on this island, there are indigenous people, this tribe called Chiameca. Years go by. John eventually falls in love with a tribeswoman."

"A tribeswoman? Really? Now, you're screwing with me. . ."

Henry burst out laughing.

"I'm not," he said over the laughter. "I swear. Anyway, John learns the tribe's language, learns how to hunt for his own food in the jungle. It's turns into like. . . like *Lord of the Flies* meets *Gilligan's Island*, only without the Skipper."

Sheila blurted out, "Hey! How do you know about *Gilligan's Island*? You don't even know who Elvis Presley is. Yet, you know all about Gilligan?"

Henry carelessly shrugged his shoulders.

"Don't know," he said. "It just came to me. I guess."

Sheila suspiciously glanced at Henry.

"Anyway, John becomes a full-blown tribesman," he said to Sheila, who still had her eyes carefully drawn to Henry. "I mean, here you have a man who spent his life surrounded by materials and when all of that was gone, he finds a new life miles away from any civilization. All he knows now are the people of the tribe, the island. There are no TVs. No cell phones or radios to contact relatives."

"I was about to say," Sheila said mindfully. "Whatever happened to his family? Or what about his friends? What happened to them?"

"After the trial, they all deserted him," he said to Sheila, who was shaking her head. "You see, John didn't need those materials anymore. He was a man who was in search for love. And love was what he found."

"Sounds like a strange story, but a good one."

"But. . ."

"Uh oh," Sheila said as she readjusted the reins around the horse. "I don't like the sound of that."

"But one morning, he wakes up. . . "
Sheila hollered out, "No! Don't tell me!"
Henry was already bobbing his head.
"He has blood covered all over his hands. . . "
"That's how the story ends."
"Yeah."
"I like it, but without the last part."
"So do I," Henry said as he turned to Sheila and looked into her starry eyes. "I just don't know why, out of all the memories, why that one came back to me."

When they got back from the picnic, Henry went upstairs to grab a record from the bedroom while Sheila hung out on the porch. On the way to Sheila's room, Henry passed another bedroom, the same room he had been warned not to enter. During his stay, he respected the rules of the house. Of course, Henry thought about it numerous times. What was behind that one door? Just one peek! The door was always closed. And that shadow! Each time Henry passed the door, he always caught a strange shadow, humanly at times, casually strolling underneath the doorway. At different times of the day, the shadow would sway back and forth and change character. Other times of the day, the shadow would sidle across the sunlight like a terrestrial creature. One time, he caught it skittishly darting across the room. Henry never asked who or *what* was behind that door. On several occasions, he was tempted to ask Sheila about the mysterious bedroom. A part of him didn't care. He was so in love with Sheila that he didn't want to ruin the special connection they had.

On a whim, Henry decided to open the door. The temperature of the room was much colder than the other rooms. The air was denser. Even the gray flannel and black jeans that he wore couldn't provide enough warmth to keep him warm inside the cool room. Rubbing his arms together, Henry gazed around the cold, empty bedroom. The walls were painted navy blue. A small bookshelf rested next to a bed. Most of the books were from late authors: Steinbeck,

Hemmingway, and Dickens. All kinds of picture frames of a young man, most likely in his twenties, same man from the picture downstairs on the piano, were mounted all over the room, on the walls, on top of shelves, dressers, armoires. In almost every picture, the man was wearing a military uniform. There were pictures of him in Iraq with other soldiers. He came across another frame. The young man was shaking hands with President Bill Clinton. Henry picked up one frame of the young man standing in the middle of Tad and Rebecca. He pulled the frame from his face and then recognized the folded American flag on top of the bed.

An object suddenly grazed over his head!

Henry flinched from the rustling overhead and looked to the ceiling.

In front of the bedroom window hung a model of a Curtiss P-40 Warhawk. The fighter aircraft, which was hanging on a wire attached to the ceiling in front of the bedroom window, was brown with a shark's mouth painted over the nose. Henry reached up to touch the model above and followed the shadow it cast on the bedroom floor below.

"He would've been around your age," Tad said from the doorway.

Startled, Henry immediately pulled his hand away from the toy. He fumbled the picture frame in his other hand. He quickly recovered, placed the frame in its rightful position on the shelf, and spun around.

"I. . . I didn't mean to. . . "

"That's okay, son," Tad said and cautiously stepped inside the room. He cautiously gazed around as if he hadn't stepped foot in the bedroom for ages. Who knows how long? "His name was Robert. We called him Robbie."

"He was your son?"

"Yes," Tad answered sorrowfully. "He died in the Gulf War. His Humvee drove over a mortar. Killed three of the four men inside. The surviving soldier lost both of his legs. Name was Edward Walton. I met Mr. Walton when he got back home from Kuwait. 'Not the same man,' they said, had issues, problems in the head." Tad turned away and sighed.

"No father should have to bury his own son. But I knew, though." He forced the thought of losing his son from his head. The act alone sent a ripple of disgust through his face. "I couldn't talk him out of it. He was adamant about joining. Rebecca did all she could to keep him here. In a way, he was already gone, mentally that is. The last couple of weeks before he left, he was extremely irritable. It was as if we were walking around on eggshells. I remember the day Robbie signed up for the Army. I was so terrified and yet so proud of him. In the back of my mind, though," Tad cleared his throat, "I knew that there was a possibility he wouldn't return home. I thought about him every night. Still do. He was a good man with a heart as big as the world. Different from the others." Tad folded his hat in his hand and pointed at Henry. "He would've liked you, Elvis."

Henry said sincerely, "Sorry to hear, Tad. He sounds like a great man. He really does."

"It's all right, son," he said and grabbed Henry by the shoulder. He forced a smile over his face. "How about we take a ride into town? I know a place that makes the best margarita? After all, tomorrow is New Years."

Henry thought about the invitation.

"You don't strike me as a margarita kind of guy."

"Trust me," Tad said, grinning. "You're not the first person who's said that to me. A man and his margarita share a close bond."

"Is that right?"

"What do you say, Elvis?"

"But what about Sheila?"

"This will be a guys day out," Tad said, carefully observing Henry. "She'll be here when we get back."

"Sure," Henry said and extended his hand. "I can use a drink."

Tad grinned once more, shook Henry's hand, and said, "It's a date then."

"Yeah," Henry said smoothly. "Just don't be making any moves on me."

THIRTY-SIX

THE drive lasted around eighteen minutes, but to Henry, felt like twice that. For the duration of the ride, Henry didn't say much to Tad, only the standard responses from Tad's questions: *How do you like working on the ranch* or *have you ever done work like this before?* Henry kept his answers short and simple. Besides that, both of them mostly kept quiet and relished the desert scenery around them. Henry never really thought of anything to say to Tad, which, in a way, earned him more kudos. Obviously, he wasn't trying to impress Tad or ramble on about something as mundane as the weather. In fact, Henry didn't even have any backup questions on standby for whenever the mood got dull or awkward. All he could think about was Sheila and getting back to her.

As Tad took a right on Morganton Road, Henry's eyes fell downward on the floor of the truck, causing him to miss the road sign. Something was etched into the frame, Henry realized, but he didn't know exactly what it was. Intrigued, he leaned forward on the bench and got a closer look. The initials *H.B.* were etched beside the door. The initials appeared as if they had been written with a blade or something sharp. Henry reached down and ran his finger across the coarse inscription.

Tad asked, "Whatcha you got there, Elvis?"

Henry uttered, "H.B.?"

Tad momentarily pulled his eyes off the road and tracked the inscription.

"This here was my daddy's truck," Tad said, now focusing on the road ahead. "His name was Hubert. I thought Becca told you."

"Yeah. . ." Henry trailed off into thought, ". . . she did."

"Yep," Tad said merrily. "Daddy had a way of putting his initials on everything that belonged to him. You know, like a lion marking his territory." He gently struck Henry on the shoulder. "It's what us men like to do, especially when it comes to our women. Right, Elvis?" Tad suddenly changed his tone. He whispered, now seriously, "But don't tell Becca that."

"Yeah," Henry mumbled.

"Well, here we are. . ."

As Henry fell into a state of disorientation, Tad pulled up to a small bar called *The Last Stop*. There were only a couple of cars (one being a truck with a hombre passed out at the steering wheel, cowboy hat covering his face, mariachi playing over the worn, brittle speakers) parked in the parking lot. From the outside, the place appeared abandoned. The flashing OPEN sign was the only lively thing on the façade of the bar and, of course, the mariachi music. Other than that, everything was either dead or old. A gaunt dog wandered from the desert and planted itself near a rusty spicket on the side of the building. The dog was so thin that Henry could see its ribcage. Somewhere down the road, tumbleweed was skipping over the cracked asphalt.

"You sure about this place, Tad?" Henry asked wearily and stepped out of the parked truck.

"On the outside, it might not look pleasing to the eye," he said. "But don't judge a book by its cover."

"Right. . ." Henry uttered, looking around the desolate place, ". . . Good advice."

"Don't worry, Elvis," he said and wrapped his arm around Henry's shoulder. "I know the owner. Nice fella."

While Tad made his way to the bar, Henry slowed down. Once more, he stopped and looked around the desert. His eyes were wet and glossy. A strange force tightened like a fist over his body. Something wasn't right, he realized. Henry could just feel it, almost taste it, in the air, in his gut. From the second he stepped foot into the truck, he knew that there was a chance that he wouldn't make it back to Sheila.

"What's wrong, son?"

"It's just. . ."

Henry turned to Tad.

"It's nothing."

"Come on," he said reassuringly and waved Henry over. "You'll feel a lot better after a drink."

They walked inside the small bar. As Tad pointed out, the inside wasn't nearly as bad as the outside. There was a Rock-Ola jukebox playing music. Henry didn't know the song playing over the worn speakers. The lyrics were muddled. The melody was out of tune. To Henry, it sounded like a country song. But he could've been wrong. A couple of folks were lounging in the dining area. They looked as if they were passing through. The owner/bartender, Chaz Steagel, waved at Tad and threw the stained towel over his shoulder.

"Hello, Tad," Chaz said. "Who's your friend?"

"Chaz," he said and pointed at Henry, "this is Elvis."

"Elvis, huh?" Chaz said with a slight snort. "Your parents must have quite a sense of humor."

"Elvis doesn't remember his parents," Tad said kindly. "Elvis was involved in an accident. He's gotta little of that ah. . . whatchamacallit. . . "

"Amnesia?"

"Yep," Tad said. "That's the one."

"Sorry to hear, friend."

Chaz reached out his hand.

Then, Henry shook it.

"Name's Chaz."

"Nice to meet you."

"Same to you, friend," Chaz said, breathing out a sigh of relief. "So, got any plans for the big night?"

"Same as last year."

"Which is?"

"Sitting at home with the misses."

"You two should hit the town."

"We're too old to be hitting the town, my friend," Tad said. "When I was Elvis's age here, I was running circles around the girls."

"I bet you were," Chaz said. "I think me and my lady are gonna drive down to Phoenix and spend the night. They're having a New Years Eve thing downtown."

"I hear it gets pretty wild down there every year."

"I didn't go last year, but I went the year before," Chaz said with a grin creeping over his narrow face. "You won't believe the women, Tad. It's like you died and gone to heaven."

"You lucky dog you," Tad said and laughed.

"So, what's it going to be?"

"Make it two usuals."

"Two usuals it is."

Chaz got to work on the "usuals."

Henry leaned over to Tad.

"What's the usuals?"

"The margaritas that I was telling you about," he explained. "They're to die for."

Tad caught Henry scanning the dining area.

"Told you it wasn't so bad."

Henry noticed a boy standing in front of the Rock-Ola with his back facing the bar. Not too far away from the jukebox, a gauntly, scraggly Native American, in fact, a Navajo, who was dressed in black leather, was exiting the restroom and making sure the zipper was all the way up on his pants. He motioned to Chaz with a flick of his head and said his goodbyes. The man was familiar looking, eyes and nose. Henry stared at his face closely and studied his eyes, nose, and then mouth. *Where have I seen this man before?* Before the man's eyes trailed away from Chaz, they crossed Henry's path. An image (a recent memory perhaps) suddenly flashed through Henry's mind. The image was of a Native American, bloody and agonized, crawling over a sparkling clean white floor in a hallway. The facility appeared military, heavily secured. There was this dark blood puddle underneath the strange man. His bloody face was filled with great terror. His frantic eyes, bloody as well, flickered, paused, and then settled on Henry.

The man uttered the words *who are. . .*

". . . *All right,*" Chaz said from behind the bar.

Henry flinched from the sudden interruption. He turned to Chaz, who was placing the two margaritas on the bar.

"Two usuals. Enjoy."

"Thanks a bunch, Chaz," Tad said casually and toasted the glass.

"Not a problem," Chaz replied.

With the strange image receding back into his mind, Henry threw a nod at the bartender.

Both Tad and Henry took a sip.

Tad let out a sigh from his mouth whereas Henry puckered his face in sheer disgust.

"It's not that bad," Tad said as he gently slapped Henry on the back.

After another sip and then yet another pucker of the face, Henry slid the drink away.

"How about something a little more stiff."

"You got it, Elvis," Tad said and shrugged his shoulders. "Well, I guess it's not for everyone." Then, he waved down Chaz. "One double of your finest liquor for my good friend here."

"Sure thing, boss," Chaz said and grabbed a bottle from the wall.

He placed the large shot glass on the bar and then displayed the bottle for Henry.

"The Gauche Lion," Chaz said. "Single malt whiskey. Over a hundred years old. Only two hundred and fifty bottles were made in the world. This will definitely put some hair on your chest."

Henry rubbed his hands together.

"Good thing you're buying," he said jokingly to Tad.

Tad burst out laughing.

Chaz followed.

Tad pulled out a cigar from his pocket, used the bar matches to light the end of the cigar, and said from the corner of his mouth, "You better enjoy every single drop of that. . . "

"Gauche Lion."

"Whatever."

Chaz waited for Tad to give him the go ahead.

Tad took several puffs of the cigar and nodded.

Chaz poured the double shot into the shot glass.

Henry pounded down half of the glass.

He jerked his head to the side.

His eyes watered a bit.

"What do you think?"

"It's got a little kick to it," he said, coughing.

"A little?"

Tad couldn't help but laugh.

"Tad?"

Chaz displayed the bottle for Tad.

"I'm fine here with my margarita."

Chaz put the bottle back on the shelf.

A new song played over the Rock-Ola, more uplifting than the last. The song started out with this pulsing electronic riff and then the beat came in like a stampede of wild buffalo. The speakers were crisper. The sound wasn't as muffled as before. As Henry sat quietly at the bar, the beat of the song lifted the weight from his slouched shoulders and immediately seized his attention. Both of his eyes pulled ahead, sharpening now. The beat sunk its way into Henry's ears, pounding and pounding, relentlessly. *That beat*, he thought, *I know that beat*. That beat, once reclusively living there in the confines of his mind, resting, waiting to find its wings, soared high and graceful. Touching the skies! That beat was his purpose, his identity, breathing, fuming, kicking, pulsing. . . alive! He suddenly grimaced. His jaw muscles flexed, making them visible, popping. His hand clutched tighter over the shot glass.

"*Elvis*. . . " Tad uttered.

His voice distorted.

The name *Elvis* shifted into the name *Henry*.

Now, that beat consumed his entire body, quaking.

Henry's eyelids fluttered.

He looked around in paranoia.

The lyrics for *Mesaterrestrial* penetrated through Henry's ears.

With a long gasp, his eyes frantically moved around his head until the whites of his eyes were exposed.

Flashes of images ran through his mind (these being much more vivid than the images before). Images of his life. . . seven years old. . . it was snowing outside. . . he and Abbey sitting in front of the television watching *Emmet Otter's Jug-Band Christmas* together. . . he and his friends laughing at Wembley from the show *Fragile Rock*. . . Zoot from the *Muppets*. . . Dorothy and her three friends, Scarecrow, Tin Man, and The Lion skipping down the yellow brick road in the movie *The Wizard of Oz*. . . Henry making sand castles on the beach with Abbey. . . watching the movie *Close Encounters of the Third Kind*, Roy Neary, who was played by the actor Richard Dreyfuss, staring into a mound of mashed potatoes that he had carved with his fork. . . watching *Purple Rain* with T.J. and Danny, dreaming of making it big that night and then Henry looking over his shoulder at his mother, who was standing with her arms crossed over her chest, smiling, not glaring. . . making demo songs in his bedroom with 2 Hot 2 Handle. . . playing the air saxophone on his bed. . . practicing the saxophone with Ms. Craft. . . his neighbor Kerri. . . Henry at the neighborhood courts playing basketball with the other kids on the block. . . Abbey embracing her son after he escaped the house fire. . . Henry reading the McGruff the Crime Dog poster with the slogan "Take A Bite Out of Crime" at the bottom in front of Principal Aires office. . . the first time he broke his wrist. . . a white cast, signatures and doodles marked all over. . . a news flash on the television about a vigilante, a strange woman with *white hair* standing on the ledge of a building with a helicopter spotlight shining down on her. . . white hair, a pair of glistening eyes in the rear view. . . white horse, flying now, soaring with wings, the name Tri-Star inside a triangle. . . the time he lost his virginity to

Amy Swearinger in the back of his silver Ford Taurus. . . watching and getting inspired by saxophone solos in music videos like "You Belong to the City". . . playing basketball for Haddon. . . starting up the band. . . traveling around the world, South America, Asia, Europe. . . Queen's Guard. . . playing songs in front of thousands, sold out crowds. . . staring down at a trashcan with T.J., bloody and beaten, inside, howling to the moon. . . standing over T.J.'s body in the hospital room. . . making love to Starlet. . . and then, finally, a photograph of his father, Henry the Fourth, sitting on a recliner with Henry held closely in his arms. . .

Henry's eyes came across a tiny red light reflecting in the liquor bottle. The atmosphere darkened around the bar. The track lights above dimmed. Henry ignored his surroundings, the music playing overhead, and concentrated on the wall before him. The red lights brightened throughout the bottles. Tad was no longer sitting next to him. He was now alone, in a cold darkness. Red brake lights flashed repeatedly through the cramped darkness. He fought and kicked. Somehow, he managed to loosen the bounds over his wrists. Suddenly, two car doors slammed shut. The slam of the door stirred yet another memory, this one closer than the others. He and Kerri were having dinner at a swanky restaurant called The Flying Dojo. After they finished the lovely meal, Henry flagged down the valet. The man who pulled up Henry's rental car wasn't the same man who he had given the keys to before. He was an older man who shared the same characteristics as a man whom the Werewolf had shot in the back not too long ago. He could remember not the older man's face but the other man's face plastered over the news the days following the shooting. Over many occasions, T.J. had talked about him. What were the odds that these two men were related? Two other men approached him from behind. Next thing Henry knew, a club was being wrapped around Henry's face.

In the darkness, he heard the footsteps over the loose gravel.

The footsteps slid.

Outside the darkness, he heard the sound of a young woman crying.

The trunk door suddenly opened and revealed a bright night sky. Three men loomed over his curled body. One of them was holding Kerri by the arm. She was gagged and bound and had a bruise over her left eye.

"Elvis (Henry)?" Tad said, touching Henry on the shoulder. "What's a matter, son?"

Officer Marson and Officer Wheaten pulled Henry from the trunk.

Henry staggered and fell onto the desert floor. Strings of blood poured from his lips and ran down the sides of his chin. A fresh trail of blood was also oozing from his forehead and around his temple.

The two cops forcibly yanked Henry upright.

"Did they touch you?" Henry asked Kerri.

Struggling to stand on her own two feet, Kerri didn't respond.

Henry ran his eyes over her body, mainly over the torn collar of her dress. One strap was hanging loosely from her shoulder while the other one was keeping the dress from falling from her body. Henry's eyes traced over the skirt and then her legs, which were both shaking. There, he witnessed the red marks over her thighs, mostly around her groin region. Some of the marks were long and narrow. Others were shaped like a hand.

"Stand up, you piece of shit," Officer Marson seethed.

As the two officers stood at each side of Henry and held onto both of his arms, Donnie pushed Kerri aside. *"Don't go anywhere, sweetheart,"* he said and stepped in front of Henry.

Donnie said to Henry, "Does my face look familiar?"

Henry spat a mouthful of blood in Donnie's face.

"I take that as a yes," Officer Wheaten said and giggled.

Henry studied Donnie's face.

Surprised from Henry's persistence, Donnie calmly wiped the spit from his face with a handkerchief.

"I can see the resemblance," Henry uttered, a trail of blood pouring from his lip. "Just like your brother, a coward."

"This man dresses up as a Halloween character and then shoots my brother in the back and I'm the coward," Donnie said amusedly to the other two. "You see, Henry. This is what happens when you try to take the law in your hands." He leaned closer to Henry. "I just want to know, Henry. Who's the other one? We both know you weren't working alone."

"What makes you any different?" Henry seethed, his voice trembling. "Because you were a badge!"

"I'm not a cop," he returned calmly. "Not anymore."

"Then what makes you any different?"

"Harding?" Donnie seethed. "Who killed him?"

Henry didn't answer.

"Who, damn it?"

"Trina Davis," Henry mumbled. "Rachael Brown," his voice slowly grew louder, "Darius King, Norman Rogers, Dwight Haywood," louder now, "Thomas Maxwell, Bo Johnson. . ."

"What are you doing?" Almost caught in a sudden daze from the many names Henry was throwing at Donnie, he turned to the other two officers in extreme bafflement. "Shut him up. . ." he said, but either officer didn't move at first command. Donnie clinched his teeth in anger. The blood wormed throughout his face, causing a vein to swell over the side of his forehead. He stepped in front of Officer Marson and shouted in his grill, "Shut him the fuck up! Now goddamn it!"

Officer Marson reared back and punched Henry in the stomach.

Henry grunted and fell to his knees, but the two officers were there to instantly yank him back upright.

"Pick him up!" Donnie shouted out as Henry struggled to stand.

". . . Monica Harris," Henry yelled with his head held downward and the blood dripping from his face, "Dwayne

Little, T.J. Livingston, and all the ones who have lost their lives because of monsters like you!"

"You don't get it," Donnie said as he shook his head from Henry's supposedly lack of understanding. "Do you, Henry?" Donnie paced around Henry, who, as before, was struggling to hold up his head, struggling to stand. The officers were mostly holding Henry up like dead weight, waiting to drop him on command. Donnie stopped pacing and squared himself to Henry, who was now slouched over. "Are you so out of touch that you can't grasp reality?" As the lines of anger carefully etched across Donnie's face, he suddenly grabbed Henry by the throat and forced his head upward. In return, Henry pulled his eyes away from Donnie and settled them on Kerri, who was weeping from behind. "LOOK AT ME!" Henry moved his eyes forward and held them on Donnie, penetrating. "You're not out there patrolling the streets day in and day out!" The spit projected from Donnie's gaping mouth as he spoke and hit Henry directly in the face. "You don't have a fucking clue what it's like to be an officer of the law! Do you? You just go by what you hear on the television, what some news anchor is reading from a teleprompter! You, you're just like the rest of them. You, Henry, you get fed the same bullshit that each and every motherfucker gets fed every single day! They've brainwashed you, Henry! Don't you get it! You're nothing more than a sheep to them! Do you hear me? A SHEEP! A FUCKING SHEEP!" Donnie pulled his face away from Henry to momentarily catch his breath. "My brother, he had his faults." Once more, he paced around Henry. "Trust me. I know. But that was no reason to kill the man! He had a family to provide for! You, *well*, you don't. You have nothing, Henry! NOTHING!"

Henry forced himself to look at Kerri, shaking.

Donnie pulled out a gun from his waistband.

Squirming around in the officers' grips, Henry yelled out, "T.J. was a brother to me! His life is now ruined goddamn it! For what? For what reason?"

Donnie didn't answer the question.

"Because T.J. owed your brother money?" Henry returned. "No! It was because your brother was a fucking COWARD! He saw a successful black man. . . "

Donnie replied, almost comically, "It's always race with you fucking people! And I thought we're supposed to be the racist ones?"

Henry grimaced, displaying a set of blood-stained teeth. The blood dripped down the side of his chin.

". . . It killed. . . " he screamed. "IT FUCKIN' *KILLED* YOUR BROTHER! IT KILLED HIM KNOWING THAT A FUCKIN' NIGGER MADE MORE MONEY THAN HIM, THAT A FUCKIN' NIGGER WAS A BETTER MAN THAN HIM! HOW IS THAT FOR GRASPING REALITY? SO WHY DON'T YOU DO WHAT YOU HAVE TO DO AND QUIT WASTING MY FUCKING TIME, YOU STUPID FUCK!"

Henry cried. His eyes rolled downward and he witnessed Donnie's finger tapping over the barrel.

"As you wish, Mr. Burl," Donnie said casually with a smile surfacing over the corner of his face and pointed the barrel at Kerri.

Henry closed his eyes.

Donnie said, "What's the saying?" He briefly thought to himself. "Right," he said. "Eye for an eye."

The first thing that came to Henry's mind: *T.J., his bloody face*.

Henry's eyes suddenly bolted open.

Before Donnie squeezed the trigger, Henry slipped his arms from the officers' grips and leaped in front of Kerri and screamed out, "No!"

A gun blast rang out!

The bullet pierced through Henry's chest and hit Kerri in the upper abdomen.

Henry, who was winded from the sudden gunshot, staggered around a bit before collapsing to the ground.

In a sudden jolt, he rotated his body toward Kerri, who, not too long afterwards, had fallen to the ground as well.

As he lay before Kerri (both facing each other), Henry watched the blood ooze from her wound, slowly now. The red dress she wore grew darker around the abdomen and spread over her breasts. She died instantly. He watched her eyes freeze, emotionless. He didn't even get a chance to say his final goodbyes, he realized, the words unspoken, always rehearsed.

As the words came surfacing over his tongue, a cloud of dust was kicked up around him.

Furious, he freed his hands from the plastic binds.

As Officer Marson reached down to flip Henry over on his back, Henry threw his curled arm upward and elbowed the officer in the center of his face.

Officer Marson blindly reached out to grab Henry, but Henry bounced to his feet and scrapped his worn fingernails across the officer's eyes.

Officer Wheaten rushed toward Henry.

Before he reared back and took a swing at Henry, Henry kneed him in the stomach.

Next, Henry drove his fist across the bridge of his pointy nose the same way he would drive a hammer into the head of a nail. The officer's nose suddenly spilt apart, now exposing the flesh and bone underneath. Thin lines of blood sprayed across Henry's face, now looking like the canvas of a drip painting.

As the bloody officers staggered around, Donnie took aim once more at Henry.

As Donnie pulled the trigger, Henry reached down to the desert floor and grabbed a handful of sand and flung it into Donnie's face.

A gunshot rang out, only this time shot in the sky!

Temporarily blinded, Donnie raked his hands over his burning eyes and screamed out with a high pitch screech.

While the three finally came to their senses, Henry had already taken off on foot.

He ran mindlessly through the dark desert.

"Henry. . . " Tad said and gave Henry another shake on the shoulder.

With half of his face, as well as neck bloody from where Henry had dug his fingernails into his flesh, Officer Marson stumbled to the rental car. He got behind the steering wheel and maneuvered the keys into the ignition. While doing so, he dropped the set of keys on the floor mat. He tried once more. Finally, he started the car while Donnie fired a couple of rounds throughout the dark desert.

One of the bullets ended up hitting Henry in the right arm, reeling him forward.

Henry regained his footing and kept running.

As he ran, faster now, he heard the sound of an engine bearing down on him.

"Oh God!" Henry cried. "Please God. . . "

He turned over his shoulder and witnessed two distant headlights—two beacons in the sea of darkness—shaking from the rough terrain. Despite his injuries, he ran as fast as he could. The car was gaining now. An image of horror flashed across his mind: T.J.'s face highlighted over a fluorescent light, revealing his grotesque injuries. The stark image inspired him and pushed him forward, faster. The car was now bearing down on Henry. The sound of an engine was just inches away from his ears.

As the car's engine suddenly revved from behind, Henry tripped over a jagged rock. His feet gave out from beneath him. He found himself rolling down into a gorge. The roaring of the engine fell farther from him.

When Henry finally came to rest, he heard the piercing sound of tires skidding over the loose dirt.

Officer Marson from above: "It's too steep."

"Find another way down!" Donnie yelled out from inside the car as he ran the backside of his hand over his eyes.

Henry eyed the slope above, as well as the lit cloud of dust kicking up over the ledge. The car sped the other way into the desert. His eyes rolled in the back of his head. Somehow, in his long journey, Henry made it to the road. Then, that cold darkness was upon him, those beacons too. The darkness was soothing, even to the touch. He ran his fingers over the dark curtain, that wall. A roaring crowd built behind the curtain. The crowd was chanting something, something beyond his comprehension. They were stomping too. The floor beneath his feet was vibrating and sending chills up his legs. Then, the curtains opened and revealed the crowd. A bright light washed over his face. . .

Henry let out a deep gasp and pulled himself from the lucid memory.

Shocked, he turned to Tad.

"Is everything all right, Elvis?"

"Elvis?" Henry uttered.

"What's gotten into you, Elvis?"

"My name's Henry."

Tad sat upright.

"Elvis?"

"Why do you keep calling me that?"

"You mean. . ."

"Yeah," Henry said with clarity. "I remember."

"Wait a second? You mean. . . you. . ."

"Yeah," Henry said. "I remember everything."

"I'll be damned," Tad said with relief and removed his hat from his head. "Becca is going to trip out when I tell her!"

"That's my song on the jukebox."

"Wait!" Tad hollered out. "You're telling me. . ." He turned to the Rock-Ola across the bar. He listened closely to the song, the lyrics, the man singing them. He looked back at Henry. "Get outta here!"

Amused, Henry tilted his head.

"Well, it sort of does sound like you," Tad said out loud. "You know all this time, I knew there was something odd about you."

"What day is it?"

"Well. . ." Tad thought, ". . . it's Friday."

Henry quickly got up from the stool.

"I need to borrow your truck."

"You what?"

"I promise one day I'll explain all of this to you," Henry begged. "But now's not the time."

Tad thought carefully about Henry's words.

"What the heck. . ." Tad said to himself, reached in his pocket, and handed Henry the key. "How am I supposed to get home?"

Henry rushed through the bar.

"Chaz will take you home," he said out of breath and exited the bar.

He got into the truck and sped away.

Next destination: Los Angeles.

Outside the dressing room, a crowd was chanting, "*Mona's Arch, Mona's Arch, Mona's Arch. . .*"

Starlet, who was dressed in a strange black getup, paced around in circles. The faint chants of the crowd made their way into the dressing room, making Starlet even more unhinged.

"Come on, Henry," she mumbled to herself as the beads of sweat raced down her forehead. "Don't you do this to us. Not now. . ."

She finally took a seat in front of the vanity and tried to calm her breathing.

While doing so, she clutched her abdomen in slight agony.

The door suddenly cracked open behind her. . .

Her eyes widened in excitement, now the both of them crossing the mirror before her.

In the reflection, James was shaking his head.

Then, Starlet turned her shoulder.

"We can't wait much longer, Star," James said, the sides of his face red with anger.

"He'll show," she said. "He has to."

"Starlet," James said carefully, "we have to make a decision.'

He waited there for a minute, waited for Starlet to say something in return, anything. She had nothing, no words, no expression on her face. James hung his head and closed the door behind him while Starlet rose from her chair. Her jaw was quaking in incredible rage. Her eyes widened, this time in a state of madness.

In a sudden uproar, Starlet—screaming to the top of her lungs—grabbed the chair from the vanity and flung it at the mirror. Glass shattered everywhere, jagged shards falling to her feet. Her eyes fell toward the many reflections on the floor. Strangely, Starlet recognized every last one of them, even the distorted ones.

As the anger settled a little, Starlet, now breathing carefully, reached down and picked up a shard of broken glass. She stared into the warped reflection. Both of her pupils were swollen, appearing like two black marbles in the reflection. The eyes stared back at her. But she saw nothing in them, only a ring of yellow light trapped in darkness.

THIRTY-SEVEN

TAD'S truck ended up overheating sixteen miles outside of Flagstaff where the snow was coming down sideways. So far, there was at least four inches of snow on the ground. Most of the roads were cleared and salted, though. A local by the name of Eugene Cornerstone (a vet who was generous enough to pick up Henry on the side of the road where he called a friend to come tow Tad's truck to the closest repair shop free of charge) provided Henry with food and shelter until the truck was given the proper coolant and repairs the next morning. Since Henry didn't have a dime to his name, the mechanic was kind enough to send Henry on his way. After Henry thanked Mr. Cornerstone for all of his hospitality as well as the mechanic (who he couldn't thank enough), he drove to Los Angeles.

During the trip through the ragged lands out West, he couldn't carry a single thought in his head. He thought about the band and what exactly they were doing right about now or if they were waiting on him or if they had given up on him; and then those thoughts turned to Sheila, her face, her gorgeous smile, the time (as brief as it might have been) they spent together. Now that the cat was out of the bag, what would she think of Henry? What if Tad told Sheila all about the band? If so, would she accept him for who he was? Would she accept the lifestyle of a rock star? They, Mona's Arch, would never believe Henry, his story. Then, he thought about Starlet and T.J. He wondered if T.J. had recovered from his injuries or made any progress or if he had stayed the same. At this point in time, all Henry could do was wonder "What if. . .

When Henry finally arrived at Gateway Coliseum in Los Angeles, the parking lot was completely deserted.

As Henry stepped out of the truck and approached the coliseum, a breeze kicked up a flyer and stuck to his shin.

He grabbed the flyer from his leg.

The flyer read: "Mona's Arch LIVE!"

He mumbled, "Great," crumbled up the piece of paper, and walked inside the coliseum. Besides the janitor sweeping up the trash from a previous concert (*not* Mona's Arch but another band), the coliseum was as silent as a mausoleum. Henry wandered through the aisles surrounding the empty seats and then made his way onto the stage. He sat there, again, thinking about the band and if they had given up on their lead singer. This was it, Henry finally realized as he stared at the many empty seats before him. They would never forgive him after all he had put them through. He let them down; most importantly, he let himself down.

After Henry left the coliseum, he walked to the nearest bar in town. A place called *Alley's Pub*. When Henry visited Los Angeles prior to recording the Machine Mistress album for a little R & R, he remembered this exact place, Alley's Pub, from the giant green shamrock on the front of the building. How could he forget? He had never been inside before, though he only passed by it while he was on the way to Venice Beach. Most of the locals inside were still hung over from the night before. One man was sitting at the bar with his hand covering his face. There was still confetti over the floor, as well as the year 2000 glasses and green glittery hats scattered everywhere. He found a spot at the end of the bar and ordered a beer. Henry told the bartender to start a tab when, again, he didn't have a dime to his name.

While Henry was sipping from the beer and thinking about the band, their future, a gray werewolf mask was slid on the bar underneath him. Henry pulled the bottle from his lips and slowly turned to Corpus, who was standing next to him.

"For a second, I didn't think you'd show up," Corpus said and sat down next to Henry. He carefully studied Henry, his exhausted state.

"What happened?" Henry asked confusedly.

"Well, the concert was canceled," Corpus said and ordered a beer. "Even a small riot broke out. There were a lot of angry fans."

After a sigh, Henry stared at the mask before him. It was the same exact one he had when he was younger, only this one was brand new and not burned.

"How did you find me?"

"I'm a cop, Henry," he said with a smirk. "I have my ways." Corpus nodded at the mask. "Pretty smart. You can't imagine the trouble I went through to find that thing. Went to nearly a dozen costume stores."

Henry snorted in disbelief.

"The thing about masks like that one is that they have a tendency to shed."

"Go figure," Henry said as he showed Corpus the label on the inside of the mask. "Made in China."

Corpus tilted his head.

"You got that right."

"So, this is it. Huh?"

The detective said bluntly, "This is the end of your road, Henry."

"For a second, I thought you were on my side," Henry said bitterly. "I guess I was wrong about you."

Henry's breath grew heavy, angry.

"Typical," Henry said with his shoulders deflated. "So, this is it. My ass goes to jail while the cops who put T.J. in the hospital walk away. You know. It's not the jail part that bothers me, Detective. It's the fact that those men still walk the streets, wearing badges."

"Not exactly," Corpus said with another sudden smirk.

Henry furrowed his eyebrows.

"Last week, highway patrol found an overturned car on the side of the Arizona Interstate," Corpus informed. "Inside were my former partner, Donnie Backer, Ted Backer's brother, and two other police officers. Donnie and one of the cops, Marson, were pronounced dead on the scene. The other cop, Wheaten, was the only one who survived. He's currently at the Fernando Park Medical Center with life threatening injuries." He took a sip of beer, smacked his gums, and made a loud *ah*. "Before you left for Sedona, a witness spotted Donnie camped outside your condo. After you caught a flight to Sedona, I went inside your condo. It was completely trashed."

"You broke into my home?"

"It's not like I stole anything, Henry," Corpus said and shrugged his shoulders. "Besides, it wouldn't be the first time. How do you think I found the hair from that mask?"

Henry shook his head in disappointment.

"Henry, the point is I have evidence that puts Officer Wheaten at the scene of the crime," Corpus said closely. "When, or if, Wheaten survives, he will be living the rest of his days in a jail cell."

"What kind of evidence?"

"Let's just say he forgot to clean up after himself," Corpus replied. "But that's not where it ends. It gets better. Apparently, Marson took his eye off the road. At least that's what the investigators are saying. Swerved into an eighteen-wheeler. Hit the truck head on. Before Wheaten went into surgery, he managed to speak a few words. 'The saxophone,' he said. Wheaten said he heard your saxophone playing in the trunk."

"That can't be," Henry drawled, his eyes slowly falling to the floor. "There was nothing left of him before I. . . "

Henry snapped his eyes back up at Corpus and then, once more, hung his head in disappointment.

Corpus pulled out a pair of handcuffs and slid them in front of Henry.

"Listen, Henry," he said. "We don't have to do this the hard way. Make it easy on yourself."

Henry noticed the handcuffs on the bar.

"We're running out of time, Henry."

"So, this is how it ends?"

"Yeah," Corpus said somberly. "This is how it ends."

"One last thing."

"Sure."

"What do you think Jennifer Snead would say about all of this?"

Corpus sighed loudly.

"You think she would be glad to hear that the right people got arrested?"

"That was a long time ago, Henry."

"I paid a visit to Ms. Snead before I left."

"She told me," Corpus said over Henry's voice. "She also told me that she told you all about Timothy and what really happened to him?"

"She said her husband died in prison," Henry said and placed his elbow on the bar and squared himself to the detective. "Murdered, Detective, by some cold blooded killer just four weeks into doing his time. She said he 'sacrificed' himself for his family, his daughter. She even used the money to pay for her children's college. So, exactly how much money did you pay her to keep her mouth shut?"

"It doesn't matter."

"How much?"

"I don't know the figures, Henry," Corpus said. "Honestly. But I know it was a lot."

"I know. . . I know Timothy Snead didn't murder my father," Henry said clearly. "Ms. Snead even said so herself. She said he was with her the night of the murder. And you guys decided to shut her up because the real killer is the man sitting before me."

Corpus glared at Henry.

"I didn't kill your father, Henry," he said.

"Then, who did?"

Corpus paused and pulled his eyes away from Henry.

"Who was it?" Henry asked. "Your partner?"

"No."

"Then who?"

"It doesn't matter anymore, Henry."

"You don't have the right to say that," Henry said, his voice raised. "Put yourself in my shoes, Detective."

"The people who killed your father are dead, Henry," he said closely. "All but one. And he's fighting for his life in Fernando Park Medical Center."

Henry struggled to look Corpus in the eye.

"Why did they do it?" he asked, his eyes directed at the bar.

"I don't know why, Henry," he said sincerely. "I don't. I wish I had all the answers, but I don't. Timothy Snead was a decent man. He had issues, as we all do. But Mr. Snead turned his life around, devoted himself to his family." Then, he quoted Henry, "For 'greater good,' Henry. If I had to go back and do it all over again, I would've fought for Mr. Snead. And your friend would've never ended up in the hospital the way he did. You have to understand. I would've done *everything* in my power to make sure that justice was served and that the true murderers were locked behind bars for good. But... but I'm tired, Henry. I just want to go home."

Henry grabbed the handcuffs, put the cuffs on himself, and said, "Then what are we waiting for, Detective?"

THIRTY-EIGHT

CORPUS drove hours into the night while Henry quietly sat handcuffed in the backseat.

As the sunrise over the distant mountains found the two riding across a desolate road in the desert, the surroundings became familiar to Henry, the road. This road, he suddenly realized, was the same one he woke up on after his escape from death. Corpus slowed down in front of a fork in the road and parked on the side of the road.

Henry leaned over the front seat and asked, "Why are we stopped?"

As Corpus let out a sigh, he turned off the ignition.

Without answering Henry, he got out of the car and opened the back door.

Henry didn't know what to do. He thought Corpus wanted him to step out, but he wasn't saying anything, not a word. He finally caught on and cautiously stepped out. Corpus unlocked Henry's handcuffs and put the cuffs back in his coat pocket. While Corpus went to the back of the car, Henry waited in the middle of the road and caressed his sore wrists. Corpus pulled out Henry's saxophone case from the trunk.

"I pulled a lot of strings to get this back," he said and handed Henry the case.

"What are you doing?" he asked and carefully slipped his hand over the handle of the case. He felt the weight of the case. It was just right.

"I chose my side, Henry."

"And what side is that?"

"The right side."

Henry placed the case on the top of the trunk and made an attempt to open it. He cracked the lid about two inches and witnessed the brass glistening from the sun above. Before he could see Harry in its entirety, he immediately shut the case.

"*No*," Henry said abruptly. "Keep him."

"You don't want it?"

"No," he said, this time more confidently. "I don't need him anymore."

Corpus grabbed the case and gazed ahead at the desolate road.

"Looks like you have two paths then," he said.

"Fork in the road," Henry replied, looking at the two roads before him. "It almost. . . poetic."

Corpus said, "I guess you can say that." He pointed to the two roads. "Back to where you came from or back home to Lansford."

"You're just going to let me walk free after everything you said?"

"I had to convince you to come with me, otherwise you'd still be drowning inside that bar."

Despite the welcoming news, a shadow of doubt ominously swelled over Henry. "But the authorities," he said, "they'll be looking for me. I can't live with constantly looking over my shoulder."

"No," Corpus said, shaking his head. "They won't. There are only four people who know what you did. Two are dead. One is in Fernando Park Medical Center. And the other is standing right in front of you, Henry."

"But. . . I. . . I wasn't. . . "

The words weren't there, even through his search.

"I know you're not a murderer, Henry," Corpus said. "And you certainly don't belong in prison. If I were in your position and my friend was beaten within an inch of his life. . ." he looked around the desert and felt a calming breeze settling over his shoulders like a cloak, ". . . I would've done the same thing." Corpus breathed in the dry desert air.

"You belong out here, in the real world." Once more, he looked around the desert. He pointed to the road ahead. "I just hope you find what you're looking for, Henry."

"I don't think that'll be too hard," Henry said with clarity.

He reached out his hand and held it there until Corpus stepped forward and shook it.

"It's be real, Henry."

"Thanks," Henry replied.

"Al," Corpus said as a restrained smile crept onto his face. "You can call me Al."

"Thanks, Al."

Corpus made his way to the car.

On the way to the car, he turned back around.

"What about the band?" Corpus asked curiously. "Will you go back to them?"

"That part of my life is over. It's time to start a new chapter."

Corpus snorted.

"Just make sure you write a good ending."

Henry nodded his head.

"I will."

Corpus opened the car door.

"Forgot," he said suddenly and reached inside the car. He grabbed an unopened water bottle from the passenger seat and tossed the bottle to Henry. "You're going to need this. . . "

Henry caught the bottle and eyed the bottle.

"No, Al," he said and tossed the bottle back to Corpus. "I won't."

"In these conditions," Corpus said, scanning around the parched desert, "you won't make it. You will break, Henry."

"I've already been broken, Al. Now, I'm just trying to put myself back together."

"Suit yourself."

Corpus placed the bottle back in the car.

Henry stepped forward and said, "There is one thing."

"Sure, Henry."

"I have this notebook. . ." he pointed at the car, ". . . It's should be inside the saxophone case."

With his trembling hands, Corpus popped open the case and found a composition notebook underneath the glistening saxophone. Attached to the notebook was a pen with the end all chewed up. He carefully reached inside and pulled out the composition notebook.

"This?" he said as he held up the bent notebook in the air.

"Yeah," Henry said. "That's it."

Corpus glanced over the composition book once more. He was about to say something to Henry, possibly about what exactly was inside the notebook or why he needed the notebook to begin with, but then after careful consideration he decided it was best to let it be and keep whatever he had to say to himself. So, the detective strolled over to Henry and handed him the notebook.

"So, I can't change your mind about the water," he said. "Can I?"

Henry shook his head and grabbed the composition notebook from his firm grip and briefly skimmed through the inside of the notebook and made sure each page was there.

Before Corpus got back inside the car, he turned back around to Henry and said tentatively, "Good luck, Henry."

Henry wasn't so experienced when it came to waving goodbye to another person; in fact, he had only waved goodbye on few occasions—none of which he could possibly remember. So, when he made the gesture, it was done more so in a robotic manner. He lifted up his arm with his fingers slightly curled, not the least waving around.

Through the rear view mirror, Corpus returned with a gesture of his own like Henry, waving almost robotically—hand raised, not moving or rotating back and forth. Then, he started up the ignition of the car and drove away on the desolate desert road never to be seen by Henry ever again.

THIRTY-NINE

SOMEWHERE between the twenty to thirty-mile mark, the tedious journey across the vast emptiness of West Sedona was starting to wear on Henry.

The desert landscape around him looked exactly the same as the last five miles. The jagged sun, now suspended highest in the sky, was hammering down on him like a newly wielded mallet over the back of his head, neck, and shoulders. Even his footsteps were long and hammering, not from the sun, but from the lack of strength in his body. There was no turning back now, Henry told himself numerous times throughout the journey, point of no return. He had to keep walking, this he knew, to keep hammering along. Walking meant moving. Moving meant surviving. His legs were extremely sore and weak. The heat was thicker too, not as dry and comfortable as it had been the previous week. His clothes had even become heavy with sweat too, which made it that much harder to walk. With each gaze throughout the desert, he felt as if Tad's ranch would manifest from across the great horizon, and then Sheila and Rebecca would be waiting for him on the porch, sipping from their glasses of iced tea, waving at him, smiling from his presence; however, the desert wouldn't allow these expectations. Henry hadn't seen a single car on the desolate road for miles. The only traces of life were from the scraggly vultures circling overhead.

Patience, vultures, he thought as he peered into the glassy blue sky above. *Your time will come.*

He said under his breath, "I'm not ready to check out just yet."

While stopping to catch his breath, Henry scanned the desert to the right and then to left of him. Not too far away he saw a unique landmark that stood out from all the other boulders and mountains. So familiar it was. The rock formation was naturally shaped like the Cathedral of Our Lady of Chartres, especially the apex, as long and conical as a spire. The sight of the unusual rock spawned another memory.

Henry reached into his pocket and pulled out the folded photograph of the two little white girls. Margaret was one of the girls' names. The other girl he didn't know. Her sister perhaps? But the name *Margaret* was first to enter his thoughts. He unfolded the photograph and recognized the same rock formation (only part of it) in the backdrop, as well as the shabby cabin, which was located not too far down the road. He held up the photograph to the desert before him and eyed the two together and then, after thorough comparison, concluded the two landscapes were identical to one another. Henry pulled his eyes back to the desolate road, the one that led directly to Tad's ranch. As before, the road stretched out like an endless blade into the horizon. Then, he turned back to the rock formation, the cabin. *More questions*, he thought. More answers. More answers led to more questions. And more questions led to other stories, more pathways. What if he was still there, alive and well? Was he writing a book? His next opus? While lying with Sheila in bed, he remembered her talking about his grandfather, an established author, Julius Hampton, and how he had two little girls and how they both disappeared and, after their disappearance, he became a recluse. Henry thought more about his grandfather, as well as the novel, *The Fire Dance*, the story about an English professor who was accused of murdering his girlfriend in his sleep, and then the other novel, *The Winds of Eastback*, which, unlike the previous novel, *The Fire Dance*, he had only read the first fifty pages. The (*Pretty Woman*-esque) story was about a totalitarian America in the year 2153 centered around two unlikely protagonists: one, a wealthy CEO for one of leading energy companies in the world called Oredine, maker of the first fully functional android, the M-1;

and the other, a penniless single mother who resorted to selling her body in order to make ends meet, and how their two lives came together after a catastrophic electrical storm destroyed both of their homes. The book was roughly around three hundred pages or so—focused heavily on the convenience of technology and the lack of connection between humanity after the merge of all races, now known as the Unican, or "Uni," for short. The short read took him no more than two days to finish before he decided to put the book aside and finish it some other time (most of the read was done in the hospital while he was sitting in the waiting room—and even then Henry had his own distractions). His grandfather, Henry gathered after reading the first novel as well as the first part of the second novel, acknowledged what downfalls could come from the rapid progression in civilization and how, in many years, decades, centuries perhaps, man would eventually become one with machine through the means of technological advancements. Unlike his grandfather, Henry knew that, in the end, the human spirit would always reign despite hardships like the ones depicted in *The Winds of Eastback*. Human beings would come together (as they always do), but Henry knew it was going to take great effort and determination. His grandfather was a pessimist who had fallen to his knees and complained about all of the bad in the world, but he never pointed out the good, a man who hid behind the walls of his house and wrote about the life he once knew when, in fact, he knew nothing about the present world. Like the character, Jacob Nadeer (from *The Winds of Eastback*), a man discarded from a life of vanity, or John Wheeler, his grandfather never hung in there long enough to give society a second chance. What could a man possibly know about the world and the wonders of it if he hadn't seen the entire world with his own eyes? What knowledge could come from a man who lived in a desert for most of his life? Sure, he wondered, he was probably incredibly knowledgeable when it came to the desert and the certain life that resided within it. But he was a recluse, as Sheila had told him. Abbey had told Henry about the time he came to visit her in Sinclair

Leprieur after he was released from prison. She told him he wasn't the same person when he left the house—he left "like a doll," she said. Then, Henry witnessed her face, not Abbey's, but Rebecca's as if she was right there in front of his eyes. The sky around him had turned to dark. The brilliant stars were winking at him from above. He was seated in a rocking chair next to Rebecca, who was sipping from a glass of iced tea: "We all deserve a *second* chance at life," she was saying to him, "that is if we are willing to move on with our lives. We have to make the best from what we got. . . "

Once more, Henry peered down the dirt road, which veered away from the main road.

"No more," he said sternly.

After serious contemplation, Henry pocketed the photograph and carried on down the road.

Another five miles in, he heard the sound of pebbles moving from a couple of boulders next to the road.

He quickly stopped in a defensive stance.

A Mexican wolf stalked up the lanky boulder and stood gracefully on top.

Henry clutched his fists.

The thin wolf had scars over one side of its face. One of his eyes was completely sealed shut while the other one remained steady on the stranger before him. Henry and the wolf shared a long stare. Having read from the stack of *National Geographics* at Ms. Craft's house during frequent session breaks, he knew in these kinds of situations to keep extremely still and not to make any sudden movements and to make himself seem larger and stronger than the animal, the alpha and not the omega.

Carefully, Henry paced forward with his chest puffed outward while keeping a keen eye on the perched wolf.

As Henry distanced himself from the scraggly wolf, the wolf howled at the bright sky.

After traveling down the same desolate road for miles, he lost track of time. At this point, he was just meandering down the road. His knees buckled a few times. Muscles cramped. He didn't have any water, energy, or strength. A couple steps in, a sudden wave of euphoria swept over his body, which caused him to stagger and stumble over the road.

Finally, he fell to his knees.

For the first time in a very long time, Henry cupped his hands together and prayed. He didn't know whom exactly he was praying to, the skies, the stars barely glistening throughout the dark blue, the desert habitat, or to a god. The One and Only God. He said a prayer for himself to safely return to Sheila and to stay strong and vigilant and to *keep* moving.

As the sun finally set, Henry decided it was best to find a place to rest.

There was no way he would make it the next day, Henry concluded, especially after having walked the entire night. He didn't have the strength to walk any farther.

After some brief searching, he ventured not too far from the highway and found a nice little rock in the middle of the desert. He gathered some twigs and shrubbery and anything that he could burn from the desert. All of the creatures of the night were out in full bloom, singing, chiming, and humming. Not too far, there was a coyote making these strange cackling-like sounds as if it was warning its friends about the meal that had been brought forth to them. He ignored such calls or warnings or various forms of communication. In order to survive the desert, he told himself, he had to become one of them, the creatures of the night. If he showed the slightest sign of weakness, the desert would get the best of him. In order to survive, he had to revert to his most primordial state. He had to catch and cook his own food and live off the land as one of them. So, Henry lived up to his word and did exactly that. He sat against the rock and used the twig to make a fire.

With hours spent twirling the twig over a flat piece of dry bark, he decided to give up. His hands were blistered. Knuckles sore.

Then, he searched his pockets. These were, after all, Tad's pants.

He lit up with both excitement and frustration.

All this time!

He breathed a sigh of great relief and used the Last Stop bar matches that he had found in his pocket to make a small fire. He didn't have to worry about running out of matches. He had at least twenty matches in here. Plenty matches to last him for the entire night and the days to come.

As he rested over the rock, he scoured the land for food.

One of night creatures came inching by his foot like a visitor saying hello, here I am, sacrificing myself for you. Henry was too tired to even flinch from the sight of the strange creature. He grabbed one of the twigs, used the sharp end, and speared the top of the tarantula. The furry thing's legs squirmed a little and then curled into a stiff position. Henry used the twig as a skewer and cooked the tarantula over the fire until it was burnt to a crisp. At first, he ate from the tarantula in bird-like pecks. The insides were much chewer than he imagined. Then, once he acquired the distinct taste of the tarantula, he proceeded with bigger bites. He forced himself to eat until the eight-legged creature was entirely consumed. Once he was done, he felt sick to his stomach. He kept the food from coming back up, though. This source of protein was going to carry him through the night as well as the next day. He did this for about an hour, spearing insects, mostly grasshoppers and beetles, and cooking them over the fire. He even managed to catch a kangaroo rat scampering back into a small burrow. Henry did this as quickly as possible before he could make sense of the idea. He placed the rodent on the ground and savagely struck it with a rock until it was no longer squirming.

Once Henry's belly was full of desert creatures, the fire started to die. So too did Henry's appetite. He preserved the little strength that he had and maintained the fire with what he had in arm's reach. He turned to the composition notebook beside him and ripped out the pages. The pages kept the fire alive for a short while. Henry keenly observed the flames, the pages, the words, and the smoke, which wreathed over the campfire like a loose string being pulled upward into the night sky. For years, Henry had kept the notebook close to him like a diary, if that was what some called it. For Henry, the notebook carried the words of *his* life. Years and years of songs, ideas, inspirations remained secret in here like a treasure chest until he exposed a part of it to the world with his band, Mona's Arch. Every once and a while either on tour or whenever he found himself alone, he would open up the notebook and bring himself back to the songs, where he was, mentally, at that point of his life, and acknowledge how far he had grown as a man. Henry continued to watch the words on each page blacken and coil and turn to ashes over the campfire. Henry ended up going through the entire notebook, each page and song, and tossed the pages into the fire. He even tossed the photograph from his pocket into the fire and watched the two girls in the photograph burn to ash. Finally, Henry was left with two pages. Out of the last two pages, one of them was unfamiliar. The words written on the page weren't from his handwriting; in fact, they were written in perfect cursive. The other page was blank, no writing or lyrics. He used the pen and decided to write Sheila a letter over the firm cover of the composition notebook:

Dear Sheila,

On July 28, 1999, I was an accessory to the murder of a Lansford Police Department Officer, Ted Backer. For years, Officer Backer controlled the streets of Lansford like a tyrant, leaving the people among them hopeless. Officer Backer was involved in countless extortion schemes, racketeering, murders, drug dealings, and everything in between. I know it's not the best way to start a letter, but it's the truth. . .

A *rustling* in the desert!

Startled, Henry stopped writing and turned toward the direction of the rustling. A coyote, possibly the same one from earlier, skittishly wandered from the brushes. The scraggly thing sniffed the lingering smoke and then went on its way.

. . . Two days prior to Officer Backer's death, Officer Backer, along with six other individuals, two of them police officers, left my best friend, T.J. Livingston, to die in a trashcan in the back of an alleyway. When I found T.J., I couldn't even recognize him. He spent days in surgery. Doctors did all they could to rearrange his face. However, he wasn't the same man. T.J. and I were like brothers. We grew up together, cried together, laughed together, and had great success together around the world. I am currently unaware of T.J.'s condition. The last time I visited T.J. in the ICU, he was fighting for his life with two broken arms and a collapsed lung and hooked up to a breathing machine. In a way, I wish those men killed T.J. so I wouldn't have to live day to day wondering whether or not he would die at any moment. So, out of revenge, I framed one of the suspects involved in the beating. His name was Jonathan Farrow. I planted the gun used to kill Officer Backer in his apartment. The remaining people who were involved in the crime were dealt with as well. You must understand, Sheila, that I did this only because I couldn't sit on my hands any longer while the real criminals of Lansford got away. I know it wasn't the right thing to do. The right thing to do was to bring these men to justice. But I had to do what I felt was best at the time. I hope one day you will forgive me. For now, I don't expect you to. Till this day, I don't have an ounce of regret from my actions. If I wasn't an accessory to Officer Backer's murder, then I would've never found you. Months after the shooting, Kerri and I took a flight to Sedona in order to clear my head from all of the craziness that was going on in my life and to find answers about my past, about the grandfather I had never met, Julius Hampton. Instead, I found love and beauty and a person whom I want to spend the rest of my waking life with. (The tears poured from Henry's eyes. A teardrop landed on the page, which caused a couple of letters from the word *past* to swell over the fresh ink.) *When I arrived in Sedona, they found us. Kerri and I were ambushed from behind and thrown inside the back of a*

car. For the first time in my life, I was scared. Avenging the death of his brother, Donnie Backer, who was also a former cop, shot Kerri in the chest, killing her instantly. Donnie wanted to kill me. But I wouldn't let him. There was something inside me telling me to hold on that much longer, that there was something special waiting for me at the end of the desert. Somehow, I managed to escape Donnie and the other two men he was with. I walked alone all night in the desert, not knowing where I was going. Guided by fate. I don't remember much after I passed out. All I remember was the darkness and then an incredible light. . .

Henry contemplated about revealing his career and how he was a famous singer, as well as saxophonist in a rock band called Mona's Arch.

I write you this letter from somewhere deep in the desert as a man who has finally accepted the crimes he has committed. Most of my memory has come back to me now. I don't have any water. Very little food. Each hour spent without you, I grow weaker. Just the thought alone of losing you is too much to bear. I don't know how much more time I have left. (Henry breathed slowly and steadied the tremor in his hand) *From the first time I laid eyes on you, I knew you were too good to be true. I was waiting for someone to pinch me or to wake me up from this dream. I was only fooling myself. Then days went by. A week. I realized that I was awake and that you were real. I got to know you better. I got to know every inch of you and yet I know deep in my heart that I have only scratched the surface. For once in my life, I feel like the planets are finally aligned in my favor and that you are there for the taking. Never have I ever met someone as special as you, the light in my darkness. Just know that even though we have only known each other for a short time, I am madly in love with you and I cannot stop thinking about you. I wish to be near you once more, to hold you in my arms, to feel your heartbeat against mine, to provide for you,* (Henry thinking) *to start a new chapter with you.*

Love, Henry Burl aka "Elvis"

As soon as Henry was done writing the letter, he tossed the remainder of the composition notebook into the fire, including the page with the names Cedric Walker, Orlando Covington, and Cedric Johnson and two police officers, Wheaten and Marson, all, of course, written in perfect cursive, not in Henry's sloppy print, folded up the letter, and placed it securely in his breast pocket. He hovered his hands over the last bit of fire. Next, he stuck his warm hands into his shirt and tried to keep warm until the sun rose.

That night at the ranch, Sheila couldn't sleep a wink. She spent the entire night staring out her bedroom window and wondering if Henry would ever return. Rebecca knocked on the door and then cracked it open. The light from the outside hallway cut through the moonlit room and shined over half of Sheila's face.

"You can't sleep," Rebecca said softly and inched her way inside the room. "Can you?"

"No," Sheila answered and turned back to the window.

"Be patient, Sheila. He'll be back."

"He promised me," she said, the tears filling her eyes.

"Don't talk like that," Rebecca replied, her tone more stern. "Have faith in him, dear."

How many more days can I last?

Henry thought: *Two more days or three?*

As Henry watched the sun rise the next morning and then set in the evening over the distant mountaintops, he could feel himself slowly fading. For miles, he had walked down the same desolate road without any food or water—the scenery the same as the day before. At night, he found another spot not too far from the highway and used the last match from his pack of matches and made a fire using the parched twigs from a desert willow and a kidneywood tree. He was too cold and exhausted to hunt for food, even though, during several instances, the food was right there at striking distance. Most of the food was insects, though. Nothing big and juicy like a kangaroo rat. But even then, if he had caught a rodent such as a kangaroo rat, the campfire was too sparse to cook the thing over. So, Henry had to make due with the little he had. Some insects crawling around him he had never seen before in his life. Some talked to him and kept him company while others just stared at him. So far, he had only caught about an hour of sleep. He spent most of the night with his eyes peeled and ears open, listening and observing nature around him. At times, the sounds, mostly the silence, were relieving and yet terrorizing at the same time. Other times, when he heard much louder and more hostile sounds cutting through the silence, sounds of animals battling to the bitter end, he kept on guard with a clutched fist and a jagged rock in the other hand, waiting for whatever beast or creature to find him. Eventually, though, the exhaustion had finally gotten the better of him.

While Henry was falling in and out of sleep, he heard an airy voice call to him throughout the darkness outside the yawning fire.

"You're almost home, Henry," the strange voice said calmly to him.

He suddenly opened his eyes and snapped his head upright.

"Who's there?" Henry said, his billowed eyes frantically searching around the dark desert.

The strange woman, who was as dark as the desert itself, stalked through the parched willows as if the desert had opened up long enough to release its likely surrogate and approached the dim campfire.

Henry groaned: "Whooo. . . I. . . I said 'Who's there?'"

Abbey manifested over the glow of the campfire and sat down on a broken tree stump across from Henry. Unlike the last time he saw her in the hospital, which he vaguely remembered from his current state of being, her face was healthy and not gaunt or sickly. She was wearing the same clothes that she wore everyday when she worked at the Depot. . . something dark and yet calming in her eyes.

As her shadowy face settled over the beating flames, she asked Henry, "Is this girl really worth dying for?"

In return, Henry said clearly, "Yes."

"Then, what are you waiting for?" She turned her head toward the sunrise building over the dark desert and said, "Go to her."

As the sun washed over his face, Henry suddenly woke with a loud gasp. Paranoid, he scoured around the desert only to find a smoking pile of burned twigs over the ground next to him.

With hardly any energy left, Henry walked on the same exact desolate road for most of the morning, hands occasionally wiping the beads of sweat falling into his eyes. But then, he realized after several swipes across his face, that he had no more beads of sweat. No perspiration, even if the temperature was much warmer than the day before. He had nothing to call his own. Nothing to show for the miles he had traveled, except the lines of his face.

When afternoon came, Henry was now dragging his feet along the road. Each step became a challenge. Still, Henry hadn't passed a single car. In fact, there were no cars on the road, which he couldn't explain. Times, he wondered if God had anything to do with the cars and the lack of them. Another mile in, his legs grew painfully tired. His eyes were now swimming around his head. Throughout his shuffle, he drifted in and out of consciousness. The darkness, so far and yet so close, was calling out to Henry. At any moment, he could drift into the darkness. How relieving it would be! He fought through the cold darkness and kept his eyes wide open. In desperation, Henry searched for saliva in his parched mouth, anything to wash down the thorn in his throat. He found none. His lips were like cracked leather, parched as well. Just when Henry thought he was about to pass out, he spotted her at a distance.

"Kerri. . ." he muttered, his racing heart nearly coming to a halt.

She was standing at the top of a mesa (familiar in size and shape), signaling to him. The dark clouds overhead parted ways. A blade of sunlight cut through the clouds and beamed down on her like a spotlight. He couldn't tell if the person standing on top of the steep, rugged mesa was Kerri. He didn't know if his mind wanted him to see Kerri, this mirage. Regardless, the sight of the person gave him that needed strength to carry on, to "go to her," as he once heard from last night's fire. He hurried toward the mesa, stumbling and staggering along the way. Before he knew it, he was trekking up the mesa. Not once did he ever question the impossibility of the climb.

Along the way, he slipped over a couple of loose rocks and tumbled down the hill. In his tumbling, he managed to grab a hold of another rock, more stable, and pull himself to safety. As he did, he found himself face to face with the razor eyes of a rattlesnake. For the shortest of time, which, for Henry, seemed to last for an eternity, he stared into the rattlesnake's primitive eyes and the reflection of himself staring back at him. In return, the rattlesnake closely studied Henry (in a way, Henry studying himself), his exhausted state. Its split tongue flickered up and down, smelling Henry and his incredible fearlessness. The rattlesnake respectfully slid back underneath the rock it had been hiding under while Henry cautiously eased himself away and continued his trek. He encountered other creatures, turkey vultures about the size of himself, feeding off the decayed leftovers of carcasses. He encountered obstacles too, steep bluffs beyond crossing, which forced him to trek up other, more unstable routes along the mesa.

When Henry finally reached the top of the mesa, all of the strength in his body was completely depleted. He reached his hand up and cupped it over the edge and tried to pull himself up to safety.

The rock below him suddenly came loose!

As his footing was about to give way, the hand of a black man reached down. His weary eyes trailed upward.

"T.J.," he said in surprise.

He reached up once more and grabbed the hand, which, over careful study, turned out to be just an old scraggy root that was in the shape of a hand. He pulled himself up the root, gripped the top of a jagged rock, and made it to the top of the mesa. There she was, standing reverently with her back turned to Henry and watching the sunset over the endless horizon. Her outfit was elegant and yet causal and comfortable. She was wearing the same red dress that she wore to dinner. However, the dress didn't have one mark of dirt or bloodstain or rip on it. The dress was blowing around in the building wind. Her dark brunette hair was blowing around her face too.

"Kerri. . . " he said with relief. "Wha. . . wha. . . what are you doing all the way up here?"

As Kerri rotated her shoulders around and took two steps closer to Henry, she crossed the brilliant rays of the sun. The glare from the sun eased from her shoulder and pierced Henry's eyes and temporarily blinded him. Henry quickly threw up his arms, shielded his eyes with his callused hands, and peered through the cracks of his fingers.

"*Kerri. . .* "

Henry's eyes wandered around in perplexity. He had used up most of his strength and willpower to climb the mesa. With no sight of Kerri around, only the pale remains of a mirage, he let out a loud and winding gasp. Then, he dropped to his knees and cried, deeply and yet quietly. At times, he cackled like a baby. And, like the sweat, Henry couldn't produce any tears from the dehydration. As he drifted into the darkness, he raked his worn fingernails over his dirty, sunburned face and yielded the tears from his eyes. No tears would come, he soon realized after he spent minutes weeping what felt like dust. The moment he became aware of his critical condition and how he was at the grip of death, a wave of panic seeped inside his thoughts, thoughts of darkness, smothering, and suffocating. Henry's sunken eyes bolted open. In small repetitions, he mouthed the words *I'm so sorry*, which spilled from his coarse lips like a whimper. Throughout each repetition, the words grew faint and distorted. His heart raced now. His breath became rapid like his heart, panting like a dog. Struggling to breath, Henry cracked open his mouth and murmured the name *Sheila* one last time. The upper part of his body suddenly fell forward over the dirt. As Henry clung to life, his hands slowly dug into the loose dirt below. His hands clutched in both agony and defeat. *This is how I die*, Henry thought. *This. . .* The wind suddenly picked up and stirred the dirt and dust from the desert all around him. The letter that he had kept in his breast pocket slipped from his wringed shirt and skipped around before his weary eyes. As he went to grab the letter, a gust of wind lifted up the note and sent it flying in the air. There, it flew like a bird flapping its wings around in the wind. Henry managed to pull up his head—just enough to watch the note carelessly fly away. Finally, he collapsed on the ground. He grunted and kicked up a small cloud of dust from his lips. Each grain of sand felt comforting over the side of his face. There, he embraced the cold presence of death, the darkness.

As soon as he closed his eyes and journeyed into the darkness, he heard the faint sounds (like a *squeak* and then a *tap, tap*) of a door closing from afar. Henry swam from the icy darkness and back into the warm light. He struggled to pull up his head. Eventually, he managed to raise his head far enough to see the land before him. Finally, he settled his wandering eyes ahead and there it was, the barn, the same exact one where he had first met Sheila. Just the thought of her holding up that scorpion in her hand had birthed life to Henry. In a frantic excitement, Henry's eyes scanned across the hazy horizon. Then, there it was, the same rock that he had sat on while gazing at the sunset. Then, there *she* was. . . a worried Sheila ambling from the house and onto the front porch with her arms folded over her chest. Henry pulled himself up to his elbows. With the wind building around him, he slid like a slug across the loose dirt.

Struggling to lift his head, Henry moaned, "Sh. . . "

The name was too hard to muster from his lips.

"Shee. . ." he cried.

His throat suddenly double clutched.

He breathed in deeply, which caused his breath to stutter.

"Sheeeee. . ."

Henry tried to speak, but the name fell short. His throat tightened up once more and nearly closed. Each time he opened his mouth, his cracked lips grew farther apart. The pain was building a foundation inside Henry, excruciating now. The pain, he gathered, was there to remind him to keep fighting, to keep surviving, to "go to her," not *her*, he realized, but the other one. Henry's upper body rose stiffly, and a thousand shades of aches ran through his body. Never had Henry longed for the pain, its bite and reassurance, until now.

In a burst of energy, the name waved throughout his body. He swallowed hard now, and even then, it felt as if a fist was being thrust down his throat.

With his raspy voice, Henry screamed the name out loudly, "SHEILA!"

Sheila miraculously caught the end of the distant voice over the horizon. The sudden call forced her to listen closely. Her breathing slowed from her chest. There was a moment when she stopped breathing altogether, only to listen over the silence, no breathing, just the faint breeze crossing the East. And if she could've controlled the winds, she would've moved the heavens and the earth to do so just to listen to that famil-iar voice once again. She pulled her sights to her right, to the West across the ranch, and spotted a small, bug-like silhou-ette kneeling over the top of the mesa. She looked twice, three times now.

"Henry. . ."

The air around Sheila suddenly went still and silent, her heart pulsing now.

She heard the shouting: "SHEILA!!!"

The name ripped through his chest.

"Oh God. . ."

As Sheila peered closely, not once taking a moment to blink or rest her eyes, Henry slowly pulled himself farther up to his knees and waved and swung his arms around in the air.

"SHEEEEE. . . LAAAAAAAAAA!!!"

With her face bloodless now, she dashed back inside the house and scrambled into the kitchen.

"Tad," she yelled through the kitchen. "Come quick!"

Tad rolled from the recliner and rushed from the living room.

They both ran back outside.

Sheila pointed up to Henry, who was crouched over.

At first, Tad couldn't see Henry.

Then, Sheila pointed closer.

Tad followed her finger.

"It's Henry," she said urgently. "Up there. Do you see?"

"I see him," he replied, his eyes widening. "What it God's name is he doing all the way up there?" Tad witnessed the panic in Sheila's face, the hurt. He couldn't stand to see her like that. He had seen that same look on Rebecca's face when they lost their son, Robbie. Goosebumps rose over his skin, mainly his arms and neck. He looked back to the house and hollered out, "Becca! Get some water! Hurry up!"

Before Tad had a chance to find Sheila, she was already dashing through the barn. She went directly to the one stall that most feared, the last one on the left.

Catching her breath, she cautiously arrived at the stall, eased open the stall door, and found She Runs With Horns snorting and stepping back into the dusty shadows. The enormous beast let out a low growl. Her big black eyes gleamed like diamonds in the shadows. The beast let out yet another growl, telling Sheila not to take one step closer or else she was getting the hoof.

"Easy, girl," Sheila whispered, holding out her hand.

She inched closer to the horse and petted the side of her scarred face. At first, the horse retracted and snorted once more. Then, Sheila shushed the horse and gazed into her big black eyes. In return, the horse steadily gazed into Sheila's eyes. *Somehow*, the horse calmed.

Sheila quickly grabbed the saddle from the mount. She carefully placed the saddle over the gray Andalusian and fastened the billet strap over her body.

"That a girl. . . "

Sheila guided She Runs With Horns from the stall, slipped her foot through the stirrup, and leaped onto the seat. She held onto the horn of the saddle and positioned herself squarely on the seat. Each breath She Runs With Horns had taken, Sheila could feel her immense strength, restrained and yet ready to be unleashed.

"Let's see what you can do, girl," Sheila said and braced herself.

She grabbed hold of the reins and thrashed them downward.

"Hehah!"

She Runs With Horns neighed and galloped from the barn and zoomed past Tad.

"I can't believe it," he said in amazement, witnessing the incredible speed of the sheepish horse. "She actually did it. Well, I'll be. . . "

Tad grabbed the closer horse to him, which was Wilmer, an Appaloosa horse, and followed Sheila through the desert.

They rode out into the desert, kicking up clouds of dust behind them.

Wilmer couldn't even keep up with She Runs With Horns.

"I'm coming for you, Henry," Sheila said to herself as she cut through the desert. "Hang on. . . "

Henry managed to stumble halfway down the mesa on his own. He tripped over a rock and rolled down the mesa and hung on for dear life over a ledge.

Once Sheila finally made it to the mesa, she didn't waste any time trekking up the small mountain.

Tad finally arrived.

He followed Sheila halfway up.

When Sheila found Henry, he was partially conscious and unable to understand any commands.

Sheila slipped her arm around Henry's torso and carried him down the mesa. Henry's weight soon got the best of her. She stumbled as well.

Then, Tad swiftly stepped in and gave Sheila an extra hand.

From there, they carried Henry to Sheila's horse, the gray Andalusian, and placed him over her back.

Out of breath, Tad exclaimed, "Get him back to the house! Hurry!"

He grabbed Sheila's shin and helped her onto the horse.

Once Sheila was on and ready to ride with Henry's body flopped over before her, Tad slapped the backside of the horse.

Sheila shouted out, "Hehah!"

By the time they got back to the house, Rebecca was already there to greet them with a pitcher of cool water and a wet towel. She helped Sheila pull Henry's lifeless body from the horse and ease him onto a flat surface on the ground. Rebecca handed Sheila the wet towel and told her to pat the sides of his face with the towel.

"I . . ." Henry slurred as he lay over the ground, his eyes moving sporadically around his head.

"Hush," Sheila said carefully and placed her finger over his cracked lips. "Save your strength."

She proceeded to dab his parched lips with the corner of the wet towel, causing a couple of droplets to seep down his throat.

With his jaw trembling violently, his eyes focused on Sheila's face above, his light.

Teary-eyed, Rebecca struggled to watch as she cupped her hand over her mouth.

As Henry's eyes rolled into the back of his head, Sheila leaned forward and kissed him over the lips. The tears fell from her eyes and landed on Henry's face.

"Henry," she begged as Rebecca placed her hand over Sheila's shoulder, "you promised you wouldn't leave me. You can't do this," she cried, louder now. "You can't come into someone's life and then leave all of a sudden. Please, Henry. . ."

Tad finally made it back to the house when Sheila was pleading with Henry.

"He doesn't have much time," he said gravely.

As Henry was drifting in and out of consciousness, Tad and Sheila slipped their arms underneath both of Henry's arms and gently hoisted him to his feet and carried him back into the house away from the sun where he finally passed out on the kitchen floor from shock.

Rebecca, who was right behind the three every step of the way, suddenly felt a gust of wind blow a sheet of paper against her ankle. She placed the pitcher of water aside and peeled the dirty, crinkled sheet of paper from her leg.

Intrigued, she unfolded the sheet of paper and skimmed through the letter inside.

"*Dear Sheila,*" she quietly read to herself, "*On July 28, 1999, I was an accessory to the murder of a Lansford Police Department Officer, Ted Backer. . .*"

Rebecca pulled her slack face from the letter, her worried eyes tracing toward the house where Tad and Sheila tended to Henry.

"Rebecca!" Tad shouted from inside the house. "I need your help in here!"

"Coming," she drawled and rushed back into the house.

FORTY

IN front of Fernando Park Medical Center, about twenty miles outside the city of Tucson, two Arizona police officers escorted former police officer for the Lansford Police Department, Chris Wheaten, from the entrance of the hospital in a wheelchair. The former officer was hunched over in shame. He was wearing a black bomber jacket over his shoulders and shielding his face from the media. Camera flashes were glimmering all around him and forcing him to seek cover behind the jacket. News reporters were cramming their microphones underneath the jacket and into Chris's face and asking him questions like "How long have you been laundering money for the LPD?" or "Why did you do it, Wheaten?" or "How do you feel about spending the rest of your life in jail, Wheaten?" Of course, the reporters didn't get any response from the former police officer. Instead, they received a stiff arm from the escorting officers.

Corpus shouldered his way through the rowdy crowd in the parking lot and walked up to Lieutenant Reed and his partner, Merrotti, who was wearing a sling over his shoulder and slightly clinching from the detective's presence.

Corpus tossed Reed the badge and proceeded past the group of cruisers.

With his face left in surprise, Reed glanced down at the badge in his palm.

Grimacing, Reed asked, "Where the hell are you going, Detective?"

"I quit," he said confidently and strolled away, never to be seen again, at least not in Lansford.

At Mount Wilson Medical Center, a small hospital about half the size as Fernando Park, where Henry was admitted after his condition worsened, Rebecca and Tad waited patiently outside the hospital room while Sheila sat next to Henry's bedside.

Rebecca said finally, "I have to tell her, Tad."

"Honey. . ."

"She must know."

Tad sighed.

"I don't think that's a good idea, honey. But. . ." he was massaging her shoulder and doing his best to downplay the situation, ". . . but I'd prefer she know now than later. I just don't want to see Sheila get hurt."

"I agree."

"If she found out about it, then—"

"I know," Rebecca interrupted. "She would never speak to me ever again." She thought for a moment, thought about Sheila's reaction. Then, she said abruptly, "I'm going to tell her, Tad."

"Are you sure?"

"Yes," she said. "I'm sure."

Rebecca quietly inched into the hospital room where Sheila was stroking the top of Henry's hand and telling him a story about the time she went skiing for the first time in Flagstaff and how she was pressured into going down the black diamond trails, which resulted in her breaking her ankle. The thought of her breaking her ankle caused her to laugh, not from the pain that she endured from the accident, but from how ignorant she was at the time for listening to her friends.

Rebecca said from behind, "How is he?"

With her eyes flickering over her shoulder, she said, "Still resting."

"Sheila?"

"Yes."

"May I have a word with you outside?"

She pulled her hand from Henry's and faced Rebecca.

"Is everything okay?" she asked.

Halfway during the question, Sheila recognized the grimness worn tightly over Rebecca's face.

"Sure," she said and followed Rebecca into the hallway outside the hospital room where Tad excused himself and grabbed a cup of coffee from the cafeteria downstairs.

Rebecca reached her hand into the back pocket of her blue jeans and pulled out a folded up letter.

"I found this outside the house." She handed Sheila the letter and then carefully took a step back. "I was wondering whether or not I was going to give it to you. But then I realized it wasn't my decision to make."

"What is it?"

"Read it for yourself."

With the letter in hand, Sheila walked away from Rebecca and read the letter to herself a few rooms down from Henry's room. She read the first couple of lines of the letter. The sudden intensity of the letter forced her to the tile floor below. There, while sitting with her back against the wall, her elbows positioned over her knees, and her rear on the floor, she read the letter closely with both intrigue and distress. By the time she reached the end of the letter, she wasn't drawn to tears as Rebecca had expected. Yet, she was left in a state of disbelief. So much had been said in so little time. The letter was filled with so much hate, she thought, and love.

When she finally finished reading the letter, she turned to Rebecca, who was nibbling on her fingernails and waiting anxiously outside the hospital room.

Using the wall behind her as leverage, Sheila stood up from the floor and walked away before Rebecca could muster out a single word from across the hallway.

Outside the emergency room, Sheila found an elderly man smoking a cigarette on a bench near the automated doors. She bummed a cigarette as well as a disposable lighter from the old man, who told Sheila to keep the lighter since it was low on butane. Sheila had never smoked a cigarette in her life. So, of course, after the first couple of drags, she coughed and nearly blew chunks all over the sidewalk in front of a couple of nurses. Somewhere between the fourth or fifth drag, the nicotine rush melted away the stress from her body and thoughts. Now, everything was clear to her. And there was only one thing left to do. Sheila sat down alongside the curb, held up the letter in her hand, and then burned the letter with the lighter until there was nothing left of it but ash.

After spending four days in the hospital, Henry was released with a clean bill of health and sent on his way. Doctor's orders: rest, plenty of it.

For the entire day, Henry did as the doctor ordered and rested in bed. During his stay at the hospital (except for the first day or two), he didn't get much sleep. Most of the time, his mind was in a fog from all of the fluids and medicine. He also couldn't sleep from the constant interruptions and noises. After visiting hours, he caught maybe two or three solid hours of sleep. One night, the nurse gave Henry a little something to ease his mind. The nurse called it the "wonder drug." Whatever the nurse had given him worked, and he caught at least six or seven good hours of sleep. The only side effect was that his head felt like a vibrating triangle.

When he woke from a solid ten-hour sleep (no interruptions, no "wonder drugs"), he felt like a brand new man.

During the walk downstairs, Henry held onto the banister and ambled into the foyer where he found Sheila calmly sitting on the front porch and gazing at the sun hovering over the tablelands. He gingerly opened the screen door and strolled outside. Before Henry could take another step onto the porch, Sheila hurried from her seat on the glider and grabbed Henry's hand.

"Did you sleep?" she asked, guiding Henry to the glider.

"Yeah," Henry said with relief and curled up next to Sheila. "A little."

She ran her hand across the side of Henry's rested face.

"Your color looks much better."

"I feel better," he said with a grin on his face. "Like a million bucks."

While they gazed at the sunset before them, they both sat—except for the faint sound of the glider's *squeak*—in a calming silence on the porch.

"Listen," Sheila said mindfully. "I never wanted to bring it up while you were in the hospital." She paused for a second. "Tad told me when you were gone tha—"

"The truth. . ." Henry interrupted. "He told you the truth."

"So your name really is Henry," Sheila said, gradually smiling.

"Yeah."

"And I was starting to get the hang of the name Elvis."

"Me too," he said and pulled Sheila closer to his body.

She squinted her eye with both confusion and curiosity.

"I just have one question."

"Sure."

"What in the world is a mesaterrestrial?"

Henry smirked.

"It's. . . it's kind of. . . how do I say. . . " he tilted his head in brief thought, ". . . complicated."

"Well, I'm not going anywhere anytime soon."

"Neither am I, Sheila," Henry said and smiled down at Sheila. "Neither am I."

As Sheila leaned over and rested her head over Henry's chest, she said quietly, "I don't mean to put you on the spot, but. . ."

". . . But you are anyway."

"Well," Sheila said optimistically, "I was hoping maybe you'd like to serenade a girl for old time's sake."

"Serenade?" Henry suddenly blushed. "Honestly, I've never serenaded a girl before."

"Really? Never?" With a smile stretching across her face, her teeth glistening brightly, Sheila gazed into Henry's eyes. "Mr. Rock Star," she said, "are you telling me that you've never poured your aching heart out to a girl before? All rock stars have a muse. Right?"

"A muse?"

"Of course, silly!"

"Well," he said, "I guess so. I guess it depends on how much of an impact that certain person made in your life or how far you fell in love."

"And how far did you fall?"

Henry said seriously, "Far enough."

With her hand, Sheila rubbed Henry's side.

"When you get your strength back," she said and smiled, "I would love to hear a song."

Henry shrugged his shoulders and said, "It's a deal."

They shook hands.

"Deal," Sheila said, pulling her hand from Henry's. Her eyes suddenly flashed with awareness. "I forgot to give you this at the hospital." Sheila reached into her breast pocket and pulled out the ballerina figurine. Pink leotard. White tutu. The piece was still together, not broken. A crack was running down one of the forearms from where the glue had loosened when it fell against the hard asphalt. "I told Tad about. . . you know. . . your special friend. . . the Kerri girl?"

"That's right," Henry replied suspiciously and listened closer.

"When you were in the hospital, Tad drove back to where he found you and found this lying on the side of the road. It must've fallen from your pocket."

Sheila handed the marred figurine to Henry.

"How about that?" he said in a daze as he carefully studied the small figurine between his fingers.

Another lost memory came back to Henry and nearly knocked the wind out of him. Sheila didn't think much of the reaction. She took it, more or less, as a man closing the door to one part of his life and opening up another. Before Henry took the flight to Sedona, he spent most of his time piddling around the living room of his condo (when he wasn't visiting T.J. at LMC). One day, Henry was putting away some of his mother's photo albums and storage boxes, as well as memorabilia from his childhood. On the way to the bedroom, his eyes crossed the tiny ceramic limb of a ballerina on the hardwood floor next to the couch. Out of curiosity, he moved the storage boxes next to the closet and went back into the living room where he picked up the limb off the floor. The limb was from the ballerina, Henry gathered after a thorough examination. He completely forgot what he had done. The night only remained in bits and pieces: finishing a bottle of wine—two or three maybe—spilling red wine over his mother's photographs that he had been riffling through all night, and then, out of rage, throwing his mother's music box against the wall and breaking it to pieces. Even more curious as to what the limb was doing on the floor, he kneeled down next to the couch, lifted up the front skirt, and found the remaining pieces of the ballerina figurine on the hardwood floor. He managed to pull out the remaining pieces from underneath the couch. Now, with all of the broken pieces in his hand, he grabbed a bottle of superglue from the kitchen drawer and superglued the ballerina back together.

Sheila nodded at the ballerina figurine.

She asked, "Who did it belong to?"

Henry was suddenly pulled from the flashback with the question. He had only caught the very end of the question—mainly the word *belong*—but he knew the answer as if it was right there on the tip of his tongue.

"My mother," he said as he gazed into Sheila's brown eyes, "it belonged to my mother."

He pulled Sheila even closer to his body and wrapped his arms around her.

"So," Sheila said, looking up at Henry, "is it over?"

"Yeah," he said closely to her ear. "It's over."

"They won't come for you?"

"No," Henry said, his voice soft and calming. "They won't."

As Henry sat quietly next to Sheila, he thought about the letter that he wrote to Sheila next to the campfire and wondered if she somehow retrieved the letter from the desert after it had been blown away from the gust of wind and if she did, in fact, retrieve the letter, did she have the letter on her person or did she destroy the letter after reading it. Would she bring up the question again? Most importantly, that one question: Is it over? Or would the question fade away and die like a bad idea?

Henry never asked her, though, about any of these suspicions that he had.

Instead, he focused on the figurine of the ballerina between his fingertips and remembered what T.J. had once told him about Screw's apartment key and why exactly he kept it on his person like a rabbit's foot. "It reminded me of the awful place I used to live at," T.J. said to Henry.

With this in mind, Henry felt it was best to keep the figurine on him, not to remind him of the awful place that he used to live at, as T.J. had once told Henry, but to remind himself of the one woman who taught him the morals of life and how to never take things for granted.

After Mona's Arch made their split official in the spring of 2000, Socks returned home to Clever and went on to become a music teacher at Dermot High School. He married his high school sweetheart in 2005 and had three kids.

Two years after the split, Deon started up his own band called Redbone. They had brief success with their debut album. In 2009, he died from pancreatic cancer.

William bought a yacht and had quadruplets, all girls. He
currently lives at Chelsea Row Bay with his family.

Geordie went back to his old band, Stella's Harbor. In 2003, they went on to win another Grammy for their hit song, "The Cat's Paw."

One year after the incident behind Frankie's, T.J. was finally discharged from Lansford Medical Center. He spent three years in a rehabilitation center where he made little progress. In 2006, he was admitted into Calvary Memorial Hospital where he died from pneumonia.

Henry and Sheila eventually moved from Arizona and relocated to Taylor's Stand where they had a daughter named Catherine and started up a local record store called Milky Way Discs.

On Saturday, March 20, 2004, four years after their split,
Henry and the rest of Mona's Arch decided to release the
songs recorded at the Hit Box. The album was called *Nothing Lasts Forever.*

E P I L O G U E

H O M E C O M I N G

So far, he had been to four pawnshops in only one month.

And this was only the second Sunday into the month of September.

Every Sunday, at the crack of dawn, Henry would high-light one of the pawnshops from the page long list that he had printed out from the Internet. He preferred the feel of paper in his hands, the coarseness and the way his marker slid grace-fully across the page, as did most people his age who hadn't succumb to modern technology. Not like that "glass. . . plastic. . . stuff," as Henry prattled to Sheila when-ever the contentious subject of modern day technology en-tered the dinner conversation. After living forty-four years with Henry, knowing all too well about his quirks and what made him tick, all Sheila could do was to avoid the subject as best she could and whenever it did come to light mistakenly or through trivial matters, brace for impact as Henry vented about the lack of quality in present day merchandise or how they had to replace a dishwasher or dryer every two years.

953

Not like the good ole days where things were built to last. "I want to hold something built with a pair of hands!" Henry would rant over the kitchen table. "I want something that a human being created, not some tin can!" Whenever he found himself alone after an argument or a debate that turned sour or rancorous with a customer or his neighbor, Flynn, who moved to Taylor's Stand two years ago from New Jersey, a part of himself knew it wasn't worth getting all worked up about and that things just happened and he had to "roll with the punches," as a good friend once told him, in order to not let change get the best of him. Henry never let the modern world touch him. In fact, Henry enjoyed the thrill of the chase, knowing that he was still out there, which meant there was still a chance that he could find him. Henry reinforced these ambitions with keeping his house stocked with everything vintage. Mainly during the summers, they would be forced to adapt with the new dishwasher or new dryer only because they couldn't find an older model from their time and if they did find one, it would've come from Hank's Junkyard, missing parts and all, and not even worth the headache. Half of the storage room was filled with boxes of paper that Henry had stocked up on before the purge seven years ago. The printer wasn't so hard to find, not like he imagined. One day at the store, a man told Henry that he was trying to sell his printer instead of throwing it away in the trash. Word had gotten around town that Henry was a man who collected things, old things like printers or machines—"toys" was what Sheila had called them. Most of the items were ancient things that had been tossed away from society and replaced with something more sleek and pretty and even worse, replaced with something that didn't even physically exist. Like the printer, Henry collected other obsolete things like typewriters, vintage record players (he even found a Crosley similar to the one Ms. Craft had loaned him), CD players, jukeboxes, DVD and VCR tape players, televisions, computers, and most importantly, paperbacks. In his study, he had an entire library of paperbacks from mystery novels to Tad's western novels that he collected (Tad passed in the winter of

2018). Most of the items, the various players and the computers, were, in fact, bought from several pawnshops around the Lansford area, as well as a couple of pawnshops clear across the country. But none of these old, fossilized things compared to the one thing that he was in search for the most. As of now, Henry had over sixty-three pawnshops crossed out on the list. A handful of them were within at least a two or three hour drive. Others were a day's drive. Henry's next search brought him to High Point, North Carolina, his farthest drive yet. He ended up driving all day Sunday and through the early half of Monday where he traveled across the Appalachian Mountains and into the Piedmont Triad. The rumor was that it was sold to a man who went by the name of Tyson Law, an avid saxophone collector firstly and American history teacher secondly, who, like Henry, spent his days off hopping from one pawnshop to another. So, like a sleuth, Henry stayed close on his trail. When Henry arrived at the furniture capital of the world, High Point, a small city outside Greensboro, he was given the same runaround as before: the saxophone was once held at the store, but then the dealer later sold the saxophone to yet another person, this Tyson person. And from what Henry had witnessed after he pursued yet another lead, this man, Tyson Law, who had supposedly bought the saxophone from the pawnshop, was most definitely sitting like a king now (a three story house, which was located in a predominantly white neighborhood in Greensboro—the wealthy residents most notably known by locals as having "Old Money"). After a couple passes through the neighborhood, it didn't take long for Henry to realize that he didn't buy the house from his teaching salary. Either that or he suddenly won the lottery. Like the others prior to Tyson, he had done the one thing that Henry feared the most. *If I was only one step quicker*, Henry told himself time and time again after he ended up falling short.

When Henry finally returned back home to Taylor's Stand on a Wednesday afternoon, he decided once and for all to give up on his search for Harry as he had promised Sheila the week before and then the week before that. Henry knew that three times was stretching his luck. Four times? Maybe? Sheila didn't mind her husband's persistence, how he wouldn't stop until he walked through that door with a saxophone case in his hand. After all, the search kept him active, which was the best remedy for his age, and his mind was as sharp as a blade. On the downside, Sheila had grown tired of seeing her husband's face when he returned home from his search every Sunday or Wednesday or whatever day he would come back from his travels. Every time Henry would return home from wherever the search had led him, either it be High Point or Topeka or Jacksonville or wherever, Sheila would ask her husband the same question whenever he would step through the door and do so with a trace of optimism in her voice, "Any luck, Henry?" In return, her husband would simply shake his head, give her the same exact expression as he did before, and then stroll back to his study. The search for Harry went on like this for three years: Henry keeping close to his trail like a bloodhound to a nasty stench. Some days, he would drive over nine hours in hope of finding Harry, but only find a handheld game console like a Game Gear for Amy or something outdated that some spoiled kid had pawned away. At the end of the day, Henry finally realized, he would receive the same outcome.

The final pages from *Missing the Edges*:

Like Heroin was in its early stages.

We recorded enough tracks to put out an EP, but not an entire album. At nights, we did the small gigs here and there, making enough money for the drive back home and maybe a happy meal if we were lucky. But it wasn't enough to make a living. So far, we had already gone through three different guitarists, all three turning out to be as unreliable as expired condoms. While I was working a couple of jobs on the side, the twins were in the works of finding a new guitarist. They said they knew a guy who knew a guy who lived in Philadelphia and that he wasn't as flaky as the other guitarists we had worked with. They told me he was the "real deal." About two months later, it turns out that the twins were right. We added two more songs, "Punch Drunk," and "The Sex Train," to the EP and distributed demos between Lansford and the surrounding cities. Even though we were hitting up the right venues and earning the right publicity, the money wasn't steady. Like most of the guys, including André, I worked my fair share of minimum wage jobs. One in particular was serving espressos to the yuppies off Park Avenue at a café called Beret. The great thing about working at an establishment like Beret was that you didn't have to worry about dragging your ass around throughout the day. Plus, you could skip the whole making-your-own-coffee thing in the morning, which shaved off at least ten or twenty minutes from the morning routine. If you needed a little "pick-me-up," the caffeine was always at your disposal. Mornings typically started out with the strongest cup of coffee, a dark roast with two bags of Sweet N' Low. The French really know how to make a robust cup of coffee. Normally, I went in at around five o'clock to do mostly prep work: cleaning counters, stocking up on merchandise, assisting bakers. If Trade Street was backed up with traffic, which typically it was on Mondays through Thursdays, then I would take Laurel Avenue and cut through two alleyways. See, the thing about the shortcuts was that you had to watch out for the muggers. And there were a lot of them, especially after my shift. I hardly had a dime to my name, so I didn't have much to worry about. Just the ones who wanted something other than money. If I took Laurel, then I passed Josette Park, which meant I passed a man whom I like to call Shark Eyes. Shark Eyes was a homeless man who loitered around the park with a German shepherd who weighed just as much as his owner. He was an older man who wore raggedy clothes, a brown coat that looked two sizes too small for him with spit marks on the side of the collar, a holey blue sweater, a pair of gray slacks, and sneakers with soles giving me the tongue. And he reeked of turpentine. Every time I passed him on my bike, his eyes were always on me like a shark. He didn't say much to anybody, nor did he carry around one of those cardboard signs or a cup full of coins like the ones on Market Street. He just stood there with a worn piece of luggage at his feet, his dog next to him, and keenly watched the cars ride by on the street. Shark Eyes. I always ignored the man and proceeded to work. One, it was way too early in the morning to deal with people, homeless or not. And two, I desperately needed caffeine. One day, the traffic was backed up as usual. I was thirty minutes late to work. So, I ended up taking Laurel Avenue. As I made the turn onto Park Street, the chain from the sprocket on my bike came loose. The backpack took most of the fall. I got a scratch on my elbow. Nothing serious. Thankfully, nobody was around to see the fall. As I was tending to my bike in a sort of an inescapable defeat, a waft of turpentine came over me. My first reaction was me rolling my eyes, followed with the word *great* projecting from my mouth. I looked over my shoulder and saw none other than Shark Eyes and his German shepherd. He was standing over me, but not looking down at me. Honestly, I was somewhat frightened by his casual nature. I had never seen him up close, never close enough to witness the years on his face. He kneeled down until he was now staring directly into my face and asked me if I needed any help. I was too exhausted to deal with the bike. Plus, he didn't appear as if he meant any harm like the ones off Laurel Avenue. So, I let him. Turns out it was an easy fix. He reattached the chain onto the sprocket and wiped his hands clean as if he was doing me a favor. After he helped me with my bike, he pulled me aside and told me that he figured out the secret to life. Despite the hangover, I was intrigued from what Shark Eyes had to say. Another part of me was pessimistic. What good could possibly come from a man living on the streets? Obviously, this "secret" hadn't done him much good. I listened to what he had to say anyway.

"Never look down," Shark Eyes told me and then pulled me even closer. "Or you might miss out on life."

This expression was something you would hear when you were a juvenile or when you brought home a bad test grade and a parent or teacher told you to keep your head up, to try harder, never look down, or before you flush the toilet, never look down, or when you're tying your shoes, never look down. When he said he knew the secret of life, I was expecting something like: Go buy a dog or make sure to exercise everyday or read a good book or eat an apple a day. But never something as vague as never look down!

When I asked him what his name was, he told me, "Harry."

He said his name was Harry.

I said, "Like the character in those movies?"

"Dirty Harry?"

"That's the one."

Then, Harry grinned and said, "But only much more handsome."

That was the last time I saw Harry. I don't know what happened to him. But what he said stayed with me, especially through T.J.'s passing, and even as I write these closing words of my story. For the rest of the day, I took what the homeless man in Josette Park said with a grain of salt. Later on in my life, whenever I found myself in a state of reflection, I thought more about that one comment. "Never look down," Harry said to me, "or you might miss out on life." In a way, Harry, a man who probably didn't even have a penny to his name or a living relative whom he could call his own, understood that all forms of life should be treasured individually. I like to think of Harry as an extraordinary man in an ordinary world who wandered the earth with goodness in his heart and who constantly kept an eye on the evolving life around him, providing his services even if it was as effortless as extending a hand whenever it was needed or looping a chain onto the sprocket of a bicycle. I would like to think of Harry as a man who was sent by God, reminding us of the little things that bring us together. From then on, I tried my best to do as Harry had told me in Josette Park, to never look down even after I crashed or stumbled along the way. Instead, I always kept my eyes ahead on the pathways I paved for myself, and no matter what came my way, I always kept moving like a hummingbird.

Starlet typed the last word of the memoir, *hummingbird*. She cracked her knuckles, exhaled greatly, and eased back in her cushioned chair with a sense of victory. She was wearing a red turtleneck sweater with a pair of reading glasses hanging around her neck. Her hair was now grown out, not shaved, white and curly and held in a silk beige bandana. Her face was layered with wrinkles.

As Starlet slid the typed page from the typewriter and placed the piece of paper on a stack of already typed pages, a hummingbird suddenly zipped across the garden window before her. Her tiresome eyes moved lazily toward the window. There, the hummingbird was sipping from the red feeder.

Before she had a chance to get a closer look, the hummingbird zoomed away.

Next to the window hung a piece of paper on the wall. On the paper, there was a poem written by Robert Frost. The poem was called *Wind and Window Flower.*

As her eyes crossed the poem, the words, a sudden feeling of morose swept over her thoughts. In a trance, Starlet sighed greatly and reflected over the book, mainly about Henry and what happened on the night of July 28, 1999, and the days following, as Starlet did occasionally throughout the day.

She redirected her attention to the stack of papers and, with her frail hands, flipped them upside down, revealing the first page, the title of the memoir, *Missing the Edges.*

"Done," Starlet said to herself and grabbed a pen from a coffee mug that she had turned into a penholder.

With two quick strokes, she crossed out the word *deadline* over the date Friday, August 26th space on the 2044 calendar.

Below deadline read, "Meeting with V at 3:30."

While easing from the chair, Starlet heard a sudden knock on the door.

"Come in," she said with surprise.

The door cracked open.

"Mom," the resonant voice said from the doorway.

The middle-aged man's skin was fairly lighter than Starlet's. He had hazel eyes, shaved head, and bulky shoulders. His outfit included a black silk shirt, khakis, and a silver watch that cost as much as the boat on the dock.

Starlet turned to the door.

"Yes, Henry."

"I was just checking up on you," Henry said and entered the study room. Each green wall, except for the one with the garden window in front of Starlet's workstation, was lined with cherry wood bookshelves. She had all kinds of books from Aesop (and his fables) to Richard Yates and then everything in between all arranged in alphabetic order by authors, excluding Z.

"So, how's it coming?" he asked, walking up to Starlet.

"Guess what?"

"You're finished."

His eyes widened with excitement.

Starlet smirked and bobbed her head yes.

Henry stepped forward and hugged his mother.

"I'm so proud of you, Mom," he said into her shoulder. "For a minute, you had me worried. You barely ate anything for lunch. I was beginning to wonder if this book of yours was making you ill."

"Well," she said finally. "I'm done." She looked into her son's bright eyes. "And what a relief it is."

"I can imagine," he said. "I bet you feel a thousand pounds lighter."

Starlet laughed out loud.

"You have no idea," she said gladly. "So much so that I could probably walk across water." She paused as her eyes crossed the time on the wall clock. The time: 2:28. "I almost forget. I'm supposed to be meeting my friend in about an hour in Taylor's Stand."

Henry furrowed his brows.

"What friend?" he said.

Starlet hesitated.

"Ah," she said, thinking. "My editor."

"In Taylor's Stand? That's at least an hour away. Aren't you going to be late?"

Starlet paced toward her desk and said, "He's a reasonable man."

"But what about Silas?" Henry said, loudly this time as he followed Starlet through the study. "We drove over four hours to see you and you're going to run off to see this friend of yours."

Starlet patted Henry on the chest and then leaned forward and kissed him on the cheek.

"I shouldn't be gone long, sweetie."

"How about I drive you?"

"No," she said abruptly. "That won't be necessary. Just because I'm an old lady doesn't mean I can't take care of myself."

As she walked from the study and grabbed her purse from the kitchen table, she glanced out the window at the weathered dock.

Dangling their feet in the lake's water were Henry's son, Silas, who was ten years old, and his wife, Celeste. In a sudden outburst, Celeste splashed Silas with water. Silas flinched and shielded his face from the water, which caused him to knock over the small clay vase next to him. Some of soil inside the vase spilled over the dock. Shock rippled over Silas's face. "Look what you did!" he shouted out almost to himself as he tried to scoop the leftover soil back into the vase. "I'm so sorry," Celeste said and helped Silas with the strange plant. The sight of the two interacting, regardless of the circumstances, drew a smile onto Starlet's face.

"Aren't you forgetting something," Henry said from the study.

Starlet turned her shoulder and saw her son pointing at the textbook-sized manuscript on the desk.

"Right," she said after a brief pause. "What would I do without you, Henry?"

As she reached down and picked up the manuscript from the desk, she came across an old vinyl record. The band on the cover was her band, Mona's Arch. The photograph was taken in New York after their success with the album *Rule or Be Ruled*. The band was all gathered around, posing in their own unique way in front of a pale backdrop. In the middle of the cover stood Starlet, who was dressed in a beige silk pirate shirt, baggy and tucked into a pair of black spandex, and silver earrings, which were like tiny hula-hoops upon her shoulders. She had a flattop—parted on one side—with both sides of her head shaved like the character May Day from *A View to a Kill*. Next to Starlet was Henry, dressed in his patent white collared shirt underneath a black blazer. His hair was shaped in the Roman Numeral 5. A smashed crown (like the ones the royals used to wear) was resting underneath his foot. Next to Henry was T.J., standing at a slant with arms crossed, wearing a gold sweatshirt with a pink unicorn graphic and a purple Lakers hat cocked to the side. To the right of Starlet was William, squatting. He was dressed in a brown suit with his greasy hair parted like a wave on one side. To the left of T.J. stood Socks, who had his bangs covering one side of his pallid face. He was wearing a red and black jumpsuit and holding a chrome space helmet down by his side. And then finally, Deon, who was standing on the far left. His beard was long and thick. He was wearing a solid black tee shirt with a green scarf wrapped around his neck.

Starlet couldn't help but smile, greater this time, from the sight of the *Greatest Hits* cover. Her eyes trailed upward and wandered around the study until they came across the cassette tape perched on the top shelf. The name on the casing read, "CYBORG."

Next, her eyes came across a strange black puppet seated on the edge of a bookshelf. The puppet was dressed in her trademark white pirate shirt and black spandex and wearing these gold looped earrings over its ears. When her son, Henry, asked her about the puppet and where exactly it came from, Starlet told him that she "burrowed" the puppet when, in fact, she stole it from the *Sesame Street* set after their second album release, *Machine Mistress*.

On another shelf perched Henry's arm guard—the brass one that he wore frequently while performing on stage—as well as during the "New Weapons" music video shoot.

From behind, Henry asked, "Is everything all right?"

"Yes. . ." she said in a trance and placed the manuscript inside a satchel.

"Are you sure you don't want me to drive you?"

Henry followed his mother through the hallway.

Starlet sharpened her eyes.

"You tell Celeste and Silas I'll be right back," she said sternly. "When I get back, we'll take out the boat. How does that sound?"

"Mom," Henry said and made an attempt toward Starlet. As he walked through the hallway, the side of his body accidentally knocked a stack of mail from the table. The mail slid over the hallway. As Henry was picking up the mail, he came across one envelope in particular. The name on the envelope read, "Buddy Egghorn."

"Who's *Buddy*?" he asked, holding up the closed envelope.

Starlet forced a sigh.

"Just a friend," she said and snatched the envelope from her son's hand. She placed the envelope in her satchel while Henry placed his hand over his hip and shifted his weight to one side of his body.

"You sure do have a lot of friends that I don't know about."

"Well, I'm a friendly girl," she said, giggling.

Starlet grabbed her wool coat from the hallway closet.

"Remember, when I get back. . ."

"Yes," Henry said annoyingly. "I heard yo— " a phone suddenly beeped from the inside of his pocket. He reached inside his pocket, pulled out the slender, glass-like phone, and peered at the face projecting from the glowing screen. He turned back to his mother and mumbled, "I have to take this call."

"Of course, you do," Starlet said disappointedly. "I won't be long, Henry. We'll take the boat out when. . ."

Even though Henry heard his mother's trailing remarks about taking out the boat when she got back from Taylor's Stand, he ignored her and proceeded to the guest room closest to the kitchen where he shut the door behind him.

In a youthful excitement, Sheila poked her head through the cracked doorway of the office room and said jubilantly, "They're here!"

Henry pulled himself away from the jigsaw puzzle, *The Last Flight of the Fable Maker*, and lit up with excitement. Throughout the puzzle, he was going over the advice that his doctor, Doctor Singh, had given him about the arthritis and how it was important for him to keep active throughout the day. Doing puzzles all day was certainly a great way to keep his mind busy. However, after a while, the joints in his hands would stiffen with excruciating pain. Henry grabbed the cane, which was made from oak (the handle was in the shape of a paw and made from brass), from the table and eased himself from the chair.

As he shuffled from the study, his daughter, Catherine, and her husband, Maurice, were walking inside the house. Sheila hugged and kissed the two, Catherine and Maurice, while Henry's granddaughter came sprinting around her father's as well as her grandmother's legs and inside the house.

"Grandpa!" she yelled out and leaped into Henry's arms.

"Hello, little angel," he said happily and lifted up his granddaughter, Amy, in his arms.

With her hand over her large belly, Catherine waddled over to Henry and gave him a hug.

"Hello, Dad," she said, smiling.

"It's good to see you, Cathy," Henry said, kissed her on the cheek, and looked down at her round belly. "How's the baby?"

"Kicking a lot lately."

"Are you eating good?"

"So-so," Catherine answered with a slight shrug of her shoulders. "Not like I did with Amy." She turned her attention to her daughter. "Speaking of Amy. You know she couldn't stop talking about you on the way over here."

"Is that right?"

"Can we go to the fun store, Grandpa?"

"The *fun* store?" Henry repeated and then glanced over at Sheila. "We can go to the fun store, but only if it's okay with Grandma."

"You two go on," she said and placed a chicken casserole inside the oven. "Just be back in time for supper."

It was roughly a two-minute drive to downtown Taylor's Stand.

Both Henry and Amy decided to walk, since the walking was good for Henry. At least, that was what Doctor Singh said.

They finally arrived at the "fun store," which was actually a small pawnshop called *Rusty's Stuff.* Henry used the paw end of his cane and opened the door for Amy. A cowbell rang out from above the doorway, which forced the jubilant owner, Rusty, to stop reading from the epaper and acknowledge the two customers.

"Hello there, Rusty," Henry said with a wave.

"Henry!" Rusty replied from behind the counter. He turned off the tablet, placed it aside, and greeted Henry.

"How are you doing today, old friend?"

"I can't complain, Henry," Rusty answered and shook Henry's hand. "Each day I wake up is a good day. Say, I heard you're selling the store. Is that true?"

"Yeah," Henry said with a sigh. "I'm afraid I'm getting too old."

"What about Sheila?"

"She says she has a couple of years left in her, but she said she'll only go in if I'm there."

"That's sweet."

"That's my Sheila," Henry said, tilting his head.

"She's a wonderful woman, that Sheila." Rusty patted Henry on the shoulder. "You're a very lucky man, Henry. So, what brings you two in here today?"

"I was looking for a gift for Amy."

"We have all kinds of gifts." Rusty looked down at Amy. "Hi there, Amy."

"Hi," she said softly, her big eyes wandering around the store.

"You remember Rusty from last time."

Amy didn't respond. She was too busy looking around the store.

"She's a little shy."

"That's no problem," he said. "Me, I remember my mother couldn't get a word out of me until I was a teenager. Now, she's says I talk way too much."

Henry laughed and glanced down at Amy.

"So, Amy," Rusty said. "Are you looking for anything in particular?"

Amy bobbed her shoulders.

"I tell you what," Henry said to Amy. "Why don't you look around and come get me when you find something you like."

"Okay," she mumbled and roamed through the pawn store.

"Cute kid," Rusty said, folding his arms over his chest.

"She's my little angel," Henry said, keeping his eyes on Amy as she made her rounds through the cluttered aisles.

Rusty extended his hand as the cowbell rang out from behind.

Another family walked into the store.

"I got to run, Henry," he said and shook Henry's hand. "It was good to see you again."

"You too, Rusty," Henry said and followed Amy through the aisles.

As Amy was looking over a section of antique clocks, at least two dozen of them, all old and dusty and varying in shapes and sizes, Henry was drawn to one particular instrument protruding from the shelf.

"Stay close, Amy," Henry's voice trailed off as he directed his attention to that one glistening instrument.

He ambled over and came across a French horn.

At first glance, he thought that he had finally found him. After all these years of searching, Henry thought this was the one. Maybe Harry had taken the shape of something else— like a French horn! Henry even checked the base of the instrument to see if his eyes weren't fooling him. There weren't any initials on the instrument. It was exactly that, an old French horn that someone had pawned off.

In disappointment, Henry placed the instrument back onto the shelf and met back up with Amy.

After they left the pawnshop, they walked over to a nearby playground where a couple of other kids around Amy's age were playing. While Henry was sitting on the bench with Amy's gift, a tarnished clock, resting beside him, he carefully watched Amy swing around on the monkey bars.

Starlet walked up from behind and sat down next to him. Henry didn't even turn toward her direction. Yet, his focus remained on Amy. Starlet placed the satchel on the bench, which caused Henry to turn.

She said casually, "Hello, Buddy."

"You know I hate it when you call me that," Henry replied, his voice carved with tension.

"Well, maybe you should pick another name."

"I see you finally decided to come out of your hole."

"I've been busy, Henry."

"Busy doing what?" Henry's eyes traced across the bench and over the leather satchel. He said bitterly, "Writing your little book."

"A memoir," she corrected, her nature still casual even through Henry's bitter tone. "I brought a revised copy if you'd like to read it."

Henry sighed.

"No thanks," he said, carefully watching Amy swing on the monkey bars. "I'll wait for the movie."

Starlet chortled.

"I see you still haven't lost your sense of humor, Henry."

"Well," he said and sighed once more, "it's hard not to have one nowadays."

"Don't be so cynical." Starlet nodded at Amy across the playground and asked, "So, how's the little one? She looks like she's growing by the day."

"She starts second grade next week. How about yours?"

"Ours, you mean," she said sternly. "He's your grandson too."

There was a silence, tenser now.

"Fifth grade," Starlet answered. "He's going to be in fifth grade."

Henry sighed once more.

"I can't do this anymore, Henry," Starlet said. "Eighteen years we've been meeting up like this every month. Don't you think Henry has a right to know who his father is?"

"T.J. was his father," Henry said calmly, "even you said that."

"T.J. was his father, but. . ." she sharpened her eyes over Henry's eyes, ". . . he wasn't his blood."

"You made a choice, Starlet," Henry said, now sharpening his eyes as well. "And I made mine. I'm happy with the way my life turned out. And there's not a day that goes by that I wouldn't change a thing." He turned toward Starlet. "As I grow older, I realize that there's not an answer for everything even. . ." his head lowered a bit, ". . . forget it."

Starlet observed the distress on Henry's face.

"I know we haven't talked much about that night. . ."

"What is there to talk about?" Henry said abruptly. "You did what you had to do, even you said that yourself."

"Well, you were certainly in no condition to bring all those men to justice."

Henry said angrily, "And killing them was the answer? That was your idea of justice?"

"You think I go about my life, never thinking about what I did," she said to Henry. "I was the one who pulled the trigger. I have to live with that, Henry." Her thoughts drifted into reflection. "Times I wonder if God will ever judge us for what we did to those people. . . "

Henry interrupted, "What you did."

"You're a part of it just as much as me, Henry."

"Don't bring me into this," Henry said closely. "I did as I was told, Starlet. I led the police away from the real suspect." Another silence built. He eased himself away from Starlet after witnessing his reflection in her glossy eyes. "I know it was you who also killed that police officer at Lansford Medical. . . "

Starlet's eyes narrowed: "He was going to kill you, Henry."

"Listen, Starlet," Henry said, the tension easing from his voice, "I understand why you did it. At the time, I probably would've burned that entire fucking police department to the ground. . . "

"You, Henry?" Starlet returned, almost amusedly. "You were in no condition. You couldn't even remember what you did the night before."

Henry sighed, loudly this time.

"I never asked you to kill those people," he said, clearly now. "*Never.*"

"Someone had to do it, Henry," Starlet said, her voice now laced with tension. "And you sure as hell weren't going to do it, not the way you were, with your drinking problem."

"There could've been another way."

"Yeah," Starlet said. "How?"

Henry pulled his attention back to Amy and ignored the question.

"So, what is Henry the Sixth up to these days?" he asked.

At first, Starlet didn't answer Henry's question. Yet, she was still waiting for an answer as to how Henry would've taken care of the ones involved in T.J.'s hospitalization.

Back at the lake house, Silas parted ways with his mother on the dock.

In one of his hands, he was carrying that same strange plant, a Venus flytrap, in a clay vase.

"Don't wander too far, Silas?" she shouted out from a distance.

"I won't, Mom." He moaned. "Geez."

Kicking through stones and branches over the ground, Silas strolled into the dim woods.

The clouds overhead swelled and created a gray wash over the sky.

Through the narrows cracks of the large oak trees, Silas spotted an old wooden shack behind his grandmother's two-story house.

Intrigued, Silas approached the shack.

Starlet grabbed the satchel and placed it over her lap.

"Henry's doing good," she answered hesitantly. "His software company goes public next week. From what he told me, he's going to be making a lot of money." She moved her eyes away from Henry, wondering whether or not to tell him about their son and how he treated Silas. With the volume of her voice lowered, Starlet said finally, "He spends more time on his smart phone than with his own kid," then, mumbled, "But what else is new. . . "

"I keep telling Sheila that it's a fad," Henry said, "that one day all of this high-tech baloney will soon fade out and that people will finally come to their senses."

"You've been saying that ever since the purge," Starlet said sourly. "I think it's time for you to be a little more realistic."

"Realistic?" Henry said, his voice raising. "You really want to talk to me about being realistic? I'm not the murderer sitting on the bench."

Starlet glared at Henry.

"How's his family?"

"They're," she cleared her throat as she tried to compose herself in front of Amy, "they're doing good. How far off is Catherine?"

"Three weeks, I believe."

"Do they know whether it's a boy or girl?"

"No," Henry said and turned his attention back to Starlet. "She says she wants it to be a surprise."

Starlet gradually smiled, which was a first throughout the conversation.

"I like surprises."

"Look, Grandpa!" Amy shouted out from the monkey bars. She was hanging upside down from the bars, her red hair dangling in her face.

"Be careful, dear!"

Starlet said, "She takes up after her mother."

"You don't know Sheila," Henry said vacantly. "And I plan on keeping it that way."

"Well, I can't say the same about Silas."

Henry scowled at Starlet.

"What do you mean?" he said seriously.

"Well," she said indirectly. "Sometimes. . . well, sometimes these things have been known to skip generations." She leaned closer to Henry. "Don't worry. I didn't put it in the book."

Henry said gravely, "What things?"

Starlet smirked.

"You know, Henry," she said, now suspiciously. "Silas, he's like. . ." she paused, ". . . how do I say. . ." then, she foolhardily shrugged both of her shoulders and gazed into Henry's worried eyes, ". . . let's just say there's a new king in town."

On second thought, Silas placed the Venus flytrap on the ground.

He untangled the chains around the door and held them in his hand for protection.

After a few sturdy tugs, the door finally swung open. On the side of walls hung all kinds of rusty tools like axes and hammers and chainsaws and anything sharp or deadly.

From the aged wood, the shack appeared as if it had been here for some time—possibly way before his grandmother's time. In the middle of the room, he found an old leather case, as cracked and worn as a hardpan desert, lying on the table.

Mindful of the many spider webs on the ceiling (ducking and dodging his way through), he carefully inched his way over to the chapped case.

Silas placed the chains over the table and didn't think twice about popping open the case.

A tiny cloud of dust spat from the case, which forced Silas to shield his face with the bend of his arm.

A stale, metallic stench wafted from the case.

Silas coughed and waved the dust away from his face.

"Whoa. . . " Silas mumbled, his eyes marveling over the dirty Jagger saxophone.

He thought: *I didn't know they still made these things.*

Without a second's hesitation, Silas picked up the soprano saxophone and scanned each part starting from the ligature to the bow.

With the sleeve of his shirt, he wiped away the dirt from the neck, the keys (the tight spaces between them), the body, the bell, and then finally the bow until the brass sparkled in the faint sunlight over the perforated rooftop.

Next, he removed his dirty sleeve from the saxophone, which revealed two initials over the base of the bow. Both of his eyes suddenly swelled with great wonder. He held up the clean saxophone before him and thought about whom the instrument belonged to. Silas didn't exactly know anyone with the initials, H.M., but soon, he would.